STORM BAY

Once the pride of the British Navy's East India fleet, the *Veritas* has fallen on hard times. She is now a transport ship, her cargo prisoners of the Crown, her destination the penal settlement of Van Diemen's Land, now known as Tasmania. Pastor Bob Cookson tries to offer solace to the convicts on board, and is shocked to discover that most of the men have committed only trivial offences. He suspects a conspiracy to empty British prisons, but finds a more sinister motive at work...

STORM BAY

STORM BAY

by

Patricia Shaw

Magna Large Print Books
Long Preston, North Yorkshire,
BD23 4ND, England.

British Library Cataloguing in Publication Data.

Shaw, Patricia
    Storm Bay.

    A catalogue record of this book is
    available from the British Library

    ISBN   0-7505-2386-7

First published in Great Britain 2005 by Headline Book Publishing

Copyright © 2005 Patricia Shaw

Cover illustration © Head Design Ltd by arrangement with
Headline Book Publishing

Published in Large Print 2005 by arrangement with
Headline Book Publishing Ltd.

Magna Large Print is an imprint of Library Magna Books Ltd.

Printed and bound in Great Britain by
T.J. (International) Ltd., Cornwall, PL28 8RW

To

John and Wendy Daniher
Peter and Jean Scott
Elizabeth and Jamie Legge
and Peter Poynton BA LLB

With love

PRESENT-DAY TASMANIA

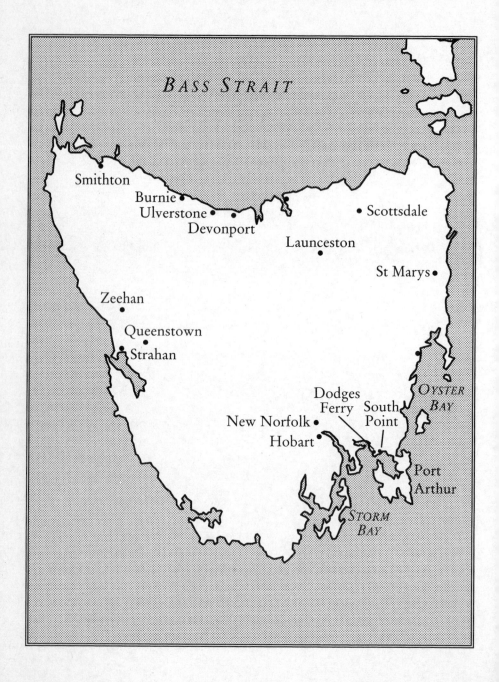

BASS STRAIT

Smithton

Burnie
Ulverstone
Devonport

Scottsdale

Launceston

St Marys

Zeehan

Queenstown

Strahan

Dodges
Ferry

New Norfolk

South
Point

*OYSTER
BAY*

Hobart

Port
Arthur

*STORM
BAY*

PORT ARTHUR

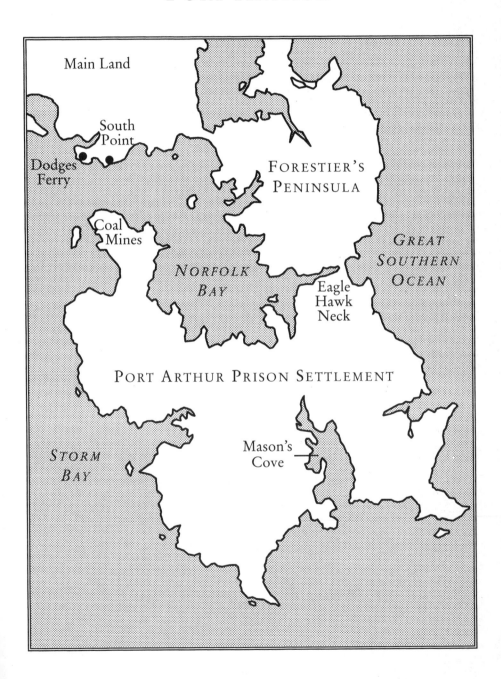

Main Land

South
Point

Dodges
Ferry

FORESTIER'S
PENINSULA

Coal
Mines

GREAT
SOUTHERN
OCEAN

NORFOLK
BAY

Eagle
Hawk
Neck

PORT ARTHUR PRISON SETTLEMENT

STORM
BAY

Mason's
Cove

PROLOGUE

October 1832

A lighter, ferrying last-minute supplies for the transport ship *Veritas*, struck out from Gravesend and ploughed into the rough seas, its crew trying to reach the old merchant ship, retired from the East India fleet, before the longboats that were heading in the same direction. They were carrying convicts from the hulk *Earl of Mar*, headed for a penal settlement on the faraway isle of Van Diemen's Land – guests of the government, the jokers liked to call them – on board *Veritas*.

She was 1,200 tons, a proud vessel in her day, veteran of the lucrative Bengal-China route, fallen on hard times nowadays, forced to ferry human cargo across the globe.

As if objecting to this humiliation, *Veritas* rolled angrily in the swell, and the men in the lighter shuddered. They had seen the timber hutches below decks, only recently installed to house two hundred of their countrymen, and they'd seen the steel rings riveted into the cheap timbers to anchor the chains.

They were glad they'd won the race, quickly unloading their cargo so they could turn their eyes and ears away from the misery of the men in the longboats that were wallowing nearby, waiting their turn, while curious seamen looked down on them in disgust. They did not condemn

13

the prisoners, nor did guilt enter their minds, just the knowledge that this was not a voyage a man could boast about.

The captain himself referred to half of his crew as trash, but he'd had difficulty recruiting ordinary seamen for this run, and beggars couldn't be choosers. As soon as the last of the fresh food was stowed, and the livestock were fed, he ordered the boatswain to clear the decks and begin taking the prisoners aboard.

CHAPTER ONE

February 1832

The magistrate furrowed his brow, scowled, peered at the packed courtroom and began to turn pages in the heavy journal on his high desk.

Carlendon was a busy little village that served the surrounding farmlands on the outskirts of London, and normally few took an interest in court proceedings, but today, it seemed, everyone wanted to hear the fate of Lester Harris, especially since this case involved not one but three of the county's leading families. And, as luck would have it, the magistrate sighed, Harris was related to his own kin, the Mudlows, by marriage.

The defendant was in the dock now, a well-built, well-fed sort of fellow with the smooth skin and even features much admired by ladies. Lester Harris was oft referred to as handsome, but to the magistrate, Jonathan Mudlow, the wretch's visage was flawed. He had always thought Lester had mean eyes – pale, calculating eyes that surveyed the world from under lowered lids. Hence it had been a wonder and a consternation to him that his cousin Josetta Mudlow, a fine young woman who, in normalcy, was no fool, should even consider marrying Lester. And he had said so. Whereupon his Aunt Ophelia had rounded on him, calling him a sour grape, claiming he was jealous because her daughter was to marry the most eligible bachelor in the district.

And so Josetta and Lester had wed. She became the mistress of Glencallan, a fine farm gifted to them by Lester's family, and in due course they were the proud parents of a bouncing baby girl called Louise May.

Jonathan had attended the christening. Josetta looked rather wan, understandable after the ravages of childbirth, but there were whispers abroad that Lester beat her.

Shocked, Jonathan asked his aunt, who brushed off such a suggestion. 'Rubbish! Where did you find a tale like that? He's got a bit of a temper, Lester has, but he'd never lay a hand on Josie. Never! And did you know she has a servant girl working for her now? How many men let their wives have servants, I ask you. None in our family and that's for sure.'

Now Jonathan studied the pages before him, coughed, rapped the desk for quiet, and turned to the prisoner at the bar. 'You have been charged and found guilty of assault and battery, a particularly brutal, unprovoked assault on a gentleman, who is now deaf as a result and has lost the use of his right arm...'

And, Jonathan said to himself, we also know now that you're a bully and a coward, since the second witness claims you've committed previous assaults that have never been brought to the notice of the law.

He saw Lester sneer and raise his eyebrows impatiently. Even now, the Harrises seemed to think they were above the law. That this guilty charge could be solved by money. They had made it plain to Jonathan that they expected him to do the right thing by his cousin's husband and levy a fine. A heavy one if he thought fit. Good of them, Jonathan reflected cynically, to assist me with my decision.

On the other hand, the victim, Matthew Powell-Londy, was the owner of a timber mill, and the permanent injuries he'd sustained constituted a serious handicap in the conduct of his business. Further to this, his brother was a lecturer in law at Cambridge, and on his advice, their father, James Powell-Londy, a powerful and bitterly angry man, expected the death penalty. They were both in the courthouse, in the front row, glaring at Jonathan this very minute.

On the other side, though, was Josie. She'd come to his door begging for clemency and he'd tried to turn her away.

'I can't listen to you,' he'd said. 'The crime has been discussed and debated in court, it is over now.'

'But he didn't mean to do it,' she persisted. 'It was just a moment of temper, Jonathan. He *was* provoked. He was being overcharged for the

16

timbers he'd ordered to build the new stables, and God knows we can little afford all that extra money.'

Jonathan shook his head. 'Now, Josie. Your farm is biding well. Don't go telling me stories.'

'Oh God, please don't regard me if I'm saying the wrong thing. But Lester is truly sorry for what happened...'

'Is he now? I hadn't noticed.'

'But he is. You have to let him go free. He'd never do such a thing again!'

'Josie, you don't understand. There are two hundred crimes on the books that incur the death penalty, many of them far less serious than this...'

'What?' She reeled back in shock. 'You're not ... you can't be thinking of such a thing! The death penalty! Are you mad? We have a daughter, she's only twelve, would you...' Too overcome to continue, she turned and ran off into the night, her wails echoing down the dark street.

Next thing, old man Harris was hammering at his door, but Jonathan refused to respond. He thought Newgate prison would be the most appropriate sentence in this case. A ten-year sentence instead of the gallows.

The night had taken its toll on his nerves as he'd dreamed of riots in the village – roisterers pillaging and burning – and seen himself atop gallows on a fine day, with the sun streaming down and children playing at his feet, a gaily beribboned noose swinging back and forth across his face, ticking heavily like a worn-out clock.

He was still groggy from those miserable dreams, and the depressing knowledge that whatever decision he made today would be met with rage by one side of the argument, at least.

Then he reminded himself that Newgate prison was not all that far from here.

Jonathan gazed into the future and saw members of the Harris family, and their friends, returning from visits to Lester in that foul prison to vent that rage on him, and his household, over and over again. There'd be no end to it. And he simply was not about to be pilloried by anyone, no matter how sorry he was that the law had Josetta's husband in the dock. He knew there was another path open to him, and he decided to take it.

He rapped his gavel and called the court to order, then, when all was quiet again, he continued: 'Lester Harris, I hereby sentence you to ten years' imprisonment for this crime, your sentence to be served in the penal colony of Van Diemen's Land. You are to be taken forthwith to Newgate prison to await transportation to that colony at the earliest.'

Harris shouted abuse at him as he was being dragged away, but his voice was drowned by the screams and shouts in the courtroom. Jonathan had other cases to hear, but he adjourned the court, taking refuge in the clerk's office until these people drifted away. It was all over and he felt relieved. In time they'd all forget Lester Harris, except Josetta and her daughter, he supposed.

But if she had any sense she'd divorce him now.

Josetta's father-in-law, Marvin Harris, came to see her that night, still enraged by the sentence.

'But I'm a practical man, Josie, so we have to

18

look at this straight. Now I know Glencallan's my son's property, left to him by his grand-daddy, but you can't run it without Lester, and he's not coming back, so we have to hang on to it.'

She was sitting at the kitchen table, too dulled by tears to care much about anything except the savage sentence her own cousin had inflicted on Lester, and the shock of seeing her husband dragged away. She hadn't begun to grasp the enormity of that sentence, she simply could not conceive of it ... that her man, her lover, was to be lost to her for ten years. It wasn't real. Could not be. It was like saying that there'd be no dawn for a decade, or that the moon wouldn't ever be seen in the skies again. She let Marvin rattle on; it was company if nothing else, for Josetta cared not a whit about the family sticking together. All she could think about was the suffering poor Lester would have to endure, locked in a grim dungeon for years and years.

Days later, when Marvin was convinced she understood the arrangements he'd outlined, he took Josetta up to London to visit Lester in prison.

Newgate was the worst, the most vile and filthy place Josetta could ever have imagined, and though she dared not say it, she was glad her husband was to be removed from there, and for the first time thought Jonathan's decision might have had some merit.

As they made their way through the stinking stone corridors, she kept the hood of her cloak closed over her face, on Marvin's advice.

'Try not to look, Josie, there's things here your

19

eyes shouldna see, nor let the foul men either side here peer on your face.'

He paid a warder to bring Lester to an empty cell, so they could talk with some privacy, but when he arrived they were shocked at his filthy appearance.

'About time!' he yelled at them. 'You'd let me rot here, wouldn't you? Did you bring me some food?'

Josetta was ready to faint, so Marvin grabbed her basket. 'Look here, son. Plenty here for you. There's spiced sausage and ham leg, and bread and pies your mum made for you...'

He broke off as Lester, ravenous, grabbed at the food, stuffing it into his mouth as fast as he could.

'Did you bring me any money?' he asked hoarsely as he ate. 'You have to have money to get food here, or clean clothes or even fresh water. They took everything I brought with me. I haven't got a stitch of my own. I can't live like this.' He grabbed his father by the lapels of his jacket. 'You have to get me out of here. Do something! Pay them whatever it costs. Sell the farm if you have to.'

Lester didn't want to hear anything else from them. He was frantic to be released and demanded his father see to it right away. He hardly spoke to Josetta, except to urge her to keep Marvin working for his freedom.

'I'm begging you,' he wept in the end, 'get me out before it's too late. They say there's a transport ship near ready to sail any day.'

Marvin took two rooms at a nearby inn, and

day after day did the rounds of legal offices on his son's behalf, to no avail. Each day, armed with a basket of food and wine, he and Josetta reported to Lester and sat stolidly, suffering his abuse. Eventually, when it did dawn on his son that there was no turning back now, Marvin broached the matter of Glencallan Farm.

'Hard for me to say this, son, but we have to mind all of our interests. You'll be back one day, but in the meantime...'

Lester sat on the bench, head down, a study in dejection, only raising it to reach for another bun and the pieces of apple Josetta was peeling for him. He didn't even appear to be listening, so Marvin pushed on.

'What I was thinking is this. Josetta can't run it with you away, so we add it to my farm and make one big one, eh? That way it's protected for you. I mean, if you leave it the way it is, then Josetta could end up bringing another man in, even marrying him!'

'No! How could you say that, Pa Harris! I love Lester, I would never...' Josetta dissolved into tears.

Lester ignored her. 'One big farm, you say?' he barked at his father. 'One big farm?'

'Yes. I've got the papers here.' Marvin fished into his vest pocket. 'If you sign Glencallan over to me, you'll never have to worry about it.'

Lester charged from the bench and slammed his hand against the damp stone wall. 'Do you think I'm stupid? Do you think I can't see what you're up to? You've always envied me Glencallan, you cursed Grand-daddy for leaving it to me, cursed him at the graveside! Now you think you'll get it! And won't my brother be rubbing his hands in glee! Well, it won't happen. Get out!'

He rushed at his father and manhandled him out of the cell.

Bewildered, Josetta tried to quieten him as the slovenly guard glanced at them from his perch at the top of nearby steps.

'Give her the papers,' Lester snarled at Marvin, grabbing them and shoving them at Josetta. 'I want to talk to you. Without him interfering.' He pulled her aside.

'Lester, you know I would never fail you...' she began.

'Sit down and listen to me,' he said. 'I've been asking around here to find out about this place Van Diemen's Land. I don't suppose any of you have done that.'

'There hasn't been time,' she whimpered. 'We've been too worried about you.'

'You let me do the worrying from now on, because this is what you do. You sell the farm, lock, stock and barrel. Sell everything. Then you buy a passage for you and the girl to Van Diemen's Land.'

She clapped her hands to her mouth. 'What did you say? I can't go to a prison. And I wouldn't know how to get there.'

'Shows how bloody ignorant you are. And stupid. Like him. I've been making enquiries. People are going to live there. Settlers. Instead of America. They go to this island, there's a town called Hobart, and they make their fortune because they get convicts to work for them free.

Imagine that! A farm where you'd not pay the farmhands!'

'But I can't go off to the wilds like that. I wouldn't know where to start.'

'Then you better learn up fast, because you're emigrating to Van Diemen's Land, with the girl and my money, and there you're buying a farm. And if you don't do that, I swear I'll come back and kill you.'

She tried to soothe him. 'Lester, dear, you're overwrought. Please ... stop a minute. I'll do everything you ask, of course I will. I am beside myself that you are being taken from me. If you go slowly and explain to me patiently what I'm to do, then I'll be with you in Van Diemen's Land as soon as is humanly possible.'

To his surprise, Marvin saw Lester take her in his arms, and thought sadly what a foolish fellow he was to entrust his farm to a woman.

When Josetta sold Glencallan to a stranger who outbid him, he was outraged.

Dublin, April 1832

Patrick O'Neill told his wife he'd keep fighting for their son as long as there was breath in him. He forbade her to despair. And indeed, it seemed at first that he was making headway.

'The first charge,' he said, 'was little more than drunk and disorderly.'

'Riotous assembly,' the solicitor corrected primly, 'assault upon a person, destruction of property.'

'Same thing. And that other charge of being a member of the Young Ireland Association, well,

23

that's not right. Our Matt was never political. He was only visiting the house.'

'They all say that.'

O'Neill thumped the wide desk. 'You're not here to take their side! I'm paying you to get Matt home. We'll pay a fine, whatever it is, but you have to pull your weight. Don't be just sitting there like a knot on a log. Do something!'

'Mr O'Neill. On the first charge, if you recall, it was I who had the sentence reduced from ten to five years, but you don't seem to understand, the second charge is far more serious.'

'Don't tell me what I don't understand!' O'Neill roared. 'I understand what they're up to, but I don't accept scooping up good with bad in a netting expedition and giving them all life! My son isn't one of them, he's never held a gun in his life.'

'He joined them, Mr O'Neill. His signature's in the book plain as day. And they were in that house plotting a raid.'

'Jesus wept! That was never proven. No one gave evidence to bear that out, not a soul.'

The solicitor sighed. 'I've done my best. Transportation to Van Diemen's Land is better than having to live in a prison cell here.'

'You're wrong. They can't wrench him away from his family like this. You have to stop him being transported! Lodge an appeal before it's too late.'

'I did appeal, it was rejected. I can do no more, I'm sorry to say.'

'And what about my nephew, Sean Shanahan?'

'His sentence was set in stone right from the beginning, Mr O'Neill. I told you that. Assault and robbery! That *is* a life sentence!'

'But it was only mischief!'

'Not to the magistrate.'

Though it was a warm day, the room seemed icy cold to Patrick. He shuddered. 'Did you read that an English ship carrying convicts went down off the coast of France, and a hundred and sixteen convicts were drowned?'

'Yes,' his solicitor said sadly. 'But they were all female. And some children.'

'God help you, man! Are you thinking that men would have a better chance? Chained in holds with less freedom than the rats?'

'I'm not saying that at all. I am simply at a loss to offer you any more advice at this stage.'

'Then tell me, how does a man draw up a petition to present to the Government?'

'On what subject?'

'On the banning of transportation of our citizens to parts unknown. Can we talk about that now?'

'It's too late for Matt.'

'Don't you think I know that? Don't take me for a fool, man. I want you to show me how to get the petition started. If I can't help my son, then I'll try for other men's sons, and daughters. I won't go back to my wife empty-handed.'

'Very well. I'll send my clerk for the official petitioning forms and when they're ready, I'll have an MP lodge them for you.'

From the lawyer's office, Patrick made his way up O'Connell Street to his hotel, where he collected the parcel of warm clothes his wife had packed for Matt. From there he trudged on to the prison, his heart as heavy as his boots.

At the gate, he was about to hand in his permit when a girl rushed over and took him by the arm.

'Mr O'Neill, wait! They won't let me go in there on my own. Could I come with you? I have to see Sean.'

He frowned. 'Ah, it's you, Glenna Hamilton. You shouldn't be here. This is no place for a young lady.'

'Oh please! Sean's being sent away too. He and Matt, it seems likely they'll go any day. You wouldn't deny me seeing him this last time.'

He looked down at the pretty, winsome face, remembering that there had been a time when Matt was keen on Glenna, but of late she'd been walking out with his cousin Sean Shanahan. And now this ... both lads sent into exile.

Patrick was distraught over the fate of the boys, but he found room for a measure of sympathy for the colleen, and thought she'd bring Sean some cheer at least.

'All right then. Pull that scarf over your face and don't be making any chatter. I'll see if I can find him for you.'

They were taken across a courtyard to the archway over the visitors' entrance, where they stood awhile, with an elderly couple and a huddled family group, until the door was unlocked and they were ushered inside, to line up before a bench and deposit belongings.

Four guards – three men and one woman – watched them; the woman was a nasty-looking beast, Glenna thought, as she handed over her purse and shamrock brooch and moved over to the female line, where the Beast actually manhandled her when it came time for her to be searched from head to foot.

She saw Mr O'Neill in his search line, looking angry at the way the woman was treating her, hands like cast iron banging up and down her person, but she shook her head at him to show that she was all right, for fear he'd cause a disorder and they'd be thrown out. But then he too was searched, and they were allowed past to join the others. They were led down a long corridor, called to a halt as if they were recruits, and left standing there, under guard.

Glenna was tingling with excitement at the very thought of seeing Sean, and was finding the whole thing an adventure, never having been inside a prison before. So far it had been not a lot different from entering any government building, with that same old lino and watery-green-painted walls.

A guard came and whisked away the old couple, then returned for Mr O'Neill, but when Glenna stepped forward she was ordered back behind the black line, the one she hadn't even noticed before.

'She's with me,' Matt's father told them, but was informed that his son was in the yard, and women weren't allowed out there.

'Then where can she see Sean Shanahan?' he asked. 'She has the permission.'

'He's out there too. Send him back to his cell. You've only ten minutes left; you should have come earlier, they'll be going in to tea now.'

Mr O'Neill jerked his shoulders impatiently

and began walking forward, forcing the guard to hurry after him. Glenna watched nervously as they disappeared around a corner, then appealed to the guard who carried a clipboard and seemed to be in charge of directions.

'What about me, sir?' she asked in her sweetest tone, but he scowled and made what she was sure was a rude remark over his shoulder to guard number three, and they both looked at her and laughed.

Blushing, Glenna turned away, and one of the women in the group said loudly: 'Don't take no notice of them, darlin'. You're too good for the likes of them.'

Then her name was called, and Glenna, counting the minutes now, was running down towards that corner, to be taken through heavy doors that had to be unlocked and locked again, with time awasting, and then sent into a bare room, with nothing, no furniture at all, only bars on the narrow window.

'Is this his cell?' she asked, incredulous, but the door was slammed shut. The guard hadn't locked it, so she sneaked over to open it just a little, because it stifled and frightened her in there, and as she reached for it, it opened and a man was pushed inside. Sean it was, shoved at her like a bag of potatoes, leg irons tripping him, hands cuffed behind his back.

He almost fell, but she caught him in her arms, and his mouth was on hers in that same minute, searching for her, needing her, and Glenna was ecstatic.

'Ah,' she said, 'you're still so beautiful and all,

no matter what they do to you.' But then she remembered he'd said, often, that it wasn't for men to be beautiful. It was for beauties like Glenna Hamilton.

'Dear God, but I love you, my darlin',' he said to her, wrestling with the yearnings of those poor clamped arms. 'I'd have died had you not come to say goodbye.'

'But it's not goodbye,' she cried fiercely, as he shuffled over to lean against the wall. 'You'll be back, I know you will. And I'll never stop loving you, Sean. Never.'

She clung to him, their kisses frantic now, as if they could hear the clock ticking. She undid her blouse, baring her breasts as she felt for the hardness of him, trying to do her best for him, though she'd never been so bold, or allowed him to be so bold, ever before, and he moaned and told her again how much he loved her and of his regrets that he had brought them to this, but then the door burst open and the guard stood there grinning. Sean moved in front of her, trying to protect her from the brute's leer, but Glenna Hamilton stood by him, taking her time to button up, astonished that she didn't care one whit what the guard had seen.

Sean kissed her, long and tenderly, and they took him away, and Glenna trooped back to the front door in a daze, in an absolute walking-on-clouds daze, to wait for Mr O'Neill and be reminded to collect her belongings.

'They leave here tomorrow,' Mr O'Neill said, his voice hoarse. 'Both of the lads.'

Glenna pulled up the collar of her coat to try to

hide the tears that were already wet on her face.

The River Thames, October 1832

One of the dilapidated hulks now wallowing in the Thames still bore the name *Earl of Mar*, but it was a far cry from its glory days as a warship, as the present ship's company would avow. They were the overflow from London's prisons, billeted aboard and sent ashore daily, to clear the marshes in a backwater known as Bosney Flats, in preparation for landfill works that would extend the shoreline to deeper water and create more accessible wharves.

No one, except the unfortunate convicts, seemed to notice that snow was falling this particular morn, and that the muddy water was caked with ice – certainly not the overseers, rugged up to the eyeballs, as they ordered the men to 'wade in and no hanging about'.

Angus McLeod, late of Glasgow, waded into knee-deep water hauling a raft to collect the reeds as they were wrenched from their beds, listening to the curses of his freezing workmates and pondering the irony of his situation. Six months ago, his support of violent protests against intolerable working conditions for the poor had seen him arrested and sentenced to be transported to Van Diemen's Land. Now awaiting the transport ship, along with a number of *Earl of Mar*'s occupants, he was enduring conditions ten times worse than those for workers in the Glasgow slums.

He'd told another convict, George Smith, about that, complaining bitterly at the way they were being treated, and George had laughed.

Irony meant nothing to him. He thought the story was supposed to be funny – but to Angus there was nothing amusing about the cruelty they were enduring, the long hours of work and the starvation rations. He claimed there had to be prisoners' rights, that they had to be entitled to lodge complaints somewhere.

'Stop worryin' about it,' George said. 'Nothin' to be done. You'd not be doin' the job so hard if you got on with it and stopped your thinking. You're making it worse on yourself, Angus.'

George was a kind man, from Wessex, listed as a farmer, but he'd stolen a prize goat, borrowed, he'd claimed, 'for to husband my nanny goat', and ended up in this foul wreck with more than three hundred other men, and inevitable fights.

Only two nights ago, a bully-boy, Lester Harris, who had appointed himself boss of a work gang, making sure they kept on the land side of the marshes, ferrying barrows of soil across narrow plank walkways, had head-butted a man over some disagreement, knocking him out for a few minutes. He'd then reached out to grab the man's blanket, decent blankets being rare, but George had stepped in and ordered him to leave it.

'Who'll make me?' Harris had challenged, but when George suddenly produced a knife, astonishing his friend Angus McLeod, the argument subsided as quickly as it had begun, and the injured man, recovering dizzily, kept his blanket.

'There are terrible punishments for carrying a weapon,' Angus felt he ought to mention to his mild-mannered friend. 'Harris will dob you in to get back at you.'

'No he won't,' George grinned. 'He ain't got the goolies.'

As rumours swept the gangs that they'd be leaving soon, Angus had managed to write a frantic letter to his cousin Ursula, asking her to bring his parents to London so he could bid them farewell. They hadn't even come to see him in the Glasgow prison, though Ursula had made the effort, explaining that they were in a state of bewilderment. 'The arrest and all, it happened so fast,' she said. 'They're not familiar with the regulations and how to go about things.'

'Aye, I understand that. Me being arrested would be a dead shock for them, but if someone would come with them ... bring them here...'

'I'll try. They might come with me, but you know, Angus, they think I'm a fallen woman because I work as a maid at the Grand Hotel and, God help my soul,' she grinned, 'I live in there. They've even got my mum looking sideways at me.'

'They've always been sticklers for the straight road, especially my Ma. She's been brought up strict chapel, but I don't think she understands they're sending me out of the country for years. It'll break my heart to have to leave without bidding them farewell. You couldn't say it to them, and I wouldn't want you to, but they could pass away in that time, and that would be the worst of all punishments for me.'

He stood at the barred window and kicked the wall. 'Do them blasted magistrates ever stop to think that these sentences are outrageous and irresponsible, in no way meant to fit the crime?' he blazed, and Ursula nodded respectfully.

It was a fact, Angus realised, that this girl didn't know what he was talking about; so ground down were poor folk that few would contemplate raising their eyes, let alone a fist, to protest. And his mother was the same. Worse even. To her, complaining about low wages was a slight to a person's own dignity.

'Do ye want people to think we're dead poor?' she'd railed at him one night, when he arrived home from a protest meeting.

'We *are* dead poor,' he'd said wearily.

'Ach! You should have seen how we grew up. A pot of gruel like mud for tea, and pleased we were to get it, no money for firewood in the freezing winter. The winters were colder then...'

She fought change, he recalled. Wore black all her life. One skirt for the winter, one for summer. And thanked the Lord for preserving them.

He tried to talk to his father. 'The bosses are stealing from us. Getting rich on our toil. Can't you see that?'

But Jim McLeod had no time for that sort of talk. 'There's plenty worse off than us.'

'Sure there are, so we have to help them.'

'I think you ought to do your own work and mind your own business.'

Ursula was standing at the cell door. 'Don't fret, Angus. I'll have my mum tell them there's not much time.'

But time had run out before they made it to the London prison, and they'd never find him here. No visitors were allowed, except for the few, like

33

Harris, who paid to be taken under guard to the coach house at the Bosney crossroads.

Harris had gone to meet his wife.

'We had business to attend to,' he'd growled when he returned to the inevitable obscene remarks from his offsiders, and had given them no further information.

After three months in the hulk, plenty of time for a letter, or a message of some sort from his parents, Angus moaned in despair when he saw several longboats approaching the *Earl of Mar*.

'You're off, me hearties!' the overseer chortled, as a roll call began and more than a hundred prisoners were assembled on the warped, uneven decks. 'The good ship *Veritas* awaits to take you to the ends of the earth, where brown maidens wearing only grass skirts sit in the sun singing songs and panting for the sight of randy Englishmen.'

'What about the Scots?' someone cried. 'We're a better bet.'

'Would you say that's right about the maidens waiting for us?' Freddy Hines asked Angus. He was a wiry little fellow who'd worked with them ashore.

'Iron maidens, maybe.' Angus scowled.

'There could be women on the good ship, though,' Freddy said hopefully. 'They're sending female prisoners too, 'tis said.'

Suddenly several of the prisoners began shouting and hurling themselves to the deck. Some wept for their families; others, in a panic, screamed that they could not swim and fought the guards, refusing to board the longboats; some tried to throw themselves into the river, and one man, frothing at the mouth, bellowed that they were to be taken and drowned in the far oceans, instilling fear in all of them.

Until then, Angus had been unafraid of the voyage, but even he was worried when it was his turn to drop into the boat beside an oarsman. That concern, however, could not be compared with the pain of having to leave his beloved parents behind, without their blessing. His heart was so heavy he had to fight back unmanly tears, and when the naval seamen, rowing hard into the wind around the point to where *Veritas* lay at anchor, cursed the weight of them, he turned bitterly to the nearest rower.

'Aye, we're heavy. I'll gladly lighten your load. You can throw me over if you want.'

Despite the cold, as soon as they were hauled aboard, stumbling and flopping, as if beached on *Veritas*'s slippery deck, strong hands grabbed them, ripping their clothes from them and shoving them forward naked, into a barrage of salt water from the hoses.

'Scrub yourselves,' an officer shouted as cakes of soap were tossed to them. 'We'll have none of your lice and filth on *Veritas*. And that means every crack and corner.'

He leapt aside as the hoses swept the deck, and several prisoners deemed it easier to do the scrubbing hanging on to the rails rather than allow themselves to be tumbled about in the confusion of bodies.

Thin cloths were thrown to them for the drying

process as they stood shivering on the dry side of the deck, allowing others coming aboard to take their turn. Then they were issued with new clothes – shirt, trousers, jerkins and canvas slippers – and no sooner were they dressed than they were lined up again for a visit to the ship's barbers to be shaved and shorn.

Freddy Hines looked about him, bewildered. 'Hey, Shanahan. How will I know anyone now? You all look blooming alike now you're bald.'

George Smith grinned. 'We'll know you, your shearer left tufts on your skinny head!'

Sean Shanahan pushed away from them, searching for a mate of his, and Freddy, sensing a rage in the Irishman, held back.

It was follow-my-leader after that, along the deck to report to an officer, who checked them off against a passenger list. This caused men who could read to comment nastily on their 'passenger' status, and the officer to shout for seamen to hurry up with the leg-irons.

Behind the officer's makeshift desk, a white-bearded cleric spoke gently to the men as they passed him by, telling them he would pray for them, and issuing a little sermon of faith and hope to those prisoners who could be bothered listening to him. Mainly they just shouldered past, too intent on stepping down into their new quarters to care.

Angus heard the cleric say that he was aboard to hold services for them and to pray for a safe voyage for the ship's company. He would only be travelling with them as far as Portsmouth, he said, and if he could do anything for them as regards last messages to their loved ones, he would be happy to oblige. Angus immediately took up the offer, as did several others including a tall, gentlemanly fellow called Willem Rothery.

The cleric, who identified himself as Pastor Cookson of the Protestant faith, took their names and promised to see each one of them before he left the ship.

Pushed along in the queue, Angus stooped to go down two flights of steps, relieved that at least this ship was clean, and seemed seaworthy. Though after the hulks, he thought, any ship would seem seaworthy.

Only then did he realise what was in store, as guards took over from the seamen, cramming their prisoners into narrow spaces along the wooden platforms that were to be their homes for the next few months. Each flat space, the length of a man, a short man, was fitted with thin bed ticking.

'These are our bunks? We have to live chained down here?' Men began to shout, and within minutes, with newcomers still filing in, there was chaos. Some attacked the guards, while others tried to storm the only exit, but the revolt was soon stilled. Obviously, Angus realised, the officers were prepared for this reaction, as the hoses were brought into play again and half of the 'passengers', wearing their clean new clothes, were left soaked and cold under the low ceiling of their crowded dungeon – one that rocked so violently that men were already wailing and vomiting, begging for mercy.

Sean Shanahan grabbed at men passing him by,

asking if they'd seen a fellow called Matt O'Neill, but they brushed him aside, fear inciting them to scramble for a bunk as close as possible to the exit. Eventually he gave up. Matt hadn't been on the hulk, but Sean had hoped he'd turn up with the other contingent, and now it was too late. He withdrew into himself then, sat passively as the ankle chains were run through the rings, connecting men to their neighbours in leads of ten. Like teams of oxen, he thought bitterly, only we have nowhere to go.

There was a sudden silence in the late afternoon when they felt the first surge of movement as the great sails heaved the ship forward, and heard the new sharp swish of the sea and the rush of the ship dipping into the tide and lifting up again in triumph. *Veritas* was on her way, and regardless of their distressing plight, more than a few of the prisoners in her hold, still boys at heart, felt a rush of exhilaration as she picked up speed. Others, too far gone in their misery, felt no such fleeting joy.

In the morning, after a sleepless night, Sean joined the group allowed on deck to see the preacher, not because he had anything to say to the fellow, but because it gave him an opportunity that he knew would become priceless as the weeks wore on – to be spared even a half-hour locked up below decks. He'd been busy preparing himself for this voyage. He'd already had enough of prisons to know to keep his mouth shut, obey the rules and keep out of prison cliques. He figured the only way to beat this system was to stay out of trouble and keep looking for the time the warders dropped their guard. It wouldn't happen on this voyage he didn't suppose, but he knew that a good record brought privileges, and privileges would open the door, some door, somewhere, to escape.

That was all Sean had on his mind. Escape. The very word would consume him.

Pastor Cookson's pity for the prisoners had him so dreadfully depressed that it took a huge effort on his part to offer solace of any sort, let alone hope. He did his best to secure some dignity for them, requiring the captain to allow him a quiet corner in the roundhouse, but when the chained men, still unused to the lift and fall of the ship, staggered to his table, they were accompanied by armed guards.

The pastor sighed. So much for privacy! But he did his best. Several men claimed they were innocent, and begged him to bring their cases to the attention of the captain so that they could be put ashore at Portsmouth, but they got short shrift from the guards, who eavesdropped shamelessly on the conversations. They were dragged off almost as they opened their mouths, and the prisoners awaiting their turn were warned to rethink their ideas. Most of them, though, did need the pastor's reassurance that the Lord had not forsaken them, and asked him to remember them in his prayers.

A few asked him to send farewell messages home for them, and he agreed to do so. A Scot, Angus McLeod, begged him to make certain his message went to the right address, because his parents hadn't been able to visit him before he'd been taken from the prison, and to be sure to tell them, in better words than the young man claimed he could find, that he loved them dearly.

Another fellow, Willem Rothery, one of a large group of educated men the pastor was surprised to find in the convict ranks, told his story and asked for assistance.

'I was a gambler,' he said, 'and my debts got beyond me. I had a very responsible position in a London bank, so I misappropriated several amounts from the bank, two hundred pounds in the end, hoping to bet my way out of trouble. It's the old story,' he sighed. 'I thought I could pay it back and no one would notice.

'Well of course, they did. I was arrested and charged. My superiors, though, did not want the matter to become public, so they demanded I repay the money immediately. When I pointed out that I could not repay such an amount, they suggested, rather firmly, that I ask my father, Colonel James Rothery, for the money. They knew he was a wealthy man ... but I couldn't do that. I was too ashamed. I refused.

'The bank did manage to keep the matter very quiet, and I went through the courts and to Newgate very swiftly. It was kept so much under wraps that my parents, who live in Cornwall, don't even know of my disgrace yet. I've tried to write and tell them but I just can't put pen to paper. They'll find out soon, they have to, they'll be wondering about me... Pastor, would you write to them for me? Tell them how sorry I am to have let them down, and ask if they can find forgiveness in their hearts.'

A guard intervened. 'Time's up. They've got to

go below now.'

'But there are still men waiting to see me.'

'Captain's orders. Ask him again tomorrer.'

'Just a minute then.' As the rest of the queue was dispersed, Cookson hurriedly took down the address of this man's parents and promised to write the letter on his behalf.

'I'll pray for you, Mr Rothery,' he said. 'But please don't give way to dejection. I'm sure your people will understand. And your letter will be in the post upon the first day I land in Portsmouth.'

True to his word, as soon as he found lodgings in Portsmouth, and took stock of his notes, Pastor Cookson set about his duties in following up the requests of the prisoners, beginning with Colonel and Mrs J. Rothery, of Loddor Estate, Truro, Cornwall.

Later in the day he heard that there were thirty prisoners being held in the Customs Hall for embarkation aboard *Veritas*, so he hurried down there, determined that these poor souls would not be denied pastoral guidance.

It appeared that the captain of the previous transport ship had refused to accept these prisoners, for fear of overcrowding, so they'd been sent back to await the arrival of the *Veritas*.

He managed to talk with several of them, assuring them that *Veritas* was seaworthy, and once again offering to take messages, and one fellow by the name of Matt O'Neill asked him if he knew of a Sean Shanahan, a prisoner who could be aboard that ship.

'Sean's a big man with dark curling hair and a

41

bit of a beard he keeps clipped,' O'Neill said. 'He's my cousin, and if we have to go to the southern oceans, I'd appreciate his company.'

'There's no one with dark or light hair among them now, Mr O'Neill. They're all shaved to bald, as you will no doubt discover before the day is out, but I do recall a Mr Shanahan with a voice like yours; he asked me about conditions in Van Diemen's Land but I'm afraid I could not enlighten him.'

O'Neill was delighted. 'Thank you, Pastor. May the good Lord bless you for ever and ever.'

The pastor moved on to try to speak to a young boy of no more than twelve, who was clutching his arms about him, his thin face white with fear.

'It's no use,' a guard said. 'He hasn't spoke to no one since he heard about the transport ship.'

'Does he have to go?'

The guard was surprised. 'Course he does. There's lads younger'n him sent off. But it ain't so bad. Out there they put 'em to school. 'Tis true,' he added, noting Pastor Cookson's surprise. 'They be better off there than here, when they get book learnin' and trade learnin' too.'

Another guard leaned forward with a leer. 'Right that is, if they last the voyage.'

The pastor was deeply saddened as he walked away from the docks, wishing he could slice thirty years from his age, for this mission had been a revelation to him. He'd been a little nervous at having to face the worst sinners of the realm, as he'd been told, on that transport ship. Men who were so corrupt and so vicious that they had to be sent to the Antipodes, as far from Britain as possible. He'd prayed all the previous night for courage when it came time for him to enter the lions' den, so to speak.

Courage? he asked himself. What a fool he'd been to believe the propaganda, even though they were the Bishop's exact words: 'The worst sinners of the realm,' he'd said.

Pastor Cookson knew now how cruel and how wrong was such talk. 'If the men I've met, bound for exile, are the worst in the realm,' he muttered, 'then we're in damn good shape. By God we are.'

He wished he could have made this the first day of his mission, to travel with the exiles and open a ministry dedicated to their well-being in the penal settlement. But then he shook his head.

'It's a sad thing,' he murmured, 'to find one's true path in life too late.'

Months passed, and Pastor Cookson received a variety of responses from the messages he'd forwarded. Had the prisoner left any money for his family? What were the visiting hours? What compensation would a wife be entitled to if her man drowned at sea? Many seemed to think Van Diemen's Land was somewhere near the Isle of Wight, or across the Channel in France; others worried that their loved ones would be murdered by savages ... one woman indulged in the gleeful hope that her spouse would meet a grisly end. But in the main, folk had no need, or the capacity, to write a reply.

He was stunned, though, to receive a letter from a public scribe on behalf of Angus McLeod's parents.

Mr and Mrs Jim McLeod wish to hear no more of their son Angus who has shamed the family Name by his arrest for Riotous Assembly and Destruction of Property. They are poor people but proud in the Kirk and God's Sight. They want no more of a son who did sacrifice his Obligations to the Care and Support of his parents and Aged grandmother in Reckless Public Disorder.

The letter was cold. Heartless. He was given no actual instructions to forward it, or indeed its content, to Angus McLeod, so after giving the matter some thought, he decided not to inform the son of his parents' attitude. It would take many months for a letter to locate Angus now, and he hoped that by then these mean-spirited people might have had a change of heart.

As a result of that experience, the pastor felt some trepidation as he sliced the seal of a letter and recognised the name of Rothery. But his fears were unfounded. The colonel had become concerned about his son, who had resigned from the bank, as he'd been told, and moved out of his rooms in Oxford Street without contacting his family, and he was greatly relieved, though naturally grief-stricken, to hear what had transpired.

His response was a lesson in compassion, Cookson thought, that the McLeods could well learn, but then he reproved himself for passing judgement on poor folk with very real fears.

In closing, Colonel Rothery thanked the pastor for his kindness and assured him that Willem would not be left to fend for himself in exile without the full support of his family.

More and more the interests of transported prisoners began to take over Pastor Cookson's life. He visited men and women with banishment hanging over their heads, in prisons or on the transport ships, and tried to comfort their families, and since fear of the unknown, of what they would encounter at the ends of the earth, was paramount among these people, he made it his business to learn all he could about Van Diemen's Land – the Government, the climate, the indigenous people, and the conduct of the prison settlement. His information was garnered mainly from libraries and government departments, but the wily preacher also sought the opinions of mariners with first-hand experience of Hobart Town and its surrounds.

By-passing the ever-present horror of shipwreck, he was able to give a fairly good account of the place to calm the nerves of prisoners, explaining that Hobart was a civilised town that employed most of the convicts in construction and farm work. And not only that, it gave them the opportunity to attend lessons even in prison.

'Only the badly behaved are locked up, in HM prisons no different from ours,' he was able to say. 'So people have a choice.'

He did not add that although officers and seamen alike, from returning ships, agreed that this was correct, there was an almost universal shudder from all but the hard-hearted as they recalled the other side of the same coin … the ill treatment of helpless prisoners, the floggings, the treadmills, the degradation.

'But who does this?' he'd asked, bewildered. 'Who are the tormentors? Whence are they drawn?'

'They're your fellow men,' an officer told him. 'From our own isles. Discipline on our ships is harsh. Floggings we regard as essential at times. In that place, they're practically the order of the day, sixty lashes and more regarded as common-place. But, ah, Pastor, they've a more diabolical punishment...'

'What could that be?' Cookson asked breath-lessly.

'Solitary, sir. A month, six months, whatever the time, that's what gets them. Solitary is the most feared punishment of all.'

The pastor would not speak of these punish-ments, but kept advocating the necessity for new arrivals to do their very best in order to achieve outdoor work as soon as possible.

'I am told,' he said, 'that some people hardly get to see the inside of the prisons there if they are on record as well behaved.'

'That is entirely possible,' the officer recalled, 'if they manage to dodge the viciousness in the ranks of the guards.'

From the pulpit, though, the pastor railed against transportation. He claimed it was a sentence upon a sentence, not only a double punishment but constitutionally illegal. He urged the Government to use the money to rehabilitate prisoners, call for volunteers to emigrate to the bonny isle, and send men and women to Van Diemen's Land with dignity. This, he argued, would eliminate the huge cost of non-productive

46

personnel such as warders, guards and military regiments, many of whom were known to harangue and torture their charges.

His reputation as a passionate voice calling for an end to mass transportation of prisoners, came to the attention of the Bishop, who rebuked him firmly, requiring he restrict his public utterances to religious matters and church business, but when a year had passed and the recalcitrant cleric was still at it, the Bishop was brought to the mat by the Archbishop. This gentleman pointed out that Cookson had it all wrong. That prisoners were desperately needed in the colonies, not only of Van Diemen's Land, but of New South Wales and others, for cheap labour. How else could the colonies flourish? Look at America! Would she have grown so wealthy so quickly were it not for the slaves? Well, slavery was banned now, and rightly so, but to take men out of prisons and give them over to farm work, for instance, was a truly humanitarian project.

'It's simple logic, something a bucolic old gentleman like Cookson could never grasp. People at high levels are becoming irritated by his amateurish intrusion into the world of commerce. The fellow simply has no idea what he is talking about.' The Archbishop yawned. 'Best thing to do, old chap. Keep everyone happy. Pension him off.'

The Bishop withdrew. Pastor Cookson was getting on anyway, it was time he retired. That wasn't a problem, but the Bishop was concerned about the stomach twinges he had been experiencing since being treated to the views of his immediate superior – twinges that reminded him all was not well. That in itself was plain enough, he pondered, but it was difficult to discern exactly what was wrong. It had something to do with what His Grace had said regarding cheap labour, the text so blurred in his mind now, that he struggled to recall the exact meaning. But surely, he told himself, surely His Grace wasn't advocating a system wherein cheap labour was a euphemism for slavery?

He shook his head as he walked away from His Grace's palace. 'I misunderstood, that's all,' he muttered.

But the twinges remained, a nervous stirring that warned the confused prelate of a looming ulcer.

Being pensioned off made Pastor Cookson's mission almost impossible. He was left with a miserable thirty shillings per annum, and the necessity to move out of the rectory as soon as possible.

His son was furious. 'You have to go back and apologise. Stop harping on that one subject.'

'I don't speak of transportation and the treatment of convicts all the time,' the pastor protested. 'Only when something new comes up, like the time I met a sea captain who said–'

'Never mind about that. You have to give your word to the Bishop that you will desist from mentioning the matter again, and if you do that he might reinstate you.'

'Ah, but I am also forbidden from visiting the prisoners either at the hulks or in Portsmouth.'

'Because they're not your parishioners, Papa.'

'Nor any other's, Leo, that's why they desperately need what spiritual help I can give them.'

'All right, but you've done your bit; leave it to younger men now.'

'I can't do that. If you would come with me to see the depths of misery they're suffering, you might understand, but you won't. Neither will my superiors, and that's why I have to leave here.'

'So soon?'

'Oh yes, I had my marching orders weeks ago. I have to find lodgings somewhere.'

'Lodgings? You will of course come to my house. It'll be a crush, with the children, but I believe it will suit for the time being.'

'Thank you, Leo, but Oxford's too far away. I intend to find lodgings in Portsmouth now: I can no longer afford to be travelling between there and the hulks, so Portsmouth will have to do. Once settled there, I shall found a Mission for the Welfare of Prison Transportees.'

'With what?' Leo demanded. 'You won't even have enough to support yourself, and I refuse to underwrite such a cause. It won't do, Papa, it simply won't do. Since you have to leave here, I'll stay on to help you pack so that you can come home with me. I'll arrange for your effects to be forwarded to Oxford at the weekend.'

His father looked at him fondly. 'It's very kind of you, dear boy, but I really would prefer you to send them to Portsmouth.'

'But you're even further away from us there.'

'I know, but it's what I have to do.'

By chance, Patrick O'Neill's solicitor heard of the Mission for the Welfare of Prison Transportees, located in Portsmouth, England, and wasted no time in informing his client, in the hope that O'Neill would stop nagging him for news of his lost cause.

O'Neill, a determined man, was not only grateful for the lead, he was on his way to England within days, looking forward to meeting members of the mission and learning more of their activities.

Another man was also on his way to Portsmouth.

Colonel Rothery had kept in touch with Pastor Cookson since their initial correspondence, and upon hearing that the pastor had founded the mission, he was eager to join.

O'Neill was disappointed to find that the mission was located in cheap rooms near the docks, and that the only member was its founder, Pastor Cookson, who did not know very much about the legalities of transportation. On the other hand, Patrick realised that the old man's work with the prisoners was important, and applauded his humanitarian endeavours.

While he was there, Colonel Rothery arrived on the doorstep.

He was taken aback to find only two members there, but O'Neill, amused by the situation, invited him to become the third member of the mission.

'We'll place you on the committee right off, Colonel,' he grinned. 'Since we both have sons over there, wouldn't you say we're entitled?'

Two days later a transport ship was in port and the pastor obtained permission to take his two 'assistants' on board with him, after presenting the captain with a box of fresh fruit provided by Rothery.

Afterwards, the pastor was sorry that he'd offered to show them the prisoners' quarters aboard ship. He'd almost taken the conditions for granted by now, concentrating his efforts on the individual in the short time available to him, but the two men, fathers of transported prisoners, were shattered by what they saw, shocked to have seen first hand what physical misery and psychological degradation their sons must have experienced.

O'Neill, backed by the colonel, turned his rage on the captain of the ship, who promptly had both men put ashore, still shouting their outrage.

They retired to a pub, where they managed to calm down after a few whiskies, comforted by the knowledge that their sons, at least, had survived the ordeal, since both had now received letters from Hobart Town. But from that experience came a resolution to give this kindly clergyman the financial support he obviously needed. Within days they had moved him to comfortable rooms near the offices of the East India Company, and established a trust with R.J. Cookson, Minister of Religion, as the sole beneficiary.

Before they departed, they all promised to keep in touch, and the pastor presented his benefactors with small ship's bells engraved with the name of the Portsmouth Mission for the Welfare of Prison Transportees.

And so life goes on, the old man thought sadly, trudging back to his new home. Everyone had to carry on with their own affairs. The faces of the exiles must dim over the years. Most of them would never see their families again, despite magistrates blithely handing out sentences of seven, ten or fifteen years in Van Diemen's Land ... sentences, taken at face value by their unsuspecting recipients, that gave no indication of how the prisoner might be repatriated when that time expired. He never had the heart to pass on that extra piece of information to families that contacted him from all corners of the British Isles.

All he could do was offer solace and pray for them.

It was snowing hard when he reached his door, and he let himself in, glad that he'd had the foresight to set a fire.

That night, as a storm raged over Portsmouth and another transport ship struggled out into the Atlantic, he thought of those lads ... Angus McLeod and the Colonel's son Willem, and young Matt O'Neill and his cousin Sean Shanahan ... and a sense of foreboding overcame him. He tried to shake it off by reading his bible aloud, but when the candle fluttered out, he found himself weeping.

'May the good Lord bless and keep them,' he cried into the darkness.

CHAPTER TWO

1837

Forty men in threadbare shirts and half-mast trousers shuffled along the busy road towards the stockade, their chains slithering and jingling in the dust, their shoulders bowed from exhaustion. A brown dog dived out from the shade of a stoop to snap at them, stopped mid-snarl, sensing this might not be a good idea, and slid back into his hollow, tongue lolling impassively. A horseman in a tweed jacket and a tall hat reined his mount about to avoid them, and two cheeky molls from the Female Factory waggled their behinds in greeting, or maybe fellowship, since they too were of the convict class, but no one else seemed to notice them. Convict road gangs were a familiar sight in these parts.

'What would you give for a handful of them dollies?' Freddy Hines muttered through closed lips.

'Not enough, the big one's Bobbee Rich,' the man behind him grunted, and next in line, Angus McLeod lowered his head even further to steal a backward glance at the woman known to be a holy terror. The steel tip of a whip seared across his tall, spare frame as the guard, on horseback, shouted: 'No talking!'

Angus didn't falter. He did not flinch. So great was his hatred of this place, these people, that in his mind he fought them all the way, every second dedicated to rebellion. Five years now he'd been in Hobart Town, enduring the ferocious summers and the cruel winters with those perishing winds hauling up from the Antarctic. It still astonished him to think that he'd been shipped from a prison in Glasgow and thrown into another prison on the other side of the world, in another hemisphere, without any notice to his family, and without the right to appeal. Exiled along with thousands of other prisoners, whose offences ranged from disobedience as a servant to criminal activities. His own crime, he pondered as he trudged along, could be put down to plain stupidity, now that he'd had more than enough time to think about it … youthful stupidity, nineteen and thinking he was a match for the bosses.

'Out of your bloody head,' Pa had yelled at him when he had joined the Workers' Party, though he had only done it for a bit of a tease, letting Joe Kirkham talk him into it. But Joe was a great talker, and the more Angus heard him sounding off outside the foundry gates, the more he'd come to think there was something in his rantings after all – that they could get more pay, better conditions and all that if they stuck together and ganged up on the bosses. Made sense to Angus McLeod. Sounded simple enough.

To simpletons, that is, he snorted as the road gang came to a stop outside a guardhouse, and two former convicts, now employed as jailers, emerged to search them before admitting them to the prison. A prison of our own making, he thought bitterly as the gates closed behind them and their chains were removed. He bent down to rub his callused ankles and looked about him.

Angus had been among the gangs of convicts who had cleared the land beyond the grim walls of the Female Factory – the prison for women and young girls – and then were put to work building cell blocks and an administration centre surrounded by a high timber fence. This was known as the Stockade, as opposed to the sombre brick Penitentiary closer to the docks. While their new living quarters were an improvement on life in that murderous overcrowded prison, their lives were still harsh. Nowadays Angus was on another road gang, working further inland, so far from the Stockade that he and his mates hoped to be reclassified and thus avoid the long marches to and from their work sites. They were Class 2 prisoners, which meant they worked in chains but were free of them in the Stockade. Class 3 men were never free of the chains; they were linked to other prisoners or wore a ball and chain on their ankles. Class 1, men with better behavioural records, were still herded in gangs but were allowed to live in huts under supervision. Top of the heap were ticket-of-leave men, who had achieved independent status, like parolees.

But anyways, he reminded himself, anyways ... after two years in the North Glasgow Workers' Party, he'd been up there spruiking with the best of them, demanding their rights, confronting bosses, leading a strike that failed, smashing the foundry windows! He'd had two years of wildly exciting times that had made him believe he really could bring some relief to the desperately poor working families ... two years that had cost him three months on a vile transport ship, hell on the high seas, and permanent exile to this mongrel of a place.

Permanent my arse, the Scot told himself. I'll be back. You wait and see, you bastards. But first I've got to get that ticket-of-leave. Then I can look to escape.

But the ticket-of-leave prize was hard to reach. Magistrates had the right to waive the incarceration sentence at any time, if the prisoner displayed remorse and had a record of good behaviour. Unfortunately, Angus was unable to even feign remorse, as many a cringing coward or clever fellow could do. If anything, he was just as outspoken in this arena, forever lodging complaints about the treatment of prisoners and the trampling of their rights.

Angus McLeod might have won the admiration of his fellow prisoners for having the guts to speak up and wear the subsequent punishments, but they preferred to stay clear of him for fear of becoming embroiled in his trouble-stirring. The guards, who normally had as much interest in the thousands of convicts who came through their gates as they would in the flocks of sheep that poured through the town from the ships, regarded him as a big-mouth, a nuisance ... a rare one who had to be taught to conform.

His ever-growing notoriety did not augur well for Angus's plans to escape, so it was about this time – such a long, weary time since he'd been shoved ashore in Hobart and looked up at that great Mount Wellington towering over the newcomers like a scowling high priest – that he decided he'd better try to wise up. It'd be hard, though, hard to watch the violence, the endless floggings, the weak bodies broken down by long toil in the coal mines and the quarries, or by breaking rocks for road fill, and say nought. And harder still to grasp that no pity was forthcoming from the free settlers, or even paroled convicts, for the plight of parched men forced to toil in chains right in front of them. It was as if the whole population had been mesmerised into believing that cruelty to prisoners was normal, that they should be treated like beasts ... though not beasts of burden, he reminded himself. Those were worth money. Convicts were worthless, a blight on the community. And yet, whose expertise designed and built their government offices and storehouses and their roads and wharves? Who made the bricks? The worthless convicts, many of them lifers whose only relief was madness. Oh yes, he nodded to himself. Everyone knew about the madhouse, hidden at the rear of the prison barracks.

Angus sighed. He had to stop fuming. Get in with some of the guards. But how? He wasn't sure, but he'd begin watching them more carefully and see what could be done.

Chores completed, they filed into the refectory for their 'Hard Labour Diet' of a pint of soup, beef and vegetable stew, it being Monday, and a bun and a lump of cheese. Every convict was aware of his daily ration entitlements in this world of officialdom, and so they would create a din if they were being short-changed in the food department, but then they also had to suffer the

57

vagaries of convict cooks who could ruin the freshest of food, grown by their colleagues who worked in agriculture. Even Angus had to admit, to himself alone, that sometimes when competent cooks found their way into this kitchen, he'd had better meals here than he'd ever seen at home.

After dinner, he joined others sitting dozing against the wall in the exercise yard.

'You! McLeod!'

Through the fog of exhaustion he heard the shout, and thought it was his father's voice, back in their cramped cottage. He groaned his resentment at being disturbed.

A cosh caught him below the ear.

'Stand up when I speak to you!' the guard, Jim Maunder, shouted at him. 'You and Hines come with me. We're low on firewood.'

'I can't go choppin' wood with my busted hand,' Hines complained. 'Look at it. I hurt it out there today, twisted it lifting them bloody rocks.'

His hand was swollen but Maunder was unimpressed. 'I said come with me. Now!'

'He won't be much help,' Angus said. 'Get someone else.'

'All right, you! Chop the lot on your own.' Maunder laughed. 'I want enough for the kitchen and the guardroom and the gatehouse for the week! Sure you don't need Hines?'

Angus stood straight and looked him in the eye. He was stuck with the job anyway, so he wasn't about to let a nasty little ferret like Maunder get the better of him.

'No!' he said defiantly. 'No need.'

Clearing away virgin bush and forests from

58

sunup to sundown six days a week had made Angus an expert axeman; nevertheless, as Maunder lit the lantern in the woodyard and set him to work, he bumbled about for a start. After watching his inept performance for a few minutes, Maunder laughed and left him to it. With his long arms and rippling muscles he flew through the chore. He remembered how he'd been a thin and sickly mess when he'd first arrived at the Hobart docks after months of seasickness on the transport ship. He'd been certain he would die, just drop dead in the street, he was so weak, but he'd held on, and now he marvelled at the transformation. He spat into his hands, rubbed them together and picked up the axe again.

Eventually the work was done and a guard escorted him through to the cell he shared with three other men, including Freddy Hines.

'I got this for you,' Freddy said, 'an extra bit of cheese.'

Angus nodded and fell down on his bunk, too tired to eat it yet.

In his corner, 'Singer' Forbes hummed a tune, the words well known to his companions:

Bye and bye I'll break my chains
And into the woods I'll go
I'll shoot the tyrants one and all
And hunt the floggers down...

As the chorus went round, Angus stuffed the cheese in his mouth. He knew all of the banned convict ballads. They were outrageous, defiant and wildly contemptuous of authority ... he wished he'd known them in Glasgow, to help with the fight. Because they did help morale. He recalled the first flogging he'd endured, for absconding from the forest-clearing gang. Fifty lashes, which had been a screaming shock to his bony back! While he was bound to the triangle in the Penitentiary yard, with the whip tearing at his freckled skin, the other prisoners, forced to watch his punishment, began to sing a song that to Angus had the lilt of a sea shanty. But then the guards had set upon the singers, bashing them fiercely and shouting at them to stop. They did stop, instantaneously, mid-beat, and that in itself was an act of contempt, the sudden silence a jeer! It was then Angus realised that the singing was in fact support from his new comrades, and he marvelled, wishing Joe Kirkham could hear it.

'We're getting reassigned tomorrow,' Freddy interrupted his thoughts.

'To what?' Angus asked wearily. 'Replacin' bullocks on the wool wagons?'

'Ah, you never know,' Freddy said. 'Lady Franklin might need dance partners. I'd be good at that, give her a twirl and a poke.'

'From a ladder, my son,' the fourth cellmate, Flo Quinlan, put in. 'She'd be making two of you.'

James Quinlan was an Irishman who'd been transported for stealing a donkey from a Limerick magistrate. 'She was a lovely little donkey,' he'd tell people. 'Her name was Flo and that wretch treated her unkind, so I acquired her and gave her to me dear old granny. The magistrate gave me seven years and doubled it when I never would

60

tell him where his donkey was sheltered.'

He told the story so often, with so many variations, that no one knew whether or not it was true, but the name Flo had stuck. It was said that he was a more accomplished horse thief.

All four men in this cell were in their twenties. Singer the eldest, nearing thirty, had been given ten years for larceny. He had a fine tenor voice, and on rare occasions he was permitted to sing for the entertainment of fellow prisoners, but he'd flatly refused to sing for anyone else. Not officers, not even important visitors. As a result he'd suffered beatings and weeks on the treadmill, but he stayed resolute, and though Singer thought nothing of it, Angus was impressed. As for Freddy, he'd been an inveterate poacher, caught so many times he'd been sent out for life. Freddy was also an expert pickpocket, and liked to show off his tricks among his mates, every so often bringing them scraps of food and tobacco.

'I reckon my hand is swelling up more,' he said plaintively.

'And by God wouldn't that be a crime,' Singer said, 'for Freddy's golden hand to be swelling. Get you to rest and we'll have a look at it in the light of day.'

Someone further down the stone corridor began to scream, and in the pitch darkness of the cells such sudden utterances still made Angus shudder, but voices yelled abuse and quiet returned. Though there were guards on duty, no one went to investigate.

In the morning, it was found the fellow had cut off four of his toes with a piece of tin and was barely alive from loss of blood.

Reassignment. They were all wearing the leg-irons again as they shambled over to the administration block to present themselves before a clerk whose job it was to make sure that prison records were kept up to date, and possibly to refer the prisoner to a magistrate for a change in status. Freddy was ahead of Angus, complaining of his injured hand, so he was sent to the medical office and ordered to return to the line directly afterwards.

'Why do I have to line up again?' he complained. 'Why can't you tick me off here and now?'

A trooper used the butt of his rifle to shove him on as Angus stepped up.

'You again, McLeod?' the clerk sighed.

'I need a new jacket, this one's falling off my back.'

The trooper spoke up. 'We've got a box of clown jackets here, nothing else.'

The clerk grinned. 'You can have one of them.'

'No,' Angus growled. Those jackets were of the same rough cloth as all the other convicts' clothing, but they were yellow one side and black the other, and they were issued to lifers.

'I see'd you bought yourself another flogging this month, McLeod,' the clerk said cheerfully. 'You'd better watch out, you'll be headed for the treadmill again.'

'No I won't,' Angus said. He'd already made up his mind never to mount a treadmill again. It was demeaning and mindless work, fit only for beasts. 'I'm entitled to lighter duties now. I've been on the roads too long.'

'You'll go where you're sent.'

The clerk chortled as Singer approached.

'You still here, Forbes?' he said as he rattled through the files, searching for Singer's papers. 'I would have said you'd be in Port Arthur by this. It's made for scum like you.'

'Then recommend me if you like!' Singer said boldly, and hearing this as he moved away, Angus stiffened.

'God Almighty,' he muttered, 'he's in a reckless mood this morning.'

A guard overheard him. 'Nah, he's safe. We need thirty of you lads for carrying. Everyone is short of workers today.'

'Then they'll have to transport more innocents, won't they?' Angus snapped, and the guard pushed him on.

Outside, he and Singer were chained into a gang of thirty men and marched away to a new building site. A large sandstone warehouse was almost complete. The workers were ready for the wooden shingles to go on, so the carriers were sent back down the hill for about half a mile, to sheds that housed building supplies.

The chains and irons were removed for this job, and every man was given a heavy bundle of shingles to carry. As usual, a runner took up position in the lead, with a much lighter load, and set the pace. The prisoners began running in line after him, but the pace was too fast and the loads too heavy. Within minutes they had dropped to a walk, deliberately staying in rank to make a point.

The mounted guards raced alongside, slashing at them with whips to make them keep up, but as one, the gang refused, and marched steadily ahead. By the time they reached the building site, where the runner waited, two men had been knocked down and almost trampled by the horses and others, like Angus, had suffered cuts across their faces. The workmen on the building site watched nervously as the shingles were dropped but dared not become involved.

On the return journey the carriers raced downhill, but back at the sheds they refused the detail.

'Lighter loads or slower pace,' Angus shouted at an officer who'd ridden down to investigate the trouble.

'Watch that feller,' Singer warned. 'He'll put the screws on you faster than an undertaker.'

But it was too late. The officer called: 'Very well. We'll compromise. Lighter loads, but you'll run fast, or you'll be fasting until the morrow.' He grinned at his pun. 'As for you, mister,' he said, pointing his whip at Angus, 'you run in irons, or they all get to fast.'

'Told you,' Singer said. 'That's Lieutenant Flood.'

'I'll run,' Angus called, wondering what had happened to his plan to keep his mouth shut.

'Right, take his number and get the irons on,' Flood instructed a guard. 'Then enter the punishment detail in the day log.'

He stood back to watch proceedings as Angus was handed a heavy bundle of shingles.

'Too heavy?' he asked with a sly grin.

Angus looked at the cold blue eyes and the thin lips under a dark moustache, weighing up his response. Affirmative would be construed as complaint; a nay as bravado.

'Could be, with the irons,' he said mildly.

'But one could try, you stinking slob, so start running.'

He couldn't run, he could only scramble, falling every so often on steeper spots when it was more a question of balance, with the wooden shingles in his arms, than making fast progress, but eventually he made it, with the elbows torn out of his already ragged jacket.

When they returned, the officer had left, probably bored with the scene, and Angus's irons were removed so that he could join the others running uphill with lighter loads.

Just another day, he fumed, when they had delivered all the shingles and were redirected by their guards to work with another road gang down by the river.

As they approached, Angus looked longingly at the beautifully clear waters of the Derwent and yearned to be able to dive in. Growing up around the Glasgow wharves, he and his mates were forever diving into the chilly waters of the Clyde, and were known as the fish boys, since his pa claimed they could swim like fish. And that reminded him, he still hadn't heard from his parents, though he'd managed to write several letters over the years. Still, he consoled himself, it'll probably take half a year for letters to get to Glasgow and another half for an answer to find me. On the other hand, there were rumours that letters to prisoners were often dumped by the bosses to maintain order. As if news from home might upset or excite the recipients. Angus wouldn't put it past them.

That evening, as he slumped in the exercise yard as usual, Angus was thinking about that officer. He called to Singer: 'Who's Lieutenant Flood when he's at home?'

'Ah, Smirking Tom! A real ladies' man he likes to think. Mean as a cut snake. He hangs about the Governor's set, always pushing for promotion.'

'Will he get it?'

'Ah yes, more's the shame. He's related to old Warboy.'

Freddy intervened. 'No he's not, he's only a neighbour. I heard Warboy's son and his family have landed on the farm, to help the old boy along. Some say they come from as far away as Mexico, and can't speak a word of English.'

'Ah, God love 'em.' Singer grinned and launched into one of his ditties:

They come they go, the tyrant class,
And look on us like foe,
But we'll be here when they pass on
And give their sons the arse.

Others picked up the tune and joined in, adding their own versions, until guards ran out to put a stop to the obviously rebellious songs with cosh and whip, but as usual the singing stopped in mid-air and the guards were left to retreat across the dead quiet yard that was suddenly alive with menace.

Angus was always fascinated by this trick, so

often played on guards who could not report silence as an offence, but now he pondered Singer's song. It was well known that farmers and businessmen came to this island to make their fortunes with government subsidies, cheap land and dirt-cheap labour – convicts. Few of them treated their workers fairly or even humanely. Yet barely any of the convicts would be returning to England, whether they were lifers or not. No consideration had been given as to how trans-ported felons were expected to return home, so they stayed, freed or paroled – free to marry and bring up their own families. They could marry convict women or free settlers, and make a life for themselves. What then? Angus thought. Would a whole generation, and generations after them, grow up suspicious, even contemptuous, of authority? It sounded so interesting a concept, he almost wished he could stay on and see what hap-pened. But Angus McLeod would not be lingering on this island; once he was freed he would take a job anywhere until he'd saved enough to go home to Glasgow, to his ma and pa. And in truth, Angus yearned to see old Glasgow again. He was heartily sick of the newness here, the pomposity of it all, as if they could make this place anywhere near as good as the great cities of Britain.

That was his plan, anyways, he thought as the bell rang, ordering them to their cells for the night. That was the plan.

CHAPTER THREE

Old Warboy's son Jubal did not come from Mexico; he came from Jamaica, and he spoke English well, though ponderously, in keeping with his self-proclaimed status as a gentleman of leisure.

Both of Barnaby Warboy's sons had been born on their mother's sugar cane plantation in Jamaica; their mother's plantation it was, because her father hated and mistrusted Barnaby Warboy, though Barnaby was a good and kindly man. He left the plantation to his daughter in his will, with strict instructions that upon her death it was to go to their elder son, Harold.

Barnaby didn't mind the arrangement; he simply took over the management and went on with living, but when she died, Harold, who was by this time, thirty years of age, laid claim to his inheritance in no uncertain terms.

'It's my place now, Father. This is my office. I run the plantation now, I'm the owner, and you have to understand that. You can remain on as an overseer if you wish, but I don't want you telling me how to run it. I won't brook any interference.'

'Ah yes,' Barnaby said, nodding his balding head. He climbed from his worn leather chair and walked to his office window to peer down at the busy work yards. He was a very large man, hands like feet, people used to say, but a quiet

68

fellow, which was why no one was surprised when he calmly accepted the situation.

'Ah yes,' he said again. 'It's your place now, isn't it? Well I suppose that ain't so bad. I can still keep my room, though, can't I?'

'Of course. You just don't have much to do any more. You can take it easy.'

'And what about Jubal?'

'He will have to earn his keep.'

Their father was well aware that Harold had encouraged his young brother to set his sights on the ministry, but the scheme failed. As Barnaby had expected, Jubal only lasted a few months at the New Orleans Academy of Theology before being assessed as 'entirely unsuited' for the religious life.

Barnaby had no quarrel with Harold's latest plan to make Jubal earn his keep.

'I don't suppose that's a bad thing,' he murmured.

'Glad you agree,' Harold said. 'It's my plantation. He'll have to mind that and knuckle down.'

Barnaby shrugged. He'd never been able to *make* Jubal complete any chores on the plantation without a barrage of grumbles, and even then, as he'd told his wife, Jubal was a 'born incompetent'. It occurred to him that maybe Harold could knock him into shape. Be firmer with him.

'All right then,' he said to Harold. 'Give me a few days to get the books in order, then we'll sit down here and I'll show you the works.'

'Righto, Father. Jolly good.'

Harold was relieved that the changeover was to proceed so smoothly. 'I told you so,' he said to his

69

wife. 'He's fifty-five now, going to seed. I've been thinking the job was too much for him for a long time...'

No one worried when Barnaby didn't come home that night, nor the following. A lady friend had a handsome cottage by the bay in Kingston, and he often stayed there for days on end.

Impatient to take control, Harold went searching for Barnaby, only to discover that he had left Jamaica – not just Kingston, but the island itself – without a word to anyone! He'd completed the sale of several properties in the town centre that he'd been negotiating for some time, closed his considerable bank accounts, and emptied the plantation coffers as well. Harold had his plantation, a heavily mortgaged plantation, and he never saw his father again.

The next few years were a serious struggle against bankruptcy until, history repeating itself, Harold's wife's parents came to the rescue. With a proviso.

By this time Jubal had married and had a daughter.

The in-laws put it plainly to Harold that they would assist him financially if Jubal and his family moved off the plantation. In other words, they refused to support a man who spent his days lazing about the plantation. And, it was whispered to Harold's wife, a man who had a penchant for very young girls. Black and white.

Jubal had to go.

So it was that the Jubal Warboys moved to another plantation, one owned and managed by his wife Millicent's father. Millicent was a wispy lady devoid of enthusiasms, who, it seemed, affected a sophisticated air of boredom but was in fact just very dim. There they stayed for ten years, until fate stepped in again. The plantation was sold and Millicent's father, sick of the sight of them, moved into Kingston, into a tastefully small house that had no room for relations.

'What's to become of us?' his son-in-law asked him and was met by these cruel words: 'Frankly, Jubal, I don't give a damn!'

After copious entreaties and letter-writing, Jubal landed a job as manager of a small sugar cane plantation near New Orleans, and there, with the bewildered assistance of Millicent and his daughter Penelope, he muddled along replacing profit with loss. But Jubal aspired to a wealthier world, and by dint of spending considerable plantation funds entertaining members of a sailing club, to his great joy he achieved membership. Some members were appalled that this fellow with his shoddy reputation should have slipped into their midst but there was nothing they could do. Mr Warboy might have been a soft and pudgy chap, but he had a hide of leather, so no unkind words or stares had the slightest effect on his swagger.

Some years later, a British frigate was in port. The commander, grateful to be ashore, made straight for the nearest sailing club for congenial company. While Jubal Warboy was not included in the congenial set, he was, somehow, introduced to the commander, who peered at him closely.

'Warboy! Warboy? Unusual name, sir! I met a Warboy in Van Diemen's Land. Jolly old chap, big fellow, bald as you, but not carrying as much avoirdupois, what? Any relation?'

'Was it Barnaby Warboy?'

'I believe so. Yes. He's a great pal of Sir John Franklin, the governor of Van Diemen's Land, who commanded frigates in the Mediterranean in his day. I served under John Franklin for many years! Imagine my surprise when we sailed up the Derwent to Hobart Town and found Franklin standing on the dock to welcome us. Small bloody world, what?'

'Indeed it is,' Jubal agreed politely. 'I do believe the Warboy fellow could be a distant relation.'

Jubal had no trouble extricating himself from the company, and once out of sight of the sailing club he held onto his hat and galloped home.

'Do stop talking so fast.' Millicent bagged her ears. 'I can't abide this fuss, you've got me all of a doodah. If you cannot address me with less frantic fanfare, then go away and put pen to paper.'

'Shut up and listen,' he shouted at her. 'I've found Barnaby!'

'Barnaby who?' she whispered, her features pained.

'My father, you dunce. My father! He's in Van Diemen's Land, moving in vice-regal circles!'

'Oh my heavens!' Millicent shrieked. 'Penn! Bring me the smelling salts before I expire.'

Her daughter came dashing in with the small moon-shaped bottle. It was empty, but she'd been asked for the bottle and here it was. She helped her mother back to the couch and waved the bottle under her nose, and Millicent recovered with a sigh. She was a thin woman and she liked to float about in layers of filmy georgettes and laces, in the belief that they gave her an ethereal appearance, though with her fair skin and fair hair they were inclined to make her look more faded than refined.

'I had a kitten called Barnaby,' Penn told them. 'It ran away.'

'No it didn't,' her mother snorted, 'you dropped it in the well. Now go away and sit in the kitchen.'

'Now tell me, Jubal, where is this place?' She fluttered her fair eyelashes and brushed tightly tonged curls away from her face.

'It's an island to the south of the continent of Australis,' he informed her. 'A long way away.'

Jubal was sweating feverishly. He sank into a chair, mopped his brow, and then made a pronouncement: 'I have decided it behooves me to forgive Barnaby Warboy. After all, Harold treated him almost as badly as he treated me. Having come to that conclusion, it would be an act of mercy for us to pay the old gentleman a visit. His self-imposed exile can be terminated if I put my mind to it.'

In the bar at the sailing club, near to closing time, he made an important pronouncement, advising one and all that he would have to withdraw his membership as he had decided to go and work among the Aborigines of the Pacific.

'Life in this kind clime is too comfortable for a man of integrity,' he told the members. 'It is time I put my shoulder to the wheel and took God's message to the heathens.'

'There's a leper colony in the south Pacific,' a

retired mariner told him. 'Are you going there?'

Jubal jumped in fright, but he covered by turning to the speaker, hand to brow. 'Before I go, I had to come here to thank all of you esteemed gentlemen for allowing me your company. I shall miss you, dear friends, but I shall never forget you in my prayers.'

He concluded by brushing aside a tear, and was rewarded with a rousing cheer and a passing around of the hat to send him on his way. Since many members of this exclusive New Orleans club were princes in banking circles, the hat was soon filled with substantial banknotes, more than enough to take a gentleman and his family into the southern oceans.

They took a ship firstly to Rio de Janeiro, and from there south around the Horn, a truly hideous voyage, the turbulent seas at the foot of the Americas dreaded by even the most experienced sailors. As their ship battled raging storms trying to make for the Pacific Ocean, it tossed and fell violently and passengers screamed in terror, but the captain and crew were too busy trying to keep their ship afloat to care about their travails. One man broke his leg, a woman had a heart attack. No meals were served, not only because of the difficulties but because most of the passengers and a few crew were seriously seasick. Fortunately Jubal found he had a stomach of cement, as a steward remarked – one that stayed firm regardless of the assaults on it by this pitching ship – and so he remained well, struggling from wife to daughter.

Millicent's vomiting and anguished complaints

disgusted him, so he fled from his cabin to Penn's side, finding her more terrorized than seasick, certain that this flimsy ship would lose the battle against the massive winds and seas. He hushed her and comforted her through the night and for the few days that it took for the Pacific to offer relative calm, and for the ship to begin to return to normal routines. When he did come back to their cabin, it stank so badly he ordered his wife to be taken up on deck, despite her protests, and instructed the stewards to scrub and air the room to make it habitable again.

As it happened, Millicent's exposure to fresh air and shy sunlight began her cure, and Penn stayed by her side to care for her every minute of the day from then on, earning smiles from the other passengers for being the dutiful daughter, so rare, they thought, in these modern times.

Eventually they landed in the quietly charming port of Melbourne where Millicent spent five shillings of their meagre funds on a navy-blue dress for Penn.

Jubal was furious. 'It's ugly. Take it back. It's too old for Penn.'

'It is not. She's nearly seventeen, she can't wear ankle-length skirts any more. She has to dress like a lady.'

They stayed in the Victorian port for two days before setting off, yet again, on a small rattling coastal ship heading south – but, as he assured his wife, 'not nearly as far south as Cape Horn, so don't worry'.

He was unaware that Bass Strait, which they crossed before heading down the east coast of

Van Diemen's Land, had a very nasty reputation as a cemetery for shipwrecks, but the weather held, the seas behaved and they sailed happily, if apprehensively, into the fine Derwent river and watched from the deck as the ship docked before a row of sandstone warehouses in Hobart Town.

'It's not a bit like Jamaica,' Millicent said, 'and there's snow on the top of that mountain. I hope it's not a cold place; this wind has a chill in it.'

'I think it's pretty,' Penn said.

Jubal said nothing. The weather was of no interest to him. He disagreed with her – this place *was* like the Jamaica ports, with the stink of whaling boats and sealers pervading the air, and the usual ruffians jostling cargo on the busy docks. Except there were no blacks. He found that surprising. But his first priority was to figure out how to locate Barnaby. He supposed he should simply ask about. It looked like a miniature town from here, creeping up into the foothills below a massive mountain that seemed out of all proportion to the landscape.

Barnaby Warboy loved Van Diemen's Land. He loved the diversity of climate, the extremes of heat and cold; he claimed the seasons were God-given, rejuvenating, unlike his former home, Jamaica, which he now dismissed as overheated and soul-sucking. He loved the strange fauna too of the antipodean island, found it all so fascinating that, were it not for his friendship with the Governor, the bureaucrats would have lowered the boom on him by this. It was Barnaby who had called for a ban on the hunting of these delightful creatures.

When he left Jamaica, he had no particular plan in mind, he simply needed to get as far away from his sons as he could, and as soon as possible; hence he boarded a ship bound for Boston. From there he moved on to Bermuda, where he dallied awhile with a wealthy widow before recalling a juvenile ambition to see the Tower of London and its gruesome exhibits, which he found rather tame after all. He was a polite man, always neatly attired, and despite his hefty frame he was an excellent dancer. The word soon went around feminine circles and so he did not lack for invitations, through which he made many worthwhile friends. He travelled about Europe, went on to stay with friends in Bombay and from there joined the good ship *Adonis* on a voyage to Van Diemen's Land, intending to complete his journey around the world by sailing on to the Americas.

By the time they glimpsed the south-west point of the Australian continent, however, Barnaby had become very depressed. He was tiring of what he called his gypsy life, bored with acquaintances no matter how amusing and cordial, and sick to death of this damned overcrowded ship. He hated his cabin, with its thin walls that were no refuge from the conceits and contrariness of the other men and women in the first-class section. Within the first week, when he could bear it no longer, he approached the captain with his complaints.

'Surely you could ask the passengers to quieten down? It's like living in a madhouse, with those shrill wives in First and the perpetual song and dance going on below decks.'

'I'm sorry, Mr Warboy, I wish I could. It really

77

is best to let people have sway, to try to enjoy themselves while they can. Boredom will soon set in, and with that, when people don't know how to occupy themselves, moodiness can cause difficulties.'

He was right. With no port to look forward to before their final destination, some of the passengers began to turn in on themselves, arguing, criticising, blaming, even fighting, while others desperately tried to keep the peace. From below, the songs lost their vigour, sighs and cries replaced the thump of lively jigs, and for that, at least, the unsympathetic Mr Warboy was grateful.

When they did sight Van Diemen's Land, it was as though a miracle had occurred. People gathered on the deck, stunned, almost disbelieving.

'They said we were here weeks ago when we first sighted land,' a woman complained. 'And 'twas not at all. How do they know they're right this time?'

'If they're not, I'm getting off and walking,' a wag said.

'It's only forests,' said the woman. 'All we've seen for miles is forests. No fields and no towns. What sort of a place is this?'

Few liked to respond that 'a prison' came to mind, since they were in the presence of military personnel and several warders, all on their way to report for duty, but the emigrant settlers were cheered by the sight of the lush green landscape. They'd been told that this island, halfway around the world and way down at the bottom of the globe, boasted countryside as green and fertile as England, and there was a possibility now that they'd been told true.

'At last! At long bloody last!' Barnaby groaned as the ship turned into the estuary of a wide river called the Derwent, en route to the capital of the colony, but even now, after all the months at sea, nature had to drag out these last days by introducing them to a furnace of a hot February day, without a breath of wind.

Confused, these northern hemisphere emigrants consulted their diaries to assure themselves that this was indeed February, and sat listlessly on the decks, fanning themselves with their hats. Some young lads, immune to the temperature, watched the shores in excitement and trepidation, in the hope that they might be attacked by savages hidden in those forests, or at the very least wild animals. Overhead a flock of curious white cockatoos swooped and screeched, and an elderly woman, taking fright, fell to the deck in a faint. Her voluminous black dress, so suddenly upended, revealed a flash of bare buttocks, and Barnaby grinned, temporarily rescued from a bout of melancholy by this spot of burlesque.

He walked over to the rails and examined the vegetation on the shores to pass the time, interested to see stands of magnificent trees and a plethora of strange ferns that constituted the undergrowth. There was smoke in the air, with a very different smell, an astringent tang, he mused. He looked up to the mountain that dominated the area but could see no sign of fire, so he strolled around to the other side of the ship. There, passengers crowded the rails to watch a huge forest fire burning only a short distance from the

79

river bank. But then the sails took heed of gusts of wind and the ship began to glide out of the doldrums.

Not so Barnaby Warboy, aged fifty-seven in this year of the Lord 1827, who felt plain weary. Had this ship been proceeding home on the Great Southern Route via the Americas, he would have stayed aboard, but instead it was returning to England the way it had come. That was disappointing, but he consoled himself that it was possible to take ship from here to Sydney and then sail across to Los Angeles, from where it would be easy to head for home. For Jamaica. Well, perhaps not Jamaica... So where? The answer to the inevitable question was causing him indigestion as well as a bout of loneliness.

Hobart was a busy little port, he mused as he strode ashore, ignoring the bustle and excitation created by his fellow passengers; not unlike Kingston with its colonial ring, except for the dry heat and the total lack of black faces. Knowing that this was Aborigine country, Barnaby had taken it for granted that the wharf labourers would be blacks, but the only natives he saw were two young girls peering shyly from behind a shed. He approached a gentleman and asked where he might find a porter, and was directed to a fellow in a suit of yellow felted cloth, arrow-marked as for government property. He remembered that jailbirds back home were identified by that arrow, and only then did he realise that most of the men working on the wharves were convicts.

Startled, he approached one of them warily. 'Are you a porter?'

'If you like,' the man said cheerily. 'What do you want?'

'I need my effects taken to a hotel. Can you suggest one?'

The convict, a diminutive fellow with a cockney accent, looked at him. 'The George Inn for you, I'd say.'

'And where would that be?'

'In Davey Street. If you hang on I'll take you. Now, where's your sea chest?'

As he sweated up the street behind the porter and his loaded wheelbarrow, Barnaby muttered to himself that he'd better take some decent walks while he was here, to get some breath back after doing so little for so long.

The porter stopped, turning back. 'What did you say?'

'Nothing.'

'You all right? You look as if you're cooking. Why don't you sit on the bench there, in the shade. I'll come back for you.'

'Come back?'

'Yes, it's not far. I can drop your stuff and come back, I'll give you a ride on me barrer.'

Barnaby blinked. 'What? On your barrow? No! Certainly not.'

'Suit yourself.' The porter shrugged, and they set off again.

At the inn, a small two-storey sandstone building, Barnaby paid his porter the penny he requested, and was surprised when the fellow introduced himself.

'You're new here, mister, so if you need anyone,

just ask for me at the docks. The name's Bailey. I'll look after you.' He winked, tipping a tall battered hat. 'Keep you out of strife, like.'

Barnaby shuddered. 'Good day to you, Mr Bailey,' he allowed.

A barman in a striped apron came out to greet him. He introduced himself as Hugh Merritt, proud owner of the inn, called to a fellow nearby to bring in the gentleman's luggage and led him through a crowded bar room to a narrow staircase, which they negotiated along with Barnaby's sea chest.

Merritt was an affable fellow, though anxious to please.

'That porter,' Barnaby asked him. 'Is he a prisoner?'

'A convict? Yes. Assigned to the wharves.'

'And they can roam free?'

The innkeeper shrugged. 'Don't worry about them. If they misbehave they're back behind bars double-quick smart.' Then he added, 'If they're caught, that is.'

That remark hardly inspired confidence in his guest, but Merritt didn't seem to be concerned at having criminals running around the streets.

'We only have the three rooms up here for travellers,' he said, 'but the missus keeps them nice and clean.'

'So I noticed. A relief I must say, Mr Merritt.'

'Call me Hugh. If you're hungry any time, just go to the kitchen, the missus will look after you. She's a good cook.'

'Excellent!'

When he left, Barnaby sat by the open window

of the bedroom and contemplated his future. He supposed he could settle somewhere in America, but the options were so vast, the choice would be more of a lucky dip than serious consideration. Besides, he needed something to do; the travelling life had turned aimless and was eroding his sense of presence. He stared down at people in the street, and saw briskness of purpose in every face, be it rough seamen, women to market, military men, child beggars, or the convict workmen like Bailey.

Damn them, he thought, envying their niche. No matter how high-placed or lowly, all of these folk would be missed if they fell off the earth. Missed by someone, even if it were the law. Tired and depressed, he loosened his collar, removed his jacket and shoes and lay down on the bed, suddenly cheered by this almost forgotten comfort. No more sea swells, no more smells, and no more noisy passengers.

'I'm in heaven for the time being,' he consoled himself as he dozed off.

When he emerged from the hotel in the morning, Barnaby was wearing one of the new white suits he'd purchased in Bombay, with a blue-striped waistcoat and a blue silk cravat with a diamond pin. He was sensibly prepared for the heat-threatening morning apart from a suitable hat. His own hatbox contained toppers and felts, but he needed something cooler, and as luck would have it, he came across a native selling hand-plaited straws. The very thing!

Walking stick in hand, to help him adjust to

solid ground again, he set off on a tour of the town. Many of the white-shuttered buildings looked familiar to him, and though all seemed quite new, the town itself had a ramshackle appearance due to the lack of any sense of order either in the standard of housing or among the general populace. There were no footpaths and he had to make his own way among roaming pedestrians and street sellers, ox carts and gigs, and horsemen who seemed to own the streets. Goats wandered about unheeded, munching on untidy tufts of grass, and a chain gang waited listlessly to allow a lorry laden with timber to pass by, on its way down to the harbour.

Barnaby, unfazed by what seemed to him to be an oversupply of convict types and poor women hanging about the streets, mingling with neatly attired residents calmly going about their affairs, trotted along peering into shops and other business premises. He circumnavigated a brick penitentiary and saw a small chapel with a side gate, where was posted a Notice of Execution, so he hurried on from there, marvelling at the constant ring of axe and shovel, until he found himself on the outskirts of the town.

Roads and buildings were under construction in all directions. He stopped to talk to an overseer at what appeared to be a new prison in the making, and was told that labour gangs could consist of three to four hundred convicts, so work stations like this one had to be provided in various districts to house them securely overnight.

The place still looked like a budding prison to Barnaby, rather than a work station, but he had no argument with the arrangements, so pressed on uphill where there was a splendid view of the river port. Eventually he found himself back in Davey Street, passing impressive military barracks guarded by red-coated sentries, so he made his way down toward the harbour. He explored an interesting area called Salamanca, where warehouses fronted the river, and a cool square to the rear seemed a popular haven for shoppers and loiterers like himself.

Several tables and chairs were placed outside a small pub for the benefit of customers, and Barnaby managed to procure one for himself, finding this a salubrious position in which to place himself and watch the world go by, a pot of cool ale in hand.

He was sitting quietly there when an entourage approached. A tribe of children were strolling along with three women, which in itself was not of any great interest to him, except that the woman in the centre of the group seemed to be attracting a lot of attention. She was a plumpish woman – no, pregnant, he corrected himself as they came closer – in a neat black dress with a white lace collar and cuffs, and a heart-shaped lace bonnet. All manner of people turned to stare at her, quite rudely, he thought, and some even called out to her. She looked rather shy but she did manage a slight wave of a gloved hand to acknowledge them, though she did not dally.

As the group progressed, the children clamouring for sweets from a vendor, the maid who had served his ale tapped him on the shoulder.

'That's the Governor's wife, sir, that's her with

her kids.'

Immediately Barnaby looked down, not wishing to be among the curious starers, but then the lady actually stopped and spoke to him.

'Why! Goodness me! It's Mr Warboy, isn't it?'

He stumbled to his feet. 'My dear lady, yes, indeed it is. Yes, Warboy it is,' he managed to say as he endeavoured to execute a bow with a chair in the way.

'And he doesn't remember me,' the Governor's wife said merrily. Surprised, Barnaby looked at her, then he gulped. 'Upon my word! Forgive me, my dear. Eliza Smith it is, her very self.'

'Not Smith any more,' she laughed. 'Don't you remember? I married Major George Arthur, who was stationed in Kingston at the time.'

'Oh Lord. So you did! But how wonderful to see you again.'

She turned to one of the women. 'This gentleman comes from Kingston too. Where I was born. I've known him all my life.'

She introduced him to the lady, a Mrs Flood, and sent the other woman on ahead with the children.

'What are you doing here, Mr Warboy?' she asked excitedly. 'How long have you been here? You must come to lunch one day. We've so much to talk about. I rarely see anyone from home. How are Harold and Jubal?'

'My dear Mrs Arthur, what a pleasure to see you again. The boys are well. Harold has taken over the plantation, so I'm clear to have a look around the world. I've come here from London. But have you been here all this time?'

'Oh no, we spent ten years in Belize. My husband was Governor there. Then we went to London and we were no sooner settled than he was appointed Lieutenant Governor of Van Diemen's Land. So here we are.'

'How very interesting. I only arrived here yesterday, but it seems an agreeable place.'

'Yesterday?' she cried. 'Only yesterday! Well you simply must dine with us this evening so we can see what we can do to make sure you enjoy your stay. It's fortunate that we don't have any other engagements this evening, so rare for us, so I do hope this fits in with your arrangements.'

Barnaby laughed. 'My dear lady, I don't have any arrangements at all and I should be delighted to accept your invitation.'

Government House was an unprepossessing, rambling building in Macquarie Street, above Sullivan's Cove, he discovered. It had a veranda along the front and extensive grounds. Barnaby came to know it well.

Sir George, a very formal fellow on most occasions, Barnaby found later, received him warmly on that first night. The three of them had an extremely pleasant time together, and the five lively children were brought in to meet him, which Barnaby considered a great honour.

He learned they'd been in Hobart for two years and were very happy with the appointment but decidedly unhappy with their living quarters.

'When we first arrived it was run-down and practically uninhabitable,' Eliza said. 'It was so dreadful we had to move out while the renovations were made. Sir George wanted to build a new, more appropriate Government House ... he even had the plans drawn up, didn't you, dear? But then he said there was a more urgent need for other public buildings. So we waited. And we still wait,' she added, wagging a finger at her husband in mock admonishment. Obviously the man could have improved matters with the stroke of a pen, but he placed duty over comfort.

Their Excellencies led very busy lives. Apart from his normal duties, the Governor hosted weekly dinner parties as well as balls and many other functions. Barnaby was invited to several of the formal dinners, but he much preferred their family get-togethers, and was even invited to a birthday party.

He was still staying at the hotel weeks later when he heard there was a berth available on a passenger ship bound for Sydney, but he passed that up because he was enjoying his stay in Hobart.

Sir George invited him, on a few occasions, to travel with him to some of the outlying villages, and gradually Barnaby came to know the settled parts of the island fairly well. So well, in fact, that one day when they were watching surveyors at work in the Derwent Valley, he remarked that he wouldn't mind owning some of that fine land.

'You ought to think seriously about it, Barnaby,' Sir George replied. 'This district would be ideal for farming, and you would be entitled to a substantial land grant if you were interested in settling here. But don't let me sway you. It's a big decision to resettle in a strange country, especially at your age. Won't you miss your family?'

There was always a possibility that Eliza would hear from her family connections that there was something odd about his disappearance from Jamaica, so he worded his response in the best light he could. 'No, I rather felt in the way there, with the young ones running the show now. I think it would be hugely interesting to start a farm from scratch in this area. It's the sort of interest I really need at my age. I'll give it some thought.'

He discussed the matter with his new friend Hugh Merritt at the George Inn.

'If you really want to do it and you can afford to hang on until your farm starts paying, you shouldn't turn your face from an opportunity like this, Mr Warboy, but make certain you choose land with water. This island can drink water like a sponge and dry out just as fast. I'd run sheep if I were you, and go in for market gardening as well, depending on the amount of land you can get. You'll be assigned convicts to work for you, and the Government supplies funds for their rations, so you'll be on a good thing.'

Barnaby was astonished when Sir George offered him a grant of a thousand acres, and sent one of his aides to assist him in choosing land and completing the necessary paperwork, and some weeks later the deed was done.

Eliza was delighted. 'Good for you, Barnaby! You won't be lonely here with us. Besides, there are many very eligible ladies who will look kindly in your direction, once they hear you've decided to stay.'

'I'm not ready for a new wife just yet.'

'That's what they all say,' Sir George smiled.

'But the ladies have other ideas.'

Within two years Barnaby was farming sheep, and oats, and the recommended market garden to supply his workforce. He built a white two-storey Georgian-style house with black shutters, and a circular drive in front. It was a gentleman's home, he told his friends, with a large bedroom and dressing room and an equally large sitting room upstairs, and downstairs a parlour, study and library and, on the other side, a drawing room and dining room. The kitchen and pantry and maid's quarters were connected to the house by a short walkway. All the rooms had fireplaces, and the windows were heavily draped to protect Barnaby against Van Diemen's harsh sun.

When the house was finished and furnished to his own taste, and an excellent (convict) cook called Dossie installed, Barnaby was a very happy man.

Folk teased him about taking a wife, but he had no inclination to do so. He struck up a friendship with a woman who lived with her daughter on Pinewoods Farm, just down the road – Josetta Harris, a handsome, forthright woman who let him know right from the start that she was not looking for a husband.

'It's right kind of you to call, Mr Warboy,' she said when he made his first neighbourly visit, with a gift of store-bought toffees. 'I find your company enjoyable, and you're welcome to come by again. You must know that being a single gentleman calling on me, you'll cause talk. Well, that doesn't bother me if it doesn't bother you,

I'm not one to care about such things, but I don't want you to waste your time on me, since I'm not in the market for courting, you understand.'

Barnaby grinned, finding her attitude flattering since he was near twice her age. 'One would never be wasting one's time in your company, Mrs Harris, and I'll abide by the rules. Any more?'

'Yes, this is my farm and I like it here. I don't want to be socialising about with local folks, if you get what I mean.'

'You prefer to keep to yourself?'

'Yes. And let folks do likewise.'

'What about the Foundation Day parade next Saturday? I was thinking you and your daughter might like to be my guests...'

'No thank you,' she said sternly.

'Then I shall have to call at a later date and tell you all about it,' he said mischievously.

'You're teasing me,' she said with a small smile. 'But we'll see.'

She did keep to herself, discouraging visitors, except Barnaby, and she even walked up to his house on occasion with her daughter Louise to have tea with him, and to borrow books from his growing library and make suggestions of what new titles he might order.

And of course there was talk. Because she was Barnaby's friend, Lady Arthur sent Mrs Harris invitations to Government House, but she always declined with a gracious note. The arrangement suited Barnaby well. It was nice, he felt, to have a lady friend, whose company he greatly enjoyed, without complications.

'She's very shy,' he told Eliza, but he felt there

was a mystery here. At first he'd thought she was a widow, but then she'd mentioned that her husband had been delayed in England, which had been a surprise to him. He'd no idea that there was a husband in the background, and rushed to apologise for his forwardness, but she'd brushed that aside in much the same way as she'd allowed him the information about the husband – without further discussion.

Barnaby's years as a new settler in Hobart were rewarding both personally and financially. The farm was doing well, though the first six months of dealing with truculent convicts had been incredibly difficult. He had to work hard himself to keep them in line without resorting to physical punishment as most employers did, and he tried hard to be patient with them. It hadn't taken him long to realise that no matter what he did, there would always be this 'them and us' attitude in the convict psyche, but if he could gain their respect, albeit grudging, he'd have a good chance of getting a decent day's work out of them, and almost be able to eliminate sabotage – a popular pastime in their ranks.

Three of his original farm workers were still with him, and three others were a lot less trouble when he promoted one of the originals, Sean Shanahan, to overseer. He was a good-looking young Irishman with thick black hair and steely blue eyes, and he had a presence about him that Barnaby recognised and utilised.

Shanahan proved to be a responsible overseer who gradually took most of the load off Barnaby's shoulders, while the farm began to run far more smoothly than before. At times Barnaby wondered how his overseer kept all the men on their best behaviour, since the Irishman was certainly no bully. But he had few complaints these days, so he chose not to look too closely for an answer.

For some time it had been rumoured that Sir George would be leaving the colony, and then Barnaby heard it was definite. After twelve years of diligence the Governor, to his great disappointment, was recalled, and Barnaby was deeply upset to see his friends depart for London. He missed them so much, Josetta began to worry about him.

'You've got too much time on your hands now,' she said. 'You ought to find something else to do, instead of moping about.'

He took her advice, and invested in an importing business with an acquaintance, Sam Pollard, who owned a general store in Elizabeth Street. They began by importing rum from Jamaica on Barnaby's recommendation, as well as other spirits, but since the duty on spirits proved exorbitant, they turned to soft furnishings. This time the investment proved successful and soon there was another Pollard store devoted entirely to curtains and chair coverings and other such materials for indoor decoration. Their stock was rather a mystery to Barnaby but he was delighted that Josetta loved the store and persuaded Sam to allow her discount for her purchases.

With the stores operating successfully, Barnaby came across a beautifully illustrated garden book and fell in love with it.

'I've always admired those English gardens,' he

told Shanahan. 'When I was in England it was my greatest joy to walk through the splendid gardens, all so beautifully kept. I had a hankering for something like that myself but wouldn't know where to start.'

'Seems to me sir, you'd start with land, and you've plenty of that. If you want a formal garden, get one, Mr Warboy. The lads will plant whatever you want.'

'I don't just want any old garden, though. They have to be designed. And you have to have the right plants, and seeds, and know where to put them,' Barnaby said dismally.

'Is that right? I never knew that. But I tell you what, leave it to me. We've got some clever trades-men here, thanks to the English Government; let me see who I can find to build your garden.'

Barnaby had been amazed when Sir George had told him that a couple of Hobart's qualified architects and several other leading lights in the town were former convicts, as were a goodly number of the colony's bureaucrats.

'Beats me that the place works at all, but it does,' he muttered to himself, and retreated to his study to try his hand at designing a magnificent garden.

As one of the favourites of the previous adminis-tration, Mr Warboy was soon to meet the new governor, His Excellency Sir John Franklin, and only a few days later, having met with vice-regal approval, he was invited to one of Lady Frank-lin's soirées. He found the lady more outgoing than Eliza, who had to measure her public duties against a succession of pregnancies; and very authoritative, having involved herself in public affairs right away, making great efforts to promote intellectual pursuits.

There was no way a landed gentleman like Barnaby could escape her ladyship's notice, and before long he was seconded to several of her committees, including the Library Support Society. He could count himself, eventually, as a friend of the Franklins, though not, as he'd had to insist to others, a personal friend, and he would never be induced to ask favours of them.

In the meantime, Shanahan had located a gardener who had been trained by masters at the Kew Botanic Gardens and who was now plucked from a Hobart road gang by the Irishman, who quietly intimated that his boss, the Governor's friend, required this man's expertise, and would not brook a refusal.

Duly, then, the man's status rose from Class 2 to Class 1. The clerks were thanked for their prompt attention to the written request from Mr Warboy with a gift of a side of lamb, and Shanahan escorted the assigned prisoner out to the farm.

His name was Zack Herring, and he was a nondescript man, aged thirty-one, with the not uncommon sour attitude towards his employer that irritated Barnaby.

'Herring will have to get that snarl off his face,' he told Shanahan, 'or he won't last long here, I don't care how clever he is. What did he do anyway?'

'Robbery. Stole a statue.'

'What did he want with the statue?'

'The records don't say. I heard it said that it was spoiling the garden he was making. Ruining the design, so to speak, so he took it away.'

'I see. I thought you were talking about a religious statue. Very well, bring him up to my study at five and I'll have a talk to him.'

Herring knew his business. Now of a more respectful frame of mind, he first enquired about the type of garden needed, and interpreted Barnaby's suggestions as being somewhere between a private park and a flower garden.

'Your trees and shrubs are the mainstay,' he explained, 'and they have to go in first.'

He looked at Barnaby's designs. 'Some of that could work, but you can't have oaks, they'll ruin the whole thing. Not enough room. You could have flowering trees, like cherries or camellias, any amount of flowering trees you could have. Then you put the flowerbeds round them and you work out paths and ornaments, but you got to get moving on your trees and shrubs now, while the winter holds...'

For the next ten minutes or so Barnaby could hardly get a word in as Herring warmed to his subject. 'You must have properly prepared shrubs, no point in planting a guinea shrub in a sixpenny hole either,' he warned. Then followed a recitation of early bulbs and the wide choice of herbaceous plants, until Barnaby called a halt.

'Thank you,' he said abruptly. 'I'll need you to draw me a suitable design, and list the requirements as well as cost, and bring it to me as soon as possible.'

'Then I'll need pen and paper. And somewhere

96

steady to work. No room in the hut we have to live in.'

Barnaby saw the scowl flicker and quickly remove itself, but he didn't react. Obviously the man wanted the job and knew he had to behave.

'Work in the kitchen,' he said curtly. 'Dossie will give you a pen and I'll give you a day to set out a plan for the four acres on the eastern side of the house. You may go now. Here, take some of these sheets of paper with you.'

Shanahan was delighted. He'd been hoping Zack would behave long enough to retain the assignment. He was known as a borderline case, and a wrong move would have seen him moved to the dreaded Port Arthur.

He had laughed when he saw Zack march up to the house for his appointment with the boss, hoping Mr Warboy didn't want statues of England's kings or queens in his garden, or they'd end up in the drink too.

Zack, of Irish descent, had been born and reared in London, and was well versed in the cruelty and injustices perpetrated on his forebears by the English landlords. Shanahan thought it was a mad move of Zack's to go throwing statues in the Thames, but that was his business. He thought it was even madder to refuse to work for Englishmen now, in retaliation for transporting him to the ends of the earth. Zack had been bitterly offended at the sentence, claiming it was his right to make a statement against royalty, whom he considered the root of evil and greed in the land. He'd protested loudly in court, which had had no effect on the judge except to lead him to stamp his file 'Political', along with the famous Frank Macnamara from County Clare and the lesser-known Scot, the socialist Angus McLeod.

'We're not singing the same songs,' Sean used to tell Zack when they'd shared a cell in the Penitentiary. 'I'm agin making slaves of us, and you're agin the King, but it's worthwhile to pull together.'

'Why should we?' Zack would argue. 'You don't give a damn about poor Ireland. You lived there, but you never lifted a finger to help the people.'

'Nor did you, me brave fella. I never noticed you rushing back to Dublin with a sword in your hand.'

'I did what I could.'

'And from here you can do nothing for the people of Ireland, but you can champion the underdog.'

'What are you talking about, you fool of a man?'

'I'm talking about us. We're all underdogs, oppressed by money and power. It's the rich who grind us down. Don't you see, it's the rich who starve the Irish, pay soldiers to shoot them down like dogs. It's all the same thing, Zack. You look around, half the mobs out here got exiled by the rich for stealin' a bit of food or a few shillings to keep clad.'

'Jesus, you've been bit by McLeod's bug. You have to calm down, matey. You're wound up tight like a clock.'

'Who says so?'

'I do. You've got a front about you, all hail fellow well met, but I know you and I can see you're still stewing over your cousin. You have to give over, he's gone, it was a terrible business, but–'

'But what? You think I should forget what they did to him?' Sean grated. 'Just don't go searching out trouble.'

'What sort of trouble?'

'Whatever it is you're up to. Whatever it is...'

Now that Zack Herring was established as a special gardener, on separate assignment from the ten workmen that Warboy was entitled to under the law, Shanahan set his plan in motion. He talked to Bailey, a cockney rogue who had served his time and stayed on in Hobart, hanging about the wharves or the town centre, looking for odd jobs to cover his operation as a forger.

'I want a certificate, like the one you've got, proclaiming that Joseph Murray–'

'Who's he?'

'Never you mind ... proclaiming that Joseph Murray has completed his sentence and is a free man. Can you do that for me?'

'Cost you ten bob.'

'What about a side of mutton and a bottle of white rum?'

'And a shillin'?'

'Don't get greedy, there's plenty more would do the job for half.'

'But not as good. The form has to be signed by a magistrate. Which name do you want? The same one what's on mine?'

'Yes. Magistrate Fallon's been moved out to Sorell township.'

Shanahan knew there was more to it than just getting the papers. Too many hopeful escapees were floating about on forged releases, but they lacked backup in the records. They couldn't simply go missing from assignments, even if farmers let them go. The farmer had to account for the number he employed to the inspectors who came to check. However, Sean planned to show the boss Joe Murray's forged papers. Warboy wouldn't know the difference, his eyesight wasn't the best, and so he would allow Joe to quit and return to civilian life. Four years too soon.

Only a few days ago Sean had met a Swedish seaman called Bengt in a pub and learned that his merchant ship *Marita* would be sailing direct to Chile after they'd completed repairs.

Chile! It was heaven sent! No ports of call to snare Joseph.

'Does your captain take passengers?'

'Legal passengers? I daresay, if they have the fare. But not too many want to go to Chile from here.'

'I know a man might be interested. He's served his time,' Sean lied. 'He's a tree man, got his papers and all. A merchantman'd be cheaper than a passenger ship, wouldn't it?'

Bengt nodded. 'Be sure he doesn't try to stow away, though. The captain's a hard man.'

'Never fear, all's well. I'll tell him to get down and book his passage.'

Sean left the pub, his face grim, though he was pleased that things were working out so well. One way and another this would be the third convict he'd sent to sea on forged papers, and that made him feel a little better. His first attempt in this business had been a calamity.

He walked quickly back to the horse and buggy he'd left in the shade behind the general store, and commenced his errands. He hated to think of the time, two years ago, that he and his cousin Matt had tried to escape the island by ship, but there it was again, his nightmare, his never-ending nightmare.

Matt had been apprehended in the town by police who'd challenged his papers. Desperate to make it to the port as scheduled, he'd tried to fight his way clear of them, wresting a cosh from a convict constable and striking him with it. He felled that one, but the other police soon subdued him, and Matt's bid for freedom had failed.

While I was safe, Sean recalled, waiting at the wharf for him, but he never came.

Sean had watched the ship sail, his freedom lost too, since he would not go without Matt. Without knowing what had become of him.

The dawn had been grey, soggy with rain, as Sean hid his own forged papers, slipped away from the docks and made for the hut that housed assigned convicts working on the Warboy farm. The plan had failed, but at least he'd made it back to his lawful abode. He hoped Matt had done the same.

Days later, though, the news was bad. The *Hobart Town Gazette* reported that a constable had sustained a broken shoulder as he was attempting to arrest an absconder, Matthew O'Neill. The convict was taken into custody and charges were laid.

Sean came back to the present and found himself standing by the buggy, sweating and feeling sick, hanging on to the side for fear he'd collapse. He dragged a rag from his pocket and wiped the sweat from his forehead, forcing himself to hum a tune, any tune, then to whistle, whistle a tune to buy time, so that he could pull himself together.

'Stand straight,' he muttered to himself. 'Stop thinking about this. Get on with what you have to do!'

It was the same every time he thought of Matt. Of the cruelty. Shaken, he strode into Pollard's General Store, half owned, he knew, by Mr Warboy, and handed over Dossie's list of requirements for her kitchen.

He no longer considered escape. That wasn't for him now. It was important to keep Matt's tormentors in his sights. Sometimes men came to him asking if they could help an escape, and he would give the same answer.

'Too dangerous, mate. There's no escaping. Just sit quiet and do your time. Life's not that bad here once you get a ticket-of-leave. Aim for that.'

But he would then begin investigating the man, in case he was a plant. And he'd consider ways and means. And occasionally, out of the blue, he would confide in the applicant that he was on his way if he wished to shake the dust of Van Diemen's Land off his boots. He himself had not actually given up on the dream of freedom when he'd done his duty by Matt, but he had no wish to return to the agonies of Ireland, where he'd be branded an escapee and run the risk of a shakedown or a tip-off to the traps. He rather thought Melbourne Town, across the strait from this prison island, might be his Utopia. A man could shake off this stain and turn respectable there, where few convicts dwelled.

'What about that bag of potatoes you've got on the tray?' Pollard asked him. 'Are you leaving that here?'

'No. Mr Warboy is donating it to the Female Factory.'

'Kind of him,' Pollard said. 'What brought that on?'

'Mrs Franklin gave the boss a heap of bulbs and cuttings for his new garden, and he wanted to pay something, so she said give the ladies up the road there some of his produce. So they get a few spuds.'

'I heard Lady Franklin is very kind to those women.'

Shanahan laughed. 'Talk's cheap. That's all she ever does. Says she's going to improve conditions, make their bloody prison habitable. Yesterday she gave them the same palaver and they gave her their bare bums.'

'Jehoshaphat! What happened then?'

'Nothing much. She bolted. They can't flog four hundred women, they'd start a war. The poor souls are starving, they're only demanding decent rations.'

'I don't think lifting their skirts at a lady will help.'

'No, but it cheered them up. Haven't you got a little spare grub for them?'

'Can't say I do,' Pollard said, and scowling,

103

Sean jumped up on to the buggy and flicked the whip at the horse. 'Get on now, my beauty, and leave the fat man to his store.'

He delivered the potatoes to the women, stole a few words in the laundry with a friend, Marie Cullen, who'd been sweet on Matt, and heard that Dr Roberts was attending to some sick inmates.

The yard of this so-called factory stank, but Sean dallied, finding a pail of water for his horse and examining its fetlock as though it might be lame. Though the women worked as laundresses and seamstresses, making the rough convict clothes, the warders ignored the insanitary conditions of the walled courtyards, and Sean hoped he could needle the doctor into lodging an official complaint.

As it turned out, his needling wasn't required. Roberts marched one of the male warders out with him, and shoved him into the disgusting overflowing outhouses, demanding they be emptied and cleaned or he'd report the situation to His Excellency himself.

'As medical officer for this area, I want it done by noon tomorrow, do you hear me?' he shouted, and Sean thought he could probably be heard at Battery Hill, such a voice the good doctor had.

After that confrontation, Roberts walked over to him. 'How are you, Shanahan?'

'In the pink you'd say, sir. I'm a farm overseer now, for Mr Warboy.'

'So I heard. Good chap, Warboy.'

'That he is. I was wondering, could you let me have a wad of writing paper and a pen, to write to my family?'

Roberts took out a handkerchief and covered his nose against the stench. 'I can't stand it here any longer, it's too foul. You're not planning to write any more letters to the Governor, are you? If it weren't for Mr Warboy's good graces you'd be locked up by this.'

'I have to write to my father. He'll be worried that I might go the way of his nephew.'

Roberts shook his head. 'Very well. Call in at my rooms on the way home and I'll give you some paper. I don't suppose you have any ink either?'

'Come to think of it now, I do not.'

Sean drove the buggy across the outskirts of the town to Battery Point, where the Doctor lived. He always tried to avoid the township itself so as to dodge the police, who took routine swings through taverns and bars to scoop up miscreants and anyone who might look like one. Though his papers were in order, he still felt a twinge of apprehension when confronted by the law. He wished he could be like Singer Forbes, who himself did the confronting and caused all manner of confusion.

'It doesn't help,' Dr Roberts had told Forbes as he stitched up the wound on his head after his last beating, 'to be aggravating them. Nor is anyone amused, so cut it out. I've better things to do than to be patching you up all the time.'

Sometimes, Sean mused, the Doc could be naïve. Because often Singer's aggravating conduct was a deliberate distraction to draw attention from some serious mischief afoot nearby. But then he was a good-hearted fellow, was the Doc, with a touch of the anarchist in him. He had made it very plain in his writings in local newspapers that many of the convicts in their midst should never have been transported, should never even have been jailed, since they'd only committed what should be termed misdemeanours, not serious crimes. 'These were,' he railed, 'but poor folks, up against power-hungry magistrates, little men with beetle brains who handed out shocking sentences for such sins as the theft of a little food, or a handkerchief, or disobedience as a servant, or as in one classic example, stealing a pair of boots from his own father.'

Roberts called these men and women, and even children, 'the luckless', and after reading his opinions and discovering that this man genuinely did try to ease their burden by contacting their families back home, and even assisting some of them to come out to Van Diemen's Land as settlers to be close to a loved one, Shanahan took a chance.

He asked Roberts if he could help with a little information here and there, in the cases of persons who were 'terrible homesick'.

The doctor was treating Shanahan at the time for an axe-cut to his leg, the result of an accident. He closed the door to his surgery quickly.

'Are you meaning escapees?'

'I'm talking of the luckless, who shouldn't ought to be here, sir. One woman I know, she's heartbroken, leaving behind her little kiddies...'

'Don't tell me any more. What information?'

106

'Could be shipping maybe. Or someplace to hide in the event of upsets ... a place like a clinic with us government people coming and going all the time, for stitches and cures...'

'No, Shanahan, No!'

'You can't help then? Ah, there's the pity. I'd have placed you for a compassionate man, but never mind. No offence, sir, if I misjudged you.'

'You certainly did. I do not entertain lawlessness. One can have concerns for people, but what's done is done. My object is to see they're treated fairly while they're here, and to encourage free settlers to support them.'

'Yes, and it's a terrible shame so few of them care... 'Twas only in hope the poor woman turned to me. And hopes die fast in this land, do they not?'

Sean turned the buggy into Cromwell Street, and took a bite of an apple, the one he'd lifted from Pollard's store.

Beautiful apples they grow here, surely the best in the world, he told himself, remembering how Roberts had helped that woman Gertrude Farrell in the end by declaring she was a lunatic, and listing her among the rare few permitted free passage home.

'There's one condition,' Sean had told Gertrude. 'Our doctor doesn't want a letter of thanks.'

Not that he'd be receiving one from Gertrude, who was as sane as anyone but a good actress. She was also a fiery speaker, determined to tell the world of her bitter experiences as a slave of the British, where women were forced into vice to survive the brutish conditions. She had told Sean

107

she already had pamphlets written in her head, and she would put them to good use in London.

But Sean had a condition of his own. She was to deliver clippings from the *Hobart Town Gazette* to the Colonial Secretary in London. Along with the clippings, which demonstrated public anger in Van Diemen's Land at the treatment of the prisoner Matthew O'Neill, was a letter from Sean Shanahan. He was outraged that the matter appeared to have been forgotten by both the public and the authorities in the two years since the shocking event. People seemed not to have noticed that no action had been taken against the magistrates who had sentenced Matthew O'Neill. He demanded that their authority be terminated and they be brought before the courts on a charge of torture.

He hadn't expected a reply. There had been no reply to the letters he'd written to Governor Franklin here in Hobart either, except a reprimand from Mr Warboy, who appealed to him to cease badgering Sir John.

'I am quietly advised that if you persist in your demands you will be sent to Port Arthur for the rest of your days, so I beg of you to desist.'

There was a well-dressed couple waiting in the small garden outside the Doc's cottage and they stared as Sean jumped down and dashed past them to knock on the open front door. They irritated him because they made him aware of the wretched state of the clothes he was forced to wear, the humiliation of it. Sometimes he thought a man would have more dignity staying in jail.

Armed with a cardboard box full of the writing

necessities, he forgot his shabby attire and headed back to the buggy, his mind racing with excitement.

This time he would eat humble pie and write a letter about the shocking business to Colonel Hastings, his father's landlord, begging him to put the matter before Members of Parliament. Joseph would carry this letter as far as Chile and then send it on. Too many letters written by convicts, especially by Sean Shanahan, went down the drain instead of into the mail bags, London bound.

'Torture,' he would say, for the umpteenth time, 'is illegal under our laws. Magistrates Sholto Matson and Grover Pellingham should be arrested.'

This letter he would send to his father, to be hand-delivered to the Colonel.

'Letter of the law, Doc,' he sighed, as the buggy skimmed past the foundations of a new church for the righteous of Hobart.

CHAPTER FOUR

In preparation for Mr Warboy's formal garden, the land was thoroughly cleared of native vegetation, which upset some of the members of the Natural History Society but Barnaby brushed aside the complaints. He was astonished that anyone should presume to tell him what he might and might not do on his own property. Such a thing would never have happened in Jamaica.

Then followed more discussions with Zack

Herring, and a great deal of striding out to decide the placement and size of the axis paths, and so the project began. Herring had been out and about, requesting donations of plants and seeds from local residents, and a goodly supply was already being nursed along in a shade house, ready for planting, but eager to have the best, Barnaby had sent lists to London with requests for plants unavailable in the colony.

He invited Josetta and Louise to view the work in progress, though there wasn't much to see as yet, and their enthusiasm matched his.

'There'll be a water feature in the centre,' Barnaby explained proudly. 'The water feature is always in the centre I'm told, and over there I'll have a pavilion, just large enough to serve tea for, say, four. And I want a rose arbour as well.'

'It sounds wonderful,' Louise said. 'So romantic.'

Barnaby noticed that Louise had filled out; she was quite the young lady now, and pretty as a picture, the lights in her blonde hair more pronounced than Josetta's.

'A garden has to have a name,' her mother said. 'This looks far too grand for a farm garden.'

'That's a good idea, but what could I call it?'

They stayed to lunch with Barnaby, tossing around all sorts of names – Garden of Eden, Oberon, Camelot, The Retreat, Heaven's Gate – but they couldn't agree on any of them.

'Think about it,' Josetta said. 'What do you want to make of the garden yourself, Barnaby? I mean, how exactly will you use it?'

'I don't understand your point, my dear.'

'Well ... would you like to view it from the house, or do you intend to work in it yourself, or bring visitors ... how would you most enjoy it?'

'Ah! I think it would be lovely to walk about, taking joy from every single thing...'

'Then it'll be your Walk,' Louise said. 'You should call it Barnaby's Walk.'

Josetta shook her head. 'That's not grand enough. What about Warboy's Walk? That sounds better.'

'Indeed it does,' Barnaby said. 'That's what I shall call it. Warboy's Walk. Are we agreed on that?'

After lunch, he walked them to the gate, just as Shanahan was passing by. The Irishman tipped his hat and stood back, but Barnaby noticed a glance exchanged between Louise and his overseer, and was sure he'd interpreted it correctly.

How long has that been going on, he wondered as he returned to the house. If Shanahan did have eyes for her daughter, Josetta should be warned. The very thought of this lovely young girl having any association with a convict sickened him, and he worried at the problem for days. Shanahan had those dark Irish looks, and eyes that could project integrity, but he was a criminal. And Louise! She had such a sweet face, and large innocent eyes, and a mop of curls which were often simply ribboned into a topknot, or tucked under a ladylike bonnet. How could she allow herself even a glance in the direction of a convict? A non-person; lower even than a servant.

The more he thought about it, the angrier he became, so in the end he had to address the

111

fellow on the matter.

'I hope you are not becoming above your station here, Shanahan. Not getting any notions about ladies in the district, especially my friends. You keep in mind that you are only on loan from jail, and a wrong move will have you back damned quick.'

'Mr Warboy, sir, I'm only too sadly aware of my situation, and never would I presume to be looking at any of the good ladies hereabouts, especially not Mrs Harris, who we do see more than most. She's a fine lady and I have the greatest respect for her. I pray she has no complaints about me, for if so I can assure you I would mean no offence.'

Barnaby was taken aback. His attempted chiding had strayed off track. Mrs Harris! He hadn't meant the mother! He'd meant the daughter! Josetta was more than ten years older than Shanahan; how could the fool think for a minute she'd even notice him? The cheek of him!

'Go!' he snorted. 'Get out of my sight. And stay out of my sight when I have visitors.'

'Ah, sir, t'other day, that was an accident that I came upon you with the ladies.'

'I said go! And don't let it happen again. Turn your back if the occasion arises again.'

'There's a good idea, sir. It'll put a stop to any embarrassment. Is that how you worked it in Jamaica?'

Barnaby stormed away. The rascal always had to have the last word.

'Well he can talk to air, for all the good it will do him,' he fumed as he puffed down to the stables, remembering that Lady Franklin had mentioned she might call in this afternoon on her way home from Mrs Flood's *conversazione*, to view progress on his garden, which interested her greatly.

The Floods were Barnaby's neighbours. Their house, a mile down the road, was a pretentious place, he thought, built like a fort, all turrets and towers as if ready for the Moors to attack.

He was never invited to any of their socials. Lieutenant Flood and his lady wife, being great status-seekers, made no bones about the fact that they did not consider Farmer Warboy's company an asset, and that suited Barnaby. At times they had differences of opinion about the borders of their unfenced properties, differences that he knew could have become nasty if he hadn't eventually acquiesced. Sometimes, he mused, weakness can be handy. He hadn't really cared one way or another about the trivial disputes, so it didn't bother him to let Flood have his way and keep the wretched pair at a distance.

Zack was in the horse paddock with his wheelbarrow, collecting manure for the garden, and Barnaby called to him: 'Leave that. Go and clean up, Lady Franklin is down at the Flood residence, she may call in to view my garden.'

'Not much to see yet,' Zack said dismally. 'Not much at all. It's a slow business on my own, Mr Warboy.'

'Get one of the other men to help you.'

'They're short-handed themselves since Joseph left.'

'Yes, yes, I suppose so, but that can't be helped. Tell Shanahan you need a permanent assistant, and he's to appoint one to you.'

Barnaby chafed at all the rules and regulations in this place. Back home if you needed more workers you simply bought them in the market-place on a Saturday morning, or managed to persuade a neighbour to lend you a good field hand for a while. But here you had to beg, even though there was a surplus of unemployed. When Joseph was granted his freedom, Barnaby had applied for an extra man and was told he had his quota. He wouldn't have dreamt of taking advantage of his friendship with Governor Arthur or Eliza, but the Franklins were different, he'd met them in their official capacity. Therefore, he concluded a word in Lady Franklin's ear might not be out of order.

He was delighted when he saw her carriage coming in the gate, determined to broach the subject, but it took until her visit was almost over to pluck up the courage.

'You mean,' she cried in that deep, resonant voice of hers, 'that you are being denied staff for a project like this? For a garden that will be the pride of Hobart when it's completed!'

'Unfortunately, Lady Franklin, that's right. I doubt I'll live to see Warboy's Walk in its full glory at this rate.'

'I have to say I agree with you, Mr Warboy.' She turned to the aide who was accompanying her. 'See Mr Warboy gets another gardener, a gardener I said, not a watchmaker or footpad. It seems so simple, but I'm appalled that the office bods here do not seem to understand how to match tradesmen with appropriate employment, even if they are convicts.

'Do you know, Mr Warboy, last week I asked for a carpet layer, a man who knew how to lay carpets. One would think that would be a simple request, but no. First I found a butcher trying to work out what to put down first, the underlay or my new carpet, with the underlay on top to protect it, and then a peasant who, I'm sure, had never encountered a carpet before, trying to stamp the rolls into place with his boots. I do declare, one can be sorely tried here. But you shall have your gardener, Mr Warboy. You shall.'

And that was how Zack Herring was brought into the conversation. Asked to recommend someone with professional gardening experience, he suggested Angus McLeod.

'Good man,' Shanahan told him, when all was quiet again. 'I've been trying to get Angus out for a long time. Well done, mate.'

Josetta Harris had not missed the way Louise had looked at the overseer, and they were no more than a hundred yards down the road when she turned on her daughter.

'I saw you flirting with Shanahan. How dare you make eyes at him!'

'Oh Mother! I was not. I merely smiled at him.'

'There's a difference between smiling and flirting, my girl, and you'd better behave yourself or there'll be trouble. You can't go around smiling at men twice your age...'

'He's not twice my age. I think he'd only be about ten years older than me. And anyway, my father is ten years older than you. You told me

115

that yourself.'

'Don't be so stupid. You're only a bit of a girl, your brains not even set yet. You flirt a smile out of a man and next thing you've got marriage on your mind. You keep away from Shanahan, do you hear me?'

'Why?' Louise pouted. 'Do you want him for yourself?'

Josetta turned on her angrily. 'Don't be so stupid!'

But Louise was amused to see her mother's cheeks flare red.

'Why did I have to come here anyway?' she persisted. 'I miss all my friends. You were stupid to sell our lovely farm back home. Why did you do that?'

'I've told you! Your father made the decision so that we could be close to him.'

Louise scowled. 'Oh yes, I remember now. So that he would be on the other side of a wall and we are allowed to visit him every three months. Well let me tell you, Mother, you can go on your own next time. I hate seeing him like that in those horrid convict clothes. It breaks my heart.'

'Very well,' Josetta sighed. Only yesterday she'd received a letter from Lester. Apparently he'd got himself into another scrape and was being sent to Port Arthur. Next time she was in town without Louise, she'd find out how this had come about, and exactly where this prison was located.

As they hurried down the road, Louise smiled. That had been close! She and Sean had been friends ever since he'd arrived at the Harris farm with a gift for her ... a gift from Mr Warboy, who

116

was at home suffering from an attack of gout, on the occasion of her eighteenth birthday. He'd brought her the most beautiful horse, a two-year-old chestnut called Tulip, and she'd been ecstatic.

Until then Louise had had a crush on Lieutenant Flood, who always looked so dashing in his uniform, the red coat with all its regalia, truly gorgeous. He was married to the snobby Antonia, and Louise was sure that he would have invited Mrs and Miss Harris to at least some of their parties had his wife not frowned on the idea. Many a time, when she'd been walking down the road on her own and Lieutenant Flood had come riding by, he'd slowed to smile at her and wish her a good day. That was rather a sweet secret, Louise reminded herself, and quite flattering. He only nodded politely when others were about.

But Sean! They had spoken a few times when she'd seen him with work parties, though only acknowledgements, but then he'd given Louise and her mother a lift in the Warboy hooded sulky one teeming wet day, taken them down the lane and right to their door, and when he helped her down ... oh my! Louise loved to think of that time ... he'd been so nice.

She used to ride Tulip out as far as Olinda Road, and then turn back following the pretty Mill Stream, stopping on hot days to allow Tulip to drink, and it was there that she saw Sean, sitting under a tree reading a book.

'Heavens!' she said. 'This is a surprise. What are you doing here, Mr Shanahan?'

He climbed to his feet. 'Well, let's see, Miss Harris. Right here is the back boundary of Mr

Warboy's property, stream an' all, and persons using this track are, by all rights and purposes, trespassing, but to keep the peace Mr Warboy has no objections. As for myself, I was just taking some time off.'

'Really? What are you reading?'

'It's nothing much. A geography book, with pictures of your island here, and the big mainland to the north, just something to look at. But tell me, how is Tulip behaving?'

'Oh, she is just lovely. Baulks at snakes, though.'

'Never mind,' he said, with a flash of anger in his beautiful eyes, 'your government will put a stop to that. They're offering a bounty on snakes, to rid the world of them.'

Louise had thought the bounty to be an excellent idea, but since he disapproved she rearranged her attitude accordingly. 'Yes. How cruel. I can't bear to think of it. They say they're all dangerous and must be killed. But there's better news, isn't there?'

She hoped he'd suggest she dismount, but he did not. 'What better news would that be?'

'Why, congratulations to you. I believe you're Mr Warboy's overseer now.'

'There's no congratulations called for.' He shrugged. 'I'm just playing the part. Promoting a slave is a contradiction.'

'Of what?'

'Of itself.'

'But you're not a slave, Mr Shanahan.'

'That's where you're wrong. But I'll not be bothering you. Look at the fish jump. I sometimes

118

come here to fish. With permission, of course.'

'Do you have permission to be here today?' she asked saucily, and he laughed.

'Possibly.'

Louise couldn't think of a reason to dally any longer, and it was awkward talking to him from horseback.

'I'd better go,' she said, 'and let you get on with your book.'

'Time for reading is up now, but 'twas well spent.' He smiled, and Louise almost swooned right off the horse.

'Goodbye, Mr Shanahan,' she said faintly, and dug her heels into the horse's flanks, too quickly and far too sharply. Tulip took off with a bound, and Louise almost lost her seat, bumping about in a horrible ungainly manner, face aflame, until she managed to regain her equilibrium, but by then she was far down the dusty track.

She saw to it that they met again after that. She took Tulip down that track as often as she could, and her efforts were frequently rewarded. She found him fishing, and that gave her an excuse to dismount and examine the catch, or commiserate when the fish were not biting. He seemed to like to talk with her about a range of things, especially the Government and the island and its history, which she had to pretend to appreciate, and in turn she began asking him questions, personal questions, politely avoiding the subject of what had brought him here. Certainly not a crime, she was sure. Some misunderstanding, it had to be. And then he asked her how she and her mother, two charming English ladies, had come to own a farm so far from home.

Louise explained that her father was ailing. He hadn't been well enough to travel when it was time to leave England, but the farm had been bought, so they'd come on ahead.

'Father will join us when he can,' she lied, thanking her stars she hadn't blurted out that her mother had been told before they came here of the situation regarding convict farmhands in this colony, and was greatly relieved that it was true. They'd never have coped without the convict workers assigned to them as soon as they arrived.

He seemed disappointed by that reply, and it made her nervous that she had, somehow, said too much, so she left rather suddenly that day.

Now she took to riding Tulip every single day, despite her mother's annoyance, heading straight for the track by the stream, but weeks went past and he was never there, though she waited for as long as she could.

There were two men working on Mr Warboy's garden by this, and Louise was so determined to speak to Sean that she kept a note in her pocket ready to slip to him next time they visited their friend.

Unfortunately, there was no sign of Sean, so she gave it to one of the workmen to pass on to him.

It simply said: 'Meet me.'

He did. He was at their meeting place the very next day, and Louise gave a huge sigh of relief.

'Where have you been?' she asked him breathlessly, as she slid down from her horse. 'I've missed you lately. I thought you didn't like me any more.'

'Ah now, don't be fussing. It's just that the boss has twigged that we're friends and he does not approve.'

'But it's none of his business.'

'I'm afraid it is.'

Louise pouted. 'Then we'll meet outside your work time. There's no law against that, is there?'

'I don't think so,' he said, his voice tinged with irritation. 'I can have time off at my employer's pleasure if I state my business and carry a permit, which, under the circumstances, I would not get.'

He was trying not to hurt her feelings. He'd enjoyed her company, she was a flirty girl – a touch of normalcy – though if the truth be faced, she reminded him too much of his darling Glenna, lost back there in time.

'I've seen you in town on your own,' she insisted.

'On errands, dear girl. Permissible.'

'Well then?'

'Well what?'

'I could meet you in town.'

'Miss Harris. You're the nicest girl I've met in a year of Sundays, but you don't belong in the company of a convict. You'll grant yourself an unfortunate reputation.'

'Oh for heaven's sake, Mr Shanahan, you sound like my mother!'

'In which case you know I'm correct.'

'I could speak to Mr Warboy. He really is the nicest man.'

'Ho now! Wait a minute!'

121

He took the reins of the horse, led it about and reached out his hand to assist her to mount. 'Now listen to me. He's still my boss. Do not be speaking to him about me. Nice as the man may be, he's indoctrinated. To him I'm only a convict, a non-person. A white nigger.'

She had no choice but to remount, though there was still argument left in her.

'Don't be so melodramatic. I know how it is with convicts. You're one of the better class and you know it. You're certain to be set free eventually.'

'I'm a lifer,' he said crossly, tiring of this. 'I could be freed, as you say, as long as I don't leave this island.'

'Is that so bad?'

'You're the very devil to argue with, aren't you? The island itself, I'll allow, is a thing of beauty, but being forced to live here is exile, not freedom.'

Louise leaned over. 'Why are you so serious about everything?' She nudged the horse back on to the track and turned to him. 'I won't bother you any more if it's such a trial,' she sniffed.

'Oh Lord!' he muttered as she rode away. He wanted to shout after her that he had rights, that the crime he'd committed didn't rate life, but she wouldn't understand. A part of the penal settlement by now, she already saw the system as normal. Just as Warboy and his ilk back in their home territory took slavery for granted.

He jumped over the low rock fence and headed across the field, where sheep were grazing quietly and everything looked so peaceful. Like a picture postcard. Except this was where the military heroes had run down and shot twenty-two innocent blacks, among them five females and three little children, in reprisal for some minor incident. This was where Sean Shanahan and ten other convicts in that road gang, all with the ball and chain on their ankles, had dug the pit and buried the bodies. One day, he reminded himself, he would place a gravestone here for them, *in memoriam*. Obviously not a Christian cross. Something perhaps, he pondered, to ease the pain left in his own soul for not refusing the duty. For his cowardice.

Angus McLeod had done so. That wild Scot. 'Bury your own sins, damn you! You bloody murderers!' he'd shouted at the officer in his red coat with the green trims.

And he'd reaped the harvest of a hundred lashes in the Campbell Street prison, the first week they'd come ashore from the transport ship *Veritas*. Most of them had had a taste of the cat since then. Sean gave an involuntary shudder. He'd been given thirty lashes, twice, but he could still see the bloody mess the flogger had made of McLeod's skinny white back that day. And the man's defiance.

There'd been a time, back home in Ireland, when he'd thought of himself as defiant. Damn fool! Playing at being a hero! Wild lads, it was said of Shanahan and his friends, and with some truth. They were the sons of tenant farmers living on the edge of disaster, forced to watch poverty stalking their families until emigrations caused a breakdown in what was left of the village as a close and abiding entity.

His brother had emigrated to America, leaving

Sean and his parents to struggle on with the farm and failing crops, and all the while the love of his life, Glenna Hamilton, kept telling him that if they could not be wed, then she'd be off and sailing for New York herself.

Sean begged her to be patient. She knew he couldn't support a wife, or even provide a roof for her, until the old people passed on and he owned the farm.

'I don't care,' she cried, in her wilful way. 'If you can't find a way, then you don't love me enough for me to stay.'

Though he did not realise it at the time, a bitterness assailed his soul over the situation, like the sudden curdling of milk when you were not paying attention.

It wasn't much of a step for Sean, the quiet farm boy, to aspire to hell-raiser, with most of his energies directed at harassing their English landlord, Colonel Linton Hastings. He and his pals regularly attacked the boys from the posh grammar school on the outskirts of the village, and poached game from Hastings' woods, but as time went on their misdeeds became more serious. They left gates open, burned haystacks, sabotaged the Colonel's vehicles, until the police became regular visitors at their farms. Then one night after a dance, with a fiery home-brew of potato spirit in their bellies, Sean and his cousin Matt O'Neill were rollicking along a dark road, singing their heads off, when along came Hastings' squire, who reined in his horse and gave them a good earful, threatening to call the police out to charge them with disturbing the peace.

Tempers flared. Sean pulled the squire down from his horse, and shooed it on its way. Matt relieved the squire of his boots. Laughing, Sean threw his hat up a tree and took his coat to dress a scarecrow. He then picked up the squire's leather satchel and found it contained a small bag of pennies and another of silver.

Enraged, he turned on the squire, abusing him for prising the last pennies out of the poor folk around here, punched him in the face and strode away with the money.

'Hey, leave the dosh or we'll be up for thievin',' Matt cried.

'Then we'll be just like them, won't we?'

The squire was standing in his socks shouting his threats, so Sean went back. 'You tell who did this and I'll burn your fine cottage down. You got that, you bloody traitor? Now get you down the road or I'll give you more of a hiding.'

The squire did tell, of course. Sean was the first to be arrested, and refused to say what had happened to Hastings' rent money. Forewarned, Matt disappeared from the village, and a week later the squire's cottage mysteriously burned down. Sean heard this news in Dublin jail, where his only real concern was for his parents. He'd let them down badly.

A few months later he took part in an attempted escape, but was caught and sentenced to be transported to Van Diemen's Land.

Before he left, his parents were permitted to visit him, and though his mother wept, his father was more optimistic.

'I knew it would only be a matter of time,' he

said, 'before you got into the wrong company, the men with guns. This jail is a breeding ground for them radicals, and this I'm guessing you already know. They say Matt has joined them.'

'What else could he do? They'll protect him, and give him a chance to fight back. We have to fight for our country now, it's the only way. We can't go on just tom-fool teasing them like I did.'

'Big talk,' Pa said. 'That's why your ma and me, we're pleased you're being sent away out of it. Too many fine lads dyin' of bullets now, and nothin' to show for it. We just see more soldiers pounding the roads.'

'You're trying to tell me it's a good thing I'm being sent to a prison on the other side of the world! Exiled! You're pleased to be rid of me, are you?'

His mother took him in her arms. 'Never. You'll be in our hearts, son, and we'll be praying for you every day of our lives. God love you.'

'What are you sayin' here, the pair of you? I'm not emigratin', you know. I'll not be pickin' up gold in the streets of New York, I'll be breakin' rocks in a bloody prison!'

'Don't be cursing in front of your mother! Prison or not, you'll be alive, and I've faith in you, Sean, you'll find your way, with God's help.'

While he was in the prison, Sean heard that Matt had been captured in a raid on a lonely Galway house that had been a refuge for Young Ireland fighters.

For the final visit, his father came alone. His mother was too overwhelmed with grief.

'You'll have to know sooner or later,' Pa said.

126

'Your cousin will be joining you in Van Diemen's Land. I went to speak to the Colonel about Matt. I reminded him it was just the times that had sent you both astray and...'

'You went begging to that bastard?'

'It's never a hard task for me to beg when it comes to your cousin's life, and don't you be judging me!'

'I know, I know. I'm sorry, Pa, it was a sensible thing you did. But listen, I promise you we'll be back. Just you hang on. And get the Molony lads to be giving you a hand, they'll be pleased to help. I'm sorry I let you down, Pa... And by the way, I can't remember where I threw down the squire's money, too far in the drink I was, but...'

'I know,' his father said wearily. 'I found it and gave it back to Hastings. I wouldna spend stolen brass.'

Later the same day, as he listened to church bells ringing and the clang of heavy boots at the changing of the guard, Sean had one more visitor. One last visitor... Glenna!

Shortness of breath caught him unawares and he reached out to lean against a tree for a few minutes as he fought to dispel that memory, moving on swiftly to thoughts of the transport ship.

It had been a voyage of despair. A terrible thing to realise you're no longer of any use to your sweetheart. Or to your family. That you'll soon be forgotten...

As he trudged back up to the house, he saw Zack Herring working at a long garden bed.

'What's happening here?' he asked.

'It's to be a box hedge that'll run to the centre

127

there, curve round it and go straight on to border the path, and the same thing on the other side there.'

'You don't say now! It'll look fine then. But listen, I've been thinking. Why can't we dig a cellar under the barn?'

'What for? It'd be easier to build another barn.'

'The "for" is to have a place no one knows about. Especially not the boss.'

'And who would we put in this private cellar?'

'Someone who might want to go missing.'

Zack nodded. 'Ah yes. As good a spot as any for someone on the run. Have you got someone in mind? Yourself maybe?'

'No! I'll not be making any moves until Matt has a proper headstone and those bastards Pellingham and Matson are behind bars.'

Zack bent down and picked up a box of seedlings he'd been cultivating. 'I'll think about it,' he said, with little enthusiasm.

Sean knew the lads were becoming wary of his escape schemes, afraid of becoming involved again in the problems of hiding escapees and spiriting them on to ships – with the added danger of the convict being picked up in a British port and being brought back. But Joseph's departure had been a dream. He'd saved for the fare, was able to buy passage and forged papers, and was headed for Chile! It would be ages before the authorities woke up to the fact he was missing, with not a soul to pin it on but the man himself.

'Let them try to find him now!' Sean muttered grimly.

CHAPTER FIVE

The laying of the foundation stone for the new Government House by Sir John Franklin was a gala day in Hobart, and Barnaby went along to view proceedings, resplendent in a new frockcoat and top hat. Before he left, his cook brought him a sprig of wattle tied with a ribbon of British blue.

'What's this for?' he asked.

'Don't you remember, sir? Lady Franklin handed them out at the regatta. She says they should be Van Diemen's Land's emblem, so you oughta have one today.'

'Should I indeed? Very well then, Dossie, tuck it into the buttonhole. And by the way, Shanahan mentioned you could do with a maid to help you with the chores.'

Dossie shook her head. 'Kind of him, sir, but it's not hard looking after you and this nice house. No need to waste money on a maid, unless you think I'm not doing things right?'

'Oh no, no. All is tip-top, ah yes, indeed. You just go along as you are.'

'Righto, sir. Your buggy's ready. Do you want one of the men to drive you?'

'No. My gloves? Where are my gloves?'

'Here on the hallstand, sir.'

Dossie closed the front door behind him and breathed a sigh of relief. 'That Shanahan!' She knew Warboy's overseer wouldn't be wanting a new maid here to ease her workload. No bloody fear. Shanahan, like men the world over, never saw cooking and houseworking as work, no matter if the little wife with a brood of bairns worked her legs to stumps. Ah no, something was up. Probably trying to move some woman in for his own reasons... 'Well not on my patch,' she muttered.

Joseph, now on his way to Chile, had been a good friend to Dossie. He'd tipped her off about the job coming up in the new house and got Shanahan to pull some strings that landed her this job working for kind old Mr Warboy. She'd been amazed when Joseph told her he would be escaping right under the noses of the police. Wouldn't hardly believe him until he showed her his papers, proving that he'd served his time and was a free man, signed and sealed by Magistrate L.M. Pettifer. It had taken weeks for a constable to come enquiring of his whereabouts, since the records showed he was still an assigned convict, not even a ticket-of-leave, but Mr Warboy had sent the constable packing, told him he'd seen the release papers, signed and stamped by a magistrate. Which one, he couldn't recall, but he'd brook no more such intrusions.

'You people have to learn to keep your records in order to avoid confusion,' he snorted. 'I will not have police charging in here asking such questions, they reflect on my integrity. My books are in order, my attitude to the employ of assigned convicts is above reproach, so get about your business.'

Shanahan had said there was a search on now for Joseph, and a Wanted poster outside the police station listing him as an escaped prisoner, now known to be a bushranger.

Dossie had laughed at that. Joseph had been petrified of horses and blackfellows. He'd have chosen Port Arthur over a career as a bushranger.

She trotted back to her kitchen. There'd be no bold bits coming into this house to upset things, or whores seeking to sneak into old Mr Warboy's bed and bankroll, him being a rich old bachelor. She often wondered why he hadn't proposed to that nice Mrs Harris, who was around here often enough with the daughter who was all gooey-eyed over Shanahan. Silly girl she was, there were plenty of eligible free men in Hobart, more than enough. Dossie, who'd be thirty-five next Christmas Day, hoped to win one herself one day. She was not too sad of face except for the one bung eye, the result of a bashing by a factory supervisor, back in Liverpool. He'd tried to rape her, a young married woman, and she'd fought him off, but then the story had got twisted and he'd taken his revenge by claiming he'd caught her stealing money from his office. Worse then, her husband blamed her for not going along with the pig.

'You knew you'd lose your job if you didn't, you stupid woman! Now look what's happened to you.'

Yes, she thought. Transported. And rid of you! When she was dumped in Van Diemen's Land, she claimed she was a widow. Wishful thinking, she laughed. But it was important to be available for a new man. Dossie dreamed of being a farmer's wife and settling down right here in Hobart, so never would she have part in any of Shanahan's plots.

He could keep clear of her territory.

Twenty-five acres adjacent to the Botanic Gardens and overlooking the Derwent River had been set aside for the new Government House and grounds, and the celebrations were well under way when Barnaby arrived.

An enthusiastic Lady Franklin had provided cold collations in a splendid marquee. Guests danced quadrilles to the music of a military band, and others took turns to examine the plans for the magnificent edifice and its surrounds that were to grace this bushland.

When Barnaby trotted in to view the plans, drawn up by James Blackburn, an ex-convict architect in the employ of the Public Works Department, he was pleased to find Lady Franklin in attendance.

She was delighted to see him and insisted on taking him to meet their special guests, Captains Ross and Crozier of the Discovery ships, who had called in at Hobart on their way to the Antarctic. Fortunately Barnaby remembered the connection, that Sir John Franklin had earned his knighthood for his gallant exploits as an Arctic explorer, and so was able to make a fair hand of conversation with these interesting gentlemen.

They all congratulated the gubernatorial couple on the success of this gala outing, and in return Lady Franklin decided to give a farewell dinner party for the two captains, to which Barnaby was invited. He rather thought the invitation came from being Johnny-on-the-Spot, but when an official card was hand-delivered to his home the following day, he sped into his study to pen his acceptance.

Having done so, and with three days to mull over his decision, Barnaby had a worrisome feeling that this was not a good idea, a foreboding that made no sense at all. Nevertheless, he proceeded as planned, but fortified himself with a couple of glasses of his best rum before setting off on the night.

Two middle-aged ladies were placed either side of him at a table set for thirty, so they made the running in the conversation stakes and soon dissolved Barnaby's apprehensions.

Sir John, extremely wide of girth, was known to require a well-provisioned table, but Barnaby, no stranger to banquets, found this menu memorable. Maybe a little overdone, he thought, feeling disloyal for even entertaining such a criticism. Nevertheless, he went at his dinner with gusto, accepting his choices of chowder, oyster fritters and scalloped crayfish, mulligatawny soup, Cape wines, roast goose, turkey, duck, port and fowls ... beef, mutton and pork chops with various sauces ... magnificent claret ... coquette, sautéed and gratined vegetables ... and a display of puddings and wine trifles.

It was a repast greatly enjoyed by all as the wine and conversations flowed with generous ease. The visiting captains were placed, naturally, near their hosts, and by them again were Franklin family members and friends. Barnaby was not a little pleased to find himself higher up the scale than his neighbours Tom and Antonia Flood. He even went out of his way, cheered by the wine, to beam a smile in their direction, but was rewarded with a scowl from the lieutenant.

Proceedings were well under way when the subject of the Government House grounds came up. What to make of the bushland? Should it be left in its natural state, with a few bush walks, or made formal?

'Formal it should be,' Sir John said eventually. 'The Botanic Gardens next door will suffice for local flora...'

Barnaby nodded. Proffered his opinion shyly. 'Formal gardens on those grounds would be magnificent, Your Excellency.'

The lady on his right, the widowed Mrs Bird, twittered a response. 'Indeed, Mr Warboy. Quite right.'

Not to be outdone, Miss Skinner on his left shook her head mournfully. 'I don't know about that. It's hard enough to find sober servants here, let alone a set of sober gardeners for a job that size.'

'The gardens would have to be carefully planned and laid out,' Lady Franklin explained, more to her husband than anyone else. 'But it could be done if we had expert gardeners. We shall have to make enquiries.' She turned to Barnaby 'Perhaps your man could recommend someone appropriate, Mr Warboy?'

Lady Franklin went on to explain to her guests that Mr Warboy was already in the process of planting a magical garden on his property, with an expert gardener at the helm. 'Are you still happy with his work?' she added.

'Oh yes, exceedingly happy,' he said. 'The man

has a good eye for aesthetics as well as a green thumb. I shall be pleased to ask if there are any more with such expertise among his ranks.'

Lieutenant Tom Flood addressed the Governor. 'I can vouch for Mr Warboy's man, Your Excellency. Being a neighbour of Mr Warboy's, I have had occasion to visit and oversee his work. The garden is coming along splendidly.'

First I've heard of it, Barnaby said to himself as he listened to Flood's surprising praise for his gardener, and wondered crossly why he had to butt in on something he knew nothing about. His land had been cleared of everything except for a few trees, to make way for crops.

'I'm pleased to hear that,' His Excellency replied. 'It's such a change to receive reports of good work being done in the colony. Well done, Mr Warboy!'

'Ah, thank you, but I have been fortunate. The man is a professional in the art of estate gardening. I did not ask what had caused his downfall, one prefers not to know.'

'Too true,' Lady Franklin echoed, and Tom Flood joined in again.

'Then you would have no objection to a fellow like Zack Herring, for that is the man's name, working on such an important project, Lady Franklin?' he asked.

'Goodness me, of course not.'

Flood smirked. 'So here's your chance, Warboy!'

'A chance?' Barnaby was bewildered. 'A chance to do what, sir?'

'To give this paragon of the plant world, this fellow Herring, to Lady Franklin and let him

135

design the most important garden in the colony!'

Barnaby scratched his ear and adjusted his spectacles. 'Let Herring do it?' he asked feebly, anxiously, hoping he had not heard aright.

'It would be a great honour for the wretch,' Flood said maliciously, 'but a most generous gesture on your part, Warboy. Would it not, Lady Franklin?'

'I could not refuse,' she said, with a forthright smile for Barnaby. 'What do you think, my dear?' she asked her husband.

'Problem solved,' he said absently, mopping his balding pate with a fresh handkerchief, which he then handed on to the nearest servant to be whisked away. Barnaby's attention was distracted from the situation by noting that the Governor's high braided collar was very tight, and in fact his splendid dress uniform must be very uncomfortable on a warm night like this.

By the time his thoughts had returned to the fold it was too late. Mrs Bird was congratulating him on his decision.

'It's so nice to find gentlemen who still know how to do the right thing,' she twittered.

Miss Skinner tapped his sleeve with her fan. 'I should enjoy to view your magical garden, Mr Warboy.'

'Then you shall, Miss Skinner.'

'We will, of course, have to promote Herring to head gardener,' Lady Franklin announced, 'and have him draw up plans right away.'

Didn't any of them understand that he needed Zack Herring? His garden was barely begun and the plan, as Herring had explained, was only a guide; he would improve on it as he worked. The end result was dependent on trial and error with certain plants, and the possibility that he might not be able to obtain exactly what he required, or that the summer might be too harsh.

'But we'll get it right, sir,' Herring had said confidently, 'bit by bit, day by day.'

'Yes. Quite,' Barnaby heard himself saying. 'Oh yes, of course. Promote him. Necessary, I daresay, for this much larger endeavour. Yes.'

He wondered if his disappointment, his bitter disappointment showed. He could not bring himself to look in Flood's direction, at his triumphant spite. The best part of his day was the discussions with Herring, who had settled down into an amiable sort of fellow. The thought of losing that pleasure and the subsequent observings of every peep of new shoots or buds left him feeling bereft.

The hearty thanks of his hosts were still ringing in his ears as he sat miserably in his buggy and allowed the horse to plod on home.

Shanahan was as annoyed as he was, and Barnaby appreciated that.

'It's no use complaining,' he said. 'Herring has to go. He's to be promoted to head gardener on that project. I imagine it will outlive us all.'

'Couldn't they get someone else?' Shanahan said crankily.

'No. Tom Flood practically threw him to the Governor. My gardener! It was all Flood's idea, the malicious wretch. He's jealous, of course, simple as that, but one could hardly disagree.'

'I would have!' Shanahan said stonily.

'You might, but you're not a gentleman,' Barnaby explained.

'Neither is Tom Flood. Though his uniform claims he is.'

Barnaby nodded. 'True ... true. Oh well, you may as well tell Herring he has to pack up and report to Government House for his instructions. But before he goes, I'd like a word with him. I need to find a replacement.'

He wrung his hands and looked about him as if someone might be found behind the desk, or the curtains in his study.

'I'll ask him if he knows anyone,' Shanahan said, but as he turned away he was already making his own plans. There'll be no asking. I'll tell him. He can recommend Freddy Hines. He's wasted in prison, a fine pickpocket like him. Between us we'll talk him up into the best gardener the world has ever seen.

I'll have to have a serious talk with Freddy when he arrives, Sean mused. Get it through his head that there's to be no thieving, not even a nail, on this farm. I can't have the boss upset over trivials. And as for Flood ... he'll keep.

Sean had been close to revealing to Mr Warboy that there was more to his remark about Flood not being a gentleman. Far from it! The lieutenant was a crook! Though officers were not permitted to engage in commerce when they were posted to the colonies, many made the most of opportunities and the governors turned a blind eye. Flood owned a saddlery in Davey Street where convicts turned out expensive but quality equipment, the very best in Hobart. The lieutenant was also a

138

smuggler. Mainly of wine and spirits, brought to his riverside property from ships anchored in Storm Bay.

He grinned. Mr Warboy would love to hear that, but the information was more valuable to his overseer.

Sean had had eyes watching Flood for a long time. His land, on the other side of the road, went all the way down to the Derwent River.

In all, Van Diemen's craggy coastline and myriad inlets were too much of a challenge for Customs, so most of their efforts were concentrated on the port. That left doors open for smugglers like Flood, who calmly carried on his own endeavours under cover of night. It was said that he dealt in all kinds of goods as well as liquor: anything that could be lifted, was the joke – and he had seaworthy boats to rendezvous with ships off the coast. The smuggling didn't interest Sean, but the location of boats with access to Storm Bay certainly did.

Ships leaving Storm Bay had to pass the Tasman Peninsula, where the dreaded penal settlement Port Arthur was located, and wherein lodged the heroic convict rebel and world-famous Irish patriot Frank Macnamara.

'Food for thought,' Sean mused aloud. 'Yes, food for thought.'

Freddy was jubilant. He had the word, he told his cellmates that night. He was being assigned to Warboy's farm.

'I'm a bloomin' gardener, and not just an old lawn-cutter, a proper one.'

Flo Quinlan laughed. 'You wouldn't know a poppy from a pea, you goat. McLeod's gone out as a gardener, you've got it all wrong.'

'It's true. Shanahan's fixing it. I've gotta say I know all about the garden business. My Daddy learned me, I have to say, and Zack Herring showed me plenty when I was working with him.'

'You were working in a bloody quarry with Herring!' Flo said incredulously. 'I never even saw the light of a daisy among them rocks. Were you ever noticing any, Singer?'

'Never. Those quarries, they'd fry plants in a second. Bloody hell-holes they are.'

'Ah yes, but that's where Freddy learnt his new trade, and who are we to contradict?'

'You can laugh,' Freddy said, 'but I'll be thinking of you tomorrer night, when I'm walking free and you're gettin' locked down in this dungeon.'

Singer stretched out on his bunk. 'What about your hand?' he teased. 'What if it gets bad again like it did yesterday?'

'It won't. It's better.'

Flo looked up. 'That was quick. Did you fake it again?'

'No!' Freddy lied.

'Have you heard the joke about the poor old bloke tramping down the road with a heavy pack on his back?' Singer asked them.

'Yes,' Flo said.

'Then shut your face while I tells Freddy here.' He took a deep breath. 'There he was, out in the middle of nowhere. Along comes the squatter in his buggy and he sees the old bloke tramping on, and it being a hot day and full of dust he feels

140

sorry for him, so he pulls to a halt and offers the bloke a lift.

'The tramp, sweatin' like a pig, looks up at him, sees a man who owns this farm that's so big he's been walking over it for nigh on two days, so he spits and he says: "Shut your own bloody gates!" And tramps on.'

Flo laughed, but Freddy was confused.

'What was funny about that story?' he complained.

'Eh, Flo,' Singer said quietly. 'How do you think we'd go as gardeners?'

'Bloody good, we would. You tell Shanahan that, Freddy, you tell him. Singer and me, we'd grow the best weeds you ever saw.'

'So what? I can learn to grow weeds too. Angus will show me!'

Sure enough, as they filed out of the refectory, Freddy was pulled from the line and sent back to collect the battered canvas bag that contained all of his worldly goods, which included some ragged clothes, a small box of fairground trinkets, a cardboard wrapper that held a picture of his mother, a knot of bootlaces and a rag tied tightly to protect three pennies.

He shot off gleefully, grabbed his bag and sped over to the administration office to join another line by the door. As he waited, he contained his excitement by casting his eyes upon a bed of flowers growing profusely by the steps.

'What sorta flowers do you reckon they are?' he asked the man in front of him.

'They're geraniums,' came the mild reply.

'And them, next to them?'

'Next to them? They're carnations.'

Freddy tucked that information away safely, hoping it would come in handy one day. He'd never had time to think about flowers – he knew gorse and blackberry and other such bushes that might hinder flight, but by sight only. Names had been unimportant.

He slouched in the door looking suitably wary – new assignments were rarely appreciated – and the clerk, known as 'Pansy' Hurley, beckoned him.

'You're going out, Hines. Step over here and start signing your life away.'

'Where to?' Freddy growled, feigning ignorance.

'Warboy's farm.'

After he'd signed the assignment register, he picked up his bag and walked through to the next office to collect his papers. While he was waiting, another clerk handed him a small booklet.

'What's this?' Freddy asked.

'Can't you read?'

'Yes, I can, but what's it about?'

'Regulations. The Governor has ordered that all assignees carry this book of rules and give it to their employers. Doesn't matter to him,' he sniffed, 'that Warboy must have a pile of these, but we have to see you got 'em.'

'I know the bloody rules,' Freddy snorted. 'Had them bashed into me, I have.'

'They're not for you, dummy, they're for your boss.'

'You don't say.'

With that Freddy studied the pages, finding that Warboy had to provide him with a new blanket, rug and bedtick, and supply him with new clothes every six months, as follows: one jacket, waistcoat, pair of trousers, shirt, ankle boots, cap. It was the same list required for all convicts, but now the clothes would be grey, not the prison shades. Freddy planned to ask for them as soon as he arrived at the farm. He also studied the rations for light labourers, and found the list of meat, tea, sugar and vegetables a bit less than men at hard labour received, but not by much. And the precious tobacco ration was the same. He nodded his approval, grinning at the page that required well-disposed convicts to be separated from the evil-minded. He also liked the bit about the right of prisoners to complain to the Attorney-General if they felt aggrieved.

'Fat lot of good that'll do,' he remarked to no one in particular.

'Put those rules in your bag, and don't lose them, Hines,' the clerk called out. 'And don't stand there all bloody day.'

More signing, more papers, more instructions, but soon Freddy was on his way out. As he returned through the first office, he saw a beautiful pack of cards, a shining new pack, sitting on the edge of Pansy's untidy desk, almost hidden under wads of paperwork, and as he stepped out into the sunshine the cards went with him, along with an overwhelming sense of joy, for they all liked nothing better than a game of cards, and the real thing, real cards, were rarities.

'Where now?' he asked a guard.

'Go down to the gate. Shanahan's waiting for you.'

143

It was a long walk down that exercise yard, a long walk, but he only had to get to the gate with the cards and he could slip them to someone else if there was a fuss, or hide them any place on the road for later. Ah yes, once he was out the gate the cards, the beautiful cards would be his.

But it was not to be.

Freddy broke into a run the minute he heard Pansy bellowing. His seabag was hindering him, slowing him down, but he dared not throw it away, the cards were inside. He could see the big Irishman, Shanahan, at the gate, could see his bewilderment as Pansy gained on him, shouting, unfairly Freddy thought, for the guards to stop him.

Pansy grabbed the seabag and emptied it.

'There they are! My cards!' he screamed.

Freddy tried. 'No they're not, they're mine.'

But everyone knew, as they all crowded at doors and windows to see Freddy dragged back and thrown down by the steps.

Pansy was still raging. 'I only got them today,' he screamed as he kicked Freddy in the ribs. 'They only came off the ship today. All the way from London. My wife sent them.'

'Your wife.' Freddy spat dust. 'What a cow she must be!'

'What did you say?' Pansy yelled. 'What did you say, you cocky little bastard!' With that he stamped on Freddy's hand with his boot. 'Let's see how light-fingered you are now! Take him away.'

Freddy was thrown into the lockup, with his seabag, to await a court appearance. He sat on the cold stone floor cursing his own stupidity ... curs-

144

ing those cards, as he nursed his hand in his shirt to keep it warm and ease the pain. His fingers were broken, he knew, but he couldn't accept it. So he just rocked back and forward like a loony, nursing the hand, telling it that this was nothing.

Shanahan bullied his way down to the administrative centre, but Pansy had disappeared. None of the other clerks blamed him. The Irishman was known to find ways to get back at any of the 'keeper' classes – warders, guards, clerks, whether they be ex-cons or not – who beat his mates.

'What happened to Freddy?' he demanded. 'I heard the man scream.'

No one was prepared to say, but someone did offer: 'He stole a pack of cards. He's in the lockup.'

'I want to see him.'

'You can't,' Jimmy Maunder said.

'And don't you go sticking your nose in, Maunder. I've heard talk about you, man. Good with the cosh on men in irons, aren't ye? One dark night someone not in irons might wish to have a word with you. Now you be a good feller and let me have a look at him.'

The lockup had a window of iron bars. Shanahan peered in.

'What's up, Freddy?' he asked.

Freddy could stand it no longer. 'He smashed me fingers,' he wept.

'Sorry about that, mate. I'll send Dr Roberts to see what he can do.'

As he walked away, Sean shook his head. What a bloody fool Freddy was. He'd been out, and if

145

Sean had had his way he'd have stayed out. Now this. And all for a pack of cards. Poor Freddy. This'd earn him weeks on the treadmill.

Mr Warboy then had to be persuaded that his overseer had found another expert gardener among the thousands and thousands of convicts on the island, and that it was sheer luck that he'd come upon him.

So it was that Angus McLeod was promoted to head gardener at Warboy's Walk, and Singer Forbes arrived at the gate with his swag, though he didn't know a poppy from a pea either.

Allyn Roberts looked in on the prisoner Hines, found he did indeed have broken fingers, and took him into the dispensary to set the bones, at the same time endeavouring to cope with the fellow's despair.

'They're not about to fall off,' he said. 'They'll be as good as new soon.'

'How good?' Hines moaned.

'Good enough, maybe a bit stiff.'

'I can't afford to have stiff fingers, Doc. You have to fix them better than that.'

'Why? Are you a piano player or something?'

'I'm an artist,' Freddy said huffily.

Roberts didn't bother to enquire further. They all had their wild stories. 'We'll give it a few months. I'm binding your hand to this piece of board and it has to stay on to protect your fingers. The bones are set now, they mustn't be moved about, so the binding has to stay for at least five weeks. Come and see me then.'

'Five weeks?' Freddy looked down at his

carefully bound hand. 'Five weeks did you say? No taking this off?'

'It has to stay on.'

Suddenly Hines was jubilant. 'They can't give me hard labour now.'

'I suppose not.'

'Will you be sure to tell them that it's Pansy put me out of action? Fixed it so I can't work at all. He should be charged, he should.'

Roberts sighed. 'If I were you I'd just shut up. You're in enough trouble.'

He felt sorry for this odd little man, knowing that the smashed hand counted for nothing in a world where sixty lashes was considered mild punishment. All the time he'd been repairing this hand, the lash had been on his mind. Hines seemed to have forgotten he still had to face the charge of theft and the inevitable flogging. Or, like so many of them, had he become immune to the looming violence?

When they took Hines back to his cell, Allyn stood at the barred window of the cold stone room allotted to the medical officers who served the local prisons on a roster system, and stared at the high grim wall. Time and again he asked himself why he did this when he could turn his back on all these crazy convicts and have a full-time private practice. It would certainly be more lucrative, given the number of free settlers, known as 'legitimates', who were migrating to the colony. And far less stressful, he reminded himself.

But then he'd seen the criminally negligent and often downright sadistic treatment of convicts by some of these doctors, and it had shocked him so much he felt he had to stay for pity's sake. So far, his complaints had fallen on deaf ears, but he could demand that rigid rules of punishment were adhered to, and not exceeded to suit the whims of whoever happened to be in charge that day. And at times he'd been able to rescue sick prisoners from callous quacks. Allyn was proud of his profession, but even now he shuddered, recalling some of the horrors he'd seen perpetrated on helpless convicts. He turned away from the window, away from those troublesome images, and began collecting patients' files, to return them to the office.

His father had visited him from Melbourne recently and was disappointed in him.

'I didn't pay all that money to send you to London to study medicine only to have you come back to this. I think you should return home and minister to decent people.'

They argued long and hard, while Allyn tried to explain that he was needed here by citing the shortcomings not only of common justice in Hobart, but of doctors as well.

'Stuff and nonsense, Allyn. That's not your business! It sounds to me as if you're making a damn nuisance of yourself, interfering. It wouldn't do for a practice back home. You can't walk into a hospital and criticise decisions made by other doctors, most of whom would be more learned than you, so what makes you think you can do it here?'

'You don't understand. It's different here.'

'What's different? Wasting your time treating murderers?'

'Oh for God's sake, Father. They're not murderers.'

'Most of them are.'

'They are not. Most murderers are hanged. Our governments don't waste money transporting murderers. They transport criminals and petty criminals and even women and children, and do you know why? Because the English jails are full and because they need cheap labour out here.'

'Bloody rot,' Roberts senior fumed. 'If that's right, what's that Port Arthur place about? They say it's a harsh prison for the worst of criminals. Don't tell me they're all innocent.'

'You're deliberately misconstruing what I'm saying. Port Arthur is for serious offenders, convicts who have committed more crimes here, so it could be full of murderers for all I know. But I'm not talking about that jail, I'm talking about...'

'The rabble. That's what you're saying. You're not a priest, nor are you a lawyer. I think this convict colony has had a serious effect on you. I don't think you're the type of person who should be here at all, in any capacity. You'll get yourself into trouble with the authorities, that's what will happen to you, my lad.

'You're too soft,' he added, placing his hand firmly on Allyn's shoulder. 'The best thing you can do is to come home with me. Come back to Melbourne and we'll see you rightly placed. Your mother will be very happy to have you home again.'

Allyn was glad when his father finally left, taking his opinions with him. Or most of them. It worried him to be called interfering. It shouldn't worry him, but it did. And that irritated him, causing him to backtrack over the arguments, sometimes thinking that maybe the old man was right.

But now he was so busy, rushing between the infirmary and his surgery, he dismissed that subject in favour of the joy he felt, to have his own horse and buggy at last, thanks to a parting gift of ten pounds from his father.

That reminded him of how he'd come to meet Shanahan, a man who could talk himself out of an iron mask. A convict who seemed to have the run of the town.

After days of haggling over the price of a covered gig with Bertie Cross of Cross Coach Builders, Allyn decided to buy it, on condition it was repainted, re-upholstered, and lightly sprung. While it seemed like a good idea at the time, to have a fine, good-as-new vehicle to dash about in, Bertie had no conception of haste, though the good doctor repeatedly reminded him that he was desperately in need of the gig. While the weeks dragged on and winter sent samples of icy winds to remind them that it was fast overtaking their mild autumn, Allyn begged, cajoled, demanded action, but always the job was 'not quite ready yet'.

As he stamped back home late one evening, after yet another fruitless attempt to bully Bertie into getting the job done, Allyn wished he'd bought the reliable old buggy his neighbour had offered him. But no, he challenged himself, gritting his teeth, you had to have something smart and fancy!

He turned up his coat collar and clung on to his cap for some protection against the cold wind, and dived into a lane, thinking to take a short cut through to Salamanca Square, but he found himself in a dead end, with no other course than to turn back and start again.

The lane, paved with flagstones, had a dip in the centre to allow for drainage, and he slipped slightly, cursing, as he began the return journey. Just then he thought he heard someone ahead of him. He peered into the darkness, shivered, and plunged on. The air tingled with the cold, as if it were made of sharp crystals, and when he heard the sound again, the crystals became pinpricks at the nape of his neck.

'Who's there?' he called, his steps slowing, but there was no answer. Perhaps it was a dog, it had been a heavy sort of sound, maybe a shuffle. Which didn't sound like a dog at all, he told himself. It was movement. Boots ... body movement.

Allyn felt fear creep on his skin as he tried to think what to do next. He should have known better than to run into a spot like this. Footpads haunted back streets on dark nights. He had a purse holding at least two pounds; perhaps he should wave it in front of him like a carrot, in the hope they might see it before they attacked him. The end of the lane was in sight, like a refuge, so there was no point in dallying. Allyn burst into a run, flying past one figure only to barrel into another, and he yelled more in fright than pain as he saw a knife flash, but he was close to the street now and nothing would stop him.

With a shout of despair, he ran right into the arms of another of the muggers, who threw him to the ground and stepped over him to welcome the rest of his gang as they came thudding out of the lane. But then the muggers were fighting and shouting at each other and someone landed a crunching punch on hard bone, giving Allyn the incentive to get out of there.

As he clambered to his feet one of the muggers grabbed him, hissing, 'Run! That bastard's got a knife.'

'I know!' Allyn said, but he was being yanked forward by this mugger, and together they bolted up the deserted road and around a corner, eventually outrunning the attackers.

'In here,' his companion panted, shoving Allyn into the shadowy reaches of a sly grog shop.

Allyn tumbled in through the door, gasping for breath.

'Nasty pair they were,' his rescuer said. 'No, let's get a look at you.'

'I'm all right. Just let me get my breath.'

'You probably are all right if you can still run like that after throwing yourself into my arms like a long-lost love.'

'I did not! I simply ran into you while I was trying to escape those thugs.'

The bosomy woman behind the counter leaned forward to get a better view of them.

'What happened to him, Shanahan?'

'He got knifed, I think, there's blood on him. Can I take him into the back so we can view the damage?'

Allyn remembered the knife and looked down

to see a bloody patch on his trousers. With that recognition came a searing pain in his hip, so he dragged his shirt aside to try and examine the wound.

'I'll send someone for a doctor,' the woman said. 'He's as pale as a pagan at the stake.'

'I am a doctor,' Allyn groaned, allowing Shanahan to edge him into a small back room while the woman lit a candle.

'Well now, there's a convenience if ever I seen it,' she said.

As he pulled down Allyn's trousers, Shanahan said: 'You can quit clutching that purse now, Doctor, it's safe in here.'

'I only had it in my hand hoping to buy them off,' Allyn snapped.

'Of course you did,' Shanahan grinned. 'Pull up your vest.'

The woman handed over a grubby towel, and Allyn winced as Shanahan jammed it on the wound.

'Seeing as you can't look round corners, Doctor,' he said, 'I can tell you that you've got a deep jab there in your bum, and a slash upwards as he pulled out the knife. You'll need some stitches to stop the bleeding, won't you?'

'And his trousers too,' the woman said sadly. 'Shame, a fine pair like this.'

'Could you take me to the hospital?' Allyn asked them.

'Too far to carry you, but Dr Jellick lives up the road. Will I get him for you?'

Allyn bit his lip and muttered: 'I'll kill Bertie Cross!'

'What's he got to do with it?'

'Nothing. Jellick will have to do if you'd be kind enough to fetch him.'

'I'll get you a good strong rum,' the woman said. 'Jellick's none too gentle when it comes to doctoring, you know.'

'Do I not?' Allyn moaned.

'Comes of him being a prize-fighter before he took up doctoring,' she continued when she came back with the rum.

Allyn drank it in a gulp and she patted him approvingly. 'That's the spirit. Have another, in case Jellick's had a few too many hisself.'

His wound healed, leaving a jagged scar decorated with uneven white dots where Jellick's needle had wandered, but by a miracle it wasn't infected, so Allyn counted himself fortunate over the whole episode.

By the time the operation had been completed, Shanahan had left, but the female serving in the grog shop, who bore the unlikely name of Majesta, spoke fondly of him. Allyn was informed proudly that the lady was a free settler, an immigrant, while his rescuer was a convict. He didn't pursue the matter further with her. He knew that since Shanahan was clad in drab grey, he was an assigned servant, in which case he shouldn't be out and about after dark. There were many rules and regulations regarding convicts, depending on their pecking order, and he was only lately paying attention to them, since he'd discovered he was expected to know. Many a time he'd been roared at by police or troopers for not reporting a patient

154

who was out of bounds, wearing the wrong garments, out after curfew, not carrying papers and so forth; and not for one minute would they accept his explanation that he was so busy he didn't have time to be checking on everyone who walked in the door. Fines, Allyn was warned, were looming if he didn't watch his step, and that annoyed the hell out of him. In fact, the endless list of regulations that confronted and confused him at every turn was the only thing that might drive him back to Melbourne. Being a medical officer employed by the Government, and therefore physician to convicts, seemed to give their keepers a reason to view him with suspicion. As if he were on their side against the stalwart upholders of law and order.

Some weeks later he was called to Tom Flood's farm to attend one of his convict farmhands, who was suffering from severe burns to his face, arms and chest.

'Fool of a man, fell into a fire on my far paddock when we were burning off.' Flood, a dapper fellow with a haughty air and buck teeth, had no sympathy for his workman. 'I want him removed tomorrow.'

'Where to?' Allyn asked. 'They can't do more for him in the infirmary. I'll attend to him here.'

'No you won't. Send him back to jail.'

'I can't look after him properly there. His burns could get infected in a cell. Sure to, the sanitary arrangements being what they are.'

'I don't care. Just get him out of here. He's useless to me. I want him replaced. It's not my business to support men who can't work.'

155

Allyn supposed he could have refused to write the necessary request for transfer of a patient, but Flood could easily obtain permission from another doctor, so he scribbled a note sending the poor fellow to the overcrowded prison infirmary. He knew that wouldn't win him any thanks from the staff, but it would stave off a filthy cell for a few days.

He was escorted to the door by a female servant, who whispered to him. ''Twas not George's fault, sir.'

'Who? Oh, George Smith, our patient. Oh yes, quite probably not,' Allyn said. 'Accidents do happen, I'm afraid.'

He brushed a strand of hair back from his forehead and took his hat, but she shook her head as she handed it over. 'No, sir. He was pushed. Nasty temper the boss has.'

Having said her piece, which had obviously taken courage, she ducked back behind the front door, hurrying him out and closing it quickly behind him.

Allyn stood, bewildered, for a few minutes before he walked over to the horse and buggy he'd finally bought from Bertie Cross when he discovered the man couldn't get the leather or the paint he needed to finish the gig. Even if she was telling the truth, he worried, what could he do? She wouldn't blame her boss publicly, and anyway, being a household servant, she'd probably only had this information second hand.

There's nothing I can do, he told himself as he drove away. Employers ill-treating their assigned workers was nothing new in the colony. That led to hundreds of them absconding, hiding out in villages or taking to the bush, sometimes seeking shelter from Aborigines, while others simply became bushrangers – all of that giving police and the military ten times more work. At one stage he'd spoken about this to the Commissioner of Police.

'If all employers were required under the law to treat their workers fairly, there wouldn't be so many absconders,' he'd said.

'But they *are* required to do so, my dear fellow,' the Commissioner replied.

'Then why isn't the law enforced, using fines or even jail terms?'

'We haven't enough police to be riding around checking on employers; the mounted police are too busy chasing absconders.'

'Like dogs chasing their tails,' Allyn muttered angrily, and as the buggy spun down the road he watched for the entrance to the Warboy farm. Now that he was in the vicinity, he could use his medical officer's hat to pay a visit, with the excuse of checking on the health of assignees. It was a way of catching up with Shanahan, and thanking him. On the quiet, of course.

The circular drive in front of the house was well laid out with a colourful flowerbed in the centre, and the low stone terrace was bordered by snug rows of pansies. Simply done, Allyn thought, but most effective.

A servant ran out to take over the buggy.

'Is your master home?' he asked.

'Yes, sir. Dossie up there will see to you.'

Almost as he spoke, the front door opened and

Allyn tramped towards it.

'Dr Roberts, Government Medical Officer, to see Mr Warboy at his convenience,' he announced.

'Yes, sir,' the servant said, and dashed back inside, leaving him standing in the cold and wondering how these stark houses had ever become popular. No veranda or portico, not even an awning to protect the man at the door from cold wind or hot sun.

She returned. 'Mr Warboy is trying to take a nap. He asks could you state your business?'

'Indeed. I am just here to see that all of the assignees working on this farm are in good health.'

'They are,' she told him. 'But I'll ask.'

He gave a good-humoured bow as she hurried away again, returning with permission.

'Mr Warboy don't much like inspectors coming round,' she said, 'but I told him you're just looking out for us. He says all right. Now me, I'm Dossie Dawkins. You can mark me as healthy.'

Allyn took out a notebook. 'Very well, Miss Dawkins. Now what about the others?'

'You can go round the back to the men's quarters and line them up, sir. And Mr Warboy said he would like your report in writing.'

'It shall be done,' he said gravely, and set off wondering what Warboy had to hide that he didn't like inspectors.

However, he found one workman who called up the rest, and spoke to each man privately in the rough log cabin that served as their kitchen. He found they were all in fairly good health except for a few colds and one case of boils that needed lancing, but most of them had the same malaise, the flat, cautious eyes reserved for persons of authority.

'I'm pleased to see you again,' he said to Shanahan, when it came to his turn.

'And you just happened to come upon me.'

'Not quite. I wanted to thank you for rescuing me from those muggers.'

'Did the police catch them?'

'No. Would you know who they are?'

'Me? Ah, no. We're all a clean-livin' lot out here, Doc. But you haven't enquired after my health.'

'You look all right to me. Is there anything I can do for you?'

Shanahan gave a great sigh. 'Yes. I'm dying in this rat hole of a colony. Get me transported home. I could be the first convict sent back for bad behaviour.'

Allyn looked around the cabin. 'Are you getting the right rations?'

'Such as they are.'

'Any complaints? I might be able to help...'

'No. Warboy's a gent. One might even say he's managed to stay sane so far. You'll want to watch out, Doc, this place'll get you. Send you cuckoo. How long have you been here?'

'Going on four months now.'

Shanahan nodded. 'Ah, bless your heart, there's time yet.' He turned to go, but Allyn called him back.

'Just a minute. There was an accident next door. A man was badly burned...'

'So I hear.'

'And I heard a whisper that it wasn't an

accident. Did you hear anything about that?'

Right on cue he saw Shanahan's face shut down just like the others. There might as well have been a brick wall between them.

'No,' he said. 'No.'

Before he left, Allyn took the time to peer into a nearby cabin to observe the sleeping arrangements, and found them clean enough, as these dormitories went: bunks jammed together on the bare boards with little space for personal boxes or bags, regulation horsehair mattresses or ticks, and blankets ... nothing out of the ordinary. They were all doing well compared to the stinking lice-ridden prison cells with the foul buckets in the corner. He hated having to visit prisoners in the cells, reminded now of his first visit, when he'd naïvely complained about the buckets, having given no consideration to a possible alternative. The guards still sneered at him over that.

Back in town he hurried to his afternoon stint at the infirmary, and gave instructions to two orderlies for the following day: they were to take the wagon used as an ambulance for prisoners, go out to Lieutenant Flood's farm and bring in a burns victim, George Smith.

'What happened to George?' Willem, one of the orderlies, cried, clearly distressed.

'He fell in a fire.'

'Ah, poor George. He and I came out on the *Veritas* together. We've been friends ever since. Is he bad?'

'He'll need care, Willem.'

'Where will we put him?' the other orderly

asked, peering in at the infirmary.

'We'll see tomorrow,' Allyn said wearily.

There was only one ward, with ten beds, and never an empty one, so patients had to be seriously ill to earn a place in this establishment. Two of this day's complement were dying of pneumonia, another had shocking head injuries, the result of a riot at a quarry. Allyn could do little for them beyond asking the orderlies to try and keep them warm and send for a minister of religion on their behalf. It saddened him that these poor fellows died lonely deaths, cut off from their families and forbidden the comfort of the few friends they managed to make during their exiles, but of late he'd noticed times were changing. Families were following transported prisoners, making their way to the colony as free settlers, and in many cases, where convicts were not required to serve their terms in jails, their home lives were renewed, even to being fully supported by former prisoners who had found rewarding employment.

The next day, Smith was brought in and placed on a mattress on the floor until Allyn could work out what to do about the poor fellow. The regulations, framed and hung by the entrance and signed by the superintendent of the prison, were clear. Bed patients only. That meant temporary bunks or mattresses could not be provided in an emergency. As far as Superintendent Moxon was concerned, 'leftovers', as he called them, had to be sent to the cells.

Willem was desperately worried about his friend, and was in and out of the infirmary all day until he could bear it no longer.

'You won't send him to the cells, will you, Doctor?'

'Looks like I'll have to, Willem. You know the rules.'

'But you can't!' Willem pleaded. 'You mustn't. Look at him, with his arms bound up like that. He's helpless.'

'I know. Someone will feed him. Look after him. And I'll get him back here as soon as I can.'

'But you don't understand...' Willem had tears in his eyes. 'Like that ... he can't defend himself. He's a big fellow, and strong, but he's helpless now if someone took it into his head to attack him. Men in the cells form their own cliques. Most of them are decent, but there are also some vile characters. George has always defended himself, and me, from them, but I fear for him now.'

It dawned on Allyn that Willem and George were more than friends.

'Please, Doctor,' Willem was saying. 'You have to keep him here!'

'I can't.'

'You have to!' Willem said fiercely. 'You have to!'

Allyn shuddered. Willem was right. If George was a known homosexual, he could be attacked in the cells. But asking the Superintendent to bend the rules to assist the poor fellow would be courting trouble.

Willem came back. 'I've got an idea. Couldn't you say George's burns are so bad that he needs full-time care?'

'I wouldn't argue with that. He does.'

162

'In that case it's not unknown to place patients into private care, when the infirmary is full. Dr Jellick does it often, for a price. I'd be willing to pay you, Doctor.'

Allyn shook his head. 'I don't want to be paid. Does the Super go along with this?'

'He doesn't care as long as the prisoners' whereabouts are known and recorded, and they are returned to prison as soon as they are off the seriously ill list.'

'Do I have to go and see him about this?'

'No, you fill in a form. I'll get it for you, and take it to the Super to be signed.'

'You sure?'

'Yes. You can ask Dr Jellick if you like. He calls them his Outside Patients.'

'But where could we send him? George, I mean.'

'To my place. I'll care for him. I have a cottage in Macquarie Street. We can take him there.'

'A cottage? How can you have a cottage?'

Willem looked at him sadly. 'I thought you knew. I'm a free man, Dr Roberts. I served my time and received my official release a year ago. We're not all hopeless cases, you know.'

'I'm sorry. I beg your pardon. If you're sure it's legal, then I'll be happy to sign George out of here.'

When the certificate that he had signed came back from the Superintendent's office, stamped *Approved*, Allyn was relieved to see George taken into Willem's care. He was not to know that the address of the carer had been altered in the mean time. A handy forger had substituted Allyn's address for Willem's after he'd signed the certificate, and sending the patient into the doctor's personal care was met with instant approval by the Super, who appreciated Roberts's dedication to his work.

Following his official visit to Warboy's farm, Allyn submitted a report on the living conditions of the staff and sent a copy to Mr Warboy. He stated that everything was in order, according to regulations, except for the cook-house, which needed a thorough clean. The form left space for recommendations, and Allyn never left it bare. In this case he recommended that a cook be employed to cater for the men, rather than have them muck in with their rations at the end of the day. This, he pronounced, would lead to a cleaner kitchen, better use of the rations, and a healthier environment.

Eventually he'd come to realise that no one ever acted on his recommendations, but he continued to issue them on principle.

Two days later Allyn went to the cottage to see how Smith was progressing and was surprised to find that Willem had gone to work but that Shanahan was there.

'You do get about, don't you?' Allyn said.

'Errand of mercy,' Shanahan grinned. 'His fellow slaves were full of concern for him, burns being horrible affairs, so I've come to find out for them. He's lucky you were about, to save him from the cells. How are you, anyway, after Jellick's operation? I forgot to ask before.'

'All right,' Allyn said abruptly. 'Will you step outside while I see to Mr Smith?'

'Surely.'

Obviously Willem was looking after his friend well. The little cottage, though sparsely furnished, was neat, and the bedroom window looked out on to a thriving vegetable garden. The bedlinen was clean, and the patient had already been sponged and dressed in a fresh nightshirt, in preparation for the doctor's visit, but there wasn't much Allyn could do beyond trying to dry out suppurating areas, and dab the edges of the bandages with disinfectant. He helped the bulky man to sit up a little higher on the pillows, and gave him a draft of opium to induce sleep.

'Are you feeling a little better now?' he asked, and Smith nodded weakly.

'Mr Smith,' Allyn continued, 'someone said you were pushed into the fire. Was that so? I mean–'

Before he could say another word, Smith became agitated, shaking his head furiously.

'No,' he cried. 'No!'

'All right,' Allyn said quickly. 'I'm sorry, I didn't want to upset you. We'll have no more of it. Now just rest there quietly and I'll come in on my rounds tomorrow.'

Smith's reaction worried Allyn. It had been too immediate. Too vehement. As if dangers were already present in this chilly room. But remembering his father's words, he told himself to mind his own business. For once.

Shanahan was in the kitchen.

'How long will it take for the burns to heal?' he asked.

'Weeks,' Allyn said.

'Bad luck, eh?' He frowned. 'Would it be too

much to ask for you to leave him a certificate in case the rozzers come busting in on him?'

'Yes, I could do that.' Allyn put down the Gladstone bag and took out an official letterhead to write the certificate.

'Make it large and clear,' Shanahan told him. 'A lot of our keepers don't know their letters at all.'

'And you do?'

Shanahan ignored that. 'I was just thinking the other day about Miss Marie Cullen. Now she's one who can read and write splendid. Taught by the nuns in an orphanage. I was wondering if you could find her a job? The Female Factory is no place for a decent girl.'

'There are worse places.'

'Shut your eyes if you like. Everyone else does. But Marie deserves some help. You could try, it wouldn't kill you.'

'Have you got the day off or something? George is asleep. He doesn't need anyone right now. You can run along, Shanahan. I'll put the certificate by the bed.'

'If you say so, sir.' Shanahan tweaked his cap in a mock salute and walked quietly up the narrow passage past the bedroom to the front door. He left without even bothering to look back, leaving Allyn both irritated and a little guilty. He had stretched the limits by ignoring the relationship between the two men now living here, but there were no thanks for that from this righteous Irishman, only criticism.

As he closed the front door gently behind him, however Allyn laughed. It suddenly occurred to him that he'd found an interferer worse than himself. The sun was finding its way through the clouds again, and a dozen ragged children were playing happily in the street. Noticing they were a bright-eyed, bonny lot, he was comforted that they would reap the benefits of a healthy life in this benign land.

Shanahan doubled back after the doctor had left, took the medical certificate and rushed it down to Bailey.

'Make me three copies of the form, quick as you can, leaving out the names, and get this original back to George at Willem's place.'

'Who's paying?' Bailey asked.

'Me, of course.'

'Ah yes, but who's paying you?'

'Never you mind.'

Sean wasted no more time in town. It was fortunate that he could get away this morning, since Mr Warboy had gone off to a boating party for the day. He knew that Tom Flood, in a fit of rage, had shoved George out of his way and sent him sprawling into the fire. And not just a campfire, as Flood had told the doctor, but more of a bonfire where they were burning off huge tree roots.

Both George and his mate Willem were so angry they were prepared to lodge a complaint with the authorities, safe in the knowledge that they had four witnesses, but as soon as he heard about it, Shanahan had rushed to beg them not to complain, explaining reluctantly to Willem that he couldn't afford to have Flood up on charges now, because he had plans for the lieutenant himself.

'To do with what?' Willem had asked sullenly.

'To do with his riverfront property,' Sean had said, rather than reveal anything about Flood's illegal activities.

'An escape is it, then?'

'I didn't say that.'

'You didn't have to. We'll shut up about Flood if you count us in. I have to get George off this island.'

'There's nothing definite going yet, Willem. I'll see what I can do. In the mean time, you'd be better trying to get yourselves away than attacking Flood. What's done is done. George will recover. You don't want to go complicating your lives by complaining. Just shut up and lay low.'

'Only if you promise to count George in if there is a move.'

'It'll cost money.'

'I've got money.'

Sean had no choice. He wouldn't renege on Willem if he could see a way to help George, but his heart was still set on that big escape. Getting Frank Macnamara out of Port Arthur would be a coup to reverberate around the world. Even planning an event like that kept Sean in good spirits – took the blight off his present exile.

'All right,' he said. 'You forget about Flood and I'll see what can be done for George.'

CHAPTER SIX

The ladies came to visit. Mrs Bird and Miss Skinner. They were greatly impressed by the landscaping that was under way, and tiptoed all over the place, marvelling at the pretty pavilion and interrogating Barnaby's head gardener, Angus McLeod. He had turned out to be a knowledgeable fellow, and more affable than Herring, the gardener who had been lost to Lady Franklin. Although, Barnaby was pleased to note, Herring came back quite often to oversee the progress of Warboy's Walk. And well he might: after all, he was the designer, this was his brainchild. No man with pride in his work would want to see anyone deviate from it.

Barnaby was happy to trundle along with the ladies, up one path and down another, taking in the beginnings of the delightful rose arbour and discussing the type of garden seat that should be placed inside, facing the arched entrance. Miss Skinner thought a plain Huon pine two-seater would be appropriate, but Mrs Bird preferred the introduction of amply proportioned cane settees in keeping with the gentle pastel shades of roses that Herring proposed for this corner. For himself, Barnaby had thought of a love seat, ample of course, that might appeal to Josetta Harris, but he soon tired of the subject and was relieved when they were able to retire to the dining room for afternoon tea.

'My word,' Miss Skinner said, as she tucked into a second slice of apple tea cake, 'you have a find in your cook, Mr Warboy. I don't know when I've enjoyed such delicious cakes.'

'Then you should come to one of my teas,' said Mrs Bird. 'I have actually been praised by Her Ladyship for my culinary treats, and Sir John loves my drop scones.'

'More tea, ladies?' Barnaby asked, as his cook came in with a fresh pot.

'There's someone coming up the drive,' she told him. 'In a hired coach.'

'Who can that be, Dossie?' Barnaby asked. 'Are we expecting anyone?'

'Not that I know of, sir,' she said, settling the silver teapot on its stand. 'I'll go and see.'

All three paused, tea cooling, cake forks resting, curiosity casting all eyes on the door. 'Who could it be?' Barnaby asked again.

'In a carriage,' Miss Skinner said.

'In a hired carriage,' Mrs Bird corrected.

They heard voices at Barnaby's front door. Muttered voices. Then, astonishingly, raised voices, and someone, a portly man, came tramping down the passageway and threw open the door, barging into Barnaby's dining room without so much as a by-your-leave.

Miss Skinner clutched her bosom and Mrs Bird reached for the last chocolate cream cake. Barnaby stiffened in his chair as if he were about to be attacked.

And then he was!

The intruder cried, 'Father!' and fell upon him,

shedding tears of joy and emotion. Hard on his heels came a tall, thin apparition of a woman in a trailing purple velour coat, a swathe of shawls and a large pink turban tied under her chin with a wide satin bow.

She too ignored the ladies, dashing towards 'Father', while a young woman in a grey coat and bonnet hung back by the door, chewing her fingernails.

'What are you doing here?' Barnaby cried in a far from welcoming tone, leaping up to extricate himself from them, and the ladies exchanged glances, recognising an interesting topic for tongues if ever they'd heard one.

'Oh Father Warboy, it is so wonderful to see you,' the woman cried, and the ladies realised that the gentleman, who only then remembered to acknowledge their presence, was Mr Warboy's son.

'Ah, ladies,' he said. 'Forgive this intrusion, but we have travelled across many great oceans to get here.'

'So has everyone else in Van Diemen's Land who isn't black,' Mr Warboy snapped.

Mrs Bird couldn't hold back. She giggled, and Miss Skinner frowned at her.

'I think we ought to be going,' she said, since introductions didn't appear to be on the agenda. 'We have had a most enjoyable afternoon.'

'Yes, forgive me, perhaps so,' Mr Warboy said. 'This is my son Jubal and his wife and daughter. I'm sorry, I was not expecting them. Dossie, call Shanahan to drive the ladies home. And Jubal, shift that vehicle from my carriageway. Send it away.'

'We can't,' he said. 'Not yet. Our luggage is on board.'

'Then send it round the back!' Mr Warboy hissed over his shoulder as he escorted his lady friends past his granddaughter and out of the room.

Barnaby experienced a pang of jealousy as the buggy spun away down the drive with the two genteel ladies aboard. He wanted to go with them, to fly from this place, from that wretch Jubal and his frumpish women. How dare they come here and upset his household! Only recently he'd been congratulating himself on the little Eden he'd managed to establish here in Hobart, with his charming house, nice respectable friends, and a farm that was running smooth as silk. Not to mention, he reminded himself, the half share in Pollard's stores, that had turned out to be an excellent investment.

'And now,' he muttered bitterly, 'they have to turn up.'

Suddenly he remembered that Jubal had said their luggage was on board, and he realised they might be decanting at his back door, so he rushed inside in time to see Dossie struggling up the passage with a large valise.

'Where are you going with that?' he cried.

'Well I don't rightly know,' she said. 'The gentleman said to take their luggage to their rooms, but what rooms?'

'Leave it there a minute,' Barnaby told her. 'Where are they?'

'In the dining room. I made fresh tea.'

Barnaby dashed down there to find the trio

finishing off the cakes. He went to the sideboard and poured himself a rum, then placed himself at the lower end of the table, since Jubal had usurped his place. Two gulps of the best Jamaican rum calmed him a little, and another gave him a gentler tone.

'Well now,' he said. 'Well now, Jubal, Millicent and, er...'

'Penn,' her mother prompted. 'Short for Penelope.'

'Yes, of course. How did you happen by this southern isle?'

'We heard you were here, Father,' his son told him, 'and we thought we should...'

'Call in? On your travels?' Barnaby interrupted, hopefully.

'We came via the Horn, a vile voyage,' Millicent sniffed. 'I shall never go back.'

'No, that route is not recommended,' her father-in-law said. 'Better to go via England, much more enjoyable, a delight actually.'

Jubal sat back in his chair and looked appreciatively at Barnaby's elegant dining room. 'As I was saying, we were concerned for your health, considering your age, and thought we should be by your side. You don't have any family here, do you, Father?'

'What? Of course not.'

'Ah, there, I knew it. You always were a gentleman of integrity. And how are you finding this colony? I have to say, it does not carry the best reputation, so you can imagine how worried we were about you. For all we knew you could have fallen in with a den of thieves.'

173

'You underestimate me, sir. Now, tell me, how long are you staying?'

Jubal undid his collar and looked coolly at his father, feigning surprise at the question. 'Why, goodness me, we've come to stay! I have been managing a plantation in New Orleans for some years, but when I learned that you resided here, I felt we should come to your side. I believe God in his goodness made sure I found you, so that we could care for you.'

'Mmm.' Barnaby considered this irritating news, wishing God would mind his own business. 'I have to tell you, Jubal, that I am not in need of care. In fact I'm in the best of health. However, since you've come this far, I'd better look for somewhere for you to stay. I think the Bluehaven Boarding House in Collins Street would be ideal for you, until you work out if you really want to stay.'

'Stay? We expected to stay here, Father.'

'I imagine you did. But this house has only one bedroom.'

'It's a lovely house,' Millicent said. 'Can we have a look around?'

'Certainly. You will see then that this is a gentleman's residence. Not a family home at all.'

He noticed Jubal frown as he began the tour, and hid a satisfied smirk. They might have come all the way across the world, but he had not invited them. God had. And God could look out for them. There was no room at this inn.

The tour ended back in the dining room, while Dossie stood by the piled-up luggage in the vestibule at the back door, waiting for her instructions. Jubal resumed his seat at the top of the table and his wife sat dutifully on his left, while the young woman sheltered behind her. Barnaby joined them, in amiable mood now.

'So,' he said. 'First thing to do is get you settled in that charming boarding house, then you must come back for dinner. I'll send my man to collect you. Then I want to hear all about your travels. You must have great tales to tell.'

Jubal shook his head sadly. 'You don't realise what I gave up to come here, Father. Passages on ships are hideously expensive these days, and we had to remain in Melbourne Town for some time before we could gain passage on the coastal ship that delivered us safely to Hobart. Therefore, we simply cannot afford to stay in a boarding house.'

Why am I not surprised? Barnaby mused. The fool has fallen on hard times. He's not here to render succour to his old man at all.

As quickly as it had come, Barnaby's amiability ebbed away. 'That is unfortunate, Jubal, but then you never were much of a hand at sums. What about you, young lady?' he asked his grand-daughter. 'Are you any good at sums?'

Penn shifted shyly from one foot to the other, twisted a long fair curl around her finger, and whispered: 'I don't know.'

'Nonsense!' Jubal threw out an arm and drew her to him. 'She's excellent at sums, aren't you, Penn dear?' He pulled a chair forward. 'Come, dear, sit here. There's no need to be shy with Grandfather Warboy. He loves you as we do, he'd never see you thrown on to the street.'

'Nor would he have taken his family to the ends

175

of the earth on the off-chance that his papa would put them up.'

'Oh but he didn't, Father Warboy. We knew that you were mixing in the right circles, a sea captain told Jubal that, and besides...' Millicent fluttered her almost white eyelashes at him, 'you were always an able gentleman when it came to business affairs. My Jubal is more concerned with the spiritual side of life. Harold, on the other hand, is more like his father.'

Barnaby detected a note of bitterness there. 'Ah yes, Harold,' he said. 'And how's the lad?'

'He's a selfish fellow,' Jubal said. 'God will punish him with the utmost severity. He evicted us, just as he evicted you.'

'Leaving us with nowhere to go,' Millicent added. 'It was pure malice. I was in a state of nerves for weeks.'

'So I took up the offer of a plantation in New Orleans, but it was a horrible place. A swamp really. So we had to vacate. For our health.'

'I really would like to go to my room,' Millicent said, removing her turban and releasing a bird's nest of fair hair. 'Where is it, Jubal?'

'Surely you can put us up,' Jubal said to his father, but Barnaby shook his head.

He shook his head a dozen times in the next hour, while father and son battled over the family's accommodation. When Jubal finally threw his purse on the table to demonstrate his poverty, Barnaby was forced to offer to pay for them at the guest house, 'for a while. Until you decide where to go.'

But that wouldn't do. Jubal dug in. There was

room in this house for them, he claimed, and Barnaby felt himself losing ground as the argument deteriorated into which rooms might accommodate them.

'Certainly not,' he said angrily as Millicent pointed out that the upstairs sitting room would suit them admirably. 'That is my sitting room; my daybed is in there, and I like to sit there and watch the men at work in my garden.'

'You have a study and a parlour and a drawing room downstairs, as well as that half-empty library,' Jubal sulked. 'Can't you sit in one of them?'

'My sitting room is private.'

'Very well. Millicent and I will take the library. And you can put Penn across the passage in the drawing room.'

'I will not have my drawing room turned into a bedroom.'

'She can sleep there, that's all,' Millicent said. 'It will be lovely, Father, you upstairs and us downstairs. So we won't be getting in your way. I'm so pleased you two have made up your minds; now really, if I don't change I shall faint. What time is dinner?'

As they moved their luggage into his library, Barnaby called for Dossie. 'I want you to get Shanahan to drive you into town,' he said dismally. 'I'll need a double bed for them, one that will fit in the library, and a bed for the girl. She'll be sleeping in the drawing room.'

'You'll need mattresses and pillows and linens for the beds, will I buy them too?'

'I suppose so. And listen, Dossie, this situation

177

is only temporary, so don't spend too much, if you know what I mean.'

'Plain stuff, eh?' she grinned.

'Yes,' he said sternly. 'As bloody plain as you can get.'

He dragged himself upstairs to his sitting room and slumped into his leather chair by the window, upset that invaders were loose in his house. He hoped Dossie would find the hardest mattresses available. And rocks for pillows.

This is my own fault, he fretted. I should have a wife. If I had a wife she wouldn't let this happen. The lady of the house can't be overridden. How did I let it happen?

Angus saw the visitors strolling in the garden that afternoon and tipped his cap as they approached.

'Tell me,' the gentleman said. 'What's going on here? Why is this such a mess?'

Well versed by Zack Herring in the plans and prospects for this enterprise, Angus was able to reply with confidence.

'We're creating an English garden, sir, very different from the local flora. It works from the central point there, where there'll be a fountain.'

'And what's over there?'

'Ah. That's to be a winter blooming garden of heathers and heaths with a sundial standing in the centre.' Angus had no idea how a sundial worked but was happy to accept whatever he was told. Not so this visitor.

'What does he want a sundial for?' he asked, turning to the woman with him, obviously his wife.

178

'I'm sure I have no idea,' she said. 'You can see very well where the sun is without having a sundial point it out to you.'

Thoroughly confused by the response, Angus wondered if he'd misunderstood the purpose of the thing. As they moved on, the young woman with them, at a guess their daughter, gave him a shy smile from under lowered lids. It was as if she sympathised with his confusion. And understood. She was a pretty girl, very pale of face, and that served to emphasise her full pink lips. Angus was entranced. He stared after her, taking in her long blonde curls and her shapely figure, but remembering mostly that rosebud-pink mouth. He wondered who they were.

He was soon to find out from Dossie that this was Mr Warboy's son and family, and according to her, they'd landed on the old man without warning, causing all sorts of conniptions. That pleased Angus. Couldn't be better, he thought. And from that day on, he endeavoured to see as much of the girl as possible.

Unfortunately, that proved to be more difficult than he'd anticipated, even though she was living right there in the house, sleeping in a room Dossie said was the drawing room, another mystery, on the ground floor. She rarely came into the garden, and when she did she was usually with her mother. On the few occasions she was seen on her own, she stayed close to the back steps or peered out at the workmen from the safety of the streaming green leaves of the big old pepper tree near the laundry.

But Angus was a determined man. And

besotted with Penelope Warboy. After a few weeks he managed to pull off a plan to talk to the women at least.

Zack Herring's workers were still busy clearing the land for Lady Franklin's garden, and Zack, being the head gardener and overseer, was not expected to lift a pick. This gave him plenty of spare time, which he spent getting riotously drunk. In sober moments, though, he still came back to Warboy's Walk to check its progress, and on one such occasion Angus, with pencil and notebook in hand, had Zack explain to him again which flowers would be growing in the perennial border to be viewed from the house. Then he learned them by heart.

Later, when he saw Mrs Warboy and Miss Penelope walking by the very spot, he sped over to explain the layout to them.

'Pardon me, ladies,' he said in his soft Scottish burr, 'I was wondering if you would be interested in knowing what is to be made of these plots.'

The woman looked through him, her watery eyes cold as ice. It was as if he were invisible. She said nothing, nor did she move. There was a viciousness about her attitude that astonished him. In all his years, no one had ever smitten him with such uncalled-for rudeness. He'd been beaten, kicked, bashed senseless by warders, but…

The girl intervened. 'I'd like to know,' she said in a shy, silky voice.

'Penn!' her mother protested. 'Really!'

Mrs Warboy turned her back as Miss Penelope asked: 'What are those green sprigs and bushes growing there?'

Angus rushed to air his knowledge. 'The plants are arranged at an angle to the border here, so that they are all visible from a distance. The perennials...' he took a deep breath, 'only bloom for about three weeks, so the bushy part holds the garden together.'

The girl said not a word. She was listening intently, though not looking directly at him, so Angus was unable to discover the colour of her eyes. Yet.

It was disconcerting to be addressing the stiff back of a woman in a black dress and the side of her daughter's bonnet, but Angus plunged on. 'At the front are low-lying fairy roses, and further along go echinacea blossoms in front of the silver grass. Across there,' he pointed, 'there'll be a whole lot of pink bee balm and behind them a wide drift of purple salvias, and over the other side the red salvias, beside the long dividers, like, of delphiniums and lilies, and behind them again, gettin' taller, more roses and...'

Mrs Warboy spun around. 'Quite enough! Go away! I can't understand a word he's saying.'

'I think he's very clever,' the girl said, with a peep of a smile, before she fell in behind her mother and marched back to the house.

'The place has gone to the pack with them here,' Dossie told Angus. 'They're a messy lot, used to people picking up after them. They eat like horses, and she's taken over the run of the place, giving me orders all day. And she won't lift a bloody finger. You tell Shanahan I've changed me mind. I need a washerwoman, and a scullery maid. I can't keep up.'

Angus conveyed this message to his boss, but Shanahan was already acquainted with Jubal Warboy. 'A bloody nuisance, that one is. Marching about sticking his nose in like he owns the place.'

'But he doesn't own the place. Dossie said the old fellow's fit to be tied. He hates having them in his house.'

'Then why doesn't he kick them out?'

Angus was mystified. 'She says she's heard them arguing. They won't go. I never heard of such a thing. If that was my old man he'd take to them with an axe-handle. Anyway, Dossie says she can't keep up and she's scared the woman will sack her.'

'All right. I'll talk to Mr Warboy.'

When Sean found an opportunity to broach the subject, the master nodded. 'Yes, you're right. Dossie can't do everything. Trouble is, they're not used to white servants. They want blacks. Do you know any trained black girls, Shanahan?'

'I've heard of a couple already placed, but they're rare.'

Warboy frowned. 'I told Millicent that. I tried to explain that the African blacks we had over there were trained from birth.'

'As slaves?' Shanahan said helpfully.

'Yes. I can't get it through her head that these Van Diemen's blacks wouldn't be any use. But she whinges that she wants a black maid. To train. See what you can do. In the meantime, send up one of the men to help Dossie in the laundry.'

Sean knew it was a hopeless task, but it was an excuse to ride into town. Winter had set in and

182

there was snow on Mount Wellington, but it was a fine clear day, as if no one had told the sun it was not his turn to shine. As he rode along the street, the constant activity, with new roads and new buildings, never failed to astonish him. He still carried the image of his home village of Rosleen like a picture postcard. The scene had been the same in his father's and his grandfather's time. And no doubt far further back than that, he mused. But this place, with more and more people coming, convicts and keepers and settlers, it could end up a real town, and then what? Sean had already heard talk that the settlers were signing petitions to stop transport ships coming to this port, and believed that to be a bloody marvel. He wished he knew where to get hold of the petitions, he'd give them a shift along. Might be an idea to get Bailey, the forger, on the job, he laughed. Sign everyone up.

'Hey, Shanahan!' a woman called, and he came up from his reverie to see the bawd, Bobbee Rich, looking a sight in a bright red dress with a huge crinoline skirt, standing in the doorway of a shop.

'Here!' She beckoned with her thumb and hurried down to the corner, so he reined in his horse and dismounted. 'What's up?'

'Freddy Hines is on the run,' she whispered.

'Why? What happened?'

'He got out of the infirmary and scarpered.'

'The fool. Where will that get him?'

'It would have got him a couple of days on the loose, I suppose, and I hear that's all he wanted. He was savage with Pansy for crippling his hand, so he lay in wait for him at Pansy's favourite

183

drinking hole, and whacked him with an iron bar. Old Pansy,' she spat, 'he got his deserves, went down with a broke leg. But now silly bloody Freddy is runnin' for his life.'

'Where is he?'

'Thereabouts. Can you get him on a boat?'

'Not enough time. He'll have to go bush.'

'How?'

'How do I bloody know?' Shanahan said angrily. 'They get themselves into these troubles and expect us to risk our freedom for them.'

'They'll send him to Port Arthur,' she warned. 'You must be able to do something.'

'What's he to you, Bobbee?'

'A mate. He done me some good turns.' She nodded towards a disturbance up the street. 'Look, the coppers are searching the town; they're true after him, Shanahan.'

'Can you send him to Bert Cross's place? The coach builders?'

She nodded.

'He has to go on his own. Bert won't trust two. I'll get over there and tell him Freddy's coming.'

She turned her rouged face to him and grinned. 'Orright, love. No hard feelins. Some other time, eh?' And strode away.

Exasperated with Freddy and with her, Sean walked back to his horse, and was just about to mount when he saw Louise Harris standing outside the general store, her eyes wide with shock. Obviously she'd seen him talking to Bobbee, of all people, the most flamboyant of the whores who worked out of the nearby brothel.

He called to Louise, but she turned on her heel

and darted back into the shop.

Sean wanted to go after her and try to explain, but there wasn't time. He had to get to Bert Cross and talk him into letting Freddy hide out in the space behind his hayloft. Apart from that, he had no idea where an escapee with police and warders hot on his trail could find refuge. They'd be tearing the town apart with one of their own struck down.

Nevertheless he rode quietly through the streets, so as not to attract attention, and on into the long tree-lined road that led to the coach builder's sheds, where his heart jolted in fear. Several police were checking passers-by and combing the buildings on each side of the road.

He couldn't turn back. Not now. So he rode blithely on, until he was ordered to halt.

'Who are you?' a constable asked him.

'Shanahan. Assigned to the Warboy farm.'

'What are you doing out here?'

'I gotta see Bert, the coach builder. My boss wants a posh new coach.'

'Aye. While ordinary folk walk.'

'Always the way. What's going on?'

'We're looking for Frederick Hines. He broke out and attacked a warder. You know him?'

'Can't say I do. Can I get on now?'

'Aye.' Two more riders were approaching from the opposite direction, so the constable turned away to question them.

Sean urged his horse ahead, worrying that Freddy might suddenly be seen crossing one of the paddocks along here. He urged the horse on to a canter, rounding the bend to ride past the coach builder's without stopping, and turned down the next side road, then doubled back to watch for the fugitive, hoping he would come this way, worrying that he couldn't hang around this area too long and end up getting pinched himself for loitering. Then he saw Freddy hurtling out of a lane as if wolves were on his tail.

Sean whistled to him. 'You can't go there now,' he warned as Freddy came puffing towards him. 'The searchers are all over the place. You'd better go back to where you came from.'

'I can't. It was only a hole under some steps. They told me to move on.'

'You still have to turn back. You'll walk into them this way.'

'Can't you hide me someplace?' Freddy said, frantic now. 'What about the wharves? You've got mates there.'

'No I haven't. It takes time and money. I've been tryin' to think where you could go. Why don't you dig into one of these paddocks till dark. The grass is high enough to hide you flat out.'

'Then what?'

'Jesus, Freddy. I don't know. You should have given this a bit more thought.'

'I did. Look at what the bastard did to me hand.'

Sean acknowledged the crabbed hand, but this was no time for commiserations. He was anxious to get out of this area, so he began to move the horse forward, with Freddy trotting alongside.

'If I were you,' he said, 'I'd head for one of the cat houses down at Salamanca.'

'That's where I've come from. Listen, I've got an

idea. Why don't you lend me the nag, Shanahan. It'll get me out of town quick from here. I'll take it straight to your farm and leave it there for you.'

'What about me? How do I get back?'

'Jeez! You could always walk, it'd only take a few hours. But someone'd give you a ride. I can't bloody ask for a ride. It's me only chance, mate. Come on, get down. Give me a go.'

'Wait a minute! Hang on, what then? You get out to the farm, and then what do you do? We won't hide you, make bloody sure of that. Not with Warboy's fawkin' son sticking his nose into everything.'

'I'll keep going!' Freddy said, suddenly optimistic. 'That's what I'll do. I'll leave the horse and keep going, I'll go bush. I'll join the lads bushwhacking!'

Sean had to agree that that was Freddy's only chance now.

'Listen.' Freddy clutched at him. 'We cleared that back road by the stream; you know, the one that goes across the back of Warboy and Flood's places. I'll take the horse down that road, and slip him into your paddock. I'll leave the saddle and bridle on the fence. They'll be safe there. Then I'll burrow off into the bush. It'll be easy, they'll still be looking for me in town. Shanahan, you have to let me have the horse. Please, mate!'

Sean cursed Freddy as he tramped back into town, making for Davey Street, where he'd last seen Louise. Hopefully, if she had the buggy, and if she was speaking to him after Bobbee's parting remarks, he could cadge a ride back to the farm.

But he shouldn't have to be doing this. Freddy was a blasted nuisance. And what was to become of him now? He had a head start on the law, but for how long? Running hell-for-leather away from civilisation was a perilous choice at the best of times. He'd get no help from farmers, who were mainly free settlers, and little from former convicts now farming outlying areas. They were determined to make new lives for themselves, which meant, in their eyes, staring straight ahead. No deviations into mischief. And no sympathy for the Freddies of this world.

Sean berated himself angrily. He shouldn't have listened to Bobbee Rich. But then he couldn't imagine himself riding away and leaving Freddy there, right in the centre of the manhunt. He'd known him since his first days in the prison ship, and had appreciated his help in getting to know how things worked in this weird world.

That brought him to musing about the even weirder world Freddy was headed for. If he managed to strike out into the mostly unexplored centre of the island, the blacks might help him. On the other hand, they might just as easily knock his block off. Then there were the bushrangers. Every man who 'went bush' hoped to join up with them, and survive in the bush by raiding villages and farms. Most were recaptured, and of the rest, few succeeded, mainly because those outlaws were hardened criminals and about as friendly as a sugar bag full of snakes. And the bush on this island wasn't mere woods and overgrown pastures. Sean had met a former prisoner who'd worked as a bearer with parties of explorers, and he'd said this bush was wild, impenetrable mountains, huge gorges and lakes, a land of bleak and secret places known only to savages and strange animals.

He shuddered as he pressed on down the street. He had been much further out of town than he'd realised, now that he was relying on shanks's pony, but eventually he crossed through Davey Street, keeping an eye out for Louise.

The thought of her dispelled his concerns for Freddy and the day seemed sunnier, the leaves on the streaming gum trees dewier. She reminded him of Glenna. His mother had written telling him that she had married Tom Fogarty, a letter that would have broken his heart had he not been in shock over Matt's death. Since then he'd tried to discourage his heart from making room for Glenna, to ward off the hurt, but sometimes, like now, she found her way in.

A runaway draught horse diverted his attention from his quest, and he dashed out to try to grab it before it reached the busier end of town, but it was too fast – too young and panicky to be sidetracked – and it galloped madly on. Sean ran too, joining other men who hoped to be of use, but they were all left behind as a rider hurtled past them, winding up a lasso. He heard the rider give a shrill whistle and saw the horse slow, pricking up its ears at a familiar sound. It provided enough time for the rider, a soldier, to hurl the rope and lasso the horse, eventually bringing it to a standstill.

Onlookers clapped and cheered and the soldier in his flash red jacket waved to them in acknowledgement.

Sean had started to clap too, but soon stopped when he recognised Tom Flood, Warboy's next-door neighbour. He scanned the crowds who had come out of the shops to see what the fuss was about, and saw Mrs Harris among them. Behind her was Louise, who turned away when she caught his eye.

He smiled. Definitely still in the bad books.

'Good day to you, ma'am,' he said to her mother, raising his cap. 'And to you, miss.' Louise sniffed, pert nose in the air, and adjusted the blue bonnet that suited her so well.

'Would you ladies be riding or driving today?' he asked.

Mrs Harris looked surprised. 'We're in the buggy. Why?'

'I was hoping for a ride home, you see.'

She could hardly refuse him. 'Very well. We were just leaving. The buggy's in the back of the feed store. I have to get some oats and some netting. I find I can grow the tomato here, but the dratty possums eat them.'

'The tomato? Is that the scarlet fruit? I've never seen one growing.'

'Then I will show you,' she said primly.

He carried her purchases out to the buggy, and was packing them on board when Dr Roberts came by.

'How are you, Shanahan?' he asked cheerily. 'Doing your good deed for the day?'

'You could say that.' Sean turned about and introduced him to the ladies, noticing that Louise found her eyes then, quick smart! She was all smiles and lash-batting for young Dr Roberts, and even the normally cool Mrs Harris had a smile for him.

'Would you be wanting me to drive?' Sean asked her.

'Yes, you may,' Mrs Harris said, walking to the front to sit by him. 'You sit in the back, Louise.'

Sean was amused when he saw the way Roberts looked at Louise. He wasn't bad-looking, if you counted his sandy hair and the sandy-coloured short beard that curled at the edges. Personally, Sean thought his looks to be wishy-washy, but apparently Miss Harris did not. And that was a good thing. He couldn't afford to be teased by a flirty girl like Louise. It was hard for a man living in limbo when it came to sex to be turning his face from her. Better she found another to concentrate on.

'Giddyup!' he clicked at the horse, taking the buggy out of the gate. Then he remembered he was supposed to be looking for a black servant girl, but he could always say he'd been making enquiries.

Allyn Roberts was very much taken with Miss Harris. He wondered how she and her mother came to be connected with Shanahan. She was the prettiest girl he'd met since he'd been in Hobart, and he couldn't make out why he hadn't seen her before, since he attended quite a few social gatherings.

He'd have to visit Shanahan again, one of these days.

Had the ladies not been present, he would have told the Irishman that he was on his way to visit

George Smith. It was three weeks since he'd first treated George's burns, and the patient was bearing up. He was not one to complain, despite the constant pain he must be enduring, but at least Willem was there to care for him when he returned from work.

Unfortunately, just as Allyn was about to drive away from the store, a policeman raced over to him, calling for help. Apparently the young draught horse's temper had flared up again and he'd kicked his owner.

'Rendered him unconscious,' the policeman said. 'And with a head bleeding sorely. Could you come quick?'

The man was in a serious condition. Allyn did what he could to staunch the blood, while calling for a wagon of some sort to transport the patient to hospital. Someone volunteered his vehicle; the man was lifted carefully aboard and Allyn climbed in with him.

At the hospital, he and the matron agreed that the man, who had been identified as Jock Disher, had such severe head wounds he would have to be operated on as soon as possible, so the surgeon was sent for.

The wait was interminable. Matron seemed to have washed her hands of Mr Disher after Dr Roberts and a nurse had prepared him for the operation, and no matter how often Allyn reminded her the patient was failing, she refused to allow a second messenger to ask the surgeon, Dr Slatter, to hurry.

'Does he know the situation?' Allyn asked angrily.

'Of course. But he can't be at our beck and call night and day.'

'I realise that. But the matter is urgent. Where is he? Perhaps I should go and get him.'

'You'll do no such thing. I'll allow you to stay with Mr Disher until the surgeon arrives so that you can assist in the operation. That would help immensely. Now just settle down, Dr Roberts. Settle down.'

A distraught Mrs Disher arrived and demanded her husband be operated on immediately, insisting that if the surgeon wasn't available, then – pointing at Allyn – 'this fellow' could do it.

'Certainly not,' Matron declared. 'Heavens, no! Dr Roberts has done his best but he is not a surgeon. Dr Slatter will be here soon.'

The miserable afternoon wore on, and Mr Disher died ten minutes before Dr Slatter arrived at the hospital.

Allyn was furious, but Slatter, a stern, grey-haired man, apologised. 'I'm sorry. I was already out of the door when your message came about this poor fellow. There was a cave-in at the West Quarry, two men killed, three seriously injured. I did what I could there and rode here as fast as...'

He hadn't finished his sentence when Mrs Disher, who had overheard their conversation, exploded.

'You ran off treating convicts before my husband! You put felons before the life of my husband,' she screamed. 'Do you know who he is? Was! He was a surveyor, a good Godfearing man, and you let him die...'

She ran forward, as if to attack the surgeon, but

Allyn held her back. 'Hush now,' he said, as she almost collapsed in his arms. 'Come with me and we'll say a prayer for Mr Disher. It's time for quiet.'

Dr Slatter nodded approval and walked quietly away.

Soon relatives and friends came to the hospital to find Mrs Disher, and to Allyn's relief she was soon absorbed into their communal grief. He was surprised to find the surgeon waiting for him when he went to collect his hat and jacket.

'Dr Roberts, I wanted to tell you that I examined Mr Disher's injuries and I couldn't have saved him. He was too badly battered.'

'Thank you. I thought as much but I hoped there was a chance. And I'm sorry about Mrs Disher's outburst. She was overcome, the shock and all.'

'Of course. Understandable. By the way, I signed the death certificate. Inoperable head injuries. I thought it would be easier for me to carry the burden if the lady decides to lay complaints than have your superiors frowning on you.'

He was right, and Allyn was grateful. Dr Slatter was the most senior medico in the colony, and as such, much better equipped to ward off the sort of trouble the Mrs Dishers of this world could cause.

As they left the hospital, Dr Slatter turned to him thoughtfully. 'I understand you have a government contract, Dr Roberts?'

'Yes, sir.'

'The infirmary and all that?'

'Yes, sir.'

'The remunerations don't go a long way towards paying the rent, do they?'

'I'm afraid not. But I do enjoy working there.'

'You do? That's interesting. There could be a much better practice coming up shortly that might suit you. I'll keep you in touch.'

He donned his tall top hat and strode off down the street. He cut a very dignified figure in his black frock coat, and some loiterers on the corner stood back to allow him to pass. Allyn gave thought again to buying a frock coat for himself, but he knew he was too short to achieve the elegance of the six-foot-two surgeon. Shrugging off the idea, he remembered he had to collect his horse from the yard a few blocks away, and he still had to call on George Smith. Any other patients who might have come to his surgery would have long gone by this, and tomorrow was his day at the infirmary. He never seemed to be able to catch up.

As he turned into Hay Lane, Allyn saw a manhunt was in progress, police moving quietly and methodically from house to house.

'Who are you looking for this time?' he asked the sergeant who was directing activities.

'An escapee. Freddy Hines.'

'Ah, no!'

'You know him, Doctor?'

'He was a patient of mine. He had an injured hand.'

'He'll get more than that when we catch the bugger.' They heard shouts further down the lane.

'Looks like they've got him,' the sergeant said,

and hurried away.

Allyn was distressed. He'd always wondered why so many prisoners insisted on breaking out of jail when so few ever managed to escape from the island. Out of the frying pan into the fire, so to speak. The punishment was always severe, and years were added to their sentences. According to his record, Hines had been well-behaved, and had served a third of his sentence, so with continued good conduct he would have been eligible for 'removal to settled districts'. In other words, assigned to an employer. Why on earth would the man bring this trouble down on himself?

He allowed the horse to plod slowly down the lane, behind about eight police who were emerging from buildings and heading towards a row of cottages. As they did so, Allyn realised that Willem's cottage was one of them. Surely Hines wasn't hiding in Willem's house?

'Ah, dear God!' he murmured. It was possible. Hines would have known Willem at the infirmary, and George Smith too, for that matter. Had the searchers found him?

He saw a group of policemen gathered outside Willem's cottage, and then he heard screams. Knowing all three men would be in trouble if Hines were found in that house, Allyn jumped down, hitched the horse to a tree, and ran.

He pushed into the group. 'Have you found him, Sergeant?'

'Better still,' the sergeant grinned, 'we've picked up a couple of queer boys. The lads are bringing them out.'

Allyn spoke sternly. 'I have a patient in there,

196

Sergeant. He is George Smith, an assigned servant to Lieutenant Flood. He had an accident and is suffering from serious burns. He can't be moved. I hope you're not thinking of arresting him?'

'That we are. I don't care if the bugger's on his deathbed.'

Willem appeared at the door, his hands cuffed behind him, his thin face grey with strain. As they dragged him down the path he saw Allyn and called frantically to him: 'Doctor, they're beating George!'

Allyn pushed some onlookers aside and rushed into the house, not surprised to find it in disarray, cupboards thrown open, drawers emptied, the floor littered with belongings.

George was sitting on the side of the bed, his eyes closed, teeth clenched, blood dripping from a wound on his forehead. He was wearing his prison issue of half-mast trousers and rawhide boots, and two constables were trying to drag a shirt over his head, despite the bulky bandages.

'Stop that!' Allyn shouted. 'This man is my patient. Leave him alone! Can't you see the note I left there?' He grabbed the paper, waved it about, trying to create an atmosphere of authority that just might trump the present command, and for a few minutes it worked. The men stood back.

Gently Allyn removed the awkwardly set shirt and draped it over George's broad shoulders.

'Look at this,' he said angrily, pointing to yellowing and bloodied patches on the bandages. 'His burns are infected. You can see where they're discharging. I will have to change the bandages and dress the wounds.'

'Yeah?' one of the policemen leered. 'Well you're too late, mister. We're arresting these gents.' He grabbed George's arm and yanked him to his feet.

Allyn saw his patient wince in pain, and was astonished that the big man could take such rough treatment without crying out. He caught George as he stumbled, helping him to the door, then turned back to snap at the policemen: 'I'll speak to your sergeant about this.'

But the sergeant wouldn't listen. He ordered that the prisoners' hands be bound and they be quick-marched to the police station.

'You can't do this!' Allyn shouted. 'There are rules covering the treatment of prisoners. If you must arrest a desperately ill man, I demand you free George Smith from those ropes, and place him in a vehicle.'

'Are you one of them?' a voice leered behind him, and he was jostled to the rear as a crowd gathered to watch the two men begin the long, awkward march to the prison barracks with their mounted escorts.

The sergeant called several of his men together, instructing them to continue the house-to-house search for Hines, before growling at Allyn.

'I'm Sergeant Budd. I'm in charge here, not you! I ought to arrest you, Dr Roberts. Obviously you knew what was going on in that house. It was your duty to report them.'

'My duty is to care for the sick. You'd better see that Smith is taken straight to the infirmary, or I'll have you up on two charges instead of one.'

Budd's coarse, florid features darkened as he

grabbed Allyn's jacket and pulled him forward.

'You do that, you young fart,' he grated, 'you just do that and you'll get that pretty face of yours shoved in so far your nose'll be stickin' out the back. Now push off!'

With that he let go of Allyn's jacket and shoved him so hard he fell back, tripping over tree roots to finally come to rest in the dirt. His horse turned its head to study him thoughtfully, flicked at flies with its tail and sighed as it resumed its usual patient stance.

Furious, Allyn collected himself, then noticed that the door of the cottage had been left open. He felt it his duty to shut the place down, since no one else seemed to have cared. He worried about Budd's words, wishing he hadn't confronted the fellow in the first place.

You could have made your position clear without threatening him, he reflected. Now you'll have to report him! Or maybe forget the incident.

That seemed the sensible course to follow, he pondered as he closed the windows in Willem's cottage and drew the curtains. Certainly the safest. As he made for the front door, he saw a flash of light on the floor of the darkened bedroom; a glimpse of something gold. He turned back, righted an upended drawer, and picked up a gentleman's fob watch that had slipped from a flat leather bag. It was a quality piece, he realised as he took it to the light and found it inscribed WWR...Willem Rothery, he supposed, not a little surprised that a former convict could own such an expensive item.

The watch seemed to have nudged him into a

little more respect for other people's goods, and he found himself tidying the bedroom in a makeshift manner, shoving things back into the wardrobe and the chest of drawers, and pulling the bed linen into a near enough shape.

There were papers in the bag that had spilled out with the watch, and curiosity roused, Allyn took them out, finding a letter to Willem on embossed paper from a Colonel James Rothery, obviously his father, written in a clear, precise hand. At a glance Allyn saw two themes in the lines: one a brief report of family affairs and estate management, which caused Allyn to raise his eyebrows; the other a plea for Willem to return home as soon as possible. Rather than pry further, Allyn bundled the papers together, dropped the watch into the bag with them and knotted the cord.

Now what? he asked himself. He couldn't predict when Willem would be able to return home, so the cottage would be uninhabited for quite a while. Thieves would be in, if only for the several pairs of good boots on the floor of the wardrobe, boots being currency in convict parlance. All but the very fortunate or the very clever relied on the pathetic government issue of clothing. Cheap boots were supplied to each convict every six months, by which time their own were dilapidated and stuffed with paper. He couldn't leave Willem's personal effects in an empty house.

The decision was made. He took Willem's bag with him for safe keeping, intending to let the man know as soon as he could locate him. As for George...

He sighed. He'd have to see what could be done for him, the poor fellow. Maybe his new friend Dr Slatter could help. It was at this point that Allyn realised that just doctoring wasn't good enough in this community. He would have to become more involved with the people who counted. Pay more attention to those social invitations instead of preferring to spend his spare time bushwalking and examining the maps of newly explored areas. To him, the virgin bush, known only to the Aborigines, was immensely interesting, and several times he'd even managed to find shy natives to guide him and show him the fascinating flora and fauna, the latter even more astonishing when viewed at night by lamplight.

As he mounted his horse, Allyn felt as if he'd just left school, though he was all of twenty-two. It was time to grow up, he reflected. His patients needed more than pills and potions; they needed doctors who could stand up for them. Doctors who had friends in the right places. His father had taken in the Hobart penal settlement at a glance, and predicted that Allyn would be overwhelmed here, and only now was his son beginning to see that on this point, at least, the old man could be right. The colony itself was rife with cruelty and a lack of respect for the poor and the vulnerable. What was it one of the convicts had said to him? Oh yes... 'Jobs here are a lottery. You get reasonable bosses and the good life is within reach. You get the others and you've come to hell. They can make life not worth the pain.'

Shanahan jumped down from Mrs Harris's

buggy, raised his cap to the lady herself, in thanks for the lift, gave Miss Harris a polite nod and made off across the first of Warboy's paddocks.

He should have asked them not to mention their good deed to Mr Warboy if the matter came up, but such a request, without an explanation, sounded too damned servile. And he hated for Mrs Harris to see him in that light. He could hardly tell her he'd been reduced to shanks's pony because he'd loaned his own mount to an escapee.

Anyway, he thought, as he cut across the paddock, dodging weedy hillocks and tree stumps, if the boss asks why I needed the ride, I can just look stupid, like I don't know what he's talking about, what with the horse snug in its stable. That'll work. We're not supposed to be too bright.

Hurrying now, he skipped between ancient moss-clad boulders and clambered over rocks to the small wooden bridge spanning the stream, the bridge that he and the other farmhands had built for easier access to the property. As he trod the boards, he thumped on them with his boots, pleased that they were strong and firm. In truth they were all quite proud of this bridge, with its raw timber railings smoothed to a shine by enthusiastic hands. Warboy had even let them christen it with a few tots of rum, and they'd called it Argus Bridge, which the boss had approved. He thought it was a fine thing to have an Argus, a giant with a hundred eyes, guarding his stock – blissfully unaware that the name was a joke, reminiscent of the good ship *Argo* that had been seized by convicts in the Derwent River around twenty years ago and not seen again. Present-day convicts were always greatly chuffed to be reminded of that event, and among themselves, their bridge was Argo.

To be riding a horse again was a marvellous feeling. Freddy wanted to throw off his cap, dig in his heels and let the nag go full gallop down the streets of Hobart, scattering folk in all directions, leaping over the barricades that had been set up to corner him, and thumbing his nose at the chumps who thought they could catch Freddy Hines. Instead he lowered his head, kept the nag moving along, sedate-like, so as not to call attention to himself, and begged God in heaven and his army of angels to give him a go.

'Jeez,' he whispered in prayer, 'I never done naught but good in me life. Pinched stuff, all right, but whose fault was that? Us Hineses have always been dead poor, lucky to get a feed a week, you know that well enough. My ma, a pious soul, was always in the church telling you that, askin' for help, but you never give it.'

He glanced around as he approached a corner, made to scratch his nose as a wagon with two men aboard came towards him, and turned into a busier street, falling into place behind several horsemen travelling in the same direction.

Two more turns and he was heading out of town, trying to keep the excitement inside him in check. The horse was trotting along quietly as if it knew its way home, so Freddy resumed his conversation with God, who, he felt, had let the Hines family down for generations.

'My ma,' he said softly, 'she keeps on reminding you but you never listen to her. Never ever. Pa says you don't care. Me, I have to wonder. You could have born us rich, or even with a bit of somethin' in the coffers, but no ... you dealt us the worst cards in the pack. Right down at the dead bloody end of the line, with barely a penny come to us without scraping. So whose fault is it, I ask youse, if I have to make a living best ways I can? Not mine.'

Time had slipped away so quickly he was nearing the well-known Argo Bridge almost before he knew it, so he steered the horse into nearby woods to watch the approach for fear of confronting someone who knew him as he crossed.

'Now, this is your chance to make up for what you've done to us,' he told God. 'I need help like I've never needed it before in all me miserable life. Once I leave the horse and head for the hills, you gotta take me to one of them bushranger gangs. I'll be right then.'

Sure that all was clear, Freddy rode the horse across the bridge and turned on to the stock route that followed the stream. Soon he saw the familiar two-story Warboy house in the distance, but kept his mount trotting evenly until he was past that point and well to the rear of the large barns.

'See that place,' he said angrily, addressing himself this time. 'You should be working there now. Living on the fat of the land like Shanahan and his mates, but no, God sees to it that even the chance of a good job gets taken from you.'

Freddy had heard often enough that God's

hand was in everything, so he had no illusions as to who was to blame for this latest disaster.

'You hear that?' he asked, as he pulled the horse to a halt. 'I'm in real bloody trouble now. You gotta help me.'

Dark clouds were gathering in the afternoon sky and Freddy shuddered as he dismounted. The weather in this place couldn't be trusted. You got lulled into forgetting the cold when they turned on days that could burn you like toast, but come June's winter you could freeze. And he didn't even have a blanket. Maybe if he waited here for Shanahan he might persuade him to find him a feed and cover for the night. This night only. Surely that wasn't too much to ask. Surely.

But he was a hard man, Shanahan. And got a lot worse since his cousin died. Freddy reckoned that Shanahan could get him off the island if he put his mind to it. Get him off altogether. No mucking about. And why not? He'd do good in Melbourne Town. Get a job on the wharves, paid this time, not bloody slave labour like the year he'd spent working on the construction of the new Hobart docks, up to his neck in freezing water every day.

He led the horse along a track to a gate as the first sprinkles of rain began to filter through the trees, then found himself eyeing the horse blanket. 'A bloody sight thicker and warmer than any issued to human beasts of burden like us,' he muttered resentfully. There was no way he was leaving quality goods like that to be worn by a horse.

As he unbuckled the belly band to remove the

saddle, he knew Shanahan wouldn't care if the blanket went missing. Why would he? For that matter, why would he care if the horse went missing too?

The enormity of the idea stunned him. Normally a simple gent with light fingers, Freddy had never aspired to horse stealing. That was out of his league altogether. But then a profound thought came to him. Came to him from God, at last, he was sure. Bloody certain! A bushranger without a horse would be worse than useless!

He hadn't thought of that before. They, them bushrangers, would spit on him. Probably kick him down a ravine or something. And keep the horse blanket.

'Thank you, God,' he said, frantically tightening the belly band again and checking the saddle, before scrambling aboard. He had to get out of here pretty damn fast. Before Shanahan loomed up. Before anyone saw him.

'Giddyup, Neddy,' he said, slapping the reins and plunging his heels into the horse's flanks.

Freddy Hines shouted with glee as the trusty steed took off down the track as if it too saw freedom ahead, and in no time they were out on the open road with the darkness of a gathering storm providing the cover he so desperately needed. He rode on for miles and miles, slowing when the road deteriorated into a welcoming bush track, his path to a new life. Shanahan was forgotten. Even Pansy Hurley was forgotten, for the time being. Freddy was on his way to find the bushrangers.

CHAPTER SEVEN

Jubal stormed into his father's study. 'What's this about a stolen horse? I only found out when I was doing a stocktake of the domestic animals.'

'It happened weeks ago,' Barnaby said wearily. 'A horse was stolen from our paddock by a person unknown, and the police have taken note. They have a description on record and will advise me if they are able to find it.'

'Person unknown! You believe that? With a pack of felons housed in your barns? I can tell you what happened to that good horse. One of them has stolen it and sold it. The answer is as plain as the nose on your face. This is not good enough, Father. How am I able to assist you if I am not told about these discrepancies?'

'You can assist me by letting my overseer do his job. He keeps the records, there is no need for you to double up.'

'That's where you're wrong. You're too lackadaisical about these matters. I checked up on Shanahan, he's the worst sort, an Irish troublemaker and a thief. They learn of sin at their mothers' breasts, those thugs.'

'That's hardly Christian of you,' his father remarked, though he knew it was a waste of breath. Jubal saw himself as a model Christian. Barnaby saw an infuriating, sanctimonious Godbotherer and blamed himself for ever allowing

Jubal anywhere near that Academy of Theology. A little knowledge is a dangerous thing, he reminded himself.

'Are you listening to me?' Jubal nagged. 'I intend to speak to all the men tonight and get to the bottom of this horse-stealing episode. They know more than they're letting on, you can count on that. And I intend to find out.'

Barnaby swung round in his chair. 'Ah, do what you like!' he said. 'But just remember, they're not niggers. Take 'em quiet.'

'Jubal dear,' his wife had ventured, as she lay on the leather sofa in the library, 'I do think, having heard that timid little vicar preach, his congregation would be far better served by a lay preacher if they can't find another minister. I mean to say…'

He knew what she meant to say, and agreed. Thorley was a scrawny little fellow with a chicken neck and a pipsqueak for a voice. It pained Jubal to listen to him.

Vicar Samuel Thorley lived in a fine sandstone cottage, set in a small garden at the rear of the Church of the Holy Trinity. Because he wasn't feeling well, he'd been hoping to have a rest this quiet Saturday afternoon before the ladies arrived for choir practice, but it seemed this was not to be.

As he passed a front window he noticed a gig, with a couple aboard, turn in the gate and make for the shade of the tall pines on the other side of the church.

Disappointed, he stood by the window, waiting to see if these people were coming to see him, or simply visiting the church. Many people called at the church to view Elias Donovan's beautifully carved altar and pews. Though he was a convict, Donovan's carvings had been declared true works of art and were greatly admired in the community, so Samuel was proud to have them in his church.

His sense of pride faded when Mr Jubal Warboy came around the corner of the church, trailed by his daughter, who was wearing a white muslin dress and carrying a huge bunch of flowers. It was with a great sigh that the vicar stepped forward to answer the knock.

'Why Mr Warboy,' he said, working hard to sound welcoming, 'and Miss Penelope, good afternoon.'

'Good afternoon, Vicar,' Warboy responded cheerily. 'We heard you'd been poorly, so we brought you flowers from my father's garden.'

The girl looked up at her father proudly. 'I picked some of them, Daddy.'

'Yes you did, dear, now give them to the Vicar.'

She handed them over and Samuel thanked them profusely. 'Bless you, they are superb, especially the roses. I do love roses.'

He hesitated, but since they made no move to leave, he asked, 'Was there anything else?'

'Yes indeed, Vicar. I did want a word with you.'

Spirits sinking, Samuel invited them into his sitting room.

'I'll just put these lovely flowers into some water, so that they'll keep fresh,' he said. 'Do sit yourselves down, I won't be long.'

He turned about and set off down the passage to the kitchen where he found a bucket, filled it with water and bundled in the flowers, then sank into a chair, clutching at his stomach to ease a sudden stab of pain. Gasping, he doubled over, waiting for this familiar pain to subside, and, as he did so, noticed he was still wearing his slippers.

'Oh dear,' he murmured, knowing he wasn't up to climbing the stairs to his bedroom for shoes, since these spasms always left him feeling nauseous.

'It can't be helped,' he murmured, dragging himself to his feet and taking a deep breath to help him on his way back to the sitting room.

As he reached the open door, forcing himself to straighten up, he was momentarily taken aback to see no sign of his visitors, but a glance through the gap between hinged door and jamb told him they were sitting on the left side of the room, facing the windows.

Samuel kept walking, kept going from sheer habit, while his mind reeled, only then registering what he had seen through that gap, in that room. Mr Warboy was seated on one of the solid black-wood chairs. His daughter was standing beside him. Mr Warboy's hand was behind the girl, most inappropriately! Shocked, the Vicar realised why. The fellow's hand was slyly moving around under her thin skirt, and worse, the girl was smiling, looking down into her daddy's smirking upturned face as if...

'Oh dear God!' Samuel coughed, almost choked, as he stumbled into the room.

They were together, looking innocent, the girl still standing by her father, practically draped over him, the vicar thought angrily, but at least both of the fellow's hands were visible now.

They sickened him, this pair, but he could not make an accusation that would surely be denied. Instead he needed them out of his house, so that he could reassess the situation calmly and fairly.

'Mr Warboy,' he said primly. 'Thank you again for the flowers. You wanted a word with me?'

'Yes I did, Vicar. I was wondering if you knew that I was once a scholar at the New Orleans Academy of Theology?'

'No I did not, sir,' Samuel said. His head ached and he wondered if he'd been hallucinating. He wished that wretched girl would move away from her father.

'Would you like to sit, Miss Warboy?' he asked.

'I'm all right,' she simpered, remaining in place, while her father rattled on about his wide knowledge of the scriptures.

'I never miss any of your services, Vicar,' he continued, 'but your ill health worries me. I do believe you should have a lay person to assist you here. As a matter of fact, I have spoken to several of your parishioners who agree with me that you have a great burden in this large parish, and that you would do well to reach out to an aide.'

'Oh I wouldn't...' Samuel began, but Warboy cut in.

'We all feel we have the solution in suggesting a lay preacher to assist you, and I have volunteered to take up the cause.'

'You, Mr Warboy?' the vicar croaked.

'Indeed, yes. Sermons take up a lot of your time. I could write them for you. And even deliver them, since I am quite an orator, though I say so myself.'

Samuel Thorley rose to his feet. 'I'm sorry, Mr Warboy, I'm not feeling at all well. You'll have to excuse me.'

'This is exactly what I'm saying, Vicar. You are just not up to this burden, and I can spare you the time...'

'Thank you.' The Vicar led them out of the sitting room. 'I am most grateful for your offer, and to you, Miss Warboy, for the flowers. I shall put them in the church and pray for you.'

He opened the front door to usher them out.

'When would you like me to start?' this arrogant brute of a man enquired, and Samuel stepped back as they exited his house.

'Next Saturday perhaps?' Warboy insisted, from the cobbled path past the doormat.

'I don't think so,' Samuel informed him. 'I am quite capable of carrying out my duties without your assistance. Good day to you, sir, and to you, miss.'

He closed the door briskly and leaned against it.

'I know what I saw,' he announced to his house. 'But who would believe me? What should I do?'

Exhausted as he made his way up the stairs, he could only reply, 'Pray for them.'

The summer was upon them again. Days of sizzling heat, dry as desert rocks. Skies bleached white by the mirrored links of caustic light that mesmerised sore eyes. The men standing in the courtyard, hats in hand as ordered, listening to Jubal Warboy's sermonising, bowed their heads, not in humility, but to lessen the impact of the sun.

Angus noticed that the neck of the man in front of him was already turning red. He pulled up the collar of his own shirt, from habit. During his first summer here he'd been working on the roads, in heat just like today, so he'd taken off his shirt and ended up sunburned to a sizzle. Blisters like plates. Got no sympathy from the bosses, though.

'Self-inflicted wounds,' they said. 'Ten days on the treadmill!'

He grunted impatiently as Warboy waffled on in that sing-song voice that was meant to denote piety, but instead annoyed everyone. Angus wondered how that lump of lard with slicked-down hair had ever managed to produce such a pretty daughter. Miss Warboy – Penn to her family, he knew – was the sweetest, shyest little pet he'd ever known. He was madly in love with her, had been from the day she'd emerged from the big house, not that he could ever tell her. It was all he could manage to have a few words with her on the odd occasion.

Sometimes he liked to think that Penn actually sought him out. It seemed like it. She'd come into the greenhouse when he was working in there, each time seemingly surprised to see him, but stayed to chat with him for a few minutes – about the weather or the garden or whatever he was working on at the time. She was like a little bird, peeping about, keeping her distance though,

213

ready to take flight. Funnily enough, that was usually the way she left, suddenly, as if she were startled by him. Frightened even. Then she'd wander about the garden, making sure she kept away from whoever was working out there. She always wore a pretty little silver cross around her neck, and mostly she wore a bonnet, but Angus loved to see her hatless; it made her seem closer to him, more familiar, when her thick creamy curls were allowed to hang loose to her shoulders. She never walked far from the house, though, only over to the farmyard fence on the other side. The workmen were cruel; they called her Creeping Jesus, and hated to look up and see her peering at them but never saying a word or even acknowledging them. Well, that was her prerogative. Angus thought they were jealous because Penn did speak to him. And he resented Billo Kemp's claim that she was a loony.

He wished Warboy would get on with his sermonising, he had work to do. Who would have believed, he wondered, that I'd get to like gardening? But he did. And he loved Warboy's garden as if it were his own ... the way it was coming to life at his hands was like opening a door ever so slowly into another world. The sanded paths were in place and the plumbing was ready to connect to the small fountain in the centre of the paths; a cane archway was waiting for the pink roses already budding at its base, and at the far end, facing the house, the carpenters were painting the light-hearted gazebo, white with a green roof. Angus's thoughts drifted then to the trees springing up in the rear, growing fast, like children, each trying to outdo the other.

There was a sudden disturbance. Billo had fainted in the heat, and his colleagues were rushing to assist, all shouting instructions until he was carried away to the shade.

Jubal ploughed on with his threats of eternal damnation for horse thieves, calling on the God above to strike down the sinner among them. He had no pity for the man who'd fainted, pausing only to shout: 'Order! Order!' and demanding his small audience resume their places, until, suddenly, the awesome truth confronted him.

God had heard him! God had indeed struck down the horse thief, before their very eyes! God had heard the words of Jubal Warboy, his representative in this earthly vale of wickedness, and acted upon them!

'Glory be!' he called, arms raised to the heavens in appreciation. 'The Almighty has spoken!'

He raced over to the sinner, shoving men aside, and struck a dramatic pointing pose. 'Behold!' he roared. 'The Almighty has spoken! Behold the sinner! The horse thief!'

The fellow on the ground, suddenly cured, sat up quickly. 'What? Who?'

'You are exposed!' Jubal was beside himself with excitement. 'The Lord himself has pointed the finger at you. Confess while there's time! Confess before he strikes you dead and commits you to eternal hellfire. Confess!'

The sinner looked about him, dazed. Dazed by the revelation, Jubal supposed. It was indeed an awesome moment.

'Confess to what?' The man blinked.

'Don't contradict the Lord!' Jubal thundered. He turned to the onlookers. 'You saw what happened! You all saw. I called on the Lord to strike down the sinner and He did! There! There is your horse thief!'

'I am not!' the sinner said, climbing to his feet, and to Jubal's horror, the other men began to laugh.

'Order! Order!' Jubal cried. 'You, Shanahan! Put this man in chains. And lock him in the woodshed.'

'Billo's never a horse thief,' Shanahan said quietly. 'He's a fainter. He often faints in the heat. You've seen him faint before.'

'I haven't seen any such thing. I know what I saw! His guilt was seen by all. You'll obey or you'll get a flogging too.'

'What?' Billo sprang to life. 'I didn't steal no horse. Get out with you! You won't be bloody flogging me for something I didn't do, mister. Who the hell are you anyway? You can go screw yourself. I don't have to listen to you. Horse bloody thief! You stupid bastard. Get out of my way!'

With that, he hitched his trousers up over his skinny hips and strode away. 'You can get someone else to do the fainting from now on,' he snarled at Shanahan as he passed.

'Get him back here,' Jubal shouted at Shanahan, who shook his head.

'I cannot. I'm a farm overseer, sir, not a sheriff.'

Jubal fumed as the rest of the workmen walked away from him. They actually turned their backs on him! He was so shocked he couldn't think what to do beyond wishing there was a flogger on

216

the farm. He'd give him plenty of work. He couldn't demean himself by demanding they come back, knowing they'd ignore him. It'd be like trying to recall a pack of wild dogs. And anyway, he thought uneasily, they might turn on him.

'You'll hear more of this, Shanahan,' he called. 'And so will that horse thief.'

No one was able to guess what, if anything, had transpired between Barnaby Warboy and his son over Jubal's claim to have God's ear, but nothing more was heard of the matter, not until Dossie tipped them off about the post.

'There's letters there for some of you lads,' she told Singer. 'Mr Jubal's got them. I heard Mr Warboy giving them to him yesterday, to hand out.'

'Letters!' Singer was excited, letters were such a rarity for any of them. 'Is there one for me?'

'I don't know. That's why I was thinking it strange. I mean, if you fellers had got letters, there'd be more excitement, but seems no one's got them yet.'

'We haven't seen any letters. Not that I know of. Where are they?'

'I think Mr Jubal's still got them.'

Singer frowned. 'The more I see of that fellow, the worse I like him. I'm going up right now to ask for them. There has to be one for me after all this time. I haven't heard from anyone back home in nearly a year. For all I know, they could be dead.'

'Ah no,' she said. 'Don't say that, Singer. It's

bad luck to be saying that. Most of the time, letters go down with ships. They get sunk.'

But Singer wasn't listening. He threaded his fingers through his hair in an effort to appear tidier, tucked his shirt into his trousers, gave his battered old boots a rub with a rag, and turned to Dossie. 'Righto. Lead the way.'

'I don't know if you should...' she said nervously. 'He might want to know how you know about them. I could get into trouble.'

'No you won't. Off you go. I'll wait a few minutes.'

Even that delay was agonising. A letter? It would be from his sister, the one with the kids, his nephews, who he'd never seen. She wrote good letters, full of news of everyone, better than the cards he sometimes got, lucky to fit a dozen readable words.

'That'll do!' Singer strode out of the stables, across the horse paddock, climbed over the chock-and-log fence, stood back impatiently, watching as Dossie picked up a milk bucket from the dairy before heading up the stone steps to the kitchen.

Forced to cool his heels a little longer, he looked up at the fine house, set high enough to be able to view the farm to one side, and that astonishing garden they were growing on the other. He thought it was madness to be spending so much time on a garden, but then supposed it was only time, and everyone here had plenty of that.

He knocked on the kitchen door and in a suitably respectful tone asked to see Mr Warboy.

'Mr Warboy Senior,' he said, having considered

218

his choices.

'He's not at home,' Dossie informed him, nervous as a cat in a chimney.

'Then the other Mr Warboy, if you please.'

'I'll see,' she allowed, and ducked away.

He peered into the kitchen. All spick and span it was, floor you could eat off if you ran out of dishes, and ho! A picture of the King high up there, as it should be, on the wall above the row of shiny saucepans.

Singer couldn't resist a grin, knowing Zack's antipathy towards royalty. And then it occurred to him that Zack was now working for His Excellency! A vice-regal! He wondered if they counted. It would be a lark to ask him.

Dossie was back. 'You are to go round to the side door, he says.'

'Didn't he ask what I wanted?'

'He did. I said I didn't know.'

The side door had a sort of sentry box attached to it, a repository for outdoor boots and oilskins, and now the preacher had joined them, standing awaiting his summoner.

'How dare you come up to the house!' he snorted.

Singer shook his head. He hated having to deal with pompous fellows like this one, who really took the cake.

'Begging your pardon, sir, but if any letters come in the mail for assignees they are sent out on the last Friday in the month, and this being the day, I have come to collect them.'

'I've never heard of that rule.'

'That's understandable, sir. We don't get many

to speak of. Not often at all. So are there any letters?'

The preacher blinked, unsure of his ground. 'There could be, and then again there might not be.'

'Am I to guess, sir?'

'No. Not actually guess. But I do have a condition, come to think of it. You bring up the horse thief and I'll see about letters.'

'So we do have some?'

'Did I say that?'

Singer shifted his stance from one foot to the other. This man's deliberate stalling was becoming unbearable. 'No you did not, sir. But would you mind having a look to see if any of them are for me? The name is Forbes. I dearly need to know, if you'd be so kind.'

'You bring up the horse thief, with his written confession, and we'll see about it. You are dismissed, Forbes.'

'Sir, I am fairly new here. I don't know of any horse thief.'

'You have my instructions! Go!'

Warboy turned about and re-entered the house.

Singer Forbes remained where he was, his whole body frozen in rage. To think there could be a letter in there for him, from his sister, or his dad even ... and that fat bastard was withholding it, was a form of torture for him. Normally he considered himself easy-going; just a stirrer, into a bit of havoc here and there for the hell of it, to pass the time, and normally he didn't get emotional, like so many prisoners did. But now he had to fight to keep his calm. He took deep breaths as he made himself turn and walk away, before he gave in to his inclination to storm that door and slam Warboy's head into the wall.

By the time he found Shanahan, he was able to speak in his usual laconic voice.

'Warboy Junior,' he said. 'We've got a right one here. As pompous as an undertaker at the Pope's funeral.'

'What's he done now?'

'Withholding our letters...'

'Letters! Are there letters?'

Singer saw the same ache in Shanahan's eyes. 'I think so. Dossie says there are, but the preacher's playing games. Won't say yes or no until we hand over the horse thief.'

'What?'

'That's the game.'

'What did you say? You didn't cheek him, did you?'

'Nearly swallowed my tongue, but no. I was afraid the bugger would burn them if I put on a turn.'

'Oh Jesus! He could too. Where's his pa?'

'Out.'

Shanahan bit at a thumbnail. 'I have to get to him before his son does. Not a word to anyone about any letters, it's no joke this.'

'Who's laughing?' Singer drew some water from a nearby barrel, poured it over himself to cool down, and then hurled the ladle high into the sky.

The meal was of a very poor standard, Barnaby thought, as he endeavoured to consume some of Mrs Bird's special recipe of tripe and onions in parsley sauce. In his opinion no amount of sauce could rescue tripe that tasted like dried cat's fur, but he chewed gamely on, frowning when one of her obnoxious sons actually spat a mouthful on the floor.

It was all Jubal's fault, this sudden and serious inclination to socialise with ladies again. He had finally decided that a wife would be infinitely preferable to sharing his house with Jubal and his women. Only yesterday, he recalled miserably, when a backlog of Sydney newspapers arrived with the mail, Millicent had started shrieking at her daughter for some misdeed, Jubal had bellowed at them to stop their noise, and she had screamed back. Barnaby himself, the owner of the house, had had to close and lock his study door in an endeavour to read the papers in peace.

He'd accepted Mrs Bird's luncheon invitation with pleasure; she was a handsome, busy woman, always on the go, rather after the style of Lady Franklin though she was critical of the explorations into the wild interior of the island undertaken by the Governor's wife. As for himself, Barnaby was hugely impressed by Her Ladyship's stamina, but he bowed to Mrs Bird's opinion on this occasion. His hostess was spirited in her attitudes, never afraid to speak up, and he fantasised about her accepting his offer of marriage with the condition that his relatives depart her future home.

The dream was shattered when he met her nine-year-old twins, a whining, argumentative pair whom she adored, and the live-in governess recruited from the Female Factory who had no teeth that he could ascertain.

Dessert was better, obviously Mrs Bird's forte, but the children's manners did not improve and he was relieved when they were sent from the table.

As he rode home, he decided that little was to be gained by substituting the Bird boys for his own son, and his thoughts duly turned to Miss Skinner for his salvation.

Shanahan was digging a drain by the gate, to allow runoff from a depression that flooded widely when it rained, and he raised his cap to the master as he approached.

'Could I have a word with you, sir?'

With his overseer's assistance, Barnaby dismounted from his horse and peered at the shallow drain. 'Will that do any good?'

'The drains will help, but tomorrow I'll bring a cartload of fill and flatten out that area around the entrance.'

Barnaby nodded approval and handed him the horse's reins. 'I'll walk up to the house.'

'Just a minute, sir. The word...'

'Ah yes. The drain?'

'No. I've a small situation here and I'm needing your advice. You see, Mr Warboy tells us there are letters in the house for us...'

Sensing trouble, Barnaby felt a pang of anxiety.

Shanahan continued: 'but he's not inclined to hand them over.'

'Why not?' Barnaby asked sternly. 'He must have a reason.'

'That he does, but the reason doesn't work. He claims young Billo Kemp is a horse thief. Now I can vouch for the lad. He's not.'

'All right, all right. But what's that got to do with the letters?'

'Plenty, sir. Mr Warboy says that if Billo does not confess, then there'll be no letters, and there you have it, sir. A stalemate, you might say.'

'Dammit! Can't you sort it out?' Barnaby was stalling for time to think this through without giving the convicts an edge.

Shanahan said quietly: 'Letters are priceless to us, sir, life's blood. The men are entitled...'

'Don't wave rules at me. I'll see to it.' Barnaby strode angrily away, wondering how to extricate his son from this mess.

As he walked in the front door, Millicent emerged from the library, her face purpled with tears.

'What's the matter?' he asked, but she wafted a large perfumed handkerchief in front of her face and flung herself across the passage to the drawing room, her lacy white dress fluttering in the breeze from the open doors.

Accustomed to her histrionics, he shrugged and yelled after her: 'Where's Jubal?'

Millicent had disappeared, but Jubal shouted from the parlour: 'In here!'

Barnaby backtracked to find his son, feet up on the couch, reading newspapers that he hadn't yet read himself. He hated that, and more so today since he hadn't had to put up with this particular irritation for years, thanks to his lovely bachelor life.

He scrabbled to pick up the pages that Jubal had consigned to the floor as he finished with them. 'Do not touch my newspapers until I have read them,' he shouted. 'I left them in the dining room, since I no longer have a library, and I don't want them touched until I say so. Are you hearing me?'

'Yes, I hear you,' Jubal said, face still in the pages. 'I was going to put them back.'

'Just don't touch them,' Barnaby gritted, as he tried to sort and smooth his collection. 'And where are the men's letters? What are you playing at now?'

'They're in the hallstand. And when they bring up the horse thief they can have them. Anyway, who told you? That blackguard Shanahan, I suppose.'

'Never mind. Just give them their letters. I don't want any trouble.'

Jubal sat up. 'There you go again. Pandering to them. What trouble? If they give us any trouble they're back in jail.'

'It's the difference between having everything working properly...' Barnaby was tired. He couldn't be bothered with this. 'Do as I say! Give them the letters or I will.'

As Barnaby wearily climbed the stairs to his rooms, below him Jubal went to the hallstand, opened the drawer and took out four letters. They had already been opened and scrutinised by a censor, and he'd cast a glance through them himself, seeing nought of interest. They were addressed care of HM Prisons, Hobart, Van Diemen's Land, to S. Shanahan, J. Forbes, A. McLeod and R. Hunter. Unfortunately there wasn't one for Kemp the horse thief, or he would have enjoyed burning it right under his thieving nose.

Which gave him an idea.

He looked up to make sure the old man wasn't hovering, and stuffed the letters in his pocket.

After Mr Warboy left, Sean dug a few more feet of useless drains, and was about to give the job away when Tom Flood came by and, to Sean's surprise, reined in his horse.

'How are you getting along, Shanahan?'

'As good as a man might these days,' Sean said, his attitude flat, apparently disinterested, though he was curious as to why the great man should address him.

'Is that right?' Flood grinned. 'I hear things are dicey on Warboy Farm with two bosses ruling the roost, upsetting everyone.'

'Not that I've noticed.'

'Well now, I may have heard wrong, Mr Shanahan. But if you find you need a change, I could do with a good overseer myself.'

Sean was noncommittal. 'What happened to your feller Jacoby?'

'He's sickly. Can't work much longer, with his consumption. I need a younger man now. What do you say?'

'I'll think about it.'

'Not for too long then,' Flood said, and rode off.

Sean stared after him. Work for you, you bastard! he thought. A man would have to be mad. Then he corrected himself. 'Only half mad, though. Think of the boats. And an influential boss who doesn't give a damn about the law!'

As he tramped back to the barn, he told himself he'd never work for Flood. Agreeing to it would be madness. And besides, here on this farm he had his own mates about him. It had taken time to assemble men he could trust, and they were glad to be here. That was why there was never any trouble on Warboy's farm. There was plenty on Flood territory, he'd heard. Fights. Booze. Women brought in. As long as his men worked hard under the whip of the overseer, Jacoby, and his two bully boys, no one cared what went on down in the men's quarters. Anyone unfit to work in the mornings was beaten up and sent back to prison.

Nice to hear it was Jacoby's turn to be booted out, though.

Nothing was heard of the letters until the next morning, when Jubal came in search of Shanahan.

'I am a Christian, a God-fearing Christian, and I cannot allow that horse thief to cause other people distress, so I have decided you may have your letters despite the wickedness rife in this company.'

The first letter handed to him was for Angus, the second for their dairyman, Bob Hunter, and the last, given with just that extra delay, was his! Sean almost snatched it, but instead took it carefully, silently, unable to thank this pious wretch who'd put them all through a night of hope and concern, and turned away. Angus and Bob would be happy, the others desperately disappointed.

Angus was separating and potting bulbs in the greenhouse when he saw Penn walking along the side of the house. He hadn't seen her for a week, at least, and Dossie had said there'd been rows in the family, so it was a relief to know the dear girl was up to taking her usual stroll.

When she stepped past the shelter of the hedge, wind whipped at her skirts and she had to bend over to walk, clutching her bonnet. Holding his breath, he watched her progress down the steps, praying the wind wouldn't chase her back inside, and then he gave a great sigh of happiness. She was coming towards the greenhouse, actually making for the greenhouse purposefully, it seemed to him, rather than just wandering past. Angus could hardly contain his excitement as she pushed aside the hessian door-flap and walked in.

At first she ambled along the outside aisle, over the other side from where he was working, and that gave him a chance for surreptitious glances at her, marvelling at how pretty she was. Her usually pale cheeks had a dusting of pink today, and Angus found that becoming. He was remarking to himself about her lashes, so thick and fair, when she looked up at him. Her eyes were the palest blue, he saw, at last ... and his heart thumped, so like the beat of a drum he was afraid she'd hear.

'It's turning cold now, isn't it?' she said, in a thin, ladylike voice, and Angus nodded nervously. 'Aye, miss.'

She was walking towards him.

'You're Angus, aren't you?' she whispered shyly. 'I'm Penn. It's short for Penelope.'

228

'Aye, miss.'

She stopped to examine some cyclamens that he intended to plant by the pavilion.

'Am I correct in thinking you come from Scotland?'

'Aye, miss.'

She smiled at him. 'I also think you like me. Would I be correct?' Her voice seemed to trip along, so daintily, so sweetly, he could have listened to her for ever.

By this he could hardly breathe.

'Aye, miss.'

With that, her fingers strayed over his, ever so gently, and he responded by giving the precious hand a tiny squeeze before she withdrew it.

'Well, there we are,' she said, almost primly, he thought, as she turned away and wandered out of the greenhouse, leaving him totally bewildered. But by no means unhappy. Ah no, his dear Penn had made her first move, in a polite and decent manner, the only way a lady could. She was no bold flirt, she was simply letting him know of the possibility of acquaintance between them. His heart soared.

Billo brought him a bun and a lump of bacon. 'There's fruit on them apple trees, what say I grab some?'

'No, they're not ripe yet,' Angus said, taking a bite of the soft, chewy bacon.

'What's the difference? They're still apples.'

'The difference is you'll get stomach pains if you eat green apples,' Angus said loftily. He'd never seen an apple tree, or indeed any sort of fruit tree, until he came here.

'Ah.' Billo lapsed into silence, appreciated by Angus, who was still in loveland with dear Penn.

'Didya hear Singer's joke about the blackfeller?' Angus shook his head.

'Well, I'll tell it to yez. This blackfellow called Moses fronts a magistrate who asks him what will happen if he tells a lie. Moses, he's been taught his Bible. He says he'll go to hell. So then the magistrate, he asks Moses what will happen if he tells the truth, and Moses, he nods his head, wise-like, and says he'll go to jail.'

When he saw Angus grin, Billo gave a yelp of surprise. 'Look at that, first time I ever seen your sour old face crack into a smile, and I haven't even finished the joke.'

'Yes you have,' Angus said amiably.

'I have, eh? I thought there must 'ave bin more to it. That Singer, he's deep. Educated too. He's gone up to see the boss about letters. Dossie gave 'im the nod, there's letters in the house for us. Wouldna be none for me. My mam can't read or write, she don't even know I'm learning my letters now. Shanahan's teaching me...'

But Angus was on his feet, swallowing the rest of his bun as he ran down the hill and over to the men's quarters.

He had to wait until the following morning to learn who had mail, but this time the wait wasn't so hard. Thinking of Penn was such a comfort. Before he fell asleep he imagined telling her all about himself, and the foundry, and his family who couldn't afford to visit him before he was dragged away by the oppressors to prevent him from telling the truth to the masses. Like that

230

blackfellow in Singer's joke, he recalled. He'd have some truths to tell about the way the oppressors were routing and killing his people. And he'd have witnesses too. Convicts would shout it to the rooftops if they got a chance.

Aye, he nodded gloomily. Moses was right. Truth gets jail. He'd found that out the hard way.

It wasn't until mid morning that Shanahan brought him his letter.

'Judging by all the crossouts on the outside here,' he said, examining the addresses, 'it looks as if it's been following you about Hobart, from the Penitentiary to the Stockade and on to here, but it's found you now, mate.'

He slapped Angus on the shoulder. 'I told you a letter would eventually get through to you!'

Angus rushed away to be on his own, to savour this longed-for moment. He dashed towards the trellis that was already entwined with young rose branches, ducked under the arch and sat on one of the new pine armchairs arranged in the arbour. The seal of his letter had already been broken by the censor, but he didn't mind and opened it with care. The date on it, at the top of the page, told him it had been on its way to him for more than sixteen months. It had been written by a public scribe, and that gave him a jolt of fear that something might have happened to his parents, but no...

To Angus McLeod
Hereunder I am requested by your Parents to advise you that they have received several Letters from you over the years, but they require you not to write

further. They can do not a Thing to assist you, nor can you assist Them in any Manner, save to perpetuate the Public Knowledge of their son's Conviction of Crimes. As Christians they bear you no Ill Will but request that you desist from further attempts at Communication.

Shocked, Angus reread the lines, again and again. Then he looked about him, anxious that someone might find him in the arbour, and with this missive of hurt and embarrassment in his hand. He stuffed it into his boot and ran again, this time to the far end of the Warboy property, down to the stream, where he threw water on to his face to hide the burning, sure that he must look as red as a beetroot. Then he wept as he tore the letter into shreds and watched them drown in the soft flowing waters.

He remembered it was his birthday today. He was twenty-seven years of age, sentenced to life, and no one to even pay for a headstone for him when he died. No one to care. If it weren't for Penn, he'd be on to Shanahan to help him escape, by God. And he'd go home, by God he would, and give them a piece of his mind! Anger, even forced anger, eased the pain a little.

He was teased by the others for not letting them read his letter.

'Too private,' he growled, and let them think what they liked.

Shanahan's letter was from his mother.

Ever since Matt's death, he knew, his letters home had been heavily censored. It had been

232

agony for him to have to sit down and write the shocking news to his father, asking him to break it gently to the O'Neills. In that letter, so great was his rage, he'd told them the cold, hard truth, and vowed he would avenge Matt by bringing the magistrates Grover Pellingham and Sholto Matson to justice for conspiracy.

The Government's refusal to bring charges against these men for torture, even after the public outcry, still tormented Sean.

He rubbed the stubble on his chin. They should have received that terrible letter from him around about August or September that year, and he had waited for their expected reaction, frantic with anxiety. And guilt too, because he'd planned the escape with Matt, he'd been part of it, but he couldn't include that bit of information in a letter without being flung back in jail and losing all his privileges. With a flogging to boot! Not mentioning that fact, in such a grave letter, made him feel like a shammer, dodging his responsibility for the débâcle, but what else could he do?

But it was all for nought, because the response from home – where else? No one else ever wrote to him – was astonishing. Not a word about Matt, though the letter was dated a full six months after they should have heard from him. Obviously his grieving exposé of Matt's capture, sentence and death had not been approved by the censor, so had simply disappeared.

'They look after their own,' he growled, recalling the anger in the newspapers over Matt's death, and the public protest at Salamanca, and his own ongoing campaign for justice – all met with a stolid silence.

'They think they can sit it out,' he'd told his ma, 'but not while there's breath in me.'

After that, he had had to smuggle mail out when he mentioned Matt O'Neill's fate, with urgent requests to be very careful in responding. It seemed the authorities were touchy about information reaching London, especially in matters concerning civil servants.

The terrible part was, he'd had to write the same grievous words all over again: that Matt was dead, that Matson and Pellingham, merciless men, had ordered him hanged. It was so difficult trying to keep up with the lapse of almost a year between communications, and dreadful to learn that Matt's mother had received letters from her son, and had written back to him, not knowing that he was long dead. It was at times like this that the grief began to overwhelm Sean again, so he slid the broken seal aside and looked at his mother's words.

Dear boy,

I'm hoping you'll be remembering your prayers for it is by the grace of God you've a decent place of work and not the dark prison we'd been seeing in our minds. Your pa is ailing a bit of late with the arthritis in his hands so I do the milking. Katie had a boy she called him Sean after you and the Christening was on Sunday, after a memorial service for Matt. Do not grieve too hard for him twill only harden your heart and the O'Neills don't want you suffering. Your Uncle Patrick O'Neill had a day at the races with Colonel Hastings, a fair fellow now, he says, and his friend from Cornwall, another Colonel name of Rothery. Your pa said colonels must be going cheap that week.

Sean reread that sentence. Rothery. Wasn't Willem's name Rothery? Could there be a connection? He was sure Willem was a Cornishman. He'd have to ask him. If he could find him after he and George had been arrested. Maybe the Doc would know.

Patrick's horse Oberon won the Guinea Stakes. A tragedy Tom Fogarty was shot dead in a Dublin street, they say he was for Home Rule and we never knew that. Poor Glenna with no husband now and baby Tom. They say she's breathing fire at the Garda, she always was terrible excitable. Hanna O'Neill wants to know more of the cemetery where Matt is buried on that Isle of the Dead next time you write. It would be a comfort. Closing now. God bless you Sean, your loving Mother.

Singer came looking for him. 'Was there a letter for me?'

'No, mate. Sorry.'

'There was. There was a letter for me. I know it in my bones.'

'No point in getting yourself in a turmoil, Singer. Wait for next time is all you can do.'

'There was a letter for me!' he said grimly. 'I saw it in the bastard's face plain as day. He's kept it out of sheer bastardry.'

'If he did, you'll never know. Best to let it go.'

'Oh Jeez, yes! That's ripe coming from you! You

carry round more payback wallop than a bloody wasp nest. And did you hear about your famous Frank Macnamara, he got out!'

'What? He escaped?'

'Not at all. He finally did his time and they had to let him go, and with his clout he was off on the first ship.'

'That's good.' Sean said glumly. Van Diemen's Land had lost its only famous prisoner and seemed an even duller place now.

'You have to talk to Warboy about my letter, Sean.'

'I can't, I've got nothing to go on.'

'My word! You have my word!'

'It won't work.'

'Then that lily-livered pious prick had better start looking over his shoulder, because I'll get him one day, Sean! I'll get him!'

'And what if you're wrong?'

'He'd be no bloody loss anyway.'

Singer stormed away. Sean couldn't do anything about that situation.

At the minute he was busy reading between the lines. They must have received one of his smuggled letters in which he'd told them Matt was buried in the Isle of the Dead cemetery, a beautiful island in the harbour off Port Arthur. Sean had never been there, nor ever wished to, though he'd heard about it from Bailey, who'd done five years at the Port Arthur prison.

'Only them as have got someone to pay get head-stones,' he'd said. 'The rest get dumped in un-marked graves on the penal side of the cemetery.'

'What's on the other side?'

'It's not just for prisoners. They bury staff members and soldiers there, along with wives and children unlucky enough to perish in the prison. There's even a gravediggers' cottage over there.' He had laughed. 'To stop escapes, eh? Get it? To stop escapes.'

Sean was in no mood for Bailey's jokes. 'What about stonemasons?'

'They work on the island too.'

'Good. Find out how much they cost. I want them to make a headstone for Matt O'Neill.'

With one thing and another, Sean had been circling the matter in his mind. He folded his mother's letter carefully and put it in his pocket.

What had she said about Glenna? Excitable? Exciting, more like it. God love her!

And now she was a widow. And her husband Tom Fogarty had died as a patriot.

That intimidated him. That hurt. That reminded him of his own worthless existence.

Dr Slatter had only recently purchased this splendid house, known as Devon Lodge, from a wealthy woolgrower, and he was busy, with his wife, deciding where special items of furniture should be placed when he saw a gentleman coming up the drive.

'Oh dear,' he said to his wife. 'It's Dr Roberts.'

'What could he want? This is quite inopportune. Shall I have him sent away?'

'Unfortunately no. He's apt to dig in. I shall have to face the music, I'm afraid.'

'What music?'

'Never mind. I shan't be long.'

He was all smiles when he opened the door to the young doctor. 'Good day to you, Allyn. The winter is receding, wouldn't you say? Come on in. Would you care for tea?'

'No thank you, sir.'

'Good-oh. We might walk then. In the garden out the back. It's quite lovely, you know. Well arranged, which is what Mrs Slatter and I have been trying to do with our furniture. Not an easy job, you know, once one has a collection; nothing seems to fit quite as we had imagined.'

He led Allyn through the low-set house, across the veranda bordered with clipped bushes that gave way to extensive lawns and neat hedges.

'A surprise, isn't it?' he asked his guest. 'Hidden at the rear like this, with only the bare essentials at the front. I don't know what the fellow was thinking of.'

As they set off, walking slowly down the main path, he added, 'He obviously wasn't taken with flowers, but my wife will attend to that. She has great plans. But of course, my dear fellow, you haven't come here to discuss our garden. Is it about Rothery and Smith?'

'Yes, sir. I hoped that Sergeant Budd would have been charged with cruelty after what he put them through, but nothing has happened.'

'Believe me, I understand that, but something did happen, Allyn. We were able to have George moved to the infirmary–'

'Where he should have been taken in the first place,' Allyn said angrily.

'Quite so. But it happened. And a word with the magistrate got Rothery off with a fine. In all

238

we did the best we could for them. You should be pleased.'

'Pleased? With all due respect, sir, I have just heard that George Smith has been sent to Port Arthur. Why? He didn't commit a crime, he was convalescing in that house. George was an assigned servant, known for his good behaviour–'

'But his employer, Tom Flood, didn't come forward, as you requested, to provide him with a reference, so there was no witness to his good behaviour.'

'It's still not right.'

'Allyn, might I give you a word of advice? The superintendent of the jail was under the impression that Smith had been removed to your house, not Rothery's. In fact he has a certificate to that extent. Yet you allowed him to be moved to an illegal location. Now you must not flout the law like that! We have to set an example!'

Roberts was taken aback. 'That's not true. There must have been a mistake. I gave the address of Rothery's cottage, because the man is an excellent medical aide and Smith was desperately in need of care. At no time did I mention taking the man to my house.'

'Well,' Slatter shrugged, 'there was a mix-up of some sort. Too late to worry about it now. But in your own words, you're telling me that you sent Smith off to that cottage knowing full well there was a relationship between the two men. What were you thinking of?'

'I was doing my job, Doctor. What I deemed was best for my patient. What else could I have done?'

'You could have shown a little more respect for

the strict regulations regarding convicts. You are a good and caring doctor, and it pains me to say this, but what did you achieve? Rothery, a free man, got a couple of days' jail, and was out by the skin of his teeth with a large fine. Smith got even worse treatment, that I am not condoning by any means, than he would have had in the town jail, and has had his sentence extended. What do you say about that?'

'I have nothing to say. I did what I thought best. If we didn't have men like Budd here, the system would work better.'

'Allyn, if you feel so strongly about these matters, you should go and see Pitcairn. Do you know him?'

'Not personally. I believe he was the first lawyer to qualify in this colony.'

'That is correct. He is also an advocate for ending transportation. Maybe that's where you should direct your enthusiasm.'

'I certainly shall, Dr Slatter.'

'Good. But do let me remind you, Doctor, that there will always be Budds in this world... All sent to try us,' he added with a wry smile.

CHAPTER EIGHT

Freddy was lost. Not lost in the sense that he didn't know his way back. He did, but that wasn't where he wanted to go. He was trying to go on, but he kept running into cliff faces and barriers of impenetrable bush, retracing his steps and ending up back where he had started. It was enough to make a man sit down and cry, except that he was hungry – starving – and this bum-walloping horse was getting as cranky as a bee in a blanket.

And he was tired. Bloody dead tired. Couldn't get no sleep at night with birds hoo-hooing and furry creatures crashing through the bush like it was a country bloody fair. If he could catch one of them he'd eat it. Light a fire and eat it. If he had matches and a knife to skin it with. He hadn't eaten for two days, not since he'd come across that hut and lifted a lump of beef out of a salt keg and grabbed a pocketful of corn biscuits like cast iron from a tin on a shelf. He hoped the hut didn't belong to a bushranger with a gun. But anyway, he was well on from there now.

He was sitting in the clearing, trying to decide which way to go next, with the horse nibbling at grass nearby, when he heard voices and instantly dived into the undergrowth to hide, but the dingbat of a horse followed him, as far as it could anyway, and there he was staring from the scrub at the horse that was staring down at him ... like raising a flag and shouting: 'Here he is, fellers. My master. You can eat him if you like.'

Behind the horse was a group of curious black-fellows, black as ink and wearing nothing but crotch covers, head bands, splotches of paint and ferocious faces. Freddy had never seen bush blacks up close before, and they gave him such a fright he wet his pants.

They, and the horse, were all staring at him

now. The blackfellows gabbled something among themselves, then the leader jerked his head for them to move on, and wonder of wonders they began walking away. Might be, Freddy thought, they think I'm a hermit. That I live here, and they're being polite not bothering me. They say they're polite people. I should call out to them, ask them for some grub.

But what if they're cannibals? And they've got me in their larder for afterwards? He began to shake in fear.

'Nah,' he whispered to himself. 'You've got the horse. They don't ride horses. You can tell 'em they can eat the horse. He'd keep them fed for a month. While you get the hell out of here.'

He saw the horse turn about, and was afraid it would trample him. It looked like an elephant to a man hid down among the spiky ferns. But it didn't trample him, it was moving away, following them, for God's sake. Then he realised the horse wasn't just wandering off, they were leading it away. His horse! They were stealing his horse.

He burst out of the bush. 'Hey! No you don't, you blokes! That's my bloody horse! Get out of it!'

The leader of the pack shook his head. 'Horse belonga Mister Plunkett.'

'No. It's mine. See.' Freddy pointed to himself. 'Me! My horse.' He went to grab the reins, but a very large bare arm barred his way.

They began to wiggle their black noses, picking up a scent, screwing their faces in disgust, then one of them pointed at Freddy, and they all started laughing as they strode away with his horse.

Freddy realised what they were laughing at but he didn't care. His trousers would dry out, but he couldn't afford to lose sight of his horse, or this gang. They didn't seem so scary now, so he'd let them lead him out of the maze. That'd be a start.

He watched in astonishment as the barefoot blackfellows shoved through the bush as if it were a cabbage patch, sometimes breaking off low branches to make way for the horse, but otherwise ignoring the prickles and barbs that clawed at the white man, and the sharp stones that penetrated his cheap boots. They seemed not to care that Freddy was tagging along behind them, and he in turn realised that despite the hazards, they were making pretty good progress, travelling north-west. There was always so much talk of escape among the convicts that it had become almost mandatory to learn compass directions from the sun. Former city dwellers like Freddy Hines, the East London pickpocket, were proud of themselves for having picked up this art, though before this he had never been sure where exactly it could be used.

Today the sun was travelling between clouds, but not offering much in the way of warmth, and so Freddy was relieved when the bushmen stopped beside a river, leaving one man with the horse while the others disappeared into the bush.

Freddy stood by, warming his hands as the lone blackfellow lit a fire, and tried to talk to him, but he was ignored. It was an opportunity to grab the horse and run, but Freddy didn't like the look of the spear leaning nonchalantly on a tree trunk nearby. He wished he had something to bargain with to get the horse back, like a piece of mirror ... it was said they prized mirrors. But this fellow was built like an ox, and Freddy doubted the veracity of that bit of folklore. In fact he decided right then that these blokes wouldn't be dills enough to fall for bits of glass or beads like the storybooks said.

Eventually the others came back with a dead kangaroo and a catch of fish on a string, so he kept back out of the way while they went about their cooking, with the aroma of meat giving him stomach pains. Eventually, when they began plucking cooked meat from the fire, he went over and asked plaintively: 'Can I have some, please? I'm bloody starving.'

The bossman shrugged, as if to say 'Go ahead' Freddy thought, and he dived in, burning his fingers but drooling over the sizzling meat. He even threw fear to the winds and went back for seconds.

The meal was over when not a skerrick of meat or fish was left, and when dingoes came skulking out of the bush to carry off the bones. The campfire was doused, stamped out and dusted over with handfuls of dirt, then they slept.

'I see,' Freddy pondered. 'I see. The day's work is over, so you get time off.'

He slept too.

He tramped after them all the next day, wondering where the hell they were going, but consoled by the fact that they were still heading away from Hobart at a pretty good pace. He discovered that they only seemed to have one meal a day, putting away as much as they could eat – meat and fish and string bags of mussels. Mussels! Fresh and lovely! Freddy ate as many as he could get his hands on, and no one seemed to mind.

They weren't interested in talking to him, though. They walked, ate, slept; had their groans and grunts and jokes as they loped along, sometimes looking back at him with a nudge, as if to say: 'He's still there.'

He'd tried to mount the horse but was barred from doing so.

'Allasame horse belonga Mister Plunkett,' he was told firmly, as if he'd wear the bloody animal out if he got on it! They didn't ride either. It just ponced along with them like a bloody pet, out for an airing, still wearing the damn saddle.

Early the next morning they came out of the bush on to a track, a real track out here in the wilds, wide enough to take a cart, so they padded along that for a couple of hours. Freddy suddenly realised that he'd been walking for days and had not had a twinge. Not an ache or a pain anywhere! What a feat! he congratulated himself. It wasn't in his soul to be grateful for the hard labour he'd put in on road gangs, the labour that had given him the fitness and strength to keep up with these men, but he understood. Without that Hobart-acquired strength, he'd have been left far behind.

Then there were fences, and cleared paddocks, and a mob of horses sheltering from the cold wind under a clump of trees and, in the side of a hill, a farmhouse. Freddy guessed this must be Mr Plunkett's place, and prayed he'd be civil.

When an old man with grey hair and a long

grey beard appeared in the doorway, the blacks gave a whoop of excitement and bounded away, dragging the horse with them, and though Freddy shouted at them to wait for him, they covered the last quarter-mile as easy as deer in a hunt. By the time he caught up, the old man had removed the saddle and was examining his horse.

'Thank you for catchin' my horse, sir,' he said quickly. 'These blackfellows stole it from me. I've been following them for days.'

The bearded one turned clear green eyes on him and Freddy saw he wasn't so old after all – maybe forty-something.

'And who might you be?' he asked, as the brown dog poised behind him added a low growl.

'Fr ... from the mainland.' Freddy had almost stumbled into giving his right name. 'Jack's the name ... Jack Barnes.'

'How do you do! I'm the Government Pound Keeper, Claude Plunkett.'

'The what?'

'Pound Keeper. This is the Pound. For holding and maintaining stray animals, sheep and cows like, but mainly I have horses. They've been roaming these parts since the first white men set foot on the island nigh on forty years ago. Real rascals to go roaming, are horses. Just like some people,' he added, examining the horse's teeth and setting Freddy to wonder if he'd been sprung, and by a government man at that.

Plunkett nodded at the blacks. 'He's all right, Juno.' And marched back into his house.

The black men rushed to the door, jigging about like kids, and next thing Plunkett came out and gave each one a small bag of tobacco.

'Hey! Wait!' Freddy yelled. 'Are they selling you my horse? Because they can't, it's mine.'

'They said they found it in the bush.'

'They didn't. I was right there.'

The black man intervened, babbling his side of the story to Plunkett, in his own language, and Plunkett smiled.

'He asks if you were holding the horse when they came across it.'

'No, but...'

The black man's grin dazzled with mirth as he spoke.

'Juno says they found the horse in a clearing but there was no white man in sight.'

Freddy couldn't bring himself to admit he was hiding. 'That dog's yours,' he said angrily, 'but you're not holding it by the collar. The same goes for my horse.'

Plunkett sighed. 'They brought in the horse. They get the tobacco. I wouldn't be fool enough to try to take it back. You don't break promises with these gentlemen, believe me.'

He shook hands with all five of them and watched as they loped away.

'Now, Mr Barnes, your horse is duly impounded. I shall have to enter it in my records. Meantime, would you like a cup of tea?'

'A cup of tea would be good, Mr Plunkett, but how do I get my horse unpounded?'

'Easily. You pay me ten shillings. And I'll record that the chestnut with the white flash brought in by Juno was recovered by its owner, Mr Jack Barnes of ... of where did you say?'

'I'm a traveller,' Freddy said, following him inside. 'But I haven't got ten shillings, so you'll have to let me off.'

'And you haven't any equipment either, eh? No food, no gun, not even a knife. You're travelling light, aren't you?'

'I've had a bit of bad luck. Bushrangers stole everything I had, and then those bloody blacks took my horse.'

'You don't say. I would have thought it'd be the other way round. But then you never know these days.'

He put plates, knives and a half-loaf of bread on the table, and took some corned beef from a muslin-covered safe that was hanging from the rafters. 'Help yourself while the kettle boils.'

While Freddy hacked into the food, he peered around him. This strange house was scrupulously clean, and sported lace curtains on the windows. There were no inner walls. The kitchen was in the middle, with a bedroom area down one end, and surprisingly, a neat office, desk and all, down the other. On the wall by the door was a government certificate which proved that Mr Plunkett was the genuine article.

Freddy was thoroughly confused about his situation now, and frantically tried to work up a plan as he sandwiched the corned beef in a slice of bread, but nothing helpful came to mind. He dropped a crust of bread and bent over to pick it up, then groaned; he had forgotten he was wearing a yellowing convict shirt. Too late to talk his way out of that. Escape had to be the next move. After the tea.

Claude was amused. Obviously the fellow was an escapee. And that wasn't his horse. The story was so full of holes he could have strained tea through it. He'd have to be careful; convicts on the run were desperate men, because they had nowhere to go. His dog, Duke, was watching the stranger, whatever his name was, while his back was turned. Duke had never been keen on strangers, not even the blacks, and he was fast. He'd once clamped his teeth on a hand with a gun in it, and made a real mess of it. Tom Tiddy, a would-be bushranger, had been trying to rob him, but he'd failed thanks to the dog. Then the blacks had done Claude a favour, marching Tiddy back to the nearest police barracks, nigh on forty miles away, and tying him to a tree where he couldn't be missed.

For that he'd given them flour and tobacco, and their business arrangements had begun. Their camp was over behind the barn, built-in protection that was. Claude never mentioned to anyone that he had a whole village of blacks within coo-ee. Living where they'd lived for generations.

He gave Freddy a mug of black tea. 'Where are you heading now?'

'Now that I've been robbed? I suppose I'll have to go back, but I thought I might get a job on a farm here somewhere.'

'Not much in the way of farms here. This used to be the Annabella sheep station. The owner took up thousands of acres, from a map. Sight unseen. Good land from here to the river but he had no idea that three quarters of his sheep run was a wilderness that only the blacks could handle. He spent a fortune trying to make a go of it, but drought finally ruined him, so he took his family and the last of his sheep and quit the property. The Government took it over then. But if you want a job, better you head across the Derwent.'

'Swim, I suppose,' Freddy said caustically.

'You could go back to Bridgewater and cross over there, once you've paid the ten shillings.'

'I told you I can't pay the fine. And anyway, it's not legal to be grabbing other people's horses like this. You and your government are no better than poachers.'

'You take it up with them, sir. But in the meantime ... the horse stays.'

'If the horse stays, I stay!'

Claude shrugged. 'You'd have to earn your keep.'

'Doing what?'

'Clean the stables, give the horses a currycomb, shine them up ready for sale.'

'I might stay a day or so. There are probably bushrangers up that track anyway.' The visitor sounded more hopeful than concerned.

'No. No one worth robbing round here.'

Freddy eyed him with suspicion. 'Them boots you're wearing, they look like military boots to me.'

'Yes. I can purchase them cheaply when I put in my order for stores. I could sell you a military shirt if you want. It'd look a sight better than the flannel you're wearing.'

'How much?'

'Two and six. That'll be twelve and sixpence

you owe me.'

'The hell I do.'

'Drink your tea, I have to feed the horses. You can come with me.'

He hadn't told anyone, much less this bolter, that the Government seemed to have forgotten about him. At first he'd ridden into Hobart every three months, collected his pay, and signed a form requesting drovers to come out to the Annabella Pound and take the horses to town. That worked for a while, but eventually it was agreed that Mr Plunkett should sell the unclaimed horses direct from the Pound, and advice to that effect was placed in various newspapers.

His present routine took him into Hobart every three months to deposit the takings from fines and sales at the Commissariat office, and sign a chit for the stores that he collected in the same building.

Claude was meticulous with his book-keeping, to the last farthing; his pages were signed off by bored clerks, and receipts issued with barely a glance. In fact these rubber-faced office lizards never gave him the time of day. They just slid the money into drawers, stamped his book and made him disappear from their view like fairground magicians. He often thought he could have pulled his ears, bared his teeth and stuck out his tongue and they wouldn't have seen him. Not that it had bothered him, but now, he pondered, an idea forming, the lack of interest could be useful.

As it turned out, with Freddy still hanging about, since they'd come to an impasse over the impounding situation, Claude found himself airing his grievance over a meal of roast turkey. His visitor's eyes popped, not only at the turkey dinner (the birds ran wild in the bush), but at the casual way the Pound Keeper was treated.

'No respect, Claude,' he said. 'That's the trouble with people these days. I don't know why you bother to give 'em the cash at all. Who's to know the difference if you just kept it? Said there weren't no horses caught lately.'

'Ah, word would get around. The folk who come out here to get cheap horses, they'd know. I have to put their names in my ledger.'

'I suppose so, yes.'

Claude lit his pipe and looked at Freddy. It occurred to him that this fellow wasn't unlike him in build and looks, without his beard, and the stranger's dark growth. They were both skinny, about the same height, green eyes and so on and so on. He nodded.

'He does an' all,' he chuckled to himself.

One day Freddy ran into a black woman outside the barn, a giant of a woman, and he nearly fainted in fright. But a better look gave him courage. She had shiny bare bosoms with thick purply nipples, and only a cloth draped across her hips. He had no idea where she'd sprung from, but she smiled at him and pushed a gourd of honey towards him.

'Claude,' she said. 'For Claude.'

'Ah yes. You want me to give it to Claude? Yes. I'll do that.'

He took the honey and was backing away when she grabbed his hand, and examined it.

'Bad,' she said, shaking her head sorrowfully.

'I'll say. A bastard broke my fingers. Stamped on them, he did.'

He tried to pull his hand away, but she wouldn't let go, raising nervous quivers in his stomach. She'd make two of him.

She examined each finger, pushing them this way and that, turning them over, until he became embarrassed. The knuckles were still swollen amid the fingers so set into a crabbed position they were too ugly to display.

Claude came around the corner. 'Ah! Lotus!' he called. 'I haven't seen you for ages.'

Freddy held up the honey in his free hand. 'This is for you.'

'Some honey? Thank you, Lotus. Much appreciated.' He turned back to Freddy. 'Isn't she something? A real live goddess.'

The black woman released his hand but wasn't finished with it. She insisted that Claude look at it too.

'She wants to know what happened to your hand,' he said.

'A bastard back in Hobart stamped on it. Broke all my fingers.'

'I'll ask you not to swear in front of the lady,' Claude said quietly. Then he continued: 'Didn't you get any treatment?'

'Yes, it wasn't all that long ago. A doctor put splints on the fingers but they got in the way and I didn't reckon they were doing any good, so I took them off.'

Claude translated, and then gave Lotus's response. 'She says she can fix them.'

253

'I dunno about that,' Freddy said warily.

'You ought to let her have a go. Come on up to the house and I'll make a cup of tea and we'll talk about it. Lotus loves a cup of tea.'

They had almost talked Freddy into her miraculous cure. Almost.

'All right, but does it hurt?' he wanted to know.

Claude discussed this with his friend. 'She says she'll go back and get some stuff for you so that it doesn't hurt.'

As Lotus walked away, Freddy couldn't take his eyes off the long, sleek body. 'Gawd,' he said. 'Just looking at that makes me think I've gone to heaven. Where did she come from?'

'She and her family are camped out back of us in the bush. Lotus likes to visit me.'

Freddy saw a tinge of red flare in those ruddy cheeks. Only for a second, but he saw it. 'You old villain. You've been holding out on me. Is that why I have to sleep in the barn? Is she your woman?'

'No, not in that sense. No. She just visits me at times. Her husband doesn't mind. It was her idea.'

'Gawd 'struth! Can you get me one?'

Claude frowned. 'I can't. But if you stay and they get to know you ... maybe. But don't take it upon yourself, whatever you do. I've told you before. You don't want to cross this mob, and never go near their camp. It's bad manners without an invitation. Other blacks can't even walk on to their territory without permission or there's war.'

Freddy thought old Claude was exaggerating, but that didn't matter for now. He had decided to stay at the Annabella Pound. Definitely. With that sort of female on offer a man would be mad to leave. He laughed at the thought of poor old Claude living the lonely life out here to all appearances, when he had a goddess like Lotus to keep him company.

'What exactly happens with her?' he had to ask, being dead curious. 'I mean, does she nick over in the night?'

'No, there's nothing sneaky about her. She just comes over and if I feel like some you-know-what, then we do it. Anywhere I happen to be. That's what's good about it. She's not shy and she doesn't mind if there's only the sky above and the birds to watch.'

'Gawd!' Freddy groaned. 'I haven't had nothin' but them thri'penny whores. You gotta help me, Claude.'

'Yes, I've been thinking about that. I've been thinking you just might have a place here.'

Lotus gave him some fiery stuff that tasted like the worst gin ever invented, and the next thing he knew, he was sitting on a chair by the fire with his head feeling as tight as a cork. Then he saw his hand. Or rather he didn't see his hand. It was covered in a bandage, but when he went to lift it, it was as heavy as lead.

'What did she do to me?' he yelped.

'She had to break your fingers again to straighten them, then she put the splints on again, then she made a mud cast to keep the whole lot in place. It has set hard now and it has to stay on for a while.'

'How long? It feels like it's set in a bloody brick!' he wailed. 'How's she gonna get it off?'

He dropped his hand towards the floor and it almost took him with it.

'Never mind about that now. You wanted your fingers fixed, now they've been fixed.'

'I never said I did. I never said that! It was your idea. Now I've got to march around carrying this rock. It's worse than the ball and chain.'

'And you'd know about that, wouldn't you?'

'Everyone knows about that.'

'Very well. Now here's the proposition. I'm about to start on a big effort to find stray horses, not just wait for them to wander around this district. And I want you to work here and keep an eye on the place while I'm away. But ... I have to account for you. If you're on the run, you're no use to me, unless I get you new papers. But I have to know the truth. What did you get?'

'Ten years.' Freddy shrugged.

'What for?'

His guest wriggled uncomfortably. 'Poaching.'

'Poaching?' Claude laughed. 'Where did you get the horse?'

'A mate gave it to me to help me get away.'

'Where did he get it?'

'From the farm where he worked. But he'll talk his way out of it. Shanahan could talk the leg off an iron pot.'

'What's your real name?'

'Freddy Hines. Cripes! What else do you need to know?'

Claude peered out the window at a curtain of rain moving across the valley. 'I need to know you're not a murderer or worse. I can check up on you, me being a government man on the right side of the counter.'

'Check all you like.'

'All right. Now. About this new identity. I figured out a foolproof one.'

'Like what?'

'Like you're my son. A free settler, come out to help his dad. I can get the forms, fill them in, even pick the ship you came in on and fill out the questions on your family background.'

As he went on to explain, Freddy was slowly coming to the conclusion that this man was a genius. Wouldn't Shanahan love to hear this bit of cunning. 'And what would you call me?'

'Why, I'd call you Penley Plunkett, to keep it in the family. I had an uncle Penley Plunkett. He was an explorer. He wanted me to emigrate with him to Canada, but he drowned over there. A big fellow, he set out on an icy lake in a kayak. Didn't know it had a hole in it and him too fat to prise himself out of his seat. Went down like a stone. I didn't like the sound of all that ice anyway, so I emigrated out here instead.'

'Can we drop the Penley then? He doesn't sound too bright.'

'All right, you can be Jack Plunkett.'

'I don't like Plunkett much either.'

'That can't be helped!' Claude snorted.

Tomorrow he'd leave Freddy here and take four horses to sell in the village of New Norfolk. Freddy could keep an eye on the other six. Then he'd go on into Hobart and set up his employee's new papers. That would only take a few days.

257

'Why don't you take all the horses?' Freddy asked him when he heard that Claude was already moving ahead with the plan.

'Because too many lowers the price, and it's hard enough for Duke and me to lead four horses. When you've got legal papers and you've grown plenty of beard for cover, you can help me take more in different directions.'

Claude thought that was enough for this bloke to digest for the time being, but he had bigger plans. Further inland there were mobs of wild horses, really wild, those fellows. And dangerous. They were called brumbies. With 'Jack' and a couple of blacks to help him, he reckoned he could round up a lot more horses to sell, horses that wouldn't go into the books at all. Brumbies were fair game.

He would then employ a horse breaker to tame his brumbies and start to advertise horse sales right here, once a month. He might even breed from the good stock, build proper stables to house the better breeds. There was no end to his dreams... This could become the Annabella Horse Farm. Famous for miles around. He should have thought of this years ago.

'Hey, Claude,' Freddy called to him. 'How much do I get out of this?'

'Wages for a start. Two pounds a year until I see how we go.'

'And keep?'

'Yes, all right.'

'And what about a hut for me? You can't leave your son in the barn.'

'I'll see to that when I get back. Now don't go

trimming that beard of yours while I'm away. Same with your hair. Let it grow.'

According to his records, Claude sold the four horses (of poor quality) to Jack Plunkett for two pounds each. On behalf of his son, he resold them in New Norfolk for a total figure of eighty pounds, which was no business of the Government.

Then he rode on into Hobart with Duke trotting along beside him, tongue lolling with pleasure, looking just like a dog on holiday.

He deposited the eight pounds with receipts made out to Jack Plunkett, and complained angrily to the clerk that he'd been accosted by the police the minute he'd ridden into town, demanding he show them his papers.

'Me? A respectable settler,' he raged. 'Been here longer than any of you lot, almost got locked up because I can't find my papers, had to shout to make them listen to me, couldn't get it through their thick heads that I'm the Pound Keeper, the Pound Keeper do you hear me? Are you listening to me?'

'What do you want?' the clerk asked dully.

'What do I want? I want new identification papers so that I can shove them in their faces.'

'All right. No need to shout at me, old man!'

The clerk pushed a form at him. 'Fill that in.'

Claude took it to a corner bench, answered the questions in his neat hand, and returned it to the counter.

'Damn nuisance for a respectable man to have to go through all this rigmarole,' he growled as the clerk stamped the form without a glance at

259

his handiwork and Jack Plunkett, farm hand, son of the Pound Keeper, was duly registered as a citizen.

Outside, Claude breathed a sigh of relief. It had been a huge effort for him to carry out that piece of play-acting, and at one stage in the middle of his rehearsed tirade his voice had actually wavered so much he'd felt his legs might give way.

But the deed was done. And since the incident with the police was a total fabrication, he had no qualms about wandering the outskirts of the courthouse and examining the long list of names of convict absconders from work duties. Then he turned to a second set of pages on the notice board. Here were listed the names of escapees from custody, a much more serious offence. Descriptions were given, and sometimes sketches of the villains. On the 'honour' board, as it was known in the town, were the faces of the elite, prisoners turned bushrangers. These 'Wanted' posters were displayed behind glass to prevent souveniring.

Claude only glanced at them; instead, he peered at the 'Escapees' list, irritated by descriptions which seemed to have most of the convicts as lookalikes, except for the occasional broken nose, or red hair, or loss of a limb, or crippled hand, or...

'Crippled hand?' he murmured. 'Who have we got here? Freddy Hines. Five foot five. Brown hair. Ha! This is our boy. Yes. Good. What did you get up to that they had you locked up? Ah. I see. Assault on a guard! Didn't think he had it in him!'

260

Pleased with his day's work, he took himself off to his favourite pub on the waterfront to watch the world go by. Claude wasn't a hermit by nature; he was simply determined to make a go of his life out here. He'd sold those horses legally, entered the sale price in the ledgers when he deposited the money. Nothing illegal about that. The sale price was at his discretion. If anyone wanted to complain, they could. He grinned.

The waitress brought him a cheery smile and his usual – crayfish with vinegar, a bun and a pint.

He saw Bailey come into the pub. This fellow was as slippery as an eel, but a reliable source of information if it suited him.

'How're you goin', Claude?' he said. 'When are you gonna give me one of them free horses of yours?'

'What do you want with a horse? You'd get the vapours if you had to go any further than a half-mile from these wharves. By the way, have you heard of a fellow called Shanahan?'

'Why?'

'I heard someone speak of him lately. Thought I might have known him from the voyage out.'

'Who was that spoke of him?'

'Farmer Jones of New Norfolk,' Claude lied.

'Nah. Don't know no Shanahan. Was he an officer, regimental?'

'Yes, come to think of it.'

Bailey shook his head and moved off, but Claude had his answer. Bailey had let a drop of truth slip out there. Shanahan existed. And the horse he'd given Freddy belonged to his boss.

Therefore it'd be listed as stolen. Not strayed. I don't want it around, thought Claude. I'll sell it cheap to one of the crofters as soon as I get back.

'Someone was asking after you.'

'Who would that be?' Sean asked

'Claude, the Pound Keeper.'

'Never heard of him. What did he want?'

'There's the tricky part. He wouldn't say Muddied the waters with a cock-and-bull tale of meeting you on the ship.' He nudged Sean in the ribs. 'That's a good one, eh? Meeting *you* on the ship! Like in the officers' mess maybe.'

'Then what?'

'Nothin'. He didn't say no more.'

'Where's this Pound?'

'Out in the bush. Old Annabella Station property.'

'Ah well. Let him be. I've got to get the boss home.'

Sean hurried over to the tailor's shop to collect Mr Warboy's new overcoat. A grand thing it was, made to order in lined tweed with a short cloak attached, for double protection of the shoulders.

As the tailor laid the coat on his shiny counter and began to fold it with great reverence, he peered over his spectacles at Warboy's servant, whose garb did nothing for the tone of his shop.

'You can wait outside,' he said.

'No I can't. It's wet out there. Just carry on.'

Finally the coat was ready for its tissued box, and Sean couldn't resist a remark to irritate the man. 'Will you look at that now,' he said. 'I hope it's well stitched. Mr Warboy is very particular.'

Bundled out with his prize, he dashed across the street to Mr Warboy's carriage – he'd bought the one that Bertie was supposed to have been making for the Doc, and was thrilled with it, gadding about daily like a little old prince. Not that Sean had any complaints. He was the only one allowed to drive it so far, so he got to join the boss on his jaunts, greatly appreciating that the driver's seat had a fair amount of shelter from the vagaries of Hobart's weather.

He opened the carriage door and placed the box on the seat beside the rest of Mr Warboy's parcels.

'Will that be all now?' he asked the boss, who was studying his shopping list.

'I think so. Yes, I imagine so.' Mr Warboy frowned. 'I haven't ever been on a day cruise before. I shall take a small valise with me for odds and sods I might need.' He looked up. 'You're getting wet standing there. Hop up and we'll head home.'

Sean needed no second telling. He swung up into the sheltered driver's seat, pulled an oilskin out from under the seat to throw over his lap, and picked up the reins. The horses that he had trained for carriage work – shades of his days at O'Neill's stables – moved off smoothly, despite the heavy rain.

Barnaby tucked the shopping list into his waist-coat pocket and gazed unhappily at the weather. The Governor and Lady Franklin were taking ship on the morrow to Port Arthur, to carry out an official inspection of the Colonial Penal

263

Establishment, and they had invited him to join their party. He was very much looking forward to this voyage, not only for the excellent company, but because few civilians had ever been permitted inside the prison walls. Not that it actually had any walls, he now knew, having studied the map when the invitation was delivered. It was located on the Tasman Peninsula, and the only land access was by Eagle Hawk Neck, a 450-yard-wide strip of land, easily guarded by the military and savage dogs. The ocean surrounds were known to be patrolled by sharks, so few prisoners ever escaped from Port Arthur.

If this weather kept up, he worried, it would certainly mean rough seas in Storm Bay, the name enough to cause a little alarm, and uncomfortable touring of the large peninsula. It was said in Hobart that this open prison held more than a thousand of the worst prisoners, men who'd continued to offend after they arrived in Van Diemen's Land. Foolish fellows, Barnaby thought, who'd been given the best chance ever to rehabilitate, and had instead earned more years of confinement.

And that reminded him. Shanahan was a good example of a man who had taken the opportunity to better himself out here, earning a Class 1 rating, and he had a surprise for him. It was right here among the papers in his tooled leather handbag.

Unbeknownst to Shanahan, Barnaby had requested his solicitor to enquire about rewarding the man with a promotion, which would allow him to apply for a ticket-of-leave. As a result, the application had been made on Shanahan's behalf, and approved by the Governor, who commended Barnaby's benevolence. The Irishman would no longer be an assigned servant; he'd be on a sort of parole system, as Barnaby understood it, free to work wherever he wished in Van Diemen's Land, and to live wherever he chose. He could settle down, make a life for himself now, and earn a higher wage. He was confident Sean Shanahan would stay on at Warboy's Farm, once he learned that extra piece of news, and looked forward to announcing it himself. Perhaps, he thought, we could have a little ceremony, something to give the other assignees heart ... a reason to continue on their present path of good behaviour. I could have Dossie make a special supper for all the lads, and then a glass of Jamaican rum all round when I make my speech and present Shanahan with his ticket.

A crack of thunder greeted the coach as it topped the hill and began its descent into the valley, but his driver kept the horses at a steady pace, neither slowing nor urging them on as the showers turned into a torrent. Barnaby couldn't see out of the windows at all by this, and the constant slosh of aggressive rain against the glass made him nervous, reminded him of storms at sea and the name of that bay they must navigate to reach Port Arthur the next day.

He kept telling himself that the Governor would have the finest of crews to take them safely to harbour, but a sense of dread persisted. To ward it off, he burrowed among his parcels and came up with a box of the Maryland Broadleaf cigars that Pollard's stores now imported at his instigation, and as he cut and lit one, he allowed himself a laugh at his son's expense. He had not told Jubal, or his ladies, that he shared ownership of the two prosperous stores with Sam Pollard, and had warned his housekeeper not to mention it to them. Barnaby had a good working relationship with Sam, who managed both stores, so the last thing he needed was to have Jubal or Millicent in there throwing their weight around. Or worse, regarding stock as family property.

'I wouldn't put that past them,' he growled, as they reached the farm and Shanahan climbed down to open the gates.

Dossie was at the front door to greet the master with a large umbrella, and Shanahan assisted him down.

'Take the parcels in,' Barnaby said to him. 'Dossie can bring them up to my rooms. And whatever you do, don't let my new coat get wet.'

'Oh, you have the coat, sir?' Dossie said enthusiastically. 'I'm looking forward to seeing it.'

Barnaby beamed, but they were all stopped in their tracks at the front door by screaming and shouting from inside.

'What the hell is going on?' he demanded.

Dossie whispered, 'I don't know, sir. Something's up. There's been ructions all afternoon. I'm glad you're home.'

'I'm bloody not! You tell them to stop that racket immediately.'

In the hall, Shanahan took Barnaby's cap and helped him out of his coat, but the screaming and weeping coming from the library seemed to worsen as Dossie appeared in the passage, shaking her head and upending her palms as if to show there was nothing she could do.

Jubal's voice, raised in rage, thundered through the house; his wife was shrieking, and there were the unmistakable sounds of someone being beaten.

Sean looked at Mr Warboy, who seemed too stunned to move, standing there with his chubby face agape, so he charged down to the library and called sternly from outside the door, 'Mr Warboy wants to know what's going on here.'

Strap in hand, Jubal Warboy flung open the door. 'You mind your own business! Get out of here!' he shouted. But behind him, his daughter was cringing on the floor, hands about her head to protect herself.

Sean moved in quickly, wrenching the strap away from Warboy, and seizing her chance, the girl scrambled to her feet and dashed out the door.

Jubal was outraged. 'I'll have you up on a charge, you scoundrel! How dare you interfere like this.'

Sean ignored him. He threw the strap at his feet and hurried out of the room. Dossie was still in the passageway.

'She ran up to the parlour!' she said breathlessly. 'She'll need looking at. Her mother's had a go at her too.'

'Jesus wept!' Sean knocked on the open parlour door as a courtesy before he entered, and found the girl crouching behind one of the leather armchairs.

Obviously appalled by all this, Mr Warboy followed him. He edged over to a window seat and plomped himself down on the soft cushions.

'What's she doing there?' he asked Sean. Then, to Penn, from across the room, 'What are you doing, miss?'

'He was beating her,' Sean said.

'Then go and get her mother.'

'I believe they were both doing the beating, sir.'

'Don't let them in here, Grandfather!' Penn called from her shelter.

'What's this all about, miss? What did you do to warrant the whip?'

'They say I'm a sinner,' she wept, and began to cry hysterically as Jubal loomed in the doorway.

'Stop this right away!' her grandfather snapped at her, then he turned on his son. 'You disgrace me, beating a young lady. Where do you think you are, sir? Do you think you're at the slave market or something? Get out of my sight!'

But Jubal refused to go. 'I'm trying to bring up my daughter in truth and godliness, something you could do with, old man, gadding about the countryside with women and panting after the Governor's lady.'

Sean had never seen Mr Warboy so angry. The old man leapt out of his seat with the agility of a six-year-old, picked up a china figurine of a hunting dog, and hurled it at Jubal striking him on the side of the head.

Mrs Warboy, lurking in the background, started screeching again as her husband tottered back, blood gushing from his temple.

'Pick her up,' Mr Warboy said to Sean, pointing to the girl, as if his son's injury was of no consequence.

Sean encouraged Penn to her feet.

'Let me look at you, miss,' her grandfather said, but she shrank from the two men, trembling in fear. 'Goodness me,' he continued. 'You've torn your pretty dress. We'll have to get you another one. Are you hurting?'

She nodded.

'Then let me see.' He walked quietly over to her, but she pulled away from him, clutching the torn white dress.

'Get Dossie,' he told Sean.

When the maid hurried in, Mr Warboy instructed her to see to the girl. 'Make sure she hasn't got any broken bones,' he added.

When it was established that Penn's back, arms and legs were severely bruised, and she had an injured hand, Warboy became even more furious.

'I should have him arrested!' he barked. 'The fellow ought to be locked up for striking a woman!'

Sean and Dossie looked at each other hopefully.

'You look after her,' Warboy said to Dossie. 'Put her to bed, give her some hot soup or something. I'll attend to her father.'

With that he strode off, and Sean went back to attend to the carriage and Mr Warboy's shopping.

Later he asked Dossie what had happened after he left.

'They had a great old row,' she told him. 'But then they went quiet, muttering in there, and things cooled down, more's the pity, because Penn's taken a nasty beating. The strap's cruel in a man's hand. But you know, Sean, that girl is light in the head. My dog out the back there's got more sense than her. She follows her ma about the house all day, never talks until she's spoke to. They give her sewing to do, and I never seen worse.'

'That's sad,' he said, for want of better words, knowing what the workmen called the poor girl.

Dossie sighed. 'She gets on their nerves, I think. Makes them cranky. They ought to take her out more. But I don't think Jubal'll be game to belt her again. He's got a lump like an emu egg on his head.'

CHAPTER NINE

The morning fog was lifting to reveal a fine sunny day, and Barnaby's spirits lifted with it. Hobarton, as the right people liked to call the town of late, was capricious when it came to weather, it could turn on three climates in the one day, but foggy morns were fairly reliable. They should have a most pleasant voyage today.

He buttoned his high-collared shirt, added a ruffled neckerchief for a touch of dash, and struggled into his new overcoat. He rubbed hair oil into his hands, massaged his bald pate into a healthy shine and, satisfied that he looked his best, stepped cheerfully out of his rooms and turned towards the top of the stairs.

Then it hit him. The family downstairs. That damned trio of misery! He had to get rid of them somehow; this wouldn't do, wouldn't do at all.

He'd slept well, with the aid of a tall glass of rum and hot milk – managed to forget about them until now. But as he descended the staircase, he could hear them in the dining room, in *his* dining room. Disarranging his unread newspapers. Their whispers were more like hisses, and he groaned as he approached the closed door. Well might the wretches whisper, bringing scandal into his home.

Barnaby was appalled that whispering was now necessary. He'd always insisted that the admonishment of 'not in front of the servants' was an admission that the family had something to hide, in which case it was the something that had to be corrected, not the level of conversation.

'Damn them!' he growled and turned away, unwilling to ruin this day by having to endure their company.

He knocked on the drawing room door, a severe irritant in itself, since it was now the girl's bedroom, and when there was no response he stormed out to the pantry and on to the kitchen, where Dossie was busy at the stove.

'Leave that,' he said. 'I will not be requiring breakfast. Get my hat and stick and gloves, and meet me at the front door.'

From there he tramped down the path to the stables, relieved to see that Shanahan already had the first horse in place and was busy affixing traces on the other.

'Am I late, sir?' the Irishman called, and Barnaby shook his head.

'No. I'll just wait here.' He saw Shanahan look up, concerned by the obvious weariness in his voice, and appreciated that because right now he was feeling very low. At least someone appeared to care.

But when he arrived in the carriage at the front door, where Dossie was waiting to hand over his hat and the rest, she also gave him a scarf.

'Here, sir, you'll be needing this out there on the ocean.'

'Thank you,' he said, and his nerves being the way they were, he almost let fall a tear for her kindness.

'Where to, sir? Straight to the harbour?'

Barnaby decided he had to stop feeling sorry for himself. 'No,' he said boldly. 'Take me to one of those fish cafés at Salamanca. I've plenty of time. I'll have my breakfast there in peace.'

He was still shocked by the revelation last night that his granddaughter was pregnant – hence the ructions – and could understand her parents' distress. But he wanted no part of the sordid story. Especially not today.

A man with a lanky grey beard was sitting nearby with his dog. He watched as the servant, a tall, good-looking fellow, accompanied his master into the square, saw him placed on an empty bench, beckoned to a girl to serve the gentleman, and retreated.

Claude Plunkett shook his head. The servant was doing his best and the gentleman accepting the assistance with an amiable smile. But surely decent clothes for the servant were in order, if not livery.

He loved to sit and study the populace and

their manner of dress. It reminded him a little of old times. For Claude Plunkett had been valet to Sir James Huxtable of Park Lane for many years. When Alice, Lady Huxtable, died, it took some time for Sir James to overcome his grief, but eventually he managed. Then he remarried.

As far as Claude was concerned, everything in the large household continued as usual with the new mistress, all the staff content except for a few mishaps here and there, until the day he himself inadvertently caused the greatest mishap of all, coming upon Lady Huxtable in a rarely used back bedroom in flagrante delicto with a gentleman.

Of course he withdrew speedily and quietly. Of course he knew who the gentleman was. And of course he would never have said a word to a soul about the incident. But sadly, Lady Huxtable thought differently, something Claude became aware of within days.

She began complaining about him to Sir James, who called him to order several times for upsetting his wife. Apparently the lady of the house now found his attitude rude and unaccommodating.

'People have different ways, Claude,' Sir James explained kindly 'What suited my dear Alice might not be acceptable to the mistress, so you should go out of your way not to displease her.'

By this Claude guessed that she wanted him out of the house, but he hung on, keeping his distance from her and behaving impeccably when in the same room.

No matter. She invented slights – such as the valet actually passing her on the stairs, or staring at her – outrageous complaints, and so untrue, but the die was cast. Finally she accused him of stealing a visiting gentleman's white silk evening scarf from the lobby.

'I saw him,' she cried. 'I was on the landing waiting for you, James, when I looked down and saw him whisk it away and hurry off through that door. I wondered what he was up to, behaving in such a suspicious manner.'

The scarf was never found. Apologies were made to the guest. Claude was fired. As he'd expected. He was no match for a woman like that. He'd thought at the time that this was the worst moment of his life. Twelve years of service down the drain and not a reference to show for it.

His friends below stairs commiserated with him, and the butler shook his hand at the back door.

'I'm sorry to see you go, Claude,' he said sadly. 'It is the household's loss, and I fear we shall all have to watch our steps now.'

As the door closed behind him, Claude breathed in the cold night air and set off up the worn stone steps to the street, as miserable as he'd ever been and with no idea where to turn now. He'd lived at this house for seven years, and considered it his home.

A constable was standing at the wrought-iron railing. 'Are you Claude Plunkett?'

'Yes. Why?'

'You're under arrest for the theft of a silk scarf, a silk umbrella, property of her ladyship here, and a shooting stick, property of Sir James. Now you come along with me, Mr Plunkett.'

'This is all wrong! I didn't steal anything.'

'You got the sack. Was that for nothing?'

'No. I mean yes. Listen, if we go back and see Sir James, I can explain everything.'

That was a faint hope, Claude knew even as he spoke. His only chance to clear his name was to spill the beans on Lady Huxtable, but that would see him kicked back into the street.

He was glad it was dark when a second constable stepped forward and he was taken into custody, but he could have died from the humiliation of that court. Of being called a liar and a thief, and sentenced to seven years' hard labour in Van Diemen's Land.

Even now Claude felt a familiar flush of embarrassment. He had never got over the shock. To this day he'd kept his face hidden from the world behind the beard. As a prisoner he was so ashamed of his situation, of the sordidness of his state, that he kept his eyes downcast, and shunned company wherever possible.

Obedience to rules and regulations was second nature to Claude Plunkett, his good behaviour automatic, so it worked to his advantage. After the horrors of the transport ship, he was so close to a complete mental breakdown that filing ashore and being told where to stand and what to do was a mercy to him. And to the authorities, trying to deal with fellow Britishers stumbling off these slave ships unafraid to shout abuse at their tormentors, Claude Plunkett was noted as mild and compliant.

At the age of twenty-seven, he was sent to live and work in the stables of the Military Barracks as an odd-job boy, later as a groom, and the world forgot Claude Plunkett.

He applied for his liberty when his term was served and a magistrate stamped his record as a free man, whereupon Claude asked for a job.

'But you have a job, Claude,' he said. 'You can stay at the barracks.'

'No, sir. That won't do. I need a proper job.'

'I see you were a valet.' The magistrate looked at him curiously. 'Could you do that sort of work again? You'd have to get rid of that beard for a start.'

'No, sir, I will not be a servant again. Never.'

'What about a servant of the Government? A public servant?'

'Yes, that is acceptable.'

'Very good. I'll enquire. Come and see me tomorrow.'

On the morrow Claude was offered the job as Pound Keeper. Offered! He felt a thrill at that! As if he need not accept if it didn't suit him. Already a little self-esteem was creeping back.

When he was advised of the duties, the Keeper's quarters and the annual salary, Claude accepted on the condition he was given a mount of his own. That achieved, he explored Hobart for a few days then, map in hand, set out for the old Annabella Station and his new domain.

It had suited him well. The Pound Keeper had simply arrived in the district, restored part of the old station homestead, fixed fences, and become part of the scenery. No one bothered him, except to complain about fines when their animals strayed. No one needed to know where the Pound Keeper had come from, or if he had come willingly to Van Diemen's Land, and Claude had acquired the privacy he so earnestly sought, to ease the burden of being branded a criminal. He still had trouble looking people in the eye. Even Freddy Hines, he reminded himself grimly. Though Freddy had a sidelong look himself, which came from dodging the truth.

In Freddy's case, though, that was survival.

Claude wondered if he could trust him. He hoped so. He needed someone like Freddy

Claude suddenly realised that while he was sitting here wasting time, he had a heap of money in his purse from the resale of the horses, and it all belonged to him.

It gave him a jolt.

While he'd been able to save a few pounds each year, thanks to his chooks and his vegetable garden, he'd never owned a wad of notes. But here they were, burning a hole in his pocket, telling him to get on and buy some land, like all the officers did. Nearly every officer stationed in the colony owned land somewhere out here; they were always talking about land, how much and where. They'd go on down to the Lands Office, study maps and come back all pleased with themselves, as if they'd bought a gold mine.

And here's another thing, Claude said to himself as he left the square via a narrow lane. If you keep on selling horses, you can keep on buying land. That seems to make sense. Anyway, he decided, I'll have a look.

But even as he approached the glass doors of the Lands Office, he encountered disdainful sniffs and stares from townsfolk and knew that his straggly hair and beard were the cause; and that called for another decision. He'd been hiding behind the beard for so long, he hadn't realised that he was drawing attention to himself. Now he would have to compromise.

The barber nodded. 'You want it cut, mate? About time. You'll be tripping over it soon. We'll cut your hair and whip the beard off altogether, eh?'

'No! No! No!'

Claude's sharp reaction startled the barber, but he laughed. 'Ah, you old bushes, you love those beards. Better than scarves, eh? So what *do* you want?'

'Make it tidy, please, sir.' Claude's voice was almost a whisper, uncomfortable at the stares of other patrons. 'Just make it tidy.'

'Right you are.'

When the barber had finished, with a flourish of scissors, he sang his own praises. 'Look at you now, mate, and tell me what you think. I reckon I've done a true sterling job on you, taken thirty years off. See, you're not all that grey after all, got plenty of dark hair left in that thatch.'

He turned to the other men. 'What do you reckon, eh? Don't you think he looks smart now?'

They all agreed, while Claude, finding himself suddenly the centre of attention, was dying a thousand deaths. He did glance in the mirror, recognising neither his grey-bearded self, nor the former clean-shaven valet, seeing only a dignified middle-aged man with neatly combed hair and a carefully clipped full beard – so like the style preferred by Sir James that it threw him off balance. As if he were trying to ape his betters, something he'd been taught to avoid at all costs.

Claude hardly recalled paying the barber. He'd been too intent on getting out of there. It was only when he'd downed a whisky in a nearby pub that he could breathe again, and his heart stopped pounding.

No one stared at him as he set off for the Lands Office, telling himself that this shyness had to cease. He was a free man. Had been for a long time now.

The whisky helped. He marched in the door, up to the counter, and enquired about purchasing land.

'Down the passage, through the third door on the right,' a youth told him. He followed the instructions and waited patiently behind two men who were studying surveyor's maps, trying to eavesdrop so that he might better acquaint himself with the process, but they soon walked away, leaving Claude to try to make sense of the maps on his own.

It took time, but eventually he worked out that there was newly surveyed land for sale at a pound an acre. It was too far north to interest him, so out of curiosity he dug up another map that showed the break-up of the former Annabella sheep station. The map was very much out of date, he noticed, since half of the area taken over by the Provost Marshall's office to serve as the Pound was still marked as for sale. This did not tie in with the map Claude had been given when he took up the post, he was sure of that. After all, he'd been living there so long, he knew every inch of that land.

He took the surveyor's map to the main counter, and in a quiet voice tried to point out the error.

'This land cannot be for sale, sir. It is the Pound,' he said.

The clerk studied it. 'No. It's for sale. The land adjoining was sold for the Pound. See here, five shillings an acre it was sold for.'

'Five shillings an acre?' Claude echoed, thinking of that northern land being sold at four times the price of these acreages. 'That can't be right.'

'It's right. Take it or leave it.'

'I'll take it,' Claude said swiftly, his usual reticence forgotten as he totted up the price. 'Twenty acres. That'll be five pounds. Is that correct?'

'Yes.'

Having paid the five pounds, and received a receipt, his instructions were to come back the next day for the deeds to his land. Claude fully expected to be told then that there had been a mistake. That that particular acreage belonged to the Provost Marshall's office, and he should look elsewhere.

He didn't have to look elsewhere. The title deeds were checked, tied with red tape and handed to him with a polite 'Good day'.

Claude owned half of the land he occupied as Pound Keeper, and he still had a wad of notes in his pocket, so another first had to be undertaken. He opened a bank account and gave his occupation as landlord.

As he rode along the track, past land that he loved and now owned, Claude's thoughts flew

280

triumphantly back to Lady Huxtable.

'What do you think of that?' he asked her. 'Do you ever look in the mirror and see the real ugliness of yourself? Or wonder what became of the valet you sent to prison? I bet you don't.'

He wished he could see her again. And thank her.

Maybe not thank her, come to think of it, but he could address her. Something he would never have dared before this.

Yes. Raise his hat and wish her good day. As if he were an acquaintance. Which he was. Claude laughed. Yes, he was, an *intimate* acquaintance!

He realised he was laughing at an episode that had shattered his life. He used to be known as quite a humorist below stairs, and even Sir James had found him droll on a couple of occasions. 'Droll', that was what he actually said. Before her, of course. Before she came in and wrecked everything. He wondered how they all were there now. How many of them had survived her? It would be interesting to go back.

Smoke rising from the chimney behind the trees told him that Freddy was still there. It wouldn't have surprised him if he had stolen the rest of the impounded horses and disappeared from the district. London had been so awash with muggers and thieves, even murderers, that Claude had learned to be aware, never take chances, especially at night. It was taking time for him to understand that but here, snakes lurking in the undergrowth were more dangerous than the human kind, be they settlers or convicts.

It had been a deliberate decision on his part to

leave Freddy here alone, unsupervised. A man had to take chances at times, and the fellow was in strife. Without a doubt, if he were caught now, he'd be rated a second offender and hence be in for harsh treatment, probably flogging and then Port Arthur, where he'd get hard labour in the coal mines. Claude couldn't, wouldn't, wish that on anyone.

But there he was at the gate, with the stubbled beard as instructed and a face as long as a wet week.

'Where have you been?' Freddy shouted, opening the gate for the rider and his dog. 'I've been marooned here for days, thinking you was never coming back. I've had to keep meself holed up in the house.'

'Why?'

'Why? Because this place is a bloody zoo, with wild animals everywhere, and some horrible screaming and fighting at night.' He ran alongside the horse. 'I reckon them blacks are a dangerous lot. I don't know what they get up to at night, but sure as hell you have to guard the place. I got your rifle out but I couldn't find any ammo, so I was stuck there...'

Claude dismounted at the house. 'When the cat's away, the mice play,' he said.

'What do you mean there's a lot of mice out there? Wolves more like it.'

'Think of Duke as a cat. The animals don't like him, so when he's away I suppose the kangaroos and their mates come closer to graze.'

'They did! They were everywhere, some big blokes too, standing glaring at me if I put my

282

nose out the door.'

Claude continued. 'All the furry animals are near to tame. Sometimes a big-fella kangaroo can get a bit cranky. The screams you hear at night would be Tasmanian devils.'

'What? Devils?'

'Only a name. They're quite small, not bad little fellas really, a cross between a pig and a dog by the look of them, but they play a lot and make a hell of a racket.'

'Do they bite?'

'I wouldn't like to test them, they're nasty-looking beasties. They were probably having the time of their lives with Duke away, chasing all the others out on a free-for-all.'

Freddy looked at Duke with new regard. 'I'll have to find you a bone,' he said. 'We're gonna be mates, Duke.'

His eyes lit up when Claude lifted down heavy saddlebags. 'What have you got in there?'

'Stores. Here, grab hold and unpack them. Make yourself useful.'

'I would have cut firewood for you but the hand's no good!'

'Yes.' Claude laughed. 'I suppose you'd have felt safe with the axe, to chase away all the wild animals.'

'Very funny! You weren't here to see them. The bloody jumping jacks were everywhere.' Suddenly he peered out the door. 'The horses? You sold them, eh?'

'Yes. I got a good price too. Put the money in the bank, but I kept enough for your pay. That's if you're staying?'

'I suppose I could stay a while.'

'Right you are. Tomorrow we start work.'

'At what?'

'I own a couple of these fields now. I'm going to farm them.' Now a landowner, Claude had decided that farming would be a lot easier than chasing wild horses.

'I'm not a farm hand. I wouldn't know what to do.' Freddy sulked.

'You will be when that hand gets better. And you can learn, like I'll have to do.'

Claude was pleased with himself, mightily pleased with himself as he sat by the fire that night, with his pipe and a fresh cup of tea.

'I've got it all worked out now,' he said. 'I've got money coming in from the resale of the horses, and I've got some good news for you.'

'What's that?'

'Here. Have a look at these papers.'

Freddy recognised them immediately. 'These are legitimate. And the identity card. It's for a free settler!'

'That's right. Look at the name.'

'Great galloping giddygoats! Will you look at this. Jack Plunkett! You did it. You've got him real papers!' He took the card over to the lamp and studied it carefully. 'God Almighty, Claude. It's no forgery neither! How did you do that?'

'It wasn't hard. It's done. So now you don't have to stay if you don't want.'

'I can't go anywhere else, not for a while anyway. Someone might recognise me. They probably got my picture up outside the courthouse by now.'

'No, no picture. But a Freddy Hines is advertised as an escapee, wanted for assault.'

'Is that right?' he answered coolly. 'That's not me. My name's Jack Plunkett, innit? Can I keep the papers? I mean, can I still be Jack Plunkett?'

'If you like. But now, another thing. That horse. It has to go.'

'You mean my horse?'

'I mean that stolen horse. The chestnut with the white front hoof. The one that doesn't even have a name.'

'It's got a name!'

'Like what?'

'I can't think right now. But wait on, I remember now – Rover.'

'That's a dog's name! You listen to me – I'll get going early tomorrow and sell it. As long as it's here it's pointing at you. And if you can't figure that out you're sillier than you look.'

Freddy pondered that.

'All right then, but I get the money.'

'No you don't. The blacks brought it in.'

The Governor's yacht sailed out of the Derwent River into Storm Bay to be met by a cold southerly that sent his guests hurrying below decks. Even Lady Franklin, the hardiest traveller of them all, was persuaded to forgo the joys of a 'good brisk breeze', as she called it, for the comfort of the well-appointed stateroom.

Though the yacht was battling choppy seas, she seemed a solid craft, so Barnaby wasn't overly concerned for their safety. He had been warmly greeted by Her Ladyship, and ushered aboard in her wake by an aide, Captain Moore, followed by Sir John and the Lieutenant Governor, who were already engaged in deep discussion about matters of state. The first couple he met on board were the neighbours, Flood and his wife! Pleasantries, stiff as starch, were exchanged, until young Dr Roberts joined them and, it seemed to Barnaby, deliberately rescued him from their company, asking him if he'd care to sit by a porthole where he might have a view of the coastline. Barnaby had the impression the doctor didn't have much time for the Floods, but then he remembered that accident where one of Flood's men had suffered serious burns. There'd been some talk about that.

They'd had to wait almost fifteen minutes for late arrivals, who turned out to be the well-known surgeon Dr Slatter, and Lady Franklin's dear friend Miss Skinner.

'I'm so sorry to have kept you and your guests waiting, Your Excellencies,' Slatter began, 'but we experienced an unavoidable delay. I hope you'll forgive us.'

Miss Skinner rushed forward. 'Oh my! Dr Slatter is such a gentleman, I cannot allow him to take the blame. I couldn't seem to get moving in my excitement. 'Twas I held him up.'

'I thought so,' Lady Franklin sniffed. She turned to the aide. 'Tell the skipper to cast off. We must be there for luncheon. And now that we're all gathered, we shall have morning tea if the boat allows, but before that Sir John wishes to say a few words.'

As the boat slewed from the jetty, Sir John grasped a railing and called to his audience to hang on. 'We can't have any bruises or sprains,' he added, 'as there's quite a bit of walking to be done today. Port Arthur is a very large establishment. More than two hundred acres, not counting the mines and outstations.'

'But very beautiful,' Lady Franklin put in, startling Barnaby, who couldn't conceive of a beautiful prison.

'Firstly now,' her husband continued, 'I'm sure you all know our esteemed Dr Slatter, and appreciate all he has done for the health of the community, so you will be pleased to know that he has been appointed Chief Medical Officer for the colony.'

That brought enthusiastic applause, to which Dr Slatter responded politely, hoping he would be able to do justice to such weighty responsibilities.

'I will do my best, Your Excellency,' he concluded. 'And one of my first duties is to fill the vacancy of medical officer at Port Arthur. We are hoping that we can persuade Dr Roberts to accept this important post.'

All eyes were then on Dr Roberts. 'I don't know if I'm up to the task,' he responded shyly, but Slatter disagreed.

'I believe you are, Doctor,' he said firmly.

Sir John added his voice. 'And who would know better, Dr Roberts, than our Chief Medical Officer? I too hope you will accept. So, what a morning! With yet another announcement. Lieutenant Flood has agreed to take up duties as my aide-de-camp, until Captain Moore returns from leave of absence, commencing next week.'

Amid the applause Barnaby hid his distaste at the latter appointment, but he did not miss the flash of irritation that crossed the young doctor's face. He hoped Roberts would not accept the Port Arthur post as, selfishly he knew, he'd prefer to have a medical man of his stature remain within reach. After all, if Slatter thought so highly of him, he would have to be more than competent.

As they rounded the point, the winds eased, allowing the passengers on deck to view the peninsula that housed the prison, and to see for themselves that escape would be difficult. The bay in which they were presently sailing Barnaby found quite lovely. He admired the dark wooded shorelines and in particular the small island in the centre of the bay.

'Does it have a name?' he asked Captain Moore.

'Yes, sir. It is the Isle of the Dead. That's the Port Arthur cemetery. It looks pleasant, but it is said to be haunted.'

Barnaby shuddered. 'Are convicts buried there?'

'Yes, they're buried in paupers' graves, unless someone pays for a headstone, which is rare. But it's mainly for decent people who have been so unfortunate as to die here – military personnel mostly, or wives, and even little children. God rest their souls.'

The yacht sailed into a sandy cove and the first direct view of the settlement was overshadowed by the huge brick penitentiary, a grim building four storeys high. Beyond that, to Barnaby's astonishment, was a lovely rural village that would have done an English county proud. There was a fine white house on the hill with manicured grounds, and other charming houses further on, all surrounded by the same neat green fields. He could even see the spire of an impressive church.

When Their Excellencies stepped ashore, they were met by the commandant of the prison, Major Farraday, in the uniform of the Royal Scots, even down to the tartan trews, a pipe band in neat convict garb, and a group of spectators who cheered wildly until the band struck up, drowning the Commandant's long-winded welcome speech.

Captain Moore darted forward to hush the band, and as he began to raise both hands in the manner of a conductor to bring their tune gently to a close, they stopped abruptly, leaving his hands mid-air and their commandant mid-shout.

From down on the beach, where some fishermen (convicts again?) were mending nets, came another shout. This time of laughter, and some of the female spectators giggled.

Formalities over, the guests came ashore and all were invited to the Commandant's house for luncheon. It turned out to be the fine house on the hill, with a small peninsula all of its own, and though it was a windy day, the view in all directions was spectacular.

Barnaby took the opportunity to turn from the sea views to look over the Commandant's realm, and was once again impressed by the neatness and precision of this penal village.

'I am looking forward to our walk,' he said to Miss Skinner, who reeled back in shock.

'Out there? Never! That's where they keep the

criminals. I wouldn't move a step from here.'

'Nonsense, Aggie,' Lady Franklin called back at her. 'After lunch we shall explore. I can't wait to have a good look around.' She drew in a deep breath. 'Look out there at all the white tops on the waves. What a view! This really is quite a magnificent setting. It is a credit to Governor Arthur! He chose an ideal location for the prison. I have never understood why prisons have to be degrading.'

The formal luncheon, as expected with such distinguished guests as Their Excellencies, was quite splendid – seven courses served by pretty girls in black dresses and mob caps.

'Compliments to your chef, Commandant,' Dr Slatter said. 'Where did he come from?'

'London. Highly regarded in the best hotels, I believe, but got himself arrested in the foyer of The Grand Duke, in Oxford Street, drunk and disorderly, and ten years for his trouble. He's married to one of our waitresses.'

'He's a convict and married to a Hobart girl?' asked Mrs Flood.

'Good Lord, no. The servants here are all convicts. They make up the entire work force, and as you'll see, Mrs Flood, we have a model town.'

After lunch Barnaby would much rather have put his feet up with another glass of the Commandant's dessert wine, but the guests were gathering on the veranda, donning overcoats against the wind blowing in from the bay, ready for their explorations. He was mollified, though, when

Lady Franklin herself noticed his new overcoat.

'It is so beautifully tailored. A London import I'm guessing?'

'Ah no, Lady Franklin. A Hobart tailor. Former convict, so whoever that magistrate was has done us a great favour.'

'Then you must whisper his name to me. I'd dearly love a new tailored overcoat. Now come along. You walk with me, Barnaby, and we'll let Captain Moore lead the way. Sir John and the Commandant can have their own conversations.'

So down the well-made road they marched, past the Commandant's offices on the left, and on past the barred windows and firmly closed entrances to the huge penitentiary. There was an eerie silence about the prison, as if everyone inside was holding his breath until the passing of this nervous group, who were thoroughly intimidated by the high walls.

Barnaby breathed a sigh of relief as they moved from the shade of that building into the pale sunlight.

When they came to a crossroads, Captain Moore pointed out that off to their left were the hospital, a policeman's residence, and the farm overseer's cottage.

'They have a large farm here, as you'll see when we walk through. They grow all their own fruit and vegetables and run sheep as well as pigs and dairy cattle, but we'll carry on down here. This is known as Champ Street.'

'Why?' Lady Franklin asked. 'Who is or was Champ?'

'I'm afraid I don't know, Your Ladyship.'

'Then you must find out and tell me later. Now who do these nice houses on our left belong to?'

'They are for the magistrate, the surgeon, and the medical officer. That will be you, Dr Roberts if you decide in the affirmative, which I hope you will do. They all have lovely gardens, do you see?'

'Yes, Captain. I'm not much of a gardener, though.'

'You don't have to be,' Captain Moore told him. 'All the officers from the Commandant down vie to have the best gardens. They search convict records for the best available gardeners.'

'That would be a help,' Dr Roberts conceded.

'Oh yes,' Mrs Flood remarked with a sneer. 'Mr Warboy knows all about that, don't you, Mr Warboy?'

Barnaby pretended not to hear her as he turned down the next street, towards a hewn-stone pinnacled church, the one he'd seen from the yacht.

'This is St David's church,' the captain told the group, looking back to see that Sir John and their host were far behind them, but obviously unconcerned.

Once again, Barnaby was astonished, not only by the fine church and its parsonage, but by the superb garden surrounds.

'This church can accommodate upward of two thousand sitters,' Captain Moore said, 'and there is a splendid convict choir.'

They all trooped inside, did their duty by the Lord and regrouped outside.

'What's down there?' Lady Franklin asked.

'That street goes off to the farm and factory

works, or down to the warehouses, stores, ship-wright's buildings and lime kiln ... nothing very interesting. They also have a tailoring establish-ment which trains apprentices in the trade, but I'm not sure where that is.'

'Yet I believe time is set aside of a Saturday afternoon for schooling. A boon for many of the poor wretches who are not literate,' Lady Franklin said.

'That's a fact, yes. Evening classes are held too; educated convicts volunteer as teachers and they get a jolly good roll-up, I hear, to beat the boredom of early lockdown. They also teach shipbuilding.'

'And yet we have hardly seen a worker. Are all the inhabitants locked up for our benefit?'

'Not all, Your Ladyship. The farm and work-shops are operating, but they wouldn't be expecting you.'

'Then that's where we'll go.'

From that moment there was a change in the air, as if a gate were to be opened and mystery lay beyond.

Sir John caught up with them, and the captain turned to him for rescue.

'Lady Franklin wishes to see the convicts at work, sir.'

'Oh no, my dear. There's no point in disturbing their routines. Workmen are the same everywhere, after all. And it would take quite a bit of walking. The Commandant and I are turning back.'

'Very well. Do you want to stop, Aggie? And you, Mrs Flood?'

'I'll stay and keep the ladies company,' Lieutenant Flood said, accepting their sighs of relief, so the troupe was reduced to four, with Captain Moore in the lead, Lady Franklin charging behind him accompanied by Dr Roberts, and Barnaby valiantly bringing up the rear.

They found the usual rural pursuits under way, except that many of the farm labourers were hindered by an iron ball and chain attached to their ankles, and forced to drag it about with them. Barnaby had tried to lift one in Hobart some time ago, and was stunned by the weight of the thing.

He called to the captain. 'May I ask a question?'

'Certainly, sir.'

'Thank you. Could you tell me why those men are anchored with the ball and chain when it is well known that escape from this establishment is impossible.'

'Ah! But they try, and a lot of time is wasted scouring the peninsula for absconders. It's amazing the tricks they get up to, trying to build rafts, even boats, or sneaking across the causeway at Eagle Hawk Neck. One man tried to sail away in a barrel, another wore a kangaroo skin to trick the dogs. No end to the ruses. The ball and chain deters repeat absconders.'

Near a sawmill they passed men in heavy leg-irons staggering under the weight of sawn timbers, and though Barnaby had seen the sufferings of chain gangs before, these men looked particularly distressed.

Roberts was moved to remark on this. 'Captain Moore,' he called. 'The leg-irons on those prisoners. They look different. Are they regulation?'

'Yes, Doctor,' Moore said airily. 'They're repeat offenders. Their punishment is flogging, a hundred of the best, then they get the hardest labour. They are wearing double irons, that's what's different.'

'Poor fellows,' Barnaby murmured.

'They bring it on themselves. There are worse punishments than that!'

Barnaby stiffened at the thought and turned away. He didn't want to know.

Lady Franklin veered to the left of the sawmill and strode towards a high fence.

'What's here?' she asked.

'Only the corn mill and granary,' their guide said, but since they could hear a loud creaking noise coming from inside, Her Ladyship strode over to a sentry.

'Open the gate, please!'

The sentry looked to Moore, but Lady Franklin banged the ground with her walking stick and he jumped to release the catch and open the gate.

They were confronted by a huge treadmill with at least thirty men mounted on it, and working very hard, as they must, Barnaby realised, or the rotary stairs would injure their shins. Their clothes were in tatters and they all looked thin and exhausted.

'How long do they have to work there?' he asked Moore, turning away from the awful sight of guards with whips standing nearby, obviously waiting for the visitors to leave.

'Usually that punishment is thirty days.'

Lady Franklin, however, had rushed off in

another direction, and was arguing with a guard.

'Release him!' she was demanding, pointing to a man crouched on the ground. He was chained to a post, with his hands resting on a wooden trestle, and appeared to be in great pain. It wasn't until Barnaby came closer that he saw the prisoner wasn't resting his hands at all; he was caught in thumbscrews, or what Barnaby imagined were thumbscrews, never having seen such an apparatus before.

'I won't have torture!' Her Ladyship shouted, this time at a guard.

'But it's orders, Your Ladyship,' he cried helplessly.

'Get him out or I'll do it myself.'

The man was released to collapse in the dirt.

'See to him, Dr Roberts! See they clean him up,' Lady Franklin instructed. Barnaby was astonished that the bruising leg-irons, the agony of men weighted with heavy timbers, and the treadmill – also mentions of floggings, which, thank God, they hadn't witnessed – hadn't seemed to bother the lady. Just the thumbscrews, bad as they were. He didn't know what to make of her. Or this place. Determined efforts to educate the prisoners and teach them trades so they could earn a living when they were released, allied with vicious punishments! On the boat the Governor had informed them that prisoners at Port Arthur were well fed because they grew their own produce in such abundance; that there was plenty to feed the thousand or more prisoners and staff housed there at any one time.

'In fact,' he said, 'statistically they are better fed

296

than the average labourer in the Old Country. Therefore they are physically much fitter and healthier than their parents or siblings back home.'

Recalling that, it occurred to Barnaby that being fitter and healthier wasn't much help if the years of incarceration killed or crippled you.

A messenger ran down to Captain Moore with a note.

'Sir John requests we return, Lady Franklin,' he told her. 'The yacht is ready to depart.'

'Very well,' she said cheerfully. 'It has been a most interesting day, has it not, Barnaby?'

'Indeed yes,' he nodded, 'indeed it has been.'

'So much so that I must tell the Commandant we will make a return visit as soon as time allows and stay a few days. We didn't even get to view Eagle Hawk Neck, the entrance to this settlement, or the coal mines, or the boys' prison. And we absolutely must visit that island, the Isle of the Dead, it looks so small and yet so majestic out there all alone.'

Barnaby hoped he would not be included in that expedition, and was busy composing excuses as they tramped back up the road, until he noticed dark clouds gathering out to sea and found a more immediate concern with the yacht bouncing about down there in the cove.

Dr Roberts caught up with them as they passed the penitentiary, commenting to Barnaby that there had been no mention of a tour of that grim edifice, not even from Lady Franklin, who had rushed on ahead to enthuse over a superb rose garden.

'I think you'll see plenty of it soon enough,' Barnaby replied.

But Roberts was troubled. 'I'm not sure that I want to take up that appointment in a place like this, but they all seem to have taken it for granted I'll accept.'

'I can understand that,' Barnaby said, 'and personally, I think you're a bit young for the job.'

'A bit soft you mean, sir?'

Barnaby nodded. 'Yes. A bit soft, as in not case-hardened in penal culture.'

'I've seen my share in Hobart.'

'You probably have, but it's a fair bet that this place is infinitely worse. It's for second offenders, don't forget. Hobart convicts are small fry.'

'I know, but Dr Slatter says I'd also have the right to put a stop to excessive discipline, and there's where I think I could make a difference. I would speak up, Mr Warboy, believe me.' He grinned. 'And it's quite a promotion. I have a feeling a refusal would not be appreciated in the right circles.'

The sun hadn't offered too much warmth so far on this day, but as it drifted behind a bank of grey clouds the wind shook off its rays and spiked the air with a sudden cold.

Barnaby buttoned his overcoat to the neck and adjusted his scarf. 'There's merit in the appointment they've offered you, as well as tribulations. It's a difficult decision to make. But with respect, Doctor, if you do accept, I'd suggest a contract for – say – one or two years, whatever you please, but set a time, a sunset on your good works, so to speak.'

'Can I do that?'

'Certainly you can. Take it up with the Lieutenant Governor. That means no petty bureaucrats can chase you off if you happen to disagree with them. And if you find you are unhappy in the service, you will be able to withdraw honourably at the date prescribed.'

'Thank you, Mr Warboy, I'll give that some thought.'

The return journey was bumpier than the trip to Port Arthur, but Miss Skinner was the only one to succumb to seasickness.

Allyn took her to a cabin and assisted her to stretch out on a bunk. He kept a bucket by her side and dabbed her face with a damp cloth while trying to convince her that a dose of laudanum would not cure her condition, but the more she cried and complained, the more she vomited, or rather dry-retched by this time.

Eventually, though, he managed to quieten her and disappeared to a corner so that he could read a letter that was burning a hole in his pocket.

He'd found it there, just a folded page, a little while after he'd attended to the prisoner released from thumbscrews. He had reset both of the man's broken thumbs, given him laudanum to ease his pain, and instructed the guards standing around to leave him be.

'He'll sleep the night, so let him have that. He'll be sore in the morning.'

'That's against the rules,' a guard said. 'He has to report in at six. He been on them screws all day, mister. He'll cop it if he don't report in.'

'Now see what you've done!' another guard growled at Allyn. 'How we gonna get him back to his cell now you put him to sleep? He's snoring like an old porker!'

Someone else suggested a wheelbarrow. 'Don't worry, mister. We'll take him up. Reckon he won't weigh more'n a bag of taters.'

Allyn tried to see their faces. Which one of them had slid this letter into his pocket? And why?

The letter itself gave that explanation. It was written on the back of a page of regulations, one of which stated that convicts at Port Arthur may not send or receive mail without the approval of the Commandant. The handwriting was large, the letters well formed but jerky, as if the writer were in a hurry. As one would expect, under the circumstances. It was addressed to Mrs L. Harris, Sassafras Road, Hobart, and was signed by L. Harris, obviously the husband. Or possibly her son.

Dear Josie you have to get a solicitor tell him to read my record sheet and get me out of here because I never did attack anyone it was round the other way so do that quick Lester.

Furtively Allyn thrust the note back into his pocket, wondering if he should deliver it. He could take it to that address and shove it under a door or leave it somewhere obvious. He wouldn't want to be seen, for God's sake! There could be charges for such activities. But if he dropped it off anonymously ... what would be the harm?

300

As he entered the lounge, he saw Flood at a table turning over cards, and Mr Warboy dozing in an armchair in a corner, and it suddenly hit him!

Sassafras Road!

A few seconds later he made another connection. Shanahan, who worked out there at the Warboy farm, had introduced him to a Mrs Harris and her daughter. Could this be the same woman? He felt a wave of guilt, as if his companions knew he had an illegal document concealed about his person and were waiting for him to give it up. He moved unsteadily to the safety of an armchair by the wall, and sank into the sanctuary of its leathery folds.

Mrs Harris, and Miss Harris. That pretty blonde girl. They were respectable ladies. Surely they weren't connected to this criminal, the fellow called Lester?

Coming closer to believing they were, that the evidence seemed to point to this Mrs Harris, he decided Lester must be the son. A prodigal son. Forgiven by his mother for his imprudent lifestyle, one that had led him to this sorry state. Back in England, magistrates would transport young fellows who had only committed minor offences, at the drop of a hat. After all, he thought cynically, workers were needed in Van Diemen's Land, weren't they? Then the mother had migrated to Hobart to lend support and encouragement to her son, to be there for him when he was released.

Allyn nodded to himself. That seemed a credible scenario.

Except, he countered, Lester had written to 'Josie'. Would a son address his mother in this way?

All right! So he was writing to the girl. To his sister. Why not? Maybe the mother wasn't up to facing solicitors.

'What do you think, Doctor?' Flood asked, startling him.

'I'm sorry, Lieutenant, I think I must have nodded off. What was that?'

'We were discussing the name change. Some people believe the Dutchman, Abel Tasman, was too modest. He was the first to visit this land, he should have named it after himself.'

Allyn turned to the conversation in hand. 'I had not heard this suggestion before, but he made the choice of Van Diemen. Who was Van Diemen anyway?'

'Ah, you young people,' Dr Slatter sighed. 'He was the governor of the Dutch East Indies.'

'Oh, I see. Nothing to do with this colony.'

'Exactly!' Flood said enthusiastically. 'He never set foot in the place. Tasman's the hero, not Van Diemen.'

Allyn turned to the Governor. 'What do you think, Sir John?'

'It's a nice thought, but it can't be changed now. It's far too late. Besides, Tasman was a great man, we should respect his decision.'

'Of course!' Flood said, changing his tune very swiftly. 'Yes, of course, sir.'

'A great pity, though,' came a deep voice from the corner as Mr Warboy sat up and peered about him. 'Tasman's explorations were too important for him to be overlooked like this. With respect, Sir John, I believe the man deserves better. It's never too late. And where are we? The seas seem to have settled.'

'On our way upriver, Barnaby.' The Governor smiled. 'In about a half-hour we'll deliver all safe and sound back in Hobart.'

'With our thanks for an interesting and most enjoyable day,' Barnaby said, but as the other guests also expressed their gratitude he settled back with a sense of foreboding.

He wished they'd turn the yacht about and take them somewhere else. Anywhere. He was not looking forward to going home. Not with the invaders in his house. And the looming scandal of the pregnant girl. What had she been up to? It was always the way, it was the quiet ones you had to watch. But the situation was a damned nuisance. A granddaughter in the family way? And who else was Barnaby to be lumbered with now? A grand-son-in-law with no morals? A bastard great-grandchild?

'Damn them all,' he muttered, and Lady Franklin looked around.

'Are you all right, Barnaby?'

'Oh yes, thank you. Just a touch of indigestion. Too much of a good thing today.'

CHAPTER TEN

For Millicent Warboy, this was turning out to be the worst day of her life. She had intended having a serious private conversation with Barnaby regarding her daughter. But he was nowhere to be found. It was so like Barnaby to stick his nose in, complaining about them giving Penn a few slaps to try to get some sense out of her, and then disappear. Simply disappear the next morning with not a word to anyone. Except Shanahan, that dirty Irishman. He knew where Barnaby had gone, but he wouldn't say, even when Jubal threatened to dismiss him.

Millicent had her suspicions about Shanahan. She had spoken to Barnaby about having a Papist on the property, as had Jubal, but he refused to accept that it was wrong. Very wrong.

'He's the best man for the job,' he had said.

Now he should take another look. She wouldn't be surprised if it was Shanahan who had raped her daughter. Who else had the opportunity? Who else had the run of the place? She felt that flush of rage come over her again and fell to her knees by the window in the front parlour, so she could keep watch for Barnaby.

She prayed to the Holy Spirit to protect her from the abyss of scandal, and to God the revengeful Father to strike down the rapist, send him to the fires of hell; and as she knelt there

Millicent could see Shanahan's hands on her daughter, she could see his naked sweating body on the bed and that mouth covering the girl's with kisses, and his strong arms holding her to him, refusing to release her until the deed was done, still holding her, his kisses warm, wet, covering her all over in gratitude.

Millicent sank to the carpet, exhausted.

When Dossie brought her afternoon tea, she was asleep on the couch, but as soon as she awoke she demanded to know if Mr Warboy had returned.

'I don't think he went out,' Dossie said.

'Do not,' Millicent warned, 'do not pretend to misunderstand me, you wretch, or I'll have you sacked. And don't think I can't. Where is Mr Warboy Senior?'

'I'm sure I don't know, madam.'

'Then since he is not at home, when he left, was he riding?'

'No, madam.'

'Then how was he travelling? I presume he was not walking.'

'In his coach, madam. It's quite a cold day.'

'And who was driving?'

'Mr Shanahan, madam.'

'Now we're getting somewhere. Send Shanahan to me.'

'He is out, madam.'

'Out where? Out womanising somewhere, I suppose?'

'I do not know, madam. He only left a little while ago.'

'Get out!' Millicent would have thrown some-

305

thing at her had not the fine china tea service been on the small table in front of her. Millicent was very fond of it.

She heaped three sugars into her tea, and took a bite of a Bath bun. Barnaby, she pondered angrily, needn't think he could ignore the situation. Obviously one of his men had raped Penn. In the mean time, Penn was hysterical, not understanding what was going on. And how could she, an innocent like her? She would have gone into marriage a beautiful untouched virgin, and now she'd been despoiled by some brute. It was a wonder the girl hadn't gone mad when the attack happened, but instead she'd simply suffered in brave silence and put it out of her mind. Thrust it so far out of her mind that she could no longer recall, or would not recall, the shock, the depravity of it.

But they'd find out who'd done this, and very soon. And Barnaby would have to face up to it.

So would Penn. When Millicent discovered her daughter had missed her monthly, she'd rushed her off to town on the pretence of a shopping expedition, and whisked her in to see Dr Jellick. And unbelievably, when Penn was told she was having a baby, she'd come out all smiles.

'A baby,' she'd said. 'Am I getting a baby of my very own?'

'It's not a doll,' Millicent had said sternly. 'Get hold of yourself, girl.'

'Oh, a tiny wee baby. I'll have to think of a name.'

'Good God! Shut up, Penn! I'm so sorry, Doctor. I think she's in shock,' her mother had said, mortified. But worse was to come.

'That's all right, Mrs Warboy. Girls like this, who are a bit simple, often don't grasp what's going on. It takes a lot of explaining. She probably doesn't relate the sex act to pregnancy either.'

Millicent was ropable. 'How dare you say my daughter is simple! She was raped by some animal and you badmouth her! What sort of a doctor are you? Penn is as smart as any girl her age. You should see her drawings of flowers, they're quite remarkable.'

'I'm sure they are. Now you run along, Mrs Warboy. I've got better things to do than listen to your rantings. I'll send the bill.'

'I beg your pardon!'

He opened the door. 'No need. You go and find someone else to yell at.' He tweaked Penn under the chin. 'Goodbye, Penn. You are looking very nice today. I like your bonnet, it's very pretty. Good day to you, Mrs Warboy.'

And that was that. Millicent had never been so insulted in all her life! But what could you expect in a brutal penal colony? What had possessed Barnaby to settle in a place like this? Then she remembered that Jubal had explained: 'Cheap land. Cheap labour, my love. He's a cunning old character.'

Well! she said to herself, as she ate her third Bath bun, I think we ought to sell up here and move to Melbourne on the mainland. It's a respectable town, no convicts, and they say it's becoming quite the hub for the right people. Barnaby might not be so popular in the vice-regal society if this scandal gets out. And I don't see how it can be kept quiet after Shanahan is arrested. They will probably hang him in that penitentiary in the centre of Hobart. They say there's more than one hanging a week at that place. Jubal says this Government culls the criminal class. Anyone who gets out of hand faces the noose. As they should.

'Where is Barnaby?' she asked Jubal as he walked in the door.

'You tell me. I'm going to line up all the workmen as soon as he gets here and find the rapist. This time I want my father standing there to witness, so they can't think I have no authority. And as the father of that poor girl I will demand the culprit be taken into custody immediately.'

'And you think he'll own up? Step forward and admit it? Fat chance of that. But if we confront Penn with them, surely she can point him out.'

Jubal stared at her in horror. 'I cannot believe that you, her mother, would even consider putting Penn through a horrible experience like that. She'd be terrified, afraid he'd attack again, and humiliated beyond reason. Could you imagine what it'd be like for the poor child to have to relive the rape in front of everyone? Confronted with the brute, she'd probably collapse.'

'I only thought it would be simpler.'

'Oh yes! Drag her out and throw her down in front of all those men and have her looking at them ... remembering?'

Millicent covered her ears! 'Stop! Stop! It's too vile, too disgusting!'

'Then let God handle this. Let Him cast up the sinner. Let him flay the truth out of him! We have to purge wickedness from our midst. We are surrounded by disbelievers and heathens. After this I'll demand that Father employs only men of the faith, that he sends all the heathens back to the cells where they belong.'

'And that includes the Papists,' Millicent spat. 'Shanahan for one.'

Jubal nodded thoughtfully. 'Interesting that his name is already in the air. I have been inclined to think it was that creature all along, but we have to be careful, Millicent. He's dodgy. He'll know he's a suspect...'

'Of course he will. He's the only one who has the run of the place. And he's a Papist.'

'I'm well aware of that. They're a lecherous lot at best. I blame Father for exposing my ladies to such villains. I'll ride into town now and request police presence so that the rapist can't dodge off on us.'

Singer Forbes was still in a dark mood over those letters, making Sean nervous that any day he might upset the applecart for everyone.

To earn a little money, Sean had persuaded Mr Warboy to allow him to work at Sam Pollard's piggery on Sundays, but on this day he'd been uneasy as he left the farm, truly beset with a feeling that trouble could erupt at any minute. When he finally rode home, in a hurry to clean up before setting off with the carriage to collect Mr Warboy, everything seemed to be calm in the men's quarters.

'What's doing?' he asked a couple of the men who were drinking their home-brew ginger wine from an old teapot.

'Nothin' much,' Hunter the dairyman said with a grin. 'The lads are fishing.'

Sean nodded. Sunday fishing was deemed a righteous occupation, and economically useful, and was encouraged as long as they remained on the Warboy property. This boss allowed them to keep their catch, but many that he knew of, including Flood next door, commandeered the fish for their own table, on the grounds that fishing was recreation for the convicts, but the catch, legally speaking, belonged to the owner of the property.

Many were the fights and rows that erupted over the grand fishing debate, he mused as he made for the ablutions shed, this island being a heaven for all sorts of fish, all worthy of a king's table. But on Warboy's farm, there was more to the recreation than met the official eye. These workers did indeed go fishing, but they also enjoyed the company of female convicts, who'd sneak through the scrub for their own form of recreation, and who expected to be paid – bartering for fish or coin. Sunday afternoons could be riotous occasions for Warboy men, but someone always kept nit, from high in a pine tree, for they were all very mindful of the terrible loss if their fishing rights were shut down.

He was surprised, then, to see Singer, normally an enthusiastic fisherman and ladies' man, sitting on a bench outside the shed with Old Pop from the saddlery and leather goods factory just outside town.

'A good day to you, Pop,' he said to the visitor. 'What brings you our way?'

'He's teaching me to make a stock whip,' Singer answered. 'Take a look at this. It's nearly finished. Isn't it a beauty?'

Pop's lined face lit up with pleasure. 'He's a good pupil, Shanahan. Patient! That's what you need to get the handle plaited right.'

Sean feigned enthusiasm as he examined the whip, to cover a groan. Making leather goods wasn't illegal: convicts often learned how to make hats or weskits, even boots, from pieces of hide rejected by saddlers, and kept the articles for their own use or sold them. Stock whips were useful and well-made ones were in great demand, but in the wrong hands a whip with a tail more than five feet long was very dangerous. In the wrong hands like those belonging to Singer.

'You're missing the fun,' Singer said. 'The fishing party will be closing down any minute. We all have to go back into our cages come sundown, don't we, Shanahan?'

Pop looked at him, surprised. 'Do they lock you down at night? I didn't know they did that here.'

'They don't,' Sean said.

Singer put down the whip. 'Come on, Pop. I'll show you the garden on the way out. It's the only way I could get him here for my lesson, he's mad for a peep at Warboy's Folly.'

'Is that what it's called?' Pop asked. 'Warboy's Folly?'

'Yes,' his pupil said. 'Nice-sounding name, if you ask me.'

'Too right.' The old man nodded. 'You tell your boss to come and look at our factory, Shanahan. We've got good stuff there. Good enough for the

Pollard Stores, I tell you.'

'I'll do that,' Sean said, wondering if he could persuade the owners of that factory to give Singer a job. Put some distance between him and the Warboys.

'A thought,' he murmured. 'And I might be able to swing Flo Quinlan in here. Poor Flo, he's had a bad trot, getting attacked by that Lester Harris.'

The censors were at work in a warm room at the rear of the courthouse, trying to catch up on the backlog of mail due to be loaded on ships the next day.

Their job was to sort settlers' mail from that of assigned or freed convicts, made easier by access to the two local registers, one for residents, the other for convicts. Settlers' mail was usually allowed through without contest, but convict mail was divided yet again. Only assigned or paroled prisoners were permitted to post letters, so that reduced the number to be checked, and many, considered so badly written as to be illegible, were cast into the fireplace.

On the whole, the censors managed to whisk through these epistles fairly quickly, since the content became of little interest after a while, and they were only on the lookout for plots and various other illegal activities.

Though most convicts were too cunning to place such efforts on paper, many felt that their lurid opinions of their betters, be they government or guards, were acceptable as literary lines. They were not. Even the mildest recriminations

312

fuelled the fire.

On this particular Sunday afternoon, one bored censor gave a grunt of interest.

'Will I let this through?' he asked his companion.

'Who's it from?'

'Number 5137 Forbes.'

'That'd be Singer Forbes. I know him. Let's have a look.'

Dearest Brother, I received your Letter number Four and am anxiously waiting for number Five to tell me how you all are and if you have heard from my Abbeyrose who has stopped writing to me it's all I can think from here and hence hard for me since I only have four years to go. Can you save the fare to get me home and if you do I'll sing at your funeral since I missed your wedding. Here I am working on a farm now and a garden and going all right. The farmer's son prays for us a lot, he is a fat fellow and wears a corset, belches and farts a lot, has a lot of hair coming out his ear and nose, and next to none on his head, eyes pinky like a pig, that being the best I can say of him. Tell Abbeyrose I'll bring her home a jewel. Tell my love and honour to the parents from your affectionate brother James.

The censor, who was a law clerk, gave a shout of laughter. 'That's Singer all right. He's a one, he is.'

'But can we pass it?'

'I don't see anything irregular. Nothing agin the Government, so to speak. Let it go. I must get a look at that farmer's son. It says here Warboy Farm. Let's keep an eye out for the Old Farter.'

In fact, the Old Farter wasn't far away. He was across the street in the newly constructed police premises, engaged in earnest conversation with Chief Constable Ernest Hippisley.

It had been a rather quiet day as Hobart Fridays went. There had been a vicious brawl in the square between the crews of two whalers, with one man killed and three arrested after the military was called in to restore order. A handful of convicts found themselves back in jail for drunkenness, a breakout at the Female Factory meant several women were still at large, and a well-attended protest at the Governor's failure to rid the outskirts of the town of blackfellows had been held outside the Governor's mansion. It was allowed to run its course, since Sir John and his lady wife were enjoying a day sailing with friends.

As soon as he heard the word 'rape', Ernest frowned, 'Ah yes,' he said cautiously, taking up a pen. 'Was it of a man or a woman?'

'A woman, of course! A woman, sir! Men don't get raped. It is about the rape of a young girl. We know who the villain is, and we should like you to come and arrest the fellow. To Warboy Farm. I'm sure you know my father. He's a personal friend of the Governor, Sir John, and also a dear friend of Her Ladyship. The thing is, this is such a vile and scandalous business, we'd appreciate it ever so much, Chief Constable, if there could be as little fuss as possible.'

'Oh yes, I quite understand. Yes. But are you sure it is rape? Women can be rather sensitive in these matters...'

'It is rape,' Warboy said firmly. 'No doubt about it. Medical opinion will bear me out.'

'Is it a white woman? I mean, black gins...'

'It is a white woman, a young innocent girl of whom I speak, sir. Trust me, on the heart of our Saviour, I would not dream of making a frivolous complaint. The matter is too serious.'

'And you know the man who committed this crime?'

'I most certainly do, but I am loath to point him out to anyone but your good self. I am not the law. We can't have him bolting until you arrive to formally arrest him.'

'And who is this gentleman?'

'He is no gentleman; the fellow is a convict, assigned to our farm.'

Only a convict! Ernest breathed a sigh of relief. Since the Warboys moved in illustrious circles, he'd been afeared that one of the lusty young officers paraded in society as escorts for young ladies might have taken certain liberties with a lass. It was rare for a girl to cry rape, very rare, but such incidents were never followed up by the police; the military saw to that. They were very powerful in Van Diemen's Land, too powerful for a lowly chief constable to withstand. But a convict...

'Where is this fellow now?'

'At the farm. Unsuspecting that we have him in our sights.'

'And the young lady?'

'You'll meet her at the farm. I thought perhaps you'd care to take tea with my wife and me before you make the arrest. She gives an excellent table.'

Tea? Chief Constable Hippisley stood to his full height and looked down at the complainant.

'I don't believe tea would be appropriate,' he growled. 'I will look into the matter and decide if any arrests should be made. So don't go off half-cocked before I get there, sir. And tell me, I need the name of the lady who is claiming to have been raped.'

'Is that necessary? No need to record it here. After all, you'll meet her...'

'The name, please?'

Warboy coughed. 'Yes. Of course. It's Penelope Warboy.'

'What relation is she to you, sir?'

The cough again, and a faint fart. 'My daughter.'

'I see. I have a few things to do here. I shall be at Warboy Farm with one of my constables at six p.m. And as I said, I shall not require tea.'

Sean drove the carriage into town and hitched the horses to a rail under trees near the wharves at Salamanca. He bought four thin, undersized cheroots for a penny from an enterprising pedlar, and lit one with a sigh of pleasure. There'd only be a few puffs to savour but the tobacco was good. Come down in the world you have, he mused, studying the butt. Once you were probably a proud Maryland cigar, and now look at you!

Drawing on the very last of it, with fingers so hardened now no pin was required, he reluctantly dropped the remnant on the ground, and as he did so, he saw a familiar face among the workmen gathered on the wharf.

'Hey, Flo!' he called, walking over to the group. 'How are you going? I heard you took a bashing.'

'Yes, that bastard Harris got me from behind, nearly broke my skull. But the head's harder than I thought and it recovered quick enough to get me this bastard of a job.'

'What's happening here?'

'New wharves. We're in that bloody freezing water half the day, lowering and settling bloody great logs into the mud. It's a job for bloody elephants it is.'

'How did you cop that with the head injury on your report? You shouldn't be on hard labour.'

'Ah, what chance have you got with that Harris? He got sent to Port Arthur for assault, but he reckoned I provoked him. Provoked the bastard? Kicked his arse for stealing my good boots. That's provoking? If it hadn't been for Doc Roberts I'd have ended up at that bloody madhouse myself.'

'I know him. I'll find him and see if I can get you pulled out of here.'

Flo shivered in his thin damp clothes, rubbing his arms. 'It's bloody colder out than in now.'

Struck with pity for his friend, Sean peeled off his patched flannel jacket and thrust it at him. 'Take this, it's worn thin but it'll keep the wind off.'

'No, no, I couldn't take your coat.'

'Yes you can. Go! The guards are glarin'.'

As he retreated from the muster of workers along the waterfront, Sean realised that he'd left the cheroots in his pocket.

'Bloody hell!' he muttered, returning to the

carriage for shelter from the wind. 'I didn't mean to be that kind.'

Keeping an eye out for the Governor's yacht, he stood watching passers-by, giving an occasional nod to people he knew and a shake of the head to whores with their questioning stares, but all the time he was thinking of Harris, the beefy farm boy. He wasn't really a farm boy, that was just his nickname. Harris had been a real farmer, and one not short of the readies either, since he was schooled and his English accent was a few notes up on the average.

Harris? His thoughts turned to Louise Harris and her mother. Their Mr Harris was a farmer too, due to follow them out to Van Diemen's Land, but so far there'd been no sign of him. They'd been living in Sassafras Road for years now. Could Lester be their farmer? Surely those two lovely women didn't belong to him? They didn't deserve him. Hell, no! He would have added a couple more years on to his sentence now, with banishment to Port Arthur, so they wouldn't see or hear from him for a while.

Come to think of it, he mused, there was never a word said of Mrs Harris being involved with any gentlemen, and as they all knew, she was more of a friend to Mr Warboy than anyone else.

He sighed, looked about, saw the yacht coming into the harbour, and hoped Mr Warboy wouldn't mind his driver turning up in shirtsleeves.

Barnaby, however, had more pressing irritations to contend with. He had really enjoyed the calmer final leg of the cruise, with Storm Bay left behind them, but his mood was spoiled by the thought of returning home. Of being sucked into *their* sordid affairs. He wished he could provide himself with an excuse to stay out a while longer.

All the passengers were on deck as they headed for the docks, the ladies ecstatic over the western skies, streaked with gold as the sun retreated, and Sir John anxiously watching the yacht's manoeuvring.

Barnaby could see his carriage, ready and waiting, and remembered he still hadn't spoken to Shanahan about his surprise, but he didn't feel up to it this evening.

He saw the Governor's coach drawing up, much larger and fancier than his own little vehicle, but not as elegant, and several grooms were leading horses from the rear of a warehouse for the other passengers.

'Are you riding?' he asked Dr Roberts.

'No, I walked down. I only live at Battery Point.'

'My dear fellow, I have my carriage. Let me take you home.'

'Thank you, Mr Warboy. That's kind of you, but the walk will do me well.'

Barnaby was disappointed. He had a sudden notion that perhaps he could dine with the young doctor, who appeared to be a single fellow and living alone, as he'd gleaned from the day's conversations.

In the end there was nothing for it. He thanked his hosts, with a mental note to write the bread-and-butter letter on the morrow, made his bows, shook hands, said his goodbyes and plunged, yes plunged, he felt, back into his own unlovely world.

'A good day then, was it, sir?' Shanahan asked in greeting.

'Yes. Interesting. Very interesting.'

'What is it really like, that place? The prison, sir. They say it's the darkest, most fearsome prison on God's earth.'

Barnaby shook his head. 'Strangely, it isn't. It looks like a model village, not in size but in layout. I have an illustrated map here somewhere, given to us by the Commandant as a souvenir of our visit. Of course the penitentiary itself is rather forbidding, not unlike the one in our town, only bigger. Much bigger...'

He was rattling on as Sean handed him into the carriage. The Irishman could see what had to be the map, a roll of parchment, sticking out of Mr Warboy's coat pocket, and was tempted to grab it then and there, but thought better of it and closed the carriage door. Another time. He'd have Dossie watch out for it.

A plan of the layout of that peninsula! Solid gold it was! Sean had no intention of letting it out of his sight.

Suddenly Mr Warboy stuck his head out of the window. 'Hang on a minute. What's going on down there? What are all those lights for?'

Sean looked back at the row of lanterns strung across the street. 'It's minstrels, sir. They play there of a Friday evening.'

'I like minstrels, they're so gay, and some of them can be quite good musicians. You can stop down there so that I can have a listen.'

Sean sighed. He was hungry, he'd miss dinner. 'I think the concert may be all but finished, sir.'

'Never mind. Hop up there and giddyup before it's too late.'

Sean turned the carriage on to the street and headed towards the crowd gathered to watch the show, but was unable to get too close.

'Will this do, sir?' he called down. 'You can hear them from here.'

'It won't do at all. You stay here, Shanahan, I'll take myself to have a look at them.'

Mr Warboy opened the carriage door, and in his enthusiasm was clambering out almost before Sean had time to assist him, but as he straightened and smoothed the old boy's coat, he saw the precious roll of parchment fall to the ground. The boss was on his way, though, bounding across to the outskirts of the crowd, finding his way through and disappearing into the multitude as tambourines jangled, songsters sang 'The Merry Merry Month of May', and Shanahan collected the souvenir map.

Dossie's heart leapt in fear as she opened the door to two policemen.

'Yes?' she asked, forgetting her training. 'What's wrong?'

'Mr Warboy,' the old one snapped – a hard-eyed copper with slapped-down hair, a clipped moustache and a parade-ground voice. The young one hung back, standing straight, his mouth tight like his pants, pinched, she thought, as she backed away and dashed over to the parlour.

'Policemen to see you, sir,' she bobbed.

'Send them in.'

The Chief Constable chose a hard chair after he was introduced to Mrs Warboy, and instructed Constable Gander to stand by the window with his pencil and notebook.

'Now,' he said. 'We'll go over the matter again, Mr Warboy. Your daughter, Miss Penelope Warboy, claims she was raped. Is that correct?'

'Certainly not!' Mrs Warboy screeched. 'She *was* raped.'

'That is true,' her husband said mournfully. 'Dr Jellick can attest to that. My wife took her to the doctor for an examination and he confirmed it.'

'Could I have a word with her, please?'

'Certainly not!' Mrs Warboy again. 'She's only seventeen. She'd be shocked having to say what happened to her in front of strange men. I forbid it. I absolutely forbid it!'

Chief Constable Hippisley nodded, and proceeded to lecture them on the necessity of an interview at some time so that the nature of the crime could be fully understood, but both parents raised so many objections, he decided to move on.

'You say you know who the rogue is?' he asked.

'We do.'

'Then I want to see him, if you could excuse us, Mrs Warboy.'

'Unfortunately that is not possible at this minute, but he'll be here soon,' she said.

'I thought he was a convict. He should not be at large after dark, and it's dark now.'

'Oh yes, I know.'

Warboy nodded his agreement. 'Ah yes, but he is my father's driver, you see. Mr Barnaby Warboy has been out visiting, and the driver has gone to collect him in our carriage. You may have noticed it in the town.'

'What's his name? The suspect rapist.'

'I'm loath to point the finger of blame as yet, even to a vile fellow like this...'

'Vile,' his wife echoed, dabbing a tear from her pale cheek.

'What we intend to do is to line up all the convicts and denounce him.'

'Seems a roundabout way of doing things! And may I remind you I have come here to investigate a crime. If there's any denouncing to be done, I will be doing it. Now, the fellow's name?'

'Shanahan.'

'Sean Shanahan? An Irishman?'

'Yes. It's Shanahan all right. I see you're aware of his activities already,' Warboy said with a nasty smirk.

'I'm aware of his letter-writing,' Hippisley growled. He didn't like this fellow or his wife, and didn't feel he was making much headway with them. To give them their due, though, as the parents of a young girl who had suffered rape, it was understandable that they'd be confused and upset, as well as being protective of their daughter. It would probably be better if he discussed this with the grandfather. Warboy Senior was well known in the town as a steady sort of old chap. And as for Shanahan, he was well known too. But a rapist? Hard to judge in this land where so many men were denied the company of women.

'I think it would be best if I come back tomorrow,' he said. 'I can talk to the convicts and to your father, sir. And perhaps, Mrs Warboy, you could prepare your daughter for a quiet little chat with you and me. Just the three of us. Constable Gander need not be present.'

'I think not,' she said firmly.

'My father should be home any minute,' Warboy said. 'Surely you could wait just a little longer. This is such an ordeal for us, Chief Constable. You can't imagine what we're going through. I never dreamt we'd be coming to an island with thousands of convicts running wild. I thought they'd be locked up.'

Hippisley shrugged. He was fed up with that argument. 'We can't lock them up, there are too many,' he said crankily. 'And the Government back home keeps sending more. And did you know that hundreds are being released every day, having served their sentences? They're free men once more, they're no longer the responsibility of the Government, so they're no longer entitled to rations or clothing!'

As he raised his voice, he saw that damn constable over there lift his eyebrows just a tinge, and knew he was beating his favourite drum again, but it wouldn't hurt this pompous moneyed pair to know the truth about this island.

'Is that so?' Warboy asked, his voice patronisingly meaningful.

'It is so, sir, hundreds every day! Hundreds of men and women who have nowhere to go! No measures are in place to return them to the old country. So we're stuck with them. There aren't enough jobs to go round, so what is to become of them?'

'I'm sure I don't know,' Warboy said. 'I do not.'

'They become paupers, sir! Paupers! Did you know we have a third class here now? A growing, multiplying class of paupers. And who has to support them? We do! Not the Government back home! They've wiped their hands of them. Our taxes have to support them! It's unfair!'

'There's a carriage coming up the drive,' Constable Gander said quietly.

As soon as she had ushered the coppers into the parlour, Dossie dashed through the house to the kitchen and out the back door, racing down towards the men's quarters.

'Coppers in the house,' she cried when she saw Billo. 'Go and tell Singer.' Then she turned on her heel and hurried back to her post.

'Coppers? What are they doing here?' Singer asked.

'Might be just a spot check on us,' Angus said. 'They do that sometimes.'

'On a Friday night? Not likely. But we'd better clean up just in case. Starting with Billo. What have you been drinking?'

'Nothin'. Only had some of Hunter's ginger wine,' Billo slurred. 'Only a sip or so.'

'Angus, shove his head in a bucket of water. He's as wobbly as a duck in a ploughed field. And see there's nothin' lying about in the sheds that shouldn't ought to be. And you. Hunter, shove your wine-making whatsits in the scrub.'

Singer strode into the cookhouse and stoked up

the fire in the stove, put the kettle on, to make the room smell normal, took his money purse and stash of tobacco and hid them under the floorboards, then went outside and looked up to the lights in the homestead.

Where was Shanahan? He'd gone off to collect the boss. He should be back by now. Had he got himself into some trouble? Not bloody hard, he mused. Coppers would pin anything on you if you happened to be the closest. And didn't Shanahan ride close to the wind all the time, with his obsession with freeing Frank Macnamara? But Frank was out, bless his heroic old heart, so that was over and done with.

Nevertheless, he did worry about Shanahan, who'd be sure to find some other plan to bend the rules.

What else could coppers be after at this hour?

As the carriage crunched up the drive, Barnaby saw the horses hitched to the rail by the garden gate, and banged on the window for the driver's attention.

'Whose horses are they?' he called.

'Police,' Shanahan said, reining to a halt at the front door.

'How do you know?' Barnaby asked as his driver jumped down.

'Police saddles and blankets. No mistaking them.'

At that, the front door opened and Dossie came bustling out. 'You've got visitors, sir. Policemen.'

Barnaby was annoyed. He caught his coat in the door handle as he climbed out of the carriage, and fussed crossly while both Dossie and Shanahan untangled him and delivered him to his door.

'What are they doing here?' he demanded.

'I don't know, sir.'

'Then get in there and find out. I'm hungry, I'm going straight through to the dining room. Have the other lot dined?'

'Yes, sir.'

'Good. I'll have some soup.'

But Jubal was in the hall to waylay him. 'We have been waiting for you, Father.'

'Who's we?'

'Chief Constable Hippisley and Constable Gander are in the parlour.'

'What do they want?' Barnaby handed his coat and hat to Dossie. 'Tell them to come back tomorrow. I'm very tired. I've had a long day.' He smiled mischievously. 'Been sailing, you know. On the Governor's yacht. Splendid day!'

Jubal waved Dossie away and turned back to his father. 'We have a serious matter to discuss.'

'Like what? I do not like people coming to my house unannounced.'

The Chief Constable was standing in the doorway. 'Mr Warboy. I am not here unannounced. I am here to investigate the claim of rape.'

Barnaby jolted to a halt, almost in mid-step since he'd been on his way to the dining room. 'What rape?' he demanded indignantly.

He could see his daughter-in-law sitting on the couch in the parlour. 'Do you not see there are ladies present?'

'Mrs Warboy has been assisting, sir.'

327

'What rot has she been going on about? Or him?' He glared at his son.

'Mr Warboy, may I introduce myself. I am Chief Constable Hippisley, I am here to investigate a serious charge of rape against one of your workers. I would prefer it if we could speak privately.'

'Hmm. I see. How do you do?' Barnaby reached out and the two men shook hands. 'Good idea,' he added. 'Come with me.'

He took Hippisley back into the parlour, nodded to the other policeman, and told Millicent she could run along.

'But the Chief Constable needs my advice.'

'Not now.' Barnaby helped her up from the couch, led her to the hall, refused entry to his son and shut the door in their faces.

'So,' he said. 'What's this all about?'

As Hippisley explained, Barnaby listened quietly. He made no attempt to interrupt, waiting patiently until the policeman turned to him with the question: 'Do you have any comments to make, Mr Warboy?'

'Yes. You didn't mention that the girl is pregnant.'

'Good Lord. I wasn't told that. It is very sad for her.'

'She's pregnant all right, but this is the first I've heard of rape. You obviously didn't meet her.'

'No, her parents felt it would be too upsetting for her.'

Barnaby nodded. 'I suppose it would be. She's a bit of a dunce. But how do we know it was rape? She could have a boyfriend for all we know. And how did Shanahan get a part in this? Has she pointed him out?'

'Apparently not. Mr Warboy had in mind lining up your workmen and demanding the rapist step forward. Though I'd hardly put the question in those terms.'

'Why can't we just ask her point blank who her lover is? And if she was raped, if she even knows what that means? And when did this happen? Did someone sneak into her room in the dead of night to attack her? In which case she probably wouldn't know who the hell it was. Or did she dally in the orchard here, or in the lovers' lane by the church. Unless we ask her, I can't see the point in this investigation.'

'Unfortunately, her parents won't permit me to question her.'

'Then I shall. Leave it to me.'

'Very good, sir. I think that should do it for now,' the Chief Constable said, and Barnaby agreed.

'I hope to God she hasn't been raped,' he said. 'I didn't get that impression from her parents yesterday when I heard she was in the family way. They were more angry with her for getting herself pregnant. Now they seem to have changed their tune.'

'Perhaps they didn't realise...'

'Or maybe it's a better story,' Barnaby growled.

He escorted the two men to the front door himself, apologising that the outer lamps had not been lit, and walked across with them to where the horses were waiting, still mulling over this wretched problem. Suddenly he saw Penn, huddled on a bench by the garden gate.

'Why, Penn!' he said, surprised. 'What are you doing out here?'

'They're angry with me,' she whispered. 'I'm hiding. It's nice here with the moon coming up. It's very big.'

Barnaby signalled to the Chief Constable to wait a little, while he sat beside her.

'I'm getting a baby,' she told him cheerfully, and he almost fell off the seat.

'Is that so?' he said, sounding as pleased as he could. 'Who told you that?'

'The nice doctor.'

'I see,' he said carefully, realising now how feeble-minded this girl really was. 'And do you have a boyfriend?'

'Yes. A very nice boyfriend.'

'I see. Let me guess. I bet he's a member of St Michael's congregation.'

She giggled. 'No, he's not.'

'Then does he live here?'

'You're getting warm.'

Barnaby was feeling very short of breath. He looked over at Hippisley, who seemed uncertain as to whether he should stay or leave. Then he looked down at his granddaughter again, and was overcome with sorrow for her, but he couldn't bring himself to ask if it was Shanahan in case she responded in the affirmative simply to please him.

'I give in,' he sighed. 'You win. Who is it?'

Penn laughed. 'I knew you wouldn't guess. It's Angus. The Scotsman. He's my friend. We're getting married.'

'Angus, my gardener?' Barnaby gulped. 'Well, for heaven's sake. I would never have guessed.

Where do you meet him?'

'In the greenhouse.' She smiled lovingly. 'He's always so nice to me.'

Barnaby sighed, sat with her for a few more minutes, then quietly walked over to Hippisley. 'Would you have your constable go quickly round the back of the house and get my maid Dossie. She'll be in the kitchen. Tell her not to come through the house.'

While they waited, he stood conversing with the Chief Constable near the horses, in view of his front door, and sure enough he saw Jubal peer out at them and then withdraw, probably wondering what was going on.

'I think we've found the father of the child,' he said heavily.

'She told you?'

'Was it rape?'

'You tell me, Hippisley, I'm damned if I know.' He glanced at Penn, who was still sitting in the shadows admiring the moonlight. 'The father is one of my gardeners. A Scot, Angus McLeod. The bastard! He ought to be horse-whipped! Penn's a simple-minded, innocent girl. For some great oaf of a labourer to take advantage of her sickens me. I want him out of here tonight.'

'Don't worry, he's headed for jail for breaking assignee regulations. He had no right to go near her. Do you think I could have a word with her now?'

'Yes, but don't frighten her.'

They walked over to Penn, and Barnaby introduced the Chief Constable. 'This is Mr Hippisley, Penn. A friend of mine. He's also a policeman.'

331

Hippisley took in this fair-haired waif of a girl wrapped in a black shawl and gave a polite bow. 'How do you do, Miss Warboy.'

'Are they your horses, Mr Hippisley?' she said. 'I wondered whose they were.'

'Yes, they are. Do you like horses?'

'Very much. I would like a pony but Mama says no.'

'What did you say your boyfriend's name is?' Barnaby asked. 'You can tell my friend.'

'Angus,' she whispered. 'But don't tell Mother. She'll get angry again.'

Barnaby saw Dossie coming. 'It's getting colder out here now,' he said. 'And here's Dossie. She'll take you round to the kitchen and make you a big cup of hot chocolate. Would you like that?'

'Yes.'

He gave the nod to Dossie, who looked more than a little bemused at this arrangement, but she took Penn by the hand and led her away.

'So?' Barnaby turned to Hippisley. 'What now?'

'You'll have to tell the parents who the father is.'

'Ah, no! *We* will have to tell them. I want you here to keep them calm. They'll probably raise the roof.'

'I wouldn't blame them,' Hippisley said. 'The poor child.'

Barnaby could hardly control his rage. He was overwhelmed with guilt that this girl had been violated under his roof, and blamed himself for too much leniency with the men, for forgetting that they were all criminals.

'By God,' he said furiously, as they tramped

back to the house, 'I'll lock the lot of them up now, there'll be no more free and easy on Warboy Farm. Do you know, Hippisley, my son has always claimed that I've been too soft on my workers! And he was right. By God he was.'

Hippisley shrugged. He just wanted to get this over with. If Warboy hadn't mentioned that his father was a friend of Governor Franklin, he wouldn't have bothered coming out. And now, the Chief Constable thought peevishly, I see Warboy Senior could have sorted it out himself and simply called the nearest police.

As he expected, Mrs Warboy went into shrieks of rage at the news, demanding the rapist be hanged, but surprisingly, her husband burst into tears.

'I couldn't bring myself to believe my daughter really was pregnant,' he wept. 'It seemed too out-rageous! Too shocking that my own daughter had been defiled! But now that you gentlemen confirm this has happened... Oh God, preserve us from evil!'

Hippisley turned to Warboy Senior. 'Would you accompany us to the men's quarters, sir. We'll arrest the fellow and take him back with us.'

'Yes, I think that's best. Get him out of the place.'

'I'll come with you,' Jubal Warboy cried angrily.

'No you won't,' his father said. 'This is my property. You stay here with your wife.'

'Then you make sure the charge is rape. I want Angus McLeod charged with rape and seduc-tion, do you hear me? Rape!'

Once outside, Hippisley instructed the constable to bring his handcuffs and pistol.

'We'll be making an arrest,' he said.

'The charge?' Warboy asked him, as he un-hooked a glowing lantern by the front door.

'Rape.' Hippisley decided he might as well, since the family would go on insisting, and as they'd said, the doctor would back them up.

Warboy nodded, leading the policemen along a paved path past the kitchen. A man was coming towards them. 'Mr Warboy,' he called. 'Is anything wrong?'

Once he'd handed Mr Warboy down from the carriage, Sean had taken the time to peer in the window of the parlour. The sight of uniformed police told him this was not a private visit, this was trouble, so he drove the carriage down the track to the stables, released the horses as quickly as he could and let them loose in the paddock before rushing up to see if Dossie could throw any light on the mystery. Forewarned is fore-armed, he told himself.

The kitchen was still lit, but there was no sign of her, nor was she in her bedroom, situated beside the laundry. Obviously she must be in the house somewhere.

Maybe there's been a robbery, he thought. Or maybe that bloody Jubal is still after Billo over the horse that Freddy pinched. The bastard! That could be it. He turned on his heel and raced down to the men's quarters to alert them, but they already knew and were sitting nervously in the bunkhouse.

'What's it about?' Hunter asked.

334

'I don't know. It's no social call. A robbery maybe. You lot got any ideas? If you have, spill it now, while we've got time to think what to do.'

Singer looked up. 'Dossie says they beat the girl yesterday and you stuck your bib in. She said you wrestled the strap off Jubal. Mad, are you? There's no saying what sonny boy will do now.'

'Mr Warboy was there. I'm pretty safe.'

'You hope!'

'Who beat the girl?' Angus cried. 'They whipped Penn? Who would do that to a harmless little girl?'

Billo laughed. 'There he goes, she's his little angel, isn't she, Angus? He's sweet on the Creeping Jesus.'

'Don't call her that!' Angus said, but Sean wasn't interested in the conversation. He decided to go back up and try again to get some information from Dossie.

She was in the kitchen, but this time with Miss Warboy, and seeing Sean, she shook her head and put her finger to her lips, sending him away.

There was nothing for it then but to wait, to keep an eye out.

Eventually he saw them coming down the path.

'Mr Warboy,' he called. 'Is anything wrong?'

One of the coppers replied for him. 'What is this man doing outside after curfew?'

'It's all right,' Mr Warboy said. 'This is Shanahan, my manager.'

'Assigned, isn't he?'

'Yes.'

'Then he should be indoors.'

Mr Warboy gave a snort of irritation, and Sean

335

recognised Chief Constable Hippisley, who wasn't a bad bloke as coppers went, though being a bit officious now.

'Right then, I'll go back.'

'No you won't, Shanahan,' Hippisley said. 'Walk with Constable Gander.'

'Certainly, sir.' As they walked on, he fell in beside the constable, whispering, 'G'day, Goosey. What's up?'

Goosey shook his head as nervously as Dossie had done, and Sean felt a stab of fear deep in his stomach. Something serious was up, no doubt about it. Mr Warboy, leading the way, was silent, puffing a little; Hippisley's hob-nailed boots clipped confidently on the flagstones, providing enough sound to wake the dead on this still night. Sean knew the men would be holding their breath too.

When they arrived at the bunkhouse, Hippisley asked Mr Warboy how many men were billeted inside.

'Twelve,' he said nervously. 'I mean eleven with Shanahan out here, of this minute.'

Hippisley then turned to Sean. 'Go to the door. Tell everyone to stay where they are.'

'Why would they not?' he asked angrily.

'Do as you're told.'

Sean strode over to the door and pushed it open. 'Chief Constable Hippisley is here with Constable Gander, lads. He says you're to stay where you are.'

He turned back with a shrug to the chorus of questions, his duty done.

Then Hippisley motioned to Gander to take up

his post outside the door before calling to Angus McLeod to step outside.

'Angus? Why Angus, for God's sake?' Sean asked, though no one answered him. He wouldn't have been surprised if Singer had been up to trouble, or Billo was being hauled out over the horse, but Angus? He was too much the dour Scot to have been involved in any mischief. Unless he'd been on his hobbyhorse again, about the rights of workers, but that had toned down some since he'd been at Warboy Farm.

The tall Scot had to duck his head as he stepped out the door.

'What do ye want of me?' he demanded.

Hippisley strode over to him. 'Are you Angus McLeod?'

'I am.'

'Angus McLeod, you are under arrest for the crime of having intercourse with a woman against her will. I am taking you to the Hobart magistrates' court where you will be charged with rape.'

There was a loud gasp from the workmen craning at the door of the hut, and Sean was speechless.

Angus, at least, had his wits about him. 'You've made a mistake, mon,' he said quietly. 'I never would do such a thing. What is this about?'

Gander reached out to handcuff him from behind, but Angus shoved him away and roared at Hippisley: 'I have just said I'm not a mon for that sort of thing! You've no right to arrest me without giving me proper reason. What woman? When was this supposed to be?'

Without bothering to reply, Hippisley took the handcuffs and expertly slammed them on Angus's wrists, but the Scot wasn't going quietly. He kept on shouting to his comrades to witness this injustice, even when Gander's pistol was pointed at him: 'Tell them what I'm supposed to have done! Tell us who is this woman? Who damns me with these lies? Mr Warboy, listen to me! I'm not a mon for that business. Sean, you tell them, I'd never hurt a woman. Never! Let go of me, you bloody fools!'

Sean strode over to Hippisley. 'He's a good man, sir. You've got it all wrong.'

But the two policemen were holding Angus strongly by this and were trying to frog-march him up the hill. Angus fought them every step of the way, digging his heels in, still shouting his innocence.

In protest, the workmen banged on the bunkhouse wall and Sean could see Mr Warboy was looking confused.

'Can't you stop them?' Sean yelled at him. 'It's a false charge. Who is it says Angus raped her?'

He was shocked when Mr Warboy turned on him, his face blotched with rage. 'He's scum! He raped my granddaughter, that poor little girl. And you people haven't heard the last of this.'

'Is that the poor little girl whose parents were whipping her? Who had to run and hide in your parlour? Did Hippisley see her bruises? Because believe me, I'll make sure he hears about it.'

Warboy stood his ground. 'You mind your own business, Shanahan! And close down. It's past curfew.'

There was talk aplenty in the bunkhouse that night. Talk that Angus idolised the brat. And maybe he did get to have his way with her. Or maybe she volunteered, she was always visiting him in the greenhouse, where nobody really knew what was going on. Argument broke out. Billo, on Angus's side, threatened to punch Hunter, but Sean made no attempt to restore order. They could fight all night if they liked, for all he cared. He slipped out the door and headed into the shadows to make his way up to the house.

Hippisley clouted McLeod with his baton as they dragged him across the front of the house, towards the horses.

'You're only making it worse for yourself,' he said. 'Resisting arrest will earn you more lashes.'

'Why should I care?' McLeod yelled. 'Who is this woman? Let me face her!'

He saw Mrs Warboy standing in the light of the open front door, and appealed to her. 'Lady! Stop them! There are liars here. Liars!'

But Mrs Warboy ran across the drive and spat on him. 'You animal,' she screamed. 'You violated my daughter, made her pregnant, and you dare to even look at me!'

McLeod reeled back. 'No! What is this? I wouldna touch the wee lassie. I wouldna. Ask her, she'll tell you.'

'She already did,' Hippisley growled, dragging him on, as Warboy Senior hustled his daughter-in-law away. 'Now you listen to me, McLeod. We're taking you into town, and you'll go if we have to drag you all the way. Mr Warboy is willing to lend me a horse for you. We can rope you on to its back if you behave yourself.'

'I'll no' ride,' the prisoner shouted, his Scottish accent becoming so thick in his rage that the Chief Constable couldn't understand the rest of his tirade, but he got the message. McLeod would have to be dragged all the way. It would take hours.

Gander threatened the prisoner at gunpoint, to no avail, while Mrs Warboy on the sidelines shouted for them to shoot the animal 'and be done with it!'

It occurred to Hippisley to suggest they chain McLeod to a tree until they could send a wagon for him, but from past experience he knew that would be too tempting for the Scotsman's colleagues. Bonds were strong among these exiles. He'd be set free by anonymous hands before sun-up, and heading for the bush.

Decision made, he took his leave of the Warboys without further ado, and they rode into the darkness with McLeod roped to Gander's horse, still shouting blue bloody murder.

There was a sawmill on the road back to town, only about a half-mile from the Warboy Farm, and as soon as they reached it, Hippisley called a halt.

'I'm not spending all night dragging you around, McLeod,' he said, turning in to the cluttered grounds of the deserted mill. 'We'll leave him here, Gander. He can yell his head off, no one will hear him in among these timber stacks. Handcuff him to a pole, a good sturdy one.'

That done, they mounted up. 'We'll ride

340

straight in now, no more wasting time,' he said to Gander as they set out. 'As soon as we get there, you find a police wagon, rouse a couple of lads and come back and collect the prisoner. I'll have laid the charges; take him straight to the lockup.'

He could see Gander wasn't impressed by the probability of losing a whole night's sleep, but that's life, he told himself smugly. And command does have its rewards, he grinned, McLeod already far back in his thoughts, as he put his splendid new mount to the gallop along the lonely road.

'What happened? What's it all about?' Sean whispered to Dossie through the open window.

'I only found out when they gave me the girl to mind, when them coppers were out there. She's pregnant and she's blaming Angus!'

'What?'

'Yes, and the rum thing about it is she's pleased as punch. She thinks it's a great thing to have a baby. Silly as a wheel, I tell you.'

'And she reckons Angus is the father?'

'So she says.'

'Angus won't have it! I heard him shouting he wouldn't touch the wee lassie.'

'Well...' Dossie frowned. 'Looks as if he did.'

'I don't know about that. He thought she was an angel... No, he wouldn't have dreamt of touching her, he's too shy of her. Had her on a pedestal. And Angus is a rare one, remember? He'd tell the truth if it killed him. You know what he's like.'

When Sean returned to the bunkhouse, he found Singer sitting outside, eager for news.

'They took him away yelling like a banshee,' Sean said. 'But worse, Dossie says the Warboy girl is pregnant and it's her what's saying that Angus is the father.'

'That'll please some of the lads; they took bets that Angus has been potting her. Me, I lost tuppence, but then I always seem to be on the losing side. What do you think?'

'I think she's lying, the little bitch. Probably been making hay with the heathens at the church they all attend.'

'It's Anglican. I know a song about them. It's called "The Merry Merry Monks of May". Do you want to hear it?'

'I do not.'

Sean sat on his bunk, too worried to even consider sleep. Angus didn't have a hope in hell if that stupid girl kept on claiming he was the father. Why would she do that? he wondered. And the answer came to him that the parish lad who'd knocked her up must have refused to admit it, so they'd had to find a scapegoat. The whole bloody Warboy family! They'd picked on a convict so they could cry rape to cover up for the girl's promiscuity. And they'd picked on a convict so that he could be made to disappear, and no one would hear a word to the contrary.

Poor bloody Angus! What could be done to help him? Sean was at a total loss.

Barnaby had told Dossie to bring his supper up to his private sitting room, and he'd so enjoyed his meal in the peaceful surrounds that he'd made a decision, there and then, to take all of his meals upstairs from now on. The sitting room was large enough to fit an extra table, which he would place over by the eastern window to meet the morning sun.

It will be very pleasant, he told himself, trying to erase the hideous events of previous hours, which, as he'd told Jubal, had knocked the stuffing out of him.

He'd also insisted to the pair of them that he never wanted the subject mentioned in his house again. He was quite adamant about it.

'And another thing,' he muttered, as he pulled on his nightshirt. 'They can keep out of my parlour too. It'll be out of bounds to them from now on. I need a place of my own downstairs as well.' In the morning, he awoke thoroughly depressed.

Dossie brought his morning tea and a jug of hot water for his basin, and seemed to be walking about on tiptoe, her silence as loud as a drum.

'I'll have my breakfast up here,' he said. 'And all meals from now on. It's more peaceful.'

She nodded. 'I'll bring it up,' and slid out of the room so quickly he didn't even see her leave.

Breakfast came and went. He even had all the newspapers to himself, set neatly on the sideboard. He didn't have to share them any more!

When he finally had to go downstairs, he shuddered at the problems ahead. He had to find a new gardener. Write a new set of rules for his convicts and see that they were strictly adhered to. Curfew would be seven p.m. from now on. No convict would be permitted to address the Warboy family members, or visitors.

So much to do, he sighed, feeling sorry for himself. And no one to help me. Another sigh was more of a sob.

He turned down the passage and let himself out of the side door, breathing in the good crisp air. Barnaby was a great believer in deep breathing exercises in the morning, when he remembered. He filled his chest and released the air slowly, and as he did so, he looked out over the garden. The last deep breath almost ended in a choke.

His garden! He recalled the noisy protests of the men as McLeod was taken away. Heard Shanahan shout at him again.

Barnaby hurried past the hedge that screened the utility shed by the side door, and ran on past the greenhouse to check his garden, now so vulnerable to attack by those angry men, who could have vandalised it overnight. He began to slow as he checked the tall lupins, and the late-flowering hellebores. Further along, rows of catmint with their blue flowers and grey foliage made way for rose bushes already showing the buds of the full-cupped apricot roses that his gardeners had promised.

Relieved, chastising himself for being so jumpy – so foolish – Barnaby wandered quietly through the various sections of the gardens, that were now linked by ground cover and artful low hedges. Still a little apprehensive, he kept an eye out for anything amiss, until he came across Forbes, who was adding manure to a new flowerbed near the pavilion. The fellow, usually a cheerful soul, turned his back, and Barnaby felt the chill, though he walked on as if he hadn't noticed.

And that reminded him, he had a busy day

ahead. And he would need a new gardener.

As he headed for his study, he called out to Dossie to fetch Shanahan.

After an unpleasant run-in with the boss, Sean strode through the garden to find Singer.

'You're on your own here now without Angus. What do we do about that?' he asked.

'Who cares? It crossed my mind last night to run a plough through his bloody garden! But then I thought 'twould hurt Angus more. He loves the place! I don't think he ever saw a blade of grass before he came here, or could call a rose a rose.'

'Warboy wants me to replace him.'

'Before he's even fronted a magistrate?'

'I told him it's not usual to call a man guilty until he's proved so in the courts. He didn't like that, said he wouldn't have McLeod back anyway, and to find someone else. Then he starts reading me the riot act. I'm not permitted into town again alone. So I said, "How do I find you a new gardener then?" And how about this? In future he will accompany me. Or his son.'

Singer laughed. 'There's a chance. Take sonny boy into the bush and lose him. I'd gladly do that for you.'

'He still wants me to replace Angus.'

'Don't do it.'

'Then he'll find someone himself. I was thinking of Flo Quinlan.'

'Flo? Another of your mob? I don't trust him. He's got a dark side, that one.'

'Who hasn't?' Sean snapped. 'He got bashed by Harris.'

345

'He probably asked for it. I tell you, there's more to Quinlan than meets the eye.'

'Ah well, I'll see what happens. I've been sent to clean out the west paddock for ploughing. My punishment. Do you want to give me a hand?'

'No fear.' Forbes started singing loudly, too loudly, as he turned back to work, flinging manure about with a pitchfork: 'The merry merry monks of May, they danced and sang all day...'

Sean shook his head. Another time he'd have told him to tone it down. Now ... he didn't care either. He began to reconsider Flood's offer. The job would have its hazards; he'd have to make it plain from the start that he could take care of himself. He wouldn't cop any rough stuff from Flood or his thugs. That would have to be made clear. And he'd want pay. Assignees were not entitled to wages, but Sean had established a good reputation as a farm overseer; maybe he could find a bidder if Flood rejected the idea. He'd have to think about it. But more importantly, he needed to find out what was happening to Angus.

How, though? He was confined to the farm and couldn't get into town; who could he ask to help him?

It wasn't until late that night that he had his answer. Louise!

CHAPTER ELEVEN

Josie Harris shut the gate of the stables and tramped across the muddy yard to the back veranda of her house. Wearily she dropped down to the steps, dragged off her boots and limped into the kitchen.

'What's the matter?' Louise asked her.

'I hurt my foot. The new cow stood on it. I thought she'd broken a bone but it seems not.'

'Let me see.'

'No, leave it. I'll tend to it later. I'll just sit awhile.'

'I've strained some broth. You must have some. It will make you feel better.'

It upset Louise to see her mother looking so tired. She ladled out some broth and placed it on the table, then sat down facing her.

'When will I get to hear about your meeting with the solicitor, Mr Baggott?'

Her mother reached for the broth, and took a sip. 'It needs more salt.'

Louise pushed the cruet towards her. 'Well?'

'There's not much to tell, Louise. I wish you'd stop nagging me.'

'You were too tired when you came home last night. You were too busy today. You have to tell me now. Was he young, old, kind, unkind? And what had he found out?'

Josie sighed. 'He's an elderly man. Very nice. He

said it's a fact your father has gone to Port Arthur prison.'

'Oh no, poor Daddy. Why?'

'A fight, something like that. He got mixed up in a fight apparently.'

'Did you give him my letter to hand in?'

'No.'

'Mother, you didn't forget!'

Josie drank the rest of the broth. 'Prisoners there are not permitted to send or receive mail,' she said heavily. 'They have to get permission from the person in charge.'

'What? That's barbaric! Can we visit him then?'

'No. I'm sorry, darling, I was utterly stunned. I had no idea, but there it is. It's the law and there's nothing we can do about it.'

Louise burst into tears, and Josie was too depressed to even offer her comfort. She just sat at the bare table, drained of emotion. It had all become too much for her. What had sounded like a good idea seven years ago had become a folly. Lester had convinced her that this would work, and she'd been too lovesick to doubt him. Too moonstruck by the romance of following her beloved husband across the oceans and making a nest for him to return to when his travail ended.

Now it wouldn't end for another eight years. She was glad Louise hadn't asked about the sentence. It hadn't occurred to her, so far, that her father's sentence would be extended after another brush with the authorities. They had learned to live with the unfairness of Lester's original sentence – although Josie still vowed she'd never forgive her magistrate cousin for it –

and to stop brooding over it, but she didn't know how her daughter would take this news. Louise, young enough to have the same romantic notions that had beset her mother, took pride in her loyalty to her handsome father. She'd had a sketch of him framed and hung in her bedroom.

Josie didn't have the courage to admit that her own loyalty had worn down over the years, allowing the stirrings of common sense to take root. Louise had no social life to speak of, and for that Josie blamed herself. She'd been so insistent on the façade of the ailing husband/father back home that they were now stuck with the lie. Which, by the way, she knew well enough was wearing thin.

But there it was. Any suitor would have to be told the truth about Lester. And Mrs and Miss Harris's little wall of respectability would come tumbling down.

'I'm sorry,' she said to Louise. 'It's been hard on all of us. I've been thinking of selling the farm and going home.'

'Home where?' Louise looked up, startled.

'To Carlendon.'

'What? Just walk off and leave him? With no one to care whether he lives or dies! You don't mean that! You can't!'

'Louise, the farm is getting too much for me. And I never seem to be able to make it pay; everything I do is wrong. The men are costing a lot more than I thought they would. They go through so much food, but I can't bring myself to cut back on their rations...'

'Neither should you, Mother. If Father was

here he wouldn't want us skimping on men who've suffered the same ill treatment that he has. Anyway, other farmers with convict workers are doing well, I don't understand why we aren't.'

Because it's a man's world, Josie thought angrily. Because they can meet at the market, and in the pubs, and make deals for their livestock, their dairy produce, their fruit – their everything, especially convict information! She wasn't privy to their knowledge of the assignees' reputations, hence she had to take whoever the Government sent her. It was years before she learned from a barrow woman that she was employing 'cast-offs'.

'But they assured me that my workers can be trusted,' she'd countered. 'And they're really not bad fellows.'

'Trusted to do what?' the woman said. 'They may have earned their Class Two stripes, and can behave themselves fair well, but that don't say they can, or will, work, missus. Most of your workers, they be cast-off by other farmers for being too slow, or too damn lazy.'

Forced to take a stronger attitude towards her farm hands, Josie had swept through and sacked men who couldn't get through their assigned work on time, and continued to do so, but it had taken a toll on the general atmosphere of the farm. The easy relationship she'd had with her first band of workers disappeared and was replaced by the more typical 'them and us' attitude of the convicts.

Farm production had improved, but her marketing ability hadn't. Her prices were being undercut at every turn, and her expenses were crippling. The Government was always thinking up ways to raise revenue, including the latest annual tax of one guinea for each assigned convict, to pay for their clothing. Josie found this outrageous, since convict clothes were made at the Female Factory and prior to this plan she'd been able to buy them direct from there for only a few shillings a set.

'It's all too much,' she'd said to the solicitor. 'I have to sell Pinewoods Farm. I have the deeds with me. Could you arrange the sale?'

He read the deed of sale, and shook his head. 'You bought it in both names. Your husband's name and your own. I understand he was transported here, and you followed. A commendable action on the part of a wife, I must say, but why did you complicate it by putting it in both names? You can't sell now without his signature.'

Josie ignored the question rather than admit that her name on the deeds had been an afterthought. She'd had no say in the matter.

'But I can't carry on, Mr Baggott. It's too difficult trying to employ convicts and cope with the competition of more ... experienced farmers.'

The solicitor scratched his beard with a tortoiseshell letter-opener. 'This is difficult. But I suppose you can't be expected to hang on for eight years. I really don't know how to get around it. I may be given permission to visit your husband. The Solicitor-General just might allow it. But think on that, Mrs Harris. What if I am able to achieve that and Mr Harris disagrees? Have you been able to discuss your plan with him?'

'I'm sorry, no. I only heard he'd been sent to that other prison through convicts working on my farm.'

'Take my advice, madam. If you're not certain he'll agree, don't send me off on this tack, because if he says no, that will be the end of it.'

'What else can I do?'

'Leave it with me.' He frowned. 'I'll find time to have a chat with the Solicitor-General. A few words. Explain your position. See what advice he can proffer, eh?'

'Thank you, Mr Baggott. I'd appreciate that.'

'What will you do when you sell your farm?' he enquired.

'I had thought of returning home. But maybe I'll have enough to take a house, and then I could find a job.'

Josie saw him raise his eyebrows and she knew instantly what that meant. That she'd be competing with convict women for employment. But she managed a smile. 'One hurdle at a time, Mr Baggott.'

Louise was the other hurdle. If they left the farm and moved into a house, preferably leased, her daughter would see that it was impossible to survive here without an income, and she would have to agree to go back to Carlendon. To the family.

'Sometimes I do get homesick, Louise,' she ventured. 'It'd be so nice to see the family again, wouldn't it?'

'It'd be humiliating! That's what it would be!' Louise shouted and fled the kitchen, banging the door behind her.

Just when Sean needed her, Louise didn't seem

to be exercising Tulip so much, so it took him three days to spot her riding down the road and whistle to her.

'You're looking a picture today, Miss Harris,' he called as she rode over to him. 'Where are you off to?'

'Nowhere, as usual,' she snapped.

'Ah, there's a waste of a day for you. Why don't you go into the markets and buy a new bonnet, that'd cheer you up.'

'Bonnets cost money!'

'So they do. I'd near forgot. But I was wondering if you do go into town, if you'd take a message for me.'

She was taken aback. 'A message? Why? You're always in town.'

'Because there's a new regime here. I'm not allowed to leave the premises.'

'You're joking? Why?'

'It's no joke. They've arrested Angus, our gardener.'

'The Scotchman? Why? What did he do?'

'That's the thing. Nothing. It's a trumped-up charge. I just thought, if you were in town, you could go to Salamanca Square and ask about for a fellow called Bailey. Everyone knows him.'

Louise was intrigued. 'And if I find him. Then what?'

'Ask if he knows what's happened to Angus Mc-Leod. We need to know, and no one will tell us.'

'That's a shame,' she said. 'Do you want me to go now?'

'If it's convenient.'

'Then I'll do it,' she said with a conviction that

353

surprised him. 'If I find out anything I'll be here after we bring the cows in.'

'Good girl.'

Louise rode back to the house, pleased her mother wasn't around, dashed inside, changed her boots and ran out to the waiting horse. In no time she was off up the road to town, delighted to be doing something to help men who shared the same fate as her dear father. Sean was luckier than poor Daddy, she lamented, he'd found a good job, whereas Lester Harris had been unlucky all the way along the line. He'd never been given the chance to show he was a real farmer, rather than one of these useless layabouts that her mother employed. Had they given him a chance, Pinewood Farm would be the best in the colony ... far and away the best. Louise was convinced that jealous guards and civil servants had kept her father in jail so he could not work his own farm, to punish him for being better than them. It all fitted. He had not seen the outside of a prison since he'd landed, yet so many real criminals were wandering loose.

'It's all so unfair,' she sobbed as she rode up the hill past the sawmill. 'The whole system is grossly unfair.'

One of these days, she pondered, I'm going to ask Sean about Daddy. No one else is able to help him. Maybe Sean can. Why not ask for information in the obvious place, for a change?

She shuddered. Her mother would be furious. Then she realised her mother would be furious anyway, since she hadn't done any of her chores this morning. And she was taking off to town without a word.

'Oh, what the heck!' she said, and gave Tulip her head on a long, straight patch of Sassafras Road.

It was market day in Salamanca Square, so all the small vendors were out in force, selling everything from home-grown tea to trinkets, scarves and knitwear, and buns and cakes. Had she known this market was on today, she wouldn't have had to run off from the farm; this was a perfectly good excuse to be in town. But there it was again. Even though Sassafras Road had been extended quite a long way and was now a busy thoroughfare, she and her mother never had much idea of what was going on around them. They didn't even buy newspapers! 'An added expense,' Josie had said.

Louise glared at customers munching on toffee apples. She loved toffee apples, but she didn't have a penny with her.

But now for this errand.

Suddenly the confident crowd intimidated her. Everyone knew exactly what they were doing, while she was dithering about trying to think who she should ask. Who might be able to point out this man Bailey. What was he anyway? Had Sean taken it for granted that she knew who he was? A vendor maybe? Or the town crier, who was making a racket with his shouts and jangling bell-ringing? Or a fishmonger? How was she supposed to find him?

She wandered about for ages, feeling like a loiterer since she certainly wasn't a customer, until she finally plucked up the courage to approach an ancient woman sitting on a step surrounded by buckets of flowers.

'Would you know a man called Bailey?' she asked.

'S'pose I do?' the woman mumbled.

'I would like to speak to him. Please.'

'Roses, tuppence for two.' The woman handed her two full-petalled pink roses, and Louise had to shake her head.

'I'm sorry. I don't have any money.'

'You don't look too poor!' the flower-seller snorted, plunging the roses back into the wooden bucket.

'Please. I have to find Mr Bailey.'

'Mr Bailey!' the woman cackled. 'Mr Bailey!' As if this were a good joke. Then she jerked her head towards a dingy shop littered with secondhand goods of all descriptions.

Louise thanked her and went over to the shop. She picked her way past the boxes of boots and used clothing around the entrance, ducked under the blackened pots and pans hanging from the door jamb and walked shyly into the musty shop.

'Do you know a Mr Bailey?' she almost whispered to the man behind the counter.

'Hey, Bailey,' he yelled to someone away in the dim interior. 'You're wanted!'

'Who wants me?' a voice came back.

'I'm not your bloody doorman,' the first man growled.

'Ah, orright! Hold your horses.'

Louise stood nervously by the grimy counter as Bailey, a wiry little man with sharp eyes, wandered out. He was wearing a close-knitted black seaman's cap with a red pompon and a long swagger coat that was too big for him, and he looked up at her with a toothy grin. He reminded her of a ferret.

'Hullo,' he said. 'What 'ave we got here then?'

Louise blushed, thankful for the poor light in the shop. 'I have a message for you, Mr Bailey. You are Mr Bailey?'

'The one and only. What sort of message?'

'From Mr Shanahan. At Warboy Farm.'

'Ah, Mr Shanahan himself. Trust him to send me the prettiest messenger-girl in town. What does he want?'

Louise shifted from one foot to the other. 'He wants to know what's happened to Angus McLeod.'

'Ah! Angus. Why didn't Sean come himself?'

'It seems there are new rules at that farm. He's not allowed to leave.'

'I thought he was getting it too good there. I knew it wouldn't last. But now, you want to know about Angus. Tell Sean they put him through the wringer fast. He's good as gone already.'

'Where to?'

'Port Arthur, miss.'

She was startled by the mention of that prison. 'It's a bad place, isn't it?'

'The worst. Some of the guards from Norfolk Island are there. When God made those guards, missy, he let devils slip into their ranks.'

'Oh!' Louise fought back tears. 'I'm so sorry. That's terrible. Sean said Angus is innocent.'

'Not according to the magistrate, miss. He got life!'

'What for? What did he do?'

Bailey glanced up at her. 'Do? Nothing, according to Shanahan.'

'But what did they charge him with?' she insisted.

He sucked his tongue noisily. 'Let's see. What was it again? Ah ... using force on someone,' he said awkwardly. 'Yes, that's what it would have been, something like that.'

'You mean getting into a fight?'

He nodded. 'Yes. That's right. What's your name, miss?'

'Louise Harris. We have a farm near the Warboy farm. But surely they don't get a life sentence for getting into a fight?'

'They do if someone really gets hurt. But now, listen here, you're a friend of Shanahan's, are you?'

'Yes.'

'Then, Miss Harris, will you tell him there's a letter for him at the grog shop.'

Louise's eyes widened. Such places were not mentioned in polite society, though she had read in the papers that there were many of these illegal dens in Hobart.

She took a deep breath. 'Will he know which one?' she asked, trying to be helpful.

Bailey laughed. 'Ah yes, miss.'

As she walked back to the horse, the sun came out from behind a bank of clouds, taking the chill off the day. Everything about her looked blue and bright, the sky, the shimmering waters of the harbour, the colourful crowds – but Louise was troubled. Sean seemed to inhabit another world, separate from his everyday farming life. He'd said she should go into the markets to cheer herself up. Which meant he knew it was market day. He knew who to ask for news, via this man Bailey, for instance. He was known at a grog shop. He even knew prostitutes. She hadn't forgotten seeing him talking to that gaudy woman! Louise realised that there was an underground convict life going on all about them, and it intrigued her.

But she had learned something helpful. That her father hadn't really hurt anyone when he was involved in a fight, otherwise he would have been sentenced to life, as Angus had been, according to Mr Bailey's information. And that went to prove, she reasoned, that he wasn't a bad man. He'd been born with a quick temper, that was all, and unfortunately it had not served him well in these extraordinary circumstances.

As she rode out of town, she passed the church and considered calling in there to say a prayer for her father, but changed her mind when she remembered that her mother had a temper too. And her chores were waiting.

Sean was not able to meet Louise that afternoon, so he'd sent Singer Forbes. He'd been called into Mr Warboy's office to read the list of new regulations that Warboy had penned on a sheet of paper to be displayed in the cookhouse.

'Do you understand them?' the boss asked.

'I do.'

'Do you have any comment to make?'

'Sure. You have ruined the life of an innocent man.'

Warboy pushed back the woolly cap he'd taken to wearing on his bald head, and glared. 'Your loyalty is misplaced. His accuser is my granddaughter and she wouldn't lie. I asked you about these regulations.'

She has lied, you old fool.

Sean looked at the page again, knowing half of them wouldn't work. Prior to this, by trial and error, he and Warboy had found a system of rules that was acceptable to all. Now the boss was resurrecting old rules, opening old sores, like the earlier curfew, banning Sunday fishing, making attendance at religious services on Sundays mandatory...

'What about them?' he said sullenly.

'Do you have anything to add?' Warboy asked.

Only that you're dealing yourself a bad hand.

'I do not. Is that all?'

'No it's not!' Warboy said angrily. 'You'd better watch yourself. I won't countenance insolence. I asked you to find a black girl to work in the kitchen. Why haven't you done that?'

Because this isn't Jamaica.

'Because there are none. But there are good women available in the Female Factory.'

Warboy took up a pen. 'I've heard no such thing. But if you say so – give me a name.'

'Marie Cullen.'

'Is she a friend of yours?'

'She was a friend of my late cousin, Matt O'Neill. The one who was tortured and killed.'

Warboy tapped the pen angrily. 'Any more of that and you'll be back in prison. No one's irreplaceable. Is this Cullen person a good woman? And clean?'

'Yes, sir.'

'Very well. Now, I need a replacement for McLeod. Do you know of anyone?'

All the good men I came with are assigned now. Or dead.

'Not off-hand,' he said, to be contrary.

Warboy gave a snort of anger and threw the page of regulations across to Sean. 'That will be all. See that the rules are displayed in the cookhouse and make sure they all read it, so there can be no arguments.'

No arguments? Jesus wept!

'Yes, sir.'

After teasing him about the young lady, Singer gave Sean the bad news about Angus, then the good news about a letter.

'I'll go in and get it tonight,' Sean said.

'That's too risky, with the famous new rules up there. You've got to collect the stores tomorrow. Wait till then. Even if the boss is along, you can disappear for a few minutes to go to the bog. But listen here, I've been talking to Dossie. She's been lumbered with minding that mad girl. She's convinced Angus did get the girl pregnant. She confided all to Dossie!'

'Get out! I won't have that.'

'Let me finish. The girl, what's her name? ... Penn. She told Dossie that Angus is her friend, and he's going to marry her. She's waiting for him to come back and sweep her up to the altar.'

'What? Doesn't she know where he's gone?'

'Apparently not. It's a bloody mad world, mate.

Could Angus have got carried away and held out the carrot of marriage? She wouldn't be the first maid to fall for that tale.'

'No! He wouldn't do it. He's a stubborn bugger. Got his principles. He'd never pull a trick like that.'

'Not even if she offered? If she did the proposing?'

'Never. If that happened, he'd be fool enough to front Warboy and ask for her hand. You can't believe it was Angus!'

Singer frowned. 'I tell you what, Shanahan, I reckon if she proposed to Angus, he would have fainted dead away. And that's a fact. See here, though, you and I might be standing up for Angus, but most of the lads are saying he's guilty. They're cranky with him for bringing this trouble down on our heads.'

'The boss is convinced too,' Sean said. 'I wish someone could knock some sense into that bloody girl. Make her tell the truth.'

'Dossie says the girl thinks she is telling the truth!'

'Then Dossie's as silly as she is.'

Singer changed the subject, and told Sean that in his opinion, introducing the curfew and the other new regulations was like dropping a cat in a fish pond.

'They're milling about agitated, looking for a fight, helped along by the gin they borrowed from Flood's cook. You'd better talk to them.'

Remembering the letter Singer claimed Warboy had held back from him, Sean was surprised. 'Since when have you turned pacifist? What do you care what they do?'

'Since you dropped the flag. What's going on with you? You haven't said a word. You don't seem to care if they work themselves up into a lather and go looking for brains to bash.'

'Why should I? Will you tell me why I should worry about keeping his farm going smooth as you like to make money for him, and I never earn a penny for my troubles?'

Singer grinned, his fair hair flopping over his face in defiance of the rules. 'Ah! You're on that soap box again! Well, let me remind you, Shanahan, the alternative is worse. Getting yourself sacked from this job will put you back in a cell, or on a chain gang, depending on Warboy's whim.'

'No it won't,' Sean growled. 'Flood's offered me the overseer's job on his farm.'

Singer's reaction was swift. 'Good! You go over to that buck-toothed reptile, and I'll have your job here.'

That was disappointing. Sean had expected an argument, or even anger, from Singer. He stamped away, strode down to the men's quarters and rang the curfew bell, ignoring the four men who'd lit a campfire out in the open, in full view of the house, and were now settling around it, inviting trouble.

Barnaby saw the blaze from his sitting room window. At first he thought it was a fire and rushed downstairs expecting to hear the alarm bell any minute, but there was Jubal, dancing about in righteous rage.

'Can you see that? It's long after curfew and

they're outside, with a campfire lit.'

'Oh, it's a campfire.' Barnaby was relieved.

'Of course it's a campfire! You can see them from here. They want us to see them. It's damnable behaviour, deliberate disobedience! To flout the new rules.' He reached for a walking stick. 'I'm going down there to put a stop to it.'

Barnaby shrugged and climbed back upstairs. He was too tired to bother with this tonight. Jubal could chase them in, let them know that the curfew would be enforced. He finished his nightcap, snuffed out the lamp and lay down on his big soft bed with a grateful sigh. In the distance he heard Jubal's voice raised in indignation.

Jubal bore down on the four men like a schoolmaster on the rampage, waving his stick about and occasionally connecting with a body in the flickering light. He bravely barged into the centre, kicked dirt into the fire to snuff it out, and, with outflung hand, ordered the men to get inside immediately.

Instead the walking stick was snatched from him and broken. He heard the snap, though in the darkness he could not make out the identity of the offender. Filled with rage, he ran towards the fellow, but suddenly he was swept up by rough hands and borne away.

'Put me down!' he screamed. 'Put me down this instant or I'll have you flogged. The lot of you.'

They carried him downhill, through the pitch black of the night, and their silence terrified him. One of them slipped on the damp grass and he thought they would drop him, given his considerable weight, but they managed to stay upright until they stopped with a jerk.

'Put me down,' he screamed again, just as they dropped him. Into water!

Jubal thought they meant to drown him, but he landed not in the river, but in a bath.

A bath. Where? He struggled to get out, slipping back, his hands finding the sides too slimy for a firm grasp, at the same time realising he was in the horse trough! The dirty, filthy horse trough! And soaked to the skin.

He shouted at them to help him out but they'd gone. Disappeared.

As his eyes adjusted to the darkness, Jubal managed to drag himself out of the trough, squelch a few steps away, and then collapse on the ground.

After a while, he clambered to his feet and began a stumbling retreat to the house. By the time he reached the bunkhouse he was crying in fear, afraid they'd come after him again, but all was quiet, so he stole forward as quietly as he could, accompanied by the swish and swash of his weighty wet clothes, and dragged on up to the house.

'What happened out there?' Sean called to Singer, who was in the next bunk.

'The preacher took a bath! In the horse trough.'

'Ah no! More trouble.'

All the candles were out. A few snorers had already found sleep, but Sean lay stretched out, thinking.

Finally he said to Singer: 'You set that up!'

'And the bastard came down right on cue!' Singer grated. 'Go to sleep, Shanahan.'

Millicent roused her father-in-law with enough banging and screeching to move Barnaby, who'd been feigning sleep.

He stumbled to the door and opened it to an apparition of wild white hair and long trailing lace.

'What is it?' he growled.

'It's Jubal! He's been attacked. Come quickly! Those fiends beat him and tried to drown him!'

Grumbling, Barnaby pulled on his slippers and dressing gown and thumped down the stairs to the kitchen, where he found his son white-faced, shivering over the stove.

'You're all wet!' he said.

'Of course he's all wet,' Millicent wept. 'Look at him! They tried to drown him.'

'Now he's trying to get pneumonia! That stove is almost cold. Why don't you get out of those wet clothes, Jubal?'

'Because I wanted you to see what they did to me! You always side with them. Now you can see their brutality for yourself. First Penn, and now me.'

'Are you hurt?'

'Of course I am. They beat me, and threw me into the horse trough! Threw me! Do you hear that?'

'Any broken bones?'

'I'm so sore all over it's hard to tell.'

'I think you'd know if you'd broken a leg.'

Jubal turned on him. 'You're so smug, aren't

you? You don't care about anyone but yourself! You never did! You stole the family money, left us destitute on the plantation...'

'Which was worth a pretty penny,' Barnaby shrugged.

'And even now you won't lift a finger to help us,' Jubal went on, almost in tears.

'He's overwrought,' Barnaby said to Millicent. 'Get him to bed. I'll see about this in the morning.'

'Trouble begets trouble, and that's a fact,' Barnaby muttered to himself after another angry session with Jubal and his wife.

He had suggested having a talk with the men, possibly even easing the rules he'd issued in haste.

'I'll explain that I was in a state over the assault on my precious granddaughter, and may have–'

'Rape!' Millicent declared loudly, from her end of the dining table. 'Rape it was.'

Barnaby chided her. 'I will not use that vile word to a company of men in the same breath as mention of Penn, and would prefer that you temper your language also, for her sake. Penn's business is not a matter for discussion with anyone outside this room, from now on. So – as I was saying – I may have been a bit harsh–'

'No you were not!' Jubal interrupted this time. 'I will not permit you to make allowances for them. I was attacked. That's the top and bottom of it. I am riding into town myself, to lay charges.'

'Against who?' Barnaby asked. 'You said it was too dark to identify anyone.'

'Yes, but I've been thinking. That fellow Billo,

he was one of them. I recognised his voice. When I get the police to him, he'll soon spout the other names.'

'Then what? Four of my men go to prison.'

'Why are you doing this to me?' Jubal cried. 'I was attacked by your staff and you want to pretend it didn't happen.'

'I didn't say that. I'm just trying to think of a way to punish them without creating more trouble. The matter is very serious, Jubal, I understand that. But if we have the police in, there'll be further retaliation. These men are hand-picked, good workers. If you send four of them to jail, the ones left behind could react badly, and who knows what we'll get in the next lot.'

Jubal stood up. 'This is ridiculous! Why don't you face up to it? You've lost control of the farm. That would never have happened with the niggers back home. What makes you think these farm hands are any different? They have to be put on report and you know it.'

'I could just talk to them. I could have them apologise.'

'Apologise?' Millicent's screech returned. 'An apology from that scum! We wouldn't lower ourselves to listen!'

Barnaby was still sitting in the dining room, worrying the problem, when Dossie ventured to put her nose around the door.

'Mr Warboy. It's stores day. Shanahan wants to know what to do.'

Barnaby remembered that according to his own instructions, Shanahan was no longer permitted to leave the farm alone. Now he was the only person available to take the fellow, since Jubal had gone off in such a huff, but he was too tired to be bothered with a long wagon ride.

'Tell him to go along,' he said peevishly. 'Collect the stores and come straight back! I don't want him hanging around the town.'

'Yes, sir.'

Minutes later she was back.

'Shanahan says, "on his own? Is that right?"'

Barnaby reacted angrily at this. 'Tell him to get a move on or I'll ban rations today!' He was fed up with his own family and with his workmen giving him so much angst. He needed to get out of the house for a while.

Sean had his letter. A carefully penned note in a hand so tiny – to fit all of her words on the small square page – that he could hardly read it. It was from his sister, and he read it eagerly. She began by telling him that Hannah O'Neill had died, and that Patrick said it was from a broken heart at the death of their son, so far away, and them never able to visit his grave.

Sean's heart gave a familiar lurch at the mention of Matt, so he leaned against the wall in the alleyway behind the store and took deep breaths to stop it thumping. Matt was still lying in his pauper's grave on the Isle of the Dead, a grave marked only with a number.

...Uncle Patrick's friends, Colonel Rothery and Pastor Cookson, have their society against transportation up and running now, with scores of members, and making a great clamour at the Government.

Good for them, Sean sighed. A bit late for us, unless the British Government goes mad and sends a great ship to bring us all back.

The Colonel asks if you know his son Willem and would like news.

Oh God Almighty! It *was* Willem! But from the word about, news of Willem would be all bad.

Patrick got never an answer from the nobs to his complaint against the Magistrates Pellingham and Matson, so he is going to London to front the Home Secretary. Says he'll never give up, even if he has to come out there and horsewhip the Bs himself.

Sean contemplated writing another letter to the Governor, but knew it was a hopeless endeavour. 'That pair have got hides like elephants,' he muttered. 'It's time I did something about them myself. They've got clear away with it. But what? That's the problem.'

Suddenly the image of Matt's last days confronted him, and he turned abruptly away, refusing to revisit the sight of his cousin in that bloody prison cell. There was a side of him that wished he hadn't gone. Bailey had warned him, but Matt was his cousin, his boyhood friend. He had to stand by him. To say farewell. He had walked in there and barely recognised the bloodied heap on the floor as a man, let alone Matt.

'What happened?' he'd screamed as he walked into pools of blood to try to pick him up. Tried to hold the slippery, sponge-like mess that was Matt's torso, blood streaming along his arms and all down the front of him.

'He got two hundred lashes,' the warder said, advancing with a bucket of water and a length of fresh sheeting to try to stem the blood.

'Why?' Sean cried as they wrapped the sheeting over the soaked bandages already in place.

'Magistrate Matson sentenced him to be flogged,' the warder said grimly.

'But he was condemned to death. To be hanged. Have they called it off?'

'No. Magistrate Pellingham gave him another hundred. And the noose!'

Matt was groaning, holding Sean's arm for support.

'He couldn't get both,' Sean cried. 'No! That's not on. Never! They can't do that!'

'Sorry, mate. They did. The first flogging for injury to the constable, and the second and the noose for attempting to escape. I've sent for the doctor. He should be here soon.'

Sean heard Matt laugh at the sheer insanity of all this. From the depths of his pain he laughed. Before he fainted.

'Are you all right, Shanahan?' Sam Pollard asked, as he threw a bucket of slops into the alley. 'You're as white as a ghost.'

'No. I'm sick. Ate the dregs of our rations last night. I reckon I got gut poison.'

'Then stay out here awhile. I don't want you spewing in my shop.'

'Bless you!' Sean took a pitcher of water from a nearby vat, and drank a few mouthfuls before squatting on the ground to ward off another giddy spell. He remembered the letter and dug it out of his shirt pocket, squinting at the last few lines.

My baby Sean is a bonny lad, even better-looking than his uncle. Glenna, being now a widow, with her son Tom, has emigrated to America but there's a story about that, that she bought passage to Van Diemen's Land instead. Do tell.

I remain your loving sister, Annie.

CHAPTER TWELVE

Unable to face the rest of the day at home, Barnaby had his horse brought round, and set off for town, passing Shanahan in the wagon on his way. He went straight to the main store, and walked in with a firm step as if he were business bound.

The attempt to give purpose to his visit was lost on his old friend Sam Pollard, who hurried out to him from behind his counter.

'Barnaby! Good to see you! But are you well? You look tired out! Come and have a seat back here in the office. I'll bet you rode in again! Now that you've got your nifty little carriage, you shouldn't be riding, not at your age!'

Sam could talk the leg off an iron pot, Barnaby mused, as he sank into a worn old armchair that knew how to accommodate his bulk. But then that was Sam's strong point as a shopkeeper: he chatted on so heartily to the customers, they hardly realised he was raising sales, and though he was known to be a tightwad, he was honest, and tried to make sure that Pollard's Stores sold the best available products.

And that, Barnaby nodded to himself, made him the ideal business partner.

'I'm quite well,' he told Sam, who had detoured to find a glass of rum and raspberry for him. 'Just a little weary.'

'This'll perk you up then. You like a sweet taste in the morning.'

Barnaby sipped his drink. 'I do indeed. Good smooth rum this. White rum, eh?'

'Your best,' Sam grinned. 'Is anything worrying you? That fire we had at the other store wasn't as bad as the newspapers said. Very little damage; and I've found a skilled cabinetmaker to repair the furniture that was burned.'

'That's good. No, I guessed the report was overdone. It's just that I'm getting fed up with my visitors. At home.'

'Ah, yes?'

Barnaby saw Sam's surprise. Normally it was not in his nature to discuss his family problems, though he'd heard plenty from Sam about his own wayward wife, Jenny, who was an audacious flirt and liked to spend Sam's money. It was Barnaby's considered opinion that these two imperfections went hand in hand, though he would never be so tactless as to wave that belief in front of Sam's concern.

'Yes,' Barnaby said heavily. 'I've got them

camped all over the place. I'd like my house back. And a bit of peace.'

'I supposed you wouldn't like to ask them to leave?'

'Oh yes I would. My heavens, I would! But I can't send them packing. They haven't any money. They prefer mine.'

Sam laughed. 'The rum's doing you good, I can see that.'

'Hit a raw spot, more like it.'

'Can't you find him something to do?'

Barnaby sat back and pondered that for a while. Then he grinned. 'I just recalled a remark my overseer made about one of my earlier farm-hands. And it applies to my son as well. Shanahan said: "He's as useless as a plough upstairs."'

When one of their employees put his head round the door to ask Sam if he could open a new chest of tea, he found both men laughing uproariously.

'Yes, go ahead,' Sam said, then he turned back to Barnaby, in a more sober frame of mind. 'We still haven't solved your problem. Are they difficult people to live with?'

'Unpleasant. Decidedly unpleasant, to tell you the truth.'

'I'm so sorry, Barnaby. I had no idea! Would you consider building a cottage on your property? That would get them out of your house.'

'No. They interfere too much with my farmhands. At least in my house I can keep an eye on them. Jubal's wife is driving my cook to distraction, and he spends his time thinking up punishments for convict sinners. At this minute

I'd say he's back at the police station trying to report them. They threw him in the horse trough.' Barnaby began to laugh again.

'They what?'

Barnaby dabbed at tears of laughter. 'Into the horse trough!' he gasped, realising it hadn't seemed so funny this morning with all the tension in his house. 'Damned fool thing for them to do, but I'll go over and see Hippisley shortly, and calm it all down. I don't want any more trouble in the place.'

Sam said quietly: 'Barnaby, I never liked to mention it before, but I heard about McLeod and your granddaughter. I'm very sorry. But if you're having problems with her parents as well, I'd say move them on. Everything was going so well for you before they came, wasn't it?'

'Yes. And that seems like years ago.'

'Get them out then.'

'How?'

'Pay them. Pay them whatever you can afford, along with tickets to the mainland. On condition they board the next ship leaving port.'

'I'll think about it.'

'Seems to me you've been thinking about it too long already.'

When Barnaby left, Sam was very concerned for his friend. He'd never liked Jubal and his pompous ways, or the wife, finding 'unpleasant' too kind a word to describe the pair. And obviously Barnaby was dreadfully hurt by the scandal of the granddaughter – that was all over town – on top of having to cope with the wretched trio in his home.

He saw Shanahan outside and asked him to wait for Mr Warboy. 'He's not feeling the best. He shouldn't be riding home. When you've finished packing the stores, go round the front and get Mr Warboy's horse. You can hitch it to the wagon.'

Not inclined to discuss Barnaby's affairs with a convict, Sam left it at that, though he would have liked to have heard more about that dunking of Jubal. Amusing it might have been, but it was a serious offence, one that Barnaby, immersed in his own problems with Jubal, could be taking a little too lightly. Any convicts turning on their master rang bells of alarm in this community, lest such mutinous conduct spread.

As he walked down the hill, Barnaby could see a grand three-masted ship at anchor in the harbour, so he pushed on, forgetting he needed to turn left to the police station. The ship looked so familiar, he thought it could be the dear old *Adonis*, which had brought him to Van Diemen's Land from Bombay, and sure enough, when he found a closer vantage point, he could see it was.

'Well I'll be blowed!' he said. 'It's her all right!'

He spotted a seat in an adjacent park that would give him an even better view, and tramped over there, shooing away the wallabies casually grazing in his path, to admire the noble ship.

'She truly is a beauty. By Jove she is,' he pronounced to the animals, since there was no one else in the park. 'A full hundred and seventy-five feet long and forty-three wide, if my memory serves me correctly. They always said she could easily be taken for a warship! I wonder who captains her now? I must enquire. Perhaps invite him to dine.'

Immediately he recoiled from that idea, with Jubal and company in the house, and it made him very angry.

'To think I'm reduced to this!' he cried out. 'Can't even invite a gentleman to my home any more. Well it has to stop. And it will damn well stop! Sam's right. They have to go. It's my house, my home. It's Jubal's duty to care for his own family!'

Furious, Barnaby sprang to his feet and set off from the park, an uphill job this time. He was puffing heavily by the time he reached the gate, but he had to keep going, so he turned on to the street and then leaned against the fence to catch his breath. His route looked daunting.

'Thank God for the tail wind,' he said, as he began again, but within half a block he was staggering, struggling...

A military gentleman took his arm. 'Might I assist you, sir?'

'Very kind,' Barnaby managed to say. 'I'm finding the hill a struggle. If I could sit down for a minute...'

'Certainly. Come on in, sir. This is the Officers' Club.'

'Oh yes, of course. Yes. Thank you.'

Soon he was seated in the smoking room, protesting that he needed no further assistance, but he was overruled by his new friend, who sent for a vehicle to transport him wherever he was going.

The vehicle took a while to materialise, but in

the mean time, calmed by the sturdy atmosphere in this comfortable club room, Barnaby firmed his plan. He had changed his mind: he wouldn't send the trio to the mainland, where they would simply spend his money and bounce back on him.

'No,' he murmured. 'I won't do that. I'll buy passage home for them. I'll buy the tickets right away so that there'll be no backing out.'

By the time the officer handed him into a gig, driven by a young soldier, Barnaby was feeling ever so much better, and was impatient to be away. He thanked the officer for his kindness and directed the driver to the nearest shipping offices, which were only a short distance away.

Less than half an hour later, Barnaby emerged on to Davey Street with a broad smile on his face, and three tickets to San Francisco in his inside pocket – first class they were; his better judgement overriding the inclination to spend as little as possible on his family. First class was his ace-in-the-hand, he crowed: they'd never be able to resist the opportunity to lord it on a grand ship like *Adonis*.

That done, he stood on the corner of the street, trying to recall what else he'd planned to do this morning.

'Oh Lord, yes!' he muttered to himself. 'Jubal's complaint.'

Barnaby seemed to have lost hours somewhere. As he marched up the steps into the police headquarters, he was surprised to hear a wall clock chime twice.

'Is that clock right?' he asked the policeman at

the counter.

'Yes, sir. Dead on.'

'Well I'll be blowed. No wonder I'm feeling a bit peckish. I'd like to see Chief Constable Hippisley.'

'I'm sorry, sir. Chief Constable Hippisley is in New Norfolk. He won't be back until next Monday.'

'Ah. Then tell me this, has Mr Jubal Warboy been in looking for Hippisley?'

'Yes, he has, sir. I had to tell him the same thing. The Chief Constable's in New Norfolk, he is.'

Barnaby was relieved. It might have been hard to convince Hippisley that the incident was just that. No harm meant. A prank. Anyway, as the owner of the property, it was his right to make complaints, not Jubal's.

The policeman interrupted his thoughts. 'Was there anything else, sir?'

'Yes. Who did Mr Warboy see? Anyone at all?'

'He saw Sergeant Budd, he did. Yes, Sergeant Budd it was.'

'Then I'd like to see Sergeant Budd myself. I'm Mr Warboy, owner of Warboy Farm. Get Sergeant Budd for me, please.'

'He's not here now. He went out to Warboy Farm to investigate a complaint.'

Barnaby was suddenly stricken with conscience. 'How long ago?' he asked, his voice wavering a little.

'How long ago did he leave? I'd say probably an hour. Yes, it would have been an hour ago. He took two constables with him. In the wagon. A bit of trouble out there, eh? Some of them convicts, they can play up merry hell...'

But Barnaby was hurrying down the steps, chiding himself for not coming here first. He would have to go home immediately and see what that fool of a Jubal was doing now.

'Dammit!' He could have done with that gig and the young soldier again. The store was more than five blocks away, in Collins Street, three back in one direction and two up the hill. He set out with a determined stride, certain the whole of Hobart had conspired to hamper his progress, pushing against him, barring his way across busy streets and causing him to detour around roadworks.

Barnaby was leaning against the solid grey wall of the Bank of Van Diemen's Land, and feeling a downright fool that he was puffing so much he was unable to take another step, afraid he would collapse if he tried, when he saw Shanahan running towards him.

'There you are, Mr Warboy!' the Irishman cried. 'Mr Pollard, he was concerned for you. Thought you should be back at the store by this, so he sent me looking, to see if you're all right.'

'I am quite all right,' Barnaby said with dignity and a deep breath. 'I was just taking a breather. I am on my way back now.'

'Good. Would you mind me walking with you?'

Barnaby gave his permission, and Shanahan reached out to take his arm, giving him the strong support he needed to make it the rest of the way

Once inside the store, though, Barnaby was

done in, and collapsed in Shanahan's arms.

They placed him on a day bed in Sam's office and sent for a doctor. Though Barnaby heard Shanahan ask for Roberts, another fellow, Jellick, arrived some time later. Not that Barnaby cared; he felt he simply needed a rest, which he would have when all his present irritants were cleared away.

The doctor diagnosed a pumping heart caused by bowel obstructions and sold him a large bottle of physic – the doctor's own remedy, made up, he assured Barnaby, of exotic herbs, though to the patient it reeked of cod liver oil and garlic.

'I'll take some when I get home,' he said, to be on the safe side.

With all this fuss, Barnaby didn't fail to notice a young woman who peered around the door a couple of times. She was a skinny piece with tufts of dark hair that could do with a comb, he noted, and large dark eyes that seemed too big for her face.

'Who's that?' he asked Sam.

'Who? The girl? I don't know. Shanahan brought her here for some reason.'

'Excuse me, sir,' Shanahan called from the door. 'This is Marie Cullen. The girl I was telling you about. To help Dossie in the house.'

'To help Dossie? What was that about? Oh Lord, yes, I remember. Listen, Shanahan, tell her I'm sorry but I've changed my mind. I don't need anyone.'

When Shanahan withdrew, Barnaby turned to Sam. 'Since *they'll* be moving out,' he said smugly.

'I'm sorry,' Sean said to Marie. 'He's changed his mind. I'll have to take you back, love, but don't be worrying, I'll find a place for you.'

By late afternoon Barnaby was feeling well enough to travel home in the wagon with Shanahan, and as the miles passed he tried not to worry about Jubal's complaints. After all, he'd be gone next week, gone and not mourned, but trepidation persisted and Barnaby felt quite ill.

Shanahan worried that the boss might fall out of his seat, and suggested he could make him comfortable on the tray of the wagon, but Barnaby wouldn't have that.

'A man would look a damn fool sitting among the stores. I'll stay here. Give the horses some hurry-up.'

As the light wagon crunched along the road, Barnaby looked about him. 'I can smell smoke. Is there a bushfire somewhere?'

'It's smoke you can smell all right. Might be someone's burning off cleared timber.'

Early the same morning, the dairy hand, Rufus Atwater, ran away from Warboy Farm.

Rufus was a timid lad, so timid he'd managed to stay out of trouble right from the day he'd been sentenced to be transported to Van Diemen's Land for stealing a book to the value of twelve pounds. He'd kept quiet through all the violence and turmoil of the frightful months chained below decks in that filthy ship, *Veritas*, and once ashore he lacked the gumption to remind the authorities that his record on the voyage was clean. As a result he was thrown into prison, and his few possessions were taken from him ... among them a warm coat his mother had made for him. Never mind that it had suffered some mildew in the steaming hold of the ship; it was his, and he treasured it.

Urged on by a fellow inmate, Rufus wrote to the chief warden, when he saw a guard wearing his coat, asking that it be returned to him. He did not know that Article 49 of the Penal Code forbade convicts confined to jails to have in their possession any article of food, clothing or otherwise, except such as should be issued to him.

His error brought him sixty lashes for insubordination.

The flogging shocked him, mentally and physically. Rufus had been an apprentice bookbinder, working in a small factory in a back street of Soho. He could not have imagined that he would ever experience such brutality in his lifetime.

He had taken the book, yes, he'd told his employers, but it was an old one. In his eyes, old and unwanted. They often threw out books beyond repair, and he'd thought this one... Had he known it was a rare book, he would never have touched it, he told them when they rushed to his digs and seized it.

But a crime had been committed. And a lesson for other apprentices had to be played out. Rufus had been charged with theft.

Now, another world away, when he was returned to his cell after the flogging, he was so terrified of his surroundings, and of the other inmates, he could barely speak, but worse was to come. He was sent to work in a quarry, thankfully not in a chain gang, but it was hard for a seven-teen-year-old who'd never done any physical work before, nor had to endure a daily battle for water and food. The Cleghorn quarry operated from dawn to dusk, and the main meal at night was a free-for-all. The last few workmen in the food queues were lucky to find a few mouthfuls left in the big cookpots, and saw nothing of the bread and rare puddings.

An Irishman, Matt O'Neill, who'd also been a prisoner in the *Veritas* hold, had taken pity on Rufus and helped him to muscle his way further up the line, until the day he fell twelve feet from a ledge to the floor of the quarry, breaking his leg.

Eventually it mended, but it left him with a serious limp, so he was reassigned to a slaughterhouse, which was to Rufus the very worst job in the world. It gave him nightmares.

After a very long time, thanks to Matt again, he was rescued from there and assigned to Warboy Farm as a dairy hand. Rufus didn't like to say so, but being nursemaid to more than fifty cows wasn't much of a job, but the boss was all right, their quarters were clean, and no one bullied him.

He was angry when Angus was arrested over that stupid girl. Really angry. Not since poor Matt O'Neill had been flogged and hanged had he been so distressed. Angus was a good chap, and if he said he didn't rape the brat, well then he didn't. That was all there was to it as far as Rufus was concerned. And now they'd flogged Angus and sent him to Port Arthur. The very name terrified Rufus. It terrified him.

After that, things were not good at Warboy

Farm. The men were restless. Cranky. They argued the point about Angus. About every little thing, it seemed to Rufus, who stayed in his corner, trying not to listen to them.

Then the curfew was pulled back to seven o'clock.

It was not so bad for the rest of them, but Rufus's last chore was to leave the dairy to feed the horses and clean up the stables before he came down for his supper. Everyone seemed to think it took a matter of minutes to rub down and feed Bonnie, the dear old draught horse that pulled the plough and hauled massive tree roots from the earth. They always brought her in covered in mud. Then there were Mr Warboy's horses, they had to be properly groomed. And last in line the four work horses. Which had been five, he remembered, until one mysteriously disappeared.

Rufus had to wait until all the horses were in before he could leave the stables and get down to the cookhouse, which was often closer to the seventh hour than the sixth.

Did Mr Warboy think he had ten hands, to get all this done by six o'clock supper? And why the early curfew anyway? What had any of them done to be punished like this?

Hunter called Rufus a grizzler when he complained there were no potatoes left in the stew, but Billo slipped him a slug of fiery gin, and that cheered him up no end. When he got a second gulp from the bottle he was giggling like a ninny. He even helped them build the campfire, and stayed out with them in the dark, after the curfew bell was rung – more in the hope of another gulp of gin than as a deliberate act of defiance.

He had been capering about the fire, having a high old time, when Warboy came down to read them the riot act. He trotted happily along behind them as they carried him down to the horse trough, and fell down smothering his drunken laughter when they threw the boss's son into the horse trough! Then found he was sitting in a heap of horse shit!

Poor Rufus. That sobered him. He knew they wouldn't let him back into the bunkhouse stinking like that, so he spent most of the night shivering over the washtub trying to clean the mess off his clothes.

They were still wet in the morning, so he had to borrow a shirt from Billo and some trews that were too tight for him and chafed his crotch like mad.

The milking was finished and the cows let out. He was cleaning the bales when Hunter yelled to him to get up to the stables and saddle a horse for young Mr Warboy.

'You can put a burr under the saddle if you like,' he added, but Rufus would never do that! It was a cruel thing to do to a horse. Cruel.

He was just strapping the girth when Warboy came thumping down the path, his black cloak flapping in the wind like a giant bat.

As soon as he saw Rufus, he started shouting at him. 'You villains won't get away with this, mark my words! I'm bringing back the police, I know who assaulted me last night. That horse thief was one of them. I'll have him flogged, I will!'

Rufus backed away, but Warboy came after

him, threatening him with his short horsewhip. 'You savages needn't think you can get away with attacking me! My father might be weak but I'm not! I'll bring the wrath of God down on you! Do you hear me?'

'Yes, sir,' Rufus said, stumbling backwards, but then the whip slashed across his head and he gave a yelp of pain, causing the horse to rear in fright.

'Hold the animal, you fool!' Warboy screamed, leaping out of the way.

Rufus grabbed the bridle again and calmed the horse, but Warboy was still carrying on and Rufus expected him to froth at the mouth any minute.

'I'll get that horse thief,' he was raving, 'and Shanahan! He was one of them. The ringleader, think I don't know. God is with me, I have the grace! Don't you turn away from me when I'm speaking to you, you scoundrel, I can see the guilt in your eyes. Stand still! Look at me! You were one of them!'

'No, sir,' Rufus cried. 'Not me. Please, sir.'

'Oh yes you were. God speaks to me. What's your name?'

'Rufus, sir.' He was shaking with fright.

'Help me up,' Warboy said, and Rufus legged him up into the saddle, standing there petrified as the angry man glared down at him. 'I see guilt as clear as day. You get ready to pay for your sins!'

As Warboy rode away, Rufus couldn't think what to do for a minute, then he remembered the mirror on the way into the stables and rushed in to stare at himself.

He still had patches of pimples, and a scar over

his lip where that dog had bitten him when he was a nipper, and his eyes, greenish they were, they didn't look any different, so where was the guilt showing? His hair, chopped with his own hand, hid his forehead so there was nothing there to show guilt, but the preacher had seen it. Or maybe he had just guessed.

'Oh Jesus.' Rufus almost peed Billo's pants. 'What bloody difference does it make whether he's guessing or not? He's got my name and he's coming after me with the coppers. Oh Jesus! There'll be floggings. Me and Billo and Shanahan for a start. Oh Jesus!'

Rufus ran. He ran about searching for Billo, but couldn't find him. Then he thought of warning Shanahan, but the Irishman hadn't been in on it. They couldn't touch him. He was too matey with Mr Warboy. They'd believe him.

He tried to calm himself. He had to get away. He could take a horse, he thought wildly. Take one of the horses now and ride for his life, there was no one about. But Rufus couldn't do that. He couldn't add horse-stealing to his crime, for fear of the shocking consequences.

So he ran away. He ran way down to the stream and followed it on to the Argus Bridge, detouring out to the road, and then he stopped, hiding behind some bushes, watching a troop of soldiers ride past.

He stayed there for a long time, realising he might as well have taken a horse, because he was now up for absconding. Another flogging offence.

He retraced his steps, wandering slowly along the bush track trying to work out exactly how many lashes they would get for dunking a boss. After they got dragged into town, like they dragged Angus. Who never did anyone any harm and them bastards up at the house didn't give a shit.

'Billo didn't steal no horse either!' he muttered, marvelling at how all this was coming together. Like it didn't matter if you did nothing, they still blamed you. Like it wouldn't make no difference when he said he'd only gone along with the jokers carrying off Warboy. For a lark was all. He was drunk.

Drunk? Another offence. Illegal to have alcohol.

'Jesus!'

Eventually he climbed over the stile into the back paddock, got as far as the haystack and hid in there, where it was warm and comfortable. But no matter how hard he tried to tell himself he'd get away with it, the fear of flogging beat him, and Billo's pants were flooded.

'Oh Jesus,' he muttered, standing there beside the haystack, shaking like his teeth were going to fall out, scared bloody stiff.

Hunter was angry. He couldn't find Rufus. The dunce had forgotten to come back and finish cleaning out the shed. He looked around outside, couldn't find him, and came back muttering to himself about his empty-headed assistant.

'I'd do better on my own,' he growled, picking up the last of the buckets of milk to go over to the dairy, where most of it was transferred into larger-lidded cans, ready for delivery to the cheese factory.

That done, Hunter hosed down the dairy himself, and took a bucket of milk up to the house.

'What went on last night?' Dossie asked him. 'Jubal was roaring like a bull. I wasn't game to poke my nose out the door. And he's gone off this morning in a proper temper.'

Hunter ran his hand through his greying hair and shook his head. 'I don't know what went on last night,' he said, 'and I don't want to know.'

'Does that mean you do know and you won't tell me?' she whispered.

'It means I'm going out to help with the ploughing.'

'That bad?' Dossie knew that whenever there were whispers of trouble on the farm, old hands like Hunter got themselves as far away from the house as possible.

She asked the same question of Shanahan, but he didn't seem to know anything either. And he was off to town to collect the stores. Then Mr Warboy himself rode off, and there was only Mrs Warboy to contend with, since Miss Penn was in bed with a cold.

And she, Mrs Warboy, came down with some of her husband's clothes – his shirt, good serge trousers, waistcoat, even boots and socks, all clammy wet and covered in mud – and dumped them on the kitchen floor.

'I want these cleaned and dried by tonight,' she said.

Dossie picked up the soggy black waistcoat and stared. 'What happened here?'

'None of your business,' Mrs Warboy said, and

pranced out.

'Then they can wait,' Dossie murmured. This was her baking day; the stove was behaving and the house quiet.

By the time Jubal came barging back into the house, she'd baked two large meat pies and one apple, one round fruit cake and a batch of scones.

Sergeant Abel Budd didn't have much time for this snivelling gent, but a crime had been committed and it was his job to investigate. Besides, he wouldn't mind a little jaunt out into the countryside today, especially since the Warboy farm was next door to Flood's property. A 'routine' check on the lieutenant's convicts, and a nod of approval, usually scored him a side of lamb or a bottle of whisky, so the day wouldn't be wasted.

The crime, dumping the boss's son into a horse trough, caused Budd and his mates to hoot with laughter in the police station as soon as Warboy turned his back, but Budd, who was also a bit of a pontificator himself, explained that the incident was serious.

'Nevertheless,' he said. 'Nevertheless. While them convicts might have been larking about – never really hurt the gent – news of a prank like that would spread like wildfire, and convicts, they'll lap it up like hot milk. They'll love it, and start thinking about trying something like that their own selves. D'you get me? They're a brainless lot, they'll forget that manhandling an employer – anyone in authority, us, for instance – is a serious crime. And I got to take it bloody serious or I'll have Hippisley down on me like a ton of bricks, not to mention the bloody magistrates, who've got more reason to watch their backs than us.

'Anyways, I'll be taking you ... Gander and Barnes. Get the wagon out and plenty of restrainers. And clean your boots, Warboy's ain't a gin mill, it's a posh place.'

When the police wagon turned in the gates, Sergeant Budd was surprised that the Warboy homestead wasn't as big and as grand as he'd expected, but everything about the place appeared to be in good order, despite the arrest of McLeod and the latest attack.

All credit to Shanahan, he supposed bleakly, wondering how the Irishman fitted into this tale. It sounded too juvenile for a hardhead like him.

Budd had no time for any convicts. 'It's them or us!' he always said. 'Them or us. That's what we're here for. They're worse than the blackfellas because you never know when the bastards'll turn on you.'

The sergeant spoke from experience. A convict had once pulled him from his horse, bashed him with his own baton, grabbed his gun and escaped with the horse. Abel preferred not to recall that the convict had been Jack Fielder, a man he'd twice beaten up in a cell for refusing to divulge the whereabouts of a woman who'd absconded from the Female Factory. Months later, Fielder had been working in a road gang, clearing scrub, when Budd came by.

He'd been taken aback when a bearded convict had started shouting abuse at him, and, enraged, had ridden over to see who this was, only to have Fielder leap up and grab him.

It was all over in seconds. The other convicts stood and watched. Not one made a move to help him. The guards heard him shout and came running, but they were too far back to get to him in time.

'They came running!' Budd told his wife when he came home battered and bruised. 'They never thought to go back and get their horses first! Pack of dummies! They went after Fielder but he was out of sight before they even rounded the bend.'

'Never mind, dear,' she'd said. 'That's why they're only guards and you're police.'

A policeman whose promotion had been postponed for two years, thanks to Fielder, who was still at large. Everyone at the police station knew never to mention the name of the infamous bushranger in the presence of Budd, who was easily provoked.

Warboy came prancing down the front steps. 'What took you so long, Sergeant?' he demanded. 'They could have absconded by this. I'll have them brought up.' As Budd climbed down from the wagon he added, 'I hope you're not leaving that vehicle at my front door. Please send it round to the rear of the house.'

With a scowl, Budd nodded to Constable Barnes to drive on. 'Come with me,' he said to Gander. 'We'll find Shanahan.'

'He's not here,' Warboy said angrily. 'He went to get the stores. Against express orders not to leave the premises alone. And he hasn't come back. He's absconded already, I'm sure.'

'What a surprise,' Budd said drily. 'Who are the others again?'

'The horse thief Billo, and a mean-looking ruffian called Rufus.'

'Their surnames?'

Warboy was impatient. 'I don't know – without reference to the journals. But that's what they're called.'

'And there were three of them?'

'Yes, I told you! Three!'

'I'll have a look around. Bring some irons, Constable.' He took his new Brown Bess gun from the wagon and loaded it. 'What's down that way?'

'It's only the garden,' Warboy called, but the sergeant shrugged and made for the timber gate.

He stood and stared at the sweep of hedges and garden beds and all sorts of floral geegaws.

'What's this then?' he asked Gander.

'It's his garden. Mr Warboy, the old man. He's had it all planted.'

'What for? Who does he think he is? The bloody Governor? Why does he want a garden this size? It looks like a bloody chequerboard gone mad.'

'Blessed if I know.'

Budd charged down a path, rounded a flower-bed and tramped down another path until he came to a dead end, faced with the locked door of a green-panelled shed.

'What's in here?' he asked, kicking a pot plant out of the way.

'I don't know,' Gander said. 'There's someone working down by that fountain. Will I go and ask?'

'No.' Budd took a short cut across a lawn to find a path going in that direction.

The gardener stood up as they approached. 'What's up?' he asked.

Sergeant Budd glared. 'Don't I know you?'

'Why would you? I'm Mr Warboy's gardener.'

'Don't get smart with me. What's your name?'

'Forbes.'

'What do you know about the attack on Mr Warboy last night?'

'What attack?'

'Ah Jesus! Here we go!'

When they had rounded up eight of the Warboy farmhands, the sergeant brought Mr Warboy down to point out the men who had assaulted him.

'He's one,' Warboy cried, pouncing on Billo, pulling him from the line by his shirt, 'and the other fellow, called Rufus!' He ran along the line. 'Where is he? He was one of them. He told me himself this morning.'

'The hell he did,' Billo shouted. 'I don't know nothing about no assault and neither does Rufus. Neither does anyone. That bloke, he's making it up, same as he made up them lies about poor Angus.'

Warboy was incensed. 'How dare you call me a liar! You a horse-thief and God knows what else!' He turned to the sergeant. 'My wife can testify. She saw the state I was in. I was soaked to the skin! They threw me into the horse trough – Shanahan, this fellow and Rufus! I want them all charged. Where is Rufus? Don't tell me you've let him get away too!'

'You talking to me?' Budd growled, but conveniently Warboy's hat blew off, and he had to chase it across the yard.

Singer whispered to Budd, 'He's a boozer, you know. A cupboard boozer. Gets into the whisky. Thinks no one knows.'

'What?'

'Those lads wouldn't have touched him. I reckon the bugger was roaming round drunk in the dark, and fell into Mill Stream back there.'

Budd gave no indication that he'd even heard Forbes. He was thinking about Shanahan. It could all come down to an interrogation of the Irishman. The bit about their accuser being a boozer didn't surprise him. He thought Warboy was a bit cracked anyway, and a whisky-sodden brain might account for it.

He stood in front of an older man. 'Who are you?'

'The name's Hunter. I'm the dairyman. Rufus works for me.'

'All right then. Where is he? Where's Rufus?'

'I don't know. He was called up to the stables...'

'That's right,' Warboy interrupted. 'I spoke to him there and he was a picture of guilt. Shook like a leaf when I confronted him.'

'He's a nervous little bloke,' Hunter snapped. 'He'd shake if the town clown spoke to him. He'll be around somewhere.'

'Go and find him then.'

Hunter headed up to the stables and searched around, but there was no sign of Rufus. It worried him that the lad might have bolted if that bastard Warboy had bullied him into admitting he was a party to the dunking. If only Shanahan was here, this could all be fixed. Warboy was guessing about

Shanahan, who hadn't been there, and Billo, who had, along with Singer and Lew Coates, a field worker. Four of them had been at the campfire, not three, as Warboy was claiming in the usual guessing game he called God's word.

From the stables, Hunter hurried down past the haystack, but something had caught his eye, so he took a few steps back and picked up the coloured kerchief that Rufus often wore around his neck.

'I reckon he's been hiding in here again,' he muttered, peering into the shallow burrow at the base of the haystack. 'The little wretch, scared of his bloody shadow! Warboy probably put the fear of God into him.'

'Hey, Rufus,' he yelled. 'Where are you? I know you're hiding round here somewhere, so come out. If you don't come out, there'll be trouble.'

He searched around the haystack, poking into possible hiding places, then turned his attention to the thick hedge leading down to the milking sheds. He'd looked in there when the call had come for them all to front up for a police check, and that had been the second time, but he'd have another look, might as well waste as much time as possible in the hope that Shanahan would get back before the whole thing got out of hand.

Down he went then. Opened the gate and tramped over to the shed, calling to Rufus again.

'This farm's huge,' he argued with himself crankily. 'He might not have bolted. He could be anywhere. It could take all bloody day to find him, and that'll raise tempers.'

'You in there, Rufus!' he shouted. 'Get out here

now! No more mucking around or Shanahan will have your hide.'

When there was no response, he walked in to check the row of milking bales, and it was then that he saw him. Saw Rufus hanging from a rafter that jutted out from the loft. A dark silhouette against the open window. Very still. As if even the mildest breeze dared not disturb the stillness.

Hunter hurled himself at the steps to the loft, reached out and pulled Rufus towards him, hoping there was time ... but there was no life left in the lad. And no more time for him.

He dragged Rufus into the loft, cut him free of the rope and laid him gently on scattered hay, then he sat down beside him with a thump, winded.

Hunter sat there for a long time. He was hurt. Disappointed that Rufus should do this, when he'd been going all right. Given time, he could have had a good life here.

What had gone wrong? Rufus had only been a watcher at that caper. Had he tried to tell Warboy that? Had he been silly enough to admit that?

'What have you done?' Hunter asked Rufus eventually. 'You didn't need to do this. Look at the years you're missing. What wouldn't I give to be your age again!'

He covered Rufus with a canvas, and climbed down from the loft. Shreds of light glimmering through the log walls seemed to have formed stark unfamiliar patterns, and Hunter found himself groping for the exit along splintered timbers, until he burst outside into the hard light, his heart burdened with anger.

Taking his time, deliberately taking his time, he began the trek back, but at the haystack he took Rufus's coloured kerchief from his coat pocket and hung it amid sheaves of hay. He also took out his short clay pipe, lit it, and sat on the nearby log fence, calmly smoking, until he heard them calling him, as he knew they would. Casually he set fire to the coloured kerchief and stuffed it into the haystack, blowing on it to help it on its errand. He moved along, striking a few more wax matches and placing them in the stack for good measure.

Once the fire had taken hold, he called: 'Here I am!' and went to meet Constable Gander.

'Did you find him?' the policeman asked.

'I have to report to Warboy,' Hunter said, leading Gander away from his fire. 'Ah yes. I have to report to Warboy.'

'About time!' Sergeant Budd shouted at him when he returned. 'Where the hell have you been? And where's Rufus?'

Hunter strode past him and confronted Warboy. 'May you rot in hell!' he hissed, before walking over to Singer: 'Rufus is dead. He hung himself.'

Barnaby sat in his kitchen with the police sergeant. He couldn't recall when he'd last sat in this place, with its warm stove, its long serving table, its pine cupboards and the framed picture of the King on the wall. But now he'd chosen the kitchen for an important talk with Budd, for the comfort it could offer, and as a compromise. He judged his parlour to be too formal for the class-conscious sergeant, who had already referred to the Warboys as 'you nobs' in the heat of the moment; and the shed,

399

where they'd had their previous discussion, to be too cold and impersonal.

He'd been shocked to come home and find the haystack on fire, but devastated to hear that young Rufus had hanged himself. He'd demanded to see the body, hoping somehow that it was all a dreadful mistake and he'd be able to will him back to life. But it was not to be.

Hunter had been extremely overcome by the death of the lad, blaming Jubal for some reason, so to cool him down Barnaby had sent him into town to bring back the mortician.

Then there was the matter of the assault on Jubal, throwing him into the horse trough, which was the reason the police were on the premises in the first place. Jubal was infuriating, insisting that nothing had changed, that Shanahan and Billo be charged for assaulting him, while Barnaby tried to shut him up.

'After today's tragedies, enough is enough. There'll be no charges,' he insisted, but that was when Sergeant Budd had intervened.

'You nobs seem to think you run the law,' he said angrily. 'I'm here to investigate, not to listen to you two arguing. Now see here, Shanahan, what have you got to say? Were you in on it or not?'

'In on what?' Shanahan said coldly, glaring at Jubal, who reacted as expected, screaming abuse at him for being a liar.

Forbes made matters worse. 'I say he was drunk again, Sean, wandering around in the night, he was, and toppled into the creek.'

And of course Shanahan came in on that. 'You could be right, Forbes,' he said with a thoughtful

400

nod, and the sergeant took it seriously.

'Is that right?' he asked. 'Had you had a few too many?'

'Certainly not,' Jubal screamed. 'It's that fellow Forbes. He's another liar. And he has been threatening me ever since that letter came.'

'What letter?' Budd asked, and Barnaby's heart sank. So there had been a letter, and his son had stolen it!

Forbes flew at Jubal. 'I knew there was a letter!' he screamed, and before anyone could stop him, he punched and battered him to the ground.

The two policemen hauled him off, leaving Jubal to drag himself to his feet and lean, moaning, against the trunk of a nearby pine tree.

'That does it,' Budd said. 'I'm taking them in. All three of them, Billo, Forbes and Shanahan, and the courts can sort them out.'

'About time,' Jubal whined. 'You can see we're not safe here among such thugs, and these three are the real troublemakers. My poor father can have some peace now. We can get some decent workers.'

'Could I have a word with you, Sergeant?' Barnaby asked, desperate to put a stop to Jubal's complaints. 'It's been a terrible day. I think if we went up to the kitchen, Dossie could find us a good cup of coffee, and some of her excellent cake.'

Dossie made good his promise, adding, at his wink, two short glasses of his best rum, all of which soothed the sergeant, placing him in a more amenable frame of mind, though he was still hell-bent on arresting the three men.

'They've broken the law,' he insisted. 'Forbes attacked your son right under my nose! Am I supposed to say I didn't see that happen while your own son is charging him? What sort of a fool are youse people trying to make of me?'

'Jubal is confused. I don't know what happened last night. He was wet when he came in, I must admit...'

'Is he a boozer?' Budd demanded. 'You tell me he is a boozer and I'll go with that story.'

Barnaby hesitated. 'No, I can't say that he is.'

'Well then. Some of your men attacked him! And he's named them.'

'Sergeant. Please. He's guessing. He really doesn't know. He's always accusing Shanahan and Billo of something. Everyone's upset. I'm devastated. I believe my son bullied young Rufus to his death, and I'll deal with that later, but please don't make it any worse for my men.'

'For your men! What are you saying? They're convicts! And they get it easy here by the looks of things. It's not your job, or mine, to let them go around attacking anyone that upsets them. Upsets? They're men, not boys. I'll tell you what you need, Mr Warboy, you need a good strong manager, not an agitator like Shanahan, to keep these criminals in order. And you need one now. I'm doing you a favour taking Shanahan off your hands.'

Barnaby reacted angrily to his lecture. 'You are not, sir. You are causing me a great deal more trouble. The one I need to get off my hands is my son! He's been stirring things up ever since he arrived.'

The sergeant downed his rum and stood up. 'That's nothing to do with me. Unless your son withdraws the charges, and fast, they're coming with me.'

No matter how Barnaby argued and threatened, Jubal refused to withdraw the charges.

'They humiliated me!' he said at length. 'They thought they could do that to me and get away with it. Now we'll see who has the last laugh.'

'Then get out of my house! All of you. I want you out of my house.'

'If you think that throwing us into the streets will make me change my mind, you can think again,' Jubal drawled. 'But if they're so vital to you, then buy their freedom.'

'What do you mean?'

'Fifty pounds each. I want fifty pounds' compensation on each count; that's one hundred and fifty pounds. And you are to tell them that I have been compensated to that amount, so that they know someone paid.'

Barnaby was about to refuse, but then he remembered the tickets now in his desk. He would have had to give Jubal and his women some pocket money for the long voyage, and it might as well be one hundred and fifty pounds. Yes, cheap at half the price.

Sergeant Budd was affronted. After hours of complaints and accusations, Warboy Junior suddenly decided to go all Christian and forgive his 'attackers'. A complete about-face, which meant the old man must have twisted his arm near off.

Wasted his time, the pair of them, they had, and while he was on the premises one of their convict workers was right there hanging himself. His report to Hippisley of this day's work was looking messy; he had to step it up a bit.

So Sergeant Budd released Shanahan and Billo Kemp, but detained Forbes.

'No you don't,' he growled. 'I'm taking you in for breaching the peace, Forbes. You attacked a man, knocking him down in my presence. I can't overlook that.'

Forbes was stunned. His face blazed with anger.

'Then I'm charging him with deliberately stealing a letter addressed to me!' he shouted.

'What letter?' Budd shrugged. 'Get the irons back on him, Gander.'

He levelled his rifle at Shanahan.

'Mr Warboy. Order your men back to work!'

CHAPTER THIRTEEN

Two days later, Jubal roused his wife at six o'clock. He was so excited at the thought of a first-class passage to San Francisco on the *Adonis*, with a hundred and fifty pounds in his pocket, that he hadn't been able to sleep a wink all night. The ship was due to sail at noon and they had to be on board by ten. Jubal wanted to see that they were well settled on the ship before then.

It mattered not one whit to him that the old

man was still angry with him. He'd ordered them out on the afternoon that Forbes was arrested, and since then had barely addressed them.

'No loss,' Jubal had said to Millicent. 'He's become impossible to live with of late anyway. And besides, this colony on the wrong side of the world is no place for people like you and me. There's no society here at all, only the dregs.'

They were packed and ready in time to have a full breakfast, and then they asked for the carriage to be brought around.

'The carriage is not available,' Dossie said. 'Shanahan has the wagon ready. Mr Warboy took the carriage early on, and said to tell you he had to go to town for a meeting with his lawyer, and he'll see you at the wharf.'

'He'd better be on time,' his son huffed. 'We're not standing around waiting for him.'

It surprised Dossie that Penn didn't seem so pleased to be leaving, wandering about with a woeful expression on her face, and she thought that maybe the girl was pining after Angus, since she still mentioned him as her 'friend' occasionally, in her vacant sort of way.

Anyway, she was as happy as a lark herself to be seeing the last of them, and didn't even emerge from the kitchen to see them off when she heard Shanahan taking out the cabin trunks and extra baggage they'd acquired during their sojourn at Warboy Farm.

As for Sean, he was coldly civil to them. He believed that Mr Warboy had thrown them out and it was all over.

When he finally had them packed on the wagon,

all but the girl, who was still hanging about the front door, he called to her to hop aboard.

'No!' Mrs Warboy cried. 'No! Leave her be. She's not coming with us!'

Sean was taken aback. 'She's not?'

'Drive on!' the mother instructed, and waved to Penn. 'Bye-bye, darling. Now you be a good girl while we're gone.'

'Write to us!' her father shouted. 'Don't forget to write.'

Sean looked back as the horses pulled away, to see the bewildered girl standing by the front door in a long white dress with a black shawl, valiantly waving a tiny handkerchief.

Hunter brought Mr Warboy to town in the carriage. It was kind of the boss to choose him as driver, so that he could be part of the arrangements for Rufus's funeral service. Also, Mr Warboy had told Hunter that he had instructed his lawyer to defend Forbes. Though he didn't sound too hopeful. Still, it was good to be told this. A kindness. Hunter was glad that the son was leaving. Had he been at the funeral service, there'd have been a riot at the farm.

As Barnaby suspected would happen, they were all well aboard the ship by the time he came down to farewell the family on the wharf. Jubal and Millicent were waving happily from the rails, but Penn wasn't to be seen. He supposed she was wandering about the ship somewhere. He returned their waves, trying not to look too smug, then found a box on which to sit out the dragging

406

forty minutes before some real activity began on the ship and the anchor chain began to move.

Barnaby felt like clapping and cheering as the great sails grew taut and the ship ducked and dipped in the fast-flowing tide before settling into its race for the coast with the wind astern. They were safely on their way. Never had the Derwent River looked so wildly beautiful with its background of deep green forest and blustery blue skies! All day he'd had a niggling worry that they might change their minds, but no. They'd taken the bait and gone.

Sean had wasted no time unloading the Warboys and reporting in to Pollard's store to collect some extras for Dossie's kitchen. He needed to find Bailey for news of Singer, but as he walked out into the street he noticed something familiar about a horse that had just passed by.

He'd continued on about five paces before he turned back to have another look, and then he gave a cry of recognition.

'By all the saints! It's Nelson!' He took off, running down the street until he caught up, and called to the rider: 'Excuse me, sir. A minute if you would.'

The rider, a young fellow, a farmer probably, Sean thought, looked down at him. 'A minute you have. What's doing?'

'The horse, sir,' Sean said. 'He's a fine fellow. Where did you get him?'

The farmer grinned, obviously amused that someone would pick this horse among so many as being a fine fellow. 'Get him? Me dad got him from the Pound, mister.'

'Is that so? What Pound would that be?'

'Annabella gov'mint Pound. Out the river road. Got him cheap too, Dad says.'

'Ah. Would there be any more good horses at the Annabella Pound?'

'Not no more. Not since the new feller came. He buys them all up now. I reckon you missed out, didn't you?'

'Reckon I did,' Sean said, patting Nelson on the rump as the rider went on his way.

So, Nelson had ended up in a pound out there! Sean mused. What happened? Did Freddy lose him? Or did the horse lose Freddy in an accident or an attack? Sean thought it interesting that there was suddenly a new 'feller' at the pound.

Ah no, he told himself. Perish that thought. Freddy wouldn't be buying horses. Stealing, yes!

As he hurried over to the square, he hoped Mr Warboy wouldn't spot the beast. Best to let sleeping horses lie.

When he found Bailey, he wasn't surprised to learn that the town was abuzz with news that a convict at Warboy Farm had suicided, and there were wild stories everywhere about the tragedy.

'Some say,' Bailey told him, 'that Rufus Atwater didn't hang himself, but got done in by that Jubal Warboy, who's escaping the law by galloping aboard *Adonis* quick smart. You carried his sea boxes, they say.'

'That I did, and good riddance. The truth being the bastard bullied poor Rufus into making the jump.'

'Ah, breaks me heart, that does. But did you

408

hear about Singer?'

'That's what I want to know. Where is he?'

'In the lockup still, but your boss has called in Lawyer Baggott to speak for him, so there's a turn-up.'

'You don't say!' Sean was astonished.

'I do say. I was thinking you had a hand in it, Singer being your mate.'

Sean frowned. 'Can't say I did, but pray it works.' He gave Bailey some strips of dried beef. 'I want you to tell Flo I'll have him out soon. I have to run now...'

'Can't you wait for a good story?'

'Make it quick.'

'While you were busy playing the lackey this morning, down at the wharf two seamen from the whaler *Titan* got in among the crowd to do some relieving.'

'Yes, I saw them. Fingers Foley wouldn't have liked that. It's his territory.'

'Neither he did. And it would have caused a riot had not one of them, being an amateur in the field, relieved old Jubal of his purse, but dropped it he did, and Fingers was on it in a flash and gone. He's crowing like Old King Cole he is. Said the purse held a fortune in paper cash. Pity it's not your field, Shanahan, you could have bought a fine headstone for Matt with that sort of money. An angel even.'

'There's nothing I can do about Forbes,' Baggott told Barnaby, 'except make a plea for leniency, due to a good record. He committed this crime right in front of Sergeant Budd.'

409

'But he was provoked!'

'Mr Warboy, every second convict claims he was provoked, even if he stole an empty tin. The magistrate could sentence Forbes to a flogging, but he might lessen the severity, taking into account your good offices. On the other hand, he's a second offender...'

'But he has a good record!'

Baggott sighed. 'I already explained to you, Mr Warboy, his first offence brought the fellow to the colony. Second offences mean Port Arthur, at the magistrate's discretion. And I have to tell you, this magistrate does lean more towards jail time rather than the flogging.'

'A humanitarian?' Barnaby asked cynically.

'No, sir. Indeed not. He believes flogging to be counterproductive, except in serious cases. He prefers to sentence them to hard labour, and there's plenty of that at Port Arthur. If you like I could make a plea for one or the other of the two sentences. What do you think?'

Barnaby was distressed. 'Good God! I couldn't make a decision like that. It's a dreadful thing to ask. I never heard of such a thing.'

'Mr Warboy, you've been here a long time. Perhaps you've never had to hear of these things before. If the sentences seem harsh, please remember convicts are in the majority here, so discipline has to be maintained at all costs.'

'I suppose so,' Barnaby said numbly.

'Don't let it depress you. They emerge from their sentences free men, introduced to a new and better life here. They have everything to gain through transportation.'

'Tell that to Forbes!' Barnaby growled.

As she walked up the wide steps of the new Franklin Building and along the colonnade with its small-tiled floor and tall fluted pillars, Josie remembered that it was built and owned by a neighbour, Lieutenant Flood. And that annoyed her. How could he make so much money on his farm, when she was barely existing? And to make matters worse, he'd taken up an appointment as an aide to the Governor!

'Damn well-paid hobby job he's got,' she muttered angrily, 'and I hardly have time to turn around!'

She pushed through the imposing glass doors, glancing again at the list of professional gentlemen installed in these offices, and headed up the stairs, engrossed in her latest worry. She'd received a letter from Lester – sent illegally, since it didn't carry a censor's mark – demanding she get him out of Port Arthur!

What could she do about that? What could anyone do? Josie fought tears as she envisaged Lester's reaction to her present plan. He'd be furious! And when she came to the landing, she hardly noticed the gentleman who stood back to allow her to pass, until he addressed her.

'Oh!' she said. 'It's you, Mr Warboy! How nice! We haven't seen you for quite a while. And, oh dear, forgive me. I am sorry to hear you had a death at the farm. How very distressing.'

'It was. It still is, my dear. I'm very upset.'

'Then you must come and have tea with us when you have time, and tell us all about it.'

'I'd like that. I really would,' he said wearily. 'But what are you up to in this miserable Flood palace?'

Josie tried to smile. She hadn't intended to tell him, but the words suddenly burst out. 'I'm selling the farm. Mr Baggott is helping me.'

'Selling the farm? Goodness me. What's this all about?'

'I have to go, Mr Warboy.' She stepped back to allow an elderly couple to pass them. 'We're crowding the stairs. I'll tell you another time.'

'Morning tea at your house tomorrow,' he said firmly. 'I've been so overburdened lately, I've missed my friends. My son and his family have gone, by the way!'

Josie couldn't resist a giggle. 'No!'

'Yes,' he beamed. 'Peace at last!'

Barnaby Warboy couldn't believe his eyes when he saw that girl, sitting on his front step nursing a rag doll.

He leapt down from his carriage and shouted at Hunter – being the nearest adult – 'What's she doing here? Are they back?'

'I don't know, sir,' Hunter cried from his perch.

The girl smiled at him through a tangle of fair hair, as Barnaby dashed in his front door, shouting for Dossie.

'Are they back?' he yelled again, looking wildly about him. 'Where are they?'

Dossie came out of the kitchen, nervously twisting at a stove cloth. 'They left her here, Mr Warboy,' she whispered. 'She thinks they've gone for a holiday.'

'Why didn't you stop them?'

'I didn't know. I swear to God I didn't know, sir, not until she came roaming in here and I thought I was seein' a ghost.'

Barnaby looked back to the front door. 'What am I going to do with her? I can't have her here! I can't send her after them! They've tricked me, Dossie. Do you know that? They've tricked me.'

Dossie could only nod.

'I'll have to think about this,' he muttered. 'I'll have to think about it.'

'Why don't you put your feet up in the parlour,' she suggested, 'and I'll bring you some good hot cocoa and buns.'

'Thank you. Yes,' he said, wandering away. 'I'll have to think about this.'

By nightfall he'd made a decision.

'Dossie. Get me Shanahan. I want to talk to him.'

When Sean came in through the kitchen, he already knew what was up and was ready for more trouble, since he was the one who'd taken Jubal and his missus to the ship, leaving the girl here. On their say-so! It would be no use for the old man to go blaming him, he'd told Dossie. He wasn't about to carry the can again. In fact, working for Flood was looking a better proposition every day.

The boss, however, merely had instructions for him.

'I want you to drive me to visit Mrs Harris in the morning, and then take me into town. And as soon as we get to town I want you to find that girl who wanted work. What was her name?'

'Marie Cullen, sir?'

'Yes, that's her. I've got a job for her. I suppose you know my granddaughter is still here?'

'Yes, sir.'

'Well, I can't have that. I want this girl Marie to be her maid. Do you understand?'

Of course I understand. She'll need a keeper. 'Yes, sir. And you want her to live here?'

'Yes, for a few days. Until I can make other arrangements.'

'Righto, sir. And can I remind you we're short-handed, what with poor Rufus gone, and McLeod jailed, and now Forbes...'

'I know the situation, thank you,' Warboy said tersely. 'These things are beyond my control. I have already warned you about insolence, Shanahan, so you be careful. I haven't made my mind up about you yet.'

Neither have I. 'I simply wished to mention a man called James Quinlan, who is looking for farm work. He's an honest man, aged twenty-seven I'd say. Plenty of muscle.'

'What crime did he commit?'

Sean was surprised. The old man was getting picky now. He'd never asked about backgrounds before. Once employers signed on convicts, their records were available to them, but until now Warboy hadn't been concerned.

Well, for a start he's not a rapist! 'I'm not too sure, sir, I think it had something to do with stealing a donkey.'

Warboy sighed and shook his head. 'All right, all right!' he said testily. 'Write the name down for me tomorrow. I'll make the applications myself.'

Sean left the house through the kitchen, after cadging a piece of cake from Dossie, and walked slowly down to the men's quarters, wondering whether Warboy's new rules still held sway. The boss would have considered the question impertinent, he supposed, so everyone would just have to put up with them for a while, adding to the general air of depression that hung like a pall over the whole farm. Homestead included.

Josie served morning tea in the sitting room; a pleasant room with French windows opening on to a flagstone terrace that looked over a small orchard. She brought in some fresh-baked apple slices for Barnaby to try, and while he pronounced them excellent, he couldn't help remarking that she should be employing a cook or even a housekeeper.

'After all,' he said, 'they don't cost you anything, and would save you so much time.'

Josie shook her head. 'No, I couldn't stand it. I like my house to myself. Anyway, I've had enough trouble with the men without employing women. Do you know I had a fellow here recently who thought he was brought here to fight Frenchmen, and went galloping around the farm with a pitchfork. I had to send him back, along with a man with a posh voice who would not stoop to doing farm work.'

'Yes, they're a dreadful worry,' Barnaby agreed. 'I remember my first batch of convicts. Very strange fellows, and all thoroughly confused.'

'But things have been better for you with Shanahan keeping them in line, haven't they?'

'Until now,' Barnaby said. 'Bad luck comes in threes, doesn't it? I had the tragedy of the lad who suicided...'

'Why would he do that?' Josie asked sadly. 'Such a young fellow.'

'It was all to do with the previous problem. I suppose you heard,' he sighed.

'About your granddaughter? Yes, I'm so sorry. It's a terrible thing. I was surprised that it could happen on your farm; the men there seemed so well-behaved, compared to mine. I seem to get the dregs every time.'

Barnaby was glad to have found an excuse to change the subject.

'Is that why you're thinking of selling?'

'That and the fact the farm isn't paying,' she said miserably. 'To be honest, Barnaby, I can't run a farm. I thought I could, because my husband insisted, but it's too hard. I'm losing money.'

'Oh, my dear! Is there anything I can do to help?'

'No. I've made up my mind. It's all too much of a worry.'

Barnaby glanced at the framed picture of her husband over the mantelpiece – the round, fair features of a typical English farmer. 'And what does your husband think about this decision?'

'He won't be too happy, I don't think, but he is still unwell so he had to postpone travelling again.'

'Oh, I'm very sorry to hear that. The poor fellow, he must miss you and Louise so much.'

There was a knock at the back door and Josie went to answer it. Barnaby heard her raise her

416

voice, and was in a quandary as to whether he should go to her aid or mind his own business, but she was back soon after, her face flushed with anger.

'Someone has stolen half a dozen bags of potatoes from the barn. It's the last straw! One night last week someone got in and stole the new long-handled shovels. I practically have to chain everything to the wall!'

Barnaby stood. 'Goodness me, come and sit down. I'll pour you a fresh cup. Just take a few deep breaths to settle yourself down. You've every reason to be angry, of course; damned cowardly of those fellows to be taking advantage of you. Have you explained the situation to your husband? I mean, a sea voyage would probably be good for what ails him, and we do have quite good doctors out here.'

Josie burst into tears. 'It's no use, Barnaby, I can't keep up the lie. My husband isn't ill, and he's not back home. He's a convict, right here in Van Diemen's Land. That's why we bought the farm, so that we could all be together when he's free. He couldn't bear to leave us behind, so he thought up this plan.'

'I see, ah, yes, I see. Goodness me.' Barnaby was treading carefully. 'I mean, it seems to me to be an excellent idea to try to keep the family together. I'm sure he's a good man.'

'He is, he really is. It's just that he has a temper, he–'

Barnaby held up his hand. 'No, Josie. You don't have to make excuses for him. If you say he's a good man, then it's good enough for me. Is there

417

anything I can do to help Mr Harris?'

'Not at the minute,' she said. 'I don't think so. Mr Baggott is enquiring.'

Barnaby needed farmhands himself, but he thought it would be in poor taste to suggest her husband might like to work for him. Best to leave well alone. It was a complicated situation. Perhaps he could have a talk to Baggott to make sure he was doing his best for Harris.

'And you don't think you could wait a little while, until your husband at least gets a work release to his own farm?'

'No,' she whispered. 'It would take too long.'

That worried Barnaby. Why would it take too long? Any experienced farmer would have achieved work release almost upon arrival in the colony ... unless a bad record kept him incarcerated.

Oh dear, he thought, and to cheer her up he turned the conversation to a discussion on what an excellent farm like this would be worth these days, with so many well-heeled immigrants coming in, looking for investments.

Sitting rugged up in his carriage as Shanahan drove him to town, Barnaby wondered about the convict, Harris. He knew Baggott could solve the mystery for him, but he would not dream of asking. What he could do, though, he pondered, was to make sure Josie was not taken in by any of the new-chum speculators looking for cheap property when she set about selling her farm. He would attend to that later, since he already had reason to call on an estate agent today.

418

When they arrived at the high brick walls of the Female Factory, he didn't feel inclined to enter the infamous establishment, so he instructed Shanahan to go in and collect the woman he'd recommended.

'I can't do that, sir,' Shanahan said. 'She's not a parcel.'

Barnaby felt his face flame. Dammit! he decided. I won't be hiring three new workers, I'll get four and let Shanahan go. I've had enough of him.

He climbed out of the carriage, went to the heavy timber gates set in the wall and reached for the bell pull. As soon as he jerked the rope, he heard a rackety clang, but nothing happened. The double gates remained firmly closed. He rang again, and again, and eventually a sullen guard opened up.

'Orright, orright,' he muttered, 'you don't have to wake the whole bloody town. Whaddya want?'

Barnaby marched forward, pushing the fellow out of his way with his walking stick. He looked up at the two-storey brick building with bars on all of its windows, and turned to the guard. 'I wish to see the manager or supervisor or whatever you have here, and right away, or I'll waken a magistrate and have you sent to the quarries.'

The guard snorted, led him across an unkempt apron of land – possibly a parade ground, Barnaby thought, since there was a flagpole in the centre – and pointed to the closed front door.

'Ring the bell,' he said, and disappeared.

This time it was a button-press bell, which apparently didn't work, because after several attempts Barnaby gave up and hammered on the door with his stick.

A grim female answered. A very large female, dressed in black, with shoulders like a fairground wrestler, and a face, he thought, that could sink a thousand ships.

She whipped off her apron when she saw a gentleman at her door, and primped oily black locks.

'Yes?' she asked.

'I have come to see about employing a young woman you have in your charge.'

'Which young woman?'

'A Miss Marie Cullen.'

She frowned. 'You know her, do you?'

'No. She was recommended to me.'

'Who by?'

'My neighbour, Lieutenant Flood,' he lied with a show of pomposity. 'Aide-de-camp to His Excellency the Governor.'

'Oh aye, sir, come through then and I'll send for her.'

The stone-floored lobby was cold, with not a stick of furniture, and as the door was closed behind him, and the bolt shot, Barnaby became aware of the barred windows, and it made him nervous.

She unlocked another door into a dank passageway, and took him through, locking that door behind her too and leading him over to a room on the left, but not before he had noticed a staircase ahead of him, a poorly built timber staircase that should have worried any resident of this place.

Shaking his head, he followed her into an office. 'Who am I addressing?' he asked.

'Me,' she said. 'I'm Mrs Roddock, chief supervisor and matron. You can sit down there while I get the right papers for you.'

Dutifully Barnaby sat on the hard seat proffered, while she sank into a chair behind the desk and began rifling through the drawers.

'Here we are,' she said affably, waving a printed form. 'Now. What's your name, sir?'

Barnaby answered the few questions required by the form and she filled it out laboriously. 'What will she be doing?' was the last on the list.

'Personal maid to my granddaughter,' he replied, and the chief supervisor and matron raised her eyebrows appreciatively.

'Lucky girl, eh? Let me know if she's no good.' She winked. 'I could probably do better for you, Mr Warboy.'

He nodded, and was left waiting, feeling uneasy, as if she were procuring for him.

From beyond the hall out there, he could hear women's voices, and then a rattle of that staircase as several ran down and around into the depths of this cold, intimidating place. Barnaby had heard rumours of ill-treatment of women in the Female Factory, and now he was here, the general atmosphere was so disturbing, he was anxious to be out of the place.

The girl was brought in, barefoot and dressed only in a thin brown smock.

'Is this her?' Mrs Roddock asked.

Barnaby nodded, and spoke to her. 'My name is Warboy. I own Warboy Farm. Would you like to

421

come and work for me, miss? As personal maid to my granddaughter?'

He heard Roddock sniff at the question, as if the girl, who was twenty if she was a day, did not rate that courtesy.

'Yes, sir,' she said meekly. 'Yes please, sir.'

'All right then, off we go,' Barnaby said. 'Where are her things?'

'She doesn't have any things,' Roddock said matter-of-factly, then she began sorting through a long box of cards, finally producing one and handing it to Barnaby.

'You keep that so she can't go running off on you. It's her identity card.'

'Thank you,' he replied.

'Good, now sign here,' she said, passing over another form. 'That's just to say you've taken her.'

Like a parcel, Barnaby thought, echoing Shanahan's words, and was angry with himself for that. After all, he was doing the woman a favour getting her out of the prison.

Mrs Roddock took them to the exit, but she did not open the door.

'Was that all?' Barnaby asked, surprised by the delay.

'It's usual,' she said, 'to offer some remunication for our work here, looking after these people.'

'Some what?' Suddenly he realised what she'd meant to say. 'Oh yes. I see,' he murmured as he scrabbled in his coat pocket for his purse and counted out ten shillings, aware from her attitude that it was more than she was usually given, but it was too late to change his mind.

He took Miss Cullen to the gate, waited for the

same guard to trundle over and open it, and hurried her outside.

As soon as she saw Shanahan waiting by the carriage, she burst into a torrent of tears.

'What's wrong with her?' Barnaby asked Shanahan.

'She's had a bad time, sir. I think she's just glad to be out of there.'

The girl agreed. 'I'll ever be grateful to you, sir,' she sobbed, with no handkerchief to stem the tears.

Barnaby turned away to climb back into the carriage. He saw her jump up to sit beside Shanahan, and nodded to himself. She can look after Penn. And the baby, he thought.

Sean tucked a rug round Marie's shoulders and looked at those sorrowful dark eyes.

She had been among a group of orphaned girls taken from the Cork poorhouse to the magistrates' court, charged with penury, and given seven years' imprisonment, to be served in Van Diemen's Land.

About as bloody cynical as you can get, he thought angrily.

'Where are your boots?' he asked her.

'Matron keeps the boots when we get jobs,' she said meekly. 'She reckons the bosses have to buy us boots and clothes.'

'Ah yes, they do indeed,' he said, so as not to embarrass her. 'Are you well, then?'

'Just a touch of the croup, but I'm nearly better. Thank you for looking out for me, Sean. Your Mr Warboy seems a nice man.'

'That he is,' Sean growled.

Being with her made him nervous. He was afraid she'd be mentioning Matt, who'd befriended her during a stint of fence-building round the Factory paddocks, and he'd have to hang back on his promise to have a headstone made for him on the Isle of the Dead. So far he'd not been able to find enough spare money, what with one thing and another, including losing his piggery job.

As he drove the carriage down the hill into town, Sean was angry with himself for baiting the old man. He was taking his own frustrations out on Mr Warboy, who, when it was all boiled down, had just been caught up in the great mess made by his son and the two crazy women. Everything was going wrong lately, plus he hadn't made any headway at all in his fight to have Magistrates Pellingham and Matson arraigned, leave alone cause the bastards to be sacked.

'We've got a funeral service at the farm tomorrow,' he told Marie, 'but don't let it be worrying you. One of our lads went to God. Dossie, our cook will take care of you, she's a good woman. No need to be afraid of her.'

'And what's my boss like? The lady? Matron said I'm to be her personal maid.'

'Her personal maid?' Sean burst out laughing. 'Dear God in heaven, Marie, she's but a girl, not too bright, and she's in the family way. She just needs minding.'

'Ah, the poor love.'

As usual he pulled the carriage in at Pollard's Store, where Sam greeted the boss warmly, enquiring after his health, and looked at Marie in surprise.

'She's back?'

'Yes,' Warboy said, 'she needs clothes. I should have brought Dossie.'

'Never mind, my wife's here. She can find her something.'

While Mrs Pollard took Marie off and Mr Warboy left to attend to some business, Sean was commandeered to pack shelves in the rear storeroom.

'By the way,' Sam said to him. 'You know that magistrate you're always going on about?'

'Which one? Pellingham or Matson?'

'Matson. He's living in Sorell now, with his new wife.'

'What! Where's Sorell?'

'Nor-east of here. A plum job for a magistrate they say, too. He's got a free rent house and servants.'

A rare thing happened. Sean Shanahan was speechless. He was so enraged, he continued moving bags of flour and rice to cleaned shelves without a word.

Barnaby was aghast. 'But did you speak for him?' he asked Baggott.

'I spoke *to* him. I said there could be a choice between Port Arthur and a flogging, and with a character reference from you I could probably get the minimum strokes there. But Forbes is a difficult fellow. He said: "Isn't it enough that you torment and humiliate us, that you have to tear the skin off our backs? I'll take my chances with

425

Port Arthur." I tried to explain that with an excellent reference from you, Mr Warboy, there would be leniency, but he laughed in my face. He insisted I tell you he wanted nothing from you, under any circumstances. Not even legal representation. I'm sorry, some of these fellows can be stubborn.'

Barnaby shrugged. 'The man attacked my son right under the nose of the sergeant of police! What did he expect? They're not just stubborn, these fellows, they're damned impossible! So what happens now?'

'It's all over. He went to court this morning. Though he was not to know, I did place your statement before the magistrate, which helped I'm sure. He was given three years in Port Arthur, on top of the remains of his present sentence, which means he'll do five years there.'

'Ah well,' Barnaby said miserably. 'I tried. I have a few other things to work out with you, including my will, but I'm busy today, so I'll come in another time.'

Barnaby strode across the street from the Flood building to a real-estate office, where he discussed the purchase of a small riverside cottage at Sandy Bay that had been advertised in the *Hobart Gazette*. This helped to take his mind off the guilt he now bore over Forbes. Though Jubal had denied it, and no proof could be found, in his heart Barnaby knew his son had destroyed that man's letter. And he knew how much letters meant to these men. He'd been too ashamed to mention it to Baggott. Not that it would have made any difference.

He sighed, because he admired Forbes, and wished to God he'd had a son more like him.

Next stop was the Colonial Offices, where he applied for four more farmhands, including one James Quinlan, to make up the loss of three under unfortunate circumstances. And terminated the employment at his farm of Sean Shanahan.

The clerk had requested the reason for sacking Shanahan, and Barnaby had brushed the question aside as he signed the various forms, but the clerk persisted.

'I need to know, sir, so it can be placed on his record.'

'Very well,' he said. 'I am not sacking Shanahan, I'm simply letting him go. You may view these papers, with the Governor's signature. And place the information on record.'

The clerk nodded, glanced at the papers. 'He's been granted a ticket-of-leave?'

'That is correct. He's free to work wherever he likes. Now when will the others be available?'

'We've got a wagonload going out your way tomorrow, so we can deliver them to you then.'

Deliver? Barnaby murmured as he left the office. Like parcels.

After a late lunch with Sam and his wife at the Ship Inn, where they tucked into roast turkey and all the trimmings, and a couple of bottles of expensive wine, Barnaby was feeling positively jolly.

Sam had agreed to inspect the cottage and arrange the purchase, and Mrs Pollard was delighted to be asked to furnish it.

427

'Not too grand, mind you,' Barnaby had said. 'Just choose furnishings suitable for my grand-daughter and her live-in maid. I am told it has a little garden and it's on the beach, so that gives them something to do, with walks and that sort of thing, without needing to be in the public eye, so to speak. Sandy Bay is a quiet area, it will be ideal for Penn when her time comes. We won't want people bothering her.

'Now, I'm good for the bill, and no argument. The meal was delicious. I haven't felt so well since I can't remember when.'

Sam laughed. 'Yes, you've really perked up since *Adonis* sailed.'

At Barnaby's request, a young priest was sent out to Warboy Farm from the Penitentiary chapel to conduct a memorial tribute for Rufus Atwater, since funeral services for deceased convicts were frowned upon, and absolutely forbidden by the churches in the case of suicide.

All the residents of the farm, some men from the sawmill and a few neighbours, including Louise and Mrs Harris, gathered around the pavilion in the garden. The priest gave a kind and sympathetic sermon, acknowledging that he was heartened by the beauty of these surrounds, and urged his audience to take heart themselves, no matter the burdens placed upon them.

They sang the hymn, 'In God's Care' and Sean wished Singer had been there to help them make a better job of it, but then it was over, and everyone began to wander away.

Louise came over to ask him if there was any

428

more news of Mr McLeod, but Sean shook his head.

'No, I'm sorry. Not a word.'

Then her mother joined them. 'You've all had a bad time here, Mr Shanahan. I hope things improve now that Jubal and his wife have gone.'

He was surprised that she would come right out and say that, but he supposed Warboy's friends must have been aware of problems.

'That's true. They were certainly sent to try us. Which reminds me, Mrs Harris, you never did show me how to grow them tomatoes.'

'We will. You come over any time,' Louise chimed in. 'They're very tasty.' She looked at him archly and added, 'Dr Roberts loves them.'

'Oh, goodness me,' Mrs Harris said, raising her eyebrows at Sean as if to say, 'these young people'. 'We'll keep some tomatoes for you, Mr Shanahan, but really, I did want to say a small thanks to you for supporting Mr Warboy through this miserable time. I don't know what he would have done without you.'

Then they were gone, two lovely women in 'becoming' black, walking sedately towards Warboy and the priest.

That was kind of her, Sean thought. He would have liked to pick some of those big pink roses for her, but it was not his place.

In the morning Sean went to the boss with a problem. 'We're very short of hay since the fire. Do you want me to take a dray and see if I can get some around the district?'

'No thank you. The new farmhands will be arriving today. Possibly your man Quinlan will be among them. I put his name down. And I won't be requiring your services any longer, Shanahan. You can get a lift back into town in the government vehicle. Here are your papers.'

Sean was stunned. 'You want me to finish up?'

'Yes.' Warboy sat, calm as you like, behind his desk.

'Then I'll finish up!'

'Yes. You've time to collect your things and take leave of the rest of the staff. You may go now.'

Dismissed, Sean backed out of the boss's office, and made for the kitchen.

'I've been sacked,' he said to Dossie.

'Oh no! He can't do that. He mustn't! What will we do without you, Sean?'

'You'll all be fine. But he needn't think he's so smart. I'll get me a job at Flood's. He's been asking. I'll be working there by nightfall. And what's all this?'

As he talked, he'd been opening up the papers that Warboy had given him, but there were more than usual. He turned over his identity card and glanced at the other pages, not once, but several times. Then he sat down on a kitchen chair with a thud.

'God Almighty!' he said, 'Will you look at this! It's a ticket! A ticket-of-leave! I'm off the bloody hook at last! Jesus, Mary and Joseph, he must have done this!'

He dashed back to thank Mr Warboy, tripping over his words, reaching over to shake him by the hand, and then: 'Is this why you're sending me on? I don't mind staying. I'm happy to go on working here.'

430

'You've done an excellent job here, Shanahan, and you've got a good reference to leave with. You can strike out on your own now. But I'm a businessman; if you stay I'd have to pay you now.'

He reached into a drawer and counted out five pounds.

'This is for you, to get you started.' He held out his hand. 'I wish you the best, Shanahan, and hope you'll find time to visit me in the near future. You'll always be welcome here.'

Dazed, Sean walked back to the kitchen, wondering if he'd be so welcome at Flood's farm once the lieutenant learned his labour would not be free. Remembering all the conditions he'd intended to put on Flood before he'd agree to work for him. All probably worth nothing now.

Mr Warboy was a cunning businessman too. Sean realised he really was out. He had to leave today. No time for fuss after work, for a send-off with the mates, no partying. Just move on and make room for the new.

While he waited for them, he took a horse and rode over to Flood's property to sound out the lieutenant, though he didn't like his chances. The first person he met was Warboy's former gardener, Zack Herring!

'What the hell are you doing here?'

'Flood wanted a new overseer, and I got the job.'

'The rat he is! He offered me that job.'

'Ah yes, my lad. So he says, but you took too long to come over. He was peeved about that, he thought you'd jump at the chance.'

'I had to think about it, there's a lot of funny

business goes on here.'

'Don't I know it! Contraband booze. And he's got some ripe bastards working here, even those cutthroats the Grigg brothers.'

'Can't you weed them out?'

'No. They're not farm workers, they're armed guards. They've even got their own hut. They're hired to keep out customs officers or anyone else who might get too sticky about what goes on down by the river. I didn't know what I was getting into here.'

'Ah well, you just turn the blind eye,' Sean said. 'But what happened to your job at the Governor's gardens?'

'They ran out of money. Had to shut down the whole show. Damned bloody shame it is.'

'If you like, I'll tell Warboy. You might be able to get your old job back with him, if Flood would let you go.'

Zack was suspicious. 'Why? So you can get this job?'

'No. I'm better off without it, now I come to think about it.'

Boats were there still, boats that might have been used for an escape, but Sean hadn't counted on armed guards roaming around. He'd have to think about that.

On the way back he considered calling on Louise, to give her the good news, but strangely he wasn't as happy about it as he should be. He supposed it was because he still couldn't leave the colony. He was a lifer.

But then the money in his pocket reminded him of a more immediate matter. He still had his pride, and paroled men didn't have to wear convict duds. The first thing he would do, would be to buy himself some new clothes. Then he could call on the ladies. That would be a fine thing. Almost like a celebration of being halfway there.

Halfway to what? The question depressed him. It would be easier to escape now. And be on the run for life! Or make a life here and never see real freedom again.

Barnaby glanced through the records of the new prisoners assigned to him, noting that the fellow Quinlan had been given fourteen years for 'criminal conversation', in other words adultery, with the wife of some magistrate. A dangerous liaison, he mused. There was no mention of a donkey.

Shanahan had told him that Zack Herring was next door, but he'd already known that. In her usual spiteful way, Mrs Flood had succeeded in petitioning Lady Franklin for his services on their farm, and made a point of crowing about it to Mrs Pollard.

'Our neighbour will be green with envy,' she'd said.

'Why would he be?' Sam's wife had responded. 'His garden is flourishing now. He only needs weeders.'

'Hardly true, my dear,' Barnaby had said later. 'But it will suffice. Thank you.'

Now he tidied his desk, sent Dossie for Hunter, who would be appointed the new overseer, and walked up to the parlour to watch the government wagon depart. Shanahan was sitting up beside the driver while the two guards were squatting in the back with a bound prisoner.

'Ah yes,' he smiled. 'There he goes. Still demanding his rightful place in the sun.'

Then he added: 'I hope you find it, my friend.'

For a while, Sean was too dazed to think straight. He sat up there beside the driver, who was rattling on about the shortage of horses in the colony, just staring ahead as the miles passed, but when they turned from Sassafras Road on to the main thoroughfare and the horses, smelling home territory, began to pick up speed, he experienced a rush of excitement. He was no longer an assigned servant, he was free! More or less.

'What'll you do now you've got a ticket?' the guard asked him. 'Go off and get roaring drunk?'

'No,' Sean grinned. 'No fear! It's the drink that got me here. I'll never go that way again. The first thing I want is to get out of these rags. I need some decent clothes.'

'Go to the back of Peeble's chancery and ask for Charlie. He'll fit you up with good new duds cheap. Real cheap. He's my brother, tell him I sent you. And if you want a horse, he'll see to that too.'

He halted the wagon at a wayside tavern.

'We can get a meal here. You coming in, Shanahan?'

'What about me?' the prisoner shouted.

'I'll bring you out something,' Sean said.

'A knife would be handy.'

Sean let that pass and followed the guards into the tavern, wondering if it might be interesting to ride out to that country pound and see who was

434

there, for the fun of it.

All was not well for poor Claude these days. Despite his great plans, Freddy was turning out to be a dud.

Now that he owned those fields out there, Claude was determined to make them pay, so he had long discussions with local farmers about the best course to take.

He was advised against a horse farm, because he lacked veterinary knowledge; told he didn't have enough land to run beef cattle; and warned that too many local farmers were already in the dairying business. When he mentioned sheep, he was reminded that one of the many hazards encountered by the former sheep-station owner had been the presence of dingoes, devils and tigers. The devils were the ferociously noisy animals, like small boars, that had scared Freddy when he first arrived, but were not as adept as the other two at killing sheep. Claude had actually shot one of the tigers when he'd seen it menacing the horses, and was surprised to find that the only resemblance to a tiger was the stripes. It appeared to him more like a large dog, but with a more beast-like head and bigger jaws than any dog he'd ever seen. Beside these two wild animals, the dingo looked more like a domesticated dog. Though it was not, of course.

So, since croppers were growing wheat and barley, he reluctantly agreed to take up market gardening, and some of the neighbours even came over to help clear the land of rocks and stumps, and assist with the ploughing.

After that it was up to Claude, who planned to begin with potatoes, turnips and cabbages, but no sooner had he planted the first seeds than Freddy began complaining.

'I can't do this, working left-handed. Get the blackfellows to do the digging and seeding. It's all a waste of time anyway. How do you know anything will grow?'

Patiently Claude explained, but as the days passed he realised that this situation couldn't be allowed to continue, so he refused to pay his 'son', and that caused a row.

'You have to pay me, you said you would,' Freddy argued.

'Not if you don't work.'

'I do work.'

Claude didn't see any point in putting the blunt truth to Freddy ... that he'd turned out to be next to useless around the small farm. He'd hoped the simple and regular work of planting and weeding might suit him, but obviously it did not.

Their argument was interrupted by hoots and yells from several blacks, who came loping down the track towards the house with two horses for the Pound, looking forward to their reward of tobacco. But when Claude brought out the tin and opened it in front of the black men, it was empty.

Angrily he turned on Freddy. 'You've taken their tobacco.'

'No I haven't. They must have pinched it themselves. You always leave the door open. I knew they'd steal it sooner or later.'

'You're lying. They'll expect payment, so they

can have ours.'

The tobacco Claude kept for their use was much better quality, and when he reached for their supply, Freddy was shocked.

'You're not giving them the good stuff!' he yelled, and tried to wrench it from him. In an instant Claude's dog leapt forward, growling angrily at Freddy, forcing him to back off.

The tribal men at the door thought this was hilarious, and fell about laughing, but Freddy did not see the joke. He stormed over to the barn, where he stayed until sundown – dinner time.

Claude watched him then. He seemed to have recovered from his sulks, and talked airily about the new horses, suggesting he could take them and sell them.

'This'll be the way to work things now. You get on with the farming stuff and I'll take the horses and sell them. That was the plan, you said so yourself. And I can buy stores with the money, we're out of tobacco.'

'We don't need to sell the horses just yet. I want to get the potato crop planted first.'

'Good-oh! Get the blackfellers on the job.'

'I told you, we have to leave them alone. They've got their own ways. They're not farmers.'

'All right,' Freddy said sourly. 'You're the boss.'

Claude heated the last of yesterday's stew, threw in some more potatoes, and turned back to kneading a bread dough.

The next day Freddy flatly refused to do the planting. 'How do you expect me to work with a hand injury? It's bloody cruelty, that's what it is.'

'Your hand is a lot better now. If you won't work, you'll have to go.'

'I'll what? You're ordering me out over bloody gardening? You don't really think you'll make potatoes grow? Or turnips?'

'Believe me, they'll grow, and planting is the most important job now. So we have to get to work. Are you coming or not?'

'All right. You go on, I'll finish collecting wood, unless you want to do that job tonight after you finish all the bendings and plantings.'

Claude set off across the fields with his wheelbarrow, and Freddy went back to the woodheap, where he sat on a stump out of the wind. He had no intention of letting Claude turn him into a farm labourer; he could keep that job for himself. The whole idea was mad anyway. What had happened to the great horse sale business? All forgotten now, and only because Claude had come up in the world! An esquire he'd said he was now, a bloody esquire, and who cared? He could call himself 'double duke' for all anyone in this godforsaken island cared.

'Come to think of it, though,' Freddy muttered, 'them farmers as came to help Claude get started with his potato garden, they got matey all of a sudden. Like they got turned into good neighbours overnight. One even brought his daughter, that girl with legs like a working bullock. She wouldn't give me a look-in, had her eyes plugged on Claude she did. And why? Because he's suddenly a bloody esquire, what owns land.'

Freddy looked about him. Claude was out of sight by this and the place was deathly quiet

438

except for the occasional rasp of crows. He missed his mates. Wondered what they were all doing, Flo and Shanahan and Singer and Angus and the rest of them. If Pansy hadn't broken his hand, Freddy fretted, he'd be sitting pretty as a real gardener at Warboy's farm. They had flowers in that garden, not bloody potatoes.

It began to dawn on him that it was time to move on. He ought to just get a horse and go. Maybe tonight, when everything was quiet, he could sneak away. But Juno and his mates were always wandering about, they'd hear him.

Freddy almost liked Juno, though he never got to talk to him much, but he was a cheery sod and could throw a spear faster than a bullet. Freddy had seen him bring down one of them hopping kangaroos in one go. Bang! Just one go. Freddy wished the lads had seen that, by God. And they caught fish with spears too, and snakes... At that thought he jumped up. Several times he'd seen snakes in the woodheap and Claude had had to get Juno to catch them.

'They're all venomous,' Claude had said. 'All the snakes here are venomous. Juno was surprised when I said that not all snakes are poisonous where I come from.'

Freddy had scoffed at that. 'My money's on Juno. If he says they're all killers, that's good enough for me.'

'I didn't mean here, I meant back home.'

'And you believe that? You can be a bit soft at times, Claude.'

Now Freddy picked up the axe and stepped warily around the woodheap, making certain that none of the slithering devils were about before he began work. Suddenly he caught sight of one! A brown snake, lying curled in the sun. It shot in among the uncut logs, but Freddy wasn't hanging about; he threw down the axe and retreated.

'This is no bloody place for me,' he muttered angrily. 'I don't have to stay here if I don't want to. I've got papers, real papers now. I'm Jack Plunkett, and I ain't got no convict haircut no more.'

He put his hand up to his head to feel the healthy growth of hair, and stroked his short beard proudly. He had the makings of a fine beard, better than Claude's. And he had clothes.

'Even Pansy wouldn't know me now,' he gloated.

His movements now were almost automatic. He collected his papers from Claude's desk; took a sugar bag and loaded it with necessities for travel: some food, matches, the knife Claude used for skinning small animals, and a blanket; grabbed his few clothes and his cap, a billy-can and a couple of turnips; then filled a pickle jar with tea.

'That ought to do it,' he said as he tramped over to the stables.

'Sorry, mate,' he said, *in absentia* to Claude, as he reached for a saddle and bridle. 'But you've forced me hand. Anyway, you don't need me now that you're an esquire farmer, with a willing wife being readied for you.'

A light dew still twinkled on the fields as the sun began to climb over the hills, and Claude nodded his approval.

440

'It's a good day for planting 'taties,' he said to Duke. 'A jolly good day.'

The dog, panting beside him, watched him work with interest.

'Pity you can't lend a hand,' his master said, raking furrows into place. 'It doesn't look as if Freddy's about to show up. Ah well, all the more for me.'

He set to work again, seeding the rich soil, undaunted by the scale of the job ahead of him, and losing track of time. The repetitive work appealed to him; he was neat and efficient, able to look back on the rows with satisfaction, envisaging ranks of green plants wafting in the breeze – his plants, his crop, his property. If Sir James could see him now!

Just then it occurred to Claude that he should write to Sir James and inform him that he had been innocent of that crime. He was no thief! And why not? There was no law against prisoners having their say. Not out here anyway. Though he supposed he could have written such a letter at any time before he was transported. It just hadn't occurred to him that he could. No, it wasn't that at all. He simply wouldn't have dared. It would have been regarded as a cheek, an impertinence, to write to Sir James for any reason, let alone question his judgement.

But not any more, by God, he determined. I'll write that letter tonight, and I won't pull any punches either. Why should I? I'll call his damned wife a liar! That's what I'll do. And – and, his face glowed with joy, 'I'll sign myself Claude Plunkett, Esquire.'

441

He was still enjoying composing his letter when Juno came running across the fields.

'Hey, boss. You lookem allasame the new fella. He gone rideabout wid your horses!'

'What?'

'Lookem, him going up dere.'

Claude could only just make out a man with two horses out on the road that passed the pound fences, but he knew Juno would be right.

'Bloody hell, where's he going?'

'He gone, boss. You want I track him?'

Claude looked at Juno, bewildered, then he laughed. 'I was just thinking I'd have to go back and saddle up and try to catch him. He didn't take my horse, did he?'

'Only dem new fellas.'

'Nice of him! So ... yes, you could track him, Juno. Catch up with him. Tell him he can keep one horse. I had intended to give him one and send him away. But he has to give back the other, or I'll set the rozzers on him.'

'Who this fella rozza?'

'That police bosses.'

'Aaaah?' Juno grinned. 'They bad fellas, eh?' He was in no rush. 'I go bring new horse fella back here, den. Go up over dat hill,' he pointed with a grin, 'sit down and wait for him. Good joke, eh, boss?'

Claude realised that the road skirted the heavily forested hill and then had to loop back, so it was possible that Juno could ambush Freddy, but even if he missed him, he could track Freddy wherever he went.

'That Freddy's a fool of a man,' he said crossly,

442

trying to take up his work where he'd left off. 'Had to steal something. Just as well there's no money in the house.'

Claude had a small tin containing his savings hidden in a tree near the blacks' camp, and of course they'd spotted it – no matter where he put it out there, they'd have found it. They'd notice if a blade of grass was out of place. The money didn't interest them, so it was safe, away from predators.

The plan had been to take a spare horse to flog, but this particular spare horse was a cranky beast, hell-bent on slowing him up. It managed to spit the bridle a couple of times, and Freddy'd had to dismount each time and fix it back into its mouth.

What kind of a getaway is this? he asked himself, as the horses trotted sedately down the road, the spare mount flatly refusing to gallop so close to its mate's hoofs. 'You should have had a longer lead,' he snapped at himself. 'You'll never get away at this rate. Claude'll be on your tail any minute.'

He twisted around in the saddle to check the road behind him, dragging the spare horse too close, causing his own mount to lash out with its rear hoofs, almost dislodging him. And so they continued on their erratic way. 'Like a bloody circus,' Freddy complained to his mount. 'You jumpin' up and down like a clown, and your mate there dragging the chain. I'm gonna get rid of him fast. To the first buyer.'

'If Claude don't catch up with me,' he added anxiously. 'And what if he brings his gun? Maybe

I oughta waited a bit.'

All of these concerns kept Freddy occupied as he came to the bend in the road and pushed the horses into a sort of lopsided gallop. That didn't last long, but at least he could see the main road up ahead. If Claude was chasing him, he would have to figure out which way Freddy had gone at the turnoff. Left or right. For that matter, Freddy hadn't decided on that himself as yet: probably back towards New Norfolk. Probably not.

He was hungry and would have stopped to get some bread and corned beef out of the sugar bag if it hadn't been for these two maniac horses that would prance around, making it hard for him to remount. Then he was thirsty, and realised with a shock that he'd forgotten to bring a water bag. Claude had had several canvas water bags hanging by the tank.

Freddy noticed a blackfellow sitting under a tree ahead of him, near the turnoff.

'The only bloke on the road,' he sighed, 'and it has to be a blackfeller what doesn't carry water. I'm bloody stuffed today, I am.'

Then the blackfellow waved, and Freddy recognised him as Juno, at the same time marvelling that blacks no longer scared him.

'What are you doin' up this way?' he asked in neighbourly fashion.

'Come for the horse,' Juno grinned. 'Boss says you keep dat one orright, me I take dis fella home.'

He reached for the bridle, but Freddy pulled it away. 'No you bloody don't,' he yelled. 'Get out of it! It's my horse now.'

Juno was confused. 'Boss say bring back dis one.'

'No fear.' Freddy gee-ed his horse, and for once both animals moved off together, lifting to a trot as he urged them down the road.

Juno, however, wouldn't give up. He raced after them, grabbed the spare horse's mane, and leapt on to its back. Then he yanked the bridle from Freddy and turned the horse about. Freddy yelled and screamed at him, and with difficulty managed to pull his own horse around, shouting at Juno to stop, but the black man had charge now and was off with Claude's horse.

Two young men riding east had heard the commotion and turned into the back road to investigate.

'What's up?' they shouted as they cantered down upon Freddy, who had just lost a bloody good horse.

'He took my horse!' he cried.

'Who did?'

'That blackfeller!' Freddy squealed, pointing urgently at the horse fast disappearing down the road towards the Pound.

'A bloody black has stolen his horse!' one of the strangers shouted. 'Let's get him!'

They both took off at the gallop, whooping like punters at a cockfight.

Freddy knew he'd never catch up with them, so he waited, grateful for their intervention. Nice to be a gentleman and be assisted by other gentlemen. Real nice.

Soon they were all out of sight around that bend, and Freddy prayed they'd catch Juno and

445

get the horse back before they ran into Claude, otherwise it'd be his turn to whoop off in the other direction.

He heard the gunshot and nearly jumped out of his skin. Then another. He froze. What had happened? He manoeuvred his horse over to the side of the road under a tree. Had Claude come along? Were they after him now? He ought to get away while he could. But they'd said they'd get his horse for him. He'd be mad to go just yet. Those blokes might just have spotted a kangaroo and tried to gun it down. That was all it was, Freddy tried to tell himself.

Fear kept him there. Shaking in the boots Claude had sold him. Wishing he had stayed potato gardening. Those two men had looked well-heeled, like they were from boss families. Maybe even military. At last he heard them coming back, hoofs pounding on the dirt track.

'There you are! Here's your horse back,' one of the strangers panted, tossing the reins to Freddy as they pulled in their mounts. 'Never let the bastards get the better of you, old chap, or they'll become even more of a pest.'

'Got him with my first shot,' the second man crowed, waving his rifle in the air.

'You did not,' his friend cried. 'You missed! I got him!'

'Give over, Charlie! You couldn't hit an elephant at five paces.'

Got what? Freddy worried, his teeth chattering.

They were still arguing as they rode away without so much as a backward glance at him. He'd only been incidental in the sporting opportunity.

He watched until they disappeared, turning right towards the town, but still he waited, unsure what to do.

If they'd shot a kangaroo, they wouldn't just leave it, would they? Kangaroos were shot for their meat and skins. No one just left them to be chewed up by other wild animals. Too much of a waste.

It'd be good if they'd left it for Juno. He'd be pleased with it; the blacks only lived on bush tucker. He'd seen one cooking on their campfire, fur and all.

Freddy wanted to ride on, but curiosity was holding him back.

He had to have a look. See what had happened. A quick look. It wouldn't take long. If they'd got a kangaroo and left it there, wild dogs would be sniffing around soon.

As he turned back along the road that Claude had said was known as the Pound Road, come to think of it, his heart was thumping for fear of what he might find, but refused to contemplate.

The two horses were behaving now, trotting smartly, like kids that had just had their ears boxed, and Freddy figured the gunshots had given them something to think about. Something that had made their hair stand on end. Like his own. Like the crawly patch on the nape of his neck that was acting up right now, warning him to turn back. Get the hell back. But curiosity dug its heels in, keeping him moving forward into the slope and round the bend.

'You can't turn back now,' curiosity nagged at him. 'You've come this far! Anyway, do you want to go on never knowing what happened?'

'I don't know if I want to know what happened,' Freddy wailed, calling a halt to their progress, because there was something in the long grass ahead, and it had moved. No mistaking the old red flannel shirt Juno wore.

Terrified, Freddy slid down from his horse and crept closer.

Juno was lying on his back in a pool of blood, flies already buzzing round his soaked shirt and trousers.

'Did they shoot you, mate?' Freddy asked frantically, dropping to his knees. 'Did they shoot you?'

The large dark eyes were wet with tears, and a hand slid across the dirt to Freddy. It clutched his coat as Juno gabbled something in his own language. The only word Freddy could distinguish was 'Claude'.

'You want me to get Claude? Yeah. Well, I suppose you do, but Jesus, he'll lock me up if I go back.'

Juno groaned. 'Go get Claude,' he whispered, and Freddy groaned with him.

He climbed to his feet and stamped back to his horse, leaving the other one, bridle drooping, to its own devices. He was doing a very bloody stupid thing and he knew it, but he couldn't leave the poor bloke, the wild dogs would attack him.

'Jesus!' he yelped. 'They still could!'

On horseback now, he stopped to stare at Juno. He was a big fellow, he'd never get him on to a horse. But he'd have to try.

Down again and kneeling on the grass. 'Can

you get up, mate? Get on a horse?'

He saw Juno stiffen, trying to move, but then the blackfellow shook his head.

'Stick,' he said. 'Gimme stick.'

This time Freddy understood fast enough not to dither. He broke a stick from a fallen branch, leaving on the foliage, and gave it to Juno for protection. From the flies at least, he thought fearfully as he ran for his horse.

Soon he was hurtling down the road to get Claude, who would hitch up the wagon to collect Juno, he supposed. Country people knew about these things. Freddy wished someone had been there to help him; it was hard to know what to do for the best.

'If I'd had any bandages, I would have bandaged him,' he said defensively, 'but I didn't have nothing. I had to leave him, he wanted me to get Claude...'

Claude heard the shouting and yelling.

Freddy was back.

Claude thought he must have misjudged him as he ran up to the house, but Freddy rode on down the track to meet him, bumping about on the fast-trotting horse. He still wasn't much of a rider.

'It's Juno,' Freddy screeched. 'Juno's been shot! He wants you to come and get him.'

'What? Where?'

'Out on the road! He's been shot, I tell you. Hurry! He wants you to come and get him.'

In no time at all, it seemed, Claude had hitched a horse to the wagon and they were careering up the Pound Road, with Claude shouting out

449

questions and Freddy, sick to his stomach, scratching round in his head for answers. By his side was Claude's medicine box, a blanket and a bed sheet. A good bed sheet, Freddy noticed.

The horse had wandered away, but Juno was still there. Claude leapt down to him, tore back the red shirt to examine his chest and then tucked the blanket over him.

'Let's see the back,' he said softly, and gently rolled Juno towards him.

'Gimme the sheet,' he called to Freddy. 'We'll wind it round him. He's got two bullets in his back.'

'What bastards did this?' he asked through gritted teeth.

Juno shook his head. He did not know.

His whole body shook violently, and he groaned in pain as they lifted him, as carefully as they could, into the wagon.

'Claude,' he rasped, his voice a whisper. Claude bent down over the tailboard to listen to him.

'What did he say?' Freddy asked as Claude drove the wagon back to the farm, trying to avoid potholes in the road.

'He says he's going to die,' Claude snapped.

'Ah gee, after all that!'

'He also said I should be gone when he dies.'

'Why? You didn't shoot him.'

'He said his people will want payback.'

'I suppose they will. But I don't know who those blokes were.'

Exasperated, Claude hissed at him, 'You bloody fool. He's a sort of chief. They'll want big payback. They're likely to break out and attack farmhouses

450

and spear anyone in sight. Including me.'

'But you're their friend.'

Claude turned to glare at Freddy. 'Yes, I'm their friend, but that won't stop them killing me. So what do you reckon they'll do to you?'

Freddy almost leapt from the wagon at that. He'd never been so terrified in his life, expecting the savages to come at him with their spears from the thick bush crowding the roadside.

By the time they reached the house, Juno was dead.

Claude washed his body, wiped away the blood and dirt, and burned the rags that had clothed it, so as not to offend the eyes of Juno's people. He called Freddy to spread a clean blanket on the tray of the wagon so that they could place the long, lean body 'in state', to be taken home. Then he put fern fronds all round Juno, but left his body unadorned, in case he might commit some disrespect.

'It's the best I can do,' he said. 'Let's go.'

'Where?'

'We have to take the body to them.'

'Not me! No bloody fear.'

'Suit yourself.' Claude jumped up to the driver's seat, slapped the reins and took the wagon down the back track, past the stables and on until trees blocked the way.

He heard voices coming from the forest, muted at first, then rising to a wail, and guessed they knew. It didn't surprise him. They were deeply spiritual people; they had ways of learning things that had often astonished him.

The wailing was coming closer, accompanied by the rhythmic click of message sticks, and a white-haired elder, his body daubed with paint, emerged from the forest.

Claude stepped back, which was just as well, as the elderly black man strode forward on his spindly legs, making straight for the wagon.

He looked down at the body, brushed it with a bunch of aromatic leaves that he'd brought with him, then, without a word, slipped his hands under the naked body and in a swift movement gathered Juno up in his arms.

Involuntarily, Claude made a move to assist, but the old man had no need of him. His sinewy arms carried Juno effortlessly back to the forest, and the noise of wailing increased.

High in the trees a wind swirled into action, picking up the voices of the mourners and lifting them into a whirlwind of sound. In the centre of this vortex, and almost deafened by the clamour, Claude hung on to a wagon wheel as the pressure built, and felt himself gasping for air, suffocating.

Then it stopped.

His ears were still ringing as he collected himself and checked the horse to see if it had been affected. Apparently it had not.

Dismally he turned the wagon about and allowed the horse to pull it slowly up to the stables, where he began to pack riding gear he wouldn't need on the road. Then he walked round the back and nervously made his way into the forest to retrieve his money tin, thankful that it was still there. He wrapped it in hessian and planted it under a horse rug before making for the shed to collect what remained of his stores.

'What happened?' Freddy asked.

'Nothing,' Claude said dully. 'An old man took the body.'

'So it's going to be all right then?'

'If you want to stay here and find out, you can. I'm off. Thanks to you, I'm ruined.'

'Ay! Fair go! You can't blame me!'

Claude wasn't exactly ruined. He had a solid bank in that tin, and he owned land, a wagon and horses. But he was devastated that his friend was dead. Shot in the back! He planned to report the murder to the police. In the mean time, he had to blame someone, so he roared at Freddy: 'You good-for-nothing bastard! If you hadn't stolen my horses, this wouldn't have happened! My friend would still be alive! I ought to horsewhip you, you thief! You useless piece of shit…'

Freddy cringed under the weight of this tirade. He could feel Juno clutching his jacket, his warm breath on his face, and he heard him groan. Then he wept, knowing Claude was right.

'You have to do this,' Claude said to him as he pulled the wagon into a paddock next door to the New Norfolk police station. 'You're safe with your new papers. Just don't forget your name is Jack Plunkett.'

'You might be right, but who's gonna believe me? Those blokes was right toffs, you know.'

'They have to believe you because I'll back you up.'

'But shooting blackfellers? Settlers shoot them all the time. Bosses don't care.'

'I care!' Claude said firmly.

'So do I,' Freddy wailed. 'I'm just saying...'

'You talk when I tell you to. Now come on, let's get it done.'

The two Plunkett men, father and son, stepped up to the counter to report a murder, and the young constable on duty was all ears, grabbing for the day-book.

'Who got murdered?'

'His name is Juno. Of the Annabella Station tribe. Age about thirty. He was shot by two men...'

'Hang on, hang on! You're talking about a blackfellow?'

'Yes, he was shot,' Claude said. 'This morning. On the Pound Road. I'm the Pound Keeper.'

As of their departure several hours ago, this wasn't strictly true, but Claude needed that extra clout.

The constable grinned. 'When the natives look for trouble, they usually get it. What were they up to? Raiding a farmhouse?'

Freddy scowled, giving Claude a 'told-you-so' look.

'This man, whose name was Juno, was riding a horse back to the Pound, on my orders. Now write that down!'

'I can't write it down, mister, I have to put the crime in this column, and it ain't no crime to shoot blacks.'

'Since when?' Claude demanded.

'Since always, and you know that as well as I do, mister,' the constable said, closing the day-book.

'Is that right?' Claude dug a small notebook from his pocket and read from a cutting pasted

454

inside the cover. 'This is a proclamation by the Governor: "Any person that shall be charged with firing at killing or committing any act of outrage or aggression on the native people shall be prosecuted for the same before the Supreme Court."'

He glared at the constable. 'You got that, fat-face? Do you want me to read it to you again?'

'No, but...'

'What's your name? I'll have you up as well if you don't do your duty!'

Claude's threatening attitude astonished Freddy. He wished Singer could hear this. He grinned as the policeman grabbed his pencil and logged the charge, then began taking the statement dictated by the Pound Keeper.

'Get it right. I'll see you're charged with failure to adhere to the letter of the law if you leave out one word,' Claude warned.

'I'm trying, but you're going too fast for me,' the constable complained. 'Slow down!'

'All right. But here's the gist of it. My son here saw them ride Juno down and shoot him in the back. Each one fired one shot. Each one told Jack that he'd got him. And that was true. Juno had two bullets in his back.

'Now I was coming from the opposite direction and I saw this dastardly act...' he continued.

Freddy's eyes widened in awe at Claude's version of events, deciding it was a definite improvement on the original.

'...those two murderers didn't even stop to check on their victim, the poor blackfellow who'd been doing them no harm. They simply turned back towards the main road, passing Jack on the way, and boasting to him that they'd shot a nigger.

'Jack was shocked to the core, and raced to Juno's aid. I did too. Juno was wearing a shirt and trousers, he was bringing the horse back, and he definitely did not have a spear, so that proves he was peaceful. Innocent. We both knew him to be of good character. I'll wait until you get all that down, because right here I've got a description of the murderers that I wrote myself.'

He'd prepared that description on the road, nagging Freddy for every detail he could remember; yelling at him to think! Until his description of their boots gave Claude some heart.

'Definitely Royal Marines,' he said.

They waited until the constable had completed his task, then handed over Claude's extra statement.

'Who were they?' the constable asked. 'What were their names?'

Claude stared at him. 'If we'd known their names, we'd have told you.'

'Then who's being charged?'

'That's your job! Find them.'

'No it's not. It says here on this column, name of person or persons being charged, and you haven't given me any names. What am I supposed to write?'

'Who's in charge here?' Claude demanded.

'Chief Constable Hippisley. But he doesn't come here very often. This is only an out-station.'

'Then you be sure to show it to Hippisley. Tell him I want them found and charged.'

'All right.'

'In the meantime, learn something about your

456

bloody job! All right, *sir!*'

The constable sprang to attention: 'Yes, sir!'

Claude had thought that reporting the murder would make him feel a little better, but it had the opposite effect. If the police did happen to locate the shooters, they'd have their own story to tell, and Juno would become a common horse thief who had got his just deserts. And now Claude was left with this anger and heartache. Juno had been such a fine man; his death was a tragedy.

As they walked back to the wagon, Claude was already missing his home and his Aborigine friends. Once again, through no fault of his own, he had been uprooted and moved on, as if fate couldn't allow him to become complacent. As if he had no right to a decent life, a nobody like him.

But it was time to make a decision, so they headed for the sale yards, and sold the spare horse.

Then Claude turned to Freddy. 'Here's six pounds. That's what you're owed, and some. And this is where we part.'

'Part? Why? Where are you going?' Freddy was shocked.

'To Hobart.'

'What will you do there?'

'I don't know. I'll figure something out.'

'Why can't you figure something out somewhere else? You know I can't go into Hobart. That'd be pushing my luck, even with the new papers.'

Claude was adamant. 'You've got cash and you've got a horse, which makes you a damn sight better off than when we first met, so you're on your own now.'

'I thought we were mates,' Freddy whined.

'Juno was a mate of mine,' Claude rasped.

Once out on the road to Hobart in his loaded wagon, he looked back over his shoulder, checking to make sure Freddy wasn't following him. The long, dreary road was empty.

Eventually Hippisley saw the charges. 'Who are these blokes? The ones who shot the blackfellow in cold blood?'

'I don't know, sir.'

'You've got their descriptions. Did you make enquiries? Ask about?'

'No, sir.'

'Then get on it, man. Do your job. Don't sit here on your dud all bloody day. Criminals are not about to volunteer.'

'I haven't been sitting around. I've been busy, I had to get volunteers to help me. That tribe of blacks out on the Pound Road have been giving folk plenty of trouble. It's been bad. They're burning farmhouses. The Pound homestead's been burned down, and another farmhouse. Two men speared in the fields. It's been terrible, sir.'

CHAPTER FOURTEEN

Magistrate Grover Pellingham was furious. He hammered on the door of Sholto Matson's hotel suite and began shouting at Matson even as he opened it.

'You madman!' he roared. 'You have to drag me

into your cocky talk! Now I've been sacked!'

'I don't know what you're talking about.' Matson stood back, ushering him in so that the neighbours wouldn't hear his ranting.

'You know bloody well,' Pellingham shouted. 'The O'Neill case. What else? Look at this! A letter from the Attorney-General, informing me that my services are no longer required. Me? Chief Magistrate!'

'That's nothing to do with me!'

'Oh no? He instructs me I may yet have to face charges of exceeding my jurisdiction in a matter under investigation by the Colonial Secretary. "The matter of pronouncing sentence of death upon one Matthew O'Neill, while in custody." Do you think that has nothing to do with you? Nothing?'

He charged into the small sitting room, then turned back. 'You needn't think I'm waiting to state my side of the matter. I'm totally innocent of any wrongdoing, and I intend to appeal immediately.'

Sholto's wife Cora, a buxom girl with black hair cascading over her shoulders, stepped out of the bedroom, still in her night attire.

'What is going on?' she cried.

'Nothing my darling, nothing at all,' Sholto said, rushing to kiss her cheek and trying to edge her away, as Grover feasted his eyes on her voluptuous bosoms while he could.

'Doesn't sound like it,' she pouted, pink-lipped. 'What is it, dear Grover?'

Pellingham almost had palpitations looking at her in that skimpy, nigh-on sheer nightdress.

He'd been mad about her ever since Sholto brought her home from the bride ship.

'I've been sacked,' he gulped. 'Sacked! But I intend to appeal. I've come here to ask Sholto to speak for me.'

She was amazed. 'Sacked? What for?'

He tried to smile. 'Our lily-livered Attorney-General's shaking in his boots because he got some sort of a missive from London criticising him. So he takes it out on me. They only have to sneeze in the Home Office and he runs for cover.'

'What do they care in London?' Sholto shrugged. He wanted nothing to do with this affair. He had no involvement in Supreme Court matters.

'Apparently someone has sent all the details to the Home Office, all about the publicity it caused. He calls it notoriety. He has also been called to order for failing to act on the petition before the hanging.'

'What petition?'

'Oh for Christ's sake, Sholto! You remember the public petition asking that O'Neill's life be spared. It was addressed to the Lieutenant Governor, who passed it back to the Attorney-General, who didn't even bother passing it back to me, so the execution went ahead. Anyway, he's trying to make me the scapegoat. I was just doing my job. He never said a word to me about it, and now I've been kicked out to save his bacon.'

'I have to say I'm sorry about that, but what do you expect me to do?'

'Make a statement to say I didn't know about the sentence you gave him.'

460

'What sentence was that?' Cora asked.

Sholto smiled and about-faced her. 'Why don't you dress, dear, so that I can take you on a tour of Hobart.'

'Can I have a new bonnet?' she asked him.

'If there's one fit for your pretty head,' he simpered, and sighed as she tripped away with a bottom-waggling exit. 'Isn't she pretty? She was a music hall dancer. You should see her Dance of the Forest Nymph.'

Much as Grover would have adored to have seen that spectacle, he had more pressing matters in hand.

'I want that statement now,' he demanded.

'What can I say?'

'You can say that I knew nothing of the sentence you imposed.'

'But you did. I told you about it. I ordered him flogged and sent him on to you, on the other charge.'

'You never told me any such thing!'

'I did so. Over dinner that night. Don't try to kid me, Grover. You knew all right.'

'I did not. The only way I knew was when I read in the paper that you'd blabbed it in your court. You, you bloody fool. You told O'Neill – don't try to deny it, it's on record – "You will first receive a hundred lashes, then be handed on to the Supreme Court where you will be found guilty, get another whipping, and I have no doubt, be hung." You said that in your own courtroom. You caused the trouble. I thought all the fuss was over ages ago, but it has started again.'

Sholto sneered at him. 'Me? I was misquoted. I

461

never said any such thing. However, let us be clear. You made the decision to double up. You gave him another hundred, on top of mine. Whose fault was it then that he got two hundred lashes before he got hung? Yours! So don't come bleating to me. I only gave him a hundred!'

'O'Neill's sentence is on record. I'll have you up on a charge of perjury if you don't admit to saying you knew I'd sentence him to be hanged. I'll commence a civil action against you.'

'Listen to me, Grover. You're the one in trouble, not me. I only ordered a flogging! The correct sentence for his crime.'

'Before the hanging? Before the hanging, you said. You're equally guilty.'

'Of what? You're the guilty one. Now get out of here and let Cora and me enjoy our holiday.'

'Enjoy it while you can,' Grover snapped. 'The agitators are still out there, they'll get you too.'

'There's nothing to get me for. I'm doing a good job in Sorell. The Lieutenant Governor himself said so when he came to visit. And he leased me a fine house at peppercorn rates. You made your bed. You lie in it. And consider yourself lucky you don't get indicted yourself. I always thought you overdid it, but I suppose the Attorney-General wanted the whole thing hushed up, to hide the fact he recruited you himself.' He laughed. 'You're poison in high places now. Watch out *you* don't end up in Newgate.'

That afternoon, while Sholto went off to keep an appointment with some bigwigs, Cora was happy to do some exploring of her own. She wore her green wool jacket over a flounced black skirt, and a green velvet bonnet that allowed her long tresses to flow freely from the back. She stood out, she knew, among the dull folk here, and it pleased her. The convict women all looked like ragbags, and the female settlers were so drab you could lose them in a fog.

She primped her bonnet as she strolled towards the square, and caught the eye of an officer in the Royal Marines, a handsome one at that. He winked at her.

Cora giggled and tapped her rouged lips with a gloved finger, whispering: 'Naughty!'

Unfortunately he was escorting two women and had to keep walking, but it made her feel happier as she strolled around Salamanca. She'd hoped to marry one of those officers, but only plain soldiers were on offer when the bride ship docked, and she certainly wasn't about to get stuck on a farm as some fellow's free cook and bottle-washer.

As a matter of fact, she'd almost had to seek shelter at the dockside Female Welfare room, rather than accept any of the mangy-looking farmers who had been hanging around the ship's gangway when it berthed, hoping to score a wife. Of course most of the women on board would have accepted anyone, they were so ugly. But not Cora Chilton; she hadn't put up with months on that horrible ship to settle for the bottom of the barrel.

Then Sholto had come along. He said he hadn't been looking for a wife – lying, of course – he'd only been there to watch the antics of all the would-be spouses. A veritable circus he said it was. He said he was standing there laughing at Reverend Pilgrim, the gentleman who'd brought the women across the world to an island desperately short of females, who was acting like a circus ringmaster in his tall top hat, trying to stop two females fighting over one gentleman, when he'd spotted Cora. And on the spur of the moment had rushed forward to seize her arm.

If he hadn't been such a plain-looking gent, Cora pondered, it would have been quite romantic, but chinless wonder though he was, he dressed like a gentleman, top hat and frockcoat and all, and that took her fancy. That spelled money or a spiv, so without hesitation she instructed him to take his hand off her arm, and enquired, straight out, no mucking about, who he was.

When she heard he was a magistrate, no less, she couldn't believe her luck. Fancy having the law on your side for a change, she crowed to a friend, while her suitor dashed off to bring her bags ashore for her.

Within days he'd persuaded her to marry him and go with him to the little town of Sorell, where, he'd told her, he had a very handsome house. That was true, up to a point. The house belonged to the Government, but it was indeed a fine abode, and new. That was the best part. Cora had never encountered a shiny new house before and so was hugely impressed from the first day she'd walked in the gate. She'd fallen in love. Not with Sholto, but with the house...

She wandered into an alley that took her out of

the square, and found herself on the wharves – where she'd stepped ashore for the first time. But there were no shops out that way, so she turned back abruptly, becoming aware again that she was the centre of interest.

She smiled at a young girl who'd stopped to stare, but when the girl scowled at her Cora tossed her head in the air and swished past.

Bailey it was who first saw Shanahan headed for Salamanca Square, and almost didn't recognise him at first.

He hurried down to head him off. 'What did you do? Rob a bank?' he asked, taking in his new clothes.

'No need,' the Irishman laughed, 'I got my ticket at last, and the boss gave me a bonus. I always said the first thing I'd do was get myself some decent clothes, so I was Pollard's first customer this morning. What do you think of these trousers? Good stuff, eh? They're cords. The shirt's cotton and this here jacket, it's lined.'

'Yes, so it is,' Bailey interrupted nervously. 'Where are you going?'

'Into the square. Thought I'd start looking about for a job.'

'You can't do that,' Bailey cried, and Shanahan stared at him. 'Why not? Are you thinking I'm too much of a toff now?'

'No. The Doc wants you!' Bailey was improvising. 'Doc Roberts, he was here early looking for you. Said in case I saw you, to send you up to his house.'

'What did he want?'

'He never told me. You better get on up there. He might have a job for you.'

'What? Do you think he's an oracle? Knows I want a job before I do?'

'I dunno, Shanahan. Don't go if you don't want to. I'm just passing on the message.'

'All right, I'll go. But you keep your ears open and there's a penny for the tip-off.'

Bailey watched him head off up the hill, then turned back to find the crowd already turning ugly. The magistrate's wife had been recognised!

Still unaware anything was wrong, Cora stepped around a puddle and was making for a shop displaying embroidered tablecloths when suddenly a woman screamed at her and hurled a handful of mud.

Shocked, Cora stood for a minute, gaping at the splatter of mud on her jacket, but she wasn't one to take that lying down.

'You bloody bitch!' she screamed, and flung herself at the woman, whom she'd already summed up as a whore. A jealous whore! 'Can't stand decent people, eh?' she yelled as she knocked the whore's hat off and grabbed her hair. 'I'll give you mud if you want some.'

She yanked the woman forward by the hair, trying to dump her on the muddy ground, but the woman fought back, kicking Cora and scratching at her, while a crowd gathered, cheering them on.

Cora lashed out, trying to beat off the woman, who was punching and slapping at her, and wrenching at her hair, and all the while she could hear voices shouting encouragement to the whore.

'Good on you, Mae!' they were yelling. 'Get the bitch.'

No one seemed to care that the other woman had thrown mud first, and it confused Cora, made her angrier still. Her husband was a magistrate, she'd have the bitch flogged. With one last mighty effort, she grabbed the whore round the waist, twisted around with her to gain momentum, and shoved her away. The manoeuvre was successful. The whore stumbled giddily forward and fell on her face in the mud.

The crowd, reluctantly, cheered Cora as the winner, but as the whore began to climb to her feet, a constable and two other men intervened.

Immediately Cora turned to the constable. 'Look at me!' she yelled. 'My clothes are filthy. They're ruined. I want that fat ginger-headed cow locked up.'

The whore was sitting puffing on a bench, and nursing a bruise on her face, being fussed over by sympathetic bystanders.

Cora was furious. No one seemed to care about her. Only then did she realise she was the one in trouble, not the whore. She could see the menace in the faces surrounding her. A woman spat at her, another woman hurled her soaked bonnet at her, and that brought a bitter laugh.

Bewildered, Cora kicked it aside and shouted at the constable: 'Do something! They can't do this to me! Don't you know who I am?'

'All too well, missus. Now you come with me, quick.' He took her hand and backed with her into a shop. He hurried her right through to the back door and out into a lane, but Cora baulked.

'I can't go into the streets looking like this. You get me shelter somewhere and find me a horse-cab to take me back to the George Hotel.'

'Cabs can't come into this lane,' he said. 'We'll go down these steps on to the wharf and send someone for one.'

Cora was so angry, she felt like punching him too. It was all his fault! He should have arrested the whore first up, pulled her into line for throwing mud at a lady. Locked her up!

'Wait until my husband hears about this,' she fumed.

She sat down on the steps, refusing to move until the constable returned to tell her a cab was waiting. Then he had four convict labourers walk beside them for protection, as they hurried along the wharves to the cab.

The driver was far from impressed by her appearance. 'She got any money?' he asked the constable.

Hugh Merritt, proprietor of the newly renovated George Hotel, was standing outside his proud establishment, passing the time of day with friends and strangers alike. He was often to be seen there, but it wasn't by choice. He really didn't have the time, but someone had to guard the premises from unwanted guests, not a job he could leave to his dullard porters, or to the housekeeper, while his wife was far too busy running the dining room.

Unfortunately, he'd stepped inside when the cab arrived with Mrs Matson, and he was return-ing to his post when she scrambled out, tripped, and fell.

Hugh thought the bedraggled woman was drunk and, horrified, was almost ready to ban her from his elite premises when a neatly dressed man stepped forward, ignoring the laughter around him, helped her to her feet, and quietly handed her over to the hotelier.

'Mr Merritt,' the stranger said, 'I was wondering if you need a concierge?'

Hugh looked at him. 'I just might at that. Come on inside.'

'That woman's been in a fight,' the driver said, following them in the door. Then, in an aside, he said to Hugh: 'She'd be better not to go out no more. Folk have woke up to who she is.'

'I have not been in a fight!' she screeched, attempting to clout the driver for that remark. 'I was attacked by a convict cow, and someone stole my purse. And my new bonnet! Someone has to pay this driver. Will you do it, Mr Merritt? My husband will repay you.'

'Certainly, madam.'

She was in a state of outrage, bordering on the hysterical, as she blurted out what had happened. Eventually Hugh managed to hand her over to a maid to take her upstairs to her room.

His wife came out of the dining room in time to catch a glimpse of the angry woman.

'What happened to her, for God's sake?'

Hugh shook his head. 'I worried about letting them in here in case there was trouble. They're in the presence of enemies, my dear.'

'Why?'

'Because he and another magistrate sentenced

a man to two hundred lashes prior to his hanging three years ago.'

'That's horrible!'

'Indeed. There was great revulsion in the colony, but despite that, neither the Governor nor the legislature did anything about it. Nevertheless, a lot of people refuse to let the matter rest. Both of those magistrates are in town at the minute, so I thought there might be trouble.'

He turned back to the stranger. 'Now ... what's your name?'

'Claude, sir. Claude Plunkett.'

Sholto was in no mood to listen to his wife's complaints. He had come to Hobart to attend the annual meeting of magistrates, chaired by the Attorney-General, but there was only a clerk in his office.

'That meeting has been postponed. The Attorney-General is in Sydney at present.'

Sholto was furious. He would never have travelled all the way to Hobart, the location of his previous jurisdiction, had it not been mandatory. Indeed, last year he'd been treated quite shabbily by the Attorney-General, who'd excluded him from the formal dinner held at the George Hotel at the conclusion of events. He hadn't dared enquire as to why he'd been overlooked, though there was a possibility the O'Neill case might be bothering some spineless wimps in the department. Wimps who were the first to complain at the lawlessness rife in the colony.

There was nothing he could do about it, so he preferred to believe it had been a simple oversight, and left it at that. Though he hadn't dallied in Hobart.

'Why wasn't I informed?' he demanded now. 'Only recently I received this letter inviting me to attend. This is very inconvenient.'

The clerk scanned his letter. 'Ah yes. Mr Matson. I'm sorry about that, but according to my list you were scheduled for an appointment with the Attorney-General at the same time. All of those appointments have now been referred to the Colonial Secretary's office, on the ground floor.'

He made a note on his list, wrote a memo and handed it to Sholto. 'Just take this down to Mr Turnbull, the Assistant Colonial Secretary. He's expecting you.'

In the light of Pellingham's news, Sholto was not sure he wanted to hear what Turnbull had to say, but then again, with Pellingham out of the way, a promotion could be on the cards. He slowed on the stairs to sneak a look at the note he was carrying, and was infuriated to find only 'Matson' scrawled across it.

'Insolence!' he muttered, then screwed up the note and tossed it away.

He announced himself to the next clerk. 'Mr Sholto Matson, Magistrate of the District of Sorell, to see the Colonial Secretary.'

Turnbull himself looked up from his desk at the far end of the room. He stood. 'The Colonial Secretary isn't available. I wanted to have a word with you, Matson. Just step over here if you please.'

Sholto frowned – he'd never liked Turnbull –

471

but he stepped over and began with: 'I have come all this way only to learn that our annual meeting with the Attorney-General has been cancelled. Might I enquire who is to blame for this inconvenience?'

'I've no idea,' Turnbull said. 'Take it up with them. The Secretary has had correspondence from London to the effect that a Mr Patrick O'Neill, father of the late convict Matthew O'Neill, has brought the circumstances of his death to the notice of the House of Commons, and the Home Office is finding this matter a great annoyance.'

'It was Magistrate Pellingham–'

Turnbull put up his hand. 'Do not interrupt me, sir. Mr Patrick O'Neill has joined up with other noisy grudge-carrying persons who have formed radical groups to lobby against transportation at a time when we need more people to colonise this and other settlements in this country. Does this mean anything to you, Matson?'

'I am not responsible for events that take place in London.'

'No, but you are responsible for your actions in the courts. And the Lieutenant Governor has instructed this office to do something about the situation.'

'You mean I'm to be the scapegoat? O'Neill was hanged on Pellingham's orders three years ago. Three years ago! What difference does it make now?'

Turnbull tapped his pen on his desk impatiently. 'When the Home Office is pushed to cast a critical eye on this administration, we suffer. Pellingham

472

has been relieved of his position. And for your hand in this débâcle you will have your land grants rescinded.'

'What? That land belongs to me.'

'At the Governor's pleasure. You will return the papers to the Commissariat Offices at earliest.'

'But Pellingham gets to keep his?'

'Pellingham has already relinquished substantial holdings.'

'I'm innocent of any wrong-doing, Mr Turnbull. You must see that.'

'No you're not, Matson. Your remarks are on record, so shut up or you'll go the same way as Pellingham. I can tell you the Governor is fed up with this matter. You will vacate the house in Sorell. You have been relocated to Port Arthur, where you will act as Assistant Magistrate.

'Assistant Magistrate? I'm being demoted as well?'

Turnbull sighed, as if this interview were taking up too much of his time. 'As I said. Yes.'

'That's unfair enough, but I won't go to Port Arthur. It's a dead end.'

'Then submit your resignation. And be advised no other government positions will be available to you. We have to be seen to have taken steps. And we have. So be it. Will you take Port Arthur or not?'

Sholto shuffled unhappily in his seat, trying to think of a way out of this situation, but in the end he gave up. 'Seems I have no choice.'

'Your decision?'

Sholto felt his face flush with rage. They were making a scapegoat of him, and they were brazen about it. But he'd have to go to that dungheap until he could figure a way out of it. 'Very well,' he muttered.

'Good.' Turnbull's smug smile was further humiliation.

Outside, Sholto turned his collar up and pulled his cap down over his face, feeling like a convict on the run. He hadn't worried about coming back to Hobart, believing the fuss had long died down, but now he was nervous. Very nervous.

'You don't care what happens to me,' Cora shrilled back at the hotel. 'I could have been trampled to death by that mob for all you care, and you're not even listening to me proper. Just sitting there in that old chair sucking your knuckles. I want to go home. I hate this town.'

'I agree. We'll go, my dear. I am outraged that you should have been attacked. We won't stay here a minute longer than we have to.'

Cora looked up, surprised. 'You mean it?'

'Of course I do. I'll find out when the next coach leaves. As a matter of fact,' he added. 'I believe we'll be a lot safer at Port Arthur, where all the convicts are kept in order.'

She turned and gaped at him. 'What are you talking about now?'

'Port Arthur. I've been relocated to Port Arthur. We'll be moving there.'

'And leave my lovely new house? We will not!'

'The decision has been made, dear. We have to go there. It's really quite nice.'

'Has this got anything to do with that stuff you and Grover were talking about?'

'Of course not, dear!'

Cora frowned and wandered into the bedroom to stare out of the window. She'd eavesdropped on their conversation earlier in the day, and though as magistrates they sounded a right pair of bastards, it had happened before her time in the colony, and so could not be her concern. But now, despite Sholto wriggling round the truth, Cora realised the past was catching up with him.

'I'll wager that's why those convict bitches attacked me,' she muttered to herself. 'It looks like I'm as unpopular as a pong in a palace, thanks to him. And I'm going to lose my house. Well, damn you, Sholto, it's time I shook you off.'

Grover Pellingham retreated to his two-storey mansion at Sandy Bay. It was a rambling sort of house with a lookout tower that gave him a wonderful view of the bay and its surrounds.

When the fuss had started, and petitions flew about the town over the fate of O'Neill, his wife had been sent to Coventry by her friends. She was shocked that this could happen, and even more upset when she realised her husband was often given the cold shoulder, and had to suffer outright rudeness from the lower classes.

Despite his promise that this unfortunate situation was only temporary, and his insistence that he'd complied with the law in sentencing the fellow, Marigold had left him. She'd taken their son and gone home to her family in Manchester, with one trunk full of her personal belongings and another packed with the silver, and her husband couldn't have cared less.

Despite the aggravation of losing his land

holdings and his job, it was a relief to be rid of Marigold and the weeping that had set in like a monsoon. She was a boring woman at the best of times, and expensive. It was she who'd found this bayside acreage, well away from the rabble of Hobart central, and insisted he buy it, disregarding her husband's opinion that the land was a worthless backblock.

She'd employed an architect, airily dismissing Grover's misgivings about the cost by reminding him that convict labour was cheap, and ignoring the bills for imported materials and furnishings that were mounting up.

In the end, though, the house was completed, and they'd moved in to their new seaside abode.

Grover marvelled at the place! He'd been raised in the back streets of Manchester, never dreaming he'd one day come to live in such a fine house. He loved the place. He loved every polished inch of it. He called it the Retreat.

But the bills were overwhelming, and he lived in fear of having to relinquish this treasure.

Gradually, though, he began to push his bank accounts into the black by leaning on litigants. Very slowly, individuals who could afford it were made aware that a few words with Chief Magistrate Pellingham might prove helpful to their cause. At Marigold's excellent dinner parties gentlemen found the magistrate to be a jovial host, and over brandies in the comfort of his book-lined study to be a most accommodating fellow.

Not only were his debts washed away by the shake of hands, Grover also accumulated stocks on the best of advice, and he found another lucrative sideline that he called discretion, though the persons involved might see it as purchasing his silence, for few knew more of the seamier side of Hobarton than Magistrate Pellingham.

For her part, Marigold knew nothing of Grover's sidelines; she had no idea that many of their respectable guests came armed with petitions and sweeteners for Grover, and she was ecstatic that her lovely home, and the bounty of her table, had sent the Pellingham popularity soaring. She was proud to boast that they entertained businessmen, bank managers, graziers, a couple of solicitors and even a doctor or two, and their wives, and she cared not a whit for the vice-regal set, whom she considered a pack of snobs.

When her close-knit group of friends began to unravel, Marigold was devastated.

Her long dining table told the story only too well. To make their point, guests accepted her invitations but failed to show, leaving gaps that neither she nor Grover had the aplomb to overcome.

Word of their dismal turnouts gave a cartoonist the inspiration to depict Marigold and Grover in formal dress, sitting at either end of the dinner table lined with empty chairs, and with a huge plum pudding in the centre. Marigold was portrayed about to cut a slice of the steaming pudding, on which was written the word BOMB.

The caption read: O'NEILL'S REVENGE.

Marigold wept for days. No one came to console her. It seemed the world had turned against them. She pleaded with Grover to leave, for all three of them to return to England, but when he refused she left anyway. Her dreams had been shattered. She couldn't face the folk in Hobart any more, especially when she realised the enormity of Grover's callousness. She was glad he'd refused to leave, because he'd become a liability. Once her wealthy parents heard the true story, they'd have turned their backs on him too. Her mother was a member of the Prisoners' Aid Society, and what was more, Marigold sighed as the ship left the wharf, she was Irish. She prayed that cartoon would never turn up in London.

CHAPTER FIFTEEN

Half a year later, the cartoon did find its way into the *Dublin Chronicle*, with a letter of explanation from one Sean Shanahan. His Uncle Patrick was pleased, but by no means satisfied. He still wanted the two magistrates to be charged with torture.

But by then, many changes had taken place in the far-flung colony.

The day the cartoon was published in Hobart, Singer Forbes was in the hold of a coastal steamer being transported to Port Arthur.

Storm Bay was kind to the shackled prisoners, with only a gentle swell, and as they crushed together awkwardly to find room to squat, Singer laughed.

'It's like old times, lads,' he said. 'Just like the

lovely voyage from the old country.'

'We shoulda jacked up,' one man growled. 'There was more of us. We shoulda chucked them all overboard.'

Another challenged him. 'There are more of us here again, mate. Why don't you 'ave a go? Only a few armed guards and crew up there.'

'Yeah, you go first,' someone else laughed. 'Let us know when the coast's clear. In the mean time, Singer, why don't you give us a song?'

Happy to oblige, Singer led them in a few well-known choruses until the raucous singing and laughter brought a pounding on the hatch. When that failed to quieten the prisoners, two guards opened it and, in the sudden glare, stood menacing the crowded hold with rifles.

At that, Singer's fine tenor voice soared into 'The Last Rose of Summer', and any thought of confrontation subsided. All was quiet on the ship as passengers above and below decks listened to his song, to the last solitary note.

The guards withdrew and were immediately quizzed by Major Farraday, Commandant of Port Arthur, who happened to be on board.

'Who was that?' he asked.

'Prisoner Forbes, sir.'

'Good. Fine voice. I'll keep him in mind.'

'Here we go lads, we're being decanted,' Singer called as the hatch opened and they were all hauled up on deck, then lined up on the jetty to be marched away.

'Single file,' one of the guards called. 'Always

single file here.'

From the minute they climbed out of that hold, Singer began observing. He stood straight, and kept in line, but his eyes took note of his surrounds in meticulous fashion, almost inch by inch. They had come ashore on the beach of a small cove with a headland to the left and cleared land to the right with some sort of building in progress, while ahead of him the port rose to a village resting under gentle hills. All about there was activity – workers, marchers, haulers, some walking free, others in irons, and he guessed that indicated a pecking order of punishments. To his right loomed the penitentiary he'd heard so much about, but there was time yet to think about that place. Four men were ahead of them harnessed to a lorry, in place of ponies, he thought angrily, and as they passed he stared into their faces, on the lookout for friends, especially George Smith and Angus McLeod, but he did not know them.

As he watched, one of the men slumped to the ground, his face grey with pain, and his fellow workers hauled him to his feet by the harness he was wearing and draped him across a T-bar to give the appearance he was pulling his weight, though his feet were dragging on the ground.

The guards in charge of the new arrivals glanced at them and passed on by.

Singer was interested that there weren't too many uniformed guards around, which meant, he decided, that prisoners could be promoted to trusties here too.

They were quick-marched down a side road past rows of workshops – tailors, bootmakers, blacksmiths, carpenters, potters and others – and around a corner to a convict entry hall, to be categorised, Singer assumed. He stood in line reading various rules and regulations plastered on the walls.

'It's a pretty place, innit?' a young lad whispered to him, and Singer's response was a growl.

Of course it was a pretty place, he told himself angrily. It was a bloody beautiful place on this marvellously sunny day. Like the prettiest English village with the greenest lawns and all manner of flowers jingling by the roadsides, and all round glimpses of the ocean blue. But it was a prison, and he would not give it a kind word. They said that the notorious Norfolk Island convict prison in the Pacific Ocean was a beautiful place too. And a place of horror.

'We'll see,' he muttered.

'No talking,' a voice boomed. 'I am Chief Constable Toohill. You are the lowest of the low. You will do exactly as ordered, or suffer the consequences. All of you will work, idlers punished, hard workers promoted. You will work from six thirty to five and you will work hard, no slacking. Any disobedience of orders, turbulence or misconduct will be punished by the lash. Badly behaved men get the severest tasks, and will work in chains. Most of you will start off living in dormitories, they're our clearing houses, then we'll see who goes up and who goes down.'

At that several of the guards laughed. A local joke, Singer surmised grimly.

Toohill continued. 'Anyone not wearing the yellow, go to the end of the shed, strip off and get

481

in line for new issue. The rest of you, stay this end for sorting.'

Sorting meant identification, examination of records to separate violent prisoners from the rest. When Singer realised what was happening, he objected, as politely as he could, marching back to the clerk who made these decisions. 'If you don't mind my saying, I am not a violent man. I don't belong with that lot of bruisers.'

'Name?'

'Forbes, J.'

The clerk shuffled back through report pages. 'You were convicted of assault,' he said drily. 'Get back in line.'

'But I only shoved...'

A truncheon, familiar in its sudden placement, sent a shock of pain across his shoulders, and he stumbled back to the queue amid the grins and chortles of fellow prisoners.

'There's a good start,' one of them commented, and the guard with the truncheon wheeled about and slammed the speaker across the neck.

'God help us,' Singer muttered, when he saw the guard. 'It's Bull Harris.'

'Who's he?' the prisoner groaned as he nursed his neck.

Singer, his head down, shrugged. 'Lester Harris. A fellow convict. Obviously a trusty now. Got sentenced for violent assault.'

'Ah Jesus,' the other man said. 'Wouldn't you know!'

The next queue was for a medical, followed by decisions on the fitness of the men for hard labour. Singer's group earned hard labour automatically, so they were marched over to the entrance to the barracks and on to the inevitable dormitory.

The berths were two-tiered. Singer's new friend took the top bunk. 'I'm Lucas Grey, who are you?'

'Forbes.' Singer didn't mind the lower berth. Looking about him, he noted that the dormitory held about sixty men, the stone walls were whitewashed, the windows were high and half open, and kerosene lamps were attached to the walls. On each berth there was a straw palliasse, two folded blankets, a rug, and a cake of soap. The whole place was clean, and it smelled of sweat and phenyl.

From there they passed by a mess hall and along a corridor to be shown bathrooms, latrines and urinals, and the tour ended as they were released into a crowded exercise yard.

Singer surveyed it quietly.

'You get one hour here every day, if you get back in time,' a guard was telling the newcomers who bothered to listen, 'then it's dinner. The silence bell is rung at eight, the morning bell at five.'

There was an archway down the far end of the yard, gated with steel bars, and Singer noticed some of the men were gravitating towards it, so he followed. He was almost close enough to look through to the adjoining yard when he heard the scream, followed by the swish of a lash and more screams.

Abruptly Singer turned away, bumping into Lucas, who seemed to have attached himself to him.

'Someone's getting the cat,' he said, disgusted,

and Lucas nodded.

'Yes, they say that's the flogging yard. They get the flagellator on the job there at the same time every night, to remind prisoners of rules.'

Singer shook his head and walked away, needing to block his ears from those screams, but Lucas hurried off to watch the flagellator at work.

Dinner in the mess hall consisted of bread and a thin stew, and as he dug his spoon into a surfeit of vegetables Singer spoke to the man next to him.

'Isn't there something missing here?'

The man shrugged. 'We only get meat every second night, but be on time for breakfast: they use up leftover meat from the main kitchen and it's served first up.' He added: 'Over there in that barrel, they put apples in there sometimes, and it's first up again. But don't hoard 'em. You get caught with any out of the mess, you'll end up on that table by the kitchen door. Those blokes are on half-rations.'

'Thanks. The name's Forbes.'

'Yeah, I spotted you. I'm Jancy. You're a mate of Shanahan's, eh?'

Singer nodded, looking about him. These 'violent' men looked a hard lot, but they were all behaving like lambs. Their only shepherds were two guards, standing at the door looking bored. Or hungry maybe.

After dinner the newcomers were called up one by one and given their work rosters for the immediate future. Singer was rostered to the iron foundry.

'And you'll work in ankle chains until you prove yourself,' the guard added.

Now that the inmates had been fed, a guard patrolled the room, overseeing various activities: lessons had begun in reading, writing and numbers before a blackboard down one end; several men were busy repairing their rough clothes and battered boots, ready for the next day's onslaught; others sat around talking, or wandering aimlessly about. Singer noticed that several men had retired to the dormitory, so he headed for his bunk too. He'd already had enough of Port Arthur and its inmates, deciding sleep was preferable, but at the door he was challenged by a guard.

'Get to the barber, you! Regulations! Clipped hair. Clean-shaven. See to it!'

'Where?'

'Down the corridor.'

Only then did Singer notice the long queue of men waiting in the corridor to be shorn.

Lights out meant just that, except for the lamplight from the open doorway into the small guardroom at the end of the dormitory that shone all night.

Singer lay on his bunk, shivering under the thin blankets, trying to encourage his brain to entertain some pleasantries in order to discourage the stronger thoughts unleashing themselves.

Five years of this, and you've yet to see the worst of it. Is this a life? And if so, is it worth living?

Angus, in solitary confinement, had plenty of time to ponder the same thing, on account of the prisoner he'd replaced.

While he waited in the breezy annexe, they dragged out the former occupant, who'd just completed four weeks' solitary, and that was the most pitiful sight Angus had ever encountered. The man was naked and covered in excrement, but worse, there were gashes in his neck, and blood streaming from them, but the boss of the prison detail was unmoved.

'Will you look at this pig! Get the hoses on to him before I sick up.'

'Looks like he's been trying to tear out his own throat,' a trusty said, awed by the very concept.

'Yeah. They often try that,' the boss allowed. 'Clean him up and get him to the hospital.'

He turned to two other trusties standing by with buckets and mops. 'Don't hang back. Get inside and clean out the cell, we can't keep this customer waiting.'

'And you,' he said to Angus as they waited, 'you've got fourteen days on bread and water for mutinous behaviour. I see the flogger couldn't teach you anything, but trust me, mate, your very own cell will. Take a tip from me, don't bother tearing at yourself like that. It hurts, and it gets you nowhere.'

While he talked, Angus glanced at the entrance to the cell, noting the unusually thick stone walls and the low ceiling, determined not to show any anxiety, though his stomach was letting him down and he was shivering with the cold.

He refused to speak, to ask any questions, to acknowledge any of them as he was ordered to strip and walk in the door. Then he discovered that 'solitary' was actually a cell within a cell, and when the second door heaved shut there was no light. None.

Shocked, Angus felt about the walls, stepping over a palliasse, hoping to find some semblance of an aperture, even a crack that might give a sliver of light if encouraged, but there was only the slot for food, carefully locked on the outside. There were only two articles of furniture in the cell, the palliasse and a smelly wooden bucket.

Determined not to panic, Angus sank down on the mattress.

'As Singer would say,' he announced to his bed, 'there's only you and me then. We won't count that old bucket over there.'

He wondered why Singer had suddenly come to mind, supposing that given the same circumstances Forbes would remain cheerful. Giving cheek even if no one was listening.

'I never gave cheek,' he told the mattress. 'Everything that happened to me was too serious. Back home they just slapped the cuffs on me and dragged me off to jail. Never even let me see my parents.'

Angus leaned back against the wall but jerked away again quickly as his back came into contact with the cold stone. He was surprised at how soon, in utter darkness, one could forget nakedness. A bonus, he decided. One less thing to worry about.

'You forgot you were naked, my good fellow?' he asked, being Singer again, but then he backtracked. 'No, that wasn't Singer, that was me. I made a joke, I did. Oh aye, not much of a joke but I did. And the bloody bad part of it is they'd never believe me. Singer and Shanahan. They always reckoned my face would crack if I laughed. That'd show them.'

He considered sleeping, to while away the time, but decided against it. Dead against it. Instead he'd fight sleep; that would give him something to do, to help beat the bastards, because they wouldn't be wearing Angus McLeod down like they did that poor bugger they dragged out of here.

Angus McLeod would be going home one day. To see the parents and tell them off.

Suddenly he stifled a wail. Going home? God help you, why are you hanging on to that notion? If they wanted no part of a rabble-raiser, why would they let a rapist in the door? A bloody rapist. Convicted! He tried to imagine situations where they could welcome him, be pleased to see him, but nothing came to mind and the hurt welled to the surface again. He needed to rail at their unfairness, to make them realise how much he loved them. Even here, in this desolate cell, he could see their faces at the dinner table: Ma with the white crocheted collar on her black dress, a clean one every night; Pa with his collar missing, shirtsleeves rolled up, braces straining...

Angus jumped to his feet and wailed, because he could here. No one was listening. No one could possibly hear a sound through those walls, they were a foot thick if they were an inch. The wailing turned into railing as he yelled at them, berated them. Called them mean, despicable, cruel. Called them ignorant. Stupid. Prepared to put up with bosses who worked the life out of them and paid them pittances.

He told them, loud and clear this time, that he loved them, but he doubted now they had a loving bone in their bodies.

When he had finished ranting his throat was sore, but he felt all right. Talking about loving had reminded him of Penn. The girl he loved. Hated. But he decided to defer thinking about Penn for a few days. There were too many other things to worry about, like that job he'd had in the quarry. That hell, where men were lashed to make them keep moving, work harder and harder. Until they dropped.

That was wrong. He'd said so, of course. Called on the bosses to think what they were doing. But no one would listen. Finally he'd exercised his rights, as stated in Regulation 46: 'If a convict shall consider himself aggrieved by any order, he is nevertheless to obey instantly, but may complain afterwards if he shall think fit, to the Commandant.'

Once more he'd complained to the Overseer of Quarries that the loads he and the other men were expected to carry up from the quarry were too heavy.

As a result, he was ordered to work in chains.

As soon as he was able to scrounge paper and pencil from prisoners earnestly learning their letters, Angus wrote a formal complaint to the Commandant. He also pointed out that if workmen were treated fairly, quite a lot of bribery and corruption would be eliminated, since it was well known that overseers took favours in return for allotting less arduous tasks.

Angus was not naïve in these matters. He'd survived incarceration long enough to know there'd be hell to pay for anyone daring to make a formal approach to the Commandant, and he expected a swift and rough reaction. But he also knew that the few real bureaucrats in the administrative section, trained government clerks, would be wary about withholding the Commandant's mail, so he did have a sporting chance that his grievance would reach the right desk.

Apparently it did not get any further than Toohill, who bellowed at him in a police cell for insubordination, then claimed that the Scot had attacked him, and sent him to a magistrate, where he was sentenced to forty lashes, and removal to one of the many single cells reserved for the incorrigibles.

Back at the quarry, struggling to keep up, his blistered back ignored by the overseers, Angus put the word out that Toohill had stolen and destroyed his letter to the Commandant, and while this story (this tactic, as Angus preferred to call it) surprised no one, he hoped it would rise to the surface, where someone might take note. One of the military officers stationed there, for instance.

'You just never know who's listening in this closed community,' he told Jancy, who thought his whole plan was madness.

'Yes, and there's an island over there full of clever dicks,' Jancy said. 'You keep your head down and your mouth shut or you'll be joining them.'

Two things, Angus decided, were important in this cramped cell: exercise and mental agility; yet despite his vigilance he lost track of the days, and found rest more attractive than running on the spot.

But rest brought an overload of thinking. It brought self-doubt, and an admission that as an agitator for better conditions, here and at home, he hadn't had much success. He even queried his own motives.

After his first flogging – when he'd protested at the cold-blooded shooting of black people – he'd suffered horribly, but had kept telling himself it was worth it. And now that same voice was a disappointment, turning into a nag, claiming nothing was worth having your back turned to pulp. Not once, but twice. Especially when his protests achieved nothing.

After the flogging he'd been singled out by overseers intent on provoking him, until Angus had used his fists on a tormentor instead of his tongue, and given the magistrate no choice but solitary confinement.

'You'll never learn,' the voice said. 'Your mother knew. If she could see you now, she'd say it serves you right.'

'And I would too,' his mother said to him. 'Look at you. You're a disgrace! Not fit to be called a McLeod. What would they say in kirk if they heard you were lying naked in a dark cell like an animal. For a crime we pray they'll never hear about.'

She slammed the front door in his face and Angus wept.

The bread and water came and he called out to the invisible servant: 'What day is it?' But no answer came, and he sat down to eat ravenously and think of Penn.

What had happened there? It was hard to remember, to view the whole picture. He was becoming confused, remembering how his father had strapped him. And strapped him again for defiance, when he'd yelled: 'Didn't hurt!'

And strapped him again when he said it yet again, hanging on to a chair for support. But then he saw it wasn't his father, it was Jubal Warboy. And Angus wanted to kill him, but he was only a small boy and Jubal was a big strong man.

Instead of saving some for later, Angus drank the whole pint of water. Defiantly.

Lester had recognised Forbes straight away but he hadn't let on. Better to let the smart-mouth work it out for himself. Lester hadn't forgotten the way those town johnnies like Forbes had treated him on the transport ship, as if he was a country oaf, a nobody, and they were the top of the heap, when it was the other way round. He could buy and sell any of them. They were all dead poor, not worth tuppence, any of them. And criminals, don't forget – thieves, mostly; men he wouldn't spit on back home.

Yes, he nodded. Forbes would keep. He'd be interesting to watch, and it was worth taking a bet on how long he'd last here before caving in, and begging for mercy.

He lined up his detail of twenty prisoners, checked their ball-and-chain irons were correctly secured to their ankles – they could be nasty weapons in the hands of convicts – and sent them marching down towards the lime pits to begin work. No sooner had he handed them on to the pit boss than a runner called to him to front up to Toohill, 'Quick smart!'

Lester hurried up to the Chief Constable's office, nervously wondering what was up. For a while he'd been working on the farm, and only recently had he been made a trusty, which meant he was all over the place, more of an odd jobber, and that didn't please him at all. Prior to that, he'd been in the butchery, where he'd been able to run a trade with some of the officers, saving the best cuts for a few shillings here and there. It kept him sweet with the military too, so he hoped they'd have enough pull to get him back to his old job.

Hopefully Toohill would see reason.

He did! To Lester's delight, he was being sent back, but to be in charge of the butchery this time. He was to be the boss!

'I understand you were a farmer, so you'd know this work,' Toohill said, glancing down at a convict record book, open at Lester's page.

Lester clutched his cap. 'Yes, sir.'

'Can you write up the ledgers? I mean, the fellow they've got now has them in a muddle.'

I could have told you that. He couldn't add two and two, and he didn't know ribs from rump.

'Yes, sir.'

'All right then, we'll see what sort of a fist you make of it.'

'Yes, sir. Thank you, sir.'

Toohill sat back in his chair. 'Now, on another matter...'

Still standing at attention, Lester waited. This

493

was the first time he'd seen the Chief Constable without his police issue cap, and he looked different. He had very thick white hair and thick black eyebrows.

'The Commandant has instructed me to look into this matter, Harris. I have here a letter written by a Mr Baggott. A solicitor. Do you know him?'

'No, sir.'

'Apparently he is acting on behalf of your wife. Mrs Harris of Pinewoods Farm on Sassafras Road. Would that be right?'

If that's what it says in the letter, dummy. But go on, drag this out. I've got all the time in the world.

'I suppose so, sir.'

'Apparently you and your wife own this farm?'

'Yes, sir.' *What's going on here?*

'Apparently your wife wishes to sell this farm.'

'Is that what the letter says, sir?'

Toohill clutched the letter to him, as if a glimpse might release a state secret. 'I believe so.'

Lester was struggling to keep his temper. 'Was the letter addressed to the Commandant, sir?'

'No, it was addressed to you. But convicts may not receive mail, except from immediate family, with special permission from the Commandant himself. Therefore you may not read it. Baggott is not a relation.'

You pack of bloody clowns.

'Then could you read it to me, sir?'

'I have no instructions to that end. But the gist of the letter, made quite plain, is that your wife wishes to sell the farm as she is unable to manage it on her own. So she seeks your permission to

494

sell. Baggott says it is losing money.'

Get that smirk off your face.

'Can I speak, sir?'

'You can.'

'Well, between you and me, sir, I'm a good farmer. I had a large and successful farm back home. I hit a fellow who was trying to dud me, and then the magistrate, a jealous relation, had me transported. They thought they'd get my farm then.'

Toohill was interested. 'You don't say?'

'But I beat them. I sold that farm and bought one here. It's worth a lot of money, what with being well stocked and with all our good imported furniture.'

Ha, I thought that would make your greedy eyes gleam.

He continued, 'I had to put half in my wife's name so she could get on with the day-to-day management, you see.'

'Yes, I see. And now the farm's losing money?'

'That's what they say, but I don't believe it. Something funny's going on here.'

Toohill pulled his chair closer. 'Like what?'

'Farms on good land don't go broke here. Not with cheap labour. I mean, back home I'd have been a very rich man if I didn't have to pay farmhands.'

The Chief Constable nodded.

'So,' Lester said, 'I think I'd be mad to let her sell until I find out what's going on. Don't you reckon?'

Impressed to be asked for his opinion by this landowner, Toohill pondered the problem for a few minutes, his hands together in a spire. 'I wouldn't rush into it.'

'No, sir. Do they expect me to reply? I mean, am I allowed to reply?'

Toohill was confused. 'I have no instructions in that regard.'

'I suppose they want me to write yes or no on that letter and send it back.'

'That won't do. You are not permitted to see the letter.'

'What if I wrote no on the back and signed it? L.Harris, Esquire.'

Toohill blinked at that small flourish of ownership, and agreed.

'Thank you, sir. I'll let you know what happens. When this is over I'll make that farm one of the best in the district, you can bet on that.'

The letter was passed to him, face down, and he bent down to write a decisive 'No' under his signature and handed it back.

'Is that all, sir?'

'Yes. You may go. And I hope you do a better job at the butchery than the last bloke.'

Outside, Lester erupted into rage. He kicked at bricks bordering a flowerbed, sending them flying, and strode away.

What was that bitch up to? Sell the farm and run off with his money? Not a chance in hell. Run off with a lover, more like it. He must have been mad to trust her. At the time he'd been so pleased that he'd been allowed to view the farm before it was purchased ... the warders in Hobart being slack, compared to this place ... that he'd signed too quickly. But also it was going for a song – good pastureland that would have cost him a fortune back home, going so cheap he'd grabbed it fast.

Too fast, he now knew. But she wouldn't get away with it.

He went to the bakery with a trumped-up message from the Chief Constable that the ledgers had to be kept in better order, picked up a loaf of bread and ate hunks of it as he headed for his new job at the butchery.

That Toohill was so stupid. He'd let him get his answer on its way, but it hadn't occurred to him to ask the convict how he was supposed to find out what was going on at his farm. What was the truth of this proposed sale? Solicitor and all. Was that meant to intimidate him? Like hell it would.

As it began to rain, he took shelter under a big leafy tree to finish off the bread, noting that it was yet another of the non-deciduous trees found in this country.

'Bloody hell,' he muttered. 'Farming in this climate's a pushover, with good virgin soil and no real winter to put up with. Does she think I'm an idiot? Trying to tell me the farm's losing. She's been stashing the money away, I'll bet, and flat strap after the lot now. No half measures for the bitch. Who's she selling to anyway? No mention of that. The boyfriend probably. By Jesus, if she thinks she can get her hands on my farm she's got another think coming. But how do I find out what's going on there?'

He stormed into the large open butchery and started shouting at the five men working there.

'You listen here, you bastards. I'm the boss now, and you do as I tell you or you'll be on the docks in a flash.'

A big man in a dirty apron strode forward. 'Since when, Harris? Get out of here.'

'No, you get out, Flynn. Here are your orders. I want the butchery, the whole place, swabbed clean now, including that stinking office, so chop chop! Get moving.'

He clouted the young fellow nearest him to make a start.

Chief Constable Toohill sat twirling his thumbs. First one way and then the other. By the way Harris talked ... an experienced farmer, mind ... operating a farm with no payroll was next to minting money. He'd never thought about that before, being brought up the son of a bailiff. It never came into question back home in England. Well it wouldn't. But things were different here.

He could understand Harris being savage about the missus wanting to sell up.

'If I was him, I'd be suspicious,' he said to the boxer pup that had sidled into his office to sit by him – offspring and successor to the leader of the pack of dogs employed to guard the narrow isthmus that connected the penal peninsula with the mainland. 'I'd be wondering what she was up to if she's so keen to sell; she's even got a solicitor on the job. And if she can sell now, she could take the money and bolt, knowing it'd be years before he could come after her.'

He peered at Harris's record again. Sentenced for grievous bodily harm. Bad record on the transport ship *Veritas* – aggressive, disobedient, violent. Most recent crime: attacking another convict, James Quinlan.

That name rang a bell. Quinlan. Ah yes, he knew Quinlan. Got transported for seducing a magistrate's wife. That was the joke of the Hobart Penitentiary when he was stationed there. But one of the new magistrates had recognised him as a former sailor turned pugilist who'd killed a man in the ring in London. A matter hushed up by well-known gentlemen of naval fame.

Tom Toohill grinned. 'Our man Harris here, he bit off more'n he could chew that time, pup. It's a wonder he didn't get his block knocked off.'

He lit his long-stemmed pipe and sucked on it thoughtfully. What if his missus is so dead keen to sell, she'd get rid of this beauty of a farm at bottom money? A man might get a good cheap buy here. And get rich like the military men do. That'd be something. That'd really be something!

But Harris won't sell.

Toohill sighed, his pipe dream of the good life on a money-making farm slipping away.

Nevertheless, he'd keep an eye on the Harris situation. He might even be able to help. For a price.

Two days later he stepped into the butchery, pleased to see clean floors, scoured chopping blocks and a muslin curtain at the door to keep out flies. There was no sign of the usual hanging carcasses, but Harris, who came out to greet him, said they would be kept in a cooler room from now on.

'I've got butchers in the back room sorting and packing the meat for all the different establishments, but it's a big job. It should be done in the slaughter-house, instead of dragging the carcasses here. We should only have meat for the private quarters here, like a normal butchery.'

'Yes.' Toohill shrugged, not the least interested in where the meat was sorted. 'I sent your response to the solicitor via the Commandant's secretary. It should reach its mark in a few days. Then it occurred to me that I'll be on leave in a week or so. I could, without breaking any rules, enquire about the proposed sale of your land.'

'It would be appreciated,' Harris said. 'By the way, I've got a spare side of lamb. Maybe I could send it over to Mrs Toohill's kitchen?'

'She'd like that,' the Chief Constable said.

Within a week Tom Toohill was in Hobart to attend informal discussions with Chief Constable Hippisley on their shared responsibilities. They exchanged the names of prisoners awaiting transfer to Port Arthur, and Hippisley took note of the prisoners who would be returning free men, hoping they'd learned a craft or skill over the years that would help him find them employment.

Tom Toohill thought Hippisley carried on too much about freed prisoners having no money and no shelter, but he promised to have the information added to their discharge papers to please the other man, who hadn't been too happy to have their meeting brought forward by ten days.

Having disposed of that duty, Tom went to the

police stables for a horse and later that day could be seen, if anyone had bothered to notice, riding past Pinewoods Farm, not once, but several times.

He was most impressed by the garden, behind which he managed a glimpse of a low-set stone cottage with black shutters. It was quite a large cottage, not as grand as several other farmhouses along Sassafras Road, but it appeared to be comfortable and well kept. There were sheep in the meadows beside the cottage, and back into the distance more fields were under crops, maize by the looks of it, but he couldn't be too sure. In all, prospects were good, and judging by the unpretentious cottage, it wouldn't be an overly expensive farm. And mind you, he speculated, as the horse trotted quietly toward home base, if it's losing money, it'll have to be going cheap.

That was all the information he needed. He'd seen the farm, he could now report to Harris.

A good day's work!

'Watch out for Forbes,' Harris told trusties and job bosses, as he encountered them. 'He's dangerous. Don't turn your back on him, he'll lay into you first chance you give him.'

Though he wasn't aware of it, his warnings pointed fingers of interest towards Forbes, from men who had no time for Harris. They saw a mild fellow with a sharp tongue who managed to keep up with his workload. They agreed that Forbes, known to many as Singer, did his job, and, like the rest of them on hard labour, was full of gripes. The only difference being that Forbes could be

501

outrageous at times.

'The things he comes out with,' a gang boss said. 'You have to bloody laugh.' And there it was. Singer amused his mates and his bosses. They came to understand that no one was safe from his ribbing, but they mostly enjoyed his savaging of the big bosses. Especially the regimental officers and their wives.

Someone remembered Harris's warning, and asked Forbes slyly if he knew the trusty.

'Harris? Aye, I know him. Knew his dad too. I used to visit him in the London Zoo. Took him bananas. He loved bananas.'

Sometimes they'd ask him to sing, but he told Jancy: 'I pushed a vicar and got sent here. That's bloody unjust. I wish I'd kicked the bugger's head in to make this place worth it. I sang my last note on the boat coming here. We're not allowed to protest, but I can, my protest is no singing. Who'd want to sing in this hell anyway? They're killing us with this hard slog. I see men dropping in their tracks every day. It's all I can do to stay on my feet and stay sane.'

Jancy nodded. He was ten years older than Forbes and he knew he couldn't last much longer cutting sleepers for the railway line. But he was a lifer. On hard labour. He'd killed a guard back in Hobart on his first escape attempt. He was thinking of making a run for it again, now that he was out of irons. This was one of the few jobs where it was impossible to work in irons. There were ways. They all failed. They either got caught or they drowned. Maybe got eaten by sharks. But they might have made it if luck had stuck with them. Jancy figured it was about time he had a share of that elusive luck.

Luck was out for poor Lester. When Toohill returned, he had nothing but bad news. He'd made enquiries and found that Pinewoods Farm was a flop. Couldn't pay their bills.

'Looks run down too,' he was able to add, from personal observation. 'I'd recommend you tell her to sell. Get what you can and keep it safe in the bank until you get out.'

'I'll think about it,' Lester said dismally. 'Thank you, sir.'

'Good. Let me know if you change your mind. We like to be able to help when we can.' Toohill fingered the silver buttons on his uniform jacket and glanced past Harris. 'That's a fine-looking saddle of beef there. Be a good fellow and send it up to Mrs Toohill.'

'Yes, sir.'

Lester was angrier still. It was Josie's fault. She'd let the place run down, the stupid woman. Well, it could run down. He wouldn't sell; a farm was land, and land was money. When he'd done his time here, he'd work the farm himself, employ convict farmhands and beat hard work out of them – put it on its feet again. So why should he worry if it wasn't earning? There'd be no sale, they could stay there, and if she and the girl were too stupid to at least grow their own food, then they could starve.

Toohill was an idiot. 'It just goes to show what sort of fools are running this colony,' Lester muttered. 'He would sell a place and tell his wife to bank the money for him. Boots for brains! No man with any sense would fall for that one. Especially not me, Mrs Harris, so stay home and stop wasting money on solicitors.'

When he was shutting down the butchery that afternoon, Lester saw Forbes in a line of chained prisoners dragging home from work, and called out to him: 'Not so bloody smart now, Forbes.'

But there was no reaction. Forbes looked right through him as if he hadn't heard a word. As if he didn't recognise who was addressing him either, but then Lester remembered something else. He had another arrow in his bow.

'Hey,' he yelled, louder this time. 'Did you know your mate McLeod's in solitary?'

That did it. He saw Forbes stiffen, off his stride for a few steps, and then keep on, trying to pretend he hadn't heard.

Lester laughed, and turned away.

Funny thing about these work gangs, Singer thought. On the way home, lightning could strike the man next to you and you'd just keep on going, step by bloody step, to make it to the end of the day without collapsing. And that was how it was now. They all trudged on, the day's addition of blisters, calluses, splinters, cuts and bruises only minor irritants for exhausted bodies craving rest.

Lester's jibe had had as much effect on Singer as a moth's flutter. He'd been hobbling along with a sprained ankle earned hours ago, so the news of Angus being in solitary didn't upset him. Right at this moment he'd give his last shilling, if he had one, for the luxury of solitary. There'd be

504

time to think of Angus later.

At least he was in a single cell now. A normal cell. Better than chancing on strangers. And it was his turn for a bath tonight. That'd help the ankle. Soak the poor thing; give it a rest too. He pictured the bathroom queues, where a guard took note of any dodgers. Was there anywhere else in the world, he wondered wearily, where a man could get the lash for avoiding his weekly bath?

The men on hard labour ate their meals in the mess with hardly a word, resenting the noise around them, so Singer was quiet, rejuvenated a little from a soak in the tin tub. Only then did he remember to ask about Angus.

'The skinny Scot with the ginger hair?' a guard asked. 'Yes, he's in the bin.'

'When does he come out?'

'How would I know?'

'Can you find out for me?'

'Cost you.'

'Go to hell.' For good conduct, prisoners were awarded credits of twopence a week, or two ounces of tobacco. Singer valued his tobacco too much to have a guard prise it from him. He'd find out for himself.

Angus was having that dream again. That he was in his grave, buried alive. But he'd stopped shouting, because no one could hear him. He knew that now. They'd all gone. Weeks ago. He knew he wasn't dead because of the pain. It had moved from his back to his jaw, and become excruciating. But it was keeping him alive. He was afraid that when it stopped, that would be the end. Then there would be nothing. Just the silence of the graveyard. He wondered where it was. Somewhere in the scrub outside Hobart, he supposed. Then he remembered the Isle of the Dead, and knew he had to be there with all the ghosts. With Matt O'Neill.

But Matt O'Neill is dead. Really dead. You're alive! You can't walk around in a coffin. Wake up to yourself. You've been dreaming.

'I might as well be bloody dead,' he growled. 'How long have I been in here? Weeks! The bastards have forgotten me.'

He banged on the walls, shouting at them that he was still in here, but gave up after a while, realising it was useless.

He began running on the spot again.

When they pulled him out, Angus was quiet. They'd won. He had to obey the rules of this prison or he'd not survive, and he had to survive. He had to find out who had raped Penn. Find the rapist and kill him. Port Arthur was different, he now knew, from the Hobart prisons, where rules didn't apply half the time and daily life was often a matter of luck. Well, luck didn't enter into this world.

As he walked out into the hall, the glare struck him like a blow, but the guards were obviously used to that reaction. They began to examine him, a humiliation Angus, in his nakedness, ignored.

'His back's covered in sores,' one of them said. 'And he's got a fever. What's happened to your jaw, mate? Give yourself a bash, eh?'

'No,' Angus mumbled. 'Toothache.'

'Ah. That'd account for the fever. Dress him and take him to the hospital. But give him a hose-down first. He stinks.'

Once out on the road, weak from lack of sustenance, Angus stumbled every so often and the guard cheerfully helped him up. Holding the chain attached to Angus's ankle, amiably chewing tobacco like a cow with its cud, he didn't seem to mind their slow progress, while Angus was treasuring every minute of the sunlight, needing its warmth and strength for reassurance that he was back in the land of the living again.

They passed the impressive church, and then he noticed an attractive cottage with a wide wrap-around veranda, set in a trim garden.

'Is that the Commandant's house?' he asked.

'Nah,' his guard said. 'The Commandant lives in a better house, up the hill there. Up by the semaphore tower. This one's where visiting bigwigs stay.'

'Lucky them,' Angus commented. He was paying attention now, anxious to learn more about his surrounds. They passed the main kitchen and the butchery, tramped up the hill past the civil officers' quarters, and he was able to observe the military barracks overlooking the hospital. He hadn't been up this road before.

'The buildings over there. What are they?'

'More prisoner barracks, the infirmary, and the lunatic asylum. The one with the high fence is the loony cage.'

The hospital looked to Angus more like a

convent than the stark hospitals back home. It was a sturdy brick building set on the green hillside; two-storeyed, with high arched colonnades that reminded him of cloisters. The roof was turreted, and Angus marvelled at the view they must have from up there.

Nevertheless, he was frightened of hospitals, and baulked as he was being led towards the front steps. 'Do I have to go in there? Why can't you take me to the infirmary?'

'Because you got a fever. You're sweaty. Rules say fevers to hospital, they could be catching. Anyway, the fang-snatcher's here in the hospital. In you go. You'll get a feed here.'

'I could do with it,' he muttered. He'd almost become accustomed to the sharp stabs that emanated from his arid stomach, but the effort of that walk had drained him. His legs were suddenly wobbly and he dropped to his knees.

As he was hauled to his feet and carried to a bed in a long dormitory Angus was only too aware that, after all this time, he was back where he had started, as sick and feeble as he'd been the day they'd cast him ashore from that evil ship *Veritas*.

'He's hungry, can he have some dinner?' the guard said to a trusty wardsman. 'He's been in the bin.'

'Too late. Kitchen's closed.'

George Smith was finally getting the hang of the place. With more than a thousand prisoners penned down at Port Arthur, it wasn't surprising that he'd come across men he knew at various times, but his face was so scarred from the burns they rarely recognised him. Bull Harris was one of those, and that was a good thing, George told himself, keeping his distance. Another time he'd glimpsed Angus McLeod, but didn't have a chance to speak to him.

When he'd first arrived here, he was sent straight to the hospital, suffering from dysentery as well as from the still-suppurating burns.

The matron lodged an immediate complaint that a man in his condition should have been sent to Port Arthur, but she did her best for him. After a few days she stopped to talk to the bulky man who only just fitted on the narrow bed.

'How are you keeping, George?'

'Real good,' he said, and she smiled. Nurses and wardsmen alike had commented that, despite his pain and discomfort, George never complained. 'Real good', they'd told her, was his stock answer to their enquiries.

As a result, she allowed him to stay a few extra days, knowing that a man his size would be needed in the fields of hard labour as soon as he was released from her care.

His crime was recorded as absconding, since he was not residing at the correct address when apprehended, and since this offence was committed in the colony, he automatically became a second offender with a mandatory sentence of two years at Port Arthur. On his release from the hospital, he was designated non-violent, and entitled to a separate cell in D barracks, a profound relief for him.

These cells were of a higher standard and better

kept than the old Hobart prison he'd endured before earning recognition as well-behaved and being assigned to Lieutenant Flood's farm, so he settled in quickly. A mild man, he knew it did no good whining.

In the mess, he made some friends, and warned off would-be comics, who thought he was retarded because of his disfigurements, not to push their luck.

For the first two weeks he worked with a gang clearing bush on the outskirts of the penal settlement, and then he was chosen to join a logging party, felling big timbers further inland. They were told by the bosses that this work was important. They would be cutting trees for the timber mills, and each day, certain trees would be marked for felling.

Unimpressed, George and his fellow workers lined up the next morning for the march to wherever these stands of timber were located, with one man whispering that they ought to chip the logs, sabotage them so they couldn't make money for the bosses. It was then, and in later talks with his mates, that George learned that convicts were also being used here to produce saleable goods. But of course he never said anything. It only made him smile; reminded him of Shanahan.

But what did make them all smile was the location of the timber.

It was at Eagle Hawk Neck! The isthmus, the slim causeway that connected the prison settlement to the mainland, with the sea lapping at either side.

They first saw it as they came over the hill,

510

unmistakably the famed exit ... from their point of view. On the other side were guards' quarters and a wide clearing, with the forest beyond, pushed well back. Anyone approaching from either side would be seen and intercepted by the guards well before they neared the causeway.

But to make doubly certain, five tall poles in the shape of gallows were lined across the causeway on the prison side. At first they seemed simply fierce warnings to convicts of the dire consequences of attempting to escape across this no-man's-land, but a closer view allowed the convicts to see for themselves that the rumour of savage dogs guarding this exit was true.

The dogs were already barking furiously at the approaching work gang, straining at chains attached to the poles. No one could hope to slip through the line of dogs without injury. Nor could they attempt to swim the shallows without the animals raising the alarm, day or night.

Guards came down to lead two of the dogs aside so the work gang of twenty men could pass by, but even then the newcomers were nervous, telling the guards to be sure to hang on to the snarling, straining animals as they hurried by.

It was an experience, the convicts all agreed. Interesting, and deeply disappointing.

George had confidence in Willem. They'd been friends for a long time, and they would stay friends. One day, in years to come, George hoped he'd run into Willem again so that they could have an ale or two and talk over old times. He'd accepted his situation now and he expected no more of his friend. Willem, he mused, should go home. He could afford his passage, and would have the joy of being reunited with his father, who had turned out to be a real gent, forgiving his son for getting into bother. George thought that would be a really good result.

As for himself, he was doing better than he'd hoped in this jail, and he'd be out in a few years. Then he would get himself a real job as a tree feller. A couple of the men he worked with now were experts, this was their trade, and they were teaching him. They kept saying: 'There's an art to it!'

Even the guards agreed. They told the new axemen that if they didn't learn the art, the big bloody trees they'd be felling now would most likely fall on them and kill them.

But Willem Rothery had not gone home. He felt he owed it to George to try to help him escape, and to make a start, he decided to go exploring.

With a full pack of provisions in case he became lost in the bush, Willem rode out into the countryside, fired up with enthusiasm for this adventure. He studied his map carefully, rode inland, crossed the Derwent, and travelled north along a surprisingly busy road for several miles or more until he came to Richmond.

This, he found, was a pleasant village with some charming houses on large estates, but he shuddered when customers at the local inn showed him the large prison complex that dominated the area.

'It has walls a yard thick,' they told him proudly.

In answer to their amiable questions, he said he was thinking of buying a property hereabouts, and that elicited quite an amount of information about the district, its climate and so forth.

But, pleasant though it was, Willem did have a destination, so the next day he rode south-east towards the coastal village of Sorell, disconcerted to be passing gangs of convict road workers.

By this time it was evident to him that this was no bush track; rather it was the overland route to the infamous Port Arthur, and it was well used. For some reason, foolish he realised now, he'd imagined that all traffic to the penal peninsula would have been by ship, but nothing of the sort. As well, this was farming country, mostly wheat, and Sorell itself was a garrison town. And the centre of bushranging activities.

Intimidated by the uniforms that paraded the narrow streets, Willem decided to take refuge in the comfortable, but expensive, Crown Inn. He signed the lodgers' book, Willem Rothery, gentleman, and was escorted upstairs to a front room overlooking the bay, which was exactly where he needed to be.

'The expense paid off,' he murmured, pleased with the outcome.

As soon as the door closed behind him, he took out his map, surveyed the view and contemplated the distance between this little port and the tip of the penal peninsula. He was trying to locate an accessible place as close to Port Arthur as possible. To date, people attempting to assist convicts to escape from that prison had set off from the mouth of the Derwent River, planning to pass by several islands and sail across Storm Bay.

'No wonder they all failed,' he said, remembering that some had drowned and quite a few had been apprehended before they were anywhere near Port Arthur.

'And probably ended up imprisoned there themselves,' he added grimly. He wanted to do what he could to get George out of that place, but he would not take foolish risks. This expedition was simply to investigate possibilities; to learn about the coast and the terrain they'd have to deal with. As he'd told himself, 'The map only gives directions. I don't want to blunder into swamps or unscaleable cliffs.'

So far, the land was flat enough not to throw up hazards, except of course the bush. Virgin bush, he'd learned, was almost impenetrable without axes and hard work, but there could be foot tracks made by fishermen or natives.

After fortifying himself with a meal of baked fish and a pint of cider, he took himself for a walk along the seafront and, visualising the map he dared not produce here, saw that it would be possible to reach Port Arthur from here in a rowboat. Better still, a few miles down the coast was Dodge's Ferry, another fishing village.

Innocent travellers didn't lock themselves in their rooms, he told himself back at the hotel, so down he went to the saloon, which was crowded with bearded bushmen and the inevitable uniforms.

No sooner had he stepped up to the counter and ordered an ale than an officer clapped his hand on his shoulder.

Willem's heart banged in his chest, but he managed to stay calm as a voice boomed: 'Mr Rothery. I say, sir, would you be any relation to Colonel Rothery, of the Royal Engineers?'

'James Rothery?'

'Yes!'

'He's my father, sir.'

'Oh, jolly good! Fine fellow. Great friend of my late papa, who always spoke highly of him. Do join us here. What are you having? An ale? Jolly good. Put it on my bill, bartender.'

He introduced himself – Neville Gilpin, Major – and Willem was suddenly swept into the company of seven officers who were already fairly drunk but in high spirits since, as far as he could ascertain, one of their number had recently become engaged to a local lass, who would be contributing a considerable dowry to the union.

Deciding that their company was as good as any, when one didn't wish to be standing about alone, inviting interest, Willem summoned some party spirit of his own, and was progressing well when he thought he spotted someone he knew among the bushmen in a corner of the smoke-filled room.

The man had matted hair and an untidy growth of beard, as if he couldn't make up his mind whether to grow the full measure or shave it off, so it was hard to distinguish him, but the eyes – the eyes were familiar. Several times Willem glanced over, but the fellow had turned towards his mates, then Willem, still unable to place him, saw him threading through the crowd, making for the exit.

At the same time as he recognised the man, Willem saw him lift a stranger's purse from his jacket and, moving faster then, disappear out the back door.

'Oh no!' a voice inside him yelled. Quickly he excused himself and headed out the back too, in time to grab Freddy Hines before he reached the horse tethered nearby.

'Ah no you don't,' he snapped. 'Give me that purse!'

'What purse?' Freddy began, then he beamed. 'Well blow me down! Willem! What are you doing here?'

'Never mind about that. Give me the purse!' Willem knew that if someone in that saloon was robbed, strangers like himself would be the first to come under suspicion.

He finally prised the purse from Freddy by threatening to point the finger at him, and left him in the yard, complaining bitterly. Once inside, he pretended to find it on the floor, held it up and asked who owned it.

The owner took it gratefully, offering to shout him a drink, but Willem went back to his new friends who, fortunately, were bewailing the fact that they had to leave to attend a dinner party somewhere.

'Meet me here tomorrow, Rothery,' the major said. 'I'll show you around. Not a bad place, a few things to see. At nine, eh?'

'Very well. Yes, thank you.'

Willem watched them depart, then hurried out the back again to find Freddy who was still there, sitting on a timber fence, smoking a clay pipe.

'Wotcha have to do that for?' he demanded. 'I never done nothing to you.'

'You could have had me arrested.'

'Why? What have you done?'

Willem sighed. Conversations with Freddy were always frustrating. 'Nothing. And I want it to stay that way. I'm here on business, Freddy–'

Freddy's hand went up. 'Wait! You're wrong there. My name is Jack Plunkett, and I've got papers to prove it.'

He slid down from the fence and produced his papers.

Willem was astonished. 'They look real,' he said. Interested.

'They are real. A mate of mine got them for me. None of your forging for my mates. They know what they're doing. These papers are the class.'

'I'd say they are. Where are you living?'

'Here. Here in this town.'

'Why?'

'I ran out of road. You can't go no further than here. Then some bastard stole my horse. Left me stranded like a pig in mud.'

'Pigs quite like mud.'

'Who says so?'

'Never mind. So what do you do here? Have you got a job?'

'Course I got a job. They don't let convicts hang about in this town, the bloody troopers run 'em out. They chase 'em back down the road with whips! Too close to that prison island! Jeez, I'd never have come this way if I'da known what's down the end.'

'What's your job?'

517

'Didn't I tell you? I'm the yardman here. Got a cabin out the back and all. Bugger of a job it is too!'

Willem didn't believe any job would please Freddy.

'I've got to get inside for dinner before it goes off,' he said, and Freddy was astounded.

'You're staying here?'

'Yes. I told you, I'm here on business.'

'All right for some people.'

'I'm a free man, I can do what I like. But I'd rather you didn't let on you know me.'

'Not good enough for you, aren't I?'

'Just see you behave while I'm here,' Willem warned, 'or they'll find out who their yardman is.'

Freddy scowled. 'Don't be like that. I thought we was old mates. I wonder you don't go home to England now you're free.'

'Nothing to go home to,' Willem lied.

'Who has?' Freddy sighed.

As it turned out, Neville Gilpin was excellent company. He was ready and waiting at the appointed time, and suggested he escort Willem on a tour of the area.

'I can assure you there are truly scenic views, and also some natural wonders I may be able to show you, all being well.'

'That's very kind of you,' Willem said, smothering nerves.

'Not at all. I should quite enjoy a leisurely ride on a fine day like this. Reminds me that such pastimes still exist.'

They rode out of Sorell, heading further east

towards the coast.

'Someone told me back there that the town of Sorell is the end of the line because this road leads to Port Arthur prison,' Willem said.

'Not quite. We can go some miles further.'

By midday, after a few detours to inspect native flora, they came to a fishing village called East Bay Neck where there was a small guard post. Willem had already noted it on his map, so it was exciting to find himself right there, on the spot.

'That's the road to the prison,' Neville said. 'These guards are only a warning of what's ahead. The next causeway is more heavily guarded than the Tower of London, so I can't take you on, unfortunately, not without paperwork and all the guff. But one day you ought to make the effort: there's a blowhole in the rocks up ahead and it's quite spectacular when the sea smashes in there, and there are several other interesting seascapes.'

While he talked, Willem studied the area, realising that this village was still a fair way across the bay from Port Arthur and, as several wagons trundled past them, too public to contemplate any sort of clandestine activities.

Neville, doing an excellent job as tour guide, was pointing out that this was the spot where the Dutch ships had landed.

'Somewhere around 1742 I think,' he mused. 'Anyway, they were commanded by Abel Tasman, who named this landmass in honour of the boss of the Dutch East India Company. Silly fellow. There's talk, though, that it might shortly be renamed after the great seaman himself.'

519

'Who?' Willem asked.

'Why, Tasman of course.'

'Yes,' Willem agreed. 'Only fair, I imagine.'

They turned back, Willem disappointed and Neville looking forward to a feed of oysters as he turned off the road and down a narrow track.

'There are great views out this way,' he said. 'Roundabout route back to Sorell, but much more interesting.'

The coastal views were certainly spectacular, and Willem couldn't help remarking on the beautiful island scenery.

'Across the bay to the west,' Neville said, 'that isn't an island. That's the mainland. At the entrance to the Derwent. You can just see one of the semaphore towers from here.'

'And what's this island here?' Willem asked, to his left.

Neville laughed. 'That's not an island either. That's Port Arthur. The main prison is further inland. We're looking over at the coal mines.'

'Good Lord! It's a wonder the prisoners don't swim away from there.'

'Few people know this area, but the sharks would scare them off. I wouldn't want to try it.'

They followed the coast to a fishing village that was also a ferry depot, and another revelation to Willem.

While Neville found a fisherman, and bought his oysters, Willem discovered that the ferry crossed over to the eastern shore of the Derwent, and he walked away with a self-satisfied smile, enquiries completed.

They ate the oysters at the ferry ramp, drank a

bottle of claret that Neville had stowed in his saddle pack, and eventually made their way back to Sorell.

Admitting to himself that he really had enjoyed the day after all, Willem thanked Neville for sparing him the time.

'Don't thank me, old chap. I enjoyed your company. It's such a change for me to get away from the military and all the gossip. Actually, I'll be resigning my commission soon. We're not soldiers in this colony, we're glorified prison guards, and it doesn't sit well with me. A comedown for the regiment, I believe. But today I didn't have to think about the job. Let's have another drink!'

'Good idea,' Willem said. 'I'll have to turn back tomorrow, since this is the end of the line, and do my exploring in another direction.'

In the morning, he found Freddy working in the stables and gave him a tin of tobacco. 'I'm returning to Hobart today, but I'll be back, so I'll see you again.'

'You're coming back? What are you up to, Willem?'

'I told you, I've got business here. And I'll probably have a good job for you then.'

'What sort of a job?'

'It pays extra well.'

'Ah! Then I'm your man.' Freddy sloshed some water around the flagstone floor, gave it a half-hearted whisk with a broom, and then put the broom aside.

'That'll do it,' he said. 'Don't go yet, Willem. I never see no one in this place. I might as well be on the moon. What's been happening in Hobart?'

'A fair bit.' Willem resigned himself to this delay. If he could put his plan into action, Freddy's help would be crucial. 'Shanahan's got a ticket-of-leave now.'

'He always was lucky. Don't tell him I'm here.'

'Why not?'

Freddy ignored that question. 'What else? How's your mate George?'

'He's still in jail.' Willem couldn't afford to mention he was in Port Arthur, and give Freddy's suspicions new life, but he could speak of others. 'Singer and Angus have been sent to Port Arthur on trumped-up charges, but the good news is that Bull Harris is there too.'

'I heard he was a trusty. How did he end up there?'

'He was sentenced for beating up Flo Quinlan.'

Freddy was surprised. 'Never! He wouldn't dare touch Flo unless Flo was gagged and tied up.'

'Why not?'

'Flo used to be a prizefighter. He beat the hell out of Bull when we first got here for double-crossing him. What else has happened?'

'Bailey's still the town voice. Zack's working for Flood. Hunter's got Shanahan's job. And, oh Lord, you remember young Rufus Atwater?'

'Ah yes, he got sent from the ship to the boys' prison.'

'Yes. Eventually he was assigned, ended up working at Warboy's farm. Then, only a while back, he committed suicide.'

Freddy was shocked. 'Ah no! What'd he do a stupid thing like that for?'

522

'I'm not sure.'

'I wish you hadn't told me that,' Freddy muttered. 'Spoiled my bloomin' day you have.'

'Then I'd better get going before it gets any worse.'

'Righto. And listen, Willem, say hello to Bobbee Rich for me. I always thought I might marry her.'

'You could do worse,' Willem grinned. 'They say she's making a mint.'

'Fair dinkum? Well, that's all right for now, but I wouldn't have my wife whoring. She'd have to quit if I was to marry her.'

'Quite right, Freddy.' Willem left him to his labours.

Willem mulled over the information he'd gleaned from this expedition as he rode back towards Richmond.

Shanahan had often said that a whaleboat with a few rowers could easily cover the distance from the mouth of the Derwent, across Storm Bay to the southern tip of the Port Arthur settlement, and pick up a prisoner. But too many had argued that it would be an arduous and risky voyage, and the whaleboat would have to pass several islands with lookouts, not once, but twice.

He remembered that someone had said it would be easier to row to England than try that trick.

But none of them had managed a good look around the district as he had. Willem felt he was going back with a foolproof escape plan, and he had to talk to Shanahan as soon as possible.

CHAPTER SIXTEEN

'You're packing, Doc?' Sean was surprised. 'Where are you off to?'

'I've been appointed Chief Medical Officer at Port Arthur.'

'Ah, God help you! How did you get stuck with a job like that?'

'Listen to you! I thought you'd be pleased. You of all people. Always out to save the world from the heavy hand of authority!'

'Come to think of it...' Sean mused.

'Don't bother. It'll be bad enough there without your complications. If you want to know, I was offered the job, but in effect could not refuse without making myself unpopular, so I'm only going for a year.'

'What about your nice house here?' Sean looked about him. 'It's a darlin' little place to be leaving idle.'

'I'll be able to take leave for a few days here and there. God knows I'll be needing it.'

'I thought this was what you'd be wanting to see me about.'

'What do you mean?'

'Bailey said you wanted to see me.'

The doctor packed medical books into a canvas bag. 'I don't know where he got that from. He's made a mistake.'

'Maybe not then. I could caretake your house

for you. Mind it, so to speak. Do the gardening,' he grinned, adding: 'And I could doctor any of the patients who came calling.'

Roberts looked at him thoughtfully. 'I heard you got your ticket-of-leave. And you're no longer at Warboy Farm. What happened there?'

'Mutual separation, you could say. No hard feelings. I'm too wound up about Angus McLeod to stay civil at the farm. And Mr Warboy employs slave labour, not half-free men. But now McLeod's in your Port Arthur, so there's an innocent man for you to keep an eye on, Doctor. You watch out for him. In the mean time I'm going to see a lawyer today. About an appeal for Angus.'

'You are?'

'Blood oath, I am. Who else will?'

'I don't know. Would you like a cup of coffee?'

Sean blinked. 'Is this to celebrate my new status?'

'Might be. Do you want one or not?'

'I'd be obliged.'

Roberts laughed. 'Good. You go through to the kitchen and make it while I finish sorting these books. The stove's going cold, I think.'

The stove was out. Sean shook ash from the grate, and set a fire with paper and kindling, adding some woodcuts to keep it alive, but after he'd boiled the kettle and found the coffee, he had no idea how to make it.

'I was just about to try a few spoons of coffee in the teapot,' he said to Roberts when he came in.

'That doesn't work with coffee. You have to boil it in a pot. Have a seat there. I'll manage. I've been thinking, Shanahan. Have you got a job yet?'

'No. There's good jobs going at the brewery they say. Paid jobs.'

'Do you know Mr Pitcairn? He's a lawyer.'

'I do not.'

'He might have a job for you.'

'Doing what?'

'He needs a clerk.'

'The devil he does! Then what would he want with me?'

Roberts put two mugs on the table and a sugar bowl. 'It's not what he wants, it's what you want.' He held up his hand. 'No! For once let me talk, Shanahan. Here's a chance to do something with your life. You're running round here playing the bush lawyer; this is your opportunity to learn how real lawyers work.'

'You want me to work in an office? At a desk? I couldn't do that!'

'Why not?'

'I haven't got the brains. I'd make a damn fool of myself.'

'You'll make a bigger fool of yourself if you don't give this a try. And in that job, sense is handier than brains. You'll like Mr Pitcairn. He's a decent chap, and one of the leaders of the Anti-Transportation Group in Hobart.'

'Is he now?' Sean was impressed.

'I thought that would spark your interest. I could take you over and introduce you this afternoon.'

'Maybe another time.'

'No. I'm leaving tomorrow. You'll forget about it if I don't take you now.'

'I'd rather be thinking on it awhile. And tell me

526

then, what would you say to renting me the sleepout back there?'

The sleepout, as he called it, had been referred to as the sunroom by the previous owners, who'd partly enclosed one end of the back veranda to make an extra room but hadn't completed the job by installing windows.

The doctor had already been thinking that it mightn't be a bad idea, after all, to have someone living in the house. In the absence of human occupation it could easily get overrun by rats or possums. He already had possums in the roof.

'Where are you living now?'

'I've got a room at Majesta's Tavern. Temporary like.'

Dr Roberts laughed. 'Majesta's Tavern? Has that place come up in the world?'

'No, but Majesta has,' Sean grinned. 'She's got a boyfriend, and he, with putting on airs, doesn't like the sound of a grog shop, so there's a grand new sign out the front.'

Roberts poured the coffee. 'When could you move in?'

'Would this afternoon be too soon?'

Sean loved to contemplate the riot of stars that inhabited the southern skies on nights like this, with no moon to steal their charm and no wind to entice a mind into distractions. He could see the silvery flush of the Milky Way, and the formation they called the Saucepan, and the bright star that was said to be the pointer to the Great Cross, which he couldn't see right now, since maybe it hadn't come into view yet. It was said it turned over across the skies, but he didn't know whether or not this was a tease. There were a lot of jokers around, for what else did most of the poor sods have but the right to jest? And even indulge in the blackest of jokes if they wished.

His mind had drifted to a remembrance of Matt O'Neill and his scornful laughter after his second flogging ... when he was in such agony...

Suddenly it came to Sean that he had to talk to the Doc. He couldn't imagine why he hadn't thought of this earlier! But from where he sat in the back yard, he could see there were no lights on. The doctor wasn't home yet.

Never mind, he told himself as he walked up to the house. You can make good use of the time.

He searched in drawers, came up with pen and paper and sat down to compose a few important lines.

After crossing out several efforts for being too militant, too long-winded, too mushy, and so on, he settled for simple, respectful words that would be approved by Matt's parents and not cause them any more heartache.

In the morning, he waylaid Dr Roberts before he left for the ship.

'I was wondering if you'd do a favour for me. I've a cousin buried on the Isle of the Dead over there where you're going, with only a number. His parents dearly wish for him to have a proper headstone, so I have the money here to pay, and would be truly obliged if you could get the request approved and pay the stonemasons.'

He handed the doctor the piece of paper:

Matthew Terrence O'Neill aged 24
Died 4th day of June, 1840
Beloved son of Patrick and Hannah O'Neill
Rest in peace

The Doc read it quietly. 'Is there anything else I should know about this?' he asked nervously.

'No, it's all above board. I couldn't afford to do this before, but here now are five shillings to cover the cost. They say the convict stonemasons there are experts at the job. Could you ask them to make a Celtic cross for him? That would please Matt. He'd be truly proud of it.'

'If it's at all possible, I'll arrange it for you. By all means.'

Allyn was tired, having worked late closing down his surgery in Collins Street and packing up files, but then a couple of his friends, accompanied by his new acquaintance John Pitcairn, had called in to bid him farewell. They came armed with bottles of wine, Maryland cigars and playing cards, so as his desk was cleared, Allyn resigned himself to finishing the job in the morning.

Now the morning was upon him, and he was feeling decidedly unwell, but he had no choice but to hurry back to his rooms and get on with it.

He'd not minded complying with Shanahan's sad request, but he did not tell him that he'd mentioned him to Pitcairn, in case the contrary Irishman disapproved.

Anyway, I've set the idea in motion, Allyn told himself as he unlocked his office, and winced at the smell and state of the usually pristine room.

It took him half the morning, in his giddy state, to clean the place and finish packing, and only then did he notice a letter on his doormat.

Wearily he picked it up, broke the seal and was surprised, and concerned, to find it was from Miss Harris.

He had been very much taken with her when they'd first met – introduced by Shanahan strangely enough – and had spoken to her and her mother in the township, even venturing to buy them lunch at the Teahouse, which had been extremely pleasant.

Mrs Harris had invited him to visit them, and he had agreed to do so when time permitted. In fact he'd been looking forward to making that a more definite appointment until that letter was thrust upon him at Port Arthur. Until he discovered the truth about them. Even then, he'd insisted to himself that these things didn't matter. What if her father was a convict? So was half the population of this town, and many of them had become upstanding citizens.

But Allyn had been unable to move himself to issue a formal invitation for them to take tea with him again, or find an excuse to call at their farm. He kept telling himself he was too busy at present. 'Later,' he said. 'Soon.'

But time fled with his excuses, and along came his appointment to Port Arthur. Where her father was incarcerated. And that had made the situation impossible. What if he came in contact with convict Harris? What could he say? If anything.

He stared at the letter in a panic. He'd have to answer, though he'd rather run for cover. What to say?

'Damn and blast,' he muttered, embarrassed by his own rather unworthy attitude, but defending himself with the claim that the situation was, in fact, beyond his control.

Eventually he dashed off a note to Mrs Harris, thanking her for her kind invitation, which he was unable to accept as he was leaving Hobart this very day to take up a post at Port Arthur.

'Damn,' he said, cringing at the last few words he'd written.

He tore up the note and tried again. This time he left out the part about Port Arthur and wrote 'elsewhere' instead. Thought it looked ridiculous.

In the end, the best he could do, considering he was already coping with haste and a headache, was simply to write that he was leaving for Port Arthur and wished them well. He stuck the finished article in his pocket and forgot about it.

Finalities in a muddle, since he'd left everything to the last minute, Allyn had to rely on Shanahan's able assistance. The Irishman unloaded Allyn's boxes of files from the buggy and stacked them in his sitting room, replacing them with the outbound luggage. He promised to look after his horse and see that the buggy was kept well protected from the elements under its canvas cover in the lean-to at the rear of the cottage.

'You'd better be off,' he said, 'or you'll miss the ship. They hate people to be late in prisons, and you'll end up a week late if you don't pick up your heels.'

'I can't find my medical bag,' Allyn snapped.

531

He was already regretting this move.

'It's in the buggy. Now hop in.'

'No, wait. My cloak. I've forgotten my cloak. Where did I put it?'

He rushed inside, found it on a chair in the kitchen, slung it over his shoulders and hurried out again.

'Are you taking a hat?' Shanahan called as he reached the gate.

'Oh yes!' Back he ran for his best topper.

And then he was in the buggy, with Shanahan driving down to the wharves at a breakneck pace.

'You don't have to kill me,' Allyn complained, hanging on to the rail and the hat. 'I'm not that keen on going.'

'Looks to me as if you're having doubts anyway. You've been dawdling all the morning. Would you care to stop for a whisky to settle your nerves?'

'No! Keep going!'

Shanahan took over the role of porter, and as they made for the gangplank of the ship they were met by a person unknown to Allyn who nevertheless addressed them both.

'G'day, Doc. You here again, Shanahan? What's he up to, Doc? Lately he's been on the wharves so much you'd think he lives here.'

'Get out with you,' Shanahan grinned. 'I have not.'

'You have so. Every time a ship comes in you're hanging about more than the matchmakers.'

'Who's he?' Allyn asked, as the stranger darted off into the crowd.

'Bailey. He's a news vendor, you could say.'

'But I don't know him, do I?'

Shanahan had stopped, his face suddenly grey, his eyes hard. 'Here's your stuff, go on board.'

He whistled to a seaman to take Allyn's baggage, and backed away into the crowd.

Shoved on board so quickly, Allyn turned along the deck to find a spot at the rails and see what had brought that sudden change in Shanahan.

A long line of convicts, chained together at the ankles, was clanking down the wharf towards the ship. The poor fellows looked so wretched that Allyn groaned, picturing them as prospective patients, wondering if he should get off this ship while he could.

But then he noticed that activity on the wharf had almost come to a halt. Most of the workmen and several women were standing very still, forcing seamen, military men and other folk to thread their way past them, causing some irritation.

Shanahan was standing still too as the chained convicts neared, and Allyn realised, astonished, that this was a demonstration – a mark of respect for comrades.

'Outrageous!' remarked a portly gentleman standing beside him, looking down at this odd picture.

And then Allyn saw Shanahan step forward to shake the hand of a convict as he passed by, but a guard intervened, shoving him aside.

When the last of the convicts had stumbled on to the ship, there was movement again on the wharf, as if nothing untoward had happened.

Shanahan was leaving. He looked up, saw Allyn, and waved to him.

'Don't forget to go to see Pitcairn!' Allyn shouted, cross with himself for not remembering to mention the matter before he boarded the ship, but the Irishman was already striding away.

Sean hadn't forgotten about Pitcairn. He'd been amused by the suggestion, and thought it was a genuine leap of faith for Doc Roberts to be visualising him as an office clerk. But well-meant. Anyway, he had money in his pocket to last a while, and a wealth of things to do. First, though, while the money was holding, he had to see Mr Baggott, the lawyer, who, everyone said, was well versed in convict claims.

On his way, however, Sean found himself reconsidering his choice. Why not go to that Mr Pitcairn? If he was clear-eyed enough to see the evil in transportation, then he'd be the man to approach on behalf of Angus, would he not?

But then, he worried, I wouldn't want him to think I'm using Angus to steer my way into his office looking for a job, a sort of back-door approach.

Deciding he'd better stick to his original plan, he sat for an hour and seventeen minutes in Baggott's office before the great man could see him, but it gave him time to study the clerk and the flurry of papers on his desk, and the comers and goers with their whispered conversations.

When Baggott appeared, ushering out clients, the clerk called Sean's name and the Irishman jumped to attention.

'Ah, Mr Shanahan,' the lawyer said. 'Come on in. Take a seat. Now, what can I do for you?'

No sooner had Sean begun to outline his concern than Baggott interrupted: 'Just a minute, Mr Shanahan. If you are trying to place blame on Mr Warboy for this calamity, as you call it, then I'm afraid I can't hear any more of this. Mr Warboy is my client.'

'So I believe. And word has it you spoke up for James Forbes, which was terrible kind of you, and much appreciated. But hear me now, sir, the blame for this is not on Mr Warboy's shoulders. It's upon a rush to judgement, like drunkards mobbing the free drinks tent, in case it's the real thing.

'In this case the real thing was that powerful word "rape". The word that sends women into a faint and men into frenzies of outrage, though it be as common as salt among our gender, and rarely punished.

'So here we have a woman who was raped. Not really a woman, though, a young girl, sadly the granddaughter of Mr Warboy...'

'Yes, yes,' Baggott interrupted again. 'I know of this. It was in the papers.'

'As it should never have been,' Sean continued, 'for the sake of Angus McLeod, and Mr Warboy, and the young girl, who is mentally lacking, to say the best of it.'

'Now just a minute, Mr Shanahan, you really must not make wild statements about the young lady, who is the victim in this case, might I remind you.'

'Of course I must not make wild statements, and you are true to your colours in reproving me, but wild this is not. The girl is mentally lacking;

535

childlike one might say, to be kind. Vacant, blank,' he added grimly, 'were one to speak the utter truth.'

'And you think speaking so cruelly of the young lady will assist Mr McLeod's case? I'm afraid it does not, Mr Shanahan. It only makes the crime more reprehensible.'

Sean pushed the heavy chair back and stood before Mr Baggott and his shiny desk.

'Didn't you hear what I just said about rushing to judgement? Or were you working out your bill? I'm asking you to represent a man who has been wronged by the courts, an innocent man, and you're already heading for the drinks tent yourself.'

'Sit down, Mr Shanahan. I cannot abide tantrums.'

'This is no tantrum, sir. I am trying to deliver the plain facts to you, and if you can't listen without interrupting, and arguing about something you know nothing about, then say so and we'll have an end to this meeting.'

Baggott was so taken aback he almost ordered the Irishman out of his office, but being a cunning man in his own way, he realised that if he did that, it would almost be paramount to admitting that he couldn't listen without interrupting. The damned fellow had talked him into a corner.

'Oh for God's sake, sit down!' he snapped. 'And I hope you realise time is money.'

'We'll come to that,' Shanahan said coolly, as he resumed his chair.

'Now, as I see it,' Joe Baggott said briskly, 'Miss

536

Warboy was found to be pregnant after a visit to a doctor. Which doctor?'

'Dr Jellick.'

'How do you know this? Did Mr Warboy tell you?'

'No. Their maid did.'

'When her parents asked the girl, she gave the name of Angus McLeod. This man was a convict, working as a gardener at Mr Warboy's farm. He did have contact with Miss Warboy because she visited him in the glasshouse, which is fairly close to the rear of the house. Is that correct?'

Sean, restraining himself from interrupting, could only nod, realising how bad it sounded put in such stark words.

'Now, you said yourself that Angus McLeod was very fond of Miss Warboy. And he was quite proud that Miss Warboy visited him at his work in the greenhouse, unchaperoned. In other words they were alone in there on occasion.'

'Yes.'

'It sounds very straightforward to me, Mr Shanahan, but we'll look at it now from another viewpoint. You say, and others will corroborate this, that One: this is a highly moral man. Two: he held Miss Warboy in high esteem, so would not have touched her without her consent. Three: you and others believe that he was in such awe of her, he would not have made any advances to her in those circumstances anyway.'

He shook his head. 'Not much here for an appeal. Your arguments are based on emotion, not fact. Argument raised against him would immediately ask what brought a highly moral man

537

to prison in the first place.'

'Angus was fighting for the rights of the working man, sir. For better pay and conditions.'

'So you said, and I understand his motives and his frustrations, but he still broke the law. Apart from that, Mr Shanahan, you know yourself that evil can lurk in the most respected of souls. You cannot see into any man's soul and say it is God's truth he is blameless. You only have his word.'

He held up a finger for silence as he continued.

'You, and others, believe McLeod, and he is fortunate in that regard. The law could not. But, on the other hand, what about the young lady? Is she as blameless as she claims? Evil does lurk in female souls as well. If McLeod is innocent, then she is lying. This is what we have to look at.'

Sean sat up in surprise. 'You'll take the case?'

'I'll see if there is a case. Since you know characters so well, tell me: of the two, which one is lying?'

Sean took a deep breath. 'Angus is not. She could be...'

'Ah, no.' Baggott smiled grimly. 'You can't have a penny each way. Is she lying?'

'Yes. She has to be. As well as being bloody stupid.'

'Next question. Do you have any idea who did rape her?'

'It wasn't any of the farmhands, so we can count them out. She had no contact with them. But she did have contact with the parishioners at Trinity church. We think it could have been one of them.'

'And as far as you know, she didn't have

538

contact with any other gentlemen?'

'As far as I know,' Sean admitted, his hopes wilting again.

'My fee for today is two shillings and sixpence, Mr Shanahan. I'll look into the case, but I can't promise anything, though I've been wondering about something else. Did Miss Warboy actually say she was raped?'

Sean frowned. 'I don't know.'

'Ah. Let's think on it. I don't suppose the young lady has had second thoughts?' he asked slyly. 'That would help.'

'I don't know if she ever had any sensible thoughts about anything,' Sean said bitterly.

'Well now, we just might look into that. Give your address to my clerk. He'll let you know when we can have another talk. In the mean time, I'd keep this discussion between us. We don't need to upset people unduly.'

The clerk stood as Sean exited the inner sanctum. 'Will that be all, Mr Shanahan?'

'Not yet. I'm instructed to give you my address.'

He watched as the address was taken down in a clear copperplate hand, then grabbed the nettle and asked a question.

'Do you like this job?'

Startled, the clerk looked up. 'Yes, sir. Yes, I do. It's very interesting.'

'I suppose it would be,' Sean said thoughtfully. 'I suppose it would. Now I have to wait for you to recall me.'

'Very well,' said the clerk. 'Good day to you, sir.'

Joe Baggott knew he would have to treat this matter with some delicacy. It wasn't that he'd be infringing Barnaby's rights by taking the case; it was simply that he liked the man, and wouldn't want to see him hurt.

He lit a cigar and put his feet up to do some pondering.

In point of fact, he mused, the worst had already happened to Barnaby. The scandal was all over town. Though Shanahan hadn't mentioned it, the girl's parents had gone home to Jamaica, leaving her behind to the astonishment of all concerned, including her grandfather. Baggott had had words with his wife over the outrageous opinion voiced by her friend Mrs Flood that the parents may have left her to Barnaby convinced he was the father.

'For what other reason would they abandon the girl?' Mrs Flood had asked Mrs Baggott.

'Don't you dare ever repeat such a dreadful thing again!' Baggott had shouted at his wife. 'Do you want to be sued for defamation? And don't bring that woman to my house again.'

'Oh dear,' he sighed. 'Poor Barnaby. From what I hear, the son and his wife were quite a burden on the poor fellow. I ought to have a talk with Jellick. See what he makes of this mess.'

'Rape?' Jellick laughed. 'I don't think so. Not before that bumptious woman brought her to me. I read about it in the papers, but I understood it to mean that she'd been raped after the consultation in my office.'

540

'So you didn't examine her after the rape?'

'No. Mrs Warboy wouldn't have brought her back to me. The woman was extremely rude, so I chucked her out.'

'That's very strange. I spoke to Hippisley, who investigated the matter – the matter of rape, you understand – and he has your name down as the consulting doctor.'

Jellick swung about in his chair. 'Then he's wrong. Or he has been given incorrect inform-ation. I only saw the girl once. Confirmed that she was pregnant. That is all.'

'That's all?'

'Oh, not quite. I did mention that Miss Warboy was obviously mentally deficient, something like that, and her mother started calling me names for saying such a thing.'

'That's what the row was about?'

'Yes. I haven't seen them since.'

Joe Baggott sighed. 'I'm sorry to have bothered you with this, Jellick, but would you mind clearing the matter with Hippisley? He will need to know that you saw no evidence of rape.'

'I certainly will. How dare that damn woman involve me in their sordid affairs! The girl certainly had not been raped from what I recall. And what's more, she was obviously no stranger to intercourse.'

'What?'

'You can have that in writing if you wish. I will tell you something else: she was pleased to hear she was having a baby. Pleased as Punch. Poor thing really didn't understand what was happen-ing.'

'Oh, good God!'

'Take my advice. If you're going for an appeal on this, get a well-qualified medical man to talk to her as quickly as possible, before she gets spirited away to a nunnery or something. And don't look at me. I'll say my piece to Hippisley and that's it. Oh, and while you're here... I've been meaning to ask you about this for some time... I need a seconder for my nomination to the Hobart Gentlemen's Club. Would you mind doing the honours?'

Baggott's heart sank. He'd forgotten that Jellick's request for a seconder had been doing the rounds for weeks.

'By all means,' he said, as cheerfully as he could manage.

That evening, at his club, having done his duty by Jellick, the lawyer sat morosely in a far corner of the members' reading room, his head buried in a newspaper, his mind wrestling with the problem of Barnaby Warboy.

Time and again he unfurled the material he'd collected over the last few days, looked at it, and shook his head. What was the point of speaking to that girl if she was retarded? It seemed everyone was agreed on that, so she hadn't been asked to give evidence in court. All she'd done was name McLeod, and that had been enough to convict him, given the circumstances.

Joe knew that Barnaby could and would block him if he tried to bring her into court. As any grandfather would. And if he succeeded in overcoming that obstacle, he would most certainly alienate judge and jury for calling up such a pitiful witness.

And that, he pondered nervously, would only be the half of it. Barnaby would be devastated if it came out in court that she was 'no stranger to intercourse', as Jellick had put it. And possibly had not been raped.

One thing a judge and jury would believe of the girl, though: were she to point the finger at McLeod again, in answer to a simple question, an appeal would be thrown out of court.

For all he knew, or anyone else for that matter, the girl being a simpleton could have lain down and accepted sex from any bounders who managed to get their hands on her. She could even have been sneaking out at night for these trysts. She had not been kept under lock and key. She was free to roam a property where lived more than a dozen convicts.

In effect, he mused, the whole sad story revolved around the sexual behaviour of a retarded girl, as Jellick had said. And trying to appeal on that basis would be marching into quicksands.

Joseph Baggott, solicitor, made his decision.

On his return to his office, he wrote to Mr Shanahan, stating that with all the good will in the world, he did not consider there was any new evidence pertaining to the conviction of Angus McLeod; therefore an appeal would not be feasible. He thanked him for his interest in this matter.

An account for his fee of two shillings and sixpence was enclosed.

Sean was happier than he would ever admit that

his hair was growing again, but he'd been keeping a cap on when he was out of the house so as not to invite the teasing that accompanied the scarecrow new growth emerging from the bristly convict cut.

Now, though, as he stood in front of the mirror in the Doc's kitchen, he could actually comb it. A little. With a comb found in a drawer, for he'd not had use for one in the colony before this. Often men warned that regrowth from the convict clip would come up grey, or even carrot-coloured, but it wasn't happening here. His hair was dark, and softening into the odd wave or two.

It's been a long time since you did any sprucing, he told himself. So don't be walking out and forgetting. You're living in a town, not on a farm any more, so every day is Sunday from now on.

And this really being Sunday, he marched off to Mass in the little church fronting Bathurst Street, sat where he pleased, gazed about him like a misbehaving child during the sermon, disdained the plate, and prayed for a myriad things, many impossible. One, though, might not be. It just might not be. His sister had written that Glenna Hamilton, now Fogarty and a widow, was said to have migrated to America, but that she had a suspicion that the woman had instead set sail for Van Diemen's Land. He'd sent a letter off the very same day, asking her to find out for sure, but it would take a year for an answer, a year of torture, if Glenna didn't find him first.

'How can you ask a man to suffer the anxieties of not knowing, Lord?' he whispered when the Mass was over and everyone else was loitering

544

outside in the sunshine for the weekly chats and exchanges. 'Has she gone there, across the Atlantic, or is she, this hour, crossing the southern seas? The more dangerous seas. Oh God, keep her safe. And her boy.'

He'd tried to put Glenna from his mind, to avoid what would be a devastating disappointment if she'd chosen New York.

'And me without a say in it at all,' he accused the Lord. 'Haven't you punished me enough? Why don't you lean a bit my way for a change?'

A woman in a startling green gown and matching satin bonnet strode down the aisle, lit a candle and was making her way back when he recognised Bobbee Rich.

'Glory be!' she grinned. 'I heard you've got a ticket now.'

'Ah yes, the Governor said, "Go forth, Shanahan and never sin again!" So here I am.'

'And I suppose he gave you the keys of the city?'

'How did you know?'

'I have my spies.'

Sean picked up his cap and walked out with her, amused that the crowd parted to allow them through, as if Moses had been at it again.

Bobbee didn't appear to notice the sniffs and glares of her betters, or didn't care. 'Where to now?' she asked him.

'I thought I'd take a walk down to the waterfront.' This was his one indulgence in the matter of Glenna Hamilton. His darling Glenna. He was always on the watch for the approach of big ships, ocean-going ships that might be carrying passengers from the old country, in the hopes that she might be aboard – but he never day-dreamed any further for fear of overstepping his luck. Which was fragile enough at the best of times.

'Would you come with me to the infirmary? They might let me in if you're with me.'

'It's not a place I'd go by choice if you don't mind. It's inside the stockade.'

'But Zack's in there,' Bobbee said.

'Zack? What happened to him?'

'He was working as Flood's overseer. He fell out with the boss and got beaten up by the brothers.'

'Ah Jesus, that's been on the cards awhile. It's a wonder he took that job, being so much agin all that Flood stands for, the King and all that.'

'Being boss, though, Sean, being a supervisor, made him feel cheered up, if you know what I mean.'

'Indeed I do.'

Zack had lost an eye in the one-sided fight. 'Will you tell Bobbee it was kind of her to try to come to see me anyway,' he said. 'They've got a hide refusing to let her in.'

'Yes, I'll tell her.' Sean dug in his pocket. 'I nearly forgot. She sent you these lemon drops. But listen to me, Zack. Why don't I bring the police in to see you? I'll get Sergeant Budd and Goosey over here, and you can give them the story on Flood. About the contraband liquor, and the arms. What have you got to lose?'

'Another eye, that's what! No, Shanahan, when I get out of here I'll be asking Mr Warboy for my job back, and never moving again. At least it's safe there.'

'Not for Angus,' Sean growled.

'I can't help that.'

'What if I get a Customs man? He won't be in uniform. No one will know.'

'Give over, Shanahan. That'd get back to Flood. If you want to make yourself useful, you could get my sea bag from Flood's farm. My horticulture books are in it, and a stock whip I'm minding for Singer.'

'Horticulture books? That's posh. Where did you get them?'

'Singer got them for me when I was working for the Governor. He said I had to look the part.'

'Where did *he* get them from?'

'The library. They're fine books, leatherbound with pictures.'

'The library?' Sean echoed. 'You're supposed to give them back!'

'Since when? Singer said I could have them. You don't know everything, Shanahan! He said it's a public library, the books are ours. We can take any we like. And I like those books, they're learning me a lot.'

Sean patted him on the shoulder. 'I'll get your sea bag.'

His first port of call along Sassafras Road was Flood's farm. What better excuse to call in on Mrs Harris on his way home, with the long-serving: 'I was just passing by.' The opportunity was not to be missed.

Flood's homestead was set back from the road,

behind a high, well-trimmed hedge. Sean would have liked a peep at it since he'd heard it had been extended into quite a mansion, but he continued on his mission, taking the tradesmen's entrance around by the orchard.

He whistled to a workman, who recognised him and ambled over.

'Hey, Shanahan!' he said. 'What are you doing here?'

'I came to pick up Zack's sea bag. Will you get it for me?'

'Sure I will. How is he?'

'Lost an eye, thanks to those bastards.'

'Ah, sweet Jesus!'

'Did you see what happened?'

'There weren't any witnesses, if that's what you're here for. They're too cunning. I'll go get the bag, they don't like strangers wandering in.'

'I wonder why,' Sean murmured as the workman, whose name he couldn't recall, trotted away. In no time he was back with a bulky canvas bag.

'What's he got in here, rocks?' he complained as he handed it over.

'Could be. Did Flood get anyone to replace Zack?'

'Yeah! Right up. He's a mate of yours too.'

'Who?'

'Quinlan. Flo Quinlan.'

'Flo? But he's working for Mr Warboy.'

'Yeah. But he wasn't the boss there. Hunter is. So when we lose another overseer, Flo marches in here, large as life, and tells Flood he'll take the job. Do you want me to find him for you?'

Sean shook his head angrily. 'No. You can tell

him I was here.'

Not calling on Flo was a snub, Sean knew. And he meant it to be. If he had his way, no one would work for Flood, let alone take on the job as his overseer after what had happened to Zack. He was disappointed in Flo. Why couldn't he have stayed at Warboy Farm where he was needed, instead of crawling over to Flood?

'You just never know with people,' he said as he turned the horse about and rode away.

He reminded himself of that at morning tea with Mrs Harris about an hour later.

The kitchen was sunny, the cake fresh and the tea strong. Just as he liked it. He'd seen the astonishing tomatoes she had growing on leafy vines at the back of a shed. Most of them were green, coming into red, plump as peaches.

'It's a marvel the vines can hold them,' he said, 'even though you've got the sticks for support. They look too heavy.'

'They manage.' She smiled proudly. 'Of course they don't have the heavy seeds like stone fruit. They're fruit all the way through.'

'Ah, they're fruit, you say? I thought I was looking at a vegetable.'

'I don't really know. I use my own measure. I say if you have to cook them they're vegetables, and if you can eat them straight from the fields they're fruit. Here you are, Mr Shanahan, you can take some home with you.'

'Thank you now. That's an honour. Though I don't know about eating them. It would be a crime I'm thinking. I'd want to show them off first. I might even charge a penny a look.'

She laughed, and her blue eyes twinkled. 'You'll have to taste them first. We'll have another cup of tea and I'll slice some for you. They're nice with bread and butter.'

The tomato was delicious. Sean couldn't help remarking on how his life had changed since he'd been given his ticket.

'I'm learning to live normal again,' he told her. 'To dress right, and take my place. It's a funny sensation after so long standing aside, branded by the flannel on your back. I got these clothes from Sam Pollard. Do you think they're all right? I mean, do they look all right?'

'They do, they're very nice. In fact I got a surprise when I saw you coming up the path...'

'You didn't know who I was?'

'For a minute, just for a minute. I'm sorry, Mr Shanahan...'

'Call me Sean. And you don't have to be apologising to me, for God's sake. I'm not out of the woods yet. This is only parole.'

He was a little bewildered that she suddenly seemed to withdraw. To be very quiet. He felt he'd said something wrong. Racked his brains to think what it might be. Ate the last slice of bread and butter. Finally broke the silence.

'Well, I'll say again, your tomatoes are top-hole. You should plant a whole crop, they'd be gold in the market.'

Her eyes were troubled when she turned to him. 'Sean, I think you've probably guessed by this – my husband is here in the colony. He was transported.'

Sean nodded. 'It crossed my mind. But why

would you be needing to tell anyone? It's no one's business but your own.'

'I think I'm just tired of covering up,' she sighed. 'Fed up with it. It seemed like a good idea at first, but now I don't care. It got to seem so wrong to be deceiving our friends. I told Mr Warboy, and it didn't matter to him at all.'

Not that you'd notice, Sean thought acidly.

'Is there anything I can do to help?'

'No. I'm selling up here and going home.'

'I see. Is your husband due to be released?'

'Lester? No. His term has been extended, so we might as well go home. I miss my family.'

Another disappointment. He felt let down that she should be talking about going home. But then the name sank in! It was Lester Harris! Bull Harris! By all that was holy, how had he managed to wed such an attractive woman? Her very nature was at odds with his mangy soul.

'I suppose you do,' he said dimly, and changed the subject. 'How is Louise?'

'Oh, she's fine. On top of the world really. Young ladies, they live at the heights or the depths, there's no middle ground.'

'Is that right?' He smiled. 'And where are we now?'

'Oh, on the heights.' Mrs Harris glanced out the window. 'There she is now.' She went to the door and called to her daughter: 'We have a visitor. Mr Shanahan!'

Louise came in, untying a large apron. 'I wondered whose horse it was. How are you, Mr Shanahan?' She smiled. 'The men said you'd got a ticket-of-leave and struck out on your own. You

551

might have told us!'

'That's why I'm here. And might I say, your daughter, Mrs Harris, is looking as happy and healthy as a hedge in May.'

'Ah yes,' Mrs Harris laughed. 'I wonder why?'

'Too many beaux on the horizon, probably,' Sean teased, and Louise's cheeks tinged pink as she tramped over to the bench to cut herself a slice of bread.

'Could be!' she allowed, with no sign of her former boldness, so Sean guessed some gentleman had tamed the flirt.

'Anyone in particular?' he asked.

Louise considered her reply. 'I can tell you he's not a farm worker,' she said mischievously, and Sean turned to her mother. 'There you go! I'm out of the running already. Give us another hint.'

'No, you'll blab. Anyway, what are you doing now?'

'Not a lot. I'm having a think about what to do.'

'Mother, you should give Mr Shanahan a job here—'

'Sean,' he said, interrupting.

Louise continued. 'Sean would be ten times better than the idiot overseer we've got now. None of the men take any notice of him.'

To avoid any embarrassment, since Mrs Harris, like Warboy up the road, was entitled to convict workers, men she didn't have to pay, he conjured up a quick response.

'As a matter of fact, I've been thinking of an office job.'

'Really?' Mrs Harris said, seemingly unsurprised. 'In what kind of an office?'

Now it was his turn for reticence. 'Well now, it's only talk, you know. Nothing might come of it.'

Louise bounced in, getting her own back. 'Come on, give us a hint!' she laughed.

He hesitated, but her mother joined in. 'Yes, Sean, tell us.'

'It's only talk, as I said. There might be a job in a lawyer's office, though what use I'd be–'

'A lawyer's office!' Mrs Harris cried. 'That's a very good idea. You shouldn't put yourself down, they'd show you what to do. And you'd have no trouble following. I think you'll do well.'

'You could learn how to be a lawyer,' Louise said. 'You read enough books as it is.'

'How do *you* know?' her mother asked.

'Because he'd sneak down by the creek to read his books. I'd see him there when I rode the back track with Tulip. But I just realised, Sean, you're not at Warboy's any more. Where do you live?'

'I had a stroke of luck. Remember Dr Roberts? I introduced you to him. I'm renting a room in his house at Battery Point while he's away.'

'Away where?' Louise asked.

'He's been appointed to Port Arthur. Medical Officer. So I volunteered to caretake his horse, his house and his worldly goods, so to speak.'

Louise's face was as white as paste. 'He never told us he was leaving,' she said tersely. 'Not a word.'

Her mother was sympathetic. 'He probably didn't have time, dear,' she said gently.

Oho. Sean picked up on the situation. Was the Doc her beau?

'That'd be right,' he said quickly. 'He barely got

a day's notice, and him unhappy about having to go...'

'Didn't he want to go there?' Louise asked, and Sean was able to give her the answer she needed.

'He did not. His very words to me were that he had no choice. The powers that be gave him the order. He couldn't refuse.'

'Oh,' she said, and sank into a baffled silence. Mrs Harris tried to minimise her discomfort by reintroducing the subject of tomatoes, but soon Louise excused herself and disappeared into the house.

'She's a little upset,' her mother said quietly. 'She'd become quite fond of Dr Roberts.'

'He's a nice feller.' Sean nodded. 'But now I won't be taking up any more of your time. I must be going.'

'You can't go yet. I want to give you some tomato seeds. Come with me and I'll get them for you.'

Sean pocketed the tomato seeds, and thanked her for the tea, and then on impulse suggested she and Louise might care to have afternoon tea with him one Sunday.

'Come to think of it,' he added, 'what about next Sunday? I'd be pleased to escort you.'

'That would be very nice,' she said. 'I'd like to see Louise get out more. We could have a picnic if you like. I'll pack a basket.'

'Now there's a splendid idea. And very kind of you.'

He was wondering about Mrs Harris as he rode down to the gate. She sounded cheerful, but the ready smile had gone, replaced by a sort of acceptance, he thought. Ah yes, acceptance! And isn't that as familiar to me in this land as breathing? But it's still a hard master.

Louise was waiting for him, standing by the open gate.

'Thank you for saving me the effort,' he grinned. 'I always said you were a dear girl!'

She shook her head and ran over to him, thrusting a letter at him. 'Sean, I want you to send this. It's important. She told you about my father, didn't she?'

'Yes, and that's fine with me. Why would it not be?'

'But did she tell you where he is?'

I already knew that. 'Your mother? No, she did not.'

'Then I'll tell you. He's been sent to Port Arthur, where we can't even visit him. My own father! Please send this letter to him. I know you can. You have ways. And you have to, because I did you the favour of finding Mr Bailey. So you have to do this for me.'

His horse shuffled sideways, and she jumped back out of the way. 'Say you will!' she insisted.

'I'll see what I can do!'

Louise beamed. 'I knew you would! And listen, will Dr Roberts be coming back to Hobart occasionally? Port Arthur's not that far away.'

'I believe he might.'

'Then you must let me know so I can happen by. And don't forget!'

'Is that all? No message for me?'

'Oh get on with you, you're such a horrible tease.'

555

And I always thought it was the other way around, he told himself as he headed back along Sassafras Road.

Flo Quinlan was sorry he'd missed Shanahan. People said Zack had lost an eye, but they didn't seem to know for sure. The Irishman would know. Anyway, he'd wanted to tell Shanahan how come he'd gone over to Flood.

Mr Warboy had been angry. 'Lieutenant Flood seems to take an unseemly delight in disrupting my staff. You've only been here a short time, Quinlan, and I thought you'd settled in well. You don't have to go over there, you know.'

'I'll be overseer there, Mr Warboy. That entitles me to extra good-behaviour points on my record, and they all count. They add up to time off my sentence.'

'But that farm is well known for violent behaviour. I believe Zack was attacked and beaten. That's why there's a vacancy, you know.'

Flo sighed. He put on his most benign face. 'Ah yes, but Zack probably provoked it.'

'I'm sorry to hear you say that. I found Zack a most obliging man, and an excellent gardener. I shall go and find him and reinstate him as soon as possible. And since you've agreed to go, I can't stop you accepting a promotion, just as Zack did, but don't say I didn't warn you.'

'Thank you, Mr Warboy.'

Flo muttered grimly to himself as he marched away. 'Zack was a mate of mine, Mr Warboy. We came out on the same hellship. Flood thinks he's smart pinching another one of your workers, but

556

this time he's picked a corker.'

Flo liked to be neat, and he had an instinctive dislike of rules, so unlike the others he'd let his brown hair grow long enough to at least cover his scalp. He worked on the premise that when challenged, he could bribe the cutter to leave more on his head than on the floor, and promise never to let such a breach happen again. Until next time.

He also still had the good jacket that Shanahan had given him, but he couldn't bear to part with it because it gave him a touch of respectability. He hoped Shanahan had forgotten it.

Having been released by Warboy, he strolled down to the men's quarters, discarded his yellow convict rags, found a bar of soap and took a leisurely bath. Then he shaved with Hunter's good razor and dressed in the treasured clean shirt and trousers given him by one of the Sunday whores.

Ready to sally forth, he detoured up to the kitchen to find Dossie, give her a kiss and earn himself afternoon tea.

'I don't see the granddaughter around any more,' he said as he quaffed the boss's coffee. 'Where did she get to?'

'Mr Warboy sent her away. With Marie Cullen. She's Penn's maid now. But I don't know where they went. The boss never said. He never told Hunter either. He was told to drop them off at the Pollard store and then go straight home.'

'They might have been sent to the mainland. Out of the way.'

Dossie laughed. 'Marie would like that. She

could escape from there. Just disappear.'

'I doubt it, she looks too frail, too much of a mouse.'

'She's surely frail, she's been starved, but she's no mouse. If she can just get some meat on her bones, I reckon she'll brighten up. But look here now, I've got you some coffee to take with you, knowing you're so fond of it.'

'Good on you, Doss. You're a treasure.'

'I wish you wouldn't go to that place. If you stayed here longer you'd get a promotion. Hunter's due for his ticket in a couple of months.'

'A couple of months is too long.'

Flo tramped the two miles along Sassafras Road to the main gate of the Flood estate, and stood to admire the gate itself. It was a grand affair, painted white and set between stone pillars; a wide gate on well-oiled hinges, like the one he used to swing on as a kid at the entrance to his uncle's manse in Windsor.

It was easy to unbolt and swing open, and he whistled a tune as he set it wide, hitching it into place. And left it open.

He laughed as he set off under a canopy of flowering gums towards the homestead.

'Shut your own bloody gates,' he said.

A fastidious man, the new overseer was appalled by the state of the men's quarters and immediately began to introduce the workers to the niceties of clean accommodation. It required a fair amount of threats and bullying to make them learn how to use soap and scrubbing brushes with some vigour, but then he realised that even more effort was needed.

He burned the thin, lice-ridden mattresses and blankets and disinfected the low-slung canvas bunks, then turned his attention to the men's clothing, most of which was worn to rags, except for the relatively new garb worn by the Grigg brothers. He solved this problem by condemning all worn-out clothes and boots to the bonfire, and sending someone up to the storeroom for replacement mattresses, blankets and convict-issue clothing. And more soap.

Then he turned his attention to the kitchen, sweeping through it, sending stale food to the pig bins, dumping filthy old cookpots and drawing up lists of required rations.

By this time the workmen had warmed to the efforts of the new overseer and began to attend to their chores with enthusiasm, until the messenger returned from the storeroom to inform Quinlan that it was empty.

'Now see what youse have done!' Max Grigg, who'd not taken kindly to the scrubbing detail, snarled. 'Now we got no bloody beds and those blokes stupid enough to listen to a bloody know-all like you ain't got no trousers.'

'Yeah,' came voices from behind him. 'Flood'll have us shot for ditching our duds.'

'And the bloody mattresses!' another one wailed. 'Destruction of property that is! Jesus wept! We're in for it now.'

Flo continued with his cleanout as if he had the matter in hand, while he tried to think what to do next. He'd seen a storeroom at the Warboy farm that was well stocked with these requirements, and he'd seen the inventory Hunter kept, marking off every item that was issued, so he'd taken it for granted that the same system applied here.

'Apparently not,' he muttered to himself as he kicked a rusted bucket out of the way. 'Flood's an even worse skinflint than I thought.'

'How did Zack let the place get into such a mess?' he asked.

'Zack couldn't do nothing,' he was told. 'It's always been like this here, and if you complain, Max tells the boss, and he cuts rations again.'

Max Grigg laughed. 'You'll go out of here faster even than Zack!'

'Another word out of you and I'll give you a smack in the mouth,' Flo said to him. He was too busy trying to think what Shanahan would have done in this situation.

Wait on now, he reminded himself. Hadn't he seen Shanahan in town in a wagon often enough? And what was he doing? Buying stores for the farm workers. He was the overseer, it was his job.

'Who goes into town and gets the stores?' he asked.

'The Lieutenant,' Max said belligerently. 'When he has time. But he's away now. And bloody lucky for you, mate. He'd have you hanging by your thumbs for this.'

'Max,' Flo said quietly, 'I am not your mate. You call me boss. Right?'

He saw Max's eyes flicker and stepped aside fast enough to dodge an attack by Owen, the other Grigg brother, who was wielding an axe handle. Not that it was any further use to him. Flo punched him on the jaw so hard, he ended

560

up on the stone floor in the corner of the kitchen, too dazed to pull himself up.

Max began shouting abuse at Flo, who warned him, very quietly once again, to back off.

'You blokes without trousers, beg or borrow, but find something to put on until I get back. And you Max, you're coming with me.'

'Where are we going?' Max scowled.

'To get the stores. Where else? I'll finish this list while you hitch up the wagon. He has got a wagon, hasn't he?'

'Yeah.'

'Well, get a move on.'

'Where does the lieutenant buy his stores?' Flo asked Max amiably as he drove the wagon into town.

'At the Davey Street warehouse.'

'Right. That's where we go. Now I've got my list written out, so I'll give the order, then I've got to duck off and see my girl. There's ten bob in it for you if you keep your mouth shut. You pack the wagon up and we'll have a few ales before we go back.'

Max was surprised by this turn of events, and readily agreed to the plan, and Flo watched him lumber into the store before he set off on his mission.

The first policeman he found at the station was Sergeant Budd, who wasted no time with niceties.

'What are you doing here, Quinlan? What have you done now?'

'Didn't you hear? I'm Lieutenant Flood's overseer!'

561

'Ah yes,' Budd said warily, the name of the Governor's aide requiring caution.

'I wanted to ask you, do you know Zack Herring?'

'Yes. What about him?'

'He was Flood's overseer before me, and he got bashed by Max Grigg. Bashed so badly he's lost an eye.'

'Bloody hell! What goes on out there? I reckon there are a few too many accidents. You'd better keep the place in order, Quinlan, or we'll be making a visit and your mates won't be too happy about that.'

'I'm trying. The Lieutenant's bloody cranky about Zack. This stuff gives him a bad name. But the thing is, Grigg's built like a bullock, and the boss didn't want any more violence, so I've been sent to deliver him to Hippisley. I'm to take out a charge against him for criminal assault and serious bodily harm, to whit, knocking out an eye.'

'I don't need Hippisley. I know the charges,' Budd said testily. 'Where's Zack?'

'In hospital still.'

'Fair enough. Where do we pick up the bruiser?'

'He's at the Davey Street store. You could send some of your lads around and pick him up now.'

'Will you stop telling me what to do.'

'I just meant the Lieutenant will be pleased to have Grigg out of the way without any ructions.'

'Yeah, all right. Can you write?'

'Yes.'

'Then fill in this form, and sign it.'

Flo took to the form with diligence, signing it

with a flourish: *James Quinlan. Overseer. Flood Estate.*

Budd sat on his horse, aware of gathering public interest at the commotion inside the store, until eventually two dishevelled constables dragged Grigg into the street and the crowd clapped.

'Good on you, Budd!' someone called. 'Now go get his brother.'

Budd appreciated the rare acclaim. Usually an arrest in this town was accompanied by spit and boos, even rocks.

They roped Grigg to his saddle, Goosey gave him a few kicks to get him moving, and the small cavalcade moved off to the lockup.

There was no sign of Quinlan, who was inside the store busily purchasing necessities for the comfort of Flood's convict workers, as well as enough rations to stock their larder for weeks.

'That's a big order for Flood,' one of the storemen said.

'If it's too much for you, I can buy the rest at Pollard's store.'

'No, we can fill it, Mr Quinlan.'

'Then get on with it. I haven't got all day.'

Three days later, when Flood and his wife returned, they were relieved to find that their new overseer had made a good start.

'However long it may last,' Tom Flood muttered sourly.

But for now, the grounds leading up to the homestead had been tidied, the hedges clipped, lawns mown, trees pruned and plants staked. The drive had been evenly raked with not a stray leaf to spoil the effect. The stables too were a pleasant surprise. The whole large complex, from the courtyard to the stalls, not only shone with the obvious spit and polish of many hands, it had a tangy, clean whiff of eucalypt, and the two stableboys, neat as pins, stood by, beaming, to welcome the master and mistress home.

They were not rewarded with recognition of work well done, but since they were spared the usual bawling-out for some infringement of duty, all was well until Owen Grigg came lumbering over with his bad news.

'Boss,' he called, 'we've got trouble. Max got hisself arrested.'

'You mean we're rid of him?' Mrs Flood sniffed.

'How did he get arrested? Were the police out here?'

'No, he went into town with Quinlan to get the stores and the police pounced on him.'

'What for?'

'Quinlan says they charged him for knocking out Zack's eye! They just marched into the store and took him away. In irons.'

'Oh dear God, he lost his eye!' Mrs Flood cried.

'Will you get him out, boss?' Owen was insistent. 'He was only doing his job.'

The lieutenant dismissed him. 'You get back to work. Leave it to me.'

As Owen slumped away, Antonia Flood turned on her husband. 'Don't you dare bail out that thug! I told you to get rid of that pair, but no, you wouldn't listen to me. You've got a new overseer

564

now. The same thing will happen to him if you don't get rid of this brother as well. People talk, Tom. There've been too many accidents here.'

'Will you shut up! I can't get rid of Owen, he knows too much.'

'So does Max.'

'Not really, he's a prize idiot. He couldn't put two and two together with four hands. Owen's the brains of the outfit.'

'Such as they are.'

Flood never went down to the men's quarters, which he called the Swamp, since they were located in an undrained area near marshes, so he had no idea that the spick and span regime now extended to the dormitories, kitchen and mess hall. And since the storeroom, which had originally held clothing and bedding for his convict workers, was in its usual state of disrepair, with large holes in the thatched roof and the door hanging loose, he tramped past it without a second glance.

Not that he would have learned anything. It was still empty. Every item that the new overseer had purchased in town, at great expense to his master, had been distributed to the workers as soon as Quinlan brought the loaded wagon to rest past the stables. And on the same afternoon another wagon had arrived, packed with new horsehair mattresses and blankets, all swiftly removed to the dormitories.

Everything, therefore, was in order as far as Flo was concerned when he heard the boss was home. The pantry was well stocked and everyone had been dining well for the past few days. He handed tobacco rations to men who'd rarely seen their quota on this farm, and who now took on their designated jobs with a modicum of enthusiasm and curiosity. They couldn't figure out why Flo wanted them to do their jobs properly and efficiently.

'I'm only trying to show you that if you get fair treatment then you should do a fair day's work.'

'For Flood?' they argued. 'He doesn't deserve a fair go.'

'Just leave that to me. It's your records I worry about. This farm is run down and you're bringing the blame down on yourselves. Bear with me awhile.'

A man called Jonah came to warn Flo that the Grigg brothers had guns hidden in the thatch of their hut.

'Like, don't turn your back on Owen, he's got it in for you.'

'I expect he has, but he'll have to fight fair now. I pinched their guns and dumped them in the swamp.'

'You pinched them? Then how come Owen isn't kicking up about that? He must be hopping mad.'

'What? And let on to everyone that he's lost them? Not him. He can't afford to scream. What if the boss finds out? He'll get hell!'

Tom Flood had soon discovered that Zack Herring might have been a good gardener, but he was no farmer, nor did he have any idea of delegating duties, which was bloody annoying. By the time he came to that realisation, Owen Grigg reported that Herring had been spying on the riverside sheds, even though Flood himself had called that area out of bounds. So the overseer had to go.

Tom wasn't concerned about Zack Herring's misfortunes, or Max's for that matter, and he was irritated to find Owen Grigg loitering by the gate of the home paddock when he rode out on his rounds the next morning.

'What's happening about me brother?' Owen asked.

'I've written a letter to the judge,' Tom lied, stalling for time. 'I'll send it to him this morning. In the meantime, you keep your mouth shut. I told you to warn Zack off the river sheds – to give him a pasting, that's all. Now get back down to the sheds. Surely you can handle patrolling a boundary on your own.'

Grigg opened his mouth to say something, but changed his mind, and Tom rode on to the main barn, where Quinlan was writing up a roster. The new overseer seemed genuinely pleased to see the boss, and volunteered to explain his roster, but Tom waved it aside.

'Just keep them working,' he said. 'They're a lazy lot.'

'I'll do that, for sure,' Quinlan said, 'but I need your approval for a few jobs. The water supply for the top paddocks is running down, you need a new well up there. And I was thinking, if we drained those marshes you'd have real good soil there for crops. It's just a waste now. And isn't it time to bring in some shearers?'

'No, let the men do it. Shearers charge the earth.'

'So they do, but from what I hear, your own men are no good at it, so what's the use of that?'

'See if you can find some at a reasonable rate.'

'I'll do that. It says here that you've got a flock of four hundred and thirty sheep in your fields,' Quinlan said, obviously impressed, but Tom gave a shout of anger.

'What? Show me that? I should have more than six hundred! Where are the rest? Where are they?'

He peered at the pages, running a finger down the entries. 'How can this be right? I can't be missing more than a hundred sheep, surely to God.'

'I don't know. I'll get out and do a proper count for you. The books could be wrong.'

'They'd better be,' Tom said. 'Get on it now and report back to me. I've got enough problems without this.'

As he headed off to his other property on the river side of Sassafras Road, he was considering chucking in his lucrative smuggling business. There were too many at it now. Besides, the Governor had plans to employ a dozen more inspectors in the Customs and Excise offices to slow traffic, since the colony's budget relied heavily on import duties.

'Might be a good time to drop out,' he murmured.

Having set everyone into their traces, Flo rode off to count sheep, which he regarded as a mildly pleasurable way to spend a balmy day, with a choir of birds to accompany him, and bread and cheese and two apples in his saddle bag. In the morning he would be able to report to the boss that the books were indeed wrong. There were only forty animals missing. He'd already had the men do a count.

So there he was, with a day in the open all to himself, riding happily across the countryside, when he saw a lady coming towards him, riding side-saddle, a pretty sight, he thought, in her black-and-white tailored attire and perky hat.

On closer inspection, though, he recognised Mrs Flood's elongated countenance, and was reminded that she was hardly any better-looking than her husband. Nevertheless, as she approached, Flo sat grandly in the saddle, gentleman-style, rejecting the accepted convict slump that was required in the company of their betters, and brushed his long lashes at her as he passed by without a word. Not a word. He simply rode on as if in a trance. Until she called to him. As he'd known she would.

'Who are you?' she enquired in a high-pitched, high-falutin' voice.

Flo came alive. Suddenly. As if she'd startled him from sleep. He reined his horse about, turning to face her. And when he did, his face lit up as if he'd been confronted by beauty. By blinding beauty!

The intended compliment was not lost on her; in fact it had such an impact that Mrs Flood smiled coyly as he responded quietly: 'Dear lady, James Quinlan at your service.'

'You're our new overseer?' she asked, her voice now gentler.

He raised finely drawn eyebrows and cast his

soft brown eyes upon her. 'That I am, and never expected to come across such style out here in the wilds, if I may say so, madam.'

'Where are you going?'

'I was heading thataway, towards the waterfalls. I'm told they're very beautiful.'

'And very hard to find,' she smiled. 'They're off to the left here. Would you like me to show you? We're very proud of them.'

'How kind you are! I should be much obliged, madam.'

And that was how Flo came to meet Mrs Flood.

And how she came to fall madly in love with him.

CHAPTER SEVENTEEN

It went against the grain for Shanahan to be forwarding mail to the likes of Bull Harris, but the letter from Louise softened his heart. Had he known the content, though, that heart would have turned to ice.

Lester was thrilled that his daughter had been smart enough to figure out a way to contact him directly, and really touched to hear that as a grown young lady now she still loved her daddy. He was determined that when he got out of this place he'd make it up to her. He'd run the farm and she'd have the best of everything, because he couldn't get over the way she was sticking by him. Lester had never expected this of a girl he'd hardly known, but there it was in her neat handwriting, clear as a bell.

You have to Refuse to sell the Farm because Mother says as soon as she sells we are going Home to England. So please do not Sign.

This from his loving daughter.

Lester was proud of her. And enraged that Josie thought she could get away with this. He'd guessed this was what she'd been up to all along. Now he knew, and he had to do something about it.

He thought of having another talk with Toohill, but remembered he'd advised selling. The snake! Lester wondered if he'd acquainted himself with Josie while he was in Hobart and seen a way to make a quick quid for himself.

For days, with Louise's warning ringing in his ears, Lester fretted himself into a state of near despair, until he awoke one morning with the answer. He threw off the despair and replaced it with an anger so fierce, his fellow workers crept about the butchery, afraid they might incur violence if they so much as stood upon his shadow.

But then they became very busy, because the Commandant had ordered the best cuts of meat for a dinner party, since he was expecting important visitors: some gentlemen from the Colonial Office in London, with their ladies. In fact the whole of the penal establishment was in for yet another of his 'shake-ups', to present the best face possible for the touring nobs.

The English visitors would be arriving on the Saturday and accommodated in the visitors' cottage. They would be dining at the Commandant's residence on the Saturday night, after which they were to be treated to a concert.

The choirmaster received a list of hymns to be sung at Sunday service, plus the news that he was to arrange the concert. Within two days he was to provide the Commandant with suggested entertainment items, and on the sixth day a rehearsal of said items, attended by the Commandant, would be held at two p.m. on the lawns by the church.

In his own hand the Commandant added some suggestions to the formal instructions written by his secretary. He wanted to begin and end the concert with band music, preferably marches. There was to be an acrobat or a juggler. A boy soprano dressed as a girl. A harmonising trio. Two solo singers, a baritone and a tenor, both to sing ballads. Also a clown, a tumbling clown.

As he handed over the instructions, his secretary explained to the choirmaster that any other items he could suggest would be welcome, and tested at the rehearsal.

'And before I forget, dig out a fellow called James Forbes. The Commandant likes his voice. And send someone over to the boys' prison for a few juvenile singers, so that we can choose the best. The rehearsal should be quite fun, what?'

The choirmaster was petrified. He didn't want this responsibility. It was hard enough trying to keep a choir of convicts in order, without letting them loose on a stage with visitors at their mercy.

As for Forbes, he'd already been recommended to him for the choir by men who had heard him sing, but had refused to have any part of it. The choirmaster had a nervous feeling about approaching Forbes for a solo performance; he sensed trouble brewing, but this was an order, no ducking it.

As a trusty, he was able to access the main prison and 'happen' upon his man in the exercise yard. Forbes was resting on his haunches, one long leg stretched forward in a stance common to the work-weary men – a sort of not quite squatting that eased muscles and kept them alert.

'I say! Aren't you Singer Forbes? I'm the choirmaster,' he began.

'Yes. I saw you coming,' Forbes said amiably. 'You do well with the choir, you've got the lads singing like sirens.'

'But they can't tempt you to join them?'

'No. Just listening to them of a Sunday morning will do me.'

'But I hear you have a fine voice. Why waste it?'

Forbes shrugged. 'Ah now, leave off, mate. It's my life being wasted here, not my voice.'

The choirmaster gave up on the tactful approach. 'Let me tell you then, you've been especially chosen to sing at a concert being organised for some official visitors. Not in the choir, if you prefer. Solo.'

'Who by?'

'The Commandant himself. That's quite an honour. And you're sure to win some points if you please his guests. It'd be a help for me too. I've got to get this right.'

Forbes climbed to his feet, and pushed his cap back on his head. 'Listen, I'd like to help, but if I don't sing for God in his church, what makes you think I'd sing for that sadistic son-of-a-bitch?'

A whistle blew.

'Time's up,' he said. 'In we go.'

The choirmaster lowered his voice. 'Listen, Forbes, I understand your attitude, but be careful. A request from the Commandant is an order. You must know that!'

'Yes. That's the best part,' Singer laughed.

They had joined the queue shuffling towards the exit when there was a sudden shriek from the far end of the yard, then another, and another. All the men stopped, their faces grim, and the choirmaster shuddered, recognising the sounds of a flogger at work.

'He's late today,' Forbes said harshly. 'Tell the Commandant I said to go to hell!'

While he waited for a guard to open the outer door, the choirmaster looked back at Forbes. He was a handsome fellow, with a cool elegance, despite the drab prison garb, and would have been an asset fronting the choir.

'A pity,' he muttered.

Days passed. The choir practised twice daily, and everything was going smoothly, until Captain Biddle, the Commandant's secretary, arrived on the scene.

He checked the list of proposed acts, the names of all the performers, and the titles of the hymns and songs to be rendered.

That done, he snapped his fingers at the choirmaster. 'I say! Where's that Forbes fellow?'

'We won't be using him.'

'Think again, choirmaster. It's not your place to say who we might and might not be using. Get him here immediately!'

'I'm sorry, Captain. Forbes refuses to sing. But I found a Welshman with a fine voice.'

'Did you not hear what I said? Get Forbes here!'

To fill in time, Biddle lined up the sixty members of the choir, checking their heights and assigning places for them to stand, with the tallest four rows back, and the shortest sitting cross-legged at the front, as if for a school portrait.

Eventually he had a formation to his liking, and instructed the choirmaster to make a note of their positions.

'That is where they are to stand for the concert. They look, aesthetically, much better this way.'

'I'm sure they do, Captain, but I can't have them sitting if they are to sing their best. And for harmony they already have their positions. I can't be mixing them up.'

Biddle fumed. 'You will stand them exactly as I say, do you hear me? Now, you fellows start calling your names so that the choirmaster can write down your places, to make certain he gets it right.'

The choirmaster saw the men smirking at Biddle's unintentional sabotage of their none-too-enthusiastic efforts, and he groaned.

But then, he thought, what did he care either? If the Commandant complained, he would have Biddle's instructions in writing. He began drawing the positions and naming them with care, remembering to note under each name whether the man was a tenor, a baritone, et cetera, to emphasise Biddle's blasphemy.

After a while guards came trotting down the dusty road, hauling Forbes between them.

'Are you Forbes?' the captain asked belligerently.

'Yes.'

'Then sing!'

'Sing what?'

'Anything!'

Forbes looked at the captain's shiny boots. 'Fine boots you've got there. Look at my footwear. The soles are falling off.'

'Never mind about that. Choose a song. I wish to hear you sing.'

Forbes looked over to the members of the choir. 'Would any of you have a spare sole?'

They laughed.

Biddle raised his riding whip and pushed the point of the handle into Singer's cheek. 'I gave you an order.'

The choirmaster peered at Singer, shaking his head, trying to convince him not to take this charade too far.

'So you did,' Forbes said quietly. 'So we might as well get this straight. I do not sing. Now go and find someone else.'

Biddle was outraged! 'Prisoner Forbes. Stand over by that fence and sing a ballad or I shall have you flogged.'

The guards rushed forward and hurried Forbes the few steps to the fence, at the same time whispering to him to sing and get it over with, but even they couldn't convince him to back down.

Forbes turned about, facing the captain. 'This is ridiculous. If you have me flogged I'll be in no condition to sing, believe me. Have you ever heard anyone sing after they've had the skin torn off their back?'

'We'll see about that!' Biddle shouted. 'Chain him to the fence, guards, then fetch the Chief Constable. While I'm waiting, choirmaster, I wish to hear the hymns you've prepared, and I don't want to hear one wrong note.'

As if you'd know, the choirmaster fumed, and took out his tuning fork. He looked for his lead singer, but had to search for him among the grinning faces.

Chief Constable Toohill hated the bumptious little captain, who was known to claim that his position as secretary to the Commandant gave him precedence over all ranks. A claim ignored by Captain McDougall, senior officer of the small band of Fusiliers based at Port Arthur, and hotly rejected by the Chief Constable.

'He's only a bloody clerk,' he would say, in his long-winded bureaucratic battle for superiority, 'and a pimp at that! Who does he think he is, telling guards to fetch me?' he roared. 'I'll give him fetch!'

When he arrived on the scene, the choir was rounding off a poor rendition of 'Lead, Kindly Light', with Biddle as audience.

577

'What's going on here?' Toohill asked, without bothering to be civil to the captain.

Biddle did likewise. 'Prisoner Forbes there persistently refused to obey an order.'

'Then why drag me down here? Why didn't you just send him up to me?'

'Because he has been ordered to sing with the choir and refuses to do so. Start him with forty lashes, then we'll get some sense out of him.'

'I can't. The flogger's sick.'

'Get someone else.'

'No one else is rostered,' Toohill informed him smugly. 'And you can't be squealing for help every time someone bucks your orders.'

'I'll have you know the order came from the Commandant.'

'Oh Gawd!' The Chief Constable turned to the prisoner. 'What's wrong with you, Forbes? Why won't you do as the nice captain tells you?'

'Because I don't want to sing.' Forbes shrugged.

Toohill was incredulous. 'You don't what?'

Biddle explained. 'I have to audition him for the Commandant's concert, but he won't sing. I'm sick of him wasting my time. A flogging will smarten him up.'

Toohill squared his shoulders and cast a wary eye upon this office-wallah. 'Did the Commandant order the flogging?'

'Not exactly. But I have the authority to do so. Forbes must obey me or accept the consequences.'

The Chief Constable removed his cap and scratched his head as if mystified by this situation. 'In the first place, Mr Secretary, you do not have the authority to order a flogging, and in the second place, refusing an order to sing is not a crime.'

'It is so!' Biddle pouted.

''Tis not!' Forbes called from the sidelines, enjoying the confrontation.

'Insubordination is,' Biddle contended angrily.

'Even so, regulations do have qualifying clauses. If the order is foolish, impractical, dangerous or, as in this case, trivial, I am required to refer the matter to the Commandant. So you must stand aside.'

'You are wasting my time, Toohill. But you've had your say, and your services are no longer required.'

'Neither are mine!' Forbes called. 'Can I go now?'

The choirmaster walked over to him. 'You're bloody mad, Forbes. Sing while you still can!'

Biddle took his outrage to the Commandant.

'The fellow is not only insubordinate, sir, he is refusing to sing in defiance of your direct order. And flaunting that defiance, making himself out a hero for standing up to authority.'

'Over a song? What's he up to? I didn't ask him to stand on his head and sing. Just sing a couple of songs. For Christ's sake! Did you ask him why he won't sing?'

'No need. He's a grandstander. Just being stubborn.'

'There is bloody need. Find out, damn you! Where does he work?'

'In the iron foundry.'

'Then get down there. He's after something, a reward of some sort. A lighter job maybe. Any-

579

way, offer it to him. It's no skin off my nose.'

There were eighteen men working in the foundry, which doubled as a blacksmith's shop, and six forges were in full operation trying to keep up with the orders. Ironwork for all the government buildings was cast under this roof, and the overseer was in a rage, having just been told that he was to cast a bell for the new church.

'Haven't I got enough to do?' he roared at the accountant who had the misfortune to deliver that message and the specifications. 'I've got these blokes working half the night as it is. If I'm to turn out satisfactory work I'll need more men, and men who know what they're doing. I can't afford any more accidents. The Commandant's already blowing down my ear, blaming me for the bloody pansies who can't lift a shovel.'

'I'll mention it to the Assistant Superintendent.'

'No you won't. You've got access to records; you dig out former blacksmiths and foundry workers, and slip the names to me. I'll do the rest.'

Among the convicts transferred to the foundry was Angus McLeod. He was disappointed to have lost his cushy job on the farm, but he cheered up when he found Singer working there.

'I wouldna have picked you for a foundry man, Singer,' he said.

'I'm not. This is the worst job I've ever had. Nearly burned my arm off last week.'

'It's a hard job to get used to, I'll allow. I was born to it, so I'll keep an eye on you. Find you a safe spot.' He sighed. 'You'd hardly believe I've come across the world and ended up here worse off, in the same job. I got transported for fighting for better wages and conditions in our foundry, and look what we get here. About a shillin' a week if we're lucky. Makes you think, doesn't it?'

'Yes, but they give us bed and board,' Singer laughed.

'Bugger their bed and board!'

A few days later Singer was pulled off the job by two guards under instructions from the Commandant's secretary. No reason given.

The overseer bawled at Singer: 'What's your game here, Forbes? You get back here bloody quick or I'll put you on report.'

'All right then, I won't go. I don't know what they want.'

The overseer had to let him go, of course, but not without a few choice words for the guards.

Singer was back within the hour, to be met at the gate by the sweating overseer, who was dousing himself with water from a bucket.

'What did they want?' he asked.

'They wanted me to sing,' Singer said, straight-faced.

'They what?'

'True!'

Incredulous, the overseer shook his head. 'Bloody topsy-turvy this place, with the maddest at the top.'

He was to be sorely tried later in the day when Captain Biddle, keeping his distance from the dirt and sweat of the foundry, sent someone inside to fetch the overseer.

'Does James Forbes work here?' the captain

asked when a brawny man in a sleeveless flannel shirt and a leather apron over battered trousers lumbered out.

'Why?' the overseer responded with matching disregard.

'Because I want to talk to him.'

The overseer stuck his head in the door and shouted: 'Get Singer out here,' over the heave and rumble of the foundry. 'Now what's this about?' he asked Singer as he approached.

'I told you, he wants me to sing.'

'He is refusing to sing,' the captain corrected. 'You listen here, Forbes. This is your last chance. If you're angling for some sort of payment or reward, you'd better spit it out now. The Commandant is losing patience with you.'

'All right. I'll sing if you release me.'

'Fat chance of that.'

'And the chances of me singing for you are just as fat. Tell that to the master.' Bemused, the overseer watched Captain Biddle storm off. He sent Forbes back to work, and then ambled over to Angus, his new foreman.

'Forbes is your mate. Tell me, why won't he sing for them?'

'Because he says he shouldn't be here. It's an injustice.'

'A lot of good that will do him.'

'Aye, don't I know it,' Angus said quietly. 'I'll try talking to him again, but I doubt he'll listen.'

Secretary Biddle could hardly believe the man's arrogance.

'He still refuses to obey,' he told the Commandant. 'A good flogging will change his tune.'

'A flogging? He wouldn't have time to recover! The man has a splendid voice. Very melodious. I want him in top form. Throw him in to solitary, with instructions that the minute he agrees to sing, he's to be released.'

The foundry overseer was having a bad day. Two men were away due to sickness, one man had fallen against a forge and sustained serious burns, another had collapsed, and while they were trying to revive him, two guards came for Singer.

'Not again,' he roared at them. 'He's given his answer, now get out of here. He's got work to do.'

'No he hasn't. We've got orders to take him to the magistrate.' The spokesman dropped his voice. 'He's headed for the bin.'

'Jesus! They're not going to put him in solitary?'

The overseer marched through the busy foundry and grabbed hold of Singer. 'You'd better give up the game now, or you're for solitary.'

Singer was taken aback. 'Solitary? Bloody hell!'

'So it is! Angus'll tell you all about it, no need to find out for yourself. You get out there quick and tell them you'll sing.'

He whistled to Angus to join them as they headed outside, but neither of them could persuade Singer to back down.

'I'll send Angus up to Captain Biddle's office right now to tell him you'll sing for them,' the overseer said. 'You've had your fun, so let go. The guards will wait, won't you, mates?'

They shrugged. Not a problem.

583

'No,' Singer said firmly. 'No.'

And that was that.

'Even though it's an order from the Commandant,' one of the guards told Singer, 'you still have to front a magistrate, so that justice looks as if it's being done. But you've got time to get out of it, mate! You only have to say the word.'

Singer had nothing to say until it came his turn to be led into the small courtroom, crowded with civilian residents, who regarded the court sessions as entertainment, given the lack of such in their tiny closed community.

He was stunned to find himself face to face with Magistrate Sholto Matson, sworn enemy of Sean Shanahan.

When Matson sentenced him to solitary confinement, 'until you repent and obey a direct order', Singer turned and shouted to the audience.

'Do you know who this man is?' he cried, pointing at Matson. 'He's vicious, a disgrace to the law. All of Hobart was up in arms at his torturing of Matt O'Neill, prior to his death.'

Even as Matson started shouting to shut him up, and bewildered guards, slow to react, began to move, Singer could see the interest he'd stirred up. The audience, especially the women, were all ears, some leaning forward, listening intently.

'That's right,' he shouted. 'Yes, that's him, that's evil in the flesh! Mad Matson! The shame of the courts.'

As the guards dragged him away, he managed to yell: 'No wonder he's here! Hidden from the public! You're a disgrace, Matson!'

His situation took another turn when Dr Roberts came to check on him in the duty room.

All prisoners sentenced to solitary had to be examined by a doctor before they were locked in, to make sure no prior condition made them unfit for the rigours of those cells, and Roberts was doing his duty when the prisoner, Forbes, asked him if he knew the regulations.

'I think so. I've been boning up on them,' Roberts said candidly.

'Then do you know the one about insubordination?'

'Is that why you're being punished?'

'Yes. I won't sing for them.'

'Sing?'

'That's what I said. Now, flogging and solitary cannot be inflicted on a prisoner for trivial reasons. Wouldn't you say refusing to sing is a trivial matter? Hardly such an offence as to warrant solitary.'

The doctor was worried.

'Believe me,' Singer added, 'they wanted to have me flogged, but the Chief Constable refused the order on the same grounds. He said exactly that, that the offence was trivial. But they've bypassed him now.'

Roberts held up his hand. 'Wait a minute. Can we start again? Who are they?'

'The Commandant and Captain Biddle. You've got some nobs coming to visit, and they're arranging a concert.'

'Ah yes.' Roberts nodded. 'Right. And that's why they want you to sing? For the concert? And you've refused?'

'Yes. And since they can't get away with flogging me, they simply ordered Matson, the crooked magistrate, to sentence me to solitary, which he did, of course. Even though the sentence is illegal.'

Obviously concerned, the doctor mulled over the information for a few minutes, then he excused himself and told the guards to keep Forbes in place until he returned.

Allyn hurried over to the office of the Chief Constable. He was seriously worried about this situation, realising that he would be disagreeing with the Commandant if he interfered. And that was what he was about – interference. The last thing he wanted to do. His job was to check on the health of the prisoner, not the legalities of the sentence.

What are you doing? he asked himself anxiously, but he knew he couldn't let this pass, even though he was prepared to overlook the obvious fact that Matson's behaviour here was outrageous. He was simply a rubber stamp for the Commandant, and the sentence itself was overkill.

Toohill was not in his office, so Allyn put the question to his clerk.

'Are you aware of the situation regarding Prisoner Forbes?'

'Refusing to sing?' The clerk grinned. 'Oh yes.'

'And did the Chief Constable state that in this case a flogging was not permissible?'

'He did, sir. He said the offence was too trivial.'

The clerk was enjoying this so much, Allyn realised he was probably a convict himself, but working here, the fellow would know the rules.

'Would the same regulation apply to solitary confinement?' he asked. 'I mean, in the same case?'

The grin disappeared. 'Doctor,' he said, 'no one other than the Governor can sentence a man to solitary for a trivial offence. And believe me, if you've come here for the Chief Constable's advice, that is what he would tell you.'

'Thank you. I'm obliged.'

Nevertheless. Allyn was nervous when he spoke to one of the guards. 'I'm sorry, I can't sign this clearance. The punishment is illegal. If you have doubts, refer the prisoner to the Chief Constable.'

'What will I do with him then?' The guard was confused.

'Take him back to his cell, I suppose.'

Once again, Singer was hobbled and led away.

'That was close,' he said to the guard.

When the Commandant heard that Forbes was not where he was supposed to be, thanks to the interference of the new medical officer, he bellowed at Captain Biddle, threatened to sack him, and issued another order.

'Very well,' he snarled. 'Give him a dose of an isolation cell, and tell him he stays there until he apologises and obeys instructions.'

To keep the prisoner report sheets in order, Biddle went first to Magistrate Matson to place on record that James Forbes's sentence of solitary confinement had been revoked and that he'd been assigned instead to an isolation cell.

'What's the difference?' Matson asked.

587

'The difference is this: they stay in Cell Block S. They're ordinary cells, but those prisoners have no contact with anyone. When they are taken out, they have to wear hoods.'

'What sort of hoods?' Matson asked.

'Leather, with slits for the eyes. They sit on their shoulders. They stay in their cells all the time except for their exercise. This is permitted once a day – walking up and down inside the cell block, wearing the hood. They are not allowed to see or speak to anyone.'

'What about their meals?'

'Food is handed into their cells twice a day. In silence. They wear the hoods to church and they sit in those wooden stalls...'

'With walls like blinkers? I've seen them. I wondered what they were for.'

'Now you know,' Biddle continued. 'That's so they can't see anyone, only the altar.'

The magistrate wasn't impressed. 'And that's supposed to be punishment? Sounds a damn waste of time to me.'

'Aha, that's what the prisoners think when they're sent into isolation, but they're wrong.' Biddle's eyes gleamed with excitement. 'It drives them batty. And it's not really a punishment, you see. No one gets hurt. So there's no need for the rules about a doctor on that watch.'

'It doesn't make any sense to me, but I'll make the correction. I hope the Commandant doesn't think this mix-up is my fault.'

'He's not pleased,' the captain said. 'He expects you to recognise legal hitches, and let him know.

'By the way, Mrs Biddle is feeling poorly. She

588

asked me to apologise to you and your lady, but we shall have to postpone our little luncheon tomorrow.'

'That's a shame,' Matson said. 'My wife will be disappointed.'

So will I, Biddle mused. His wife's a real eyeful. However, his own wife had seen and heard the commotion in the courtroom when the magistrate had sentenced Forbes.

'It's bad enough we have to suffer Matson's common wife,' she said, 'but after what I heard today, I refuse to entertain the man.'

Angus soon learned that Singer had been sent to the 'Hoods', and tried to contact him, but it was too late.

'All that over a song,' he told George Smith when they met in the exercise yard.

'He'll give in as soon as that concert is over,' George said. 'He's only got a day to go.'

'I hope so,' Angus said gloomily.

What George didn't tell Angus, not yet anyway, was that Willem had managed to smuggle a letter to him, telling him he would keep his promise soon, and that he hoped George was able to attend church on a Sunday morning. The letter was signed: *Your loving Mother.*

George had been stunned when the letter was slipped to him by an elderly lifer, who worked in the church as a janitor. It happened so quickly, with the letter suddenly in his hand, that he almost gave the game away by staring at it before he shoved it out of sight.

He took it to mean that an escape plan was in

the wind, one that necessitated his attending church on a Sunday, and thinking it over, he agreed it wouldn't be a bad time and place to try for a break. Jobs were switched around so often, it'd be hard to nominate which end of the peninsula a man would be on any given day. Not that it would be easy, he worried. He'd really have to set his mind to figuring out how to abscond. Willem could only arrange to get him off the island, to pick him up from a spot yet to be named, but George would have to get himself there.

Attempts to escape from Port Arthur were so common, they'd become almost a pastime for a number of lifers who had nothing to lose. Some of them simply dodged away from work parties and hid in the inland forests, hoping for a miracle, and were only listed as absconders. Either way, escape was always a favourite topic of conversation.

George yearned to be free of this prison; it was a dangerous place for men with his reputation. To make matters worse, the scars were not healing. The thin skin on his face was deteriorating into weeping sores and scabs. Some men found them disgusting and refused to sit near him in the mess. The doctor had given him some ointment, but it wasn't helping much. He'd written away to a specialist for advice. George didn't put much store by that idea.

The important visitors arrived and the convicts began taking bets on Singer Forbes. Would he sing or would he not?

Toohill bet Matson five shillings that the prisoner would not fold in time, and after the concert he went in search of Magistrate Matson to claim his winnings but was unable to find him.

When he met up with Biddle, he learned that the magistrate had not been invited to the concert, or to the dance to be held afterwards.

'We had that fellow dumped on us,' Biddle fretted. 'I had no idea who he was, and now the Commandant is livid. Blaming me, saying I should have checked on him before he rubber-stamped the appointment.'

Toohill couldn't care less about Matson. 'And Forbes still didn't sing for you,' he gloated.

'No. But he will. The orders are now that he stays in isolation until he apologises and volunteers to sing for the Commandant. The man is nothing but a damned nuisance.'

This Sunday morning was as warm and lovely a day as he'd ever seen, Angus thought, as they marched along towards the church. He found himself admiring the flowerbeds that bordered the road, and the native trees with their gaggles of chattering birds, and thinking of Mr Warboy's garden and how well it must look after the spring rains.

They turned into the long avenue of trees, and as he glanced about, Angus saw that a contingent of 'Hoods' was right behind them. He managed to hang back as they were filing into the church to get a glimpse of them as they shambled by in their grotesque head coverings, and was at least able to pick out Singer's tall shape, though he was unable to contact him.

I'll do better next time, he vowed, interested to

591

see that those men had their hands bound and were roped to the man in front, but were not wearing ankle chains. Angus was very aware of those chains, because he'd had to wear them himself until the overseer demanded they be removed. But they made the chains here, in the foundry, and went to great lengths to make them as flawed as possible whenever they could.

Singer seemed fit. Obviously he hadn't been flogged, which was a relief, but having to live like that was ugly and degrading. Angus prayed his friend's ordeal would soon be over.

Sometimes, in the mess, he'd have a yarn with George, who was surprised to find that Angus's fury had subsided quite a bit since his time in solitary. When George asked how he'd ended up here, a lifer like him, Angus was at last able to talk about it, and he supposed that was a milestone.

'God save us!' George said, on hearing Angus's story. 'That's a grievous thing to happen to a man. Why wouldn't the Warboy girl tell the truth?'

'Damned if I know.'

'Where is she now?'

'Still at the farm, I suppose.'

'Looks to me as if she deserves the strap.'

'Oh no!' Angus cried. 'Someone has shamed her. Raped an innocent girl and left her with a baby. I worry about Penn, and wonder how she's getting along.'

Shanahan was curious too, but more interested in how Marie Cullen was faring in her new job as lady's maid.

Unable to find work as yet, he went fishing and

caught more than he needed, so he decided to take a few out to Mrs Harris, who was delighted at his thoughtfulness.

He spent a couple of hours at the farm, helping to repair holes in the roof of the barn, then went on his way again, meaning to call at Warboy's, but he met Billo on the road.

'Been making the delivery to the cheese factory?' he asked.

'Ah yes. Nothing much changes.'

It seemed all was going well under Hunter's supervision, and the Sunday day off had been restored. As had the later curfew.

'And how is Marie Cullen getting along?'

'Was that Miss Warboy's maid?'

'Yes. Why?' Sean asked anxiously. 'Is she not there any more?'

'She's gone. And Miss Warboy too.'

'Where to?'

'No one knows. Dossie said Mr Warboy packed them up and took them away himself.'

'Who drove the carriage?'

'Hunter did, but he only got to take them as far as Pollard's store. He never saw them no more after that. Dossie thinks it's a nunnery has got them.'

Sean shook his head. 'They could put Miss Warboy in a nunnery, but she wouldn't need a maid there. I hope they didn't send Marie back to the Factory. Dammit! I'll have to see about that.'

Billo was on for a yarn now. 'Did you hear about Flo Quinlan?'

'No. What's he up to now?'

'Well, you know he's the overseer at Flood's?

Well! It didn't take long for him to fall out with the Grigg brothers, but he had their measure. First he gives Owen a punch in the face, then he gets Max arrested for bashing Zack. That's him out of the way, and Owen too scared to take on Flo.'

'Good work! What did Flood make of it?'

'He was away. It was all over when he got back.' Billo grinned. 'Nothing much he could do. But guess what?'

'What?'

'Word has it Flo's romancing Flood's wife!'

'No!' Sean roared with laughter. 'What would he want with that ugly shrew?'

'I suppose he doesn't have to pay her,' Billo said thoughtfully.

As he rode away, Sean was still chuckling about that, until he remembered the two boats the lieutenant had in that shed. He almost turned back to have a word with Flo, but decided it wouldn't be a good idea to be seen on Flood's property, given that those boats could be useful one of these days.

Instead, as soon as he was back in town, he went in search of Bailey to find out where Marie had got to.

First, of course, Sean detoured around the wharves to check shipping arrivals, but there were only a few new whalers and a merchant ship from Singapore. No tall ships from the Old World today, and no coastal steamers; the latter were important, because most of the big ships ended their journeys in Sydney or another mainland

594

port. The penal settlement of Van Diemen's Land was not a priority for settlers, miners or travellers; or the gentlemen of various nationalities eyeing possibilities for investment. It occurred to Sean that if Glenna did come to Hobart, there was every likelihood that she'd step ashore from a coastal ship. If she came. If...

Strangely, he found himself thinking of Josie Harris, and how she'd brought her daughter and followed her husband to the Antipodes. To the ends of the earth, it could truly be said. He wondered how a man like Harris could inspire such love and loyalty in his wife. And her a fine, attractive woman any man would be proud to wed. Sean admitted he was a little jealous of Harris, because he himself had never been able to inspire a lover to reach such heights.

But then he felt he was being unfair to Glenna. How could she even consider tearing off to the other side of the world after a man whose own foolish deeds had turned him into a convict? No matter how much she loved him. And her knowing how much he adored her. What would she have done when she got here? There was no use at all in his plodding over these fancies. Such a move would have been impossible for a young lady.

No matter how much she loved him.

Suddenly those words sounded shallow, against the depths of loyalty Josie had shown towards her man. Pinpricks of envy raced back to unsettle him. To remind him that it hadn't taken long for Glenna to fall into the arms of another man. To marry him.

'Ah, to hell with it!' he murmured. 'Why do I have to keep brooding over all this, getting nowhere? As if I haven't got better things to do.'

Bailey was absorbed in conversation with a seaman, in a quiet corner of the square, so Sean signalled that he wanted to see him, and propped himself on a stool by the door of a pub to wait for him.

A nip of cheap overproof rum fired his spirits, so he was feeling better when Bailey approached him with a face of gloom.

'What's the matter with you?' Sean asked. 'You look as if you've lost a pound and picked up a penny.'

'So I bloody should. I don't know what the world's coming to when a bloke wants me to pay for information.'

Sean laughed. 'He's new to the village, is he?'

'Yes. A whaler.'

'But is the information worth it?'

'Could be,' Bailey allowed, thoughtfully.

'Ah. So what's doing?'

Bailey sighed. 'Nothin'. It's probably nothin'.'

'All right then. I wanted to ask you about Marie Cullen. Do you know where she and Miss Warboy have been taken to?'

'The pregnant girl? The potty one? No, I haven't heard any more about her. And I haven't seen Marie Cullen at all. But see that gentleman in the tall hat, coming towards us, that's the lawyer, Mr Pitcairn. He's been asking about you.'

'Good afternoon, gentlemen,' Pitcairn said, raising the hat.

Sean was surprised. He'd been expecting to meet a white-bearded sage, not this middle-aged fellow of average height with dark hair and a dark clipped beard, like those pictures of Spaniards of old. And in a quirk of nature, Sean thought, he had lively brown eyes. To his mind it had always seemed that brown eyes were more serious, they lacked the twinkle of the lighter colours. Pitcairn's eyes, though were bright, sharp and brimming with intelligence, and they intimidated him from the first moment they were cast upon him.

'I'm Pitcairn,' he said. 'Could I have a word with you, Mr Shanahan?'

He was wearing a dark suit with a dark satin waistcoat, but though web cut, the clothes seemed untidy to Sean, as if he'd dressed in a flurry. Even his shiny black cravat was askew.

'To be sure,' Sean said, rising from the stool to find a spot for the newcomer, but the lawyer handed him his card.

'Good. My office at four o'clock. Would that be suitable?'

Sean blinked at the suddenness of the arrangements. 'Yes. Well ... yes. All right. I'll be there.'

Pitcairn took his leave politely and they both stared as he marched off.

'Ah lookee there, you Irish reprobate.' Bailey grinned. 'Going up in the world, are we? Or going down maybe. What have you been up to?'

'I don't know. I'll find out later, I suppose. But what about this mysterious news you nearly have?'

'Maybe I don't want to know,' Bailey growled.

The office turned out to be three rooms at the front of Pitcairn's large house. Children could be heard somewhere inside. The front garden was large too, and suffering from neglect.

As he made his way to the door, Sean thought he might find a few hours' work here, gardening, but he reconsidered as Pitcairn himself opened the door, remembering that convict gardeners were free and freely available. Obviously Mr Pitcairn was not much fussed by an untidy garden.

'Ah, Mr Shanahan! Come in and I'll show you around, then we'll have a talk.'

They passed through a small reception room which made Sean shudder. A high desk was surrounded by tall closets and packed shelves. Overwhelmed by them, he thought, but the bow windows with fancy lace curtains saved the day.

'This is where my clerk works,' Pitcairn said. 'But he's leaving me to return to Sydney.'

Across the passage they entered the other front room, which had the same bow windows, a long desk piled with files, and hundreds of important-looking books lining the walls.

'This is my lair,' he said. 'Please sit yourself down, Mr Shanahan.'

He placed himself in the chair behind the desk. 'I was expecting you to call on me, not to have to search you out,' he frowned.

'Ah yes,' Sean said. 'I'm sorry. I didn't get around to it.'

'Why not?'

Sean hesitated. 'I don't know, sir,' he said. 'I just wasn't sure what I was to do, or what it's all about.'

'Very well,' the lawyer said briskly. 'I will have an opening for a clerk. Dr Roberts said I should give you a chance at it.'

'So he said, sir, but I don't know if I'd be up for somethin' like this. 'Twould maybe be a bit over my head. I think the good doctor might have got carried away in his enthusiasm to help, now I'm on a ticket-of-leave.'

'He said you're of good character, and enterprising,' Pitcairn said. 'But let's start. You can read and write, I presume?'

'Yes, sir.' Sean felt he was up before a headmaster. A headmaster to beat all headmasters. The king of them all. He tried not to slink down in his chair.

'And you've never done office work before?'

'No, sir. I've worked on our farm, and at my uncle Patrick's racing stables. And I kept some books for Mr Warboy's farm. Stock sheets, dairy produce and the like.'

'It's much the same here, on the financial side. What comes in, what goes out. The clerk makes my appointments, sees that people are correctly charged and that I am fully paid for my services. He keeps files on all correspondence, makes sure they are up to date and files away completed cases. There will be contact with the courts, though not a lot, and some protocol to be learned, but overall it's basic and he can always ask me if unsure.'

Sean resisted remarking that he'd already had contact with the courts, this being a serious occasion. He really wanted this job, though he knew that getting it was a long shot. A very long shot. But he listened intently to Pitcairn's every word. Somewhere in the distance, beyond all the filing and the corresponding, there lay that other door Dr Roberts had spoken of so vaguely, and Sean was determined to try for it.

For quite a while, Pitcairn continued to explain the ins and outs of his law office, and at one stage he left the room to bring back samples of correspondence, to demonstrate the correct style of address and the types of cases he handled. He spoke in a rather long-winded way, and even repeated himself several times, but Sean didn't bat an eye. He listened. Desperately.

'Oh. Just a tick,' Pitcairn said suddenly. 'I nearly forgot something. Good clear handwriting is very important.'

He pushed over a blank page. 'Take up a pen, Mr Shanahan, and write something for me.'

'What will I write?'

'Whatever you like. Just do your best.'

Sean remembered the many times Brother Thomas had rapped his knuckles with a stick, causing his chilblains to weep, all for the glory of God, and for the eventual emergence of a readable hand.

He wrote: *Order is Heaven's first law.*

'Ah.' Pitcairn nodded. 'Excellent. And whence the quote, Mr Shanahan?'

'To give you the truth, sir, I can't recall.'

'Pope. Alexander Pope. The poet. Now let me see. What if I give you a month's trial? At the end of the month I'll pay you two pounds, and then we'll decide yea or nay, with no hard feelings. Would that suit?'

'It would.' Sean nodded. 'And thank you, sir.'

Pitcairn escorted him to the door. 'Monday week, then. You will need to wear a shirt and tie, and a waistcoat. And have a jacket in case you have to deliver messages to the courthouse.'

The lawyer shook his head as he reported the interview to his wife. 'I don't think he'll be any good, but I gave him a trial to please Roberts. I owe him that much, since our little Sally is doing so well now thanks to him.'

'That's good. Every time I think of how we nearly lost our darling little girl I say a prayer for Allyn Roberts. But why don't you think the Irishman will be any good?'

'My dear,' her husband said. 'That man is twenty-nine going on seventy. He's very much what the Irish call a "bosso" type. Born to it. I'm not at all surprised that Roberts saw a bush lawyer in him; he's smart. But what I saw was a man flat out keeping his personality well hidden. Even though he's a convict, he's still not at home with his servile status.'

'But he's to be your clerk, John. Not actually a servant.'

'It's much the same thing to him.'

'But you'll give him a chance, won't you? If he's smart, you said that yourself, he'll know what to do. Intuitively.'

'I don't know,' Pitcairn said gloomily. 'I really should be looking for a younger man.'

Sean forgot about the neglected garden as he closed the gate behind him, because an unfamiliar sense of well-being was flooding over him. He'd have taken the month's trial for free, for the opportunity to learn how to do that job and discover inroads to the forts and castles of the legal profession!

Of course, he warned himself, you'll have to hold your tongue this time. One wrong word and you'll be out on your neck.

But I can do that, I can! The work, if you can call it that, doesn't look too hard after all. I'll be the best bloody little clerk Pitcairn ever had.

I hope.

'Good afternoon,' he said gleefully, raising his cap to two ladies coming towards him. 'It's a wonderful day, is it not?'

So was the next day: trees everywhere were glowing with golden wattle, choirs of large birds were warbling their astonishingly true notes, and there was a fragrance of lilacs in the air as Sean strode over to Pollard's store in search of information about Marie Cullen.

He was still feeling very happy, though he'd rather not tell anyone he'd soon be working for Pitcairn, for fear he'd fail the test. Then again, he supposed, word would get around. But wouldn't he just love to be able to write the family of this great turn-up! If only he could hold the job. They'd be proud of him, surprised out of their wits, and he'd be making them happy at last. And Glenna! She'd be proud too.

'Ah!' he muttered, disgusted with himself. 'Get off this daydreaming. What will happen will happen.'

Sam Pollard couldn't give him any information about Marie or the Warboy girl.

Nor could the women he spoke to at the Female Factory, and that left him mystified. He decided he'd have to ask Mr Warboy direct. Marie Cullen was a dear friend, she shouldn't simply be whisked away like that. Her friends had a right to know her whereabouts.

CHAPTER EIGHTEEN

Late that night, Sean had a visitor.

Willem came around the back to knock on his door, needing to talk to him urgently. He had a plan to rescue George and Angus from Port Arthur, but Sean was reluctant to even discuss a breakout.

'It's too hard, Willem,' he said. 'Too many have tried it. They say there's hundreds of men in that place wearing the ball and chain for life after trying the run. You can't help George now, and you're putting yourself at risk. Take my advice: pack up and go home. God, man, you've got a life away from here, you can go home free as a bird. How many wouldn't give their eye teeth to be able to leave when they've done their time? You can afford to go! I don't know why you're still here.'

Willem stared at him. 'What's happened to you? You got four people out of here that I know of. You plotted for years to free Macnamara from

603

Port Arthur, and now you won't even help your friends!'

'I am trying to help. Angus is innocent. I hired Baggott to get him off on an appeal. He says the case is hopeless, but I'm not giving up.'

'But what about George? He shouldn't be there either. It's my fault they caught him out of bounds. I organised for him to be at my place. George was too sick from the burns to know where he was.'

He stopped, looking about him. 'Hey! I just realised, this is the Doc's house! Someone pointed it out to me, said you were boarding back here.'

'Nothing's sacred,' Sean grinned. 'But since you've got me up, I'll find us a drink. I've got a quart of ale in the pantry.'

He lit a lamp and took Willem into the kitchen.

'Where's Roberts?' Willem asked, bewildered that they should be entering the man's house.

'He's been appointed the medical officer at Port Arthur. I'm caretaking here.'

'What? The Doc's over there? Do you think we could use him somehow?'

'We?' Sean raised an eyebrow. He poured the ale. 'Fresh from the brewery.'

'Are you working there?'

'No.' Sean didn't enlarge. 'I've been thinking, about George. He's only got two years at Port Arthur. He's not a lifer. Why do you want to take such a risk when he'll make it out of there on his own?'

'You said so yourself. I'm one of the lucky ones. I'm free to go home and I've got the money to do it. But I'm not leaving George in the lurch. I've made enquiries. If I can get him out of there I can get him to the mainland. And Angus with him. Everyone knows how tough that prison is, they can get flogged for looking sideways. I'm not leaving George there for two years. Never! And I can't believe you're shilly-shallying about Angus! He's bound to get himself into strife and you know it.'

'I've told you, I'm trying to get him out.'

'And I *can*. Will you at least look at my plan? Or is that too much trouble?'

Guilt forbade Sean from reacting angrily to that taunt. He was sorry now that he'd offered Willem the drink. He should have sent him away first thing. But he hadn't wanted to offend his friend; they'd been through a lot over the years. On the other hand, he couldn't bring himself to tell Willem the truth: that he was afraid to become involved in any of these schemes because they would kill any chance he had of working for Pitcairn.

It was only a sense of shame that pushed him into relenting.

'What plan?' he asked.

'First of all, have you still got that map of Port Arthur? I want to match it up with my own.'

Sean shrugged, lit a small lamp and carried it to his sleepout. When he returned, Willem had a much larger map spread out on the table.

'Now see here,' he said quickly, as if he had to get his information out before Sean changed his mind. 'This is a map that takes in the whole area from Hobart across Storm Bay to Port Arthur.

Look here, this is the mouth of the Derwent.'

'I can see that.' Sean was terse.

'And we can see all the mainland north of the Derwent, with its bays and inlets. By no means a straight shoreline looking over to the Port Arthur peninsula, is it?'

'No.'

'And here is the entrance from the mainland to Port Arthur. It's called Eagle Hawk Neck. It's on a thin strip of land.'

'So it is,' Sean said impatiently. 'And it's guarded heavier than the Tower of London, with vicious dogs thrown in for good luck.'

'Right. Quite right. And what's more, civilians can't even approach it by road, for miles back, without papers. And the area surrounding that same road is all rough bush, right down to the shores.'

'I imagine it would be.'

'Then look here.' Willem stubbed a finger. 'I have been here, following an old bush track south from the road to Eagle Hawk Neck to this spot on the beach called South Point. I've stood there, looking across at the Port Arthur coal mines. It's right there. It's only a mile or so across.'

'That can't be right. Where's the mouth of the Derwent?'

'Way over here. Too far to be useful. I plan to pick the lads up from the backside of Port Arthur, at the coal mines, whisk them across to South Point on the mainland by small boat, and take them on from there.'

Sean looked at his colour-enhanced map of Port Arthur, courtesy of Mr Warboy, with its green parks and farmlands, and buildings lining streets just like any village.

'There's no coal mines marked on here,' he said.

'Of course not. They wouldn't want visitors to see conditions there. But trust me, I had a guide, an officer if you don't mind,' he grinned. 'I played the gentleman and we had a pleasant day exploring the opposite coast.'

Sean was rather put out. All of his plans had envisaged sailing upriver, and across Storm Bay to the prison settlement, collecting the prisoner and returning to the same point. A long and arduous journey, hopefully under cover of darkness. But this plan of Willem's was less dangerous, and less strenuous. Too simple.

'Has anyone else tried that route?'

'Not that I know of. It's a long ride all the way around there from Hobart, through a couple of villages, not to mention one is a garrison.'

'God Almighty! You're looking for trouble.'

'No I'm not. I've been there, I told you. People don't bother travellers. Life can be normal, you know. Anyway, I've got Freddy to help me.'

'Who?'

'Freddy Hines.'

Sean sat up with a jolt. 'What's he doing there?'

'Working in a pub.'

'Ah! I always wondered where the bugger got to. He stole my mount. It belonged to Warboy. I had some fun covering that. And Jubal Warboy nearly had Billo arrested for stealing it.'

Willem laughed. 'You get what you give. Someone stole it from him.'

'Rats! He probably sold it. But say now, he's on the run without a pass. How's he getting away with a job?'

'Believe this! He's got papers. No forgeries either. His new name is Jack Plunkett.'

Sean was amazed. 'How did he do that?'

'Damned if I know. But anyway, I told him to stay put. I've got a job for him.'

'Whatever it is, don't rely on him. And have you contacted George about this great plan?'

'Sort of. I'm testing a steward on the steamer that ferries passengers and supplies back and forth to Port Arthur. He needs money badly, been gambling with a couple of whalers, so he'll do his best. I'm trying for a Sunday morning escape, when the prisoners are not all over the place in work gangs.'

They discussed the plan for more than an hour. Willem was so enthusiastic that Sean had to remind him there were a million details to be sorted yet.

'What will you do with George if you can get him over to the mainland?'

'George *and* Angus,' Willem said firmly.

'I don't know about that.'

'The answer is simple. Give them good clothes, some money and our horses, Freddy's and mine, and tell them to ride to an address in Richmond.'

'I see. And leave you stranded?'

'No. There's a ferry. Dodges Ferry, near South Point. Freddy and I can get a boat to another part of the mainland.'

'And from Richmond? Where will the lads go from there?'

608

Willem sighed. 'Try not to be so negative, Shanahan. I'm heading north shortly, to the top of Van Diemen's Land, where there are fishermen aplenty I believe. If so, I'll buy a fishing boat so that we can be transported across the strait to Victoria. That's a free colony, no need for passes and papers! What do you say to that?'

Money talks, Sean thought dully. Probably, if Willem threw enough money about, and was blessed with enormous luck, he could pull it off.

'I don't know. I honestly don't know whether I'd be doing Angus a favour or a bad turn if I go along with this.'

'Ah well.' Willem got up to leave. 'There's time yet. Can I call on you if I need help?'

'You can,' Sean said with a firmness he didn't feel. By the time he returned to his room, depression had chased away his elation.

'I knew things were too good to be true,' he muttered.

The Sunday picnic wasn't entirely a success. Sean collected the two ladies in Dr Roberts' buggy, and drove them to a scenic spot he'd already noted along the river, overlooking Sullivan's Cove, not a little disappointed to find he wasn't the only one with that plan. In fact it had become so popular that it bore a sign: *Picnic Point*, and several families were already settled.

'Oh no,' he groaned. 'I'm sorry, I didn't mean to deposit you in the middle of a bun fight.'

'We don't have to stay here,' Louise put in quickly. 'We can go into town and have our picnic in the square.'

'We will not,' her mother said. 'This is just lovely. I don't mind a few people about.'

She'd brought a basket of cold cuts, bread and pickles and various other delectables.

'Oh my,' Sean said. 'I haven't seen a spread like this since my granddaddy's wake. Though I do remember there was a fair bit of poteen about as well.'

'Is poteen a cake?' Louise asked, opening a round tin. 'I made this cake. It's chocolate.'

'Ah! I'm in heaven! All I can offer is some cider.'

'And that will suit us beautifully,' Josie said.

Louise was restless. After they'd finished lunch, she wandered off, leaving Sean and her mother sitting quietly in the shade of a flowering gum.

'When your time is up here,' Josie asked him, 'will you go home?'

'I can't. I'm a lifer.'

'Oh, I'm sorry. I forgot. But tell me, have you heard any more about working for the lawyer?'

'I start tomorrow,' Sean said. Off-handedly. As if it didn't mean an iota to him. As if he could take it or leave it any old time.

'How interesting. Which lawyer is it?'

'Mr Pitcairn. Mr John Pitcairn. Do you know him?'

'I haven't had the pleasure. But I'm sure he's very good if you chose him.'

Sean laughed. 'Ah, my dear, I have to tell you I was never the chooser. It was Doc Roberts who threw me in head first.'

He saw a tinge of pink in Josie's cheeks and, for

610

a second, thought it might be sunburn, but then he recalled that he'd said 'my dear' – hardly appropriate for a married woman. At the same time he had a flash of gratitude that Louise hadn't heard that lapse.

Rather than embarrass her further by apologising, he carried on. 'I think the Doc is determined to make a respectable character out of me.'

'I never thought you not to be a respectable gentleman,' Josie said. 'From what I've seen here, the division is not between the convicts and the settlers, but the usual mix, the good and the bad. Look at Barnaby's troubles. The son and his wife were dreadful people, leaving the poor granddaughter behind.'

'Ah yes. Miss Penn. She's no longer at the farm. Where is she?'

'I'm not sure. I don't see much of Barnaby lately. He's concentrating on his garden again. But I did ask him how she was, and he seemed quite happy about her now.'

'Why? What did he say?'

'He was rather vague. He just said Penn and her nurse are getting along fine.'

'Mmm.' Sean nodded. The news *was* vague, but somehow he felt better about Marie. 'I think he's probably placed them with folk in another town,' he said, 'to avoid any more embarrassment.'

'Yes. I think so. He was acutely upset at the thought of sharing a house with a pregnant lady.'

'And a single one at that,' Sean grinned.

She smiled. 'Oh heavens, we shouldn't laugh at other people's misfortunes. I don't find my own amusing.'

'What are yours?'

Josie hesitated, as if weighing up whether or not to share this with him, but then she shrugged. 'You might as well know. Mr Baggott had a response from my husband, via the commandant of the prison, and it has taken a couple of weeks to get to me. All he said to my request for his approval of the sale of the farm was "no". Just "no"! Obviously he won't even consider it. That means I have to stay there until the bills mount up and the bailiffs come in.'

She was almost in tears from the telling, and involuntarily, Sean put an arm about her. 'Come on now. There's an answer to everything. Let's talk it out. Think where you could do some saving for a start, perhaps.'

Josie nodded. 'I thought of sending back all the workers. Just keeping one for maintenance. At least I won't have to keep providing their food and clothes.'

'But your crops will suffer.'

'I know. I've almost lost interest in them.'

Sean eased away from her and reached for the cider. 'I think it's time you took another glass here. For medicinal purposes,' he smiled. 'Pity we've no poteen, it would chase away your worries for the afternoon.'

They were still discussing the pros and cons when Louise returned. 'There are some ladies staring at Sean from over there by the campfire,' she giggled. 'Do you know them?' she asked him.

He looked over. 'No. I don't.'

'They're saying he's good-looking,' she said to her mother. 'I suppose he is, now that his hair's

612

growing,' she added, teasing Sean.

'Louise!' her mother exploded. 'You apologise to Sean. Personal remarks are unforgivable!'

She pouted. 'I was only joking. Sean knows that.'

'Apologise.'

'All right. I'm sorry, Sean.'

'Thank you,' he said. 'Accepted.'

'Well, it's boring here now. We've had lunch. Why don't we leave?'

'Do you want to go home?' Josie asked.

'No. It's too early, and we're close to town. Why don't we go into Salamanca Square. They always have entertainers there on Sundays, singers and musicians and things. Don't they, Sean?'

He looked at them uncertainly. 'Well ... they do. But it's for your mother to say...'

'I'm quite happy here,' she said, but in the end Louise won the day, and next thing, the basket and cloths and glasses were packed in the buggy and they were skimming through town towards the square.

Sean escorted them through the crowds to view the fat lady in her tent, and have a gypsy tell their fortunes, but he baulked at having his own fortune told.

'You're too superstitious, Sean,' Josie laughed. 'It's only fun.'

Louise differed. 'It is not, Mother. It's real. Come along, there's a queue.'

As she turned away, she almost bumped into Bailey, who raised his old bent topper to her. 'Good afternoon to you, miss!'

She giggled. 'Good afternoon, Mr Bailey,' and

Sean groaned.

Then he heard Josie's abrupt question. 'Who was that fellow? How do you know him?'

Sean had to agree with the motherly concern. Bailey still wore outlandish poorhouse clothing, and matched it with a cheeky attitude. But Louise shook off the question and raced over to the gypsy who was sitting at a table by the wall, reading a set of cards to an elderly customer, and Josie must have decided to let it go. She hurried after her daughter, hair the colour of wheat flowing from under her straw hat, and her face shining with excitement at this caprice.

'What a pair of beauties!' Bailey materialised beside Sean. 'Which one's yours?'

'Neither, they're friends of mine.'

'I would have thought the young one, since you had her running your messages.'

'No, she just did a favour for me.'

Bailey puffed on a foul-smelling cigar. 'They wouldn't be the Harris women, would they?' he asked, frowning.

'They are. Why?' Sean was still watching them as they stood in the line. In their full-skirted summer dresses they looked a picture ... Louise in yellow cotton, Josie in white.

'Somethin's up there,' Bailey said, interrupting his pleasure. 'I heard some bad stuff about them. The Harrises.'

Sean whirled about. 'What bad stuff?' he demanded. 'You'll never hear a breath of scandal about those ladies.'

'No, no, 'twasn't that. No. Gawd! It was only a whisper, get me? I didn't know it was your nice

614

young lady. She called me Mr Bailey. None of your boldness about her. I gotta go.'

Sean grabbed his arm. 'You'll not be going anyplace until you tell me what's up here.'

'I don't know, Shanahan. True I don't.'

'Yes you do. A whisper has words. It's never bloody mute. Now you tell me the whisper, the words.'

'Let go, you're hurting. I heard the name Harris put about, never thinking... Payback, the word was. Someone's after payback.'

'What for?'

'I dunno. Someone's trying to buy payback, I reckon. But it can't be them. Not them ladies. And that's all I heard yet.'

Sean agreed. 'No, it can't be them, but I wonder what it's about.'

'I might hear if anyone buys in.'

'You mean someone's looking for a hand to strike the blow?'

'Sounds like it. They're looking for a doer.'

'And who said the words?'

'I dunno. I told you, I heard them, whispering in the dark by a bog. Seamen outside the Whalers' Return. Could be bad blood among them, someone called Harris did the wrong thing.'

Sean nodded. Bailey was famous as an eavesdropper. They said he could hear a pin drop at twenty paces.

'But it wasn't over women?' Sean asked anxiously.

'No. Here come your ladies. I'll tell you if I hear anything, but these things, they mostly come to nought.'

He scurried away, and Sean was left worried. Did Bailey know that Bull Harris was Josie's husband? She kept her cards close, and she and Louise rarely socialised, so they weren't well-known in town. No need for Bailey to notice them except for the day Louise met him.

She ran over to him. 'I'm going to marry a handsome officer and live in India,' she cried, 'and Mother is to be wildly rich and all her grey hairs will turn to gold.'

'I didn't know you had any grey hairs,' Sean said to Josie, peering at her fair hair.

'They're not far off, the way I'm going,' she laughed, 'but if they turn into gold they'll be welcome.' She looked at the clouds gathering in the southern skies. 'It's been a lovely day, Sean, but if you don't mind, I think we should be getting home. It looks like rain.'

'So it does,' he said, 'and we'll say a prayer of thanks that the Doc thought to put a fine roof on his buggy.'

'Does it belong to Dr Roberts?' Louise asked.

'Yes, I thought I told you that.'

'Sean,' she said, producing a winning smile, 'do take us and show us his house. We'd love to see where he lives.'

'We do not need to see where he lives,' Josie said, and Sean added: 'Some other time, Louise. I'd better get you home.'

'Have you heard from him?'

'Not since he left,' Sean said, 'but I guess he's busy now.'

On that same Sunday, two women were strolling

barefoot along the beach at Sandy Bay as pushy seagulls squawked and squealed around their feet. The birds made such a clamour that one of the women, Marie Cullen, ran up to a grassy verge, calling to Penn to feed them.

'They know you've got food there,' she laughed, 'and they won't give way until it's all gone.'

'But I wanted to teach them to take turns,' Penn shouted over the fuss and flurry of wings. 'I want them to be good, like chickens. This way some of them keep missing out.'

'They're not chickens! They're wild birds!'

'Oh, dash!' Penn opened the paper bag, and a bird snatched at it, almost ripping it from her hands, so she gave up and began to toss the bread in all directions.

Marie dug herself a shallow seat in the coarse grass of the shoreline, and watched her mistress, pleased that she had improved since they'd been here.

At first, back at the Warboy farm, Penn had missed her parents so much she was constantly weepy, and had begun to wander round the house at night looking for them. That annoyed her grandfather, and he'd threatened to lock her in her room if she didn't stop disturbing him.

Marie shared a staff room with Dossie, and when they came in at six o'clock they'd find the silly girl sitting in the kitchen by the cold stove, waiting for them. It was easier to give her breakfast and send her back to bed for the morning.

In the afternoons Marie would try to take her for a walk, but she'd only go down to the greenhouse, which was mostly bare of plants these days, hoping to see her friend Angus.

'What with fretting for her parents at night and fretting for the boyfriend in the daytime,' Dossie complained, 'it's like having a ghost in the house. A pregnant ghost,' she added.

But that didn't last long. One morning Mr Warboy told Dossie he was moving them out. Both Miss Penn and Miss Cullen.

'Where to?' Marie whispered.

'He hasn't told me yet.'

Nor did he.

The day dawned only a week later. 'Pack them up, I'm taking them to town,' he said.

'Yes, sir,' Dossie said, seizing the chance. 'For the day, is it?'

'No. For good. They'll be living elsewhere.'

'And where would that be, sir?'

He was in too good a mood on the sunny morn to tell her to mind her own business. He simply ignored the question.

'I'm sorry,' Dossie said to Marie, who was worried about the change but too afraid to ask. 'I couldn't get any more out of him. But he'd do you no harm, girl.'

'He might be sending me back to the Factory, and I could not deal with that place ever again. I'd die there, Dossie.'

Dossie too was worried. 'I tell you what. If they send you back there, first chance you get, run away. Run out here. It's a long way, but you could do it in a day, easy. We'll hide you and tell Shanahan. He'll look after you. So now don't you be frettin' too. Between the both of you, you'll start a flood.'

618

So with that lifeline to hang on to, Marie set about packing up Miss Penn, who could not, or would not, accept they were leaving the farm. She seemed not to notice the luggage. Her trunks were packed on the roof of the coach, with the small sea box that held Marie's own belongings, all the lovely new maid's outfits, from 'tip to toe'. She prayed they wouldn't take them away from her and wished she could have her sea box in the coach, on the seat beside her, with Miss Penn on the other side, and Mr Warboy opposite them. He was facing the way they were going, towards town, and they had their backs to the horses. Marie had clutched her hands together so tightly, all the way to town on that frightening ride, that her knuckles had ached for days.

'And all for nothing,' she said gaily, sifting warm sand between her fingers and keeping an eye on her charge, who was now paddling and splashing in the shallows with no care for the soaking of her dress.

Nor should she. Marie smiled indulgently. She's like a bird been freed here. And if she makes a mess of her dress, hasn't she got one of the best laundresses around to set all the flounces back in place like new? She thought back to the long days of toil in the Factory laundry and could have screamed with delight for the joy of the present life.

But poor us, she recalled. Me thinking I was to be dumped, and her thinking it was just an outing, cheerfully counting the horses we passed.

'You get ten for white horses,' she'd told her grandfather, who grimaced impatiently. He hated to be reminded of her childish state.

Eventually Penn thought to ask where they were going, the very question that was nagging Marie.

'To the beach,' Mr Warboy said shortly.

'Oh.' Penn gave no indication as to whether this pleased her or not. She went back to counting horses.

'I have a house at a place called Sandy Bay,' he told Marie. 'It's by the beach. You will be living there with Penn as her housekeeper. I suppose you can cook?'

'Yes, sir,' Marie said eagerly. She had done stints in the big stinking kitchens so she supposed that counted. 'Will it be just the two of us?'

'That is right. You will behave as young ladies should, and at the first complaint you will be replaced. Is that understood?'

'Of course, sir.' Her heart was hammering. She could not believe this until it was set before her, and not just a pleasing posy of words playing on her willing ears. To come from the hell of that overcrowded factory of women, all fighting to survive, to be housekeeper for this sad little person was a leap to another world. A world she was only now learning to understand. She'd never lived anywhere without bosses, though. From the poorhouse to the orphanage and the hideous ship... She stopped there. She was erasing that gradually, fiercely, from her mind.

'You are to be kind to her,' Mr Warboy said suddenly. 'You seem a kind young woman. Under no circumstances are you to hit or strike her. I will be keeping an eye on you. Don't forget that.'

As the coach spun along the road, he explained that their stores would be delivered by Mr Pollard each week, and if there was anything else they required, they were to ask him.

'Will you come and visit us, Mr Warboy?' Marie asked nervously.

He coughed. 'Well – yes. Yes. I'll see.'

'Oh look,' Penn called. 'Look at the wallabies. Can we get out and pat them?'

'No,' her grandfather said. 'We haven't time.'

'Oh, that's right. We're going to the beach. How far is it now?'

Hunter was driving. He took them to Pollard's store, and to Marie's surprise they were invited to step down from the carriage. Then Hunter unloaded their luggage.

Penn walked into the store. 'This isn't the beach,' she cried, jamming her thumb in her mouth.

'You'll be there soon,' her grandfather said nervously. 'I have to get back home.' Then, obviously feeling he should do more, he patted her on the head, grabbed a gaudy tin of toffees from the counter and handed it to her. 'Now be a good girl for Miss Cullen.'

Then he turned to Marie and handed her a small purse. 'Here's five shillings to go on with, Miss Cullen. It's your pay. Mr Pollard will pay you each week from now on. Now, you will look after her, won't you?'

He glanced at Penn, who was already trying to open the tin, and strode quietly out to his carriage. Hunter slicked the whip at the horses, and it pulled away.

'Isn't Grandpapa coming to the beach?' Penn asked.

'No, he's too busy,' Mr Pollard said. 'But if you two ladies would come along and hop into my buggy, I'll take you there. It's all packed now, ready to go.'

'Oh good!' Penn said, rushing over to him. He lifted her up and put a hand out to Marie. 'Ladies, I'll be looking in on you every Friday. So you can call me Sam.'

He drove them through town at a smart trot, on past Salamanca Square, where Marie had worked for some weeks with two other girls, scrubbing the floors of inns and taverns, at the time when the Governor had ordered cleanups and forbidden spitting.

When they topped a hill outside town, they looked down on a glittering blue bay.

'That's it,' Sam said. 'There's Sandy Bay, and your house is down there in Blaze Road. It's called Blaze Road because they had a bushfire through here some years back.'

There was a mansion on the corner of Blaze Road, a beautiful two-storey house with a lookout tower.

'Is that our place?' Penn asked eagerly, and Sam laughed. 'Not likely.'

There were a few other houses along the short road that ran parallel to the beach, but they were well separated by thinly forested vacant allotments that still bore the scars of fire. Mr Warboy's house was at the very end.

'This will be a nice neighbourhood one of these

622

days,' Sam said, 'now that the smugglers have gone.'

He climbed down to hitch the horse to a tree. 'Here you go, ladies. This is it!'

Marie stood at the edge of the unfenced block and stared at the small white house with a red roof that nestled among the trees. It had a veranda across the front, quite a wide veranda, neatly finished with a low white railing.

'It's a dolly's house,' Penn cried, 'a dear little dolly's house.'

She picked up her skirts and raced across the uneven grass, and Marie rushed after her. 'Don't run, Penn! You mustn't. You might fall!'

Unpacking their luggage and supplies, Sam nodded his approval. He liked Marie, remarking on how different she looked now, in the neat black skirt and white blouse, from the first time he'd seen the poor wretched convict girl in his store, introduced by Shanahan. He must congratulate his wife for finding just the right clothes for her.

Marie had taken off her hat and was standing at the door waiting for him, and he noticed her dark hair had been rescued from its wiry tangle – Dossie, he supposed. In all she looked quite presentable now. A few more square meals should finish the job, he grinned.

They'll be all right here, he told himself. They're a lot closer to town than out at Barnaby's house, though Barnaby didn't want them roaming about.

He'd felt sorry for Barnaby when he heard the pregnant girl had been abandoned by her parents and dumped on the old man. Having never met Miss Warboy until today, he'd been inclined to think the hussy should have been taken straight to a nunnery – on the mainland, if there wasn't one of that kind here – and he'd quietly mentioned something of the sort to Barnaby.

'No, Sam. I can't do that,' he'd said wearily. 'That would make me as cold-hearted as my son. I've bought the cottage, I've got to give this a try.'

'But what will people say?' Sam had worried. 'I mean, two young women in a house on their own. Unchaperoned. That will raise eyebrows.'

Barnaby managed a wry smile. 'My granddaughter's reputation is already in tatters, and those poor convict girls, they don't have any to defend.'

While Penn roamed about on her own, Sam showed Marie the house.

'My wife fixed it up at Mr Warboy's request,' he said proudly. 'It belonged to an old fisherman who died. She had it painted in and out, picked the curtains and the furniture and a new stove, and Mr Warboy was really pleased with it.'

'It's all beautiful,' Marie breathed. 'Beautiful!'

'There are two bedrooms,' he explained. 'The first one is Miss Warboy's. Mr Warboy worked all this out. He said the second one is yours, and when the baby comes along, it will be a nursery as well.

'The sitting room is to be kept neat at all times, as Mr Warboy will be visiting. You must not have strangers in the house.'

Marie nodded, trying to contain her excitement. 'Don't be worrying, Sam,' she said. 'It's not hard to see what this is about. I'm to keep Penn happy here, minding her own business, and if I can say so, that's fine with me. We're both truly blessed to have such a peaceful home.'

'You won't be nervous?'

'Not at all.'

Looking back now, Marie was amused by the question. Most folk had no idea of the travails of convict women. From a young girl, she'd learned to sleep with one eye open for fear of assaults emanating from the madness around her. She'd never before slept as well as on the last few nights she'd spent at Mr Warboy's house, when she realised she was safe. Really and truly safe.

'Oh no,' she laughed. 'I won't be nervous. I might look like a piece of string, but I can protect myself now. I've had plenty of practice.'

She dozed in the sun until Penn called to her.

'Can I go for a walk?'

'Sure you can.' Marie roused herself. 'I'll come with you. But we'll only go a short distance, then we have to be turning ourselves back for lunch.'

'Oh no, I want to walk down to the big house.'

'Oh, all right.'

'What are we having for lunch?'

'Stew and bread.' Then she waved both arms wide, and shouted, 'Bread with loads of butter!'

Penn reacted gleefully. 'And jam!'

'Why not?'

'And biscuits?'

'Sure! We'll raid the pantry!'

Penn whirled about. 'That will be so much fun!

Quickly. Let's run back now.'

'No running! I thought you wanted to look at the big house.'

'I'm too hungry.' She took Marie's arm. 'I like living here, it's the best place. And you're nice. Where are your mother and daddy?'

'They've gone to heaven.'

'My goodness. That is sad. Is that why you are a nobody like Dossie?'

'Dossie's not a nobody. She's a person. A truly good person.'

'No,' Penn countered firmly. 'My mother said all convicts are nobodies.'

'Your mother's wrong,' Marie said kindly, though she was not well disposed towards the mother. 'She's very wrong, because we're all God's family. Convict folk are loved by the good Lord just as much as he loves you.'

'I'm glad,' Penn said thoughtfully as they walked back up to the house. 'I'm glad he loves Angus too.'

Oh God, Marie sighed to herself. Not that again.

Dossie had told her the story of Angus McLeod, the rapist, when she'd first arrived, but Sean had disagreed. He wouldn't have it for a minute that Angus had even touched her.

'That girl's lying,' he said.

'Then it's a cruel thing for her to do, blaming an innocent man. And for what reason?'

'God knows,' he'd said. 'See what you can find out.'

But now that she'd come to know Penn better, Marie couldn't bring herself to be questioning

626

her. It hadn't taken long for her to see the poor girl's brain was as fragile as a sparrow's. She didn't feel it would do for her to be delving into it. Better to leave her go along her own little way without inviting concerns.

Marie had seen women like this, born near mad, or sent this way by ordeals and confusions. It was clear Penn was one of them, but though she had about as much attachment to the real world as that doll she carted around, she could still sail along fairly well. Just the same, Marie knew it wouldn't take much to rock her boat, even tip her overboard, and with the drama of childbirth to come, she determined her role was to try to prepare Penn by keeping her days smooth and even. She didn't want her upset.

The girl never mentioned any man other than Angus, which left Marie with little doubt he was the father, with all due respect to Sean's opinion. On the other hand, she was almost certain that Penn had not been raped. Marie knew about rape all too well, and this girl had none of the terror, the lasting terror that the pain and fear brought with it, the remembrance that could still make you jump at a man's voice. Penn had been open and friendly with Sam when she met him, never in the least alarmed.

'But that's all history now, and I can't be biding with it,' she murmured. She needed to keep Penn calm, and never backtrack into her past with questions. Instead she gave her small enlightenments about looking after herself properly, about not romping, and once she'd tried to talk about the baby in her swelling tummy, despairing when

Penn immediately rejected that information in total disbelief.

In the first shopping list she'd handed to Sam, she'd ordered wool and needles so that she could teach Penn how to knit; and pens and plenty of paper for educational purposes. Sam was delighted to hear that Marie was taking her duties so seriously, unaware that Penn was teaching her to read and write. It was Penn who wrote the orders!

They ate their lunch in the kitchen, and as she cleared up Marie sent Penn off for her afternoon nap, but after a few minutes Penn called to her. 'Will you come and lie down with me. I'm lonely.'

'No, you need your rest. Go to sleep.'

The first night they were in this house, much the same thing had happened. Penn had come knocking on Marie's door. 'Can I sleep in your bed?'

'No, you have your own nice bed.'

'But sometimes I get lonely.'

'Then you say your prayers again and you won't be lonely any more.'

'But I will.'

'No you won't,' Marie had said firmly. Nevertheless, she'd climbed out of bed and taken Penn back to her own room.

'Now you get into bed and I'll tuck you in.'

She recited the Our Father and a few more prayers, staying by the bed in the dark until Penn's breathing steadied and she could steal away.

This happened several times, but Marie was

firm in her refusal; the child was no more. Penn had to begin the climb to womanhood somehow.

Finally, one morning, Penn was cross with her, complaining that she didn't care about her bedroom lonelies, leaving her in the dark like that.

'If it upsets you so much, I'll leave a small lamp in your room tonight.'

'I'll still be alone,' Penn pouted. 'But I tell you what, Marie-know-all, when I marry Angus I won't be lonely! So there! He'll let me sleep in his bed.'

'Whatever you say,' Marie sighed. She knew better than to try to unravel Penn's pronouncements, especially when they concerned the saintly Angus who, according to Sean, had never touched her.

'Glory be to God,' she said as she refilled the kettle with fresh water. 'Like as not we've got a virgin birth on our hands. Let us hope the Bishop doesn't get wind of it.'

But Penn was still grizzling about being sent to bed on her own.

'It's like trying to mind a naughty kid,' Marie muttered. She remembered the curtains were open in Penn's room and the sun beaming in, so she marched up the passage. 'If you don't go to sleep, there'll be no cake for tea.'

There were lace curtains over the windows and side curtains of brown velour. Marie loved the feel of the velour; there were dark green ones in the sitting room. She yanked the velours across, darkening the room and bringing an immediate complaint from Penn.

'Now you've made it dark. You know I get

lonely. You've got nothing else to do! Why don't you get into bed with me and look after me like my daddy used to do. I don't think you care about me at all.'

For her age, Marie Cullen was a worldly woman, who'd seen more of life's maladjustments than most would ever encounter. But now she froze. Then she put her hands over her ears and fled.

Early in the morning, the day after the Warboys had visited him with their flowers, Vicar Thorley was rushed to hospital with a mild stroke. He was forced to take a month's leave of absence, which he spent recuperating at his sister's farm near the seaside town of Sorell. But now he was back, fully recovered, even from the debilitating illness that had plagued him beforehand.

His parishioners were delighted; they had missed their gentle cleric, and were unhappy that their church had been closed for those weeks, as no substitute was available. Prior to his return, they'd held working bees to expand and rejuvenate his garden, and on the big day he was welcomed with a splendid morning tea and an opportunity to sit and chat with folks about all the changes and happenings during his absence. Though he listened carefully, he was unable to pick up any news of Jubal Warboy, which was unfortunate, because he was very interested in the gentleman.

Eventually he asked Mrs Flood how the Warboy family was faring, and heard news that troubled him.

'They left,' she said. 'Warboy and his wife. They went home to Jamaica. But, my dear! They left the daughter behind. You know, the little fair girl. Quite a surprise that was. I'm not one to talk, of course, but I could tell you, the girl is...' She looked about her, and then whispered: '*Enceinte!*'

'Oh! She's married!'

Mrs Flood gazed at him round-eyed. 'No. She's not.'

'Oh! Goodness me!' he said, and changed the subject.

Determined not to let the matter rest, he ferreted the rest of that story from his housekeeper, who told him that young Miss Warboy had been raped by one of the convicts employed at Warboy Farm.

'The convict swore blind he never did it,' she told him, 'and there's plenty say he spoke the truth and the girl was lying.'

The vicar had to keep in mind that his housekeeper was a former convict, so she could be biased. He decided to call on Mr Barnaby Warboy.

Unfortunately he was out.

'Perhaps I could see Miss Warboy?'

The maid's face coloured. 'She doesn't live here any more.'

'Where could I find her?'

'I don't know, sir.'

He was surprised. 'She is not residing with her grandfather?'

'No, sir.'

'I'd like to wait for Mr Warboy. Do you think he'd mind if I took a stroll in the garden? I have a little time to spare.'

631

'Not at all. Mr Warboy's ever so proud of his garden.'

Given this opportunity, Vicar Thorley wasted no time in striking up a conversation with a gardener by the name of Zack.

'Do the workmen here attend church services?' he asked.

'Jubal Warboy used to give us some sermons,' the man said bitterly, 'but he's gone, thank God.'

'It seems strange to thank God that you've lost him.'

'No it's not, he was a nasty piece of work, if you don't mind me saying. He'd put you off God for life.'

'Amen,' the vicar said softly. 'Then perhaps Mr Barnaby Warboy might allow you to come to Trinity church on a Sunday?'

'He probably would. He's pretty good with things like that. He don't fuss, like.'

Thorley looked about him. 'The garden is quite beautiful. But I believe it has suffered tragedies.'

Zack nodded.

'Is Miss Warboy about?' the vicar said. 'I had hoped to have a word with her.'

'No.'

'I believe she was the victim of an assault.'

'So she says. And she blamed an innocent man.'

'Did she now, and who would that be?' he asked quietly.

'Angus McLeod. A good God-fearing man sent to rot at Port Arthur, and I can tell you, Vicar, it ain't fair. It ain't fair at all.'

'I'm sure Mr Warboy wouldn't allow an innocent man to be charged.'

632

Zack sighed. 'It ain't for me to say what he allows, sir. But things have never been the same here since they took Angus away. Some say the garden's cursed.'

'Dear, oh dear,' Vicar Thorley murmured as he walked back up to the house to inform the maid he could wait no longer.

For days he worried about the Warboy scandal, and prayed for guidance, and in the end he went to the bishop.

Initially he mentioned that the convicts on the Warboy farm would like to be included in the Trinity services.

Bishop Hankers turned his nose up in disgust at the Warboy name. 'There have been some strange goings-on out there.'

'So I hear. I wish I had come back sooner.'

'There was nothing you could have done. But I commend you for taking an interest in the rest of the convicts working on that farm. They must have gone through a very trying time. Some pastoral help wouldn't go astray there.'

'But I might have been able to help, Bishop.' He looked earnestly at his mentor. 'I am very concerned about Miss Warboy. She accused the convict McLeod of being her attacker. What if it was someone else?'

'Then she would have pointed to someone else. And she did not. Plain as day.'

'But there was someone else in the picture.'

'There was?' That caught the bishop's interest. 'By Jove! Did she have another boyfriend?'

Thorley shook his head sadly. 'I don't think that little girl had any boyfriends, Bishop. Something

633

I saw before my illness has been preying on my mind. I have to speak up or I'll never get any rest.' Nervously he began to relate the incident in the house, when Warboy and his daughter thought they were not being observed.

'Good Lord!' the bishop was stunned. 'What did you say to the fellow?'

'I didn't say anything, I was too shocked. Totally taken aback.'

'So you said nothing?'

'Yes.'

'And this was a month ago?'

'Yes.'

'Do you think you misinterpreted their actions? That you could be wrong? It sounds to me that by not saying a word to him, you were not too sure of the situation at the time. And brooding over it for so long has you convinced you are right.'

'Bishop, I know what I saw.'

'You saw some sort of movements in a glance. I would be very careful of blackening the names of two people on guesswork. Your interpretation sounds like guesswork to me. You have no real proof. Leave it be, my dear fellow. Don't be imagining sin where none exists.'

'But what about the convict McLeod?'

The bishop stood. 'You said Miss Warboy accused him! That'd be enough for any judge. She should know. Now I'm sure you have many more pressing matters to attend to in your parish, so I won't keep you any longer. I'll pray that you remain in good health now.'

Samuel Thorley was a quiet and self-effacing

man. Reasonable too. And that was his problem now. He understood why His Grace had taken this stance. On reflection, the case he'd put forward did sound weak. And maybe he should have taken Warboy aside and spoken to him on the matter there and then. But had he done so, it would have caused denial and outrage. Bishop Hankers would realise that, too, given time to think about it.

But why would he? Samuel asked himself, as he left the manse. *He thinks you imagined it.*

His face flamed when he recalled being asked not to imagine sin where none existed. He'd never before been accused of being over-zealous.

But then he thought of the sufferings of the convict McLeod, condemned to life in Port Arthur.

Vicar Thorley did not lack gumption.

For McLeod's sake, he decided he should mention his misgivings about Warboy to a civil authority. *I realise now it's not much to go on,* he said to himself, *but you never know...*

The second telling of the incident he had witnessed was not so difficult. Chief Constable Hippisley listened politely, making no comment. He certainly did not express shock, which, the vicar thought wearily, only served to show him that such depravity was not unknown to the policeman.

'Now, let me see, Vicar,' he said at length. 'You believe that what you saw could be relevant to the rape case.'

'I do. Sad to say I am not unacquainted with cases of incest. I was unable to come forward before, and on my return to Hobart I fully intended to speak with Mr Jubal Warboy about the matter, but unfortunately he had already left the colony. But the young woman is still here. She would have the answer. It is my opinion, sir, that there could be a miscarriage of justice here.'

'I see.' The Chief Constable nodded, not discouragingly by any means.

'Yes, a man was convicted of her rape on her testimony, but many people claim he is innocent. I believe Mr Baggott even considered an appeal.'

'With no grounds because the victim identified her attacker.'

'Exactly. But what if rape were cried when they discovered she was pregnant? She had to identify someone, to remove suspicion from what was happening at home, so to speak. I hope you don't think I enjoy having to rake up such a sordid matter, Mr Hippisley, but I would like to make sure the right person has been convicted. It would be a tragedy were it otherwise.'

Hippisley took his time. He put his right elbow on his desk, and rested his chin on his hand, while he tapped the desk softly with the other hand. Minutes passed. The vicar did not interrupt his train of thought.

Finally Hippisley said: 'Did you know that the girl was ... is simple? I mean, a bit mental.'

'I thought she could be. Yes. Rather juvenile for her age, I thought.'

'That of course makes this business even nastier. Incest is bad at the best of times. And it often results in pregnancies that the parents cover up by accusing someone else. Which is what could have happened here.'

'It could have,' Vicar Thorley agreed. 'That's all I have to offer, Chief Constable. I do verily believe it was my duty to advise you of the family situation.'

'Thank you, Vicar. It was good of you to come. I will look into it further, and let you know the outcome.'

Hippisley was intrigued. He couldn't ignore this piece of information. It was too important.

So that rat of a father, Jubal Warboy, was the fly in the ointment. But what could be done now? The fellow had fled. Unless the girl could be persuaded to have a rethink. To talk about it. After all, she had just blurted out a name, if he recalled correctly. And she hadn't appeared in court. Barnaby Warboy's standing in the community had kept her out of the limelight.

He wondered what Barnaby knew about his son.

No use going down that track. Yea or nay, he'd never say.

He had to find the girl. She'd left the farm, gone into seclusion, he supposed, to discourage gossip.

He'd send Goosey to snoop around.

Dr Jellick always enjoyed Hippisley's company; he was a most interesting man, formerly with the British police in Calcutta. So he was quite pleased, after a hard day, to be invited to join the Chief Constable for a drink at his favourite pub.

'So, what's up?' he asked. 'Why the sudden call

637

to arms?'

'I've got a favour to ask of you.'

'Shoot.'

'It's about a patient of yours. Miss Penelope Warboy.'

'She's not my patient.'

'She was.'

'That's true.'

'Well, since she's having a baby, I hoped you might call in on her, see how she's getting along.'

'I can't do that. What brought this on?'

'It's to do with that case of rape. It won't go away.'

Jellick scowled. 'I'm not surprised. I never believed she was raped.'

'I know. But another possible contender as father of the child has entered the field.'

'Really? Who would that be?'

'Keep this quiet now. The father.'

Jellick whistled his surprise and heads turned.

'Quiet, I said. Yes. Someone has come forward with a statement. He saw them in a compromising situation.'

'What the bloody hell has taken so long?'

'He's been away. This is why I want you to visit her in your capacity as her doctor. She's living out at Sandy Bay with a maid. She's not quite all there, and I think a visit from a medical man would be very much in order.'

'She might already have a doctor.'

'No she hasn't. I asked about.'

'Her parents aren't around any longer, but Barnaby is still with us. He could object.'

'She's of age, closer to nineteen now, I think.

He can't object. You were her doctor. You could call on her. See how she's coping. And ask a few subtle questions, but don't lead her on, if you get what I mean. And you could have a chat with the maid, too.'

He ordered two more gins. 'If not, the case is closed for good. People still say McLeod is innocent. I'd hate to think Jubal Warboy let an innocent man pay for his crime.'

'From what I heard, he didn't just let him pay, he was busy shouting guilty.'

Marie welcomed the doctor. She'd been starting to worry, as Penn hadn't been well lately and had had stomach pains, but Dr Jellick said she was hale and hearty and the odd pains here and there were caused by the skin stretching.

He was a nice man, and he had a little chat with her at the door after he'd examined Penn, commenting that they had a fine tranquil spot here. He also asked if Miss Warboy had experienced any after-effects of the rape, and Marie had hurried off that subject.

'No, Doctor,' she said. 'It doesn't seem so.'

But Jellick, not known for his delicate approach, had been interested when Penn started telling him about Angus, the man she intended to marry. He took the opportunity to ask her a few blunt questions, while he was examining her, and she answered freely. In all innocence.

'This will interest Hippisley,' he muttered angrily.

CHAPTER NINETEEN

Sean was far from happy in this job, but he did as he was told like a little marvel. Like the best-behaved schoolboy in the class. He seated the customers, called clients, took them across the passage to Mr Pitcairn on the stroke of their appointed time, returned to his clerk's tasks, copying letters, writing receipts, filing diligently, taking messages from court runners, ushering clients out, ushering more in.

It seemed to him a demeaning way for a man to fill in a day, but he knew, vaguely, that it was important for him to go forward along this road. To stick it out.

There was a saving grace, though – the problems that presented themselves to Mr Pitcairn. This side of the business, which, sadly, had nothing to do with Sean, was fascinating. Blessed, or cursed, with great curiosity, Sean was mightily interested in the clients' affairs ... in their desperate pleas that Pitcairn defend them from the arms of the law, and their outraged demands that an adversary be sued forthwith.

Most of the background he learned from the lawyer's notes and letters, because the average client usually sat po-faced, tight-lipped, in the presence of the lowly clerk. As he had done himself at Baggott's rooms, he recalled. Others, though, couldn't keep the drama in. They boiled over, unable to hold back as they awaited Mr Pitcairn, pouring their outrages and their entreaties into the ears of Mr Shanahan, who had to fight to keep aloof, he who all his life had been a purveyor of advice.

That was tough, really tough, because to ignore people's feelings and get on with his work like a drone, unable to make comment of any sort, brought hard looks from the waiting room. Tears sometimes. Sneers even.

He'd been warned about that by Pitcairn, warned that even nodding when being regaled with a tale of woe in that room was unwise. Seriously unwise, he'd added with a frown, and Sean understood the reason, but it didn't make it any easier. The Irishman was not accustomed to unpopularity. Once again he had to remind himself to keep his mouth shut.

Towards the end of the second week, as the sun was setting, Sean was walking home when Bailey stepped out of the shadows.

'You never told me you was pen-pushing for Pitcairn,' he complained.

'It's a job. Why? What are you doing out this way?'

'Can't I even have a talk with a mate? Or are you too uppity now?'

'No.' Sean grinned. 'Took you a while to find out, didn't it? I got you beat this time.'

'That you didn't,' the little man leered. 'I know a lot of his customers, don't forget.'

'All right. There's a pub on that corner, I'll buy you a rum and you can tell me why the visit.'

'It'll cost you more than a rum,' Bailey warned,

suddenly very serious.

He wouldn't stay in the dingy bar, but wandered out the back door, so Sean bought the rums and took them outside to find him over by a water tank, blithely sucking on a pear collected from a nearby box.

'The nights are getting nice and warm now,' he said, taking his drink. Then, suddenly: 'How are your ladies? The Harris ladies?'

'They're well, I suppose. I haven't seen them awhile.'

'Why didn't you tell me they are Bull Harris's wife and kid?'

'Why should I?'

'Because somethin's up,' Bailey said fiercely. 'I heard a doer was found for that payback job, and only just now, down on the wharves I hear the name Harris again, Bull Harris, and I did some asking about your ladies, you bloody fool.'

'Jesus! Do you think he's hawking a payback on his wife? What the hell for?'

'Are you romancin' her?'

'No!'

'What if he thinks you are? I tell you, somethin's up and I wouldn't mind bettin' they're the target.'

'They can't be.'

'Please yourself. Nice ladies like that. You never know where it's coming from. But I'd bring 'em to town. Could be one of their own convicts might have a go for pay.'

Sean tossed down the rum. 'I'd better go and see.'

'I'd say it's worth a look around.'

'I'm off then. You get a message to Hippisley.'

'Not on your life. God spare me days, you jest!'

But Sean was gone. He elbowed through the bar, ran across the road, rounded a corner, where he was nearly run down by a water cart, raced through the narrow streets and up the hill to the Doc's place. He whistled the horse from a paddock at the rear of the house, threw on the bridle and strapped on the saddle, and then he was off, worrying for the women, worrying that he could be making a damn fool of himself.

'It wouldn't be the first time,' he said, keeping the horse to a trot as it wove through the busier streets. 'But I just have to make sure they're all right.'

'But surely,' Josie said, 'if there's trouble on Sassafras Road, the police and the military can handle it. I mean, it's very kind of you, Sean, to be so concerned about us, but everything is all right here.'

'How do you know?' Louise challenged, her voice shrill. 'Sean comes out here to warn us of trouble and you won't even listen to him.'

'I am listening. I'm sorry, Sean, but it's not as if we're alone here. We have our own workmen, we can alert them to be on their guard if you like. Even so, I'd have to get you to speak to them, because I'm mystified. It's not the blacks, is it? Not in this district, surely?'

Sean had known it would be difficult trying to dislodge the two women with his flimsy tale, but he could not tell them of Bailey's warning. Louise was all in favour of going into town with him right away, but unconvincing in her motives. Neither Sean nor her mother had any doubts that the attraction was more a visit to Dr Roberts' house than a dash to safety. Her mother determined not to budge.

He'd been sitting in their kitchen for more than an hour now, finally discussing other matters over a cup of tea, but he refused to believe he'd over-reacted. He had a gut feeling that Bailey's information could be right, if the trail led back to this woman's husband. There was also the possibility that Lester Harris, never a popular bloke, had wronged someone and the payback was to be directed at his property, if not necessarily at his women. Trouble is, he worried, that's not too palatable a story to put to Josie either.

'So you started work in the lawyer's office?' she said.

'That's right.'

'And are you liking it?'

'Ah now, it's easy enough. I have to do a fair bit of writing, copying like, and the words bewilder a bit.'

'Are they too long?' Louise asked.

'Aye, there's a little of that, but it's more the sentences go round in circles, taking a week of insomuches to get to a point. If you can find it at all. But I don't dare leave a word out, even them as not needed.'

'You'll get used to it,' Josie laughed.

'Don't tell me I'll end up talking like that. My mother wouldn't understand a word from me.'

'Is your mother still alive?'

'Yes, back in Ireland, and my pa. I have a sister,

Annie, and she's a son called Sean.' He turned to Louise. 'And a good-looking fellow they say he is too, like his uncle.'

'Oh, get on with you!'

They were only making conversation by this, so Sean had no choice but to leave, but as he opened the back door, Josie relented a little.

'I'm really grateful to you, Sean, and if it would make you feel better, we could take a turn around the house to see if anyone's about, and then you might have a word with the men.'

Sean carried the lantern as they tramped through the gardens that surrounded the house, and then walked back to the house through the orchard.

'Would you go down to the men's quarters?' Josie asked. 'It's a warm night. Modesty prevents me from intruding on them at this hour.'

'All right. But you go on inside.'

'Very well.' She mounted the back steps. 'Take the lantern, I don't want you falling over something. They're always leaving tools lying about.'

Sean frowned at that, but carried on. 'I won't be long,' he said.

Josie was impressed with his kindness, but she still couldn't raise any concern about these vague dangers. She hadn't liked to say so, but she would have heard if there was trouble in the district; she wasn't exactly isolated from her neighbours.

'Anyway,' she muttered as she waited for him, 'I've got enough troubles of my own. Including you!' she added when she saw a possum looking down at her from an apple tree. 'Shoo!' She ran down the steps. 'Get away from my apples!'

But the large luminous eyes peered calmly at her, their owner making no move to obey.

Josie searched about for a stick, moving away from the apple trees to the base of a gum tree, where she spotted the dry white remains of a branch. She dived towards it, but just as she grabbed it, she felt a sharp blow to her arm. At the same time she smelled sweat, and a heavy figure lurched at her. Josie spun around with the stick, and clubbed the man with all her might. She thought she heard dogs barking as she tried to escape from him, fighting strong hands, but he punched her in the neck and she stumbled. The glint of a knife released a scream from her. Immediately a clammy hand closed on her mouth as he wrenched her backwards, and she felt a thump in her side.

Still screaming, Josie tore herself away from him and ran, but she hit her head on a tree branch and went down in the damp undergrowth.

She heard men's voices raised in alarm, heard them running, and waited for the attacker to come at her again, but he was gone. Or he couldn't find her in the dark. She didn't know. Her head ached so much, and the grass smelled so sweet. Then she could hear Louise screaming and prayed to God he hadn't turned on her.

Sean carried Josie up to the house, while the men raced after her attacker, their dogs coursing ahead. They tore down the road, yelping and baying after a horseman, but were unable to catch him, he had too much of a lead on them. Nevertheless, some of the men mounted up and took on the chase, while others roused neighbours.

Josie was bleeding profusely from a wound in her side, and another in her upper arm, so Sean laid her on her bed on her side, and called to Louise for cloths to stem the blood, but she was hysterical, clinging to her mother, who was only semi-conscious, begging her to wake, to speak to her!

Impatiently, Sean pushed her away, snapping at her to do as she was told.

With help from Louise, he tried to keep pressure on the wound as he cut away Josie's blouse, but he was shocked when he actually saw the bloody raw cut in her side, so he applied the cloths as tightly as he could, using a pillow to keep them in place.

Louise started weeping again. 'We have to get a doctor,' she cried. 'Go and get a doctor, Sean.'

'No,' he said. 'Go out and tell the overseer to hitch up the buggy. We'll take her to the hospital.'

Josie tried to protest, but he soothed her, telling her not to worry, everything was all right, thinking that the bed was narrow and they could carry her out to the buggy, mattress and all, for a more comfortable journey.

When Louise came back, a little calmer now, he told her he needed strips of sheeting to bind up the wound and bandage Josie's arm before they could move her, and sent her off to attend to that chore.

'Who was it?' he asked Josie quietly. 'Did you know him?'

'No,' she gasped.

A few minutes later she managed to whisper:

'He was horrible, a heavy man, sweaty, no shoes. He stank.'

Sean saw her grimace in pain. 'Don't worry then. We'll find him.'

She looked at him angrily. 'How did you know?' It was more of a demand than a question, and then she closed her eyes, shutting him out.

The only doctor available was Jellick, who buzzed by the hospital, sleepy-eyed, and announced he would sew her up in the morning, in better light. Matron herself washed and bandaged Josie's arm, then sent the visitors on their way.

'Let your mother get some rest now,' she said, but Louise refused to leave.

'I'll just sit here with her. I won't get in the way.'

That suited Sean. He took the matron aside. 'She'll be quiet if you let her stay, ma'am. To be truthful, I don't know what to do with her. I'm only a family friend. It wouldn't be fitting to take a young lady to my house with only me there.'

'It certainly would not! I thought you were the husband!' Matron sniffed.

'No. He's away. In the morning I'll find Miss Harris some digs. She can't go home with a knife-wielding bandit roaming about out there.'

'Very well, she can stay.'

'Ah, God bless you. You're kindness itself.'

The matron smiled. 'Thank you. One doesn't get much appreciation in this place. Too many patients and too little money.'

After he left the hospital, Sean rode over to the large brick police station, disappointed that the red lamp over the heavy front door was burning. He'd been hoping the place would be closed so that he could get some sleep, but a report had to be made, so he hurried in, looked about for a familiar face and, failing that, giving the details to the surly constable on duty.

'What do you expect us to do about it at this hour?'

'Nothing,' he growled. 'I'll be back tomorrow when the live ones are on duty.'

'What's that supposed to mean?'

Sean didn't bother to answer. He marched out into the deserted street, telling himself he could spare three hours for sleep, then he needed to see Sam Pollard, and then he had to get to work. On time. He couldn't allow private matters to interfere with his duties in this crucial month.

Sam was surprised to see him waiting outside the store when he opened up. 'How are you, Shanahan? I heard you were working for Pitcairn. If I'da thought you wanted a job as a clerk, I could have put you on here. Helluva job keeping the books in a business this size. But then Mr Warboy mightn't have–'

'It's all right, Sam. I'm here for a favour. There was trouble out on Sassafras Road. Mrs Harris was attacked by some bastard with a knife. She's in the hospital.'

'Good God almighty! Mr Warboy didn't have any trouble, did he?'

'Not as far as I know, but he'll be upset when he hears of this. They are friends of his.'

'Yes, I know.'

'Well, the thing is, I brought Louise Harris to

649

town with her mother last night but she's stuck at the hospital now, with nowhere to go. I can't send her home, the attacker could still be in the area.'

'Oh, the poor girl.'

'I was wondering if you and your missus could put her up for a couple of days. Just while her mother's in the hospital.'

'Of course we will. No trouble at all. Will you bring her here?'

'I can't, I'll be at work. Could I ask you to collect her?'

'We'll scoop her up. Don't worry. How did you come to be working for Pitcairn? He's a bit of a radical, you know.'

'Is he now? I'd better watch me step. Thanks, Sam. You're not such a bad feller after all.'

'Phew!' he murmured, as he rushed away again. 'That was a shot in the dark. But them being Warboy's friends saved the day, I'm thinking.'

Sean didn't say a word to Pitcairn about the night's events, but all morning he was expecting someone from the police station to come barging in on him with questions; dreading the interruption in case it would irritate his boss. But when it did come, the interruption was only a timid knock on the door. A young constable handed him a note from Chief Constable Hippisley, instructing him to present himself at the police station after work.

'Glory be,' he grinned as he sent the constable on his way with his answer 'in the affirmative'.

That's what Mr Pitcairn writes, he mused. A fine turn of phrase it is. But what a turn-up that even Hippisley fell short of lead-footin' it in here

650

after me! The things a man learns!

Nevertheless, Hippisley wasn't in the best of moods when Sean kept his appointment, nor did he waste any time.

'Mrs Harris tells me you knew she would be attacked last night. She said you came out to warn her! Now you can tell me, Shanahan, how you knew a crime was about to be committed, and you don't leave here until you do.'

Sean went over the story, placing himself in Bailey's shoes, claiming that he had heard a rumour in a pub.

'Which pub?'

He named the biggest, busiest pub, the Whalers' Return. It was always packed with seamen.

'I didn't know you drank there.'

'I call in often when I'm down on the wharves,' he lied.

'Why are you often down on the wharves?'

Bloody hell, Sean thought. If I don't come up with some truth here I'll be in a tight corner. Reluctantly he admitted: 'I've been watching the ships for my girlfriend from Ireland, who's coming here.'

Hippisley laughed. 'You expect me to believe that?'

'She's coming here with her little son, Tom,' he said angrily, and the truth of it was plain.

The Chief Constable wouldn't admit that, however; he simply moved on, and Sean breathed a sigh of relief. He was a bit cross that Josie had said so much, but then he supposed she had good reason. He wasn't too popular with her now.

'Right then,' Hippisley said. 'What's your best

guess here?'

'Bull Harris. Either someone's taking payback out on her, since he's not the nicest feller in town. Or he wants her dead.'

'What?' Hippisley was taken aback.

Sean himself was surprised at the way he'd come out with that accusation. He'd hardly entertained the thought before, too busy looking at payback.

Hippisley picked up on that.

'Why would Harris want to pay her back? What for? Has she got a lover? Is it you?'

'No!'

'Is it the old boy, Warboy, then? I heard she's always been matey with him.'

'I don't think so. No. The poor woman and her daughter have been minding their own business there for years, just trying to run the farm. They're well respected, I can tell you, and it's only lately that they're about admitting Lester Harris is her husband.'

'And now she wants to sell the farm?'

'Yes. But he won't give consent.'

Hippisley frowned. 'All right, that'll do for the minute. No, hang on. You're working for Pitcairn?'

'Yes.'

'What? He's recruiting you to join his anti-transportation mob, eh?'

Sean wished he could agree with that, but Mr Pitcairn had never mentioned the subject. They rarely had any conversations at all, outside work-related matters, and then only about the weather – the congenial climate in comparison to Ireland, which Mr Pitcairn hoped to visit one day.

'No,' he said flatly.

When Sean had left, Hippisley sent for Constable Gander.

'I've been talking to Shanahan about this attack on Mrs Harris,' he said, and went on to explain the situation to date. 'Shanahan doesn't ring true,' he concluded. 'He's no ferret. I believe he got that information from his mate Bailey. I want you to talk to Bailey, tell him Shanahan dropped him in, so you want some names. Don't mention Lester Harris, just see where your chat takes you. Put the arm on Bailey if you have to. Warn him it's attempted murder, and he's involved.'

'Could Lester Harris have ordered that attack from Port Arthur?' the constable asked Sergeant Budd later that morning.

'That mob of convicts can arrange messages, give orders, buy stuff, do anything, as long as they've got the money to bribe seamen and civilians who come and go,' Budd said. 'There's nearly a thousand convicts in the place, and it's spread out like Hyde Park. The authorities can't watch them all the time.'

'Why don't they escape then?'

Budd laughed. 'Fear, Goosey my lad. Plain bloody fear! The Commandant, he don't care about their messages, but try escaping and the sky'll fall in on you. What did Bailey have to say?'

'Nothing. He didn't believe Shanahan had dropped his name. He said I was just trying him on, and he didn't know nothing about the whole thing. But then when I was giving up on him he says, just the same, if there was a money trail he'd be guessing it'd lead back to Harris.'

'Why?'

'He says because he's got money. He owns that farm, he could offer top money for a doer. But why would he want to kill his wife? I asks him, and he says he's not a bloody mind-reader!'

'Did you tell Hippisley?'

'Course I did.'

The constable's report sent Hippisley around the corner to visit Baggott, and when he learned that Lester Harris had flatly refused to allow his wife to sell the farm, he had to agree that the attack was based on a domestic quarrel. But how to deal with it? Convict undercover activities were hard to infiltrate without an agent, and this domestic business wasn't worth employing an undercover man. In the meantime, as Shanahan had observed, Mrs Harris could be attacked again.

'One thing I could do,' Baggott offered, 'is to go to the Attorney-General requesting permission for her to sell the property on the grounds that she fears for her life there. And that she wishes to return to England.'

'Away from his murderous clutches?'

'Well, I couldn't say that, but one could imagine it as given.'

'Good. Give it a try, and let me know as soon as possible.'

As Sean left the police station, a young man called to him: 'Remember me? I'm Mr Baggott's clerk.'

'Of course. What can I do for you?'

'It's this way,' the clerk said apologetically. 'Since you've joined our little group of law clerks, Mr Shanahan, and with great respect, may I give you a little hint?'

'You may,' Sean smiled.

'Well, we have to be careful not to upset people, and give ourselves a bad name so to speak. For instance, we try to pay our bills on time.'

'Ah, I see. Do I owe someone money?'

'I'm afraid you do. You owe Mr Baggott two and sixpence.'

'What for?'

'I sent you the bill, with Mr Baggott's letter.'

'What did the letter say?' Sean asked him urgently.

'I'm afraid I can't discuss that, but you would have had the letter for some time. Weeks.'

'No I haven't. I didn't receive any letter from him.'

'Oh well! That's different. I shall have to enquire at the post office, for I posted it myself.'

'Ah, wait!' Sean said. 'When letters come for Dr Roberts, I don't look at them, I put them in his office. Your letter could be there!'

'Not my letter, Mr Shanahan. Mr Baggott's! Well now, I'm glad I spoke to you. I didn't want to put your name on a rendered list.'

'Thank you,' Sean said absently as he tried to decide what he should do first, go home and search for Baggott's letter, or visit Josie.

Baggott won.

From habit now, Sean checked under the front

doorstep, where the postman usually left mail, safe from the vagaries of weather and marauding magpies, but on this day the cupboard was bare, so he sorted through the dozen or so letters in the doctor's office and found the one he was looking for.

He was ashamed that with one thing and another he'd forgotten about Angus lately, but angry when he read the letter. Baggott would not help. He'd found no grounds for appeal! And had charged two and six.

Sean sat down with a thump! What now?

He worried about that all the way back into town, but set it aside as he walked into the hospital.

Josie had been moved into the crowded women's ward. She looked coldly at him as he approached her bed.

'There was no need to come,' she said. 'Louise has been here for hours. She has just left.'

'Then you're all right?'

'The doctor stitched the wound. As long as it doesn't get infected I can leave here in a couple of days.'

'That's good. I'm terrible sorry this has happened to you.'

'A bit late for that.'

'I tried to get you to come to town, but you wouldn't listen to me.'

'Listen to your lies, you mean?'

'They were not lies.' He glared at the grey-haired woman in the next bed, who was leaning over perilously so as not to miss a word of this conversation. It did no good, though.

'I simply did the best I could, considering I'd only heard a rumour.'

'Oh yes, of course. I forgot. You and your rumours!'

He looked about him. 'Is there anything I can do for you?'

'Yes. You could let me rest, I'm very tired.'

'Poor thing,' the eavesdropper added. 'She's in pain. She only had her stitches done this morning. You ought to leave her alone.'

'I'm sorry,' Sean stammered. 'Yes. I'll go.'

The next evening he was earlier, and Louise bailed him up in the hall outside the ward.

'What are you doing here?' she demanded. 'Haven't you caused enough trouble? The police were here again this morning and my mother's very upset.'

'What about?'

'You've got a damn cheek to even ask. I thought you were our friend, but what do you do but run to the police and blame my father for that shocking attack!' She raised her voice. 'I'll never forgive you for that, Shanahan. My mother is distraught that you should invent such lies. Isn't it hard enough for her that Daddy is in prison, an innocent man, and now you're trying to blame all this on him. Makes me wonder what you're really up to.'

'Louise,' he tried, 'you've got it all wrong. Let's go in and see your mother and I'll explain.'

'You will leave my mother alone,' she cried bitterly. 'There's nothing to explain. You're just another convict trying to better yourself by sucking up to your superiors. You won't last long in that job! Anyone can see that.'

'In that case,' he said quietly, 'I'll leave your mother to rest, and you to maybe grow a little sense. I think there's still time.'

As he walked away she shouted at him: 'And don't come back.'

A few days later, Chief Constable Toohill of Port Arthur broke the news to Louise's father that a man had attacked his wife at the farm and she had been hospitalised with knife wounds.

'Is she all right?' he asked breathlessly, hoping for the worst.

'Yes, she's all right now, and back home, so there's no need for alarm.'

'Did he steal anything?'

'Who?'

'The robber, who else?'

'No, apparently she disturbed him on the premises. But the Hobart police think it may not have been a robber. Do you know of anyone who would want to injure your wife?'

'My wife! For God's sake, no! She's a fine respectable woman. A good country woman, not like the hussies that overrun Hobart.'

'Then it's a great mystery.'

'How can you say it's a mystery?' Lester grated angrily. 'It's no bloody mystery. Josetta is also a good-looking woman. In the prime. Obviously some bastard took a knife to her to subdue her. To rape her! Thank God she escaped.'

'No, *he* escaped. She fought him off, I believe.'

Lester groaned. 'Do you know how hard it is for me to hear things like that? My wife attacked, and me not able to lift a finger to protect her. Can I apply for leave, for only a couple of days even, to make sure she's all right?'

'I doubt it, but I'll ask.'

'If you would,' Lester said plaintively. 'If you would, sir.'

Lester didn't get his leave, but Toohill's report affected Hippisley's decision.

He spoke to Baggott. 'I can't go along with the story of Lester Harris arranging a "doer" to attack his wife. She vehemently refuses to have that, on any account. And my man over at the prison believes it's more likely that it's attempted rape by some hooligan in the district. And there are plenty of them. So there's no point in approaching the Attorney General on her behalf.'

'Drat,' Baggott said as he made an entry in the Harris file. 'The woman has just wrecked her own case. Oh well!'

His clerk came in. 'I thought I should tell you, sir, Mr Shanahan paid his account. His letter was mixed up with Dr Roberts' mail, and he only recently found it.'

'Yes, yes,' the lawyer said testily. 'Very well.'

Sergeant Abel Budd was interested. 'Attempted rape?' he said to Goosey. 'Could be. Might be the same one that raped the Warboy girl, if it wasn't Angus.'

'I dunno,' Goosey said. 'How come Shanahan got wind of it?'

'What you said. Bailey tipped him off.'

'Hang on. I never heard of a rapist boasting

before the deed. After, yes, but before? I don't hold with that stand.'

'Forget it. Hippisley's looking for a rapist. It was probably one of the convicts working out that way.'

'Out of curfew? On a horse?'

'Wonders will never cease,' Budd laughed.

Lester was not amused.

Neither was the lifer, a coal-miner who'd set it up for Harris, with a mate who worked on the coal barges. The latter had put the word out among the whalers in Hobart that a doer was needed for an easy job with big pay. A whaler from New Zealand had volunteered for the job, but required payment first, so he could choose the night before his ship sailed.

Since his mate was holding an IOU from Harris for twenty pounds, the bargeman paid the would-be assassin his five pounds from his own pocket. He was pleased with himself that he'd beaten the tough whaler down, arguing that Harris wouldn't pay any more. He hadn't meant to drop the name Harris right there, but he supposed it didn't matter since Mrs Harris was to be the victim. It'll be right! he told himself.

But it wasn't right. The whaler's ship had sailed on the early tide the morning after the attack, as he'd planned.

And Mrs Harris had survived. Which didn't bother the bargeman one way or another. He'd carried out his side of the bargain.

It didn't bother the coal-miner either, when his mate's barge slid into the Fort Arthur coaling wharf, right across the bay from South Point. He agreed they'd done their job. And what was more, he laughed, he had the IOU, which he would now call in.

Unfortunately, Bull Harris did not see it that way. He demanded the return of the IOU because the job had not been done. Simple as that.

'What sort of a mug do you think I am?' he asked. 'She's still there. Nothing's changed, so I'll have my IOU back. I'll have to start all over if I can't figure out another plan.'

'You're forgetting. My mate paid the doer. He gave him fifteen pounds, and the other five was for our part of the job.'

'He paid him before the job? What does he use for brains, paying one of those bastard whalers a farthing in advance? If he's that stupid you ought to stuff him in a bag and chuck him in the river.'

'Say what you like, Harris! He's still out of pocket fifteen pounds, and the whalerman, give him his due, he tried.'

'And failed. I don't pay for nothing. Give me back the IOU.'

'Not on your life! I'm claiming it. If you won't pay I'll put it into that bank you've been skiting about.'

That spurred Lester into action. He couldn't afford this to happen, not so soon after Josie had got stabbed. He hurled himself at the miner, landing a heavy fist on his jaw.

'You'll give it back,' he hissed, 'or you won't live to use it.'

The miner, easily a match for Harris, retaliated

with a head butt and a fist to Lester's solar plexus. He crashed to the ground, and at the same time a guard felled the miner with several heavy blows to the back of his head.

The fight over, bystanders were ordered to throw buckets of water over the two men, then more guards arrived to drag them off to their cells.

They were both put on report, which didn't bother the miner, but Convict Harris lost his trusty status. He was livid with rage when it was announced at the morning muster, protesting that the miner had attacked him for no reason at all.

'Yes, they all do,' the gang boss chortled. 'Marvellous the way they all attack Harris for no reason! It was Flo Quinlan last time, wasn't it?'

Lester was quiet. Flo Quinlan? He'd almost forgotten about him. You just never knew in the convict ranks who was mates with who. He owed Quinlan a payback too, and he'd get him one of these days, but for now he'd have to knuckle down and earn that trusty spot back. It wouldn't take long, if he saved his tobacco ration and the measly shillings he earned to bribe the right guards.

But then disaster struck. He was pulled out of the muster and ordered to the coal mines with a fresh gang.

'I've never worked in a coal mine,' he complained. 'I wouldn't know what to do.'

'You're not picked for your brains, Lester. Just like the rest of these jokers, you're here for your brawn. Now march!'

Although Lester hadn't noticed, George Smith was marching behind him. George had surprised the bosses by offering to work in the mines, claiming they couldn't be worse than tree felling or toiling in those open quarries where the sun damaged his frail skin more than he could bear. The burns had served him well for a change.

George had been astonished to find that illegal convict contact with the mainland was widespread through a complex system of message channels, and that Willem had managed to infiltrate one of them. But then Willem always was a smart fellow, he allowed.

Already a plan of escape was under way, for George and for Angus. The messages were delivered to him hidden in the base of small tins of tobacco, and the rule was that the man who handed him the tin received the tobacco as payment.

So far, George knew the escape was to be on a Sunday morning, and that they would be quitting the island by boat, near the mines. When the time came, both he and Angus were expected to create diversions by starting fires. Angus could start one in the woods, he mused, and he'd start one somewhere else ... which was another reason why Sunday was essential. Everyone would be on church parade.

It would be easy enough for a man to go missing for a little while, as long as he was free of chains, George knew. The Sunday crowds, marching to the church from all directions, were often chaotic; the Papists deliberately disrupting, demanding their own services, and the everyday troublemakers joining in for the hell of it. Experienced guards just kept their convicts moving, but the more sadistic enjoyed nothing better than to lay into anyone within reach of whips and clubs.

So it seemed, he reflected, that Willem really could pull off an escape from this peninsula prison, by picking them up from one of the lonely bays near the mines. And, no doubt, he'd have those arrangements well in hand by the time he named a definite day.

At first George was scared. He was scared he'd get caught and his sentence would be extended to life. He had hoped to serve the extra couple of years here and be done with it. Walk out a free man. But he'd soon come to realise that no matter how hard a man tried to keep his nose clean, trouble lurked. From the Commandant down the bosses ruled by violence and, he reflected, violence begat violence. One of the guards, a weasel of a man, had taken a liking to George, too much of a liking, and when George rejected his advances he made an enemy who wasted no time in telling everyone that the prisoner had molested him.

Clouds were gathering now. Willem, bless him, would have been aware it was only a matter of time before his friend came under attack. Now he was afraid of staying. He had to escape.

The coal mines weren't the safest place either, but that was a risk he'd have to take.

'For how long, Willem?' he murmured. 'For how long?'

George was surprised when Harris claimed him as a mate and commandeered the bunk next to him in one of the long sheds that housed miners during the week. He soon learned, though, that Harris had fallen out with a bargeman called Taffy, and needed a mate for protection, though as George mused, he hadn't outright said so.

But then, when he was introduced to the hard life as an underground miner, George had no time to be concerned with Harris or his problems. He worked his shifts, watched for a man with a tobacco tin, and looked forward to Sundays, not knowing that Willem was, once again, just across that stretch of water at South Point.

Freddy was still working at the Crown Inn in Sorell when Willem rode in, and he soon gave him a piece of his mind.

'About time you turned up, Willem! You needn't think I was goin' to sit about waiting for you for ever. Where have you been?'

'Sorry,' Willem said patiently. 'I had to wait for some money to come from my father so that I could get on with my business.'

'Your father sent you money? What are you gonna do now?'

'Attend to my business.'

'Ah yes, that's right. How do you do that?'

'First I have to buy a block of land.'

'Go on!' Freddy breathed, impressed. Then he remembered. 'I've got another mate owns land too,' he said. 'Name of Claude.'

'Around here?' Willem asked hopefully.

'No. A long way off. The other way. Where's

your land?'

'I'm thinking of a place where I could build an inn, not far from here, on the coast, near the ferry depot.' He didn't bother to add, 'Down there near South Point.'

'Then will you live there?'

'Maybe. I always wanted an inn of my own.'

'Me too,' Freddy enthused.

'I could call it the Ferry Inn. You can get across the bay to Hobart via that ferry so easily. And it's a lot quicker than going all the way up and around Richmond.'

'So they say. I never been down to that ferry, because someone stole my horse. But listen, hey! You was back in Hobart?'

'Yes.'

'You didn't tell Shanahan where I am, didja?'

'Me? No! Of course not.'

Willem didn't ask Freddy not to mention his business plans. He deemed it better to let the yardman do his own talking. Which Freddy would, with or without permission. So that afternoon he drifted off around the sparse little town; took a nap in his room; and then went down to the bar, where he was greeted with a frown by the previously genial mine host.

'Are you startin' up in opposition to me, Mr Rothery?' he asked, red-faced, belligerent.

'Good God! Who on earth would dare to open another Crown Inn? Mr Havelock, sir, you do overestimate me. I could never hope to match this exclusive establishment. Ah no. I was thinking more of a travellers' rest, a small cheap inn, by the ferry depot.'

Havelock, slightly mollified, was listening.

'But then,' Willem said, 'then I had an idea. It's obvious this area will grow fast, with that road to Port Arthur under way. It's all very well for travellers to start coming over on the ferry, but what then, if they're not local people? I'll tell you what! They're stranded.'

'And what good would your inn be to them?'

'I was thinking of a small coach service to meet the ferry and take folk up to Sorell. I was even thinking that between us, you and me, we should own that coach service.'

'Why me?' Havelock leaned over the bar. 'Why would I be interested?'

'My dear fellow, if you're not, I wouldn't dream of trying to persuade you. I wouldn't have enough funds to build my inn *and* invest in a sturdy public coach, so I intend to discuss the matter with other Sorell townsfolk–'

Havelock interrupted him. 'Hold your fire. I didn't say I wasn't interested. I just asked.'

'There's plenty of time to discuss it, Mr Havelock. I'll have to find land first.'

'Find land?' he laughed. 'They'd give it away down by Dodges Ferry. It's run by a family of backwoods yokels. A real mongrel mob. They'd steal the hair off your head! Here, have a brandy on the house Mr Rothery.'

The next morning Willem rode out of town with a bottle of rum in his saddle pack. A band of yokels were about to become his best friends.

Henry the shaggy-haired patriarch of the family,

with his twisted foot, gained on a treadmill, took a while to warm to the visitor. The clincher was Willem's rum, drunk out of tin mugs on the dilapidated deck of the ferry, which in another life had been a coal barge.

'Whaddya want with land here?' Henry asked. 'Different if you was a fisherman. My oldest son back there's a fisherman.'

He jerked his head at a brawny fellow striding along the shore with several ragged boys all carrying fish baskets. They cut across a scrubby field, making for some humpies at the edge of the bush.

'You live up there?' Willem asked.

'No. There's too many of them there now, and the women get my goat. I live on my ferry.'

'Why I asked, I was thinking about the land next door to them. Who owns it?'

'No one,' Henry growled. 'The bloody Governor, I suppose. And it just hit me, it did. I seen you here once before, with one of them redcoat pigs.'

'Yes,' Willem said coolly. 'He came in handy, showed me around.'

'And now yer back. On yer own, eh?' His rheumy eyes glittered with suspicion.

'Is there a law against it?' Willem asked boldly, and Henry shrugged.

Changing the subject, Willem asked what time the ferry left.

'When there's customers.'

'What if there are customers on the other side of the bay?'

'They throw up a flag.' Henry pushed forward

his mug. 'That's good rum.'

Willem obliged. 'What's over there?' he asked.

'Just the depot, and a wagon trail to the other ferry.'

'What other ferry?'

'The one that takes you across to Hobart!' Henry jeered. 'What do you think I do? Dump me customers over there among the bloody mutton birds? The smell'd knock 'em down for a start. Just as well you wasn't thinking of putting your bloody pub on that side,' he grinned, baring blackened teeth.

Willem decided not to linger; he was starting to feel the effects of the rum, even though Henry had drunk twice as much as he had.

'You comin' back tomorrow?' Henry asked.

'Yes, after I see who owns what here.'

'Bring me a loaf of real baker's bread, willya? I've got a fondness for proper bread, not the muck these women make.'

'I'll do that.'

The police station in Sorell doubled as a licensing bureau and Lands Office, as well as a number of other government services, so that was where Willem went to continue with his enquiries. He learned that the area around Dodges Ferry had only recently been surveyed. Previously it had been part of a grant of land to some magistrate who had blotted his copybook and had his claims rescinded.

'You'd have to chase them up in Hobart, sir,' a clerk told him, 'but if you look around you'll find surveyor's markers out there. They wouldn't have had time to get overgrown.'

Willem wondered why Henry hadn't told him about the markers, but he wasn't concerned about that at the minute. If he had to, he would buy one of those blocks; they were only worth a few shillings anyway, a small price to pay for providing his presence with legitimacy. People were already taking him for granted in Sorell.

'Still going to build your pub?' Havelock asked him.

'My word, yes,' Willem said. 'I'm very taken with the site.'

'They're talking about building a causeway so folk can cross straight to Sorell,' the publican said spitefully. 'That'll be the end of the ferry.'

Willem couldn't have cared if they built ten causeways. 'I'll worry about that when the time comes,' he said cheerfully.

Mindful of the possibility that he could face another rum marathon to keep sweet with Henry, he ate a hearty breakfast in the Crown Inn dining room the next morning before setting about his business. Then he bought two large loaves of bread from the baker.

'Don't they feed you enough at the Crown?' the man asked.

'This is lunch,' Willem said.

'Then you'd better take some of my German sausage to go with it,' the baker said. 'You wouldn't get better in Hobart. That'll be a shilling in all.'

Back at the one-family town of Dodges Ferry he searched through the straggly bush but couldn't find any markers.

'The surveyors must have blazed trees instead,' he told himself, and set about examining the trunks of trees, with mosquitoes buzzing and over-protective magpies swooping at him. Determined to locate something to indicate where the blocks began and ended, he kept on until a snake reared up at him from the long grass.

Willem knew he was supposed to stand still when confronted by a snake, but he found this impossible. Instead he turned about and bolted, still puffing when he emerged on to the seafront track.

He could see the ferry labouring back across the bay, belching smoke from its thin chimney, but there was no one else in sight. The place seemed deserted with the ferry missing from its landing, but there was activity up at the humpies, and he thought he might ask up there about markers. In the end, he simply sat on a bench and waited for Henry. As he sat, he thought about his plan to get George and Angus here safely. He intended to buy another horse and to instruct Freddy to secure both animals deep in the bush until he rowed back with his two friends. He would have civilian clothes ready for them, and money, as well as forged passes.

Then he would give both horses to the escapees and tell them to ride north straight away. Exactly where they were to go was not yet clear in his mind. Last week he'd visited two small northern villages and found that George and Angus could easily hide in the bush until he caught up with them, but he was not able to make contact with any helpful fishermen because the villages seemed to be overrun with customs inspectors. He'd been warned that crossing the strait between northern Van Diemen's Land and Port Melbourne was hazardous, and they would need a good reliable boat, but he was unprepared for the atmosphere of suspicion that spelled failure to any chance of bribing fishermen for assistance.

In the meantime, having given away their horses, he and Freddy would catch the ferry, which would take them out of the district. Both of them had legitimate papers; no one would bother them. Then they could simply make their way back to Hobart, where they could purchase remounts, and he would head north to catch up with the others.

At this point, Willem's plan was falling apart. He'd thought the greatest difficulty would be the actual escape from Port Arthur, and that was hazardous enough, but then what? He was still worrying about the problem when a wagon trundled down to the seafront, turned about, and came to a halt at the ferry landing.

The driver lit his pipe and waited as the ferry sashayed into place and two women hurried ashore with four children. In no time they were all bundled aboard the wagon and the vehicle pulled away.

Obviously, Willem mused, there was to be no hanging about this remote spot.

He began to reconsider. He could take them to Hobart on the ferry once they were decked out in civilian clothes, but people would wonder where they had come from. How had they got here?

What if, he asked himself, you and Freddy stayed out of sight, and gave them your horses to ride down to the ferry?

And they head off to Hobart leaving their horses behind? Not likely.

With no safe house in Hobart ready to take them in? Madness!

'You got the bread, mate?' Henry shouted from his ferry.

They sat on the deck again for a few swigs of rum, and this time Henry was in a better mood. He produced a small bin of oysters and shucked so many for Willem that he had to call a halt to the bounty. Then they drank some more rum and polished off the sausage with one of the loaves of bread, though Henry was cautious and locked the second one in a wall cabinet.

He was interested in Willem's plan for a travellers' inn. Who would build it? Where would it be placed? How big? Who would work there? And Willem's imagination was kept busy answering all the questions until Henry dropped his first bombshell.

'Problem is, Willem, if you buy a block here, the other folk will come along and buy blocks here and what'll become of us?'

Willem looked back at the nest of humpies and realised what he was saying. The family was just camped there, they didn't own any land.

'We'll get chucked out!' Henry added. 'And we like it here. So you see, mate...' he puffed heavily on his pipe, 'you won't be buildin' no inn here, if we have any say in it.'

Willem searched for some excuse to keep his plans afloat. 'But surely...' he tried.

'No surely about it,' Henry growled. 'I'm lettin' you off light, seein' as you seem to be a good bloke, lettin' you know good and early you don't get to build nothin' here.'

'Is that why all the markers have gone?'

'They've gone the same place as pit-sawn timbers that find their way here, out to sea! You get my message?'

'I do, and it's very disappointing,' Willem said, for want of a better response, but Henry went off into shouts of laughter.

'Disappointing, he says! You're a real fancy man you are, Willem, but I'll tell you something for nothing. It takes one to know one. You've got a gent's way about you, but your eyes are hard. You don't fool me.'

'About what?' Willem said angrily.

Henry shrugged. 'About what ship you come out on. I reckon you was a guest of the Gov'mint same as me. You want to take your boots off?'

'No,' Willem snapped. His ankles were permanently scarred from the irons. 'No, it's none of your business.'

'And that's right, sonny boy. It ain't my business at all, but what you're really up to could be my business.'

'I don't see how,' Willem said, controlling his nerves. 'They'll put the markers back, you can't hold up the world.'

'Markers be buggered! I've been wondering how long it would take for someone to wake up to how close we are to that stinking prison over there. Do you know why I come to live here, brought my family here? So I could spit at it every day. I told you I did my foot in on a treadmill and you didn't even ask where. You know where it is, don't you?'

'So what?'

'So, you get me what I want and I'll get you what you want.'

'What *do* you want, Henry?' Willem asked carefully.

'That block of land where we got humpies. I want that best block for me and me family so none of the buggers round here can chuck us off. They bin trying to smoke us out for years.'

'You'd have to put the markers back,' Willem said.

'Done.'

'You're gettin' a bit ahead of yourself, aren't you?' Havelock asked him when he returned to the Crown Inn.

'Am I? How did that come about?'

'That good-for-nothin' yardman, Jack Plunkett! He's getting too cheeky for his own good. He says he's going to work for you when you open your pub. So I told him he can start now.'

'You sacked him?'

'Yes! He's all yours.'

'What can I do with him?' Willem was genuinely bewildered.

'You could make him manager,' Havelock hooted.

Willem ran up the stairs to pack. From his window he could see Freddy sitting by the horse trough across the road, but couldn't bring himself to feel sorry for him. Now that Henry had taken charge of arrangements in his jurisdiction, Willem had no need of Freddy. Indeed, he was relieved that he no longer needed to rely on someone like Freddy. Surely the idiot had realised by now that an inn wasn't built in a day. A real inn!

He would have a talk to him, though. See if he could drum some sense into him. Try to get his job back for him.

But when he looked out, Freddy had disappeared.

As he paid his bill, Willem tried to persuade Havelock to re-employ Jack Plunkett, but the innkeeper was adamant.

'Very well!' Willem shrugged. 'I shall see you again shortly, Mr Havelock. I do enjoy the comforts of this hostelry.'

He slung his pack over his shoulder and headed for the stables, hoping he wouldn't come across Freddy.

'Your horse isn't here, Mr Rothery,' the stablehand said. 'Jack Plunkett said you wanted it. He came to get it for you.'

'Where did he go with it?'

'He must have taken it round the front.'

There was no sign of the horse. Or Freddy. Gone.

Jack Plunkett was now on record as a horse-thief, and Mr Rothery was forced to purchase a new horse so that he could return home to Hobart.

CHAPTER TWENTY

Louise was sorry she'd offended Sean, when she remembered where he lived. He was the only person she knew who could arrange for her to see Dr Roberts again. Unless, of course, Allyn fulfilled her dreams and came seeking her. But he was over there at Port Arthur and would soon forget all about her. Perhaps Sean would put in a good word for her. It was a shame Allyn hadn't received that invitation. How were they to know he was shutting down his surgery in town?

She really worried about the best thing to do now, huffing at herself for not contacting Sean sooner. But Mother was a lot better and they were going home today. One of the men was coming to collect them. She'd have to do something soon or, the way things were now, she'd even lose touch with Sean.

The idea came to her in a flash. She hurried across town to the cottage, glanced at the brass plate by the gate, and ran up the path, almost colliding with Mr Pitcairn himself.

He raised his hat. 'Good morning, miss. What can I do for you?'

'I wanted to see Sean Shanahan.'

'On a legal matter?' he asked, eyebrows raised.

'Well, actually no. I'm Miss Harris.'

He frowned. 'Ah yes?'

Louise could see a refusal looming, and she

blushed. 'I won't be long. It's a private matter.'

'This is highly irregular. Couldn't it wait?'

'I'm afraid not, sir. My mother and I are going home soon. I just wanted to thank Mr Shanahan before we go,' she improvised. 'He ... saved my mother's life!'

'What did he do?'

'My mother was attacked by a thief, and Mr Shanahan saved her ... from him.'

'Oh! Miss Harris! It was your mother? Yes, I read about it, but I had no idea Mr Shanahan was there to help out. I shall call him, he may be able to spare a few minutes.'

He strode back into the house, and came out just as quickly. 'Do sit here on the veranda, Miss Harris,' he said, offering her a cushioned chair. 'We enjoy a pleasant breeze at this spot. Mr Shanahan will be with you shortly. Now I must rush. Good day to you.'

Mr Pitcairn had hardly turned the corner when Sean poked his head out. 'What are you doing here? I'm not supposed to have visitors in my work hours. Especially not...' he said coolly, 'little girls.'

'I am not a little girl!'

'Then you are a woman, and a very ill-mannered one at that! What do you want?'

'I didn't say I wanted anything. I just came to say I'm sorry for being rude to you. I was overwrought.'

Sean looked at her, surprised. 'What brought this on?'

'We're going home today.'

'I don't think that's wise.'

'You think the thief could come back?'

'He wasn't a thief. I believe he was sent to harm your mother.'

'Don't say that, you're frightening me. And we have to go home. Where else can we go? I was lucky the Pollards had a spare room.'

As she spoke she thought of his temporary accommodation, but knew he couldn't offer someone else's home. Unfortunately. It would have been dreamy to stay at Allyn's house.

'I don't know. Is your mother still angry with me?'

'Mother? No,' she lied. 'She's not upset any more. She's just looking forward to going home. Dr Jellick doesn't care about her at all. I wish we'd had Dr Roberts looking after her.'

'Yes,' he said absently, and Louise warmed to that little glimmer of light.

'By the way, Sean, guess what? I know where they've got little Miss Warboy stashed away.'

That woke him up. 'You do! Where? How do you know?'

'I heard Sam Pollard and his wife talking about her. He delivers their groceries. To Miss Warboy and her maid.'

'Where are they?'

'Out at Sandy Bay. They've got a house there. Mr Warboy pays the bills to be rid of them.'

'Ah dear God, is that all? Well that's a blessing. Listen to me, you tell your mother to go see Mr Baggott before she leaves. She must seek his advice, if she won't listen to me. Now off you run. I think it's the crime of the century for a law clerk to be receiving folk at the office.'

Louise giggled. 'Mr Pitcairn seems very nice. Is he married?'

'Yes.'

'Pity. Well it will still have to be Dr Roberts. I did you a favour telling you about Miss Warboy. You ought to say some nice things about me to the doctor, and don't forget.'

Sean watched her cross the street and thought how attractive she was looking these days, even from the rear, with that full skirt swinging happily from a neat little waist. He wondered if Roberts really was interested.

The Duck Inn was a sedate little hotel hidden away behind the courthouse, mainly patronised by members of the legal profession. Sean had been there many a time over the weeks, to collect or deliver legal papers for Mr Pitcairn, since several small alcove rooms off the bar were often used for meetings.

He was never invited in for a drink, of course, being only a messenger boy, but he loved the leathery smell of it, and the portraits and cartoon characters that filled the walls, all of them once much-loved customers of the Duck.

It was late on a Friday afternoon when Mrs Pitcairn came tiptoeing into 'the rooms', as they were known to her family, to apologise to Mr Shanahan, who was about to leave, for asking a favour of him.

'Mr Pitcairn went off and forgot this parcel,' she said. 'He was supposed to give it to a gentleman at the Duck at six o'clock, but he's forgotten it. Would you be so kind as to take it to him?'

'Certainly, Mrs Pitcairn. It's no trouble at all.'

'Thank you, Mr Shanahan. And please, you must give it to Mr Pitcairn by hand, yourself. Do not leave it with anyone else.'

'Of course, ma'am.'

As he headed for the Duck Inn, with the book-sized package, he wondered what it might contain. Interesting secret information regarding transportation? he mused. Too important, too clandestine maybe, to be given into the wrong hands?

He went to the side door of the Duck as usual and asked for Mr Pitcairn, who took the parcel and said, 'Thank you, Mr Shanahan. Good of you. Come through.'

It was a crush, being this hour, but they managed to push out of the passage and into one of those alcoves, where several gentlemen were waiting.

Sean recognised Baggott and his clerk and, of all people, Dr Roberts! But before he could say a word, Mr Pitcairn spoke up: 'It is my fortunate duty, gentlemen, to introduce Mr Shanahan to you, formally, as my clerk, and to present this book to him as a memento of the day – Mr Shanahan, welcome to the fold.'

Sean was so taken aback, he looked at the slim leatherbound book but couldn't take in the title. 'Does this mean I'm hired?' he burst out. 'For permanent?'

'It does indeed,' Mr Pitcairn beamed. 'It's been hard for him,' he told the others, 'kept in with his head down! But he's done well.'

He turned to Sean. 'If you wish to stay on, Mr

681

Shanahan, I'll be keen to have you.'

'And none more pleased than me, sir.'

'Good! A drink for Mr Shanahan,' Pitcairn called. 'And one for Dr Roberts, who got here only minutes before him. It was the good doctor who suggested Mr Shanahan for the post, so we couldn't leave him out of this. Bottoms up, everyone!'

Sean knew that his presence in the holy of holies parlour was a one-off privilege, so he made himself scarce as soon as Baggott's clerk slipped away, and he didn't see Roberts until the next day.

The doctor was working in his office, so Sean knocked gently, not wishing to disturb him.

'Come in,' Roberts cried. 'I'm just sorting things out here. And first things first. We should be on Christian names by this. I'm Allyn.'

'Then I'd be pleased to be called Sean.'

'Good, that's done. I got a surprise to see the garden looking so trim. Have you been busy?'

'The least I could do. And I've got tomatoes growing. Mrs Harris gave me some seeds. But tell me, I'm dead curious, how are you going over there at the prison? Is it as bad as they say it is?'

The doctor shut down. 'I'm not permitted to talk about it.'

'That figures,' Sean said bitterly. 'But have you seen any of my mates? Angus McLean? Singer Forbes?'

He saw a slight change of expression at the mention of Singer, just a flicker, but enough to push for an answer.

'You remember Singer,' he said. 'Didn't you meet him out at Warboy's farm?'

'I don't think so. If I did, I don't recall him.'

'But you have met him in that prison, have you not?'

'Only for a few minutes. He's another bush lawyer like you. Overturning rules.'

'That'd be him,' Sean smiled.

'Yes, he seemed a decent fellow. He's very popular. But I've a lot to do here, Sean, I've got to go back tomorrow. Is everything all right?'

'Sure it is! Good as gold. I was thinking of visiting some ladies this afternoon, it being Saturday. The Harris ladies, you know, the beautiful Louise and her sweet mother.'

Roberts burrowed his nose in a side drawer of his desk. 'No, I don't think so.'

'There's a shame. They need a bit of cheering up. Mrs Harris was attacked in her own orchard. It was a terrible thing to happen. I was there, trying to look after her, and turned out to be useless. I let her down badly. She was knifed!'

'What? She was knifed? Mrs Harris?'

'She surely was, and now only just out of hospital.'

'Who did it? Who would attack a nice woman like that?'

'Some thug. An attempted rape, 'tis said. If you believe a word of it.'

'Who then?'

'A doer, I'd say.'

Allyn frowned. 'What the hell's a doer?'

'Someone who does a dirty deed for another person. Who's paid to strike the blow.'

683

'Surely there must be some mistake? This person must have attacked the wrong woman.'

'Not in my book,' Sean growled.

'Then who?'

'We'll talk about it later. I want the women to move to town for a little while, and I need your help to persuade them. I don't think they're safe out there. Even with their workers on alert, they'll be better off in town.'

'You do know Mrs Harris is a married woman, Sean? She's not a widow.'

'Of course I know that.'

The doctor grinned. 'Just thought I'd warn you. I had a feeling you're interested.'

'I'm interested that you know she's not a widow, and you also know who the old man is. Have you come across him over there?'

'No!' The answer was harsh. Adamant. Sean chose to ignore that for the minute.

'What about it then? What about coming for a ride this afternoon. It'll do you good after being confined to that place.'

'I'd rather not.'

'But I need your help, I want to bring them to town.'

'What can I do?'

'Ah, use your charm, they'll be putty in your hands.'

The next day, Sunday, Allyn caught the coastal steamer back to the place he'd come to loathe. Even if permission were given, he couldn't describe this prison to anyone. It reminded him of those beautiful tropical plants with foul-smelling

684

depths, used to trap insects.

Were he not committed to a contract, he would not have returned this afternoon, despite the fact that he had been able to assist quite a few convicts – make their lives just a little easier – because there was too much suffering all about him. Too much! The all-pervading air of menace gave him nightmares. The inhumane punishments for minor offences gave rise to even more violence, as prisoners with some spunk left in them fought back, tried to abscond. Allyn had seen men crippled for life in this much-acclaimed rehabilitation depot; driven to madness, hence the asylum on the north shore, or suicide. He never should have come here, he reflected angrily. When one scraped away the posing, he only had his insufferable ego to blame. The do-gooder had stepped forward, stepped into the limelight, totally unequipped to cope with such a situation. He didn't have the guts to make a stand against the ill-treatment of convicts that he had witnessed; he would only call a stop, for instance, when the flogger reached the specified number of strokes. And the Port Arthur magistrate handed out vicious sentences.

Several times he'd mentioned to the Commandant that he considered some sentences too harsh, but his timid approaches were brushed aside as typical new-chum attitudes. The last time he'd raised the subject, the Commandant's secretary had intervened.

'If you're so worried about them, Doc,' he'd said, 'give them some help. We're short of aides at the hospital, Matron would be glad of your expert assistance.'

685

'Good show!' the Commandant agreed, with a mean grin on his face. 'I'll tell her you're volunteering.'

Allyn could have said that serving as an aide was not the role of a doctor, but their attitude was so loutish, he'd had to call their bluff. Now he took on the night shift Sundays and Wednesdays.

He tramped angrily up to his sandstone cottage with its high shingle roof and the flourishing garden behind its white picket fence, annoyed that it was twice the size of his cottage in Hobart. And the furnishings were far more expensive. It was shut-down time, and long lines of despondent convicts were being marched back to their cells, but he trudged past, unaware that he barely noticed them any more.

His mind on other matters, Allyn opened the doors and windows and stepped out on to his veranda to take in the spectacular views – to his left, past the huge parade grounds, the green and wooded hills at the centre of the peninsula, and to his right a sweeping panorama of the windy seas.

He would love to show Miss Harris this view. She'd find it stunning! But of course that could not be. Any more than he could or should consider a romantic adventure with Louise. That this situation had arisen again was all Shanahan's fault. Allyn had ended up visiting Pinewoods Farm, to be welcomed royally by the ladies, though the handsome Irishman didn't appear to be too popular with Mrs Harris. She'd thawed after a while, until mention was made of moving the ladies to town.

'We can't leave here,' she said. 'We simply can't.'

'There's a nice little boarding house for ladies in Argyle Street,' Sean told them.

'That sounds nice,' Louise said, as Allyn recalled. She'd looked absolutely dazzling, her beautiful blonde hair loose, just tied with a ribbon, and she was wearing a cornflower-blue dress that matched her gorgeous eyes.

'Why does her father have to be a convict?' he moaned. 'That's bad enough, but Lester Harris! Good God!'

He had sought out Harris. Of course he had. Kept his distance, though, just had him pointed out. And sadly, he could see the resemblance. Harris was a fair-haired, well-built man, blessed with the smooth skin that welcomed sun, Allyn reflected enviously. He himself freckled and burned in the long southern summer.

He tried to picture Louise's face. She had skin like gossamer, and long eyelashes. And the fullest, pinkest of lips. Kissable lips, he sighed.

And he'd sentenced himself to a year out of Hobart.

He sincerely believed it was for the best, but he yearned for the convict's daughter. Really yearned, like never before.

Anyway, he thought morosely, they wouldn't move into town. Mrs Harris made it plain she had no intention of paying for accommodation when they had a perfectly good home of their own.

Allyn had agreed with her. It'd be a waste of money. The farmhouse was comfortable. And, as she'd said, her workmen would protect her. That dreadful attack could never happen again.

It was only on the way home that Sean had told him his theory: that Lester Harris could be at the back of this, because there was friction between the pair. Mrs Harris wanted to sell the farm and return home to England. *And take Louise?* But Harris refused to agree to the sale.

'With his wife out of the way, there'd be no contest,' Sean had said drily.

'Surely the man wouldn't go to those lengths?'

'I know Harris well. I came out on the same transport ship with him. He's a treacherous piece of work. God knows what she saw in him.'

Allyn knew that. When he first came to Port Arthur, he looked up Harris's record. Conviction: grievous bodily harm. He would have been languishing in an English prison had he not been a healthy young farmer. A prime candidate for the Van Diemen's Land workforce. That was the first thing Allyn had noticed about the prisoners here. Most of them were young, the eldest heading for forty now, after years on the island.

Harris was just another of His Majesty's subjects who'd stumbled into this flytrap.

The book was Sean's prized possession. He'd hidden it away without so much as a glimpse at its precious pages until he had the house to himself. Until the Doc left.

Then he took it out, stroked the soft aged leather and, almost like an intruder stealing through proud mansions wherein he had no place at all, turned to the first page:

All far too clever for him, but there it was, and he owned it. The honour staggered him.

Gently he turned the pages, glancing at the double columns packed with mighty words, reading a line here and there, until he was forced to return it to the box under his bed.

When time permitted, he would read every line, but the remainder of Sunday gave him time to look for Marie and Miss Warboy.

He rode out to Sandy Bay, new territory for him, but a pleasant excursion. There were farms aplenty on that road, but he was looking for a house, and found himself riding along a road near the beach only to find it was a dead end.

Turning back, he walked the horse hoping to sight them, but in the end he had to enquire. On the corner was a mansion called The Retreat, with an uninviting iron gate, so he crossed over to the opposite house and called to a man working in a garden.

'I'm looking for two ladies, living out this way. A Mrs Warboy,' he said diplomatically, 'and her maid. Would you have seen them at all?'

'I don't know them but I think they'd be the ladies living in the last house down there. Friends of yours, are they?'

'Relations,' Sean said, tipping his hat.

Marie opened the door. She blinked, stood staring at him for a minute and then threw herself into his arms.

'Sean!' she cried. 'Sean! What a joy it is to see you! Oh my heavens! What are you doing out this way?'

'Looking for you! And what do I find? A new Marie, with rosy cheeks and glossy curls...'

She laughed. 'And a smile on her face, eh?'

'True. You're looking so well, the job must be suiting you. How is Miss Warboy?'

'She's well. She's having her nap now, so I'll leave her be. Can I get you some tea, Sean?'

'You can indeed.' He went to follow her inside, but she indicated the table and chairs on the veranda. 'Sit yourself down there. I won't be a tick.'

For a minute he thought that strange, but then he realised: Marie wasn't the lady of the house, it wasn't her place to be inviting anyone in. He appreciated the respect she showed for the girl.

She brought out a tea tray, and some biscuits.

'Penn and I made them,' she grinned. 'They're a bit hard. We're not good at it yet. You can dip them in your tea if you like.'

'Never. They're too good, they taste like toffee biscuits.'

'Yes. Too much sugar. So tell me, how are you and where are you working?'

'Marie, me love, you'll never guess where I'm working in a million years, but first I've a picture to show you. A prisoner sketched it at the Isle of the Dead and a doctor mate of mine brought it here from Port Arthur.'

She stared at the sketch that Sean had pasted on to a rectangle of cardboard to preserve it.

'What is it?'

'Look here now, it's a lovely grave on a pretty slope with a backdrop of wattle tree and a darlin' view, and if you look hard you can almost read the inscription. It says: "Matthew Terence O'Neill aged 24. Died 4th day of June, 1840. Beloved son of Patrick and Hannah O'Neill. Rest in peace."'

Marie burst into tears. 'Oh Sean, it's so beautiful. And Matt's buried there, is he?'

'Yes, they say it's as pretty a place as ever you could find. I'm sending it to Uncle Patrick, but I wanted you to see it first.' He frowned. 'I'll have to warn Uncle that it wasn't me spelled the Terrence with only one r. I suppose them stonemasons over there wouldn't have had much of a schooling.'

'I don't think he'll mind,' she sighed, mopping her eyes.

'No. I suppose not. This is a nice house. Just the two of you living here?'

'Just us, and I love it. Come round the back and I'll show you the beach.' He followed her around the path to find that the house sat high above the beach on a rocky ledge.

'Penn and I go for walks every day,' she said, her voice full of enthusiasm, 'and we paddle and we even throw ourselves right into the waves, for there's no one to care! It's the happiest I've ever lived, bless you, Sean. I'll never be able to thank you enough.'

'There's no need for thanks. Sounds as if the girl is even more fortunate, to have a dear one like you minding her. Did she ever say who's the father of the child?'

691

Marie shook her head. 'No, but she still thinks Angus is coming for her.' She couldn't bring herself to mention her suspicions for she could be wrong, starting more trouble.

'If he did he'd knock her down,' Sean said. 'She sent him to hell.'

'Oh Sean, don't be too hard on her. She's simple.'

'Have you asked her who got her pregnant? Made her stand there and tell you?'

'I have not, for would you be wanting her to say Angus again?'

'Surely to God you could get the truth out of her?'

'She knows she's getting a baby, but she won't believe it's inside her. Will not! Yells and screams, "Lies!" when I try to prepare her for what's coming. So how do I ask her who put it there?'

'Get her a mirror!' he snapped.

'Come on now, don't be getting upset. We'll go back and you can tell me about that job. And what else? Have you got a girlfriend?'

He stopped at the corner of the house. 'Yes and no. I had this girl in Ireland, but I lost her to another man. But now she's a widow, and my sister Annie writes that she has left Ireland and may have sailed for Van Diemen's Land with her little son.'

'Coming here to you? Oh, that's lovely. So romantic. And when's she coming?'

'Annie's letter took months to get here. It was sent after Glenna left.' He shook his head. 'She should have been here by this. I don't believe she's coming now.'

'That's terrible. Enough to break your heart, that waiting.'

'No it's not,' he laughed. 'It was wishful thinking. She's forgot me long ago.'

Penn appeared at the back door, her dressing gown flapping. 'Marie, I thought you'd gone. Can I have tea? Who's that down there?'

'It's Mr Shanahan. From the farm. You remember Mr Shanahan?'

'I think so. Is he your boyfriend?'

Marie smiled. 'He's not. You get dressed and come out to the front veranda and I'll make fresh tea.'

After that Sean only stayed long enough to give Marie his news, and his address if she needed him. He found it difficult to have to listen to Miss Warboy's chatter when he'd prefer to talk with Marie.

His first glimpse of her looking so lovely had taken his breath away. It was as if she'd gone from girl to woman overnight; from a waif-like servant to a dignified lady in her fine black dress with the lacy collar, and black beaded buttons all down the front. He wished he hadn't rattled on about Glenna. It had been pointless to even mention her. Marie must think him a damn fool.

Is he your boyfriend? Penn's voice echoed.

She'd been quick to deny that. And that set Sean to wondering...

Penn was in a jolly mood when Sean left, pepped up with excitement from playing her role as lady of the house. She was skipping along the beach, swinging her arms and twirling about until, of course, she almost fell in the shallows.

'No more dancing about,' Marie said. 'We'll turn back now.'

'I want to go right to the end so I can look at the big house. I suppose they'd have lots of visitors.'

Marie nodded, plodding along beside her, thinking about her visitor. She was still over the moon with happiness that Sean had come to call.

'Mr Shanahan was my first visitor,' Penn said. 'I don't count Sam. He's only my grocer.'

'Then we must tell the grocer to bring a length of cotton material so that I can make you some new summer dresses.'

She hoped the girl Glenna *had* forgotten him.

'What's wrong with this one?'

'It's too tight.' Marie shivered. He'd called her 'a dear one'. That was so nice of him.

'Oh, all right. But I want a white one this time, with lots of lace, like Mummy wears. And coloured ribbons.'

'Whatever you say,' Marie murmured, as Penn took off again, heading for a mound of rocks down the end of the beach. She liked to climb over them. Being the king of the castle.

I'll make her some white smocks, Marie decided, and bung a bit of lace on them to keep her happy, and a couple of prints for running about.

She was startled to see that a gentleman had appeared ahead of her and was helping Penn down from the rocks. He was a squat-built fellow with swarthy skin, a large nose and long dank hair, far from comely, she thought as she approached. But she noticed that his shirt, open at the neck, was silk, and the trousers were well-cut, expensive. He was wearing open sandals, quite an innovation, and Marie thought she wouldn't mind a pair herself.

Penn called to her. 'This gentleman lives up there in the big house! Don't you?'

'Indeed I do.'

'We live down the other end,' Penn told him. 'I'm Miss Warboy, and this is Marie.'

'How do you do, ladies. Might I also introduce myself, since we're almost neighbours.' He bowed. 'Mr Pellingham at your service. Mr Grover Pellingham.'

Penn nodded. She was more interested in his house. She gazed up at it. 'Can you get right to the top there?'

'Yes. It's my lookout. I have beautiful views.'

'Can you see as far as Hobart?'

'No, but I can see upriver and watch the ships coming and going.'

'How marvellous.'

For an instant there Marie thought Penn was about to invite herself into his house for that view, so she stepped in. 'Miss Penn, we must go back now, there's a breeze blowing up.'

'Do we have to?'

'Yes.'

Pellingham's gaze was on Marie. 'I'm delighted to have met you, miss. Perhaps I might see you again when I take my constitutional?'

'Perhaps,' she said, as mildly as she could muster. She'd never seen him taking a 'constitutional' along this stretch.

As they walked back, Penn worried. 'Do you think he noticed my wet skirt?'

'No.' *But the bastard would have noticed the little pot belly, Miss Warboy.*

She plunged on. Pellingham! The magistrate who'd sentenced Matt to another hundred lashes. And death!

Tears were coursing down her cheeks when Penn turned to her.

'I should have invited Mr Pellingham to come to tea one day.'

'No you won't! You must never speak to him again or I'll tell your grandfather. Never! He's a very bad man.'

'He's got a nice house,' Penn sulked.

That night a storm raged over the bay, waves crashed on the shore and a high wind battered the house. Marie hardly noticed. She was too distressed at having met Pellingham, upset that she didn't have the power to strike back at him somehow. Finally, though, she was almost falling asleep when she heard Penn crying and calling out to her.

'I'm frightened. Come into my bed with me. I'm frightened, Marie. Daddy would never leave me alone in a storm, he'd come into my bed and make me feel better. I miss him so.'

Marie leapt out of bed and slammed her door against the weeping.

Once the job was his, Sean felt calmer, more able to concentrate on his duties and understand what they were all about. Prior to this, he realised, he'd been working by rote. Like a puppet. Now he could do what he had to do without having Mr Pitcairn looking over his shoulder; and he could talk to the clients, put them at their ease without nosing into their business.

He was humbled by the number of secrets entrusted to lowly law clerks. That was something unexpected. As was the book he was rereading. His book of Common Law.

And there were other unexpected things to think about as well. Ever since he'd found Marie happily settled, the weeks had been kind. First he'd had a letter from Josie, apologising for her rudeness and her 'lack of faith', as she called it, in his good intentions. Mainly, though, she wanted to thank him for his kindness to Louise in bringing that so-welcome guest to her door.

My daughter is fond of Dr Roberts. What his inclinations are I do not know, but you gave them the opportunity to meet again, and it was much appreciated.

Sean grinned. He had taken Roberts to please Miss Harris, but it was also a way of throwing his hat in the door before he dared venture inside, since he'd been dropped from Josie's good books.

And then there was last Saturday. The most unexpected of all. Josie and Louise had come to town to hear the military band play at an open-air concert on the wharves, so he'd joined them. It was the regiment's farewell concert, as it was due to return to England. And good riddance, Sean thought, but he enjoyed the music.

The concert was over at seven, but Louise, never

satisfied, insisted on staying to watch a Punch and Judy show, so Sean and Josie went on ahead to find seats at the busy fish café in the square.

On the way there they were jostled by crowds hurrying from the concert, and Sean pulled Josie into a small alcove out of their way.

Looking back on it now, he shrugged. Proximity had caused the fuss. One minute they were angry at being shoved and pushed by a crowd of louts; next minute they'd found shelter, and next, Josie had her arms around his neck and was kissing him furiously! There was so much passion in that sudden embrace, he was completely taken by surprise. Fortunately the crowd cleared and Josie stepped back, primly adjusting her hat, and he smiled at her more in embarrassment than appreciation.

He took her arm then, steering her towards the café, every step of the way trying to think what to do or say that wouldn't cause hurt, blaming himself for the situation, for surely he must have given her the wrong impression. But whether or no, the piper had to be met quick, to smooth this over.

When they were seated in a snug corner, he took her hand, but she snatched it away.

'I shouldn't have done that, should I?' she snapped, a strand of blonde hair falling forward on her face. 'You're not interested in me at all. That was obvious!'

'Aah...' he wavered, searching for a diplomatic response, but Josie charged on.

'It's Louise, isn't it?'

'What about Louise?' he asked, startled.

'You'd rather her than me. Wouldn't you?'

Sean groaned. 'Is that what you're thinking?'

'Why not? Why else would you be calling on us? I thought you liked me, but all the time...' she tugged a handkerchief from a pocket, 'you were after Louise.'

'Ah God help us, I'm not a suitor at all. I thought we were friends.'

'We were,' she said angrily. 'Now you've spoiled everything.'

God spare me from her logic, he muttered to himself, but aloud he said: 'Ah then. I see. Have you got so many friends you can afford to toss one away over a kiss, and a nice kiss at that?'

Josie turned away in a sulk.

'Do you know what I've missed most here? Family. The hearth. I've plenty of mates, but I yearned for folk I could call on. Folk who would invite me into their kitchen to sit awhile, like normal people, and you were kind enough to allow me that pleasure. If I've misled you, Josie, I'm terrible sorry and hope you'll forgive me.'

'Besides, I'm a married woman, aren't I?' she sniffed, to continue the argument.

'There's that too,' he said, with a twinkle in his eye. 'Do you want to talk about it?'

'No I don't!'

'Then that's all right. Are we still friends?'

'I suppose so,' she muttered.

'Try yes. It'll make life easier for us all.'

'All right. Yes.'

'There you go. Now, what can I get you, milady?'

On the way home he passed the Penitentiary and was reminded of Marie.

The night Matt was hanged, Sean had obtained permission to hold a vigil in the Penitentiary chapel with one other person, so he'd brought Marie in with him. It was the worst night of his life, but she'd helped him to get through it.

They'd prayed, saying the rosary, litanies, every prayer they knew, over and over to keep their vigil strong until the hour passed and Matt was gone. And they'd wept together in the cold, desolate chapel with not even a candle to be lit, until they were shown the door.

Marie Cullen. She was a friend. She had a kitchen now, bless her heart, but even that little haven was out of bounds.

'Never you mind,' he murmured as he paced up the hill. 'Time you went out to see her again.'

He realised he could think of Matt now without his heart seizing up, and there seemed to be some content in his soul this strange old Saturday.

It didn't last, of course. It would have been too much to ask, he told himself as he sat across the table in the Doc's kitchen, for a second time, from Willem and his plans.

He had a foolproof plan, he'd said.

'There's no such thing,' Sean growled.

'Then stop interrupting and I'll tell you about it. George and Angus are to be at this point,' he poked at the map, 'next Sunday morning, during the services. I'm not saying it can't go wrong there. It's up to them. But we'll have a boat waiting for them. I'll keep it out of sight until I spot

700

them. If, God forbid, they can't make it to the beach, then I'll just have to try again some other time. A fisherman called Mort will be with me.'

'Is he the son of the bloke called Henry?'

'Yes. He's a big strong fellow, he'll make short work of rowing across that stretch of water from South Point to Port Arthur, near the mining areas. It's maybe only a couple of miles.'

'Storm Bay,' Sean said. 'It could be heavy going.'

Willem glared at him. 'It's not Storm Bay. We row them back to South Point. George and Angus change clothes in the scrub. Mort rows his boat on home. We walk through the bush to the ferry and calmly step aboard. It takes us directly west across an inlet to land at the mouth of the Derwent.'

'Where's this?' Sean couldn't believe it was so easy.

'Look on the map. We don't have to go near the main part of Storm Bay, we're only using inlets. From there we get across the spit to another ferry that plies up and down the river. We'll be legitimate customers; we just step on board. No one asks for papers on ferries anyway. We can get off where we like.'

Sean had to admit he was impressed. Willem had worked it all out without his help.

'As easy as that?' he breathed.

'A few things went wrong. Henry had his price, but then Mort wanted a new boat.'

Sean whistled. 'Costly!'

Willem shrugged. 'What could I do? Finally I agreed to pay him fifteen shillings. After my friends were landed. And one other thing. I had to buy a new horse.'

'Your band of gypsies! They got land and a boat! And your horse as well?'

'No. Freddy Hines stole my horse.'

'Freddy?' Sean burst out laughing. 'The little bastard! I told you not to trust him. Does he know your gypsy mates?'

'No, thank God. I didn't introduce them. They're a tough lot, I think they'd cut off his hand if he pinched anything from them.'

'Where's Freddy now?'

'I've no idea. But let me get on. By this I've got them here, at Hobart, and they've got forged papers.'

'How will you get them out?'

'I met the skipper of a whaler. He'll take all three of us, for a price. He's going to New Zealand via Sydney Town. He says there are too many whalers working out of this port.'

'I have to hand it to you, Willem, it's a pearler of a plan.'

'Except for one thing. I haven't got a safe house.'

'What's wrong with your place?'

'I've got the nosiest neighbours in the world.'

'Couldn't Flo set you up?'

'No, he wasn't that helpful. I was thinking of here. This house. Only for two days.'

'What?' Sean jerked back. 'No. Definitely not. In the first place it isn't mine. The Doc trusts me.'

'The Doc's not to know,' Willem said quietly.

'I couldn't do that. No.' Nor could he bring

himself to tell Willem he was threatening his new job, his new life. It was asking too much.

There was a stalemate for a while. They discussed the ins and outs of the plan again.

'But it's Angus,' Willem pleaded. 'Surely you can help a mate. George says Angus has already been in solitary–'

Sean put up his hand. 'Don't. Please. I can't have them here. There are eyes all around these narrow streets too. Not possible, Willem, but I might know a place, out at Sandy Bay. I'll check. They could probably get off the ferry there and stroll up the beach to the house.'

'Are you sure?' Willem asked eagerly.

'It's worth a try. I'll ride out tomorrow night and ask. She'll help, I'm sure.'

'Who's she?'

'You don't know her, and better you don't.'

'Good man,' Willem sighed. 'I knew you wouldn't let me down.'

Marie did say no. Strongly and firmly. Reflecting his own reasons for not wanting to be involved. 'Mr Warboy made the rules. No visitors in the house. The man took a chance on me, for all he knew I might have started a knock shop here, with his back turned. But he trusted me to look after Penn...'

'Penn!' Sean cried, 'Lord, wait a minute! What was I thinking of? Angus can't come here!'

Marie was stunned. 'Don't tell me Angus is one of them,' she whispered. 'For God's sake!'

'I'm sorry, truly sorry, Marie, I should never have come here with this. I forgot about the girl,

703

I really did. I was just thinking of it as a possible safe house, with no proper thought. We'll just have to find somewhere else.'

Marie looked about her to make sure Penn wasn't listening. 'Wait, Sean. I've an idea. I'll tell you something but I don't want you going off like a cracker. Promise me you'll sit quiet till I have my say?'

'All right, I promise.'

'Well now, there's a house up the street. A big place. And only one man lives there and no one goes near him. I've been watching the house when we go for walks up the street, and I can look at it from the beach too.'

'You mean the mansion on the end, with the room on top?'

'A lookout. That'd be handy, wouldn't it?'

'Maybe. Why are you watching this feller? Got your eye on him, have you?'

'No, but he's given me the eye a couple of times. So ... you could hide your friends at his house.'

'Ah yes,' he said patiently. 'I could knock on his door and tell him I've got a couple of escaped convicts on my hands and I'd like him to put them up for a few nights.'

'Something like that. But it wouldn't be you. I want you to keep away. You shouldn't be mixed up in this stuff, Sean. Not now, when things are looking up for you. It'd be too cruel to falter at this stage.'

'Don't I know it,' he said miserably.

'And the same goes for me. I can tell them what to do, but keep me out of it.'

She was trying his patience. 'What should they do, girl?'

'He goes out most days. Some days when he's home he walks on the beach. But he's home at nights. Drinking. I've slipped down there and peeped in the windows.'

'You spy on him?'

'Yes. Just because I know who he is. But listen to me. Your friends, they go to his house when he's on his own. When he opens the door, they bash him, and push in.'

Sean almost toppled off his chair. 'They bash him?' he laughed. 'Then they ask him to put them up for a few days.'

'That's it. That's what they do.'

'Have you turned into an anarchist or something? Plotting to bash good citizens.'

'He's no good citizen. That's Grover Pellingham.'

'Holy Mother of God!' Sean strode down from the veranda and out to stand in the darkness and stare down the road at that house.

'You promised you'd take it quiet,' she reminded him, 'so you get a grip on yourself.'

She stepped down and stood behind him. 'We can't touch him, Sean. He's an evil thing, poisons everything around him. But we can use him. The lads can bind him up and keep him quiet till they're ready to leave.'

'Which is when he starts screaming for the police?'

'Not if he's still tied up.'

'You'd leave him there? Tied up? To die?'

'No, I suppose not.'

'That's right,' he said firmly. 'But maybe a day or so to let the lads get clear, and you might notice doors left open or something, and mention it to other people in the street.'

Sean knew it was dead against his own instincts to be preaching to her like this. He wanted to go down there now and bash the lights out of Pellingham. He wished she'd not told him who it was.

'You're a genius,' he cried, hugging Marie. 'I'll put the plan to Willem, never mentioning your part, and I'll explain why I can't go near Pellingham myself, without jeopardising the whole operation. But his house is a Godsend.

'Now I suppose I'd better be getting back and give Willem the good news. But suddenly I don't want to go.'

He bent down and kissed her.

He held her in his arms in the velvet darkness of the trees and the sweet girl brought him a love he'd almost forgotten existed.

As he rode home, being reminded of Pellingham broke the spell of that evening. He wondered if the lads would consider flogging Pellingham while they were at it, for good measure.

Lester could see something was brewing.

For weeks now he'd stuck to George like glue, letting everyone know that they'd come out on the same transport ship and therefore were mates, but not sissy mates. Lester didn't care that George, the country bumpkin, had a sissy reputation, because what George also had was six foot two of brawn. Combined with Lester's own formidable reputation as a head-banger, they made a good team, and so far, the barge men were keeping their distance.

George hadn't been too enthusiastic when he'd first claimed him, but he'd been polite. Probably, Lester thought with lofty pride, because he was upper class compared to a peasant like George. But anyway, George was a hard worker, and an amiable sort of fellow, and they were managing to keep out of trouble. That was all Lester needed of him, because he was desperate to get out of these dangerous mines and have his status upgraded to trusty again.

For the present, he couldn't be worried about the farm; it was hard enough trying to cope with these filthy underground caves. How anyone could volunteer, in civilian life, to work in these bloody mines, deep in the earth, deprived of God's fresh air, was beyond him. And yet men did, back home, and they took their sons down into the pits with them. He'd met a couple of real coal-miners working here and they boasted they were no worse off here than at home. On Saturday nights, workers from the Port Arthur mines were allowed to swim in the warm sea, to cleanse themselves of the ingrained dirt, and that bath, to them, was a real bonus.

Strange world, Lester thought. You meet all sorts of weird characters here.

As they came up from the sea on this Saturday night, Lester saw someone pass a tobacco tin to George just as he was pulling his clothes on, and then George disappeared into the crowd for a while and he couldn't find him until he saw him up ahead, lining up for the supper meal.

He didn't let on that he'd seen George getting his hands on extra tobacco; he simply asked for some later on.

'I'm out of tobacco. Could you lend me some, George?'

'No. I haven't got any neither.'

'I thought you did.'

'No. Wish I had.'

So there it was. George was lying to him, and that angered Lester.

Early the next morning, while George was at the bog, Lester rifled through his sea bag. Some men had sea bags, others had small boxes to hold their few permitted possessions. He couldn't find any tobacco and there was nowhere else to look, unless he'd hidden it in the thin horsehair mattress. Which was against regulations. Tearing or cutting mattresses incurred punishments. George's mattress was intact.

He began to notice, then, that George was apt to hang back and get into whispered conversations with two particular men, so he gave him the word.

'Take it from me, George. Don't you go joining in any sissy games here, if you know what I mean. There's too much of that going on, and too many dobbers. It's worth a hundred lashes if you're caught, and it'll put me in bad too. The bosses will think I'm a sissy too, because we're mates. And I can't have that, you see what I mean?'

'Yeah. All right,' was all George had to say, taking no offence.

But the following Saturday night Lester

watched and saw another tobacco tin change hands. And he saw the provider clearly. It was a guard, and he was no sissy.

Lester sped across the beach, gave George a small shove, and grabbed for the tobacco tin, completely unprepared for the effect of his actions.

George's punch sent him flying backwards into the sand.

Angered and insulted, Lester's reaction was swift. Friend or no friend, no one could be allowed to punch him and get away with it! He clambered up and went at George with a shout of rage, but he was no match for the bigger man, who just threw him aside and marched away.

For starting a fight, Lester was chained to a wall in a pit for the night.

George, deemed to have been attacked, was not punished, but he was petrified. Lester had nearly got the tin. With the date. Sunday week.

He handed over the tin, minus the message, which he chewed and swallowed, and the go-between guard winked his appreciation. Then he awaited Lester's wrath.

But Lester had had all night to mull over the event. By now he'd worked out that George's sly activities had more to do with tobacco than sissy meets. But when he'd searched that time, he hadn't found any tobacco, and what was more, George never smoked any more than anyone else. They were all on minute tobacco rations.

So what was it all about? What would cause a mild man like George to react like that over a very small tin?

What was in those tins?

Eventually it came to him. George had a lot of outside mates, He was on for an escape.

That information was worth plenty. They might make him a trusty again if he could catch them out, because you could bet your life, with that mob, he won't be going alone.

Then again, he could get in on it and escape too. What the hell? It could take him years to get out of here. He could die of suffocation in those bloody mines. He was already coughing like an old woman.

For the first time the reality of Port Arthur struck him like a physical blow. Lester had always been so sure of himself, so ready to manipulate people by treachery or physical force, that he hadn't been able to accept how far he'd slipped down the ladder.

George was popular. If he informed on him – cost him a flogging, and the ball and chain for life – his mates would retaliate. They would, Lester reflected nervously. Tit for tat – payback – was rife among convicts, and approved by Toohill. He said it helped keep order.

As the night dragged on, and his stomach rumbled for the missed meal, and rats scuttled around him, Lester looked into his future.

He should tell Josie to sell the farm. Quickly. Get some cash in the bank. He'd even pay that IOU to the barge men, and more, to get himself on a ship. But if George had an escape plan, it wouldn't help just to get out; they had to have a plan to get off this island as well. Be rid of Van Diemen's Land once and for all.

He'd get a message to her to sell the farm and go home to the family. My dad'll sort things out for me once I get myself back to England, to a civilised country, not a bloody prison.

His mind was racing with such great plans he hardly heard the guards who came to set him free; he didn't even bother to blast them with complaints. Instead he hurried over to grab some breakfast, locate George – and apologise.

'What's that?' George said, staring at him as he filled a bottle with water.

'I'm saying I'm sorry I grabbed at your belongings like I did, but I was only joking, mate. No hard feelings?'

'Ah ... all right,' George said. 'Here's your coal hat, I brought it along for you.' He handed Lester a leather cap with a flap over the neck, which gave some protection from coal dust, and Lester thanked him as they trooped off to work.

When Angus heard that an escape was on, and George had included him, he couldn't believe his luck, but he had to keep stony-faced as they talked, for fear of giving something away.

'What's Harris doing hanging about all the time?' he asked. 'Is he in on it too?'

'No, but he's got me worried. He couldn't have picked up a word, there's been nothing said, and I've got reliable runners, but I can't seem to shake him.'

'You may have to deal with him,' Angus warned as they walked up and down the long recreation yard.

'Could you start a fire somewhere on the Sunday morning?' George asked him. 'A diversion? I won't have any trouble starting one in the woods. They'll go up like paper. But I need you to light another one nearer here.' He grinned. 'For the fun of it I've got some mates of mine, loggers, starting a bush fire on Saturday night, near Eagle Hawk Neck. A real good one. That'll give the bosses the jitters for a start.'

Break away from the church detail and start a fire? Angus worried about that day and night. He couldn't see how it might be done, but he was anxious to obey every instruction. If they were good enough to include him, then he should do his part to the letter.

It was hard to hide the tension that was coiled up inside him now, making him break out in cold sweats. He kept telling himself there was no need for anxiety. Put it simply, he reasoned, you've made a decision. A man's decision. If you're caught trying to escape they'll hang you or make you wish you were dead; but the way things stand now, I'd rather be dead than live like this. So what's to lose? If this break fails I'll try again and again until I get what I want – freedom. In this life or the next.

Not that being reasonable helped to control the sweats, once George gave him the day – the very next Sunday. He was immediately struck by a sudden onset of the trots that kept him on a pot half the night, since they had no access to the outside bog once the doors were locked. He wondered if George felt as tense as this. He didn't seem to. He'd just dropped the day to him. Said not to forget to create the diversion, split away from the mob, and leg it through the middle woods of the peninsula to the coal mines. Run round the back to the second bay from the coaling wharf and the boat would be there. It would wait until eleven o'clock. No longer. One hour before noon.

On the Monday night, to ease the strain, Angus joined Jancy in the exercise yard. Jancy had been a gardener back home, and he loved to talk about gardens, so Angus enjoyed his company. He remembered Jancy saying that he had his favourite plants in the estate garden that he and his father used to manage, and often wondered what had become of them, as if they were children.

But Jancy was also a mate of Singer's and he was worried. 'He's still wearing the hood,' he said. 'He doesn't go to work, just sits in the cell all day, only gets a little exercise, and church, still with the hood, and the guards say he's breaking down.'

'What do they mean?'

'They reckon he doesn't know where he is. Mumbles, talks to himself, going a bit mad I think.'

'When does he get the hood off? It must be soon. We've been expecting him back at work any day.'

'When? Who bloody knows? He still won't sing.'

'Yes, but that's no reason. That was weeks ago. We thought he must have bought himself another penalty.'

'No, it's the same one. He could be there until Doomsday.'

713

'The hell he will!'

Angus put in a request to be permitted to see Chief Constable Toohill, but it was refused. He asked the guards if they could slip him in to visit Singer. Once again refused. He wrote to Toohill, asking him to investigate Convict Forbes's punishment.

The guards told him there was no reaction from Toohill, and Singer was now refusing to eat. They had reported the situation to Toohill, but as this was a common form of protest among prisoners, he replied that, in his opinion, refusal to eat was a form of self-inflicted injury, and therefore punishable by flogging. He was of the opinion that Forbes was a malingerer anyway, and instructed the guards to report back to him if the prisoner was not eating by Monday.

Nagged by Angus, though, the guards fulfilled their duty by notifying Dr Roberts.

Allyn, insisting the hood be removed, was shocked by Forbes's haggard appearance.

'How are you, Mr Forbes?' he asked, taking his bound wrist to check his pulse.

The prisoner peered at him with a dazed expression.

'I'm Dr Roberts. Do you remember me? We've met before. I'm sorry to see you stuck in here. I came to see if I could help in any way. Is there anything I can do for you?'

Forbes shuffled around the cell, obviously pleased to be rid of the hood. Allyn noticed severe chafing on his neck and thought he should rub some salve into it, but that would only make matters worse when the cumbersome hood was replaced.

'Would you free his wrists, please?' he asked the guard.

'Sorry, not permitted. Last time we did that he wrecked his hood. Now that they stay bound, he won't eat.'

'Is that what it is?' Allyn asked Singer. 'If they untie your hands, will you eat?'

'Yes.'

Calmly Allyn took a clean cloth, dipped it in the mug of water on the floor by the food, and wiped Singer's bearded face.

'I know you feel you're being treated like an animal,' he said quietly. 'And maybe you are. But you know, Mr Forbes, animals don't have hands, but they have the sense to get food into themselves.'

Singer turned about and whispered to him, 'Possums use hands. And kangaroos.'

'So they do. I'd forgotten that. So why don't you?'

'I can't.' His voice shook with woe. He held up his hands and stared at them. 'I can't. They won't do it. See!'

Both of his hands swept down and knocked over the mug of water.

'What? Your hands won't work?'

'No. They can't feed me. They're tied up! Can't you see that?'

'If I feed you, will you eat?'

He opened his bag and took out the bread and pieces of chicken that he'd brought along as a treat for this prisoner, and began to feed him,

715

while the guard stood watching. Singer ate the food greedily.

'Well I never,' the guard said. 'Don't tell me you expect us to feed you, Singer, 'cos that ain't on. We got better things to do.'

'It's all right,' Allyn said. 'Leave him be.'

He began to talk to Forbes, about everyday things. The weather, how it was getting so much hotter here, and dry, with not much rain about these days; about the farm he'd seen on this settlement that had amazed him, everything growing so well. And gradually he got around to Forbes's present situation.

'I'd like to take you out of here. Would you come with me?'

Singer stared at the hood.

'No, without the hood. You shouldn't have to wear it. What does it matter if you just sing a little song for the bosses? Who cares? I could tell the Commandant you will allow him to hear you sing, Mr Forbes. Shanahan says you've a truly fine voice.'

Allyn stood, trying to tell him everything was going to be fine. 'You could come with me, and the guard too.'

'Not without his hood,' the guard warned. 'I'll get into strife if I do that.'

Allyn took Singer's hands. 'This can be all over now. You'll be back with your mates this evening. Out of here. Come on, Mr Forbes, a song is all the Commandant wants. Surely–'

'No,' Singer said firmly. 'No.'

'I coulda told you that, Doc,' the guard said. 'He's not a bad bloke, are you, Singer? We ask him to give over every day, but not him. No, not him.'

Convict Forbes turned away from them to stare at the wall.

Allyn patted him on the shoulder, and left.

He lodged a complaint about the inhumane treatment of Convict James Forbes. He claimed that the reason for the prisoner's prolonged punishment was trivial and unfair, and he should be released immediately, having already served far more punishment days than his offence warranted.

On the matter of his refusal to eat, he stated, the prisoner was mentally unstable due to this inhumane treatment, and unable to accept a new ruling, such as feeding himself with bound hands.

Because he was not qualified to discuss such matters, he did not enlarge on the negativity that seemed to be controlling some of Singer's non-actions. But he was very concerned that Forbes's refusal to sing had triggered the inability to feed himself, and more problems could follow if the thought processes were not interrupted. It was only a theory, of course, but he believed the hood and the hostile environment were disorienting Forbes.

Toohill took great delight in forwarding Dr Roberts' bold report to the Commandant. In fact he walked up and handed it to Biddle himself, so that he could watch his reaction at the outright criticism of his boss.

Biddle squinted at the page. 'Who wrote this?'

'Dr Roberts, of course. You note he is asserting that the Commandant himself is out of order. That's interesting, isn't it? I wonder where that places me? You might ask the Commandant. It will save me having to delve into books to find the answer. I'm not a lawyer either.'

Chortling, he strolled away.

As expected, the Commandant was furious. 'How dare that whippersnapper doctor criticise me!' He threw the report into a bin. 'I'll fix him. I'll have the fool recalled for overstepping his duties. Take down a letter for the Governor.'

'Don't you mean overstepping the mark, sir?'

'Whatever! Write it down. And for interfering in matters not of his concern. And for being too free with his ill-informed opinions. And for lack of any understanding of discipline. Think of a few more, I haven't the time. Bring it back for me to sign. I want the busybody out of here before he causes real trouble. I don't know whose idea it was to send him here.'

On the Saturday there was a huge fire on the Forestier Peninsula, on the mainland side of Eagle Hawk Neck. Willem could see the smoke from his camp in the bush near South Point. He'd bypassed the town of Sorell this time, paid his respects to Henry and set up camp within sight of Port Arthur. In his saddle packs he had civilian clothes for George and Angus, papers, and enough cash to see that they each had some money in their pockets.

He wished he could go on the ferry with his two

friends when the time came, but he couldn't leave the horse. He wouldn't! Henry and Mort and Freddy had gotten enough out of him. Besides, he reasoned, it was more sensible for him to return the way he'd come. People had seen him on the road. He liked to think that the beauty of his plan was in keeping everything as normal as possible. He had ridden here. He had to ride out.

That night as he stood by the shore and looked over at the dark, foreboding woodlands of Port Arthur, he had an attack of nerves. What if they were caught? What if someone saw them in the boat? What if he ended up in prison there? All the what-ifs ruined any chance of sleep. He was worried about George, who was inclined to be a bungler, but not so much about McLeod. The Scot was a wily fellow, and sharp. He'd help George, see that their plans worked. Keep him moving.

But Willem was wrong. Even now, McLeod was pulling George's neat plans apart.

'I need your help, Jancy,' Angus said, breaking his promise to George not to tell anyone.

'To do what?'

'To get Singer out of here.'

'What? Why?'

'Because even Dr Roberts said he was going mad. And the Doc up and blamed the Commandant.'

'Jeez, that'll get him nowhere fast. But if the Doc can't get him out of the Hoods, what hope have you got?'

719

'Not just out of the Hoods, out of Port Arthur.'

Jancy laughed. 'Your brains are getting scrambled too.'

'No they're not. I can get him off the peninsula, I just need help cutting him out of his mob when they get to the church in the morning.'

'Is this something to do with last night's bushfire?'

'Could be.'

'I heard they had all the lads from B Sector trying to put it out, and some places are still burning.'

'It's this hot wind,' Angus said.

'Aye, yes, that'd be right.' Jancy grinned. 'So, are you going too?'

'No. Only Singer. We have to get him out. They'll kill him here.'

'What do you want me to do?'

'Start a diversion. A fire. That's all.'

'Where?'

'I don't know. I'm hoping to grab Singer when they're shoving the Hoods into the church. And please, Jancy, not a word.'

'You didn't have to ask, mate.'

'I know. Sorry. Do you think you could do this?'

'I'll burn the whole place down if you like. You sure Singer won't need someone to go with? Like me, for instance?'

'No, he'll just have to do it on his own.'

'It's a tall order.'

'Can't be helped.' Angus saw George coming towards him and frowned, so George detoured to the other side of the yard. Followed by Lester Harris.

'Bloody hell!' he said, and Jancy looked up. 'Something wrong already?'

There wasn't another chance to talk that night and Sunday toppled on them so quickly, it seemed, that neither George nor Angus had time to think; they just went straight into their plan.

The wind was a scorcher, and some said the heat was up round ninety degrees, a good day for a fire. Because George should be marching towards the church with the miners, Angus had no idea if he'd made a break until he saw a fire raging up in the woods behind a magistrate's house, and he guessed, hoped, George was on his way. He'd have the cover of those woods for the cross-country run of about thirteen miles to get him to the mines, and he already knew the area well.

Lester couldn't believe it! They'd only just left their barracks and were marching up Champ Street, past the penitentiary, when a runaway donkey came hurtling towards them, its keeper hard on its heels. The animal seemed to come from nowhere, crashing into their ranks, knocking down a few of the men, including a guard, which brightened the morning.

By the time the donkey was caught and dragged off, and the miners lined up to resume their march, he'd lost sight of George. He was still trying to see if he was in the front ranks when they came to Tramway Street and had to wait for some civilians to stroll by. This gave him a chance to slip forward, causing irritation to some prisoners who objected to being shoved aside, but he still couldn't find his friend. This church party was two hundred strong, so Lester figured he could, maybe, have joined the tail end after all, but somehow he knew in his bones that George was missing. That made him so angry he almost raised the alarm, but he decided to look first, and keep an eye out for McLeod.

Angus was already in the church. He was standing just inside the door handing out hymn books, and as the large church was filling up with more and more convicts he peered out to see if the Hoods were on their way.

As usual they were herded quickly up the steps in single file. Angus dropped the hymn books on a table and watched for Singer, who was taller than most of his colleagues.

Then he saw him, and as Singer came in the door, crowded along by other hooded men, Angus grabbed him and yanked him aside.

'Quick,' he hissed, dragging Singer behind the tall wooden individual pews designed for the Hoods. He pulled the hood off him, sliced his bonds with a well-sharpened kitchen knife and rushed him towards a side door. A mild panic grabbed him, for there was no sign of Jancy and his diversion, so he kept pulling at Singer, who was completely bewildered, until he heard several bangs.

At the same time he could smell fumes, like paint or something, but there was no time to waste now, so he grabbed Singer and ran for the woods.

Jancy was pleased with his mates as he swished

the turps along an aisle by the wall. The innocent paper bags they'd exploded on the other side of the church had guards running in that direction.

'I'll give Singer a real good send-off,' he muttered. 'You needed a diversion, mate. How about this?'

Jancy set fire to the church.

Angus and Singer were among the many people running up the hill towards the fire in the woods, Angus explaining what Singer had to do as they ran. When they had almost reached the outskirts of the fire, which was now bearing down on the magistrate's house, he began a detour that took them away from the flames.

'Do you know what to do now?' he asked, when they were moving south under cover of the trees.

'Yes,' Singer puffed, his eyes bright with excitement. 'Head for the coal mines. Beach. Second bay from jetty. Look for George and a boat.'

'Right! He'll take you to the mainland. Good luck.'

'Aren't you coming?'

'No. I can't, it's only you and George.'

'Big George?'

'Yes. I have to go, there's someone following us.'

'Jesus!' Singer stopped, confused.

'Run, you silly bugger!' Angus shoved him on. 'Get going!'

Angus himself turned off to the left, dodging in behind the asylum, heading for Masons Cove, the actual port for the township.

Lester had ducked out of the line and hidden in the parsonage gardens as the rest of the men marched on to the church. He saw Angus go past in another mob, so at least he had him tabbed. Then he saw flames shooting up in the woods, taking hold fast. Some people started running up there, but the guards stuck stolidly to their jobs, herding their charges into the church.

There was still no sign of George, and that fire had him suspicious. He'd begun to move in that direction when he heard some sort of commotion in the church, but he was sure he was on the right track now, so he joined the growing crowd hurrying up the hill towards the fire.

The magistrate's wife was standing outside in her nightie, screaming her head off as men raced about with buckets, trying to keep the fire at bay, and Lester was enjoying the spectacle when someone handed him a bucket and shouted at him to give a hand.

Amused, he ran forward, almost choking in the smoke, hurled the empty bucket into the fire and dodged away from the scene.

It was then he saw them, McLeod with his carrot-coloured skull, and another bloke, racing wildly through the trees, heading south. He took off after them, wondering where they could be going, running inland away from the cove, where they might have a boat, and away from a chance at Eagle Hawk Neck. There was still no sign of George.

He raced after them, but once he caught up it was hard to track them at this pace and keep out of sight at the same time. They too could hardly stay together as they dodged trees, and he lost sight of them for a while and had almost given up when he spotted Angus moving back towards the asylum.

Lester congratulated himself. He'd been right. The fire was a diversion. Those men could not have escaped from the church and run calmly through the open streets to the cove, so they'd joined the mobs, made the run from the church up to the fire among the crowds and were now taking a detour.

He looked back to see the magistrate's house well ablaze, and laughed.

It was an easy job to follow McLeod now; he wasn't bothering to hide too much, and why would he? Half the population of the island was tearing up Tramway Street to the great fire.

There was hardly anyone at the cove when McLeod slid down under the guard tower, and ran across the road to the shore. He turned over a small boat, dashed up to a shed, grabbed oars and ran back. By which time Lester was lying in the sand by the boat.

'Where do you think you're going?' he growled.

Angus was startled. 'Get out of the way. This is nothing to do with you.'

'The hell it isn't. You're making a break. Where to?'

'There's no time,' Angus said frantically. 'Get out of here or I'll break your bloody neck.'

'Touch me and I'll raise the alarm.'

Angus tried to think what to do next. He couldn't allow an escape alarm; they shouldn't discover that anyone was missing until roll-call tonight. That would give the lads plenty of time to get off the peninsula and get clear, wherever they were going. That part of the plan hadn't been relayed to George; it was difficult enough to get short messages through without adding unnecessary information, so Willem had been spare with words.

On the other hand, he could belt Lester with an oar.

It was Lester who solved the problem. 'I'm coming with you. If not, you'll be in the flogger's sights come noon.'

Angus stared at him. 'You're what?'

'Get moving, you bloody fool, or we'll both get caught.'

He shoved the boat into the water and jumped in. Angus followed, wondering how long this farce could go on, but started to row anyhow. Rowing hard.

'Where are we going?' Lester asked excitedly, now that they were skimming out of the cove, where most of the sea business of the island was carried on.

Angus nodded. 'Round that point.'

'That's the Commandant's grounds,' Lester said.

'Aye, it is. You don't think he'll be sipping tea with half the settlement burning under his nose?'

'Gawd, eh?' Lester said. Mightily impressed.

But by then they were well out in deep waters and Angus had had enough of rowing. He threw the oars overboard and watched them float away.

'What the hell did you do that for?' Lester screamed.

Angus didn't bother to explain. 'I think I'll have a swim,' he said.

He tied his boots round his neck and slipped into the warm water, remembering the freezing Glasgow mornings of his youth, when their skin had turned blue with the cold. This was bliss.

'I can't swim!' Lester yelled at him.

'Aye, I know,' Angus laughed. He laughed so much he nearly swallowed half the bay, but then he straightened up and set off for the shore with long, smooth strokes, interrupted only by the awkwardness of his necklace of boots.

'I hope the sharks get you, you bastard!' Lester screamed.

Angus set his boots free and swam faster.

Singer was running. Dodging trees and running and dodging trees until he didn't know where he was. He hoped he was running in the right direction because he had to find the coal mines. It was hard to make out what had just happened, and he thought he might be hallucinating, which was on the cards the way he'd been lately, but his hands seemed to be behaving. He slapped at a tree as he passed and they obeyed, so that was all right. And the hood was gone! He touched his head to make sure. The bloody hood really was gone. Angus had it. That was right. And someone was chasing them. Oh Jesus!

Surprise, surprise, he told himself. What did you expect when you're running away? Get a hold of yourself! George is waiting for you, go faster, that's all you have to do.

He tripped and fell. Climbed to his feet, and his

ankle gave way.

'Sorry about that,' he muttered, 'but you haven't got time to look at it.'

Singer staggered on. At times he felt dizzy with the blue sky swinging above him and the treetops trying to hold it still. When he broke out into open country, parrots screeched and sped away from gaudy bushes. He seemed to be going downhill then, and judged that a good sign. Since he'd never visited coal mines of any sort he didn't exactly know what he was looking for, but he thought they had to be around here somewhere otherwise he'd end up in the sea.

And that was when he stumbled on to a wild and rocky beach. With no sign of a coal mine, let alone a wharf.

But right across the sea from where he was standing, Singer saw land! He knew it wasn't part of this peninsula, it couldn't be. It was the mainland!

'God Almighty!' he said. 'If I can't find George I'll make a raft and sail myself across, I swear I will.'

He put two fingers to his lips and gave a long, shrill whistle, causing seagulls to flap away from him, but otherwise nothing stirred except the waves lapping the shore.

Singer sat staring at them, at the endlessness of them, at their bloody indifference to his plight.

He looked along the beach, one way and then the other, trying to decide which direction to go. Thinking more clearly now, he remembered that the peninsula came to a point on the southern end, and that point housed the coal mines. So they had to be south. He lifted a hand against the glare of the sun, climbing high in the east, and pointed.

'I think it's that way, lads,' he said,

Willem finally dozed, wrapped in a strip of canvas that was to have been a ground sheet. He was wakened just before dawn by the soft brooding hooing of a kookaburra, that he knew was only a prelude, and he found himself poised, tense, waiting for that burst of maniacal laughter. When it came, hooting governance over the bush dwellers, it intimidated him and made him feel very nervous about being in these strange and lonely surrounds.

Suddenly the noise stopped, and the silence rattled him too. By the time he shook out the canvas and folded it away, a red dawn was colouring the sky and a pungent smell of burned eucalypts lingered over the beach. He drank some water, threw off his clothes and went for a swim.

Within minutes he felt better, exhilarated by the crystal-clear water as he watched the surface of the sea change from pink to a glittering blue.

His day had begun. A very important day.

He knew he'd have to wait hours for Mort, since he hadn't planned to meet him until seven, but every long minute that passed filled him with dread, and until he saw the fisherman rowing towards him, Willem was convinced he wasn't coming.

'How you goin'?' Mort asked, as he pulled off a heavy-knit jumper.

'I'm well, thank you, Mort. Were there any strangers in the town yesterday?'

'Not even a possum. There are a few black-fellers around, that's all, but they don't bother no one. You got yourself all sorted out?'

'Yes.' Willem was staring at the boat, a battered dinghy only about twelve feet long.

'Is that boat safe?' he asked. 'It doesn't look too safe to me.'

'Why do you think I wanted a new boat? This is the best I've got; if you think it's no good, we don't have to go!'

'No, no, no,' Willem said firmly, though his heart was pounding. 'It's all right!'

'Good-oh, then, let's away.'

Mort was highly amused that he had to teach Willem how to row, and quite pleased that his passenger picked up the rhythm fairly quickly.

'See, it's faster with both of us rowing,' he said. 'We can't be plodding along today, we gotta get moving.'

As the dinghy nosed forward in what was, fortunately, a small sea, Willem groaned at the pain already besieging every muscle in his body. He had expected Mort to row him over there, so he could make sure everything went to plan. Not for a minute had he envisaged himself caught behind the oars, straining to keep up with the skipper.

'This old boat's slow, I hafta say,' Mort told him. 'When I get the new one it'll be a lot faster.'

'Oh good!' Willem said, crankily.

The boat suddenly switched about, and for a

minute Willem thought that Mort had lost control.

'Hang on, Willem, there's a bit of a swell,' he called. 'And pull hard. We gotta get across the channel, the tide's runnin' out.'

To Willem, the bit of a swell was a very strong current that was trying to tear the oar from his already blistered hands while Mort was yelling at him to dig deep, deeper!

It was windy out here in the open, halfway between heaven and hell, he mused as he struggled to keep up with Mort, so he fastened his eyes on the forested shores ahead, and tried not to think how far he could swim if this flimsy boat sank.

But after all that Mort took them into the calm waters of a shallow bay without batting an eyelid.

'Thank God, I thought we'd never get here,' Willem said as he sat limply in the boat, at the end of his tether.

Mort glanced at him in surprise. 'That was a bloody good run, mate. Not often she's as calm as that.'

His companion was searching the shores, though, praying for George to appear from the woods, or along the beach. George could row back; Willem depended on him now.

As soon as he reached the outskirts of the coal-fields, George cut away to the left, knowing that guards patrolled at weekends. He'd forgotten to tell that bit to Angus, and worried that his friend would barge straight into them.

He moved up to higher ground and climbed a

tree to see if he could spot Angus coming through the woods, but there was no sign of him. Turning about, he looked out to sea, and saw a small boat heading his way.

'Oh God help us,' he wept. 'I'm saved.'

In his heart of hearts, George had never really believed this would work. Not for an ordinary bloke like him, who never had any luck, he worried as he ran; as he waited for something else to go wrong. In his panic he fell into a ditch, he almost collided with a deer, and he slipped, hitting his head, as he clambered over boulders that barred his way to that beach. Wild horses wouldn't have stopped him now.

Willem and another man were pulling the dinghy up the beach when George came tumbling down to greet them.

Mort stared at him. 'Gawd! Who's he?'

'This is George,' Willem said quietly. He had forgotten how badly scarred George's face was, but it seemed worse now, and he was almost as shocked as Mort had been.

'Where's Angus?' he asked,

'He'll be here. He's coming,' George said, and overcome with emotion, he shook Willem's hand. 'How can I thank you for this?' Then he turned quickly to Mort and shook his hand too. 'You're a good man, sir. I'll be lifelong grateful to you.'

'It's orright,' Mort said. 'It's orright. Now where's your mate?'

They pulled the dinghy into the woods and stayed with it in case they were spotted by a passing boat, and every so often Willem ran along a ridge to look towards the mining area, but there was no sign of Angus.

They waited a long time. Hours. Until the sun was almost overhead, until Mort made the decision.

'I'm not waiting any longer. If that convict mate of yours has troopers on his arse he'll bring 'em here.'

'Can't we give him just another ten minutes or so?' Willem said. 'George is keeping a lookout up there. He'll call us.'

'Nope. I'm off. You blokes is on your own.'

He pulled the dinghy free and shoved it into the water, and Willem had no choice but to signal to George to come down.

In response he heard a shrill whistle. 'It's Angus,' he shouted. 'Can you see him, George?'

'No.'

'Here he comes,' Mort said, the dinghy swaying in the water now. 'The other way,' he called to them. 'He's coming the other way.'

A tall figure walked up the beach and said to them: 'I've been walking for hours and I couldn't find any coal mines.'

'What are you doing here, Singer?' George wanted to know.

'I've no bloody idea. Angus sent me.'

'Where is he? Angus. Where is he? We have to go.'

'He's not coming.'

'He was. What's happened to him?'

'I don't know. He pulled me out of the church, unveiled me. Dragged me off into the scrub, told me to look for George, coal mines, wharf, beach. I don't know, George! He just said to get going.'

733

'And he's not coming?' Willem asked.

'I told you. No. What are you doing here, Willem?'

Mort yelled at them: 'Get in the boat, you lot, or I'll go without you.' As George climbed in he said to Willem: 'You didn't say you were bringing a giant!'

'He'll row.'

'He'll need to!'

'Angus said someone was chasing us,' Singer told them helpfully as he climbed calmly into the dinghy.

'Then we're off!' Mort said. 'Grab the oar, mister, and pull hard.'

Willem gave George a hat, but he didn't have one for the pale-faced Singer. Then he handed the two men over to Henry and watched the ferry chug across the bay. He paid Mort, and rode on to Sorell. He didn't bother to stop at Havelock's pub this time; he was on his way back to Hobart.

'Where the hell are we?' George asked, when Henry put them ashore.

'Keep walking straight ahead there,' Henry pointed, 'and you'll be looking at the Derwent, and across at Hobart. You go over on a ferry. Do you know where you are now?'

'Yes.' George gaped.

'Right. Tell them to put you off at Sandy Bay and a woman will meet you. That's all I know. Now get goin'.'

'What woman?' Singer asked George as the second ferry swung out into the river.

'I dunno.'

'It's all very strange, that's what I say. But we're free, George! Or I'm madder than I thought. Maybe I should sing a song.'

George looked at the other two passengers, an elderly couple who'd come over on Henry's ferry with them.

'Not now!' he hissed.

He was worried about Angus.

On that Sunday, Sean made it his business to be in the square for most of the day.

He sat outside a pub in Salamanca Place talking amiably to one and all. Bailey joined him and they shared a meal of fish and potato cakes. Then Bobbee Rich came by for a chat.

'Do you remember Claude, the Pound Keeper?' she said. 'Well, his house got wrecked in that blackfeller raid out past New Norfolk, so he came to town. Now he's working at the George Hotel as, get this, a con-sierge.'

'What's a con-sierge?' Sean asked.

'A high-class porter. And Mrs Merritt says he's a star. She says he was trained by aristocrats.'

'Do they have to train porters?' Bailey was astonished. 'But listen here, Shanahan, you heard about Flo Quinlan?'

'No, what's he up to now?'

'You wouldn't want to know,' Bailey grinned. 'He's took off with Mrs Flood.'

'Go on!' Sean said, disbelieving.

'Took off to where?' Bobbee asked.

'Well that's the thing. No one knows. Flood's gone bush with her Governorship and her exploring party, and the farm's headless so Hippisley was searching for Flo and Mrs Flood. He was thinking foul play at first, but Goosey says the police now think they've eloped to the mainland under Mr and Mrs Someone-no-one's-ever-heard-of.'

'Oh shoot me dead now!' Bobbee screamed with laughter. 'The lieutenant'll be fit to be tied. And what do you reckon her chances are?'

'Whose chances?' Bailey asked.

'Mrs Flood's, of course.'

'Nil.' Sean gave the answer. 'If she was silly enough to help him escape to the mainland, that's the last she'll see of Flo.'

'I'll miss Flo,' Bobbee sighed. 'He was such a rascal.'

She moved on, and Bailey wandered off, but Sean stayed. He played cards in the square for the rest of the afternoon, and joined some friends for supper at a long table in the Irish pub. They sang old tunes and ballads until late, and all the while he worried about George and Angus.

The ferry set them ashore at the Sandy Bay landing, but there were few people about on this hot dry day.

George saw two ladies, who watched the ferry come in but did not board. One was a small fair woman in a white dress and a large hat; the other was in a maid's uniform. They appeared to be more interested in the ferry than the passengers, but as they turned to walk away, the maid nodded to Singer.

They let the women walk well ahead, and then

followed them, keeping their distance as Willem had instructed.

'I hope we've got the right ones,' George worried.

'We have,' Singer smiled. 'That's Marie Cullen from the factory. Where did Willem say we're going?'

'To a house owned by Magistrate Pellingham. A real bastard. No one will think to look for us there.'

Singer saw Marie pick a flower, a red geranium, and as they turned into a street she dropped the geranium at a large wrought-iron gate.

'This is the place,' he told George. He picked up the flower and placed it in his pocket, then let George walk ahead and ring the doorbell. It was his party now.

Three days later, the gardener heard muffled thumps coming from inside Mr Pellingham's house.

'On investigation,' he told Goosey, 'I found the master roped to a post in the cellar, and he had a hood on his head.'

'What sort of a hood?'

'It was made out of a flour bag. It had eyeholes and a cut for the mouth and the breathing, I suppose.'

Pellingham could not give a description of his attackers. He was punched in the face as he opened the door, a coat thrown over his head, and he was flung into the cellar. That night, one of them brought him food and secured the hood over his head. For two days they gave him water and food, without removing the hood, but never spoke. Then they were gone.

'What did they steal?' Goosey asked.

'Nothing, it seems,' Pellingham growled.

Hippisley was well aware that Pellingham was a blackmailer, but as yet he hadn't been able to pin anything on him. When he read Goosey's report, he figured the former magistrate had been given a warning by one of his victims.

'I think it's time to get rid of him,' he told the Attorney-General. 'Kick him back to London before someone gets really nasty and we have a murder on our hands. He's got to be the most hated man in the colony.'

CHAPTER TWENTY-ONE

The church was saved from serious damage and the fire in the woods had been contained, but not without the loss of Magistrate Matson's house and all their belongings.

Mrs Matson was taken to hospital suffering from smoke inhalation, but was still there several days later in a state of hysteria, refusing to leave the bed until her wardrobe of clothes was replaced. That, of course, was impossible, but some ladies did donate dresses, which at first she refused to wear, calling them dirty cast-offs.

Finally Allyn managed to convince her that she must dress in something, by bringing her the news that a ship was leaving Port Arthur that afternoon.

'Good,' she said. 'Tell Sholto to get me on it. I'm going back to Hobart to purchase some clothes, and I'm staying there until he finds me somewhere decent to live.'

As the story went, Allyn heard later, she found somewhere to live without his help. A friend, former magistrate Grover Pellingham, stepped into the breach, inviting Mrs Matson to stay with him in his mansion at Sandy Bay. Not too long after that, Pellingham, who was said to be a wealthy man, sold the mansion and departed Van Diemen's Land for parts unknown with Sholto's wife on his arm.

On the Sunday afternoon of the fires, the Commandant himself spotted a man out in the bay in a small boat, and called the guard to bring him in.

Though he knew he shouldn't be, Allyn was horribly embarrassed to find that the absconder was none other than Lester Harris. With that news, his budding romance with Miss Harris was treated to a cold shower, and he vowed not to see her again. Then things took a turn for the worse when he was forced, as medical officer, to witness her father's flogging.

By now he'd been present at many such punishments, to make certain the sentence was legal and the prisoner could cope. This time, listening to Lester's screams, he stopped the flogger at thirty strokes, halfway through the sentence. He simply couldn't stand it any longer, and he felt even worse when the prisoner fell at his feet in gratitude.

'That does it,' he said to the guard who

escorted him from the yard. 'I've had enough of this place.'

'Me too,' said the guard, and Allyn realised he'd been talking to a convict trusty.

But then sirens began to blast. 'What the hell's that?' he asked.

'Someone's missing. Full roll-call out on the parade ground. There goes supper.'

This time the twenty or so mounted troopers stationed in Port Arthur were patrolling the streets to keep order, as all the prisoners were turned out of their various abodes. They were quick-marched to the parade grounds, where their identities were checked against their records while their cells were searched. Once they were given the all-clear, they were returned to their sectors.

At a hurriedly convened meeting chaired by the Commandant, it was established that George Smith and James Forbes, prisoners from two different sectors, were the only men missing.

The Commandant was both amazed and outraged that a convict from the Hoods should have escaped, and demoted all of their guards on the spot.

Only one of the prisoners had attended church services in the morning, and various convicts gave evidence that they had seen a guard behaving oddly in the church. But they'd had no idea he had spilled a flammable liquid prior to lighting a fire, endangering all their lives, until it was too late. In the confusion, they did not see him exit the church.

How Forbes had escaped was no mystery to Chief Constable Toohill. 'Bringing hooded prisoners into the church, unless they're chained together, is asking for trouble. You wouldn't know who was there and who wasn't.'

The Commandant instructed his secretary to make a note of that advice, and to see to it that all hooded prisoners wore the ball and chain, and Biddle nodded, keeping his head down. He had no wish to be included among the searchers out in that inclement bush in the dead of night.

'So where are they?' the Commandant shouted at the Chief Constable and the regimental officers. 'I want them found. I don't care if it takes all night, and tomorrow as well. No prisoner leaves his cell for any duty whatsoever until they are found, and when you do find them, bring them to me. Personally. I'll have Forbes flogged within an inch of his life.'

Biddle looked up as if to remind him there were two absconders, but decided not to bother. At the minute, the two men were only absconders. If they were found to be missing, casting a slur on the Commandant's reputation, there'd be hell to pay. He had always boasted that no one could escape from Port Arthur.

It was thought that Convict Harris might have been part of the escape plot, but under serious questioning, with the assistance of thumbscrews, it was clear he had no knowledge of it. He had accused Convict McLeod of being involved, but McLeod had been accounted for as a volunteer with the firefighters. However, the two troopers who had left their recreational dinghy unattended on the beach, giving rise to Harris's foolish attempt to head for the notorious Storm Bay in their frail craft, were each punished with forty lashes of the cat. Their excuse, that they had rushed away to fight the fire, was not deemed relevant.

Not for two days would the Commandant allow a signal to be sent to the Comptroller-General of Convicts in Hobart. When he did, it reported only that it was believed that two men may have escaped from the penal settlement, but that a full-scale search was under way, and had been extended to Eagle Hawk Neck, the adjoining Forestier Peninsula, and the Isle of the Dead.

Boats were sent from Hobart to search various islands in Storm Bay, and by the end of the week, an irate Comptroller-General arrived on the Governor's yacht to castigate the Commandant for withholding news of the escapes.

'Earlier notice,' he fumed, 'would have alerted mainland police. By this they could be anywhere.'

'I am convinced they are still here somewhere,' the Commandant said. 'And I will find them.'

'You do that, sir. In the meantime I want a full report on both men. And their descriptions. Delivered to the yacht within the hour.'

The *Colonial Times* raced into print:

ESCAPE FROM PORT ARTHUR

Two convicts escaped from Port Arthur last Sunday. George Smith and James Forbes, both regarded as dangerous, according to the Commandant, went missing from a morning service at the church. They are believed to have attempted to swim the narrow channel of water at Eagle Hawk Neck during the night, despite the expected barking of guard dogs, but a search of the area has failed to find any trace of them. Local folk are of the opinion that the convicts would have been taken by sharks if they attempted to swim away from Port Arthur. Nevertheless, police are maintaining their vigilance and asking settlers to watch out for strangers who might be lurking on their properties.

The Governor pushed the paper aside. He was unable to concentrate on escapes or anything else happening here today, since only recently he had been given the disappointing news that he had been recalled to London. Sir John and Lady Franklin's days in Van Diemen's Land were coming to an end, and there were a number of odds and ends he must attend to, among them the matter of Convict McLeod.

Only last week the Attorney General had brought the case to his notice, believing it could require the Governor's attention. On reading the report, Franklin instructed his secretary to thank the Attorney General for his interest in this matter. 'Then send for Chief Constable Hippisley. I need to talk to him. He wrote most of the material in this file, so, to save time, I'll go straight to the source.'

When Hippisley was ushered in the Governor asked him, 'Did my secretary tell you what this is about, Chief Constable?'

Hippisley stood straight, with his chin up, as if he were on the parade ground. 'Yes, sir.'

'Distasteful business, what?'

'Yes, sir.'

'Take a seat there,' Franklin reread the top page as Hippisley sank on to the sturdy chair facing his desk. 'Tell me this, Hippisley. You believe Convict McLeod to be innocent?'

'I do, Your Excellency,' the Chief Constable replied nervously. 'As you might have seen, I also enclosed written evidence from Dr Jellick to the same effect. I had my suspicions beforehand, having been approached by Vicar Thorley with certain information.'

'Yes, I have the vicar's statement. And this girl, Miss Warboy, actually told Jellick that McLeod had never touched her?'

'Yes, sir, she volunteered that it was her father, seeing nothing wrong with...' he coughed.

'Why didn't she speak up at the trial?'

'She wasn't asked to give evidence.'

The Governor clucked his disapproval. 'And her parents simply abandoned her without notice? Left her with her grandfather?'

He turned pages over, checking facts. 'It's awkward, damn awkward. On the face of this I'm inclined to believe your findings are correct. Problem is, if I encourage an appeal on these grounds, it will be a major embarrassment to the judiciary, and a dreadful thing to do to Barnaby Warboy. I mean, he's a dear old chap. Had he known what the son was up to I believe he would have taken the horsewhip to him.'

'Yes, sir.'

'But if we don't release the truth, as we see it, Convict McLeod will remain over there for life.'

'Yes, sir.'

The Governor sighed, tapping his fingers on his

desk for an eternity, it seemed to the Chief Constable. At last he said: 'I tell you what. Let's keep this between ourselves. I think I'll pack the whole business away. Not to be released.'

'You mean Convict McLeod, sir?' Hippisley hoped the Governor did not notice the sudden hard edge to his voice.

'No, no! I meant the file. If you have any more notes on this matter, you are to destroy them. Understood?'

'Yes, sir.'

'Now, McLeod. He's had a hard time of it physically, and his reputation has taken a battering. Hard to recover from that sort of thing, you know. Damned hard! But I'm granting some pardons this week to convicts who have proven themselves to be worthy citizens and have contributed to the betterment of the colony. I think I'll slip McLeod's name in among them. No fuss, no fanfare, he simply walks free.'

'Yes, sir.'

'I want you to take the pardon to Port Arthur and hand it to the Commandant. He will of course want to know what it's all about. You will simply say you are acting on orders, and you are to escort McLeod back to Hobart. You then hand him over to the Comptroller-General's department for official release. They will have their instructions. I have looked at McLeod's record and he seems a decent sort of a chap, so he will be forgiven the balance of his original sentence. He'll be free to go.'

'Thank you, sir,' Hippisley stammered, though it was not his place to do so.

Sir John nodded. 'Don't forget, your answer to any questions is that you do not know.'

The Commandant was insulted. Not only had the Governor denied his request for the recall of Dr Roberts, but here was the Chief Constable with an order to escort Convict McLeod back to Hobart to facilitate a pardon, without even consulting him.

He bombarded Hippisley with questions, to no avail. The Chief Constable had been made aware that promotion was in the wind since he'd had a *private* meeting with the Governor himself, so his lips were sealed.

Angus McLeod was not pleased to be delivered to this Chief Constable, the man who'd hauled him out of Warboy's farm and dragged him down the road like a bag of spuds.

'What do you want?' he growled.

Hippisley took him aside. 'Get your things, McLeod. The Governor has granted you a pardon. I've got orders to take you back to Hobart.'

'The hell you have! What sort of trickery is this?'

'Don't you understand English, you dumb Scot? You've been pardoned!'

'I don't trust what you English buggers get up to. Show me the papers.'

'The Commandant has them. He's not pleased! If you want to go up and tangle with him, do your worst, but you'll miss the boat.'

'What boat?' Angus was so bewildered, he was losing the gist of this conversation, but when Hippisley barked at him to collect his things from his cell, and Toohill stood by, looking as confused as Angus felt, he ran. He ran giddily up the road, past work parties, past the tailoring shop and the bootmaker, past the wheelmaker's, to the foundry, where he raced through shouting: 'I'm out, lads!'

They could only stare as he tore out through the far door and on to the penitentiary, where he was detained by guards who thought he had lost his wits.

Then in a daze, with no shackles of any sort, Angus was aboard the small steamer as it sailed out of Mason Cove. He was on deck, able to walk about at will and look up at the Commandant's handsome white house as they rounded the point and set off across Storm Bay.

It was a hot day, a magnificent day, and Angus exulted in it, standing at the rails of the ship, looking out into the blue, breathing in the free air while he could, for so far this was all a dream.

'Why?' he said to Hippisley.

'Them as ask no questions get told no lies. You're free. You've been pardoned your previous outstanding term as well. The slate's wiped clean. You can go home to Scotland now if you want.'

'Are they paying my passage?'

'You're not that popular.'

Angus thought about that. Going home? With a pardon! That was something to show them. A clean slate! That'd put them back in their boxes.

As the ship made its way upriver towards Hobart, it hurt to recall that in all these years he'd not had a letter or even a message of some sort from his ma and pa, and nothing from any other soul in the district. It was as if they'd all forsaken him, and now it was hard to see their faces, to conjure up any faces; they seemed to have been left behind in a dark mist, where it was damp and cold. And clammy. And miserable. He shivered, but then he realised the sun was beating down on him, burning him. And Angus laughed.

'Are you sure there are no guards waiting for me on the wharf, or another work boss?'

'No one. Now listen, I shouldn't be telling you this, it's against orders, but take a tip from me and stay the hell away from Miss Warboy. She's not worth another sentence.'

'I never touched her,' Angus growled.

'Good. Keep it that way and all will be well. I have to take you up to the Comptroller's office to sign you out, then you can do what you like.'

The day he walked free, with a couple of shillings in his pocket, Angus was stunned. He wandered down to Salamanca Square, bought himself a pint and stood outside the pub door, staring at the world. Everything was so familiar. People he knew came past, nodded to him. Gave him a smile. Asked how he was going. And he nodded back.

His news was too big to share just yet, there was too much adjusting to do. Too much to think about.

Bailey went past. He went right on past until he realised who the lanky bloke was, the one leaning against the pub wall. He doubled back, stood and stared. Squinting to make sure.

'I'm out,' Angus managed to say to him.

'God Almighty, man, so you are, or you've got a double. When did this happen?'

'Today.'

'Good on yer! You got somewhere to sleep?'

'Not yet.'

'I can put you up behind the shop till you get a job if you like. It's not much, but...'

Angus fought down emotion to reply. 'I'd appreciate that, mate.'

It was Bailey who brought the news, waiting for Sean outside Pitcairn's gate. Almost jumping out of his skin with excitement.

'Guess who's in town?'

For a moment there Sean's heart sank. Oh Lord, he fretted, don't be saying it's Glenna, just when Marie and I are... He surprised himself by the admission that Glenna had faded from his life. Had been replaced.

'Who?' he asked.

'McLeod!'

'Angus?'

'The very one. He's out.'

Sean looked up and down the street and pulled Bailey aside. 'He did get out then, with the other lads?'

'No, he's carrying a pardon as big as your arm, and a grin to go with it.'

'That can't be.' Sean had been relieved to read that Willem's plan had worked and he'd managed George's escape, and brought Singer out as well. But what had happened to Angus? He'd not dared ask anyone, just been left in the dark worrying about his innocent friend doing life in that prison.

''Tis true. He's in town. Free.'

'No!'

'Then come and see.'

The two of them sat in the pub, celebrating with Angus. They bought him crayfish and oysters with bread and cheese, but he could tell them no more than that he had been granted a pardon.

'That's all they said, and I'm never one to argue, am I?' He grinned.

'They woke up you didn't do it, that's all,' Sean said. 'And it's easier to give you a pardon than apologise.'

'Then who did?' Bailey asked.

'Leave it,' Angus said. 'I don't care any more.'

Sean was so pleased for him; he could hardly believe his friend was actually back with them again. But then he remembered Singer, and spoke very carefully.

'When I heard two men had escaped from Port Arthur, I thought one of them was you, Angus, you were so savage at being charged.'

'It wasn't me mixed up in that escape.' He winked. 'But they say Singer was getting a real bad trot. The Commandant had it in for him, so his mates sent him out with George.'

'By jingo,' Bailey said. 'You coulda knocked me down with a feather when I read that poor old George, and Singer too, had scarpered.'

'What news of them?' Angus asked anxiously.

'None,' Sean said. 'Maybe they've gone bush-ranging. Joined up with Fearless Freddy Hines.'

'Is Freddy a bushranger now?' Angus was astonished.

Bailey laughed. 'An apprentice, more like it.

But you haven't heard Shanahan's news, Angus. Wait till you hear what he's doing!'

'It's a long story, how it came about,' Sean said.

'I've got the time,' Angus said. 'I've got all the time in the world.'

A few weeks later, Sean received another letter from Annie to say that times were bad in Ireland these days, and that she and her husband were joining up with three families from the village and all emigrating together to New South Wales.

So we shall all be able to ride down to see you, she wrote, and Sean laughed.

'I hope your horses can swim, Sis!'

Then she told him that Uncle Patrick had news. The Government in London had agreed to suspend transportation of prisoners to Van Diemen's Land for two years.

'And the rest, as well as prisoners,' Sean muttered. 'Don't forget the orphans and poorhouse folk that got snatched away from their homelands.'

But it was very good news, just the same.

Almost in the same breath Annie wrote that Glenna and young Tom were now living in New York and she'd married a rich American. His sister seemed to have forgotten her previous suspicion that they were on the way to Van Diemen's Land, Sean mused. Were I not over Glenna by this, I'd have been crushed to have this dropped on me! But Annie's words ran on without the hindrance of full stops and commas, and Uncle Patrick was featuring again. He was coming to Van Diemen's Land to visit Matt's grave. Then there was talk of the village and the great sadness that old Mrs Ryan and her daughter had died of starvation, and the priest was placing food baskets at the door of the church for them as they were too proud to ask for a crust.

We are trying to take the Mater and Pater with us to New South Wales but they're too set in their ways they said this is no slight on you for they love you dearly and look forward to you coming home one day but we should see you within the year and Uncle Patrick even sooner your affectionate sister Annie.

These days Mr Pitcairn was not quite as formal with his clerk, though he still referred to him as Mr Shanahan, more to impress clients, Sean realised.

When an opportunity arose, he asked his employer if it was true that transportation was to cease, and if so, why only for a couple of years?

Pitcairn was delighted. 'I hadn't heard yet. That's wonderful! But only for two years? I think that's a compromise. Half the settlers here want the convict traffic stopped, others want to retain the cheap labour; and not just settlers, the Government wants them too. There are plenty of public works on the books. The only government income of this colony is still earned from the rent of Crown land and duty on spirits and tobacco. They won't be keen on losing the workforce. Which reminds me. Do you know Lieutenant Tom Flood?'

'Yes.' Sean was wary.

'Most peculiar case. Baggott has it. Flood is

being prosecuted for possessing a quantity of illegal spirits. Apparently his own overseer reported the cache to Customs. Even showed them where they were hidden. There's loyalty for you!'

'That is unusual,' Sean said virtuously, thinking of Flo. 'I suppose he'd be out of a job now.'

'Of course! So is Flood. He's no longer an aide, that wouldn't matter with the new governor already on his way, but he'll get a heavy fine.'

Sean was surprised that Pitcairn appeared not to know the real gossip about the Floods, or maybe these things were not discussed by gentlemen. Which reminded him, Baggott had come through for Josie, obtaining permission for her to sell the farm, approved by the Attorney-General because of the hopelessness of her present situation. Her husband had been convicted of absconding and another ten years had been added to his sentence.

Strangely, it was Angus who held the key to that story, which Sean couldn't pass on to Josie. Apparently Harris had discovered that George was involved in an escape plan and was on the lookout. He'd seen the connection between George and Angus and had followed Angus, who tried to give him the slip by taking to sea in an unattended dinghy. Harris had jumped in with him and ended up alone in the boat without oars.

While Josie was relieved that she could at last give up the farm, Louise was devastated that her father would be imprisoned for many more years.

'He is a hero!' she wept. 'He was trying to escape, to get back to his family. Only a man like my father would have the courage to do that.'

She wrote a long, emotional letter to Allyn Roberts, insisting her father was a good man, and requesting that Allyn seek Lester out, to tell him she would never forsake him.

The two women were in a desperately unhappy situation, and there was nothing Sean could do to ease the growing tension between them.

Roberts came home for a few days, complaining bitterly about life in that penal settlement.

'I am forced to watch men being flogged,' he cried. 'It's dreadful.'

'They can't make you,' Sean said.

'If I don't go, there's no one to stand up for the prisoners. It's the same here, you know that. I found out that the last medical officer didn't care; he rarely attended them, never challenged the count or checked the condition of the prisoners.

'It turns out,' he said bitterly, 'that's why I got the job. Because nobody else wanted it. And here was I thinking it was an honour. And I'll tell you something else. I had to witness Louise's father being whipped, and listen to the man scream. Imagine how I felt. I was nearly sick!'

Sean gulped. That wouldn't do a lot for the romance. He'd been hoping Allyn's arrival would have a calming influence on Louise, but the doctor made no attempt to see her. He didn't even ask after them.

'Harris isn't well, anyway,' Roberts added. 'The flogging broke his nerve, you know. It happens quite often.'

'You don't have to tell me,' Sean growled.

'Oh yes. Sorry. Well, his back was badly infected

when they brought him into hospital a couple of days ago, and he had a fever as well. Several men have the same sickness. It's damn hard to break a fever in this heat, hard to keep them cool. I felt terrible having to treat him, knowing he is Louise's father.'

'He wouldn't be feeling too good either by the sound of things.'

The doctor changed the subject. 'How are you getting along with Pitcairn?'

'Doing well. I can't thank you enough. I never knew a clerk's job would be so interesting.'

'At least someone's happy,' Allyn said with a frown.

I don't know about that, Sean pondered. If Lester's sick, shouldn't Josie and Louise be told? Surely he'd want to see them. Sean didn't know what regulations applied to this circumstance, with family nearby, but he supposed it was all up to the Commandant. The very thought of that tyrant made his blood boil. Angus had told him about the standoff between Singer and the Commandant, and he was proud of Singer sticking to his guns, even though he'd been consigned to the infamous Hoods.

'So he wouldn't sing for them,' he laughed. 'He must have driven the Commandant mad.'

Angus shook his head. 'Who cares about that bastard? Singer nearly drove himself mad. When I saw him his face was as white as a sheet and his eyes were all over the place, wobbly as peanuts in a shell they were. I'm amazed he found George at all.'

The weeks passed and Sean became more and

more involved in town life. He visited Marie, who told him quietly that she had seen the two men, recognised one of them as Singer Forbes, and shown them Pellingham's gate as discussed. She didn't want to talk about it further, but Sean was now able to reassure Angus that both men had made it to Hobart. And he was certain in his own mind that Willem had managed to ship them out.

'Well done, Willem!' he murmured. 'Well planned and executed. Looks like you take after your dad after all.'

He didn't mention Miss Warboy's whereabouts to Angus, and fortunately he didn't enquire. Maybe he thought she was still at the farm.

As for Marie, she was looking bonnier by the day, but Penn was a woebegone little figure with her belly out of shape.

'She can't grasp what's happening to her at all,' Marie said, 'so I keep telling her that if she eats her meals and don't run about too much, her tummy will get better.'

'Poor lass,' Sean said. 'I saw there's a new church up on the hill. Would it be one of ours?'

'It is,' Marie smiled. 'I've been wanting to go to Mass, but I don't know if I'm allowed to take Penn, and I can't leave her here on her own.'

'Why didn't you ask Sam?'

'I didn't like to. He'd have to ask Mr Warboy, who, he says, isn't one for religion these days.'

'Tell you what. I'll borrow the Doc's buggy and take the two of you next Sunday. It'll just be a morning out for Penn.'

'That would be lovely. We'll look forward to it, Sean.'

Pinewoods Farm was sold! Mr Toohill was an eager buyer, Josie said, but in the end a new settler outbid him, and she was pleased with the result. The settler had paid a lot more than she'd expected to receive.

On Baggott's advice, though, fifty per cent of the sale money had to be banked in Lester's name. Unsurprisingly, Josie wasn't happy about this.

'That's not fair,' she railed. 'What can he do with it? He doesn't need money where he is.'

'It helps,' Sean said. 'Money can buy a little comfort.'

'Like what?'

'This and that.' He wasn't about to mention that bribes could buy anything

'See, you can't think of a thing. It's not fair. It's my farm now, he hasn't lifted a finger to help me.'

Rather the opposite, Sean thought, but he said: 'The farm was in both names. What did you expect?'

'Whose side are you on?' Josie snapped.

'No one's. That's the law.'

'Oh, so now you're the expert, are you?'

'Mother, he's right. Don't be so rude,' Louise chipped in.

But as they were packing to move into temporary accommodation at a Hobart boarding house, Baggott sent his clerk out to the farm with a message for Josie. He had heard from Dr Roberts that Lester Harris had suffered a heart attack and was seriously ill, so he'd lodged an official request that Mrs Harris and her daughter be granted permission to visit Convict Harris in the Port Arthur hospital. The Commandant had approved the request.

'We aren't going there,' Josie told the clerk. 'How dare Mr Baggott take it for granted we would visit that place! I want my husband brought to the Hobart hospital.'

'I'm afraid it's not possible. Against regulations,' the clerk said.

'Then please thank Mr Baggott,' Louise said quietly. 'We appreciate his kindness, and we'll go to Port Arthur as soon as possible.'

'The next boat leaves the day after tomorrow, ten a.m.'

'We will not,' Josie hissed as the clerk mounted his horse for the ride back to town. 'What will people say?'

'I don't care. He's dying, Mother, we have to go,' Louise wept. 'How can you be so cruel?'

'Are you sure this isn't just an excuse to see your friend Dr Roberts?'

Louise slapped her face and rushed out of the room.

Louise made a lonely, nervous little figure walking down the busy wharf, in a full-skirted blue dress with a buttoned-up bodice and a very becoming bonnet, and Allyn felt sorry for her.

He'd come in on the steamer that had arrived only an hour ago, to break the news to Mrs Harris, and to Louise, that Lester had died that morning.

When she saw him coming towards her, she

758

burst into tears and ran into his arms.

'Where's your mother?' he asked, hoping for support in breaking the news.

'She's not coming. How is my father, Allyn? Is he still very ill? When did you last see him?'

'This morning,' he said quietly, taking her aside.

'You did? How was he?'

'Louise, your father died peacefully in his sleep early this morning.'

'No!' She shook her head, disbelieving. 'No. I was going out to see him.'

'Yes, you were. But I think it's best that we turn back now. Just a minute, let's sit in the park up there. It's very nice, and the roses are all in bloom.'

As he talked, he shepherded her up the path. He hadn't counted on seeing Louise on her own, and he'd only made this effort to break the news to them from guilt. Witnessing her father's pain and humiliation had left him with a deep sense of guilt, and he'd made it worse by cowering away from telling the man, even when he was his patient, that he was acquainted with his family. It might have given him some solace at the end.

But it was Matron whom Lester had turned to when he was at his lowest ebb, asking her to write his last will and testament. One line only.

Lester Harris left all his worldly goods to his daughter, Louise Harris.

These things Allyn didn't mention now. Louise was weeping quietly, and he had his arm about her and he could smell the faint perfume of her and feel her warmth; and that love he had for her, that truant love, returned, chastened. He felt unworthy that he'd treated her so badly, and hoped he could make it up to her.

Since his estate was able to pay, Lester Harris was permitted a tombstone, but he was still buried among the convict graves on the southern side of the island, not far from the grave of Matt O'Neill.

Feeling more confident these days, Sean escorted Louise to Port Arthur, where they were met by Dr Roberts, and rowed over to the tiny Isle of the Dead by trusties. At last he was able to view Matt's grave, marvelling at the beauty of his surrounds, and put an end to the misery that had plagued him, for Matt was surely at rest now and nothing more could be done.

When Josie learned that her husband had left his half of the farm to Louise, she was furious. Sean was shocked at her reaction, and tried to mediate, because Louise was still upset over the death of her father.

'No matter that they were to you just pipe dreams,' he told Josie. 'To Louise they were real. She truly believed her father was hard done by, and that he would secure his release and come home to the farm. Now all of those dreams have come tumbling down, and she has to build new ones, so don't be too hard on her.'

'I'm not being hard on her. I'm tired of her crocodile tears. He never gave a damn about her. He's left her all that money to get back at me, that's all. She's got no right to it, and I will forbid

Mr Baggott to give her a penny.'

'He won't have any choice, Josie.'

'Then you get your lawyer to challenge the will.'

'I can't do that.'

'You mean you won't! You're still on Louise's side!'

'I told you before, I'm on no one's side. It's sad to see you ladies at odds.'

'Then tell her to sign the other half of the money over to me.'

Sean gave up. Rather than face more arguments with Josie, he retreated. By this time they'd settled into the boarding house – two single rooms, he'd been pleased to note, for the sake of peace and quiet. And what was more, he reminded himself, Josie had announced she was returning to England as soon as the money from the sale of the farm was paid.

'I'm not surprised,' Louise had said angrily. 'She's been wanting to go home for years. That's why she wanted to sell the farm. I never believed it was in such bad shape as she claimed.'

'But she's never been happy here. It was a terrible strain to put on a woman.'

'On me too, don't forget. Now she's going off without me.'

'Ah, dear Lord, can't you two agree on anything?'

'Rarely. Do you know she hoped you'd go with her? But I told her you couldn't, you've got a lady friend. That didn't please her either. She'd help you escape, you know. You've still got time!'

'Louise, give over.'

She laughed. 'Walk with me to the bank. I have to sign some papers.'

'You're too late. They close at noon on Saturdays.'

'Oh well, never mind. Isn't that your friend McLeod?' As Angus neared them, she called to him: 'I was just asking Sean when he intends to introduce me to his lady friend.'

'I've been asking the same thing,' Angus grinned.

'It's a bit awkward now,' Sean said, frowning at Louise. 'She can't leave her job. How's yours going?'

'It's a good job. Fancy me working in a brewery.'

'The family back home will never believe it!'

'I'll no be telling them. I've never said before, but they disowned me, me being a convict.'

'Wait until they hear you've been pardoned, though!' Sean said.

'They'll never hear that from me. They can go to hell. I've made up my mind. I'm never going back.'

CHAPTER TWENTY-TWO

Barnaby came to visit, and hardly recognised the maid. She'd been transformed from a skinny girl with wispy hair and eyes too big for her head into a typical Irish colleen. There was life in the girl now, and her dark curls were tinged with red.

He thrust a toy rabbit, a pink furry little thing, at Penn and gave the maid a packet of chocolate powder to be stirred into hot milk, because Sam had reported she was doing a good job.

He tried to talk to Penn but she wasn't feeling well, and grizzled about the heat.

'I don't like it here any more,' she added. 'I want to go back to the farm. It was much cooler there.'

'It was winter then,' he laughed. 'And I thought you'd like the heat, coming from Jamaica.'

'We came from New Orleans, and it was a horrible smelly place, and we were as poor as church mice, my mother said. Do you like this dress?'

She stood back for him to admire her pink and white cotton smock. 'Marie made it for me, and she put the lacy flounces on the bottom of the skirt too. It's my favourite dress now. I wore it to church on Sunday.'

'What church?' he asked mildly, an eye on the maid.

'The one on the hill.'

'I wanted to speak to you about that, Mr Warboy,' the maid said.

'Yes?'

She flushed. 'It started when Sean Shanahan came to see how we were getting on.'

'Shanahan? How did he know you were here?' He shook his head then, as if shaking off that question. 'It doesn't matter, I might have known he'd turn up.'

'You said we were not permitted to invite callers into the house, and so we did not. Sean understood you have your reasons. He sat on the veranda awhile, he did, that's all. And then he came another time, and that was when he saw the new church. It's a Catholic church.'

'So you dragged Penn up there, eh?'

'Mr Warboy,' she said quietly, 'I would never drag Penn anywhere. It's a long walk up to that church. I mind not being able to go to Mass sometimes, so Sean solved the problem.'

'He would! I suppose he comes out and takes you.'

'Yes,' Penn cried. 'He comes and takes us in the buggy and I get to sit up the front.'

Barnaby scratched his head, stalling. He was sorry he'd been short with the maid, thinking the worst; that was wrong. This was just the sort of thing Shanahan would do, and there was no harm in it. Probably good for them to get out.

'I hope you don't mind,' the maid said. Marie. He must try to remember her name.

'No. It's all right. But tell me this. I believe Shanahan has a job in town now.'

'Yes,' Marie said proudly. 'Isn't it grand! He works for a lawyer gentleman.'

'How did that come about?' Barnaby had been dying to know what Shanahan was up to, and this was a fine source of information.

'Well!' she said. 'It was all one thing after another, I think. First he's minding Dr Roberts' house, then the doctor sends him on to the lawyer ... not Mr Baggott. Sean had to visit Mr Baggott to see if he could get his friend off, whose name we can't mention here, and that didn't work. And then the other lawyer, Mr Pitcairn, gave him the job. And then lately, glory be, if that friend whose name we're not mentioning didn't get off anyway.'

Barnaby was trying to keep up with this rush of a story but he grasped the last sentence. 'He what?'

Marie looked to Penn. 'Why don't you take the little rabbit and make a hutch for it with pillows?'

'I could do that,' Penn said. 'And give it some pretend milk.'

'Yes.' Marie watched her run inside, then turned to him. 'You didn't know?'

'Are you telling me he was pardoned? McLeod?'

'That's him. Indeed he was.'

'Why?'

'They proved he didn't touch her, Mr Warboy.'

'This is ridiculous. How could they?'

'God works in mysterious ways. I'm sure I don't know. Neither does Sean. But he says the Governor did, which was why he pardoned him.'

'Why wasn't I informed?'

She shrugged. 'I don't know. I was more worried that the man, being proved innocent, and back here in town, might come here pretty cranky with Miss Inside There, so to speak. But Sean says no. He's a good man, and forgiving. It's all over.'

'Did they find the man who did it?'

'No one seems to know whether they did or not. I think it's best forgot, for the sake of our girl here, Mr Warboy.'

He left the stifling little sitting room and went out to the veranda, appreciating the sea breeze. He supposed she was right, but he'd like to have a talk with Shanahan about it one day.

His carriage was still waiting in the shade of a

fine old elm.

'I have to go,' he said as Marie followed him out.

'I'll call Penn,' she said.

They both bobbed respectfully as they said their farewells to him, and he put on his hat.

'Tell Shanahan it's a good thing, that job,' he muttered to Marie. 'Very good.'

She beamed. 'So it is, Mr Warboy. We're proud of him too.'

It was four Sundays after that when Sean came to take them to church.

'I had a letter, smuggled from my friend Willem,' he told Marie. 'He was a free man, having done his time. He's on his way home to England. He said he had two companions. One had just died, God rest his soul. Apparently he became very ill with sores erupting on his face and chest. The doctors said they were incurable tumours.' He sighed. 'That would have been poor George. He died in Sydney, that's New South Wales. A damned shame, with him past freedom's door. He said his other companion had now left for America.'

'And that would be Singer?'

'Yes. He made it.'

'That's a relief. I got the surprise of my life to see him there at the ferry.'

'He wrote a note on the bottom of Willem's letter. Typical of Singer, havin' to have the last word. He wrote: *Make them shut their own bloody gates.*' Sean laughed. 'He'll always be a rebel.'

'What did he mean? About the gates?'

'It's only a joke. I'll tell you another time. We'd

better get going. Where's Penn?'

She liked to sit up front in the church so that she could see better, and add her voice to the hymns whether she knew them or not, which Marie found embarrassing, but there it was, Penn really enjoyed Sunday Mass.

When they left the church, Penn walked proudly through the small gathering, holding high the yellow parasol Sean had bought for her, and people turned to smile. By sheer good fortune it matched the tiny yellow roses that Marie had appliqued on the cuffs and collar of her white muslin dress.

They proceeded down to the buggy, and Sean was just about to lift Penn aboard when she saw a tall kangaroo standing in the middle of the road leading to the church.

'Oh look,' she cried. 'Isn't he lovely!'

With that, she took off, running down the steep gravelly road, calling out to the animal.

Marie yelled at her to stop, but it was too late. Penn tripped and fell forward, only to slide further and tumble head over heels into a culvert.

The kangaroo fled into the bush as Sean and Marie raced down to her, followed by half the congregation, all anxious to help.

She didn't appear to have any broken bones, but she was dazed, her dress was torn, and she'd suffered numerous cuts and bruises, so Sean lifted her gently and carried her up to the buggy.

A woman came forward. 'I'm Bea Warner, I'm a midwife. She's pretty far along for a fall like that. Would you like to bring her to my house? I live in the farmhouse down the bottom of the hill.'

'I'd be grateful,' Marie said nervously. 'Would you hop up for a ride down there?'

'Yes. I'll come with you.' She turned back to four young children who were standing watching them. 'You kids come on straight home, you hear? And stick to the road.'

Mrs Warner took Penn into the tiny farmhouse, and laid her on the plump covers of a small iron bedstead.

Sean waited nervously in the hallway until the children came home.

'Is she going to die?' the elder boy asked cheerfully.

'No, no, no. She just fell over.'

Curiosity satisfied, they wandered away.

Mrs Warner came out of the bedroom. 'You're Mr Shanahan? A friend?'

'Yes.'

'Where's the husband? I think you should get him.'

'There's no husband, missus.' He felt he ought to defend Penn's honour. 'She was raped by someone unknown.'

'Ah God help us and save us! The poor little thing. Well listen now, she's not too good. She's gone into labour, ready or not. But I think she's twisted her neck and that's got me worried. Would you mind going for Dr Jellick? Marie says he's her doctor.'

'Not at all. I'll go right away.'

Jellick wasn't home, the maid said. 'Gone to church.'

'Which one?'

'St James's. Where they've got the organ.'

He rode on into town and hurried up to the packed church, all the while unnerved by having to call on Jellick for assistance. That man not being his best choice.

Peering in, Sean caught the eye of an usher. 'Is Dr Jellick in there? He's wanted urgently. Will you tell him?'

The usher returned. 'The doctor says the service is nearly over.'

'But this is urgent.'

'He said the service is nearly over,' the usher hissed.

So Sean could only cool his heels outside, waiting impatiently, crankily.

When Jellick appeared, he seemed to have forgotten the urgent message. He stood talking to parishioners outside on the street, bowing and chatting to others as they came from the church, until Sean was beside him, reminding him.

'In a minute,' Jellick snapped, waiting until the minister came out to farewell his fold, and wasting more time in conversation.

Almost the last to leave, he told Sean to go on ahead. 'I have to go home and get my bag first. I am not in the habit of taking it to church. I know the place.'

'No you don't. It's the midwife's house at the base of the hill, where the Catholic church is.'

'What? She's got a midwife? Then she doesn't

need me. Some of these women are just fusspots!'

'It's the midwife who asked for you. Miss Warboy fell over and hurt her neck.'

'What do you mean, she's hurt her neck? How could she have hurt her neck? What was she doing?'

'She had a fall,' Sean said stubbornly. 'You can ask all these questions when you get there, can't you?'

'Kindly remember it is Sunday, sir. I am doing the woman a favour, though if she has a midwife, I'm sure I don't know why I am needed.'

He stalked away. Sean felt like following him to hurry him along, but thought better of it and headed back to Sandy Bay.

The doctor came eventually. Penn was in labour and in intense pain, so he decreed that she not be moved. He told the midwife that Miss Warboy had not twisted her neck, despite the swelling, but that she was suffering from concussion.

'I think it's only a small infant in there,' Mrs Warner said, 'but she doesn't seem to be making any progress. And she keeps complaining about her neck. Maybe she's broken a bone.'

'We'll see when the swelling goes down. It's more important to attend to your job. I'll be at the hospital tomorrow if I'm needed.'

When he'd left, Sean went to fetch Mr Warboy, and by midnight they were keeping vigil in the midwife's kitchen, fortified by copious cups of black tea.

At four in the morning, after a night of convulsions, Penn gave birth to a baby boy. He was born lifeless, but his mother had lost consciousness by then.

With her grandfather holding her hand, Penn Warboy died as the sun was coming up on another day, and they all kneeled to pray for the two sad little souls.

'They'll meet in heaven,' the midwife said.

Few knew that Penn and her baby son had died. Barnaby chose to have a private funeral, with a pastor from St James's church in attendance; then he went home and wrote the letter.

He'd heard nothing of Jubal and Millicent since they'd left, so he addressed his letter to his other son, Harold, asking him to pass on to them the sad news that their daughter Penelope, whom they'd abandoned so callously, had departed this life as a result of a fall.

My respects to you and yours, he wrote in conclusion, deeming that to be as much civility as he could muster.

Then Shanahan came to call.

'I was wondering how you are,' he said. 'It's a hard blow to see one of your own go, especially one so young.'

'That's true,' Barnaby said. 'I had not expected it to hit me so hard. Old age, I suppose. Makes me think of my own hold on life's ropes.'

They walked about the farm, as they had done for so many years, discussing the crops and the day-to-day operations, and Sean said: 'It's getting on to Christmas. Are you giving the lads the treat this year?'

'I'd forgotten all about that,' Barnaby said wearily.

'They look forward to it, and it'll cheer you up too. You only have to tell Dossie and she'll get it all going.'

'I suppose I could.'

'You might as well. And there's something else. What's to become of Marie Cullen?'

They walked through an archway into the garden and Barnaby sat down on the nearest bench. 'My legs are getting old and lazy,' he wheezed. 'Marie Cullen? I don't know. Penn's gone. There's nothing more for her to do.'

'Mr Warboy, there has to be something. She'll get sent back to the Factory! You can't do that to her. She looked after Penn better than a mother. You can't just pack her off now.'

'What else can I do? There's nothing for her to do here.'

'There must be something,' Shanahan said anxiously. 'I can't let her be sent back to that prison. Her only crime was being one of the orphans they scooped up and brought out here.'

Barnaby looked up, amused. 'Ho now! What's this I'm hearing? It sounds to me as if you've got more than a passing interest in her.'

'I just might have, you know. But I don't want her to think I'm feeling sorry for her if I speak up. That's if she's sent back to the Factory. A lot of help it will be for me to be coming along to her at the Factory and asking her if she'll be my wife. Can you understand what I'm saying?'

'No! You're always so damned complicated, Shanahan. Why can't you just ask her straight out? She's still at the cottage.'

'Because she's sitting out there scared you're about to sack her. It'd be bad timing.'

'Oh, all right. Leave it with me. I'll see if I can work something out.'

'I'd be obliged, sir.'

'Your manners are improving,' Barnaby said. 'Pitcairn's influence I suppose. Tell me about your job. It must be very interesting.'

'I hear a lot,' the clerk whispered with a theatrical wink, 'but none as good as what's going on next door.'

'At Flood's? What's happening there?'

'Aha, you're really missing out lately. Let me tell you...'

Barnaby went to bed that night still laughing about Flood losing his wife to a convict.

Things were looking up, he supposed, and he made his own joke: 'After the flood!'

'I think I've had too much rum,' he murmured as he blew out the lamp.

Within days Sam was given instructions to deliver Marie Cullen to Warboy Farm, where she was to be employed as kitchen maid and assistant gardener.

'Gardener?' she said to Sam. 'That's never a job, is it? Just gardening?'

'Ah yes, it's a very important job,' he grinned. 'Very important.'

'Is that right?' she breathed.

'I'm to have a day off a week,' Dossie cried, full of excitement. 'I've never had a day off before.

And you're to do my work on that day. We'll get along well, Marie. But where's Penn?'

Marie took her aside, whispering what had happened, and how it was to be kept quiet so as not to upset Mr Warboy any further.

'He got a bad shock, he did, poor man.'

Sean was invited to the treat at Warboy Farm – picnic fare with a plum cake made by Sam's wife. Barnaby had invited a few of the neighbours as well, including Josie and Louise Harris, but Josie declined.

'She's packing, going home to England,' Louise told him. 'She hates it here since my father died. But I'm staying.'

'Yes, I'm so sorry. I did send my condolences.' But Barnaby was surprised. 'Leaving you here on your own?'

'Not exactly. I'm staying in the boarding house, but I won't really be alone. Dr Roberts and I are to be married.'

'Heavens! Congratulations, my dear, that is excellent news.' He turned to Sean. 'You didn't tell me this!'

'She wanted to tell you herself.' He didn't add that he'd asked his own love, Marie Cullen, to marry him this very morning, and she'd agreed with so many tears that he'd begun to think he'd upset her. They needed to treasure this time for themselves for a while.

The newly-weds took up residence at Port Arthur, and with apologies to Sean sold the Hobart house. After Dr Roberts completed his term of duty at the penal settlement, they planned to live in Sydney.

'I'll be glad to leave here,' Louise said. 'And so will Allyn. Too many bad memories.'

In other words, Sean thought, as far as Louise was concerned, Lester Harris was never a convict. He was a settler. If people dared to ask. But her husband wouldn't forget. Nor would folk here forget him. Dr Roberts was one of the righteous.

Sean moved into a rented room and was able to see Marie at weekends. They planned to marry at Easter, and his gift to her was the right of a bride to stay home and keep house, though their house would be only two rooms for a start.

Then the great day came, and Barnaby, who was to give the bride away, was more nervous than she was. For weeks he'd been checking with the George Hotel that everything was in order for the wedding breakfast.

'I want the very best for my friends,' he said to Hugh Merritt. 'I haven't been to a wedding breakfast in years. I've always had a soft spot for them.'

Hugh introduced him to his new partner, formerly his concierge, Claude Plunkett.

'Claude worked for the aristocracy,' he said. 'There's nothing he doesn't know about these things. He'll look after you.'

So Claude took over the arrangements for the wedding day, and Barnaby was delighted, but curious about Claude's sudden elevation to partner.

'How did this come about?' he asked.

'Simple. I sold some land and needed somewhere to invest. Hugh needed funds to buy the old house next door so that he could expand the hotel, and here we are.'

And Claude certainly knew his job. The dining room was a picture of elegance that morning, with tables set for forty guests, and an iced wedding cake in pride of place at the bridal table. There was even a lady piano player and a violinist.

It gladdened Barnaby's heart to be taking the bride to St John's church in his carriage, and Marie looked beautiful in a softly simple dress of Indian muslin, with sheer sleeves and an underskirt embroidered with sprigs of flowers. Her dark auburn hair was swept up, with long ringlets framing her face under a light mantilla of lace, and as he walked her down the aisle he witnessed Shanahan's joy, and felt as if his own life was back on track again.

Even the best man, Angus McLeod, who Barnaby thought would never forgive him, had a smile for him.

As the wedding ceremony proceeded, Barnaby pondered the last couple of years. From the minute Jubal had walked back into his life, causing havoc and embarrassment, he had gradually lost confidence in his place in the community. It had ebbed away, along with invitations that had failed to materialise.

People were still kind to him, he'd noticed, ladies smiled, hats were raised, but over the last year he'd become more and more lonely, with no one to turn to. Even the easy camaraderie he'd once had with his workers had gone, and he'd been too lonely to reach out.

By Jove, he said to himself as they all stood for a hymn, that's a line straight out of Sean's vocabulary, if ever there was one. But loneliness can corner a man, it can.

The Christmas treat for his workers had broken the ice a little, but not much. They were still an arrogant lot. Since the new men had joined his staff, they'd fallen back into the old 'Jack's as good as his master' attitude, so fiercely held by this army of British transportees. It was their accepted method of protest, wildly at odds with those who saw no fault in their banishment and use as cheap labour.

Barnaby himself wasn't bothered that he was one of the bosses. It was just a way of life to him, as slaves were back home. Though slaves were a lot worse off than these people. But he had come to understand their attitude, and he often wondered why they didn't rise up and revolt, for there were any amount of leaders about.

He looked up at the bridegroom, who was repeating his vows to the priest, and then Marie, starry-eyed, had her say.

Then Shanahan, the black-haired Irishman who could indeed have been a rebel, took his bride in his arms, and a wave of emotion swept through the church.

Barnaby was the first to arrive at the hotel and he stood in the hall by the dining room, with Claude, ready to welcome the guests.

A tall, distinguished-looking gentleman, about sixty years of age, not a guest at the wedding breakfast, strode by them, on his way into the hotel.

Suddenly he stopped, and walked back. 'I say,' he said. 'You're Claude, aren't you? Weren't you Sir James Huxtable's valet?'

'Yes, I was, Your Excellency. You have a good memory!'

'Well I'll be blowed. And what are you doing here?'

'This is my dining room, sir. Set for a wedding breakfast.'

The gentleman walked calmly in the door and peered about with an experienced eye. 'Ah yes. Well done. Not a hair out of place, Claude.'

'Sir, may I introduce Mr Barnaby Warboy, one of our leading citizens. Mr Warboy, this is our new Governor, His Excellency Sir John Eardley Eardley-Wilmot.'

The gentlemen exchanged greetings, and the Governor winked at Barnaby before he walked away. 'Did you hear that? Claude even got the name right. Rare!'

Barnaby blinked, a little awestruck by that chance meeting, but then the wedding guests were arriving and he rushed forward with open arms to greet them.

It was a beautiful morning, the happiest wedding breakfast Barnaby had ever attended, and before the bride and groom left he slipped an envelope into Marie's hands.

'This is your wedding present, Mrs Shanahan,' he said. 'Now run along.'

'Well done, Barnaby,' Sam said. 'It was a wonderful breakfast. But what about having a cup of tea with us before you leave?'

Sam was the only one who knew that Barnaby had just given Sean and Marie the cottage at Sandy Bay.

Not long after that happy day, anxiety rekindled, Barnaby withdrew to his study to read a letter from Harold.

My Dear Father,

I received your sad note upon the passing of my young niece Penelope Warboy and so am given to express Deep Sympathy to you from our Family and Friends in Kingston. I was greatly shocked but also confused that I should be the Conveyor of the sad News to her Parents as I assumed their Daughter would have been with them in New Orleans. My sister-in-law later explained that you all agreed it would be best for Penelope to remain with her wealthy grandfather who would see the young lady well placed in Society.

At this point, I must congratulate you Father on your rise to prominence and financial success in Van Diemen's Land. We are all proud of you, none the least your elder son.

Barnaby's irritation at Millicent's outright lie about her daughter remaining in Hobart was tempered by that message from Harold.

'Proud of me?' he snorted. 'I'll bet you are. I suppose you'll be next to visit. Up with the barricades!'

He poured himself a rum and continued.

I am now to come to New Orleans to break the news to her Parents who took up Residence again here upon their return from Van Diemen's Land, then did writ me for a Loan of Money at which I did allow them Twenty Pounds, but now I find them in a Sorry State living in an evil Slum. I put aside my Revulsion whereupon I knocked upon their door.

Upon opening the Door this fright of a Woman whom I declare I should not have recognised had she not shrieked my name threw herself at me demanding I take her back to her Parents in Kingston immediately. I quelled the urge to escape after suffering a blur of hysteria from Millicent and ascertained that Jubal was abed, further he would neither leave his Bed nor entertain my presence. It was then that I approached the subject of dear Penelope with care and eventually managed to break the sad news.

Not unexpected then was an attack of weeping Hysteria and Screams almost bringing down the Roof, an undignified Performance which tho did bring Jubal from his Bed. At first sight of him I thought he had the Plague he was so covered in red blotches and it wasn't until the weeping subsided I learned the nature of his ailment. By this time Jubal had found a half bottle of cheap rum, served three Glasses, taken his share back to his Room and shut the Door, ignoring me as if I were no more than a travelling salesman.

Barnaby shook his head sadly. 'Not a note of grief or remorse anywhere. No questions about Penn's death or her burial,' he sighed, placing the pages on his desk as if they'd become too weighty to hold. He took a box of matches from a drawer, to burn this burden, but curiosity had him read on.

Shocked, my Duty done, I begged my leave but my sister-in-law began packing with immediacy, resolving to accompany me to Jamaica, leaving her Husband behind. So said her that Jubal had committed an offence at the New Orleans Sailing Club, the details of which are too sordid to put on paper, and the gentlemen of the Club were so incensed they did tar and feather Jubal and throw him into the street. Perchance me to remark that Jubal's blotches were caused by adherence of tar and nothing catching as I had feared.

I am temporarily ensconced at the Bristol Hotel which is still utilised by the right people and have placed my sister-in-law in a boarding house until I can arrange passage for the woman and give her back to her family.

'Like a parcel,' Barnaby commented.

I hope you don't expect me to take Jubal in... Harold continued.

'At your own risk!' Barnaby interjected, glancing at the next few lines from his 'affectionate' son as he lit a match. He watched the pages flame and crumple into his large ashtray and then scattered the remains out of his window.

'Ho!' he called to Zack, his head gardener. 'What are you doing there?'

'Dossie needs some flowers for the house.'

'Very good. Everything seems to be in bloom today. The garden's a credit to you, Zack.'

'Thank you, sir,' Zack beamed. 'Thank you, sir.'

Almost twelve months later, after a short illness, Mr Barnaby Warboy, much-loved elder citizen of

Hobart, passed away.

Mr Baggott duly read Barnaby's will to his heirs.

He asked that he be buried beside Penelope Warboy and her son.

He left a large sum of money to his friends Mr and Mrs Sean Shanahan.

He gave over to his business partner, Mr Sam Pollard, his share in the stores and related warehouses.

His property Warboy Farm he left, lock, stock and barrel, to Mr Angus McLeod, with his humblest apologies for the grief and humiliation that had been caused by the Warboy family.

There were various other small legacies and donations.

The will was signed:

Barnaby Warboy.
God bless you all.

The publishers hope that this book has given you enjoyable reading. Large Print Books are especially designed to be as easy to see and hold as possible. If you wish a complete list of our books please ask at your local library or write directly to:

Magna Large Print Books
Magna House, Long Preston,
Skipton, North Yorkshire.
BD23 4ND

This Large Print Book for the partially sighted, who cannot read normal print, is published under the auspices of

THE ULVERSCROFT FOUNDATION